ANYTHING?

She huddled in the snow, crouched over her brother, stroking the fair hair. His face was untouched, snowflakes coated his dead, green eyes, and she felt the hot flow of blood soaking her own parka. More blood bubbled at the corner of her mouth, and her strength was going fast.

A side party, Stevie, she thought. *At least I sent you a side party.*

But it wasn't enough. Never enough. The bastards behind it were beyond her reach, and she gave herself to her hatred. It filled her with her despair, melding with it, like poison and wine, and she opened to it and drank it deep.

She raised her head, glaring madly after the vanished shuttle. *Anything! Anything for one more shot! One more—*

<*Anything, Little One?*>

She froze as that alien thought trickled through her wavering brain, for it wasn't hers. She closed her eyes on her tears. Mad. She was going mad at the very end.

<*No, Little One. Not mad.*>

Air hissed in her nostrils as the alien voice whispered to her. It was soft as the sighing snow, and colder by far.

<*You are dying,*> the voice murmured, <*and I have learned more of death than ever I thought to. So tell me—did you mean it? Will you truly give* anything *for your vengeance?*>

"*Anything!*" She raised her head and screamed it to the wind, to her grief and hate and the whisper of her own broken sanity, and a curious silence hovered briefly in her mind. Then—

<Done!> the voice cried, and the darkness took her at last.

Baen Books by David Weber:

Honor Harrington:
On Basilisk Station
The Honor of the Queen
The Short Victorious War
Field of Dishonor
Flag in Exile
Honor Among Enemies
In Enemy Hands
Echoes of Honor
Ashes of Victory
War of Honor
At All Costs

Honorverse:
Crown of Slaves (*with Eric Flint*)
The Shadow of Saganami

edited by David Weber:
More than Honor
Worlds of Honor
Changer of Worlds
The Service of the Sword

Mutineers' Moon
The Armageddon Inheritance
Heirs of Empire
Empire from the Ashes

In Fury Born

The Apocalypse Troll
The Excalibur Alternative

Bolos!
Old Soldiers

Oath of Swords
The War God's Own
Wind Rider's Oath

with Steve White:
Crusade
In Death Ground
The Stars At War
The Shiva Option
Insurrection
The Stars At War II

with Eric Flint:
1633
1634: The Baltic War

with John Ringo:
March Upcountry
March to the Sea
March to the Stars
We Few

with Linda Evans:
Hell's Gate
Hell Hath No Fury

IN FURY BORN

DAVID WEBER

IN FURY BORN

This is a work of fiction. All the characters and events portrayed in this book are fictional, and any resemblance to real people or incidents is purely coincidental.

A Baen Books

Baen Publishing Enterprises
P.O. Box 1403
Riverdale, NY 10471
www.baen.com

ISBN 10: 1-4165-2131-3
ISBN 13: 978-1-4165-2131-0

Cover art by David Mattingly

First Baen paperback printing, August 2007

Distributed by Simon & Schuster
1230 Avenue of the Americas
New York, NY 10020

Library of Congress Cataloging-in-Publication Data: 2006000096

Printed in the United States of America

10 9 8 7 6 5 4 3

IN FURY BORN

DAVID WEBER

BAEN

Book One:
The Empire's Wasp

Blackness.

Blackness over and about her. Drifting, dreamless, endless as the stars themselves, twining within her. It enfolded her, sharing itself with her, and she snuggled against it in the warm, windless void that was she. The blackness was all, and yet, beyond the comfort of her cocoon, dimly perceived, the years drifted past. They were there, beyond her sleep, recognized, and yet not quite real.

Deep, deep at the heart of her the fiery coal of purpose still glowed, but dimly, dimly. A once-fierce furnace, drowsing its way towards ultimate extinction.

A tiny fragment of her being watched sleepily as the white-hot coal cooled into a dimmer, fading red, and under the thick, soft blankets of blackness, that fragment wondered if she would ever be called again. Those she had once served were long vanished, she knew without knowing how she knew, yet every once in a while, floating in the dreams, an echo summoned her close, close, to the surface of her sleep. They were few in number, their existence fleeting and flickering like tiny mirrors of her own fiery essence. Not so many of them, perhaps, and yet, in so many endless years, the numbers were enough to trouble her slumber.

There. Another one flickered on the very edge of her dreams—another tiny flash of potential, of possibility. All the myriad futures in which she and that echo might meet, their purposes become one, shifted and shimmered about her, like the floating constellations of the zodiac . . . and so did the futures in which they never would.

Which would she prefer, her sleeping mind asked itself drowsily? To rouse once more—perhaps one last time—or to sleep, sleep, until there were no dreams, no echoes and mirrors?

She had no answer, and so she snuggled deeper under that soft shroud of non-being, and simply waited for whatever would be.

Or whatever would not.

PROLOGUE

"Just who *is* this child?" Colonel McGruder asked, gazing at the psychological profile floating in his holo display. "And how did we come to have this information on her?"

"Her name is Alicia DeVries," Lieutenant Maserati replied, "Alicia Dierdre DeVries, and she's in her final form. Education administered the standard exams to her class six months ago, and her results popped straight through the filters. So they retested last week. As you can see, the retest only confirmed the original results."

"Final form?" McGruder turned away from the display to look at his aide. "It says here that she's only fourteen!"

"As of six weeks ago, yes, Sir," Maserati replied. "She's, ah, in the accelerated curriculum. If you'll notice here—" the lieutenant flipped a command into his computer through the neural linkage, opening a window in the colonel's display to show him the girl's academic transcript "—she's already made the guaranteed cut for admission to Emperor's New College next year under ENC's gifted students program."

"Jesus." McGruder gazed at the transcript for a moment, then looked back at the psych profile. "If she looks like this at *fourteen* . . ."

"That's why I felt she should be brought to your attention, Sir," Maserati said. "I don't believe I've ever seen a stronger profile than this one, and, as you say, she's only fourteen."

"Too young," McGruder mused, and Maserati nodded. Scholastically, young DeVries was four standard years ahead of the vast majority of her age cohort. The test results had been forwarded to Colonel McGruder's office because the results of *every* Fourth Form student whose profile cracked the filters were sent here. But imperial law positively prohibited actively recruiting anyone—however high their test results, however severe the need, and even with parental consent—before he or she turned eighteen . . . among other things.

"Besides," McGruder continued. "Look at the genetic profile." He shook his head. "Couple the Ujvári gene group with this academic profile, and she's never going to come our way, anyhow. If she's already accepted for ENC, you *know* that's where she's going." He shook his head again, his expression sour. "It's too bad. We could really use her."

"I agree, Sir," the lieutenant said. "And I also agree that she's undoubtedly going to be under a lot of pressure to accept the ENC slot. But I think this may be one of the ones we want to flag to keep an eye on anyway. Especially when you consider this."

He sent another command over his headset, and his computer obediently opened yet another window.

"You've already noticed the genetic profile, Sir. But she gets that from her father's side of the family, and I thought you might find her maternal grandfather's résumé . . . interesting, as well," he said blandly.

". . . so I told the Lieutenant it was a Bad Idea." Sebastian O'Shaughnessy chuckled and shook his head. "And she told *me* she was the platoon commander and I was only the company first sergeant. The way she saw it, that meant we'd do it *her* way. So we did."

"And after you did?" his granddaughter asked with a huge grin, green eyes sparkling.

"And after we did, and after the post-exercise critique, the Lieutenant called me into her office and told me the Captain had . . . counseled her on the proper relationship between a brand, spanking new lieutenant, fresh out of the Academy on New Dublin, and a company first sergeant with nineteen standard years in the Corps."

O'Shaughnessy smiled back at the girl.

"I'll say this for her—she took it like a Marine. Owned right up and admitted I'd been right without ever letting either one of us forget she was *still* the Lieutenant and I was still the First Sergeant. That's harder than it sounds, too, but she was a good one, Lieutenant Chou. Stubborn, like most of the good ones, but smart. Smart enough to recognize her mistakes and learn from them. Still, I don't know if she ever did figure out that the Captain'd deliberately let her screw up by the numbers just to make the point. But it's one a good officer never forgets, Alley. There's always someone who's been in longer, or knows his job better, and the trick is to *use* that person's experience—especially if he's a long-service noncom who's been doing his job since about the time you were born—without ever surrendering your own authority or responsibility. That's why any *good* officer knows it's really the sergeants who run the Corps."

His granddaughter looked at him for a moment, her eyes much more thoughtful, her fourteen-year-old face serious, then nodded.

"I know how much I hate admitting it when I'm wrong," she said. "I bet it's a lot harder for an officer to admit that. Especially if she's new and thinks looking 'weak' will undermine her authority."

"Exactly," Sebastian agreed. Then he glanced at his chrono. "And speaking of being wrong," he continued, "isn't there something else you're supposed to be doing right now instead of sitting here encouraging me to gas on?"

The girl blinked at him, then looked at her own chrono, and sprang to her feet.

"Omigod! Mom is gonna *kill* me! Bye, Grandpa!"

She bent to plant a quick kiss on his cheek—at fourteen she was already a full head taller than her mother—and disappeared magically. He heard her thundering up the short flight of steps to her cubbyhole bedroom and shook his head with a grin.

"Was that Alley, or just a runaway air lorry?" a mild tenor inquired, and Sebastian looked up as his son-in-law poked his head into the room.

It was easy to see where Alicia's height had come from. Sebastian stood little more than a hundred and seventy centimeters, but Collum DeVries was better than twenty centimeters taller. He was also broad-shouldered, and powerfully built, even for his towering height. In fact, he looked far more like the holovid's idea of a professional Marine than Sebastian ever had. Of course, appearances could be deceiving, Sebastian reflected with, perhaps, just the slightest edge of smugness.

"Alley," Sebastian told him with a chuckle. "I think she'd forgotten all about that exam."

"You mean she was too busy pestering you for stories to remember it," Collum corrected. He smiled as he said it, but there was a faint yet real edge behind the smile.

"She doesn't see that much of me," Sebastian said, and Collum nodded.

"True. But I'm afraid that aura of martial glory of yours can be a bit overwhelming for a teenager."

Sebastian leaned back in his chair, regarding his son-in-law with fond exasperation.

"I'm sure an 'aura of martial glory' *could* be overwhelming," he said mildly after a moment. "That wasn't what we were talking about, though. In fact, she's a lot less interested in war stories than she is in picking my brain for the nuts and bolts of how the Corps really works."

"I know."

Collum looked at him for a moment, then sat down in the armchair Alicia had abandoned in favor of her upstairs computer workstation. The chair shifted under him, twitching into the proper contours, and he leaned forward, propping his elbows on his thighs.

"I know she is," he repeated, his distinctive slate-gray eyes unwontedly serious. "In fact that's what's worrying me. I'd almost prefer for it to be an adolescent fascination with the idea that combat can be 'glorious' and exciting."

"Would you, now?" Sebastian gazed at him thoughtfully.

Sebastian was more than merely fond of his son-in-law. Collum DeVries was probably one of the most brilliant men he'd ever met, and he was also a very *good* man. Sebastian suspected that it was rare for any father to believe any man could really be worthy of *his* daughter, and he admitted that there'd been an additional edge of concern in his own case when Fiona brought Collum home for the first time. Those gray eyes, with their oddly feline cast, coupled with his height and fair hair, had been impossible to miss. The Ujvári mutation's combination of physical traits was as well advertised as its *mental* traits, and Sebastian had braced himself for the inevitable confrontation. But that confrontation had never occurred, and over the years, Collum had amply demonstrated that he was, indeed, worthy of Sebastian O'Shaughnessy's only daughter.

Which didn't necessarily mean they saw eye-to-eye on every issue, of course.

"Alley—unfortunately, I sometimes think," Collum continued "—is exactly like *both* of her parents. She's smart—God, is she smart! And stubborn. And the sort who insists on making up her own mind."

"I agree," Sebastian said, when the younger man paused. "But this is a bad thing in exactly what way?"

"It's a bad thing, from my perspective at least, because I can't get away with telling her 'because I'm your father, that's why!' Or, at least, because I'm smart enough myself to know better than to try."

"Ah." Sebastian nodded. "A problem I had a time or two with her mother, now that you mention it."

"Somehow I don't doubt that for a moment." Collum grinned, his face momentarily losing its unusual expression of concern. But the grin was fleeting.

"Oh," he went on, waving one hand, "if I tell her not to do something, she won't. And I've never been afraid she'd sneak around behind my back to do something she knew Fiona or I would disapprove of, even now that the hormones have kicked in with a vengeance. But she'll make up her own mind, and if she thinks I'm wrong, she's not shy about letting me know. And when the time comes that she decides it's right for her to make a decision, she *will* make it—and act on it—even if she knows it's one I'd strongly oppose."

"Every child does that, Collum," Sebastian said gently. "At least, every child who's going to grow up into a worthwhile human being."

"You're right, of course. But that doesn't keep me from worrying about one of those decisions I don't want her to make."

He met his father-in-law's eyes—the same green eyes he saw when he looked at his wife or his older daughter—very levelly.

"It's a decision we all have to make, one way or the other, even if we do it only by default," Sebastian said after a moment.

"Sure it is," Collum agreed. "But I'm afraid of how quickly she's going to make it. I want her to take time to really think about it. To consider all of her options, all of the things she might be giving up."

"Of course you do," Sebastian said, but Collum's eyes flickered at the ever so slight edge he allowed into his voice.

"I'm genuinely not trying to pussyfoot around the issue, Sebastian," his son-in-law said. "And I think you know how much respect I have for the military in general and you in particular. I know exactly what you did to win the Banner, and I know how few other people could have done it. I think it's unfortunate that we still *need* the Marine Corps and the Fleet, but I'm fully aware that we do. And that we'll go on needing both of them—and thanking God we *have* them—at least until the Second Coming. If anyone knows that, those of us who work for the Foreign Ministry do."

And that, Sebastian reflected, was nothing but simple truth, despite the fact that Collum DeVries was an Ujvári, with all of the ingrained personal distaste for violent confrontation which went with it. No one would ever confuse Collum with a weakling, but like the vast majority of Ujváris, his entire worldview and mental processes were oriented towards consensus and pragmatic compromise. As one prominent geneticist had put it, the Ujváris suffered from an excess of sanity, compared to the rest of the human race, and Sebastian had always thought that summed it up quite well.

They did have their detractors, of course. Some people saw their bone-deep—actually, *gene*-deep—aversion to confrontation as cowardice, despite all of the evidence to the contrary. Personally, Sebastian had always viewed their attitude as more than a little unrealistic, but he was prepared to admit that that could have been his own prejudices talking. And whether it was unrealistic as a personal philosophy or not, it was definitely one of the things which made them so effective in the diplomatic service, or as analysts and policymakers, capable of standing back from personal, adversarial approaches to policy debates. And it was also the reason why, despite their intellectual prowess, Ujváris as a group had a well-earned reputation for looking down their philosophical noses at other people who were readier to embrace . . . direct action solutions to problems. And at the people, like the citizens of New Dublin, where the tradition of service to the House of Murphy ran bone-deep, who were called upon to implement those direct actions at the command of the Emperor.

But Collum had never shared that private, unstated Ujvári disdain, possibly even contempt, for the military. It was not a career he would ever have chosen for himself, but that was largely because he recognized how supremely ill-suited for it he would have been. Not to mention the fact that his own greatest potential contribution had lain in other areas.

"At the same time," Collum continued, "the fact that I respect the military—and you—doesn't mean I want my daughter to charge into your footsteps before she's had the opportunity to look around and consider all of the other equally valid, equally important things she might do with her life."

"*Equally* important, perhaps," Sebastian said, his New Dublin accent surfacing with unusual strength. "But there's not a single thing she could be doing that would be *more* important, Collum."

"I never said there was." DeVries' eyes never wavered under the green gaze which had weakened the knees of generations of Marine recruits. "But there are sacrifices involved in the life you've chosen, Sebastian. Don't tell me you didn't hurt inside when you saw how much Fiona and John had grown up—how much of their lives you'd missed—when you came back home from a deployment. Or how much it hurt when you lost one of your friends to the Rish or some Crown World lunatic or Rogue World merc. I respect you for being willing to make those sacrifices, but that doesn't mean I want my daughter to make the same ones without thinking about it long and hard."

And you hate the very thought of getting the personal letter from the Minister of War, Sebastian thought. *You're terrified your daughter won't come home one day. Well, you've a right to be . . . but she's the right to make the decision herself anyway, when the time comes.*

"Are you asking—or telling—me not to answer her questions?" he asked. "Not to discuss my life with my granddaughter?"

"Of course not!" Collum's vehement denial was genuine, Sebastian realized. "You're her grandfather, and she loves you. She wants to know about your life, and you have every right in the universe to share it with her. For that matter, you damned well ought to be proud of it; God knows I'd be, in your place! I'm just . . . worried."

"Have you discussed it with Fiona?"

"'Discuss' isn't exactly the verb I'd choose." Collum shook his head with an expression Sebastian recognized only too well. Fiona, after all, was *very* like her mother had been.

"I've voiced my concerns," Collum continued, "and she shares them, I think. But she's got that damned O'Shaughnessy serenity. She just shakes her head and talks about leading horses to water, or tying strings to a pig's back leg."

"'Serenity' isn't exactly an *O'Shaughnessy* characteristic," Sebastian said dryly. "Trust me, she got it from her mother's side of the family. But she's a point. You'll not convince Alley to do anything she thinks is wrong. And you'll not convince her *not* to do anything she thinks is right."

"I know that." Collum inhaled deeply. "And I know it's not something that's going to happen tomorrow, too. But she adores you, Sebastian, and she's not immune to that New Dublin tradition. I'm not saying she wouldn't be considering the Corps even if her grandfather had been a mousy little civilian and not a genuine military hero. I think she would. But I'll be honest. It scares me."

"Of course it does," Sebastian said gently. "And you know I've never tried to glamorize it, or underplay just how ugly it can really be. But I adore *her,* too, you know. If this is something she's seriously thinking about, then I want her to know what it's really like. The bad, as well as the good. And I promise, I'll never encourage her to do anything behind your back, Collum."

"I never thought you would." Collum stood, and touched his father-in-law lightly on one shoulder. "I guess as much as anything else, I just needed someone to lean on for a moment about it."

CHAPTER ONE

The command sergeant major, 502nd Brigade, 17th Division, Imperial Marine Corps, looked up at the crisp, traditional double-tap knock upon his office door.

"Enter!" he said, raising his voice slightly, and the door opened.

He watched critically as the tall, broad-shouldered young woman marched through the doorway, braced to attention, and saluted smartly. There was still just a bit too much of Camp Mackenzie in that salute, he reflected. Too much spit and polish and new, unworn edges. But that was only to be expected in such a recent graduate of the Corps' premier training camp on Old Earth herself.

"Private DeVries reports to the Sergeant Major!" she announced crisply.

He tipped his chair back slightly, examining her with the same, thoughtful expression which had greeted literally generations of new Marines. Her red-gold hair was short, almost plushy, just beginning to grow back out from the traditional close-shaved smoothness of boot camp. Despite the fairness of her natural coloring, she was tanned to a dark, even bronze, and he noted the sinewy strength of the forearms bared by her fatigues' precisely rolled up sleeves. Her boots were mirror bright, the creases in her fatigues sharp as an old-style razor, and a smile hovered invisibly behind his evaluating eyes as he reflected on how happy she must have been to be issued her smart-cloth uniforms. It had been quite a while since his own days at Camp Mackenzie, but he remembered perfectly how . . . irritated he'd been by the Corps' insistence that boots had to experience traditional old-style uniforms which actually had to be ironed—and *starched*—to maintain precisely the correct appearance.

For all of her height, the young woman in front of his desk was younger than he usually saw. He doubted that she would ever be a full-breasted woman, but at this particular moment, she still had quite a bit of filling out to do. Despite her solid, hard-trained physique, she still had the "not-quite-finished" look of adolescence's last gasp in more than one way, yet despite that, the black, single chevron of a private first class rode her right sleeve, just below the crowned stinging-wasp shoulder flash of the Imperial Marine Corps.

He completed his leisurely examination while she held her salute. Then he returned it, with the less punctilious, well-oiled ease of long practice.

"Stand easy, Private," he said.

"Yes, Sergeant Major!"

She dropped not into the stand-easy posture he'd authorized, but into a precisely correct parade rest, and despite his many decades of service, his lips twitched, hovering on the brink of a smile, as she stared straight ahead, a perfect regulation ten centimeters over his head.

He let her stand that way for a couple of seconds, then climbed out of his chair and walked around his desk. He stood directly in front of her, half a head shorter than she, scrutinizing every detail of her appearance one more lingering time. It was, he was forced to concede, perfect. There wasn't one single thing about it he could have faulted, any more than he could have faulted the perfection of her non-expression as she stood statue-still under his microscopic examination.

"Well," he said finally, and opened his arms wide to envelop her in a crushing hug.

"Hello, Grandpa," the private said, her contralto voice huskier than usual, and wrapped her arms about him in return.

"I tried my damnedest to get home for your graduation formation, Alley," Sebastian O'Shaughnessy said a few minutes later, half-sitting, with his posterior perched comfortably on the corner of his desk and his arms crossed. "It just wasn't on."

"I knew when they assigned you out here that you wouldn't be able to be there, Grandpa," she told him, and smiled. "I'm just glad my own movement orders left me enough slack to stop in and visit you on my way through.

"I am, too," he said. "On the other hand, my spies kept me informed on your progress." He frowned portentously. "I understand you did *fairly* well."

"I tried, at any rate," she replied.

"I'm sure you did. And I guess I'll just have to be content with your graduating second in your training brigade. But by a full *tenth* of a percentage point?" He shook his head sadly. "I mean, I *had* had my heart set on your graduating *first*, but I suppose that was unrealistic of me."

His eyes flickered with laughter, and she shook her head.

"I'm sorry to disappoint you, Grandpa," she said politely, "but I *was* at a certain disadvantage, you know."

"But *nineteenth* in PT?" he said mournfully. "It's a good thing you maxed everything else, that's all I can say!"

"Only two of the boots who beat me out in PT were from Old Earth," she told him severely, "and both of them were male, and one of them was a reserve triathlete in the last Olympics. The others were all from off-world. From heavy-grav planets, as a matter of fact. And only three of *them* were female."

"Excuses, excuses." He chuckled, shaking his head while he beamed proudly at her. "If it hadn't been for that small arms record you set, you'd have only graduated *third*, you know!"

"But I'd still have topped my regiment," she shot back.

"Well, I suppose *that's* true," he conceded with a chuckle. Then his expression sobered. "Seriously, Alley. I'm proud of you. Very proud. I expected you to do well, but you've managed to exceed my expectations. Again."

"Thank you, Grandpa," she said, her voice softer. "That means a lot to me."

Their eyes met again, and O'Shaughnessy smiled warmly. Then he straightened slightly, with the air of a man about to change the subject.

"Did you know that Cassius Hill and I have been friends for the last twenty or thirty years?" he asked.

"You and Sergeant Major Hill?" She blinked, then shook her own head. "No. I suppose I should have wondered—you seem to know just about *everyone* in the Corps. I guess one reason it never occurred to me was that he was such a . . . fearsome presence, let's say. It's sort of hard to picture him *having* friends, actually. I mean, I know he must, but it's just hard to imagine from the worm's eye view of him I had. In fact, there were times all of us boots were positive he had to be something they'd cooked up in an AI lab somewhere. We figured they were field testing autonomous combat remotes and using us for guinea pigs."

"Well, a boot isn't really supposed to like his DI, and that goes double—or triple—for his battalion sergeant major. But Cassius rather *liked* you. I had four letters from him while you were at Mackenzie. He said you'd managed to impress him."

"I did?" Alicia laughed. "I didn't know that. I knew *he'd* impressed *me*, though! Scared me to death, a time or two."

"He was supposed to. On the other hand," O'Shaughnessy looked at his granddaughter thoughtfully, "he told me that nothing ever seemed to faze you. I think he was almost a little worried. Thought he might be losing his touch, or something. In fact, he said he sometimes thought you were actually *enjoying* Mackenzie."

"I was," she said, her tone surprised.

"Enjoying *Mackenzie*?" O'Shaughnessy looked at her, and she shrugged, as if surprised by his attitude.

"Oh, parts of it weren't exactly among the most pleasant moments of my life," she admitted. "And I had more trouble with the augmentation surgery than I'd expected. But overall? I had a blast, Grandpa. It was *fun*."

O'Shaughnessy leaned back, eyebrows arched. The most astonishing thing about it was that she seemed perfectly serious.

Camp Mackenzie, on its island off the southeastern coast of Old Earth's United States Province, had been a training site for Marines for over a thousand years—since long before there'd been an Imperial Marine Corps, or even an Empire for it to serve. It still was (although there were some on New Dublin who felt that their home world would have been a better site), and he knew why that was. Old Earth remained the imperial capital, the heart of the

Empire, after all. And no location on the mother world could have been better chosen to provide the maximum summer heat, humidity, mosquitoes, and sandfleas to test a new recruit's mettle . . . or to melt him down into the properly malleable alloy required for the Empire's steel.

Not that the Corps hadn't found ways to make it still better than nature alone had intended. O'Shaughnessy had always more than half believed the rumors about the Corps shipping in alligators to make sure the Mackenzie population was maintained at ample levels, for instance. But whether that was true or not, there was no question but that the merciless training regimen was deliberately designed to create a hell on Earth. Not out of the institutional sense of sadism some of the recruits—the "boots"—who experienced it were certain was to blame, but because the Corps had spent so long learning to take civilians apart and rebuild them as Marines. No one survived something as grueling as Camp Mackenzie without being brought face-to-face with what was *really* deep down inside him. It was *supposed* to be the hardest thing a boot had ever done. It was supposed to teach him what he was, what he could accomplish and endure, and the often grim, frequently harsh difference between any daydreams he might have cherished about the military and its truth. It taught him how to meet the challenges of the reality of what it meant to be one of "the Empire's Wasps," and above all, it gave him the discipline, devotion, and self-confidence which went with those lessons. And in the process of learning those things, those who survived the teaching were hammered into true Marines on the Corps' anvil.

But while Mackenzie was many things, including the avatar of the Corps' very heart and soul, one thing it most definitely wasn't supposed to be was "fun."

"You're an even more peculiar young woman than I thought you were, Alley," he told her, after a moment. "You thought Mackenzie was *fun*. I don't think I have the heart to tell Cassius that. It might finally break his spirit."

"I didn't say it was *easy*, Grandpa!" she protested. "It wasn't. In fact, it's the hardest thing I've ever done. But it was still fun. I got to learn a lot about myself, and like you say, I did graduate second overall in the entire brigade." She grinned. "I earned this the hard way." She touched the first-class stripe on her sleeve. "I not only survived boot camp in *August*, but I got to kick ass and take names along the way!"

"I see." He shrugged. "Well, that's the sort of thing a sergeant major likes to hear out of any larva, even if it does raise a few minor concerns about the larva in question's contact with what the rest of us fondly call reality. And I really am proud of you. But don't go around admitting you actually enjoyed boot camp. We're stretched enough for personnel that the Corps couldn't afford to replace all the senior noncoms who'd drop dead on the spot when they heard you."

"Yes, Grandpa," she promised demurely, and he chuckled.

"Your parents?" he asked then. "Clarissa?"

"All fine, and they all send their love."

"Even your Dad?" O'Shaughnessy asked with another half-smile. "He's forgiven me for 'encouraging you'?"

"Don't be silly, Grandpa." She shook her head fondly. "He was never really *that* mad at you, and you know it. He loves you. In fact, once he'd calmed down, he even admitted it wasn't your fault. And you did get me through college first, you know."

"Somehow," O'Shaughnessy observed, "I don't think he'd really expected you to burn through the entire five-year program in only three and a half years. I think he'd figured you'd slow down a little bit once you were out of high school."

"No," she said. "What he figured was that once I'd gotten my undergraduate degree under my belt, those Ujvári genes might kick in the way they already have with Clarissa and I'd forget about the Marines and pick some other career." She shrugged. "He was wrong. As a matter of fact, Mother knew he was wrong about that going in. She told him so when I told them I hadn't changed my mind."

"She would have," O'Shaughnessy said wryly. "A lot like *her* mother, your mother. So you don't think your Dad is going to shoot me on sight the next time he sees me for proposing my 'compromise'?"

"Of course he isn't. He wouldn't even if he weren't Ujvári. I took the scholarship, I got my degree, and that was my part of the bargain. He didn't even wince when he signed the parental waiver for the recruiter. Not once, I promise. He's tough, my Dad."

"Actually," her grandfather said, his expression and tone both suddenly more serious, "he is. I may tease him sometimes about being Ujvári, but I've always known it keeps him from *really* understanding what drove me—and you—into this sort of a career. And on top of that, his ministry duties mean he's in a position to know exactly what sort of crappy jobs the Corps gets handed, and just how hard we can get hammered if it falls into the pot on us." Sebastian shook his head. "It's not easy for any father to see his child go off to something like the Corps, knowing she could be wounded, or captured, or killed in action. Especially not when she's only seventeen. And extra especially not when you love her as much as your parents love you."

"I know," she said softly. She looked away for a moment, then back at him. "I know," she repeated. "And that's probably what could have come closest to making me change my mind, really. Knowing how much he—and Mom, whether she's willing to admit it or not—are going to worry about me. But I couldn't, Grandpa. I just couldn't give it up. And," her eyes brightened again, "like I say, Mackenzie was a blast!"

"I really need to check your psych profile," he told her. "In the meantime, though, I suppose they've gotten you squared away for your first assignment?"

"I got to request the duty I wanted because of where I graduated in the Brigade," Alicia replied. "I got it, too. Well, I didn't get to pick the actual unit, of course."

"I'm reasonably familiar with how the process works, Alley," he said dryly, and she laughed.

"I know you are. Sorry. But in answer to your question, I'm on my way to the recon battalion of the First of the 517th."

"Recon?" O'Shaughnessy frowned slightly, tugging on the lobe of his right ear. Recon Marines were generally considered, even by their fellows, as among the Corps' elite. Normally, a Marine couldn't even be considered for Recon until he'd pulled at least one hitch doing something more plebeian. Even Mackenzie honor graduates were supposed to get their tickets punched before they were considered for Recon.

"Sergeant Major Hill warned me that I probably wouldn't get it," Alicia said. "But I figured I might as well ask for what I really wanted. The worst they could do was tell me no."

"I'm surprised they didn't," O'Shaughnessy said honestly, but even as he did, a sudden suspicion crossed his mind. He tried to brush it aside as quickly as it occurred to him. After all, the very idea was preposterous—wasn't it? Of course it was! No one would be thinking that so early. Not even about *his* Alley!

"Well, let me see," he said. "I know Brigadier Erikson has the 517th, but who has the First?"

"There's something about the Corps you don't *know?*" Alicia's green eyes danced, and he made a face at her.

"Even I can lose track of the minor details, girl," he told her.

"Well, your secret is safe with me, Grandpa," she assured him. "And I'm not sure who has the Regiment right now. According to my orders, though, Recon belongs to a Major Palacios. Do you know her?"

"Palacios, Palacios," O'Shaughnessy murmured. Then he shook his head. "I don't think I've ever actually crossed paths with her. There are at least half a dozen officers in the entire Corps whom I've never met. Just your luck to draw one of them."

"Might be a good thing, now that I think about it," she said. "I love you, Grandpa, but your shadow can be sort of overwhelming."

"Yeah, sure!" He rolled his eyes, and she chuckled. "And now that you've pandered to my fragile ego," he continued, "when are you supposed to report to Martinsen?"

"Martinsen?" Alicia looked surprised.

"The 517th *is* stationed in the Martinsen System," O'Shaughnessy pointed out, and she shrugged.

"That may be where the Brigade is headquartered, Grandpa, but it's not where they're sending me. According to my orders, I'm going to Gyangtse."

"Oh?" Fortunately, Sebastian O'Shaughnessy's face and voice had had a great deal of experience in saying exactly what he told them to. But that didn't do much about the sudden chill which danced down his spine.

"I didn't know the First had been reassigned to Gyangtse," he said after a moment, keeping his voice merely thoughtful. "Still, from the intel reports I've seen, sounds like things might get 'interesting' out that way, Alley. Do me a favor and remember what they taught you at Mackenzie and not all the bad holo dramas you've seen."

Alicia DeVries gazed at her grandfather, and her own expression was as calm as his. Not, she suspected, that either of them was actually fooling the other. Obviously, he knew something about the Gyangtse System that didn't exactly make him happy. She was tempted to ask him what it was, but the temptation was brief lived. It was hard enough being Sebastian O'Shaughnessy's granddaughter without letting herself fall into the habit of trying to take advantage of their relationship. Not that her grandfather would be likely to let her. In fact, she'd be lucky if he didn't take her head off if she tried, she reflected.

"I'll remember, Grandpa," she promised him, and he gazed into her eyes for a moment, then nodded in obvious approval of what he'd found there.

"Good! And," he pushed himself up from the desk, "since you're in transit, rather than reporting in for duty, a noncommissioned officer of my own towering seniority can permit himself to be seen in public with a mere PFC without unduly undermining military discipline and the chain of command. So, I was thinking we might head off-base for an hour or two. There's a really good Thai restaurant I want you to try."

CHAPTER TWO

"So, you're our new warm body, are you?"

Sergeant Major Winfield managed, Alicia noticed, to restrain the wild spasm of delight he must have experienced at her arrival. He tipped back in his comfortable chair, contemplating her across his desk in the armory barracks the Gyangtse planetary militia had made available to the 1st/517th's reconnaissance battalion's command section, and shook his head with a galaxy-weary air. She wasn't certain whether or not his question had been purely rhetorical. Under the circumstances, it was probably better to assume that it hadn't been, she decided.

"Yes, Sergeant Major," she replied.

"And straight from Mackenzie." He sighed, head shaking harder. "We ask for nineteen experienced replacements, and we get . . . you. There *is* only one of you, isn't there, Private?"

"Yes, Sergeant Major," she repeated.

"Well, at least we won't have to break in more of you, then," Winfield said with the air of a man trying desperately to find a bright side so he could look on it. This time, Alicia said nothing, simply standing in front of his desk, hands clasped behind her in a regulation parade rest. Somehow, this arrival interview wasn't going quite as well as she'd hoped.

Winfield regarded her for several more seconds, then allowed his chair to come upright.

"I presume that you noticed Sergeant Hirshfield on your way through to my office?"

"Yes, Sergeant Major."

"Good. In that case," Winfield raised his right hand and made a shooing motion towards the office door, "trot back out there and tell him you're assigned to Lieutenant Kuramochi's platoon."

"Yes, Sergeant Major."

"Dismissed, Private DeVries."

"Yes, Sergeant Major!"

Alicia came to attention, saluted crisply, waited for Winfield's somewhat less crisp response, then turned and marched briskly out of his office. As she closed the door behind her, she wondered if she'd ever be allowed to use more than a three-word vocabulary in Winfield's presence.

Staff Sergeant Hirshfield looked up with a faint smile as Winfield's door clicked ever so carefully shut. The staff sergeant was a wiry fellow with dark hair, and he wore a neural link headset.

"Welcome to the Battalion, DeVries," he said. "Did the Sergeant Major extend the approved Recon welcome?"

"I believe the Sergeant Major may have been somewhat . . . underwhelmed by my arrival, Sergeant," Alicia said carefully.

"Sar'Major Winfield is always 'underwhelmed' by new arrivals," Hirshfield told her with a faint twinkle. "Mind you, his disposition really is almost as cranky as he'd like you to believe. That's why he has me. I'm the little ray of sunshine that brightens up the day of everyone he rains on."

"I was given to understand," Alicia said, emboldened by Hirshfield's small smile, "that he'd hoped for someone with more experience."

"He always does." Hirshfield shrugged. "No offense, DeVries, but Recon isn't usually considered a slot for newbies. Not to mention the fact that we're always shorthanded, and right this minute, with things heating up here in Gyangtse with the runup to the referendum, we're feeling it a bit more than usual. So even if he gives you a hard time, I'm sure he's really glad to see you. After all, even a brand new Mackenzie larva is better than nothing," he added, somewhat spoiling, in Alicia's opinion, the reassurance he might or might not have been attempting to project.

"Thank you, Sergeant," she said. "Ah, he told me to tell you that I'm supposed to be assigned to Lieutenant Kuramochi's platoon."

"Figured that." Hirshfield nodded. "The Lieutenant's nine people short. I imagine you'll go to Third Squad—that's Sergeant Metternich's squad. It's shortest right now, and Metternich's the senior squad leader. He's pretty good about bringing the babies along, too. No offense."

"None taken, Sergeant," Alicia replied, not entirely honestly.

"Good." Hirshfield's eye gleamed with a certain gentle malice. Then he spoke into the boom mike attached to his headset. "Central, Metternich." He waited perhaps half a heartbeat, then spoke again, smiling up at Alicia. "Abe, got one of your new people here. You wanna come by the office and pick her up, or should I just give her a map?"

He listened for a moment, then chuckled.

"All right. I'll tell her. Clear."

"Sergeant Metternich is sending someone to fetch you," he told Alicia, and pointed at the utilitarian chairs against the wall opposite his desk. "Park your fanny in one of those until whoever it is gets here."

"Yes, Sergeant," Alicia said obediently, and parked her fanny in one of the aforesaid chairs.

"Yo, Sarge. You got somebody for me?"

Alicia looked up as the short, almost squat PFC poked his head in through Hirshfield's office door. The newcomer was even darker than Hirshfield, with broad shoulders, heavy with muscle, and a thatch of unruly black hair.

"Medrano!" Hirshfield beamed. "If it isn't my favorite Marine! And I do, indeed, have somebody for you. Right there."

He pointed, and Private Medrano turned his head in Alicia's direction. He looked at her for a moment, then looked back at Hirshfield.

"Golly gee, thanks," he said. "Did you tell Abe what you had for him?"

"And spoil the surprise?" Hirshfield arched his eyebrows.

"Thought not," Medrano said, and shook his head. Then he looked back at Alicia and jerked a thumb over his shoulder. "Come on, Larva."

He pulled his head out of the office and headed back the way he'd come without even looking to see if Alicia was following him.

Which she was, of course, if not precisely cheerfully. So far, she reflected as Medrano led her briskly out of the office block, *none* of this day seemed to be going exactly the way she'd hoped it would.

"Where's your gear, Larva?" he asked without turning his head.

"They're holding it for me at the pad," she replied.

"Guess we'd better head over there and collect it, then," he said, then turned left and headed down one of the walkways.

His greater familiarity with the local geography quickly made itself apparent. Alicia had followed the map the arrivals sergeant had loaded into her personal com to find her way across Gyangtse's capital city of Zhikotse to Sergeant Major Winfield's office in the planetary militia barracks the battalion had taken over. The path Medrano picked to get them back to the field and her arrival shuttle pad was far more winding and complicated, making much more use of twisty back alleys rather than following the newer, wider thoroughfares. It was also much shorter, and they got back to the capital's smallish spaceport in little more than half the time it had taken her to get to Winfield's office *from* the pad.

"Fetch," Medrano said dryly, parking himself comfortably in one of the chairs provided in the baggage-handling section. He pointed at the single manned window, then leaned back in the chair and crossed his ankles.

Alicia glanced at him, then crossed to the window and the local civilian standing behind it. On most planets, baggage claim would have been handled by an AI, or at least a self-serve computerized system. But she'd already realized that Gyangtse's poverty was pronounced, at least by the Empire's generally affluent standards.

"What can I do for you?" the short, wiry (like most Gyangtsese she'd so far seen) civilian inquired genially.

"I need to collect my gear," she told him, sliding the electronic claim ticket across the counter to him. "I came in on *Telford Williams*."

"No, really?"

The Gyangtsese grinned at her, and she felt herself color ever so slightly. Of course he'd known she had to have come in aboard the *Williams*. The transport was undoubtedly the only ship to have made Gyangtse orbit in the last several days. But although the man was obviously amused, he didn't make a big thing out of it as he accepted the claim tag and slotted it into his terminal.

"DeVries, Alicia D., right?" he asked as the data came up.

"That's me," she confirmed.

"Okay." He tapped something into his keypad, then nodded. "Bay Eleven," he said, pointing at the numbered baggage bays against the rear wall. "It'll be up in a couple of minutes."

"Thank you," she said, and he nodded at her again.

"You're welcome," he said. "And, by the way, welcome to Gyangtse, too."

"Thanks." She nodded back, and headed over to the indicated baggage bay.

Her baggage arrived almost as promptly as the clerk had suggested it would, and she dragged her foot locker clear and checked its security telltales to be sure it hadn't been tampered with. Then she hauled out the pair of duffel bags which went with it and checked them, as well. She piled the bags on top of the locker, pulled the web strap taut across them, then switched on the foot locker's internal counter-grav unit. It rose obediently, and she gave it a push to make sure she had its mass distributed evenly. It bobbed gently, but stayed on an even keel, and she nodded in satisfaction.

She activated the tractor leash, tethering the locker to the small unit on her belt, and turned back to Medrano. The locker and duffel bags floated obediently across the floor, staying precisely the regulation meter and a half behind her.

"Everything?" the older private asked, coming to his feet.

"Everything," she confirmed. He glanced at the baggage critically, but seemed unable to find anything to pick apart.

"Then let's grab some transport," he said, and she followed him out of the pad waiting area.

Medrano commandeered one of the field's limited number of jitneys and punched destination coordinates into the onboard computer while Alicia loaded her baggage into the cargo compartment. She closed the compartment door and climbed in beside him at his brusque gesture, and the jitney hummed rapidly away.

Alicia glanced sidelong at Medrano's profile. She badly wanted to ask questions, but everyone she'd met so far today seemed far too interested in depressing the newbie's pretensions for her to offer him the opportunity to do some more of it. So she switched her eyes back to look straight ahead through the jitney's windscreen, possessing her soul in patience.

Medrano leaned back without speaking for a minute or so, then smiled ever so slightly.

"It's all right, Larva," he said.

"I beg your pardon?" She looked at him a bit warily, and he chuckled.

"Oh, you've still got a *long* way to go before you're a member of the lodge, Larva," he told her cheerfully. "And all us growed up Wasps're gonna make your life hell before we let you forget it, too. But there's just the two of us right now, and I know you've got questions. So go ahead. 'S all right."

"All right," she said. "I'll bite. Staff Sergeant Hirshfield said something about things heating up here in Gyangtse. What's going on?"

"That'd be good to know, wouldn't it?" Medrano's grin turned crooked. "The Lieutenant can answer that one better than I can, but the bottom line is that this whole sector used to be League systems. Which means we've usually got someone making trouble and generally showing his ass, and half the time they seem to think they can actually kick the 'Empies' back off their planets. It's not gonna happen, of course. But the local idiots manage to forget that from time to time, and it looks to me like that's what's getting ready to happen here."

"There's actually some sort of underground cooking away?" She was unable to keep the surprise totally out of her tone, and he chuckled again, more harshly.

"Larva, there's *always* 'an underground' someplace like this. It's usually fairly small, sort of a holding pattern for the cream-of-the-crop loonies, but it's always there, and sometimes it's not all homegrown, know what I mean? Most times, the rest of the locals are happy enough to have us around that they make the loonies' lives hard. But sometimes, like now, that's not so much the case."

"Why not?"

"Who the hell knows?" Medrano shrugged. "I mean, I guess the Lieutenant does. She's pretty sharp . . . for an officer. But the bottom line is that Gyangtse's right in the middle of moving from Crown World to Incorporated status. Mostly, folks seem to think that's a good idea when it happens; this time, it looks a little shakier. Dunno why—maybe it's the economy, because that's not so great. Or maybe the Gyangtsese are just dumber'n rocks or just don't like the Governor. Or maybe it's the Lizards or the FALA poking around." He shrugged again. "Whatever. The point is, Larva, that we've got exactly one battalion on the planet, there's these GLF yahoos announcing how opposed they are to 'closer relations' with the Empire—like they had a choice—and the locals who'd usually be sending us quiet little messages about the bad boys are keeping their mouths shut at the moment."

"Oh."

Alicia considered what Medrano had said. The older Marine's apparently casual attitude and manner of speaking had fooled her—initially and briefly—into underestimating his intellect. That hadn't lasted long, though, and even if it had tried to, what he'd just said would have knocked it on the head, because it made sense out of a lot of things she'd noticed without really recognizing.

The Terran Empire had grown out of the ruins of the old Terran Federation, following the League Wars and the Human-Rish Wars which had come after them. The huge, physically powerful Rish-athan matriarchs weren't actually "lizards," of course. In fact, they were far closer to oviparous Terran mammals, in most ways, although the slang term for them was probably inevitable, given their looming, saurian appearance. But if they weren't lizards, they weren't exactly the best neighbors in the galactic vicinity, either. More militant even than humans (which, Alicia was prepared to admit, took some doing), they had not reacted well to mankind's intrusion into their interstellar backyard in 2340. And their reaction had gone downhill steadily from there, especially after their analysts realized just how much more productive human economies were . . . and how much of a technological edge humanity possessed. The fact that humans were far more fertile and liked lower-density populations, which produced a more enthusiastic and rapid rate of exploration and colonization, only made the Rishatha even less happy to see them.

Which explained why the Rishathan Sphere's diplomacy had played upon the lingering tensions between the rival Terran League and Terran Federation with such skill and persistence. It had taken them a century of careful work, but in the end, they'd managed to produce the League Wars, which had lasted from 2450 until 2510, and killed more human beings than the combined military and civilian death tolls of every other war in the recorded history of the human race put together.

Those sixty years of vicious, deadly warfare had turned the Federation into the Terran Empire, under Emperor Terrence I of the House of Murphy. They had also led to the League's utter military and economic exhaustion . . . at which point its Rishathan "friends and neighbors" had launched the First Human-Rish War with a devastating assault into its rear areas. Their victim had been taken totally by surprise, and in barely eight years, the Sphere had conquered virtually the entire League.

Unfortunately for the Rish, whose plans had succeeded up to that point with a perfection which would have turned Machiavelli green with envy, the Terran *Empire* had proved a much tougher proposition. Especially because the time the Sphere was forced to spend digesting its territorial conquests in the League following HRW-I gave Terrence I time to put his own house in order and reorganize, rebuild, and expand his navy.

The Second Human-Rish War had lasted fourteen years, not eight. And despite its war weariness and the political chaos which the six decades of the League Wars had produced, the Empire had been solidly united behind its charismatic new Emperor. Besides, by that time humanity had figured out who was really responsible for those sixty horrendous years of death and destruction. By the end of HRW-II, the Empire had taken two-thirds of the old League's star systems away from the Rish and driven the Sphere to the brink of total military defeat. Under the Treaty of Leviathan, which had formally ended the war, the Rishathan Sphere had been required to return to its pre-HRW-I borders, and the remaining third of the old League which had not already been incorporated into the Empire had found itself at least nominally independent—the so-called "Rogue Worlds" which served as a buffer zone between the two interstellar great powers and belonged to neither.

But those sixty years of human-versus-human warfare, followed by the "liberation" (or forcible occupation, depending upon one's perspective) of so many League star systems by the imperial armed forces, had left the Empire a festering legacy of resentment. Even now, four hundred years later, Alicia knew, that resentment provided at least two thirds of the Marines' and Fleet's headaches.

All too many of the old League worlds were still Crown Worlds, directly administered by Ministry of Out-Worlds governors appointed from off-world by the Empire, despite having population levels high enough to qualify them for Incorporated status. But making that move from a Crown-administered imperial protectorate to full membership, with senatorial representation, was always a delicate process. Especially in a case like Gyangtse, where the planet's original association with the Empire hadn't exactly been voluntary.

"This GLF you mentioned—that stands for what? Gyangtse Liberation Front, or something like that?" she asked after a moment, and Medrano glanced at her.

"You got it, Larva."

"And it's opposed to Incorporation?"

Medrano nodded, and Alicia made a face. Of course it was. And, from the name, it was probably doing everything it could to hamstring the local planetary debate on whether or not to seek Incorporated status. Some ex-League worlds, she knew, had voted as many as twenty or even thirty times before their citizens finally decided to forget the past. Or, at least, to forget it sufficiently to become willing subjects of the Emperor.

"Have there been any actual incidents?" she asked, and Medrano grunted.

"More than a couple," he acknowledged, just a bit grimly.

"What kind?" she asked, frowning thoughtfully. Medrano raised an eyebrow, and she shrugged. "I mean, have they been more of the 'we want to make ourselves enough of a pain that you'll negotiate with us and give us what we want so we'll go away' sort, or of the 'we're dangerous enough nuts that we actually think we can kill enough of you so that *you'll* go away' sort?"

"That's the big question, isn't it, Larva?" Medrano replied, but there was an odd light in his eye. As if Alicia's question—or the insight behind it, perhaps—had surprised him. "Nobody much likes the first kind of loony, but it's the *second* kind that fills body bags. And right this minute, I don't have the faintest idea which variety we're looking at here."

"I see." Alicia's frown deepened, more pensive than ever, and she leaned back in the jitney's seat.

Medrano glanced at her again and half-opened his mouth, then closed it again, his own expression thoughtful, as the self-possessed larva at his side digested what he'd just told her. It wasn't the response he'd expected out of someone that young, that fresh out of Camp Mackenzie. Maybe this kid really did have something going for her?

Well, Leocadio Medrano thought dryly, *I guess we'll just have to see about that, won't we?*

CHAPTER THREE

"So what do you make of our new larva?" Lieutenant Kuramochi Chiyeko asked. The slightly built, dark skinned lieutenant was tilted comfortably back in her chair, nursing a cup of coffee. Gunnery Sergeant Michael Wheaton, her platoon's senior noncom, sat across the paperwork-littered desk from her, sipping from his own battered, much-used coffee mug.

"Um." Wheaton lowered his mug and grimaced. "Gotta admit, Skipper, I wasn't very pleased to see her." He shook his head. "I'm a little happier now Abe's had a chance to look her over, but still—! Things are getting hot, and they're sending us *one* warm body at a time? And a larva straight out of Mackenzie, at that?"

"Take what we can get," Kuramochi said philosophically, but Wheaton's eyes sharpened.

"I know that tone, Skipper," he said, just a trifle suspiciously.

"And what tone would that be, Gunny Wheaton?" Kuramochi's expression was innocence itself.

"That 'I know something you don't know,' tone."

"I don't have the least idea what you're talking about," she asserted.

"Skipper, it's my job to make sure all our round little pegs are neatly fitted into round little holes. If there's something about DeVries I should know, this would be a pretty good time to tell me."

Wheaton's tone was completely reasonable, but he gave his lieutenant a moderately severe look to go with it. Kuramochi Chiyeko had the makings of a superior officer, or she would never have been given a Recon platoon. And she and Wheaton had established a tight, well-oiled working relationship. But she was still only a lieutenant, and one of a gunny's most important jobs was to occasionally, with infinite respect, whack his lieutenant up aside the head with a clue stick.

"You mean aside from whose granddaughter she is?" Kuramochi asked.

"I know all about her grandfather, Skipper. And I know she graduated second overall from Mackenzie. And I know she's got a five-year college degree under her belt when she should still be home shooting marbles, that she's smart as a whip, and that Abe Metternich is impressed with her. None of which changes the fact that she's still a newbie less than eighteen standard years old in a slot she shouldn't have qualified for for at least another standard year. But you already knew I know all of that, so what is it that I *don't* know?"

"Well, I don't actually *know* anything," Kuramochi said. "But take a look at what we've got. As you just pointed out, she's got a five-year degree—from ENC, no less. Plus where she graduated from Mackenzie. *My* record was nowhere near that good, but the Corps was already recruiting me as an officer before I was completely through Basic. And I've looked at her jacket's available profiles, Mike. She's better qualified for a commission, in terms of basic ability, than I am. In fact, she's probably better qualified than at least two-thirds of the Battalion's officers. And, like you say, Recon isn't a slot they normally offer a newbie, no matter how good her Mackenzie performance might have been. And although I've never met Sar'Major O'Shaughnessy, I've heard enough about him to seriously doubt that *he* pulled any strings to get her what she wanted. So, why did they give her to us, and why haven't they started gently suggesting to her that OCS lies in her future?"

"I don't know," Wheaton replied, but he was frowning as he spoke. Then his eyebrows rose. "No way, Skipper!"

"Why not? You know they like to use Recon as the final filter for the selection process."

"Of a Mackenzie *larva*?" Wheaton shook his head. "I dunno, Skip. I've never heard of their even looking at someone who didn't have at least one complete tour under his belt!"

"Maybe not, but I've been trying hard to figure out any other explanation for why we've got her. And like you say, Abe is impressed with her, and he's seen a lot of larvae over the years." Kuramochi shrugged. "Nobody's told me anything officially, of course. They wouldn't. And I don't have access to her complete profile, even if I knew exactly what the selection criteria are. But it's pretty obvious she's a special case—both in terms of native ability and where they sent her for her very first active-duty tour."

"Wonderful," Wheaton said sourly. "You know, Skip, sometimes I get *so* tired of those overly clever . . . professional colleagues of ours. Let them do their own damned recruiting and testing! And leave us—especially Recon—the hell alone. I hate the way they keep skimming off our best people even after they've served their time, but if they're planning on poaching someone *this* early in her career, it really frosts my chops. If you're right, they're gonna give us just long enough to get her trained up right, bring her along nicely, and then they're gonna steal her from us. You wait and see."

"My, my." Kuramochi grinned. "Such heat, Gunny Wheaton!"

"Yeah, right," Wheaton grumbled. "Tell me you won't be just as pissed off as I am if it turns out there's anything to this."

"Of course I won't," Kuramochi said virtuously. "The very idea is ridiculous."

Wheaton snorted, and she chuckled. But then her expression sobered.

"Like I say, Mike, no one's told me anything, and it's entirely possible I'm completely wrong. But I think we—specifically, you and I—need to bear the possibility that I'm *not* wrong in mind. No corner-cutting, no special treatment—God knows, nothing to suggest to her that we think she's anything more than just one more, possibly above average, larva. But anything we can throw at her to give her that little extra edge of experience would be a good idea, I think."

"Understood." Wheaton drank some more coffee, then shrugged. "I may not like the idea of playing schoolmarm for someone besides the Corps, Skipper, but if you're right, then I have to agree. Want me to talk to Abe about it, too?"

"I don't think so." Kuramochi rubbed one eyebrow thoughtfully. "Not yet, anyway. He's going to be too close to her, and we've all got a lot on our minds right now with the local situation. We both know how good he is at bringing newbies along, anyway, so let's not jog his elbow. Let's get her settled in before we suggest to Abe that we may want to keep a special eye on this one."

"Something new from Gyangtse, Boss."

Sir Enobakhare Kereku, Governor of the Martinson Sector in the name of His Imperial Majesty Seamus II, looked up as Patricia Obermeyer, his chief of staff, walked into his office.

"Why," Kereku inquired after a moment, "does that prefatory remark fill my heart with dread?"

"Because you know what an idiot Aubert is?" Obermeyer suggested.

"Maybe. But while you, as a lowly member of the hired help, are casting aspersions upon the capabilities of my less-than-esteemed junior executive colleague, let us not forget the incomparable talent *his* chief of staff has for making things still worse."

"Point taken," Obermeyer said, after a moment, and grimaced. "To be honest, I think Salgado may be even more of a klutz than Aubert. Not that achieving such monumental levels of incompetency is easy, you understand."

"And now that we've both vented, suppose you tell me exactly what new bad news we've got from Gyangtse?"

"It's not actually from Gyangtse itself." Obermeyer crossed the large, luxurious office to lay a chip folio on the corner of Kereku's desk. "Brigadier Erickson's intelligence people handed it to us, as a matter of fact. According to their reports from Major Palacios—which Colonel Ustanov strongly endorses—the situation in Gyangtse is headed straight for the crapper."

"I've always known Wasps were bluntly spoken," Kereku observed with a crooked smile. "'Straight for the crapper' in official correspondence is a bit blunt even for one of them, though, don't you think?"

"I may have taken a few liberties with the exact wording, but I believe the basic sense of the Colonel's comments comes through my own pithy choice of phrase."

"I'm afraid you're probably right about that." Kereku sighed. He looked at the chip folio with a distasteful expression, then back up at Obermeyer, and pointed at a chair. "Go ahead and summarize,

Pat. I'll read the gory details for myself later, assuming I can find time."

"Basically," Obermeyer said, seating herself in the indicated chair, "it's more of the same, only worse. Ustanov is actually pretty careful about his choice of words, trying to avoid any sort of polarization between the military and civilian authorities, I think. But he's strongly behind Palacios on this one, and it's pretty clear—especially comparing Ustanov's dispatches to the last ones we've had from Aubert himself—that Aubert doesn't have a clue about the way things are starting to come apart on him. He thinks he's still completely in control of the situation, Eno. He's consistently playing down the threat of this Gyangtse Liberation Front's open avowal of 'the armed struggle' to drive 'the imperial oppressors from the soil of Gyangtse' as little more than a negotiating ploy. And, despite that, and despite what he and Salgado both know imperial policy has been for centuries now, he's actually *welcomed* Pankarma's 'participation' in the public debate over the Incorporation vote."

The sector governor's chief of staff shook her head, her expression grim.

"He doesn't seem to grasp the fact that the GLF's 'participation' can only be as a voice of opposition. Or that he's talking to criminals as the Emperor's personal, direct representative. Or that the GLF might actually mean what it's saying about armed struggles. I can't tell from here exactly what sort of local contacts and intelligence sources he may have, or think he has, but *Palacios'* sources indicate that weapons are being stockpiled. In fact, she's got some reports of at least a few arms shipments coming in from off-world, maybe even from the Freedom Alliance, although she admits she's been unable to positively confirm that. Despite that, though, her threat assessment is that things are getting steadily—and rapidly—worse. And Ustanov's reported to Erickson—*not* to any of his civilian superiors—that his requests to Aubert for permission to reinforce Palacios and authorize her to take a more . . . proactive stance have been persistently denied."

"So he's keeping it in his own chain of command, trying to avoid any appearance of going over Aubert's head," Kereku mused.

"I think that's exactly what he's doing," Obermeyer agreed. "At the same time, though, he's been expressing himself pretty strongly, for an officer of his seniority, in his 'in-house' reports to Erickson. And Erickson clearly takes his concerns seriously, since he handed Ustanov's *and* Palacios' raw reports over to me without sanitizing them."

"Wonderful."

Kereku's expression was not that of a happy man. The fact that the team of Jasper Aubert and Ákos Salgado probably would have had trouble zipping its own shoes under the best of circumstances—which these weren't—only made a bad situation worse. The Terran League and the old Federation had never seen eye to eye, even before the Rish got involved. The League had originated in the off-world migration of primarily Asian peoples who had resented the "Western" biases of Old Earth's immediately pre-space first-world cultural template, especially in light of how much of the home world's population had been Asian. The fact that the Asian Alliance had lost the last major war fought on the mother world's soil had only made that resentment still worse, although the sharpest edges had finally begun to fade . . . before the Rish came on the scene.

But after more than a century of careful manipulation by the Rish-athan Sphere, followed by sixty more years of bloody warfare, the bitter resentment many citizens of the ex-League planets felt towards the Empire had attained a virulence which persisted with religious fervor. The sort of fervor which was far, far easier to create than it could ever be to overcome. A point which certain individuals—like one Jasper Aubert—seemed capable of missing completely.

Obermeyer watched his expression for several seconds, then sat forward in her chair.

"Governor," she said, with unusual formality when just the two of them were present, "we've *got* to get rid of Aubert. I sometimes think that if we could just get rid of Salgado, we might be able to get through to Aubert—whatever he may *act* like, he's not a total idiot. But Salgado's been 'managing' him for so long that he might as well have the brains of a carrot. By this time, he and Salgado're like Siamese twins. Where one goes, the other automatically follows, and we can't afford anyone out here who's as persistently blind to reality as they are. Not any longer.

"I think Gyangtse really is just about ready to move over to Incorporated status. Mind you, I don't think the local oligarchs realize just how bad a deal that's going to be in terms of their ability to control the folks they've been exploiting for so long, but it did look like the climate was just about ripe to carry the referendum when Aubert was sent out here.

"But that very fact was what lit a fire under Pankarma and his extremists. They were afraid that *this* time their friends and neighbors really were going to vote to become full subjects of the Empire, and they didn't like that idea one little bit. So they decided to do something about it, and their appeals to the Gyangtsese poor—especially the urban poor—have fallen on some fairly fertile ground. Class resentment and wondering how the hell you're going to feed your family will provide that, especially if the propagandists know how to use them. Which is a pity, since the people Incorporation would help *most* would be that same urban poor, if they only realized it.

"That would be bad enough, but Aubert's decisions are making the situation incomparably worse. I know it's hard to conceive of any mistakes he could make that he hasn't already made, but I'm sure he'll be able to come up with some more if we just give him time. And we both know Salgado's too busy being 'pragmatic' and practicing '*real politik*' to rescue him from himself. Hell, he's probably out inventing brand new mistakes for Aubert to make! I don't think the situation on Gyangtse is past the point of no return yet, but between the two of them, they're going to push it there—or let the GLF do it—and I don't think either one of them has the least clue of just how much trouble they're headed into."

"I know, I know." Kereku ran a hand through his tightly curled silver hair. "Unfortunately, the only way to get rid of Salgado is to dump Aubert, and I can't get rid of Aubert on my own authority. His appointment came directly from the Ministry, the same way mine did. And it was confirmed by the Senate, the same way mine was. The *Emperor* could get away with removing him on his own authority, but I can't. And if I tried . . ."

Obermeyer nodded unhappily. Enobakhare Kereku had been selected to govern one of the Empire's crown sectors—the frontier sectors, most of whose planets had yet to attain Incorporated World status and senatorial representation, and which thus came under the administration of the Ministry of Out-World Affairs—because he'd amply demonstrated his qualifications for the position. Jasper Aubert had been selected as a planetary governor in that same crown sector solely because of his political connections, however. And, she suspected in her darker moments, as a means of getting him safely off Old Earth and away from any *important* policymaking position. Which was all very well for Old Earth, but left Kereku with a hell of a problem in his sector. And as Kereku had just more or less observed, a sector governor who started doing little things like firing Senate-approved appointees on his own authority would not remain in his position long. But still. . . .

"If we can't get rid of him, then we'd better start getting ready for things to go from bad to worse on Gyangtse," she said gloomily.

"Ustanov is suggesting that there's been a genuinely significant buildup in weapons by the GLF?"

"Yes." Obermeyer's tone was flat. "So far he's had reports primarily of small arms, but there are persistent rumors, from what Palacios' intelligence people consider reliable sources, that at least some crew-served weapons are already in place. We're close enough to the frontier that all sorts of people can slip through unnoticed, and Palacios says that she thinks the GLF's been in touch with the Freedom Alliance."

Kereku grimaced at that; the so-called Freedom Alliance was the most persistent, and dangerous, interstellar umbrella organization devoted to supporting "planetary liberation" movements within the Empire.

"Palacios doesn't know for certain that the weapons are actually coming from the Alliance," Obermeyer continued, "but she's sure they're there. And that others are in the pipeline. And," she added even more flatly, "reading between the lines, Palacios is pretty damned worried that the local authorities—civilian and planetary militia both—are persistently disregarding and discounting the sources *her* people are tapping."

"Damn." Kereku's jaw tightened, and he shook his head. "What exactly does Ustanov have on-planet? And available for quick reinforcement out of his own resources?"

"That," Obermeyer admitted, "I don't really know. Not positively. I know he's got his reconnaissance battalion actually on the planet. Those are the only troops, aside from the planetary militia, we have in-system. The rest of his regiment, which is at least a little understrength—they always are, aren't they?—is split into battalion-sized detachments covering not just Gyangtse but also Matterhorn and Sangamon. That leaves him, at best, one battalion in reserve, and he's headquartered in Matterhorn, over a week away from Gyangtse. As for additional supports, my impression is that the Fleet's presence in Gyangtse is limited, at best, and the planetary militia—especially its leadership—doesn't appear to produce a great deal of confidence in him or Palacios. For that matter, Ustanov would be stretched awful thin trying to keep a lid on an entire planet, if something does go wrong in a big way, even if he had everything already on the planet and all of his battalions were technically at full strength."

Kereku nodded. A full strength Marine line regiment, exclusive of attached transport and artillery, had a roster strength of just over forty-two hundred. Its reconnaissance battalion, on the other hand, had a nominal strength of just under one thousand. That wasn't a lot of warm bodies, even with Marine training and first-line equipment, to cover a planet with a population of almost two billion.

"The problem, of course, is whether or not we want to reinforce him," the sector governor observed. "Or possibly just authorize him to redeploy. He could at least get his reserve into Gyangtse if we gave him the discretion to put it there. But if we send in more troops, then we risk making the locals even more antsy than they already are, especially the hotheads who already regard us as foreign occupiers. That's not the way to encourage them to vote in favor of Incorporation. Worse, the additional manpower might actually make Aubert feel more confident, give him a sense of additional strength."

"But if we *don't* reinforce Palacios, and if it does hit the fan, then it's going to take Ustanov at least two weeks to get any support to Palacios—and we'll need at least another month to get Ustanov additional backup," Obermeyer pointed out.

"Agreed." Kereku nodded, lips pursed. He stayed that way for several seconds, then brought his chair back fully upright with an air of decision.

"We can't put any more warm bodies into Gyangtse," he said. "Not yet. But I want to do three things.

"First, sit down with Erickson. I want him to plan now for an immediate redeployment to support Ustanov if the situation comes apart. I want graduated options. On the low end, I want plans to send in an additional peacekeeping presence—maybe another battalion, a company or so of military police, some additional air assets, that sort of thing—direct to Gyangtse to back Palacios up against low-level incidents. On the upper end, I want plans for a full-scale reinforcement designed to handle a general guerrilla movement on the part of the GLF, maybe with FALA involvement, as well." The FALA—the Freedom Alliance Liberation Army—was the so-called Alliance's operational wing, and its members were among the galaxy's more proficient terrorists. "But tell Erickson that I very definitely do *not* want the knowledge that we're considering reinforcing to leak out. Specifically, I don't want Aubert or Salgado to know a thing about it, although Erickson can inform Ustanov, for his personal and confidential information, about what we're working on.

"Second, I think I need to get on the starcom and 'counsel' Aubert on his situation. I'll want to think about exactly what I say to him, and how I say it, and I'd like *you* to be thinking about that, as well. I want to talk to him within the next twenty-four hours and see if we can't find some way to make him at least a little bit aware of his situation.

"Third," Kereku's face hardened, "I need to draft a formal request for Aubert's recall and get it starcommed to the Ministry. And I want to do that within the next *twelve* hours."

"Eno, I know I'm the one who just said we have to get rid of him," Obermeyer said after a moment, "but he really does have some influential patrons at Court."

"I have a few friends of my own, Pat, especially in the Ministry. I may not have his clout in the *Senate*, but the Earl—" Allen Malloy, the Earl of Stanhope, was the Minister of Out-World Affairs "—trusts my judgment. He also has direct access to the Emperor, and he doesn't want the situation to blow up out here anymore than you and I do."

"I know that. But he—and the Emperor—both have a lot of balls in the air simultaneously. I'm sure you're right that neither of them wants to see some sort of bloodbath out here, or even a low-level insurrection that's no more than moderately messy. God knows how long something like that would hang up Gyangtse's eventual Incorporation! And that doesn't even include all the people who might get themselves hurt or killed in the process. But the dynamic they're going to be looking at back on Old Earth isn't going to be the same one we're looking at here in Martinsen. There's a reason they shoved Aubert out to the backside of nowhere in the first place, and that same reason may make them want to go ahead and leave him here. And if you strongly recommend his recall, Aubert's patrons are probably going to hear about it, whether the Emperor acts on it or not."

"Maybe. And Gyangtse may be the 'backside of nowhere.' But there are still two billion people on the planet, it's still an imperial possession, and we've still got a responsibility to the people living there. Not to mention the fact that imperial policy on League separatism is perfectly clear and not subject to renegotiation. If we don't get Aubert out of here, he's going to create a situation in which it's going to be *my* responsibility to demonstrate that point to the people on Gyangtse, and I'd just as soon not be forced into the position of spanking the baby with an ax."

"Yes, Sir," Obermeyer said quietly, and he nodded to her.

"Good. Go get Erickson started on that preliminary planning. Then pull all of our interoffice memos on Aubert and Gyangtse for the last, oh, year or so. Bring them back over here, once you've got them all pulled together, and you and I will spend a couple of delightful hours putting together our best case for getting his sorry ass fired."

"—and *Governor* Aubert suggested that we all go piss up a rope," Namkha Pasang Pankarma snarled.

The founder and self-elected leader of the Gyangtse Liberation Front had never been noted for his fondness for the Terran Empire. At the moment, however, his normally impassive expression had been replaced by a mask of fury. Ang Jangmu Thaktu, his senior adviser, had seen that expression from him more often than most of his followers, but that didn't make her any happier to see it at this particular moment.

"Namkha Pasang," she said, "that doesn't sound like Aubert's usual style to me." Her tone and manner were both much firmer than most of Pankarma's followers would have been prepared to show him, especially when he was obviously so angry, but she met his irate glare calmly.

"I know he's an unmitigated pain in the ass," she continued. "Even more so than most Empies. But one of the problems I've always had with him is the way he talks his way around problems instead of addressing them directly. Personally, I've always suspected that what he's really got in mind is just to keep us talking long enough to keep us out of the field until after the Incorporation vote. Either he's spinning things out to accomplish that, or else he really is a complete and total idiot. Or maybe it's a combination of the two. Either way, I've never heard him say anything quite that . . . direct."

"It's what he meant, whatever he may have *said*!" Pankarma shot back.

"That may be true. But if we're going to expect our people to follow our lead, we've got to be certain that what we tell them about our contacts with Aubert and his people doesn't get dismissed as exaggeration," Thaktu said firmly. "We can interpret all we want to, but we've got to give them the original text the same way it was given to us."

Pankarma's glare intensified, and she shrugged.

"Sooner or later what he actually said—his exact words, I mean, not what he may really have meant—is going to get out. Better that our people should hear those words from us, and not start to wonder if we've been . . . embroidering all along."

"All right," Pankarma said finally. He inhaled deeply, then let the air out explosively. "All right," he repeated. "You're right. I know that. But he just pisses me off with that sanctimonious, oh-so-civilized, nose-in-the-air attitude of his."

"Namkha, he'd piss *you* off no matter what his attitude was," Thaktu replied, smiling at him at last. "Admit it. You've never met an Empie yet that you didn't hate on sight."

"Maybe. All right," Pankarma actually chuckled, "certainly. But he's a special case, even for an Empie." The Liberation Front's leader shook his head. "At any rate, he did agree to sit down and 'discuss my position' with me again. But that was as far as it went. He's ready to 'discuss' till the sun goes nova, but he's not about to meet any of our demands. He's not even willing to come halfway! Basically, we can talk all we want, but in the end, we're going to go right on doing things *his* way."

"To be fair—which I don't want to be any more than you do—he may not have a lot of wiggle room," Thaktu observed. "The Empies' fundamental policy towards people like us is pretty well established, after all."

"But there's always been some room for local adjustments, Ang Jangmu," Pankarma argued. "He could modify the more objectionable aspects of his own policies if he really wanted to!"

"Probably," Thaktu allowed. "But Out-World Affairs has to sign off on that, even if it's only by looking the other way, and the Ministry won't do it unless the local governor convinces his boss that he's not going to get a vote in favor of Incorporation anytime soon."

"Exactly," Pankarma growled. "It's how they try to bribe the poor benighted locals into voting in favor next time around. Getting them to do that in our case is the whole point of the Movement!"

Thaktu nodded. Despite the fact that she was the senior of the dozen or so GLF leaders who'd gone off-world for training under the FALA's auspices, she didn't actually share Pankarma's belief that they could ultimately convince the Terran Empire that Gyangtse was enough more trouble than it was worth for it to simply go away and leave them alone. Whatever the Freedom Alliance might think it could ultimately accomplish, that simply wasn't going to happen. But if the GLF and its adherents could produce enough resistance to Incorporation, they might at least be able to win enough concessions to prevent the total disappearance of their traditional way of life and liberties into the Empire's voracious maw.

"From what you're saying," she said, after a moment, "Aubert made it pretty clear he doesn't intend to give any ground at all, right?"

"I think you might say that," Pankarma agreed in a tone of massive understatement. "From what I can see, he expects the Incorporation referendum to pass this time. Which means there's not a chance in hell of our ever getting our independence back, as far as he's concerned. And there's sure as hell not any reason for him to ask his own masters to let him grant us any greater local autonomy as a Crown World if he thinks we're all about to vote to become good little helots living on an *Incorporated* World."

"Well," Thaktu said, her expression suddenly darker, "I suppose that means it's time we decided just how far we're really prepared to go to change his mind about us, isn't it?"

CHAPTER FOUR

"I don't think this is exactly what the mission planners had in mind, Leo," Alicia said, looking out across the rugged valley.

"Sure it was," Medrano said with a slow grin. The thickset PFC lay comfortably on his back, head pillowed on his backpack, chewing on a strand of the local ecosystem's tough alpine grass. Gyangtse was a mountainous planet, the river valley below them was high in those mountains, and their present perch was almost two hundred meters above the valley floor. That put it high enough that Alicia's lungs felt a bit tight, even after two weeks of acclimating morning runs, as they labored to provide her with sufficient oxygen, but it also gave them an outstanding field of view.

"I thought we were supposed to be pretending to be guerrillas," Alicia said, looking over her shoulder at him.

"Which we are," Medrano said virtuously, and waved one hand at Gregory Hilton, Bravo Team's senior rifleman. "Tell our larva we're being good guerrillas, Greg."

"We're being good guerrillas," Hilton said obediently, turning his head to grin at Alicia.

"With *plasma rifles*?" Alicia raised one eyebrow skeptically, and Hilton chuckled.

"Hey, I'm not in charge—he is!" he said, and jabbed his thumb at the reclining Medrano.

A rifle squad normally consisted of thirteen Marines, divided into two fire teams, each built around a plasma rifle, a grenadier, and three riflemen, all under its own corporal, and a sergeant to command the squad. At the moment, Third Squad was still three warm bodies understrength. Alicia's arrival had brought Bravo Team's riflemen up to strength, but Alpha Team was short a grenadier, and Sergeant Metternich was also short one corporal. Which was why Medrano, as Bravo Team's plasma gunner, was filling in as the team leader.

"Anything worth doing is worth doing well," Medrano said now, with a grin.

Alicia looked at him, still more than a little dubious, but she decided it was time to keep her mouth shut. Despite the degree of good-natured grief the rest of her squad had visited upon her as part of the initiation process, Sergeant Metternich—and Medrano—had proved quite approachable. At the same time, she was the newest newbie imaginable, all too well aware that she was grossly inexperienced compared to all of her fellows.

Medrano watched her expression, then sat up with a sigh.

"Look, Larva," he said patiently, "you were there when the militia got their brief on what's supposed to happen today, right?" Alicia nodded, and he shrugged. "Did they strike you as real competent?"

"Well . . ."

"What I thought," Medrano snorted. "Overconfident, undertrained, thickheaded 'weekend warriors,' right?"

"I'm sure they do the best they can with the training time available," Alicia replied, but she heard the edge of excuse-making in her own voice, and Hilton and the other Marines on the position with her chuckled harshly.

"You really are fresh out of Mackenzie, aren't you?" Frinkelo Zigair, the team's grenadier said, shaking his head. There was a tiny edge in Zigair's voice—he had the most cantankerous disposition of anyone in the squad, and he also seemed most aware of Alicia's total lack of field experience—but this time it seemed directed less at her than at someone else.

"There's militia, and then there's militia, Larva," the grenadier continued. "Some of 'em are pretty damned good, better'n most Wasps I've served with, really. Others, well, you wouldn't want *them* trying to take on a good troop of Imperial Cub Scouts. This bunch," he jerked his head in the general direction of the valley below them, "would have trouble just *finding* the Scouts."

Alicia felt that she ought to say something in the militia's defense, if only because of how strongly her instructors at Mackenzie had stressed the importance of planetary militias in the self-defense scheme of the Empire. Unfortunately, Zigair's scathing evaluation tracked entirely too well with her own observations here on Gyangtse.

"The truth is, Alley," César Bergerat, Bravo Team's other rifleman, said, "that Frinkelo's probably right. These people are pretty damned pathetic. Worse, I don't think they know they are."

"Hard to blame them for that," Hilton put in. The others looked at him, and he shrugged. "Oh, you and Frinkelo're both right, César. But given how dirt poor these people are, and how unpopular the Empire is with some of them right now, the militia's not really what you'd call motivated, is it?"

"And it gets shitty equipment and a training budget that wouldn't buy e-rats for a family of gnats," Medrano agreed. He shook his head. "Lots of reasons for it, and I'm not looking to kick any of them—well, not *most* of 'em, anyway—for how bad the situation is. But the point, Alley, is that their people, starting with their officers and working down, really need to get themselves shaken up enough to realize just how bad it is. That's why we're up here, waiting for them."

Alicia sat back on her heels and thought about what they'd just said. She didn't notice the approving light in Medrano's eye as she engaged her mind to consider the new information before running her mouth further. She pondered for several seconds, then looked back at the acting team leader.

"So you're saying that what *they* heard at the briefing and what *we* heard at the briefing wasn't exactly the same thing?"

"Give the larva the big brass ring," Zigair said, and this time his tone held only approval.

"Exactly," Medrano said, without mentioning that he was relatively certain Bravo Team had caught this particular portion of the squad's assignment because Abe Metternich had wanted her, specifically, to see how it really worked.

"The militia's gonna scream when it comes down," he continued. "But when they start raising hell, the lieutenant's gonna be able to say they were warned the 'guerrillas' might have 'military-grade' small arms. 'S not *her* fault if they figured that meant just combat rifles, because technically, even this—" he reached out and patted his long, heavy plasma rifle comfortably "—ain't *officially* a heavy weapon by the Corps' standards. Too bad if they didn't think about that ahead of time."

"And at least we're not in powered armor," Hilton pointed out with a virtuous air. "After all, no wicked bunch of terrorists is going to have access to *that*, and we've got to play fair with them, don't we?"

"Of course, like Leo says, they can't hold us responsible for their own misinterpretation of the original mission brief. For that matter," Bergerat said, grinning wickedly, "if they happen to've jumped to the conclusion that *all* the nasty old guerrillas have to be out here in front of them somewhere, instead of back in Zhikotse, then that's their problem, too."

"But there's more to it, isn't there?" Alicia said, still frowning thoughtfully. "Lieutenant Kuramochi wants them to get hammered, not just to lose, doesn't she?"

"She never actually said that," Medrano said, "and neither did Abe. But I think it's pretty clear the militia's been giving itself basically 'gimme' exercises for quite a while now. One of the problems with a lot of militias, when you get down to it. They don't seem to realize you learn more from losing than you do from easy wins. Well, they're gonna learn a *lot* this afternoon."

"Well, isn't *this* a lot of fun," Captain Karsang Dawa Chiawa, commanding officer, Alpha Company, First Capital Regiment, Gyangtse Planetary Militia, muttered balefully as he watched his lead platoon slogging along the constricted valley's rugged floor.

It was remarkable. The bare, tumbled rocks—none of them particularly huge—which the spring floods had left strewn about were more than enough to make this hike thoroughly unpleasant, yet they offered absolutely no effective cover. And, of course, the chilly, damp weather of the last few weeks had left the ground suitably soupy and mucky.

Personally, Captain Chiawa could have thought of dozens of things he'd rather be spending one of his precious days off doing.

"Whose idea was this, anyway?" a voice asked, and Chiawa looked at the militia lieutenant standing beside him. Like Chiawa himself, Tsimbuti Pemba Salaka, Chiawa's senior platoon commander, was a self-employed businessman. In Salaka's case, that amounted to partnerships in and partial ownership of half a dozen of Zhikotse's grocery stores.

"Colonel Sharwa's," Chiawa replied, and Salaka rolled his eyes. Ang Chirgan Sharwa was one of the capital city's wealthiest men—in fact, by Gyangtse's standards, he was almost obscenely rich—and a well-established member of the Gyangtsese political elite. Unlike Chiawa, he enjoyed a position of great status and political and economic power, and he regarded his post as second in command of the planetary militia as both the guarantor of that power and a proof of his natural and inevitable importance. It also put him in a position to toady properly to Lobsang Phurba Jongdomba—*Brigadier* Jongdomba, the militia's planetary commander—who was probably one of the dozen or so wealthiest men on the planet. Chiawa knew Jongdomba had found lots of ways to profit from his militia position (as Sharwa probably had, as well), but the Brigadier was still one of the biggest political fish on the planet, and Sharwa never missed an opportunity to suck up to him.

None of which, however, meant that a busy man like Sharwa had enough time to waste any of it actually getting his own boots muddy, of course. Which didn't prevent him from putting the *rest* of the militia out into the mud whenever it crossed his mind.

"Why am I not surprised it was the Colonel's brainstorm?" Salaka said dryly, and Chiawa chuckled. He couldn't really fault Sharwa in at least one respect—*he* didn't have the time to waste out here, either. Especially not with the way the GLF's economic boycotts were beginning to hammer the business community even harder. In fact, he was seriously considering resigning his militia commission in order to pay more attention to his own two-man engineering consulting firm. If it weren't for his nagging concern that those idiots in the GLF might actually *mean* some of the lunatic things they were saying, he probably would have sent in his papers already. As it was, though . . .

"Bravo, Alpha," a voice said quietly, sounding clear and composed over the com speaker implanted in Alicia's mastoid as she lay at the edge of Bravo Team's prepared position.

"Alpha, Bravo," Medrano replied. "Go."

"Bravo, be advised the target is just passing Alpha's position. it should be entering your engagement range in about two hours. Map coordinates Baker-Charlie-Seven-Niner-Zero, Québec-X-ray-Zero-Four-Two."

"Alpha, Bravo copies. Coordinates Baker-Charlie-Seven-Niner-Zero, Québec-X-ray-Zero-Four-Two."

"Confirm copy. Expect visual contact within one-five mikes."

"Alpha, Bravo copies visual contact in approximately fifteen minutes."

"Confirm copy," Sergeant Metternich repeated. "Alpha is moving now. Repeat, Alpha is moving now. Alpha, clear."

Alicia turned her head, looking to the left and the eastern end of the valley. She could see a long way from up here, despite the valley's narrowness, and she brought up her sensory boosters.

She hadn't counted on how . . . uncomfortable the surgery to implant the standard Marine enhancement package would be. In fact, it had been more like physical therapy for a recovering accident victim than anything she would have thought of as "training" before she actually experienced it. But she'd made up for that by the speed with which she'd adjusted to the new abilities once she was out of the medics' hands and free to start training. And she wasn't about to complain about the downtime for the recovery—not when she could see with the acuity of a really good pair of light-gathering binoculars, even without her helmet's sensors, just by triggering the right command sequence in her implanted processor. She supposed she shouldn't be using her augmentation, either, since the exercise parameters had specifically denied the "guerillas" the use of their helmet systems, but she figured no one was going to squash her like a bug for it.

Hopefully.

The distant terrain snapped into glassy-clear focus. Nothing at all happened for quite some time, and then she spotted a flicker of motion.

"I've got movement," she reported over the fire team's tactical net.

"And who might you be?" Leocadio Medrano's voice came back dryly, and she blushed fiery red.

"Ah, Bravo-One, this is Bravo-Five," she said, thanking God that no one else was in a position to see her flaming face. "I have motion at two-eight-five. Range—" she consulted the ranging hash marks superimposed on her augmented vision "—eleven klicks."

"One, Two," Frinkelo Zigair said quietly. "Confirm sighting."

"Acknowledged," Medrano said. Alicia heard the quiet scrape and slither as the plasma gunner moved closer to the edge of their perch. He was silent for several seconds, obviously studying the situation. Then he came back up over the fire team's net.

"One has eyes on the target," he confirmed. "Looks like they're coming along right where we expected them, people. I'd say another ninety minutes or so, given how slowly they're moving. Four."

"Four," César Bergerat acknowledged.

"I think you'll have the best line of sight. When they get here, you'll be on the detonator."

"Four confirms. I have the detonator."

"Three, since they're coming in from the east this way, you and Five have perimeter security. Move to the gamma position now."

"One, Three confirms," Gregory Hilton replied. "Moving to gamma."

Hilton reached up and slapped Alicia on the back of her left heel. She nodded sharply and wiggled back from her position at the lip of their perch, careful to stay down and avoid silhouetting herself against the gray, drizzling sky or making any movement which might be spotted from below. Then she turned to follow him at a brisk, crouching trot to the previously prepared secondary position which had been carefully placed to cover the only practical access route from the valley floor to the fire team's primary position.

They reached it in just over ten minutes and settled down into the carefully camouflaged holes. Alicia's Camp Mackenzie instructors would have been delighted with the field of fire they had, and she'd been impressed by how carefully Medrano had insisted that they camouflage their positions. She was sure quite a few people would have been prepared to take a certain liberty, given the capabilities of the Corps' reactive chameleon camouflage and the knowledge that they were up against only a planetary militia—and not a particularly good one, at that—in a mere training exercise. Leocadio Medrano didn't appear to think that way, however, and for whatever a mere "larva's" opinion might be worth, she approved wholeheartedly.

"One, Three. Three and Five are in position at gamma," Hilton reported, even as his hands ejected the magazine from his M-97 combat rifle and attached the four hundred-round box of belted training ammunition in its place.

Alicia opened a second ammo box, but she didn't attach it to her own weapon. Hilton was the heavy fire element, but attaching the weight of the bulky ammunition box to transform his combat rifle into what amounted to a light machine gun cost it a certain handiness. It was Alicia's job to watch their flanks while he dealt with laying concentrated fire where it was needed. If necessary, she could quickly attach the second ammo box to her own weapon; otherwise, it would simply be ready for Hilton to reload a bit faster.

"Three, One confirms," Medrano replied over the net. "Now everybody just sit tight."

"Any sign of them at all, Sergeant?" Captain Chiawa asked, looking around a valley which had gotten only rockier, muddier, more barren, and colder over the last several hours.

"Nothing, Karsang Dawa," Sergeant Nursamden Nyima Lakshindo replied, and Chiawa hid a scowl. Lakshindo's casual attitude was—unfortunately, Chiawa often thought—the rule, rather than the exception among the personnel of Gyangtse's militia. In civilian life (which was to say for ninety-nine percent of his time), the sergeant was a pretty fair computer draftsman. In fact, he worked for Chiawa's consulting business. That had certain advantages in terms of their working relationship in the militia, but it made it difficult to maintain anything remotely like proper military discipline.

"Unless they decided just to skip the exercise after all," Lieutenant Salaka offered, "they've got to be somewhere in the next ten klicks."

"Maybe." Chiawa scratched his chin thoughtfully, eyes slitted as he peered up the valley. The sun was settling steadily towards the western horizon as the day limped towards late afternoon, and he had to squint into its brightness.

"What do you mean, maybe?" Salaka asked. "We're supposed to be pursuing a bunch of guerrillas ready to turn on us, aren't we?"

"That's what the Colonel said," Chiawa agreed. "On the other hand, according to the mission brief, the 'guerrillas' we're chasing are supposed to've wanted to take out a target somewhere in Zhikotse before they were 'spotted' and had to run for it. And Wasps are supposed to be sneaky, right?"

"So?" Salaka looked puzzled, and Chiawa snorted.

"So suppose they've actually been planning on carrying out an 'attack' in the capital all along?"

"But that's not what we were briefed for," Salaka protested.

"So what? You know Major Palacios has been hinting for weeks that our training scenarios haven't really been realistic. Suppose she decided to do something about that? These 'guerrillas' we're supposed to be chasing could have found some place to drop out of sight and hide while we went floundering past them. They *could* be three-quarters of the way back to town by now to carry out their 'attack' while we're still wandering around in the boonies looking for them."

"But that's not how the exercise is supposed to work," Salaka pointed out again in a tone which hovered somewhere between incredulous and affronted at Chiawa's suggestion.

"No, it isn't," Chiawa agreed, suppressing an ignoble desire to point out that that was exactly what *he'd* just said. He stood a moment longer, drumming on his thigh with the fingers of his right hand while he thought. Then he waved his radioman closer.

Unlike the Marines, the militia's older, less sophisticated individual communication equipment lacked the range to punch a signal reliably off one of Gyangtse's communications satellites, especially out here in the mountains. That took the larger, heavier backpack unit the radioman got to lug around, and Chiawa gave the sweating, tired youngster a faint smile of sympathy as he reached for the microphone and the radio's directional antenna deployed and locked onto one of the satellites.

"Base, this is Scout One."

There was no answer, and Chiawa scowled.

"Base, this is Scout One," he repeated after two or three seconds.

Eight repetitions later, someone finally replied.

"Scout One, Base," a bored voice said. "What can we do for you, Captain?"

"Base, I'd like to speak to the Colonel, please."

"I'm afraid Colonel Sharwa isn't back from lunch yet, Captain," another, much crisper voice said. "This is Major Cusherwa."

Chiawa rolled his eyes heavenward and inhaled deeply, wondering why he wasn't more surprised to hear that Sharwa was still off stuffing his face somewhere.

"Major," he said, once he was confident he had control of his voice, "I've just had a nasty thought. We've had zero contact so far. No sign of them anywhere. I'm beginning to wonder if maybe they slipped back past us, in which case they could be headed for whatever their target in the capital was in the first place."

"That *is* a nasty thought," the major said, and his voice was thoughtful, not dismissive.

Despite the fact that he was only one of three majors in Sharwa's regiment, and the most junior of them, at that, everybody knew that Ang Chembal Cusherwa was the person who really did the colonel's work. It was unfortunate that the bookish major—Cusherwa was a voracious reader and a pretty good self-taught historian—didn't have the authority to cut Sharwa completely out of the circuit, in which case things might actually have gotten accomplished.

"Have you seen any evidence to suggest that that's what happened?" Cusherwa asked after a moment.

"No," Chiawa admitted. "But we haven't seen *anything*, either. And we're getting close to the end of the exercise's scheduled time block. I'm thinking about the fact that Major Palacios mentioned in passing that too slavish an attitude towards expectations can bite you on the butt even in a training exercise."

"I see." Cusherwa was silent for another few seconds. Then, "I hope you're just being paranoid. On the off-chance that you aren't, I'm going to go to Red status on our patrol elements in the city. Meanwhile, complete your sweep as quickly as you can and get back here."

"Understood. Scout One, clear."

Chiawa returned the microphone to the radioman and looked at Salaka and Lakshindo.

"You heard the Major," he said. "Let's get these people back into motion."

* * *

"Do those guys look just a little more suspicious to you, Sarge?" Evita Johansson asked wryly.

"I think they look like they're *trying* to be a little more suspicious," Sergeant Abraham Metternich replied. "If I thought they could find their asses with both hands, I'd be a little concerned about it, too," he continued. "But look at them."

"Be nice, Sarge," Corporal Sandusky said. "Remember, we're guests on their planet."

Sandusky, the leader of Third Squad's Fire Team Alpha, had a gift for verbal impersonations, and he sounded exactly like one of the narrators from a Corps training holovid, or from one of the travelogues the Imperial Astrographic Society produced. The other members of his team chuckled appreciatively, but none of them disagreed with Metternich's assessment.

The three militiamen who had occasioned Johansson's comment were at least out of their vehicle, standing on the corner and looking up and down the street. The last time Colonel Sharwa's regiment had carried out what it fondly described as a "security readiness exercise" here in the capital, most of the teams assigned to the street checkpoints had stayed parked comfortably on their posteriors in their troop carriers. Metternich suspected that most of them had seen the "exercise" primarily as an opportunity to catch a little extra sleep, although he was aware that his disgust for the militia's senior officers might be coloring his interpretation of their subordinates' actions and attitudes, as well.

Be that as it might, this time around the militia infantry, in their unpowered body armor, were out in the open air, positioned to give themselves clear sightlines up and down the street. This particular checkpoint was in the heart of the business district, on one of Zhikotse's major downtown traffic arteries, not the twisting, narrow streets and alleys which served so much of the city. That meant the militiamen could see quite a ways, which probably gave them a heightened sense of security. But that very sense of security translated into a casual attitude. They were out where they were supposed to be, and they were going through the motions of doing what they were supposed to be doing, and yet it was obvious from their body language that their minds weren't fully engaged on the task in hand. Their rifles were slung, two of them had their hands in their pockets, and none of them exuded any sense of urgency at all.

"Think they'll stop us?" Johansson asked. The private was at the wheel of the civilian delivery van Metternich had appropriated to transport his first fire team into the city. Her question was well taken, but she knew better than to do anything which might draw attention to them—like slowing down—and she continued to approach the militiamen at a steady forty kilometers per hour.

"Tossup," Metternich said, with a shrug, from his position in the passenger seat. He looked back over his shoulder. "If we have to take them, make it quick," he told the rest of the team, and Sandusky nodded.

Like all of the other members of Metternich's team, the corporal sitting on the floor of a cargo compartment wore *militia* fatigues, not the Marine' chameleon battle dress and body armor. Given the fact that Gyangtse's population was even more genetically homogenous than that of most of the old League worlds, only Johansson looked very much like a local. Certainly no one was going to mistake any of the *rest* of Third Squad's people for natives if they bothered to really look at them! But even competent people had a tendency to see what they expected to see, and these yahoos weren't exactly poster children for We Are Competent, Inc. Thus the militia fatigues.

Of course, if the checkpoint actually stopped the van and looked inside it, they would certainly realize what was happening. Except, equally of course, for Sandusky. His posture would have deceived anyone who didn't know him well into believing he truly was as relaxed as his expression looked. Metternich knew better. The silenced M-97 in the corporal's lap was ready to "neutralize" the militia checkpoint in a heartbeat if it proved necessary.

But it didn't. One of the militiamen looked up as Johansson turned the corner right in front of them. The local's expression was bored, and he waved her on around the corner with little more than a glance at her fatigues. It was obvious that the thought of checking her ID or asking her where she was going had never even occurred to him, and while Metternich was grateful for the way it simplified his own life, that didn't keep him from shaking his head in disgust.

"Now *that* was what I call slack, Sarge," Johansson said sourly, and Metternich shrugged.

"Can't argue that one, Evita. I guess they're busy looking for us to come sneaking in on foot or something. I mean, after all, where could we possibly lay our hands on a vehicle, instead?"

"Then God help us if the GLF gets serious," Johansson muttered.

"All Bravos, One," Medrano said quietly over the net. "Standby to execute . . . *Now!*"

César Bergerat pressed the button on the detonator, and the flash-bangs the fire team had carefully planted amid the tumbled rocks below popped up head-high on their pogo charges and erupted in brilliant, blinding flashes and abrupt thunderclaps of sound. The radio transmissions they sent out simultaneously activated the sensors on the Marine training harnesses Major Palacios had distributed to the militia for the exercise, and visual alarms flashed brilliant amber as well over a third of Captain Chiawa's company became instant "casualties."

"*Shit!*"

Karsang Dawa Chiawa didn't know exactly who the strangled shout came from, but it summed up his own feelings quite nicely. He'd seen flash-bangs detonate on training exercises before, but only in ones and twos. He'd never been this close to a *dozen* of them, all going off at once, and the paralyzing effect of the sudden visual and audio assault was far worse than he'd ever realized it could be.

Then he saw the flashing lights as the training harnesses reacted to the lethal patterns of pellets the old-fashioned claymore-style mines the flash-bangs were pretending to be would have sent out in real life.

"Cover!" he shouted. "Get everyone under cover before—"

"Ouch," Gregory Hilton said mildly, watching the chaos into which the leading half of the militia company had abruptly disintegrated. "*That's* going to leave a bruise," he added in tones of profound professional satisfaction.

Alicia nodded in agreement, watching the hapless militia bumbling about. At least half of the people whose harnesses were telling them they'd just become casualties seemed too stunned and confused even to realize they were supposed to sit down and play dead.

They got the message a moment later, though. She could see the instant at which the training harnesses' built-in processors realized their wearers weren't responding properly and activated the tingler circuits. People twitched as the harmless but *most* unpleasant neural stimulators reminded the "casualties" that they had abruptly become deceased. Alicia had experienced the same sensation—once—in a training exercise at Mackenzie. Once was all it had taken for her to resolve to *never* ignore the initial warning signals from her own training harness, and she winced in sympathy as the militia men dropped their weapons and sat down abruptly.

"My, my," Hilton murmured. "I wonder if they're going to be as enthusiastic about borrowing frontline equipment for the *next* exercise?"

Chiawa swore as his battered eardrums registered the yowls of indignant anguish coming from his tardier people. He didn't have very long to think about it, though. Because, suddenly, his own harness was flashing at him. He looked down at the light on his chest for just a moment, then sat down quickly, before the harness decided to admonish him.

Salaka was a bit slower, and despite himself, Chiawa felt a sudden mad urge to laugh out loud as the lieutenant squawked and abruptly clapped both hands to the seat of his trousers. Salaka danced in place for a heartbeat or two, then flung himself to the ground a few meters from Chiawa's own position.

The captain hardly noticed. He was looking beyond Salaka, watching as his remaining personnel's harnesses began to flash.

Alicia watched harness lights spring to life all across the valley floor. For the exercise, Major Palacios had made at least one concession to the "guerrilla" status of her Marines and forbidden them to use their helmet sensors or synth-link driven HUDs, but she didn't really need them for this. Her own eyes—and their enhancement processors, of course—were more than enough as she watched Medrano walk the simulated fire of his plasma rifle methodically down the length of the stalled militia column. He had the simulator attached to his rifle set to maximum dispersion, and each shot set off every harness in a circle almost twenty meters across. The technical term for what she was seeing, she thought, was probably "massacre."

"Whups," Hilton said conversationally. "Looks like we're going to get some business after all, Larva. Keep an eye out to the right."

"I'm on it," Alicia confirmed, focusing her own attention on the rapidly disintegrating main body of the militia column. What looked like one of the militia's outsized squads was coming almost straight at their position from the left, but that was Hilton's responsibility. Her job was to see to it that no one interrupted him while he dealt with it.

Exactly what the approaching squad had in mind was impossible to say. It was remotely possible that whoever was in charge of it had figured out where the plasma rifle ripping their column apart was located, in which case he might actually be moving to flank Medrano. After all, Alicia and Hilton were where they were precisely because it was the only practical way to get from the valley floor to Medrano's position. It was more likely, she thought, that it was simply a case of any port in a storm, since the militia men were also headed for one of the few spots Medrano couldn't target directly from his perch high up on the cliff.

Unfortunately for them, Gregory Hilton had no such problem. The senior rifleman settled himself comfortably, bracing his combat rifle on the rest he'd carefully built when he first dug his hole. Then he squeezed the trigger.

The belted blanks from the ammo can clipped to his M-97 were there to provide the visual and audio clues which might have allowed someone to spot his position when he fired. In this case, though, the clues were strictly pro forma, because none of his targets had time to react to them. The rifle's laser range finder was capable of doubling as a target designator for precision guided munitions . . . or for activating the sensors on a training harness.

Hilton swept his "fire" across the oncoming militiamen, who stopped abruptly, staring down at the flashing lights on their chests in astonishment. Some of them looked up again, as if trying to figure out exactly where the fire had come from. Most of them, however, were otherwise occupied in getting themselves and their posteriors into contact with the ground before their harnesses goosed them.

"Remarkably good hunting around here, Larva," Hilton commented, looking up from the dozen-plus militia he had just encouraged to become features of the local landscape. "Especially for some," he added with a grin as he watched Medrano's fire, coupled with a judicious sprinkling of "grenades" from Zigair's launcher, finish what the flash-bangs had begun.

The simulated carnage was as complete as it was sudden, and Hilton shook his head, surveying the "body"-littered valley.

"Next time, train harder," he told the hapless militiamen. "We be serious out here."

"Don't be ridiculous, Cusherwa!" Colonel Sharwa said impatiently. "Even if Chiawa were right—which he *isn't*—just how do you think a dozen obvious foreigners would get all the way into the city without any of our people spotting them?"

Sharwa snorted in disgust. He supposed it was at least partly his own fault. His favorite restaurant's wine list had been known to entice him into extending his lunch hour often enough, but he really shouldn't have let it do it today. Not when there was an exercise underway. And especially not when, as Cusherwa's account of his conversation with Chiawa made abundantly clear, his subordinates were prepared to jump at imagined shadows without his firm guiding hand to keep them focused.

"Now," the colonel said, "the first thing to do is—"

"Excuse me, Colonel."

Sharwa looked up, scowling at the interruption.

"What?" he barked.

"I'm sorry to interrupt, Sir," the communications tech said, "but we're picking up some confused traffic from Captain Chiawa's company."

"What do you mean—confused?" Sharwa demanded.

"We're not certain, Sir. It's only snatches from their short-range coms, and we aren't getting much even of that. But it *sounds* like they might be under some sort of attack."

"There!" Sharwa glared at Cusherwa. "See? This is what happens when an officer—a *junior* officer—in the field lets himself get distracted from the task at hand by wild fantasies!"

"Now," Sergeant Metternich said, and the Marines of Alpha Team, Third Squad, Second Platoon, climbed out of of their borrowed van. They moved without any particular haste, calmly, as if they had every reason to be there. They were three-quarters of the way from the van's curbside parking slot to the building before any of the militia men even glanced in their direction.

They covered most of the remaining distance before anyone realized that whatever they might be wearing, the van's occupants weren't Gyangtsese.

"Wait a min—" someone began, and Sandusky casually tilted his silenced M-97 to the side and opened fire.

The rifle's silencer was remarkably efficient, and the militiamen looked down in astonishment as their harness lights began to flash. Then the tingler circuits kicked in . . . at which point the "dead" sentries suddenly started making rather more noise than the rifle had and got their posteriors into contact with the sidewalk with remarkable speed.

Sandusky and one of the fire team's riflemen had already peeled off, finding positions which let them dominate the sidewalk and street immediately in front of the building with fire. While they did that, Metternich, Johansson, and the rest of Alpha Team opened the front door, tossed a pair of flash-bang "hand grenades" into the building's lobby, and followed them in a moment later with their own weapons ready.

"What the—?" Colonel Sharwa began as the ear-splitting "CRACK!" of Metternich's "grenades" shook the office building he'd appropriated as his HQ for the exercise. He glared at the communications technician, still standing in the doorway.

"Go find out what the hell is going on!" he barked.

"Yes, Sir! Right away!" the tech replied. He spun on his heel to sprint away, then, suddenly, stopped.

Sharwa's glare grew even more pronounced as the tech stepped slowly and carefully backwards into the office. He opened his mouth to flay the unfortunate man, but then he froze, his mouth still open, as Sergeant Abraham Metternich, Imperial Marine Corps, followed the com tech into the room.

"Good afternoon, Colonel Sharwa," the Marine said with exquisite military courtesy.

Then he raised his combat rifle, and Sharwa's harness began to flash as the Marine squeezed the trigger.

CHAPTER FIVE

"God damn that son of a *bitch*!"

Planetary Governor Jasper Aubert slammed himself down in the comfortable chair behind his desk. He was a tallish man, who normally had the well-groomed, smoothly dignified good looks of the successful politician he'd been back on Old Earth. At the moment, however, he looked much more like a petulant child throwing a temper tantrum than like Seamus II's personal representative from the sophisticated old imperial capital world itself.

"Pankarma?" Ákos Salgado asked, as he followed the governor into the office.

"What?" Aubert looked up from his scowling contemplation of his desk blotter.

"I asked if you were referring to Pankarma and his GLF idiots."

"As a matter of fact, no," Aubert half-snarled, his cultured Earth accent notably in abeyance. "Not that Pankarma isn't a son of a bitch in his own right. Not to mention an ambitious, possibly traitorous bastard. But I was 'referring,' as you put it, to that *other* son of a bitch, Kereku."

"Ah." Salgado nodded. He wasn't exactly surprised, even if the governor of a Crown World wasn't supposed to talk that way about the sector governor for whom he theoretically worked. Given the fact that Salgado's opinion of Sir Enobakhare Kereku closely paralleled that of his own immediate superior, however, he felt no particular urge to point out the inappropriateness of Aubert's comment.

"May I ask just what the good sector governor has done this time?" he inquired after a moment.

"He's decided to 'counsel me,'" Aubert snapped. "Jesus! He's talking to me as if I were some sort of political intern! God *damn,* but I *hate* these career bureaucrats who think they understand how politics work! You think that ivory-tower asshole Kereku would have survived six months in real-world politics back on Terra?"

"Sir Enobakhare?"

Salgado laughed at the thought, although, despite his own intense dislike for Kereku (and his officious chief of staff, Obermeyer), he had to admit privately that one thing Kereku *wasn't* was an ivory-tower intellectual. True, Kereku was firmly aligned with the reactionary bloc which had gathered around Sir Jeffrey Madison, the current Foreign Minister, and the Earl of Stanhope, in the senior levels of the Out-Worlds hierarchy. Salgado was, of course, a protégé of Senator Gennady, like Aubert himself, which meant that Kereku was far more likely to adopt confrontational policies than either of them were. And, equally true, the sector governor was also technically a bureaucrat, never having won an elective office. But, for all that, he was scarcely a typical example of the breed.

Kereku had started out in the diplomatic corps and done superlatively there, then moved over to Out-World Affairs decades ago. Salgado didn't have much faith in Kereku's judgment where Gyangtse was concerned, and he'd done his best—generally successfully—to steer Aubert into a more pragmatic policy. But he had to admit that Kereku had at least gotten his ticket punched. If he'd never won an election himself, he'd put in his own time in exactly the sort of positions that *Salgado* currently held—not to mention holding five separate Crown World governorships and overseeing two successful Incorporation referendums himself—before rising to his present rank.

None of which made the effort of imagining Kereku as a successful *politician* any less of amusing.

"I think you can safely say that the sector governor . . . wouldn't have prospered in *real* politics," he agreed once he'd stopped laughing.

"Of course he wouldn't survive it," Aubert agreed viciously. "But he's lecturing *me* on the 'political dynamic' here on Gyangtse. Lecturing *me*! As if he'd ever visited the damned planet more than once himself or had the least idea what these frigging neobarbs are trying to pull!"

"Lecturing?" Salgado repeated. "Lecturing how, Jasper?"

"He obviously thinks I don't have a clue," Aubert said bitterly. "On the basis of his own vast, personal experience—with *other* worlds!—he seems to think this entire planet is about to go up in a ball of plasma! He's even talking about the possibility of some sort of serious armed, open resistance movement—as if these GLF clowns could find their backsides with both hands!"

"It sounds like that insubordinate piece of work Palacios has been running around behind your back," Salgado said, his own expression turning ugly. Ákos Salgado had had precious little use for the military even before he and Aubert arrived on Gyangtse. The military was no more than a necessary evil, at the best of times . . . and in Salgado's opinion, it was most often the military's ham-handed approach to politically solvable problems which produced the sort of disastrous situations that same military then used to justify its own existence.

More to the point, in this instance, Major Serafina Palacios was exactly the sort of Marine he most loathed. She looked so tautly professional, so competent. So utterly devoid of a single thought she couldn't fire out of a rifle's barrel. Although Salgado had absolutely no interest in learning how to read all of the ridiculous 'fruit salad' Marines—like the anachronistic, lowbrow primitives they were—insisted on draping all over their uniforms, she'd obviously had her ticket punched by the senior members of her own xenophobic, militaristic lodge. That was they way they groomed their own for accelerated promotion, and her arrogant attitude showed that she knew it. Worse, he was certain she spent all of her time looking down her nose at him, as if her experience carrying a rifle and bashing in neobarb skulls was somehow superior to his own hard won understanding of the horse-trading realities of practical politics.

He'd taken pains to depress her pretensions and put her in her place when she first began hawking her particular brand of alarmism, and her apparent inability to grasp the fact that he was her superior in the Gyangtse pecking order infuriated him. She'd simply ignored him—just as she'd ignored or disregarded the intelligence reports of the militia, which *lived* here and might thus be reasonably expected to actually *know* a little something about the planet—and asserted her right as Aubert's official military adviser to go right on repeating her mantra of doom at every meeting with the governor. Until Salgado had taken to arranging creative schedule conflicts whenever Palacios tried to corner Aubert and pour her paranoia into his ear, that was.

"I don't know for sure that it was Palacios," Aubert said, in the tone of a man manifestly trying to be fair. "But *someone's* obviously been feeding the most pessimistic possible interpretation of our own intelligence sources to Martinsen. To listen to Kereku's message, you'd think someone was shipping in HVW launchers! And," the planetary governor's voice turned suddenly harsh and bitter again, "I'm pretty sure from the way he's talking that this isn't the only place he's been starcomming messages to."

"What do you mean?" Salgado asked sharply.

"What do you *think* I mean, Ákos? Where else would he be peddling his unhappiness with the way we seem to be handling things here on our mountainous little ball of mud?"

"You think he's taking his concerns to the Ministry?"

"I'm almost sure of it." Aubert shoved himself up out of his chair and turned to look out the window of his office, hands clasped behind him. "He didn't say so in so many words, of course—no doubt because he doesn't want to get into a public pissing contest with me when he knows how many friends I have back at Court and in the Senate. But trust me, I could hear it. It was there, behind the things he actually did say."

"I see."

Salgado frowned, and his mind shifted into high gear. It was true Aubert had a great many contacts and allies back on Old Earth. Not as many, or as powerful, as he might choose to believe he had, perhaps, but they were still impressive, or he wouldn't have been here. Politics had its own rules, its own tickets which had to be punched, and for all its headaches, Gyangtse was still a plum assignment for a man of ambition. There were far cushier, less strenuous ones available, but anyone who aspired to the higher offices Aubert sought had to have a planetary governorship, or its equivalent, in his résumé. And, frankly, the process of successfully steering a planet like Gyangtse through the transition from Crown World to Incorporated World would give Aubert tremendous clout in his future political career—far more than a simple, "routine" governorship on some planet full of placid farmers might have. Whatever he might choose to say about his "need to serve the Empire," that was the only reason Jasper Aubert was out here. Which was fair enough; it was also the only reason Ákos Salgado had attached himself to Aubert. And Ákos Salgado had no intention of having his own career plans derailed because his chosen patron's career stumbled.

The problem, he realized, was that neither he nor Aubert could know exactly what Kereku had actually said in any of his messages to Earl Stanhope. And without knowing how Kereku had chosen to present his criticism of the situation here on Gyangtse, they couldn't know what *they* had to say to rally Aubert's Old Earth patrons in his defense.

"Exactly what did Kereku have to say about our current policy?" the chief of staff asked after a moment.

"He *suggested* that we made a mistake in agreeing to 'negotiate' with Pankarma in the first place," the governor growled. "Which, of course, overlooks the fact that that wasn't what we actually did at all! Pankarma's a citizen of Gyangtse, whether we like it or not. He may be associated with the GLF, and the GLF may be a proscribed organization, but he's here, and he has the ear of a significant number of locals, so how the hell were we supposed to keep him out of the Incorporation debate? But that's not the way *Kereku* sees it, of course! *He* says that by not protesting Pankarma's participation, and by actually daring to attend referendum debates and conferences I knew Pankarma would also be attending, I gave him *de facto* recognition as 'a legitimate part of the Gyangtse political process.' He's insinuated that by doing so we've violated the basic imperial policy against negotiating with 'terroristic movements.' Without, by the way, ever mentioning that *he* was the one who classified the GLF as 'terroristic' on the basis of the *vast* insight into local conditions he garnered on his single two-day visit to the damned planet when he first assumed his post! And he also had the gall to inform me that talking to the GLF has only 'exacerbated' the situation by 'raising unrealistic expectations' on Pankarma's part."

Salgado's lip curled. Maybe he'd been a little too charitable when he dismissed the ivory-tower label in Kereku's case.

"Neither the sector governor nor his *esteemed* chief of staff seems to have the least grasp of what we're actually doing," Aubert continued, glaring out the window across the streets and roofs of Zhikotse's Old Town. "They want me to refuse to sit down across a conference table from Pankarma, or even engage him in public debate on the holovid, because the GLF has blown up a few bridges and a power transmission tower or two, but at the same time they want me to keep a lid on the situation. I've explained to them, repeatedly, that getting Pankarma involved in the debate—offering him a shot at real local political power, after the Incorporation goes through—is the best way to wean him away from his previous extremism. And that even if he and the GLF don't see that and continue to insist on our complete withdrawal, I can keep them from carrying out further attacks as long as I can keep them talking. That it's a case of showing them enough of a carrot that they decide they've got too much to lose if they abandon the negotiating process."

"I don't understand how he and Obermeyer can fail to grasp that point, Jasper." Salgado shook his head. "The incidence of the sorts of attacks that inspired the two of them to classify the GLF as a 'terroristic' organization in the first place dropped off to almost nothing when you offered it a seat at the table. And it's not as if we're actually proposing to give the lunatics what they say they want! Hell, for that matter, Pankarma himself has to realize he's not going to get what he's demanding. Sooner or later, he's going to have to tell us what he's really prepared to settle for."

"I suppose," Aubert said, "that it's possible Pankarma truly doesn't realize that. That's what Kereku seems to think, anyway, even if the local political leadership disagrees with him. Somehow, I don't think people like President Shangup and the Chamber of Delegates would be going along with us if the people who actually live here thought we were making a serious mistake! But what do I know? I've only been here a year. We've been over this again and again, and my own analysis is the same as yours, of course. Get them involved in the existing system, co-opt them by showing them how they can benefit from it, and they'll lose interest in getting rid of it soon enough."

In fact, as Salgado knew perfectly well, Aubert's analysis *was* Salgado's. But that wasn't a point a successful manager made to the man he was managing. And especially not when that man's superior had just rejected the analysis in question.

"But even if Kereku were right," Aubert continued, "we're in a position to keep Pankarma talking forever, if we decide to. Or, at least, until the Incorporation is a done deal and he and his crackpots become the responsibility of the local authorities."

Salgado nodded, because what Aubert had just said was self-evidently true. Oh, Pankarma was continuing his movement's economic boycott of any off-world-owned businesses—or, for that matter, any Gyangtsese business which 'collaborated' with off-world firms. And he continued to spout the sort of fiery rhetoric which had been his stock in trade for so long. But that was only to be expected. He had to at least appear to pander to the prejudices and paranoia of his lunatic fringe followers lest one of his more radical disciples end up deposing him. But all the winning cards were in Aubert's hand. He was the one who could call upon the full coercive power of the Empire at need . . . and also the one who controlled all of the possible concessions Pankarma and his followers could ever hope to obtain. Unless and until the Incorporation referendum succeeded and those goodies fell into the hands of Gyangtse's new senators, of course. After which any continued hooliganism on Pankarma's part also became someone else's problem.

"Unfortunately," Aubert continued in a quieter, flatter voice, "Kereku doesn't see it that way. He thinks we've 'legitimized' Pankarma in his own eyes, and the eyes of his followers, by agreeing to talk to him and allow him to participate in the public debate instead of regarding him and all of his people as common criminals. And he seems to believe Pankarma is genuinely likely to resort to fresh and even more violent acts if he decides we're not going to give him what he wants. And, of course, we *can't* give him what he claims to want."

Which, Salgado admitted unhappily, was true. If Pankarma was far enough out of touch with reality to genuinely believe the Empire could ever be induced to withdraw from Gyangtse, he was doomed to ultimate disappointment. Once a planet was taken under imperial sovereignty, it stayed there—especially out here, among the old League systems closest to the buffer zone of Rogue Worlds between the Empire and the Rishathan Sphere.

But the Empire had also made it clear that it was prepared to involve the inhabitants of those worlds in their own governance. A substantial degree of local autonomy was available, especially once a Crown World qualified for Incorporated World status and the senatorial representation which went with it. Seamus II and his advisers felt no pressing need to exercise dictatorial power, nor were they interested in promoting the economic rape of frontier worlds by the Empire's transstellar giants. But that local autonomy would be exercised only from a position firmly inside the Empire.

"Pankarma knows that, Jasper," the chief of staff said now. "He has to. He's what passes for a well-educated man out here, and he's never struck me as an outright maniac."

"I agree," Aubert said. But he also turned in place, putting his back to the window to look hard at Salgado.

"I agree," he repeated. "But what if we've been wrong?"

"Wrong?" Salgado blinked. "Wrong to have involved Pankarma in the Incorporation debate? Or in our estimate of what he really wants?"

"Both—either!" Aubert shook his head and snorted harshly. "Kereku has a point when he says Pankarma's never wavered from his ultimate demand of complete Gyangtsese independence. He may be 'participating' in the debate over the Incorporation referendum, but what he's really saying—over and over again—is that he and his followers are completely opposed to the ultimate success of the Incorporation process. And he *has* gained a much more public, much more visible platform for his rhetoric since we let him into the debate process. I disagree with Kereku's view that that amounts to 'legitimizing' the GLF somehow, but it has brought him closer to the forefront of what passes for the political process out here. And if he's really as fanatical, deep down inside, as his rhetoric suggests, then when he finally realizes we intend to complete the Incorporation process regardless of anything he says or does, he just might provoke exactly the sort of incident Kereku is so damned concerned about."

"We both know how unlikely that is," Salgado said reasonably.

"I didn't say it was likely. I said it was *possible*. And if it does happen, Ákos, it's going to look really, really bad for me. For us. Especially after Kereku's been running around warning everyone that the sky is falling!"

"That's true enough," Salgado admitted unwillingly.

"But what the hell do we do about it?" Aubert growled. "Pankarma does have a seat at the table now, and we gave it to him. If we suddenly snatch it away from him, the way Kereku seems to want us to, we're just likely to push him into some sort of violent reaction. But if I *don't* remove him from the process, and if Kereku can convince Stanhope we're in violation of standing policy, then it really is possible I could find myself recalled to Old Earth."

He looked levelly into his chief of staff's eyes, and Salgado heard the unspoken corollary.

"Well," he said, after a moment, "since neither one of us wants to go home with our job half done, I suppose we've got to find a way to fix the things Kereku thinks are wrong." He grimaced. "Mind you, I still think he and Obermeyer are jumping at shadows. But be that as it may, he's got the whip hand just now, so I suppose we're just going to have to satisfy him somehow."

"That's easier said than done, Ákos."

"Yes, it is," Salgado agreed. Still, he had no more desire than Aubert to see the planetary governor—and himself, as Aubert's chief of staff—recalled as failures. "On the other hand, it's not an impossible challenge, either. I mean," he smiled nastily, "Sector Governor Kereku *is* the one who's just pointed out that 'terrorists' are common criminals, not legitimate political figures."

"I don't like this. I don't like this at all," Major Serafina Palacios said flatly.

"Skipper, it's not like either one of us thought we were Aubert's favorite people in the known universe, anyway," Captain Kevin Trammell, the commanding officer of Alpha Company, pointed out. Trammell was Palacios' senior company commander, which made him the executive officer of her understrength battalion, as well. He was also a good eight centimeters taller than she was, and as dark-complexioned and haired as she was fair-skinned and Nordic blond.

"Under the circumstances," he continued now, "is it really that surprising that he's communicating directly with the planetary militia without going through you? I mean, if you look at the organizational chart, as planetary governor, he is the militia's CO. There's no reason he *has* to go through us."

"It's not the fact that he's talking to Jongdomba and Sharwa directly. It's the fact that he hasn't even *mentioned* to us that he's doing it. Whether he likes it or not, that same organizational chart says I'm his imperial military adviser. He's supposed to keep me informed and actually seek my input when he deals with the militia, and he sure as hell isn't. And he wouldn't be sneaking around this way unless he was up to something he and that prick Salgado don't want us—or anyone in Martinsen—to know a thing about."

"Skipper, that's sounding just a little paranoid," Trammell said. She glared at him for a moment, then snorted.

"If all I am is a *little* paranoid after dealing with Governor Aubert and Mr. Salgado for the past eleven months, then I'm obviously even more mentally stable than I thought I was!"

They both chuckled, but then Palacios' expression sobered again.

"Seriously, Kevin," she said, "I'm concerned. I don't like the way Aubert's looking these days. I think he's suddenly realized just how shaky the Incorporation vote's in the process of becoming. And I think he's also finally realized that talking to Pankarma at all was a serious mistake—career-wise, at the very least. I'm even starting to wonder if he's not more than a little afraid Governor Kereku is going to get him recalled if he doesn't get this mess straightened out in a hurry."

"And you think he's actually going to come up with some way to use the *militia* to fix his problems?" Trammell raised both eyebrows. "That sorry bunch of stumblebums is going to get his ass out of the crack he's been so busy wedging it into?"

"It's the last thing *I'd* try," Palacios conceded. "On the other hand, and with all due respect for our civilian superiors, I have a functional brain. Which means I *know* the militia is a 'sorry bunch of stumblebums.' I honestly don't think Aubert—or Salgado—recognizes that little fact. They don't realize what an incompetent, graft-hungry little empire-builder Jongdomba really is, either, I'm afraid. Of course, if they did, then they'd have working brains, too, and they wouldn't have let themselves get into a mess like this one in the first place. In which case they wouldn't be looking for desperate expedients to get them *out* of it, either, now would they?"

"But even if Aubert's thinking that way, and even if Jongdomba and Sharwa were willing to go along with him, what good would it do him?" Trammell countered. "The planetary government and the militia haven't been able to put the GLF out of business on their own hook for the last six local years, so unless he's come up with some sort of magic bullets to issue them, I don't see them miraculously solving his problems overnight at this point."

"I don't either," Palacios said grimly. "What I am afraid of, though, is that he may think he *has* managed to come up with some sort of 'magic bullet.' Don't forget that he's got that poisonous little twerp Salgado whispering in his ear. In fact, Salgado's at least two-thirds of the problem. Aubert's not the sharpest stylus in the box by any stretch, and he's as ambitious as they come, but he doesn't have the same sort of tunnel vision ambition Salgado does. Or not to the same extent, at least. But when the chief of staff thinks he's the reincarnation of Niccolò Machiavelli and thinks the governor is almost as stupid as he thinks *we* are, you've got all the ingredients for a total cluster fuck. Especially when Salgado's so used to seeing himself as the puppetmaster pulling the governor's strings that he's convinced himself he's some sort of infallible Svengali."

Trammell winced internally at the sheer venom in Palacios' tone. Not that he disagreed, but having so much naked hatred and contempt between a governor's chief of staff and senior military adviser was *not* an ideal situation.

"Skipper, I don't much like Salgado either. But—"

"But I'm supposed to shut up and buckle down to do my own job, whether I like him or not," Palacios interrupted, and nodded sharply.

"I know that. And I've tried to. But Salgado's controlling access now, and he's got the governor's ear all day long, whereas I have trouble even getting Aubert to take my messages. Salgado's really the one forming policy by now; I'm sure of it. And his bias against the military, coupled with his misplaced confidence in his own brilliance, is going to produce a frigging disaster if we're not *damned* lucky. Especially since he's been so blithely treating Pankarma like one more machine politician from Old Earth he can cut some sort of deal with." She grimaced unhappily. "If he thinks that's blowing up in his face, then he's going to be looking for a quick fix to save his ass. And let's face it, Kevin. After what we had Kuramochi's people do to Sharwa and his regiment in that last training exercise, he and Jongdomba both hate our guts. And they're both likely to be looking for some way to redeem themselves, prove that what Chiyeko's people did to them was some sort of 'fluke,' as well. So if the governor's resident genius and political seer has come up with some plan they think might make them look better at *our* expense, they might just jump at it."

CHAPTER SIX

"So, do you really think anything's going to come of it?" Ang Jangmu Thaktu asked.

"I doubt it," Pankarma replied. "On the other hand, looking reasonable doesn't hurt us a bit when it comes to public opinion."

"Maybe not, but this is the first time he's specifically invited you—and me—to sit down privately with him. I think that's a significant change, don't you?"

"It may be."

Pankarma walked across his office in the building the Gyangtse Patriotic Association, the "legal" parliamentary branch of the GLF, had rented in the capital. It was near the spaceport, and when he stopped at the office's outside wall and looked out the window, he saw almost exactly the same vista Jasper Aubert had contemplated from his own office. Pankarma gazed at the sight, rocking gently on his heels, and his expression was pensive.

"No," he said after a moment. "You're right. It *is* a significant change. Whether its significance is anything more than symbolic, though—that's the question you're really asking, isn't it? And the answer is that I don't have the least idea at this point. The polls all suggest his majority is beginning to slip. Maybe he feels a need to shore up his support by indicating that the Empies are willing to talk even to 'lunatics' like us. That doesn't mean he actually intends to give any ground, though."

"In fact," Thaktu said, watching his back as he stood before the windows, "I don't think he does, Namkha. Like I said before, I don't think he can. That's why I'm not sure actually accepting the invitation is the smart strategic move. If we sit down in private discussions with him, for instance, and if he claims later he offered us concessions, even if he really doesn't, and that we rejected them, it would be our word—the word of a 'terrorist group'—against the word of an imperial governor. That may not be exactly what he has in mind, but if I'm right, and he knows going in that he isn't going to be moving towards our demands, then I have to suspect that he's up to *something* he expects will benefit him at our expense."

"I think you're probably right," Pankarma said, then snorted with bitter humor and turned back from the window to face her. "Actually, I'm pretty sure you are. The problem is, this is a pretty shrewd move on his part. Since he invited me as the head of the Patriotic Association, *not* the GLF, and since the Association is supposed to be participating in the free home-rule democracy the Empies have so graciously theoretically permitted us, I really don't have any choice but to accept."

"I don't like it, Namkha," she said flatly, in her strongest statement to date. "It doesn't feel right. It doesn't *smell* right."

"Well," he crossed back to his desk and sat down behind it, tilted back his chair, and looked at her seriously, "I've always trusted your instincts Ang Jangmu. On the other hand, I've already sent Salgado a formal communique to the effect that that we accept the invitation. I'm sure he'll announce our acceptance as soon as he gets my response, so we can't change our minds now."

"I'd feel a lot happier if we could," she said, and he shrugged.

"I can see you would. In this case, though, I think I have to override your instincts. But given how strongly you seem to feel about this, I think it would probably also be a good idea to take Chepal along instead of you." He raised a hand and shook his head when she frowned quickly. "Not because I think you'd let your feelings get in the way of anything we might actually accomplish. No. I'm thinking that I want you in charge of our own tactical arrangements. I know what kind of advice you'd give me if you were there, anyway. So in this case, knowing that you're watching our backs, as it were, will probably be worth more to both of us then having you actually at the table."

* * *

"They've accepted," Ákos Salgado said.

"Good!" Lobsang Phurba Jongdomba said, with a most unpleasant expression. "I take it that they've also accepted the location?"

"They have," Salgado confirmed, and smiled pleasantly at the Gyangtsese officer.

No one could have told from his expression that he felt even more contempt for Jongdomba than he did for Palacios. Jongdomba was not simply a representative of what passed for the local military forces, which would have been enough all by itself to put him into the "brains of a rutabaga" category, but also a thoroughly venal member in good standing of the local oligarchy.

But any good politician knows that you don't have to actually like *someone to work with him. And at least Jongdomba isn't a hysterical paranoiac like Palacios. Of course, he is even more convinced of his own infallibility than she is.*

Which, of course, was one of the very reasons Salgado was sitting in this palatial office in one of Jongdomba's Zhikotse office buildings. The expensive wooden paneling, artworks, and imported off-world liquors in the amply stocked wet bar were all ostentatious declarations of Jongdomba's wealth. They were rather tacky, too, in Salgado's opinion, which made them an accurate reflection of the basic stupidity which was the main factor in Salgado's decision to rely upon Jongdomba for this particular operation. Someone with a more . . . realistic appreciation of his abilities might have figured out where Salgado intended to deposit any official responsibility, should anything go wrong.

"I wish we could have held out for someplace a bit more isolated," Colonel Sharwa said. In Brigadier Jongdomba's presence, he spoke almost diffidently, but the militia's planetary commander frowned at him anyway. "I'd really prefer for the operation to go down somewhere without quite so many civilians in the vicinity," the colonel continued, despite his superior's expression.

"Your concerns are laudable, Colonel," Salgado said smoothly. "I'm confident, though, that the operation will go without a hitch under your command. And suggesting that we use the Annapurna Arms was a stroke of brilliance on Brigadier Jongdomba's part, if I may say so myself. It's the biggest, most luxurious hotel in Zhikotse. That makes it a logical venue for Governor Aubert to meet with Pankarma, and it's big enough for us to preposition our surprise without its being spotted. And the fact that it's right in the middle of town has to have been very reassuring to the GLF, too. In fact, if we'd suggested someplace more 'isolated,' Pankarma might have been suspicious enough to reject the invitation entirely."

"Exactly," Jongdomba said heartily. "Don't be an old woman, Ang Chirgan! Or are you still brooding over that busted exercise?"

"I'm not 'brooding' over anything, Sir," Sharwa said a bit stiffly.

"Nor should you," Salgado said firmly, and looked at Jongdomba with an air of mild reproval. "I've had my own reports about that exercise, Brigadier. It's hardly the Colonel's fault that Major Palacios deliberately misled him—and, I might add, all of the other militia officers involved—as to her own intentions. It's all very well to argue that the enemy will try to surprise you in actual operations, but it's quite another to create your own surprise advantage by lying to your own personnel and allies." He shook his head, his expression turning sad. "I'm really quite disappointed in the Major, and I've made that point to the governor, as well."

"As well you should have," Jongdomba growled, clearly diverted from his pique at Sharwa's apparent criticism. "I've made the same point myself, let me tell you—and not just to Governor Aubert. I've addressed my own protest to President Shangup, as well."

"I appreciate that, Brigadier. But I also assure you that I'm not letting what happened affect my judgment in this case," Sharwa said. "My only concern is that the GLF has already demonstrated that it's capable of carrying out violent actions. However unlikely it may seem, it's still remotely possible that we could wind up with a violent incident on our hands here. That's why I'd prefer not to have any more civilians than we can help in the potential line of fire."

"If they're stupid enough to resist," Jongdomba's expression was grim, "then there damned well *will* be a 'violent incident.' But, first, I don't think they are that stupid. And, second, if they are, you'll be well placed to contain any violence that happens. And, to be brutally honest, if there *are* a few civilian casualties, it will probably work to our advantage."

Sharwa, Salgado saw, didn't much care for Jongdomba's logic. In an odd sort of way, that actually caused the chief of staff to feel at least a minor twinge of respect for the militia colonel. Of course, Jongdomba was right about the practical consequences of any civilian injuries or fatalities, especially once they were spun the right way for the news media. Still, Salgado supposed it was to Sharwa's credit that he wanted to avoid those casualties in the first place. Unfortunately, making omelets always used up a few eggs. And, of course, since it was the militia's operation, acting in the name of the planet-ary government, and not that of Governor Aubert, if there was any … unfortunate fallout it wouldn't be falling on Jasper Aubert or Ákos Salgado. Although Salgado would be happier if that particular point never occurred to either of his present guests.

"I feel confident that the Brigadier is correct, Colonel," the chief of staff said now, making his firm voice radiate assurance. Sharwa looked at him, and he shrugged. "I've read over your plans, and it's obvious to me that you've considered every eventuality. Under the circumstances, not even Pankarma is going to be stupid enough to buck the odds and provoke any sort of violent confrontation.

"After all," he allowed more than a little contempt to edge into his smile, "people like the GLF are always a lot more willing to kill *other* people for their beliefs than they are to die for them themselves."

"What d'you make of this meeting with the GLF of Aubert's, Alley?" César Bergerat asked.

"What?" Alicia looked up from where she'd been cleaning the trigger group of her M-97. They'd been to the range that morning, and the smell of solvent as they cleaned the residue from their weapons was like an oddly pungent incense as she worked.

"I asked what you think of this meeting between Pankarma and Aubert," the rifleman said, and Alicia frowned thoughtfully.

Sergeant Metternich watched the conversation from the corner of one eye, carefully hiding a mental smile. Young DeVries had been with the platoon for almost two standard months, now. She still wasn't an official "Wasp"—she hadn't smelled the smoke yet—but she'd slotted into place surprisingly smoothly for a Mackenzie larva. Largely, he thought, that was because she had the trick of keeping her mouth shut and her ears open. And, he admitted, because she didn't make very many mistakes . . . and *never* made the same one twice.

At the same time, it hadn't taken long for the rest of Third Squad to figure out she was the best educated of them all, despite her youth. She'd never said a word about it herself, but it had quickly become painfully evident that there was an agile, fully engaged, and remarkably well informed brain behind those jade eyes of hers. And while she was careful about showing off, as befitted someone as junior as she was, her squadmates had developed a surprisingly acute respect for her judgment as they discovered that she seldom answered a question without thinking about it carefully, first.

"Well," she said finally, her long, graceful fingers continuing to work with independent skill while she focused her thoughts elsewhere, "I know I haven't been out here anywhere near as long as the rest of you. Still, I'd have to say I'll be surprised if anything comes of it." She shrugged. "You know, my dad's a senior analyst with the Foreign Ministry. I was never that interested in that sort of a career myself, but I've heard a lot of table conversation about situations like this one. I don't think there's very much room in either side's positions for any sort of compromise. In fact—"

She broke off, shook her head, and smiled, then turned her attention back to the trigger group.

Several of the other members of Third Squad looked at one another, then at her.

"Don't stop there," Bergerat said.

"Excuse me?" Alicia glanced back up.

"I said don't stop there. You were about to say something else, and then you thought better of it, Larva."

It was the first time in at least a week that anyone had used the term "larva" in addressing Alicia, and he used it now with an almost humorous air. But his tone was still pointed. His question was obviously serious, and she sighed.

"I was just going to say that I don't think Dad would approve of this meeting of the governor's," she said, just a bit reluctantly. "The GLF's officially designated a terrorist organization. That means people like planetary governors aren't supposed to talk to them at all. The Empire officially excludes them from the political process under any circumstances."

"She's right," Metternich said quietly. All eyes swivelled in his direction, and he snorted. "Come on! All of you know that as well she does! We're Recon, remember? Who always gets handed the dirty end of the stick when some League neobarb gets a wild hair up his ass, or some bureaucratic puke from Out-Worlds screws the pooch? You mean to tell me you've all been over the river and through the woods as often as I know you have without learning how many ways the politicos can fuck up?"

"Well, yeah, Sarge," Gregory Hilton said. "But, I mean, he *is* the planetary governor. Doesn't that mean he can shave the rules, even bend them a little, if that's what it takes to get the job done?"

"Of course he can," Metternich agreed. Alicia watched him, trying not to look wide-eyed. She was surprised at how bluntly the sergeant appeared prepared to speak his mind about the Empire's appointed governor for Gyangtse.

"The point, though," Metternich continued, "is that he's supposed to do it to 'get the job done.' And also that there are some rules he's not supposed to bend, ever. You know how thoroughly it's pounded into *our* heads that we don't negotiate with terrorists. Never. Oh, sure, we do it anyway, in a sense. But there's a difference between trying to talk a bunch of terrorists holed up with a batch of civilian hostages into surrendering on the best terms they can get and sitting down to talk political deals with the bastards! And that's supposed to be just as true for a planetary governor as it is for a Marine first lieutenant."

Several other Marines were looking at Metternich as if his acid tone had surprised them almost as much as it had surprised Alicia. Leo Medrano, she noticed, was not one of them, and she felt an inner chill at the realization that the two men she had decided were Third Squad's most thoughtful observers felt nothing but contempt for Governor Aubert.

No, it's worse than that, she thought. *They're not just contemptuous. They're* worried. *They think* he's *going to be one of the politicos who 'screw the pooch.' And Grandpa wasn't too happy about my getting sent out here, either, now was he?*

She finished cleaning the trigger group, set it aside, and picked up the bolt, and her brain was busy.

* * *

Namkha Pasang Pankarma smiled for the cameras in front of the Annapurna Arms Hotel with a pleasure he was far from feeling, as he stepped out of the first of the three ground cars into the brisk autumn morning. Gyangtse's news media was scarcely what he considered a standardbearer for freedom of the press. Too many of the local newsfaxes and public news channels were owned by members of the planetary elite for that. Their editorial staffs—to their credit, he supposed—made no real secret of their own biases when they pontificated on local politics and events, but everyone pretended that they at least tried to be neutral in the way they *reported* those events.

Pankarma was willing to concede that at least some of the street reporters tried to be neutral, but it would have required something very much like a miracle for that effort to succeed. And miracles, he thought, were in short supply upon Gyangtse these days.

Nonetheless, the newsies had turned out in strength to cover this series of private discussions with Planetary Governor Aubert. There was a lot of speculation in the editorials, and it was even possible some of the newsies covering this meeting actually believed something might come of it all. At any rate, it was incumbent upon all of the participants to pretend *they* believed it.

So he stood there, smiling and waving through the blustery gusts of wind, while Chepal Dawa Nawa and the rest of his delegation followed him out of the ground cars. Although he was the one who'd suggested to Ang Jangmu that she not be a member of the delegation, Pankarma still missed her presence. Nawa had been with him almost as long as she had. His seniority had made him Pankarma's second ranking lieutenant, and the GLF founder had no doubts about the man's loyalty and determination. But for all his many virtues, Nawa was a plugger, not really a thinker, and he lacked Thaktu's quick, alert intelligence.

Still, it wasn't as if it were going to matter. Pankarma had come to the conclusion that Ang Jangmu had been right from the beginning. This entire meeting was nothing more than a bit of political theater, something Aubert had arranged because he expected it to benefit his own political agenda.

* * *

"I think that's all of them," Lieutenant Salaka said softly. He was speaking over a secure landline link, but he kept his voice down anyhow, as if he thought Pankarma might somehow overhear him.

"You *think* that's all of them?" Captain Chiawa repeated from his command post.

"I mean, it's the right number of bodies," Salaka replied a bit defensively. "I can't see them all that well from here. You know that."

Chiawa rolled his eyes, then made himself inhale a deep, steadying breath. Salaka, he knew, hadn't been any happier about drawing this assignment than he'd been himself. Unfortunately, Brigadier Jongdomba had been willing to call up only two companies for the operation, and Colonel Sharwa had decided that Chiawa's company deserved the chance to show its mettle as a "reward" for Chiawa's alertness during their last disastrous exercise against Major Palacios' Marines. Personally, Chiawa suspected that it was also a form of punishment for what those same Marines had done to his company despite his alertness.

"I realize you may not be able to see their faces, Tsimbuti," the captain said after a moment, his tone much more relaxed. He even managed to inject a little humor into it as he continued, "On the other hand, we're supposed to get this right, and I'm sure the Colonel will be grateful if we manage to pull that off."

"I know," Salaka said. "All I can tell you for sure, though, is that the right number of people got out of the cars. They're headed into the hotel now, and the cars are pulling off towards the parking garage."

"Understood."

Chiawa nodded, even though there was no way Salaka could possibly see the gesture. The militia captain's belly muscles tightened as he felt the moment rushing towards him. A part of him—most of him, really—was eager. Pankarma and his lunatic fringe followers had caused enough grief for Karsang Dawa Chiawa's planet, and for him personally. Their boycott had cost him business, making it harder to put food into his own children's mouths, and if their constant prattle about "the armed struggle" ever amounted to anything, guess who they'd be actively shooting at? Besides it was one of the militia's jobs to suppress criminal activities, wasn't it? And decapitating the only organized association of violent felons opposed to Gyangtse's Incorporation into the Empire obviously fell under the heading of suppressing criminals, didn't it?

The one question in Chiawa's mind, the concern that awoke a tiny kernel of internal doubt, was the *way* they were doing it. Gyangtse was a planet where people who gave their word were expected to keep it . . . even when they gave it to criminals and traitors.

None of which mattered very much at this point, he reflected. He sat for a moment longer, then nodded to his communications tech.

"Send the execute," he said.

"Yes, Sir!" the corporal said crisply, and keyed his microphone.

"All units, this is the command post. Execute Scoop," he said clearly. The transmission went out over the militia's radio net, because it simply hadn't been possible to establish landline connections to all of Chiawa's people.

"I say again," the corporal repeated. "Execute Scoop."

". . . cute Scoop."

Ang Jangmu Thaktu's head snapped up as her com unit picked up the transmission. The GLF had its sympathizers even in the ranks of the militia. Even if it hadn't, there was always a militiaman somewhere who needed a little extra money and was prepared to "lose" equipment for the right price. Which was the reason her com was official militia issue, with the same signal encryption protocols as the one Captain Chiawa's com tech had just spoken over.

Thaktu had no way of actually knowing what the code word "Scoop" signified, but she could think of at least one ominous application of that particular verb. More to the point, she hadn't picked up a single hint of its existence from any of their militia sympathizers, nor a single scrap of communications chatter up to the moment the order to execute the operation was transmitted, which represented far tighter security than the militia normally achieved. There had to be a reason for that, and she snatched up her own civilian com.

"It's a trap!" she barked. "It's a trap! Breakout! I repeat, Breakout!"

* * *

Namkha Pasang Pankarma froze between one step and another as the doors to the elevator at the end of the hall slid smoothly open. The uniformed militiamen in the elevator car sat behind a tripod-mounted calliope, and the multibarreled autocannon was aimed straight at him. At almost the same instant, four more doors opened—two on each side of the corridor—and more militiamen, armed with combat rifles, appeared in them.

"This is Captain Chiawa, of the Planetary Militia," a hard voice announced over the luxury hotel's intercom system. "You are surrounded. You are also under arrest, as directed by President Shangup in the name of the Planetary Government, for treason and the commission of terroristic acts. I call upon you now to surrender, or face the consequences."

Pankarma simply stood there, unable to believe what was happening. Despite Ang Jangmu's fears, despite his own reservations, he'd never anticipated anything like *this*. Surely even idiots like Jongdomba and Shangup knew better than to violate a promise of safe conduct this way!

"You will surrender *now*," Chiawa's amplified voice said harshly. "If you do not, we will employ deadly force."

Sergeant Lakshindo nodded to the troopers of his militia squad.

"You heard the man," he said. "Let's go!"

The squad filed out of its place of concealment in the Annapurna Arms' basement and took up its planned position to cover the hotel's main entrance. That entrance led to the hallway in which, Lakshindo knew, the GLF delegation was being taken into custody at that very moment, and under Captain Chiawa's ops plan, Lakshindo's squad was responsible for crowd control and for blocking the only possible path of retreat for Pankarma and his fellows. They were also supposed to be alert for any external threat, though exactly what sort of "external threat" they might face was more than Lakshindo could imagine. After all, operational security had been so tight on this one that even the members of Lakshindo's squad hadn't known what was going to happen until they reported this morning.

The sergeant stood with his back to the street, watching his people take up their posts, and grimaced in satisfaction. He would have preferred an opportunity to rehearse it all at least once, but his militiamen moved briskly, their expressions and body language calm enough to disguise their excitement from anyone who didn't know them as well as Lakshindo did.

He nodded mentally as they settled into place, then keyed his own microphone.

"Command post, Lakshindo," he said crisply. "We're in position."

"Command post copies you are in position, Sergeant," the com tech replied.

Lakshindo released the transmission key with a sense of profound relief. He'd been more than a little anxious when he was first briefed on Operation Scoop, and it was a vast relief to discover that his anxiety had been misplaced.

"Excuse me, Sergeant?" a voice said politely.

Lakshindo turned to the man who'd spoken. It was one of the reporters, he saw, taking in the other's press badge and the camera crew behind him.

"Yes, Sir? Can I help you?" Lakshindo said, equally politely, mindful of Captain Chiawa's admonition that everything had to be kept as calm and low-key as possible.

"Could you tell me what's happening?" the newsy asked, extending a microphone in Lakshindo's direction.

"I'm afraid not," Lakshindo replied. "Not yet, at any rate. I understand a statement will be issued shortly by Brigadier Jongdomba's headquarters. In the meantime, however, I'm afraid I'm going to have to ask you to step back from the lobby entry."

"Of course, Sergeant," the reporter said, with a respectful nod.

He stepped back and to the side, gesturing for his camera crew to follow him. But the cameraman and his two assistants appeared to have been taken by surprise by the gesture. They started to follow their newsy, but as the cameraman turned hastily, he bumped into the closer of his assistants and dropped his camera. It hit the pavement and shattered, and the sudden disaster to such an expensive piece of equipment drew Lakshindo's eye like a magnet.

Which was why the sergeant was looking in exactly the wrong direction as both the cameraman's assistants produced sawed-off combat rifles from under their jackets and opened fire.

Lakshindo felt the impact of at least half a dozen rounds. The tungsten-cored penetrators of the discarding sabot ammunition penetrated his antiballistic, unpowered armor effortlessly at such point-blank range. The sledgehammer blows battered him backwards, and he went down, eyes huge with disbelieving shock and agony as the penetrators—tumbling after slamming through his armor—shredded his heart and lungs.

The rest of his squad was frozen in total disbelief. They were still staring, brains numbed by the shock of their sergeant's sudden, brutally efficient murder, when the cameraman and reporter produced their own machine pistols. Then all four of the "newsies" opened fire, even as two nondescript civilian vans screeched to a halt and at least a dozen more armed men and women began erupting from each of them.

Three of Lakshindo's troopers actually managed to return fire before they died. None of them hit anything, and as the last of them was slammed to the ground, Ang Jangmu Thaktu led her attack force across their bodies and into the building.

CHAPTER SEVEN

Serafina Palacios was in the middle of a conference with her company commanders when the com on her desk beeped softly.

"Just a second, Kevin."

She raised one hand in Captain Trammell's direction, then activated the com implant in her mastoid instead of walking across to her desk.

"Palacios," she said. She listened for a moment, and Trammell and the other company COs watched with casual curiosity—which became abruptly *uncasual* as she stiffened suddenly in her chair.

"Repeat that!" she said sharply, then shook her head as if the person at the other end of the com link could actually see her disbelief. "And then?" she prompted. She listened again, then said, "They did *what*?"

"No," she said after a moment. "No, I believe you. I only wish I didn't. All right. This is going to turn into the mother of all cluster fucks, and it's going to do it fast. I've got all the company commanders right here. I'll pass the heads-up to them and get them back to their companies ASAP. In the meantime, get all of our people stood to. Transmit the Blockhouse alert now—my authority."

The five captains sitting in her office looked at one another. Then they looked back at her, as her eyes refocused on them.

"I take it you heard," she said in a desert-dry tone.

"Blockhouse, Ma'am?" Trammell asked for all of them, and she nodded grimly.

"Our esteemed militia colleagues have just screwed the pooch by the numbers." Her tone was no longer dry; it was harsh, biting. "Not that they didn't have help. It would appear that Governor Aubert's invitation to Mr. Pankarma wasn't issued in good faith after all."

"Jesus," somebody muttered, and Trammell pursed his lips in a silent whistle.

"That's right," Palacios said. "When Pankarma and his delegation arrived at the Annapurna Arms, Brigadier Jongdomba had Colonel Sharwa's regiment waiting to arrest them in the name of the planetary government."

"After they promised safe conduct?" Trammell sounded like a man who very much wanted to disbelieve what he was hearing.

"Ah, but they didn't," Palacios said bitingly. Trammell and the others just looked at her, and she laughed harshly. "*Governor Aubert* promised them safe conduct, not President Shangup. And, if you'll notice, the military forces directly answerable to the governor as His Majesty's representative—that's us, by the way—had nothing to do with the arrest attempt."

"And who's going to believe Shangup and Jongdomba would even have dreamed of doing something like this without Aubert's approval?" Captain Adriana Becker, Bravo Company's CO, demanded incredulously. But Kevin Trammell had zeroed in on another part of Palacios' terse explanation.

"You said 'attempt,' Skipper," he said. "*Please* tell me they at least managed to pull it off."

"No, they didn't." Palacios shook her head, her expression equally disgusted and apprehensive. "Apparently the GLF wasn't quite as trusting as Governor Aubert—excuse me, as *President Shangup*—hoped. They had a strike force of their own ready, and they must've been tapped into the militia's com net. They came crashing in while the militia were still trying to take Pankarma's party into custody."

"How bad was it, Ma'am?" Captain Shapiro asked softly.

"We don't have much in the way of details yet, Chaim," Palacios told Delta Company's commander. "What we do have, though, sounds pretty damned bad. Apparently, the GLF punched out an entire militia squad on its way in—no survivors. Then they shot their way through another couple of squads to pull Pankarma out.

But about the time they got there, the idiots who'd been trying to arrest Pankarma in the first place, seem to have opened fire themselves. According to the preliminary reports, they killed a half-dozen or more of their own people, but they did manage to kill at least half of the GLF delegation, as well . . . including Pankarma."

"My God." Captain Kostatina Diomedes shook her head, her face ashen. "The GLF will go up like an old-fashioned nuke!"

"And a good chunk of the rest of the planet will be right behind them," Palacios agreed grimly. Then she shook herself. "All right. All of you know everything I know at this point. Get back to your companies—now. I'll pass everything else I get to you the instant I have it. Now *go*, people."

She watched her subordinates gather up their computer chips and memo pads and head for the door. Most of them went straight through it at something between a brisk jog and a run, but Trammell paused in the doorway and looked back at her.

"Yes, Kevin?" she said.

"Boss," he said quietly, "you went to Blockhouse on your own authority."

"Yes, I did," she said flatly. Then she inhaled and gave her head a little toss. "Sorry, Kevin. I know what you meant. But there's no time to clear it with Aubert ahead of time—assuming that asshole Salgado would even let me talk to him in the first place! Besides, this whole fucking mess is the result of their brainstorm, and it's obvious they went to considerable lengths to lay the blame off on the militia and Shangup if anything went wrong."

"But, still—" Trammell began.

"No." She cut him off with a sharp shake of her head. "I know what you're going to say, and I can't risk it. Right this minute, they're probably in a state of shock over there. And you know as well as I do that the only thing they're going to be thinking about right now is how to save their own asses. Their first instinct is going to be to try to keep their heads down and let someone else—*anyone* else—take the fall. Which means they're going to be busy trying to shove all of this off on Jongdomba, too. And Jongdomba couldn't organize a bottle party in a distillery on this kind of notice. Or do you actually think he had a contingency plan in place for something like this? Because, if you do, I've got some nice beachfront property on the Mare Imbrium I'd like to sell you!"

Trammell opened his mouth in fresh protest, then closed it. For just a moment he was deeply, selfishly—and guiltily—grateful that *he* wasn't in command of the battalion.

"No, Ma'am," he said. "I don't think the militia ever even *heard* of contingency planning. But going to Blockhouse without the governor's authorization is going to raise a shitstorm. If anything—anything at all—goes wrong, Aubert's going to try to hang *you* for it."

"My mother always told me the real test of anyone's character was the enemies they made," Palacios said with a cold smile. "I'll take my chances, Kevin. Now, go."

"Yes, Ma'am."

Trammell surprised them both by coming briefly to attention and saluting formally. Then he obeyed her order and vanished.

Captain Karsang Dawa Chiawa stood in the corpse-littered hallway and stared about him in shock.

This wasn't supposed to happen, his brain told him numbly. *They were supposed to surrender!*

But they hadn't.

"Sir." He looked up dully from the contorted bodies and the death-stench of ruptured organs and blood. Somehow, he thought distantly, it was the *smells*, far more than the sights, which were going to live in his nightmares.

"Yes?" he said.

"Sir," his com tech resolutely looked away from the bodies himself as he held out a handset, "Colonel Sharwa wants to speak to you."

Oh, I'll just bet he does, Chiawa thought bitterly, but he only nodded and held out his own hand.

"Chiawa here, Colonel," he said into the handset.

"Chiawa, you fucking *idiot*!" Sharwa bellowed into his ear. "What the *hell* did you think you were *doing*?!"

"Colonel, I—" Chiawa began, without much hope that he'd be allowed to finish the sentence.

"Shut the fuck up!" Sharwa shouted. "I don't want to hear any goddamned excuses! It was a simple enough mission, and now, thanks to *your* fuckup, God only knows what's going to happen!"

Chiawa shut his mouth and gritted his teeth while the com rattled against his ear.

"Just how bad is it?" the colonel continued.

"Sir, I've lost at least thirty men," Chiawa said harshly. "They ambushed my outer security squad—apparently they had their own armed people mixed in with the newsies." *The newsies which you specifically told me we couldn't bar from the hotel approaches without "giving away the game,"* he thought bitterly. "Then at least another twenty or thirty of their people shot their way into the hotel. I lost more of my people on their way in, and several members of the hotel staff were killed or wounded in the crossfire. And—" he drew a deep breath "—Pankarma's group hadn't surrendered when the shooting started outside. I'm not sure exactly what happened. According to one of my people, one of the GLF delegates produced a pistol. I don't know if that's true. If it is, I haven't seen the gun yet. But whatever happened, my people opened fire."

"You mean—?" Sharwa seemed unable to complete the question, and Chiawa's lips twitched in a humorless smile.

"I mean Pankarma himself is dead, Sir," he said flatly. "At least half his 'delegation' is also dead."

"But you have the others in custody," Sharwa said.

"No, Sir. I don't." Chiawa turned, looking away from the bodies and the puddles and pools of gummy blood. "The gunmen coming in from the outside shot their way through to the 'delegation' too quickly for that. As far as I know, they got all of the survivors—some of whom may have been wounded—out with them."

"*Shit!*" Sharwa exploded. "Couldn't you do *any* fucking thing right? Now the bastards know their precious leader is dead, or at least wounded, and we don't have a single goddamned bargaining chip!"

"Sir, when this operation was planned, I was assured that—"

"Shut up! Just shut the fuck back up!"

"Sir," Chiawa continued, despite the order, "however we got here, the situation is coming completely apart. We need more—"

"I told you to shut your trap, *Captain*." Sharwa's voice was suddenly icy. "Of course you want more men. And just what in your *brilliant* handling of the situation to date suggests to you that I'd trust you with a kindergarten class? If I give you more men, you'll just make this disaster even worse!"

"Sir, we've got to get a mobilization order out before—" Chiawa began, then looked up as Lieutenant Tuchi Phurba Nawa, Second Platoon's commander, came running into the hallway.

"We've got trouble out front!" Nawa was breathing hard, his eyes wide. "The crowd's getting ugly. They're starting to throw bricks and paving stones. And they're demanding to see Pankarma—now."

Chiawa closed his eyes. Then he opened them again, held up one hand at Nawa in a "wait" gesture, and drew a deep breath.

"Colonel," he said into the handset, interrupting a further tirade. "The mob—" he used the noun deliberately, hoping it might break through to Sharwa "—outside the hotel is turning violent. And it's demanding to see Pankarma."

"And what the hell do you expect *me* to do about that?" Sharwa demanded. "You're the genius who killed the bastard! If a mob's gathering, disperse it!"

"Sir, I don't know if that's the best approach," Chiawa began. "If we—"

"Goddamn it, Chiawa! Get some people out there and get those sons of bitches under control! I don't care how you do it, *Captain*, but you damned well better do it now!"

Chiawa lowered the handset and looked back at Nawa.

"Take your platoon," he began, then stopped. Sergeant Lakshindo's squad had been from Nawa's platoon. Emotions would probably be running high among their platoonmates, and Nawa would be understrength without Lakshindo, anyway.

"Tell Salaka to take *his* platoon out there. Tell him I want those people dispersed."

"Yes, Sir!" Nawa began to turn away, but Chiawa's left hand shot out and grabbed his equipment harness.

"I want them dispersed," he repeated in a lower voice, simultaneously pressing the com handset against his thigh with his right hand to muffle the microphone, "but I don't want any more escalation if we can avoid it. You tell Salaka that no one fires a shot, except in direct self-defense. If he can't move them back without that, he's to tell me so and get my direct, personal authorization before he opens fire. Clear?"

"Yes, Sir!" Nawa repeated.

"Then go!" Chiawa released Nawa's harness and watched the lieutenant disappear. Then he raised the handset once more.

"I'm sending troops out, now, Colonel," he said. "With your permission, I'd like to go take personal charge of that and—"

"I'll just bet you would, Captain!" Sharwa snarled. "Unfortunately, I'm not quite *done* with you yet. In fact—"

Lieutenant Tsimbuti Pemba Salaka drew a deep breath and looked at his platoon sergeant.

"All right," he said. "Let's get this done."

Sergeant Garza nodded, but his expression was less than confident. Salaka didn't blame him. The lieutenant had tried to project as much confidence as he could, but he knew he'd failed. This wasn't the sort of situation he'd envisioned in his worst nightmares when he'd decided to join the planetary militia.

He gave the taut-faced men behind him one more glance, then hefted his bullhorn and started towards the shattered glass doors.

The luxury hotel's palatial main lobby was a shambles. Huge shards of broken glass glittered in the patches of blood which showed where the GLF gunmen had shot their way in. The hurled bricks, paving stones, and beer bottles which had produced most of the breakage laying amid the rubble like curses, and the snarling sea of voices from the furious mob was like the sound of some huge, hungry beast.

Something else came flying in through one of the demolished glass walls. It hit the floor and shattered, and a gout of smoking flame erupted from the crude Molotov cocktail. The hotel's sprinkler system activated almost immediately, and Salaka and his platoon found themselves advancing through a pounding downpour.

Just what we needed, the lieutenant thought. He swallowed again and again, fighting the useless urge to wipe his sweating palms on his breastplate.

Another Molotov cocktail crashed into the lobby, sputtering flame, and two or three of his people flinched.

"Steady!" he said, wishing his own voice sounded less tentative, less frightened. "Steady!"

We need riot police, not militia, he thought. *Why didn't they deploy riot cops to handle the outside security in the first place?*

Then he was at the doors, and he drew another deep breath and stepped out of them, wishing he had something considerably more lethal, or at least intimidating, than a bullhorn in his hand.

The mob voice surged suddenly higher at the sight of his men and their uniforms. He could actually *feel* the hatred pulsing behind that deep, harsh, snarling sound, and a bewildered part of him wondered where it had come from. The militia had only wanted to arrest a batch of self-proclaimed criminals. The vast majority of Gyangtse's people *condemned* the GLF—that was what all the militia's intelligence briefings, all of the editorialists, had been saying for years! They should have *wanted* to see Pankarma and his people taken into custody. And surely they must understand that no one had wanted this sort of carnage—that it was the *GLF*'s fault for coming in shooting this way!

"Citizens!" he shouted, the bullhorn giving him sufficient volume to make himself heard even through the bellowing chaos. "Citizens, disperse at once! You are engaged in an illegal activity, and people—*more* people—are going to get hurt if this continues! We don't want any more injuries, so please—"

Tsimbuti Pemba Salaka never heard the sound of the three shots. One round struck his breastplate and was deflected. The second struck his left arm, shattering his upper arm instantly.

The third struck him almost exactly midway between his left eyebrow and the rim of his helmet, and his skull exploded under the impact.

"—and after *that*, Captain, I'll personally see to it that you spend the next five or ten years in prison!" Sharwa raved in Chiawa's ear.

The colonel was into full rant mode. Even at the moment, he had to know as well as Chiawa did that most of his threatened extravagant vengeance wasn't going to happen. Or maybe he *did* think it would. Maybe he was even right. Depending on how badly this turned out, the planetary government might just decide that one Captain Chiawa would make a suitable scapegoat for how all of his superiors had screwed up.

Chiawa didn't know about that. He just knew there were things he needed to be doing besides standing here listening to this idiot scream in his ear. Unfortunately, the idiot in question had the rank to *keep* him standing here.

And then Chiawa looked up from the handset as Nawa came charging back into the hallway.

"Sir, Salaka's down and—!"

The sudden crackle of rifle fire cut Nawa's report off. The outburst of fire was as brief as it was sudden, and then Chiawa heard the baying howl of hundreds of voices as the mob outside the Annapurna Arms charged the building.

"—and I trust you have an explanation for your high-handed, *illegal* actions, Major!"

Ákos Salgado's voice would have blistered battle steel, but the golden-haired woman in the Marine uniform on his communicator's display simply looked back at him calmly.

"With all due respect, Mr. Salgado," she replied after moment, "any explanations are due to Governor Aubert, not you."

"I'm the governor's *chief of staff!*" Salgado snapped furiously. "He's delegated the authority to get some sort of explanation for this idiocy out of you . . . and I'm still waiting for it."

"Then you're going to have a lengthy wait, Mr. Salgado," she said coldly. "For an explanation of my 'high-handed, illegal actions,' I mean. Because, Sir, they were neither."

"The hell they weren't!" Salgado glared at her. "You had no authority—none at all—to occupy the spaceport, or the city's water plant and power station, *or* to declare martial law here in the capital in His Majesty's name!"

"Under Article 42 of the Imperial Articles of War, I have not merely the authority, but the responsibility, as the senior ranking military officer on this planet, to take any action I believe the situation requires in the absence of direction from competent superior authority," she said, and Salgado's face turned puce.

"God damn it, the governor *is* your superior authority!" he bellowed.

"I'm aware of the legal chain of command, Mr. Salgado. However, I had no direction from the governor—or even from you—of any sort, and at the critical moment—due, no doubt, to the confusion engendered by the sudden outbreak of violence—I was unable to contact either of you. And," she looked him straight in the eye, "since I've been unfortunately unable to contact Governor Aubert for quite lengthy periods on several occasions over the past few weeks, despite what you've assured me are your communications people's best efforts, it was apparent to me that I might not be able to reach him for some time. Under those circumstances, I felt I had no option but to take action immediately on my own responsibility."

Salgado's teeth ground together. The bitch. The backbiting, conniving, rules-lawyering *bitch*!

He started to open his mouth for the verbal flaying she so amply deserved, but then he made himself stop. She was recording this. He knew she was, that she *wanted* him to say something she could play back for her own military superiors—or *his* superiors in the Ministry—to justify her own actions and hang him.

Well, Ákos Salgado wasn't going to give her that particular soundbite.

"You may have acted within the letter of your own authority, Major," he said icily. "You did so, however, without any consultation with or authorization by your civilian superiors. Given the current state of confusion and the heat of emotions on Gyangtse, your personal decision to resort to the iron fist approach may very well have elevated what would have been a minor, purely local matter into a direct confrontation with the authority of the Empire. Should that happen, I warn you, Governor Aubert and I will do everything in our power to see to it that you suffer the consequences you will so amply merit."

"I'm sure you will, Mr. Salgado," she replied, her tone cool while contempt flared in her blue eyes. "Time, of course, will tell whether or not my actions were justified, won't it? And, speaking of time, I find myself rather pressed for it at the moment. Will there be anything else, Sir?"

"No," he grated. "Not at this time, Major."

"In that case, good-bye," she said, and cut the circuit.

"My, my," Gregory Hilton murmured as he and Alicia stood on the roof of the Zhikotse spaceport's northernmost shuttle pad and watched the dense columns of smoke rising above the Old Town. "That doesn't sound good, does it?"

"That" was the staccato crackle of automatic weapons fire, interspersed with the occasional explosion of hand grenades, mortars, or chemical-explosive rockets. There were other sounds, as well. Sounds Alicia's sensory boosters could sort out of the general bedlam if she tried. The yammering surf of a howling mob, the wail of emergency vehicles' sirens, individual screams and shouts, and the clatter and roar of the militia's old-fashioned, unarmored troop carriers.

How? she wondered. *How did it all happen so fast?*

She didn't have an answer for that question. So far as she knew, no one did. And as she watched the smoke billow, heard the cacophony grinding steadily closer to the spaceport, she knew it really didn't matter. Not now. Perhaps it had once, and no doubt it would someday matter once more. But what mattered right this moment was *dealing* with it, not understanding it.

"How long before they hit our perimeter, do you think, Greg?" she asked, and the calmness of her own voice astounded her. It seemed to belong to someone else, someone whose nerves weren't tied into knots and whose belly muscles weren't clenched.

"Hard to say," Hilton replied after a moment. "They're obviously headed our way, and those militia sad sacks aren't going to stop them. Might slow them down a bit, I suppose." He frowned judiciously. "Of course, I imagine quite a few of our noble militiamen are busy finding new and compelling loyalties at the moment."

"You really think many of them will go over to the other side?"

"Don't sound so surprised, Larva." Hilton chuckled harshly. "First, it's pretty damned obvious from the remotes that the mob is gonna roll right over anything that gets in its way, and these poor militia pukes *live* here. They're going to be thinking about that, in between pissing themselves. They aren't gonna want to get rolled over, they don't have anyplace to go, and they aren't gonna want to kill a whole bunch of their friends and neighbors. Especially not if they're gonna go on living here . . . and if doing that won't stop the mob, anyway.

"Second, I'd be *real* surprised if there weren't quite a few GLF sympathizers in the militia to begin with. They're going to go over to the other side in droves, and they're gonna take as many of their buddies with them as they can." He shrugged. "Frankly, in their shoes, I'd probably be thinking the same way. What're we gonna do about it later? Shoot 'em all? Especially if we can't *prove* what they were up to during the present . . . unpleasantness? Oh, a few of them might catch it in the neck, but even so, that's somewhere off in the future. They're thinking about right now."

"Well, *someone's* still putting up a scrap," Alicia observed, waving a hand as a fresh wave of weapons fire chattered and thundered in the distance.

"Yep." Hilton nodded. "There's gonna be some who stick it out all the way to the end. Some of 'em because, frankly, they're good troops, even if they are stuck in this useless militia. And like good troops everywhere, they're gonna be the ones who take the heavy losses while the rest of their sorry outfit packs up and bugs out behind them.

"And some of them are gonna stick because they don't have anywhere else to go. You think maybe Jongdomba or Sharwa is gonna be especially welcome in the bosom of the Revolution?"

"They can't possibly expect to win, not in the long term," Alicia murmured.

"The mob? The GLF?" Hilton said. She looked at him, and he shrugged. "Alicia, this isn't—none of this is—what you might call a reasoned response." He waved one hand in the direction of the smoke and thunder and shook his head. "When Pankarma got his ass killed, 'reasoned' went right out the window. Neither side ever expected it, and neither side had any kind of plan in place in case it happened. And now the whole damned situation's completely out of control. No one's in *charge* of this, Alley. It's just happening, and by now it's feeding on itself. I've seen it before."

"Well," Alicia said after a minute or so, "at least we managed to get most of our people inside the perimeter."

"There's that," Hilton agreed. Then he sighed. Alicia looked at him, and he smiled sadly.

"Think about what you just said," he told her quietly. "We've got 'most of our people' inside. Who *are* 'our people'? Just us offworlders and our dependents? What about all the people here on Gyangtse who supported the Incorporation? The ones someone in that mob is going to *know* supported Incorporation? What happens to them? And, for that matter, what happens to the mob when it does hit our perimeter and finds out the difference between the local militia and the Imperial Marine Corps?"

Alicia looked at him for a moment longer, then turned back towards the distant wall of smoke.

Somehow, at that instant, that rising breath of destruction was far less frightening than the questions Gregory Hilton had just posed.

"This is a frigging disaster," Ákos Salgado said bitterly as he strode into Governor Aubert's office. Aubert stood by the window, back to the door and hands clasped behind him, gazing out at the same smoke Alicia could see from her own position. "I warned Palacios that this knee-jerk, iron fist approach of hers can only make things worse, and the goddamned lunatic basically told me to go fuck myself! I swear to God, I'll see that bitch court-martialed if it's the last thing I—"

"Ákos," Aubert said levelly, "shut up."

Salgado's jaw dropped, and he stared at the Governor's back with the eyes of a beached fish. For at least three full seconds, that appeared to be all he was capable of doing. Then his mouth started to work again.

"But . . . but . . ." he began.

"I *said*," Aubert said, turning from the window to face him at last, "to shut up."

Salgado closed his mouth, and Aubert walked across to seat himself behind his desk. Then he leaned back in his chair, his expression grim.

"This isn't the result of any 'iron fist' on Major Palacios' part," he said flatly. "This is the result of *our* stupidity."

"But—"

"I'm not going to tell you again to keep your mouth *shut*." Aubert's voice was an icicle, and Salgado felt a sudden stab of very personal panic as he looked into his patron's eyes and suddenly read his own political future with perfect prescience.

"Palacios has been trying to tell us for months that something like this was coming," Aubert continued. "I thought she was wrong. I thought she was an alarmist. I thought Jongdomba's so-called intelligence analysts knew the local situation better than she did. And, God help me, I thought *you* knew your ass from your elbow. I wish—you'll never know how *much* I wish—that I could look in my mirror and tell myself this was all your fault. You're the one who's been manipulating my schedule to keep Palacios from bending my ear with her 'alarmism' and her 'paranoia.' You're the one who's been 'losing' messages from her to me. And you're the one who came up with this brilliant plan to arrest Pankarma. But the only problem with blaming it all on you, is that I knew exactly what you were doing when I *let* you do it. I even agreed with you, despite everything Palacios tried to tell me, which makes me just as big a fool as you. No, a *bigger* fool, one who kept his eyes closed and his fingers in his ears so I could go on ignoring all the warning signs. Kereku was completely correct in his reading of what's been happening here on Gyangtse, and he's twelve light-years from here. Which means, much as I hate to admit it, that he was also absolutely right to try and get my worthless ass fired."

"Governor—Jasper," Salgado began desperately, "of course this is all a terrible—"

"Get out," Aubert said almost calmly. Salgado goggled at him, and the governor pointed at the office door. "I said, 'get out,'" he repeated. "As in get your stupid fucking face on the other side of that door, and out of my sight, and keep it there. *Now.*"

Ákos Salgado looked at him for another heartbeat, recognizing the utter and irretrievable ruin of his career. Then his shoulders sagged and he turned and walked blindly from the office.

CHAPTER EIGHT

"Fall back! *Fall back!*"

Karsang Dawa Chiawa's throat felt raw as he shouted the command.

Even now, he could scarcely believe how explosively the mob had reacted, how quickly it had gathered and how violently it had grown. Nothing in any of the intelligence reports *he'd* seen had suggested that anyone in the planetary government or the militia had believed the GLF enjoyed any real support among the general population. Apparently, they'd been wrong.

And sending Salaka out to face it had been exactly the wrong move, he thought grimly. Although, to be fair to himself, even now, he couldn't think of anything which could have been considered the "right move." Especially not given Sharwa's demand that he "disperse" the mob immediately coupled with the colonel's refusal to allow Chiawa to take charge of it personally. After all, it had been *so* much more important for Sharwa to continue ripping a strip off Chiawa than to let the captain do anything constructive about the situation. Or for the colonel to call up more of the militia. Or even to inform President Shangup of what had happened.

But Chiawa knew that, however badly at fault Sharwa might have been, he would never forgive himself for not telling the colonel to shut the hell up while *he* handled the dispersal. Of course, he hadn't realized there were weapons in the crowd any more than Salaka had, but he should have allowed for the possibility.

Salaka's death had been the final straw. The brick-throwers had turned suddenly into a screaming tide of enraged humanity, and most of Salaka's men had been just as confused, just as shaken, as anyone else. They hadn't expected *any* of this, and when Salaka went down, they'd hesitated. Maybe that was Chiawa's fault, too. He was the one who'd specifically cautioned Salaka against the use of lethal force. He was sure he'd go on second-guessing himself for the rest of his life, but the truth was that he didn't know if it would have made any difference if they'd opened fire the instant the crowd-become-mob started forward. In any case, they hadn't. They'd tried to give ground, to avoid killing their fellow citizens, and those fellow citizens had swarmed over them.

As far as Chiawa knew, not a single member of Salaka's platoon had survived, and he didn't know, frankly, how he'd gotten *anyone* out of the hotel as the howling mob seemed to materialize out of the very pavement. They'd had to shoot their way out, and he knew at least some of his people hadn't even tried to. He didn't know how well they'd made out with their efforts to join the mob, but he knew some of them had at least made the attempt.

Those who'd stuck with him had tried to reach some sort of support, some haven from the typhoon. It hadn't been easy, with the capital's streets infested with rioters—more and more of whom appeared to be armed—screaming their hatred for anyone in uniform. They'd managed to link up, briefly, with Echo Company, the only other militia unit Brigadier Jongdomba and Colonel Sharwa had mustered for the "routine" operation. But Captain Padorje, Echo Company's CO, had insisted on attempting to carry out Colonel Sharwa's order to retake the Annapurna Arms. Exactly what Sharwa had hoped that might accomplish escaped Chiawa, although the colonel had apparently believed even then that a sharp, successful show of force would "whip the street rabble back to its kennel."

Whatever Sharwa might have thought would happen, the orders had been a mistake—*another* mistake—but Padorje had refused to take Chiawa's word for that. And so they'd gone back against the tide . . . and disintegrated like a sand castle in the face of a rising sea. Chiawa had seen it coming, and he'd done his best to pull his own people out of the wreck, but they'd been hit from three sides as they entered Brahmaputra Square, three blocks short of the hotel.

Padorje's lead platoon had simply disappeared, and the rest of Echo Company—and Alpha Company's survivors—had splintered into desperately fighting, frantically retreating knots with the mob baying savagely in pursuit.

And now, after what seemed an eternity but couldn't have been more than a few hours in reality, he was down to this. He'd been trying to work his way towards the spaceport, where the Marines were supposed to be holding a perimeter, but every time he headed east, he ran into a fresh surge of rioters who drove his remaining people back to the west. By now, they were almost halfway across the city from the port, but he couldn't think of any other objective which might give his people a chance of survival.

The two dozen-plus militiamen still holding together under his command—only eight of them were from his own company—actually managed to obey his latest fall back order. The jury-rigged squad under the sergeant from Echo Company rose from its firing positions and headed back past Chiawa's own position at a run. The captain had managed to select the location for their next no-doubt-pointless stand from his map display, and the sergeant—whose name Chiawa couldn't remember—flung himself back down on his belly behind an ornamental shrub's ceramacrete planter. The other members of "his" squad found spots of their own, most with decent cover, at least from the front.

"Position!" the nameless sergeant announced over Chiawa's com.

"Copy," Chiawa responded, then looked back to his front. "Chamba! Time to go!"

"On our way!" Sergeant Chamba Mingma Lhukpa replied, and rose in a crouch, waving for his own men to fall back.

They obeyed the hand signal, moving, Chiawa noted, with a wary care they'd never displayed in any of the militia's exercises. He couldn't avoid a certain bitterness at the observation, but he made himself set it aside quickly. These people were the survivors. The ones who'd possessed the tenacity to stick when everyone else bugged out . . . and who'd been fast enough learners—and nasty enough—to survive. So far. If Chiawa had had a single full platoon of them under his command at the Annapurna Arms, none of this would have happened.

Bullshit. You—and Sharwa and that idiot Jongdomba—still *would've fucked it up, and you know it,* a small, still voice said in the back of his brain as Lhukpa's exhausted, grim-faced people fell back around him. Bullets whined and cracked overhead, skipped across the pavement, or punched fist-sized holes in the façades of buildings, and he heard a sudden scream as one of his remaining privates went down.

Lhukpa started back, but Chiawa pointed back to the position from which the nameless sergeant and *his* people were laying down aimed covering fire.

"*Go!*" the captain screamed, and once again, the sergeant obeyed.

Chiawa turned back. An icy fist squeezed shut on his stomach and twisted as the incoming rifle fire seemed to redouble. He heard the thunderous, tearing-cloth sound of a firing calliope added to the cacophony, and he felt like a man wading into the teeth of a stiff wind. Except, of course, that no wind he had ever faced had been made of penetrators capable of punching straight through the breast and backplates of the unpowered body armor he wore.

He went down on one knee beside the fallen private. Chepal Pemba Solu, he realized. One of the handful from his own company, like Lhukpa, to stick by him. He rolled Solu onto his back and checked the life sign monitor. It was black, and he bit off a curse, grabbed Solu's dog tags, and went dashing after Lhukpa.

And even as he ran, he felt a fresh stab of guilt because a part of him couldn't help thinking that they were better off with Solu dead than trying to carry a badly wounded man with them through this nightmare.

Something louder than usual exploded ahead of him. The shockwave caused him to stumble, still running, and he tucked his shoulder under, grunting with anguish as he hit the ceramacrete full force, still driving forward at the moment of impact. He rolled as he landed, flinging himself sideways until his frantically tumbling body bumped up over the curb of a sidewalk and he slammed into a city bench. That stopped him . . . and would have broken ribs without his body armor.

There was another explosion. And another.

Mortars, his brain reported even as he gasped for the breath which had been driven out of him. *The bastards have gotten their hands on some of our own mortars!*

A moment later, he was forced to revise his initial impression. If that was an ex-militia mortar, it wasn't a bunch of untrained rioters using it. The initial rounds had landed long, well beyond his people's positions; the follow-up rounds were marching steadily and professionally up the avenue towards him. Someone who knew what he was doing was on the other end of those explosions, so either it was one of the weapons Sharwa had assured all of his people the GLF didn't have, or else it *was* one which had once belonged to the militia . . . and was being operated by a mortar *crew* which had once belonged to the militia, as well.

Not that it mattered very much. His double handful of people had semi-adequate cover against small arms fire, but not against indirect fire that could search out the dead spots behind planters, parked cars, and ceramacrete steps.

"Inside!" he shouted over the com. "*Into the buildings!*"

He was already up, running for the broad flight of steps to the main entrance of the office building behind his bench. Someone else was running up them with him—at least two or three someone elses. That was good; at least he wouldn't be alone. But this was the one thing he'd tried to avoid from the beginning of the nightmare retreat. Once his people were broken up into tiny, independent groups he couldn't coordinate and control, their cohesion was bound to disappear. And even if that hadn't been the case, as soon as they split up, they could only become complete fugitives, unable to rely on one another for mutual support.

"Everybody, listen to me," he panted over the com as he burst through the office building's door into the incongruously spotless and peaceful lobby. "Keep going. Break contact, scatter, and get to the spaceport somehow. I'll see you all there. And . . . thanks."

He said the last word quietly, almost softly. Then he looked over his shoulder at the four militiamen who'd managed to join him. None of whom, he noted, were from Alpha Company.

"All right, guys," he said wearily. "That goes for us, too. You—Munming," he read the name stenciled on the other man's breastplate. Munming was a corporal, armed with a grenade launcher, and he still had half a bandolier of grenades. "You're our heavy fire element. You stay behind me. Load with flechette for right now. You two," he indicated two riflemen, neither of whom he recognized. "You and I are point. You," he tapped one of them on the chest, "right flank. You," he indicated the other, "left flank. I'll take the center. And you," he turned to the fourth and final militiaman, "you've got our backs. Clear?"

Gaunt, smoke-stained faces nodded, and he nodded back to them.

"In that case, let's get our asses moving."

"Well, this truly sucks," Sergeant Major Winfield said. Major Palacios looked up from the tactical display table and quirked an eyebrow at him.

"I take it that that profound observation reflects some new and even more disgusting turn of events, Sar'Major?"

"Oh, yes, indeedy-deed it does, Ma'am," Winfield told her. "We've just received a priority request for assistance from none other than Brigadier Jongdomba."

"Why am I not surprised?" Palacios sighed. She shook her head, gazing down at the map display in front of her, and grimaced.

The response to the bungled arrest attempt had been even swifter and uglier than she'd feared. She still didn't think the GLF had planned any of this. In fact, her best guess—and the take from the Battalion's sensor remotes seemed to confirm it—was that the Liberation Front's remaining leadership understood just how suicidal something like this was. All indications were that Pankarma's surviving lieutenants were doing their damnedest to shut everything down before it got even worse. Unfortunately, if the GLF ever had been in control, it was no longer.

What had begun with the shootout at the Annapurna Arms had turned into something with all the earmarks of a genuinely spontaneous insurrection. There were conflicting reports—rumors, really—about who'd done what first, and to whom, after the initial exchange of fire. Her own best guess was that the reports that the Liberation Front people had only tried to pull back and disengage with the handful of their delegation they'd managed to get out alive were accurate. She couldn't conceive of them having *wanted* to do anything else. Aside from that, though, she had no idea what had transpired. Except, of course, for the fact that a sizable percentage of the capital city's population was out in the streets, armed with everything from combat rifles, calliopes, grenade launchers, and mortars to old-fashioned paving stones and Molotov cocktails.

A lot of it doesn't have anything to do with what happened to Pankarma, she told herself. *This is the politically voiceless urban poor of a depressed economy scenting blood and the opportunity to get some of their own back against the people they blame for their poverty. Sure, there's separatism stirred into the mix, and anti-Empire feeling does run deep out here, especially with the people who feel most crapped on by the system, but that's not what's giving this the fury we're seeing.*

The Gyangtse oligarchy was no worse than some she'd seen, but it was still worse than most, and it had generated a lot of resentment among the lower strata of Gyangtsese society even before it embraced the current Incorportation referendum. She knew it had, because she'd seen something like this coming for months. One of the reasons her battalion had been assigned to Gyangtse in the first place was that Recon was—in addition to being specifically trained to pull information out of chaos in a situation like this—also supposed to specialize in identifying trends and keeping a handle on even restive planetary populations in order to *prevent* a "situation" like this one.

Unfortunately, that assumed their civilian superiors would let them do their job ahead of time. Speaking of whom . . .

"Have we heard anything else from Governor Aubert?" she asked.

"No, Ma'am," Lieutenant Thomas Bradwell, her S-6, the officer in charge of her communications, said expressionlessly. "Not since his secretary commed to tell us that we're supposed to go through him, not Mr. Salgado, if we need to reach the governor."

Palacios nodded, her face as expressionless as Bradwell's voice, and wondered once again whether or not Salgado's apparent fall from grace was a good sign, or a bad one. If it *was* a bad one, at least it had plenty of company on that side of the ledger sheet.

Once it all hit the fan, her people had quickly gotten their sensor remotes deployed. The small, independently deployed drones were extraordinarily difficult to spot, even with first-line military sensors, as they hovered silently on their counter-grav. She didn't have as many of them as she would have liked to have—no CO ever did—but she had enough for decent coverage, and their own sensors, designed to deal with the smoke, confusion, camouflage, and electronic warfare systems of a full-scale modern battlefield were more than adequate to keep an eye on something like this.

That meant she had a depressingly clear picture of what was happening, and as she looked at the map, she knew that unless they were all far luckier than they had any reason to expect, the madness was still building towards its peak.

"What sort of assistance is Jongdomba requesting, Sar'Major?" she asked harshly.

"According to his message, Ma'am, he and the loyal core of his brigade are at the Mall. He says his men are prepared to die in defense of President Shangup and the planetary government, but he urgently requests assistance in order to insure the safety of the President and the delegates with him."

"I see."

Palacios managed not to roll her eyes. At the moment, her people had a solid perimeter around the spaceport, as Operation Blockhouse had specified. They also had control of the city's main power station and water plant, which put them in a position to preserve its core public services, and the governor's residence and most of the Empire's official offices on Gyangtse were inside the spaceport perimeter. But the Presidential Mansion was located amid the Capital Mall's parks and fountains on the far side of the city, beyond the chaos and bedlam.

It ought to have been relatively simple—*even for Jongdomba*, she thought acidly—to organize a semiorderly evacuation of the President and the members of the Chamber of Delegates from the Mall's public buildings. They should have been gotten out of the capital the instant the shooting started, but no doubt Jongdomba had given Shangup his personal assurances that the mob couldn't possibly threaten the Presidential Mansion or the adjacent Chamber and executive office buildings. And, of course, no Gyangtsese politician could afford to radiate anything except steel-jawed determination to stand his ground at a moment like this.

Until, of course, it turns out Jongdomba can't *protect them, that is,* she thought, then frowned as another, distinctly unpleasant possibility crossed her mind.

"Did the Brigadier provide us with a situation report, Sar'Major?" she asked after a moment.

"He says the situation is 'unclear,' Ma'am. He says he has the equivalent of about two battalions, and his current estimate is that he's pinned down by an undetermined—but large—number of heavily armed GLF guerrillas. He says they're equipped with military-grade weapons and that his own ammunition is running low. He also states that without assistance, he doubts he can continue to resist effectively for more than another two or three hours."

"I see," she repeated. "I take it he didn't include a list of exactly how many civilians he has inside his lines?"

"No, Ma'am, he didn't." Winfield frowned at her, and she showed her teeth in a humorless smile.

"Now, isn't that interesting," she murmured to herself.

"Excuse me, Ma'am?"

"Just thinking aloud, Sar'Major," Palacios said, and found herself forced to suppress a chuckle, despite her thoughts, at the look Winfield gave her. But the temptation to humor disappeared quickly.

"Tom."

"Yes, Ma'am?" Lieutenant Bradwell replied.

"I need to speak to the Governor, please."

"Are you serious, Major?"

Serafina Palacios' eyes narrowed, and she started to open her mouth quickly, but the man on her com display raised one hand, palm out, before she could speak.

"Forgive me," Jasper Aubert said, and despite herself, Palacios' narrowed eyes went wide at the sincere tone of his apology.

"I owe you—all of your people, really, but especially you, I suppose—a sincere apology for not having listened to you earlier," the governor continued. "For the moment, let's just leave it at that. Hopefully, I'll have an opportunity later to deliver it more appropriately. But I'm not trying to simply dismiss what you're saying now. I'm just trying to get my mind wrapped around it."

"Governor," Palacios said, "I'm not sure I'm right—not by a long chalk. But if I am, then we may have an even worse problem than anyone thought we did.

"It's clear from our remotes that only a minority of Zhikotse's population is actively involved in all this, but even a minority of an entire city's an enormous absolute number. I doubt that as much as twenty percent of the . . . call them "rioters," started out with modern weapons, and most of those were civilian-market, not military. But it looks like most of the weapons from the two companies Sharwa deployed for the . . . arrest attempt are in somebody else's hands now.

"That's bad enough, but an overflight of the two main militia arsenals indicates that they've been looted, as well. So, by now, in addition to anything that may have been out there to begin with, there's probably at least the equivalent of a couple of militia regiments' firepower floating around in the streets."

Including, she thought grimly, *shoulder-fired SAMs.*

The militia surface-to-air missiles which had found their way into someone else's hands (*or,* she made herself admit, *which the GLF had in its possession all along*) had already reduced the original three sting ships of her attached air support to only *two* sting ships, and she'd lost the pilot along with the ship.

Which wouldn't have happened, if I'd allowed for the possibility that they had surface-to-air capability from the beginning. But I didn't. I fucked up, and I wanted a live *set of eyes up there to supplement the remotes. Stupid bitch.*

She pushed that thought aside, too. For now, at least; she knew it would be revisiting her in her dreams.

"I've called on the Fleet for support, but there's not much Lieutenant Granger can do for us at the moment. He's the senior Fleet officer in-system, and all he's got is his own corvette. Corvettes are too small to carry assault shuttles, so he can't assist us with airstrikes or troop drops, and while his vessel's armament could take out the entire *city* with a kinetic strike, heavy HVW aren't very well suited for fire support missions in a situation like this one.

"That leaves it all up to us, and with those SAMs out there, my tactical flexibility's badly cramped. I've got an attached company of air lorries, but we never got the counter-grav armored personnel carriers I requested, and this is exactly the wrong environment for what's basically an unarmored airborne moving van. The 'terrain' makes it effectively impossible to get a detailed read on what might be waiting down there, even with the remotes. There's no way to know with certainty where SAMs or antiarmor weapons actually are, especially if they hide them inside buildings, until the moment they open fire. And even if I knew roughly where they were, the firepower required to suppress them without *precise* locations would be devastating." Palacios shook her head. "At this moment, the majority of the people out there're undoubtedly simply trying to keep their collective head down. I'm not prepared to use that sort of fire when it could only inflict heavy noncombatant casualties. Killing that many innocent bystanders isn't what the Corps does, Governor."

"Of course not," Aubert agreed so quickly and firmly that Palacios had to suppress a fresh flicker of surprise. "Even if you'd been prepared to contemplate that on a moral basis, the political consequences would be totally unacceptable."

Despite herself, Palacios couldn't keep her disdain for his last sentence out of her expression. He obviously saw it, because his own eyes hardened briefly. But then he shook his head.

"I'm not being 'business as usual' about this, Major. I've already admitted that my own judgment and decisions here on Gyangtse have been . . . badly flawed, let's say. But however we got into this mess, eventually, the Empire's going to have to stabilize the situation down here. I've already made that difficult enough for whoever catches the job, but if we kill hundreds, maybe thousands, of people who *haven't* been up in arms against the Emperor's authority, 'stabilizing' Gyangtse once more will take decades. At best."

He said it unflinchingly, and she felt a stir of respect for him. *It seems he's got a brain—and some guts—after all,* she thought. *Some moral integrity, for that matter. Pity he couldn't have shown any sign of it early enough to keep all of this from happening, but this is definitely a case of better late than never. None of which alters the fact that my options are so damned limited.*

She contemplated the tabletop map display again.

After it had finished massacring every militiaman it could catch (except for those who declared their change of allegiance quickly enough), the mob's greatest savagery—so far, at least—had been reserved for the downtown business district. At least a third of the main financial buildings clustered in the district, including the Stock Exchange and the home offices of the Gyangtse Planetary Bank, were already in flames. In addition, the sensor remotes had shown laughing, chanting looters—most of whom weren't armed and had no apparent political axes to grind—smashing shop windows and stealing everything they could find. And then, inevitably, someone set fire to the emptied shops, as well, of course.

What is *it about pyromania and civil insurrection?* she wondered. *Can't* anyone *stage a riot without bringing the matches?*

The thought provoked a bitter chuckle, but she pushed it aside and ran one finger across the top of the display.

"We're in agreement about the need to minimize noncombatant casualties, Governor," she said, looking back at the com display. "At the moment, I believe all of our Blockhouse positions are secure. Certainly that's true unless there's some new, major influx of weapons and *organized* manpower on the other side, and I see no sign of that. But unless I miss my guess, they're going to run into our spaceport perimeter sometime fairly soon. When that happens, there *are* going to be Gyangtsese bodies on the ground. I'm sorry, but there's nothing in the universe I can do to prevent that now."

"I understand, Major," Aubert said heavily. "For what it's worth, you have my official authorization to proceed in whatever fashion seems best to you on the basis of your military judgment and experience."

"Thank you, Sir. But that still leaves us this other minor problem. Do you have any directions in regard to that?"

"At this point? Frankly, no. As far as I can see, we simply don't have enough information at this moment."

"I'm afraid I concur." Palacios glanced at her map display once more, then looked back at Aubert's com image. "With your permission, Governor, I'll see what I can do about acquiring that information we don't have. And I'll also engage in a little contingency planning."

"That sounds like an excellent idea," Aubert agreed. "Please keep me informed of your findings and your plans."

"I will." She nodded courteously. "Palacios, clear."

She cut the circuit and turned towards Lieutenant Boris Adrianovich Beregovoi.

"Boris!"

"Yes, Ma'am?" The lieutenant was her S-2, her battalion Intelligence officer, and he looked up at her call from where he'd been buried in the consoles managing the remotes.

"They're still pushing in harder from the south and west, right?"

"Yes, Ma'am." Beregovoi didn't point out that the display in front of her had already confirmed that. Then again, he'd always been a tactful sort.

"What about confirmed GLF leadership elements?"

"Most of the ones we had positively IDed and localized have dropped off our plot, Ma'am," Beregovoi admitted. "Our intercept birds are picking up fewer and fewer com messages between them, which may indicate that they're meeting up with one another somewhere—close enough together they don't need the com traffic to tie them together. And once they stop actively transmitting, it's awfully hard to keep track of them in a mess like this one."

"Understood." Palacios drummed the fingers of her right hand on the display, frowning.

"You say we're getting fewer communications intercepts. Is there any indication from the traffic we did intercept as to where their leadership cadre might have been heading?"

"No, Ma'am. Not really. There was a lot of 'join so-and-so at location such-and-such,' but their security is pretty good. I think they took it as a given that we'd be listening in once it all hit the fan. They're using code names for both people and locations, and we haven't got enough data yet for the computers to crack the code names for us."

"What about a general indication of their movement from position fixes on their last transmissions before they dropped out of sight?"

"I already ran the projections on that, Ma'am. There's nothing statistically significant in what we've got, but there *is* a slight trend of movement away from downtown and the spaceport."

"Away." Palacios looked up and met Sergeant Major Winfield's eyes. "Like they're giving up their efforts to control the mob and get it back out of the streets, do you think, Sar'Major?" she murmured.

"Might be." Winfield frowned. "Question is, why. Are they just throwing in the towel? Giving it all up as a bad deal? Or are they headed somewhere else?"

Palacios nodded, then looked back at Beregovoi.

"Any sign of additional rioters moving into the area north or east of the Annapurna Arms, Boris?" she pressed.

"Not from the last remote overflight," the lieutenant said. "That's about thirty minutes old, though; we've been concentrating our assets on covering downtown and the approaches to our perimeter. I can schedule another sweep of that area immediately, if you want, Ma'am. Take about five minutes to set up, and another fifteen for the sweep itself."

"Do it," she said. "I want the hardest numbers and the best locations you can give me on everything between us and the hotel, between us and the Mall, and between the hotel and the Mall. Map them and drop it onto my display here. And see to it that Lieutenant Ryan gets the same info."

"Yes, Ma'am." Beregovoi started to turn back to his panel, but Palacios stopped him with a raised forefinger. "Ma'am?" he asked.

"I want you to do something else for me, too, Boris. I want a bird's-eye of the Mall. In particular, I want your best estimate of how many civilians are still there—and who they are."

"Excuse me, Ma'am?" Beregovoi looked puzzled, and Palacios grimaced.

"Brigadier Jongdomba wants us to come rescue the members of the planetary government. I want to know how many junior officials, bureaucrats, secretaries, file clerks, and janitors are caught inside the Mall with them."

"Yes, Ma'am." Beregovoi still looked a little confused, but he nodded and this time Palacios let him turn back to his Intelligence section to get on with it. Then she looked up and met Sergeant Major Winfield's eyes.

"Skipper, I'm not sure I like what I think you're thinking," he said quietly.

"You mean the fact that I'm getting ready to call on Ryan's services, Sar'Major?" she asked.

Ryan commanded the heavy weapons platoon which had been attached to the Battalion when it was sent to Gyangtse, and his single mortar squad's two tubes were the only indirect fire support weapons they had. That might not sound like a lot, in a situation like this one, but the sophistication of the rapid-firing weapons' munitions made it far more impressive than it might seem to an uninformed layman.

"Ma'am, I'd be just as happy as you are to not kill any more people than we have to," Winfield told her, "but you and I both know we're not going to get any of our people into the Mall without somebody getting seriously dead. I'll be sorry as hell if that happens to a batch of poor, ragged-ass rioters who get caught in a mortar concentration, but not as sorry as I'd be if it happened to some of us. That's not what I meant, and you know it."

"Yes, I suppose I do," she acknowledged, then shook her head, her expression briefly sad. "Why *do* some people insist on fishing in troubled waters, Sar'Major?"

"Because they're frigging idiots," Winfield said bluntly, and she snorted in bitter amusement.

"I suppose you've got a point, even if that is pretty damned cynical of you. In the meantime, though, we may have a small additional problem here."

"Yes, Ma'am."

"All right. Inform Captain Becker that I need to speak to her and to . . . Lieutenant Kuramochi, I think. She's levelheaded, and she's a hell of a lot tougher than she looks. Tell Becker I want to see her and Kuramochi here in the CP, personally."

"Yes, Ma'am!"

Winfield turned away to obey her instructions without another word, and Palacios smiled thinly. Becker's Bravo Company held the northernmost, least threatened arc of the spaceport perimeter. Palacios hated to thin that perimeter any, but her only other choice would have been to weaken some more seriously threatened part of it or call on Captain Shapiro, whose Delta Company formed the Battalion reserve—and which had already given up one of its platoons to hold the capital's power station and the water and sewage plant. And, frankly, it would be better for Becker to hold her part of the perimeter with two platoons, instead of three, than to fritter away Palacios' tactical reserve by slicing off still more detachments.

And if what she was beginning to suspect about Lobsang Phurba Jongdomba happened to be true, she was going to need someone with Kuramochi's qualities on the ground.

But that's not something you tell someone over the com, Serafina Palacios thought. *The least you can do when you send someone out into a shitstorm like this one is look them in the eye when you do it.*

CHAPTER NINE

"Sniper! Eleven o'clock, tenth floor!"

Alicia DeVries flung herself sideways, plastering her back to a wall of old-fashioned brick building, as Corporal Sandusky's barked warning came over the com net and a sudden, crimson threat icon flared at the corner of the immaterial, helmet-driven heads-up display her neural feed projected into her mental vision. Sandusky's Alpha Team had the overwatch as Bravo leapfrogged past them up the city street, and she heard the distinctive whickering "snarl-CRACK" of a plasma rifle.

The packet of plasma smashed into the façade of a building perhaps a hundred meters farther west with an ear-stunning blast of sound. Brick and mortar half-vaporized and half-shattered as the energy bolt hit. The second plasma strike slammed home an instant later, and flames and smoke poured from the demolished stretch of wall as thermal bloom ignited the building's contents. Then, slowly, the entire tenth and eleventh floors crumbled, spilling out into the street below in a stony avalanche of dust and debris.

"Clear," Sandusky announced, and Alicia's helmet computer obediently erased the threat from her mental HUD.

"Acknowledge," Lieutenant Kuramochi said. "All right, people. Back to the salt mines."

Alicia was astonished at how reassuring she found the lieutenant's matter-of-fact tone. Intellectually, she was confident that Kuramochi didn't know much more about the immediate tactical situation than she did, but at least the platoon commander *sounded* like she did.

The thought was distant, little more than a flicker far below the surface of Alicia's conscious mind as she kept her eyes glued to Gregory Hilton's back. Third Squad was Second Platoon's point, and at the moment, that meant that Gregory Hilton, personally, was the entire recon battalion's point as they advanced towards the Presidential Mansion.

The older rifleman seemed much calmer about that than Alicia could have been in his place, but no one would ever have confused "calm" with "relaxed." Hilton moved warily, cautiously, head swiveling. Like all Marines who were Recon-qualified, he was (like Alicia) one of the sixty-plus percent of the human race who could tolerate and use a direct neural computer feed. And, also like Alicia, his surgically implanted receptor was currently locked into the computer built into his combat helmet. It linked him to the helmet's built-in sensors, drove the HUD which it kept centered in his mental field of view, managed the free-flow com link, and connected him to his M-97's onboard computer. In his case, it wasn't a full-scale synth-link, the ability to actually interface directly with a computer. It still had to work through the specially designed and integrated interfaces, but the effect was to provide him with continuous access to all of his equipment. That gave him a huge "situational awareness" advantage over any nonaugmented foe, and after so many years of experience, all of that extra reach was as much a part of him as his heart and lungs . . . which didn't keep him from using his own booster-augmented vision and hearing to supplement his other senses.

Alicia, on the other hand, *was* synth-link-capable. Only about twenty percent of all humans fell into that category, but that was enough to give the Empire a tremendous advantage over its Rishathan opponents, *none* of whom could handle neural receptors, at all. Even Alicia had never been qualified for a *cyber*-synth-link, however, and she was just as happy about that. Fully developed AIs were . . . unstable, at best, and any unfortunate soul in a cyber-synth-link with an AI when it crashed normally went with it. That struck her as an unreasonable price to pay, even if the fusion of human and computer would have given her a subordinate of quite literally inhuman capability.

Because she was synth-link-qualified, though, she had an even greater "natural" situational awareness than Hilton did. At the moment, she had every bit of those capabilities on line, searching for power sources, weapons signatures, com transmissions, or movement to the flanks or rear, but three-quarters of her attention was focused on Hilton, watching for *his* reactions, looking for hand signals.

"Keep one eye on *me* all the time, Alley," he'd told her quietly when they started out. "You've got my back; I'll worry about what's in front of us. Clear?"

"Clear," she'd said, happy that she'd been able to keep any obvious tremor out of her voice. Not that "keeping an eye on him" was the easiest thing in the world to do. Like her, Hilton wore reactive chameleon camouflage. It wasn't as good as the more sophisticated system built into powered combat armor could produce. Then again, powered armor radiated a much fiercer emissions signature, which made any sort of purely optical camouflage useless against front-line military grade sensors.

The fabric of Hilton's uniform and the surface of his helmet and body armor—his entire equipment harness, for that matter—was covered in smart fabric which produced an illusion of semitransparency. The sensors in his helmet maintained a continuous three hundred sixty degree scan, transmitting the results to his uniform, whose fabric then duplicated that same imagery across its surface, merging him visually with his background. The result was rather like looking at a humanoid figure made of absolutely clear water, with everything beyond it sharply visible, yet subtly distorted.

The effect wasn't perfect, and in good visibility, any movement tended to give away the wearer's position. But even under optimum conditions of visibility, the reactive camouflage made someone virtually invisible, as long as he held still. In the sort of smoke and dust hovering in Zhikotse's air at the current moment, it was far more effective. Except for the other members of the platoon, that was. Their helmet computers kept track of what their fellows' camouflage was doing and effectively erased it from their vision through their neural links.

Which meant Alicia could, in fact, keep her eyes focused on him, and that was precisely what she was doing. Gladly, as a matter of fact, because she realized that she needed as much of the benefit of his experience as she could get.

Her current position, she knew, was at least partly a sign that the rest of her squad recognized her newbie status. César Bergerat, with his own far greater store of experience, was in charge of keeping a protective watch over Frinkelo Zigair and Leo Medrano as they followed along behind her with the team's heavy weapons. But in another way, Hilton's attitude was a testimonial to his confidence in her. After all, she was the one he was trusting to keep him alive. Of course, he might figure he might as well appear confident in her, whether he was or not, since he was stuck with her anyway. Still—

Her M-97 snapped up to her shoulder without any conscious thought on her part. The muzzle tracked slightly to the left, then steadied, and the sensor built into the combat rifle's laser designator popped a crimson crosshair into her HUD. The crosshair moved slightly as her synth-link dropped a command into the combat rifle's simpleminded computer, selecting grenade, and the helmet computer adjusted for the grenade's different ballistics. She compensated for the change automatically, holding the crosshair on target. And then she squeezed the trigger.

The grenade launched with a mule-kick blow to her shoulder. The rifle-launched weapon was slightly less powerful than those in Zigair's grenade bandoliers, but its advanced chemical explosives were far more potent than anything pre-space Terra might have boasted. The instant it cleared its safety perimeter, its tiny, powerful rocket kicked in, and it went screaming down range. Its exhaust drew a fire-bright line across her vision as it streaked across the street to drop dead center through a window on the fifth floor of an office building.

My God, did I—?

The question ripped through Alicia's brain even as she rode the M-97's recoil. It had happened so quickly, so suddenly, that her conscious mind hadn't had time to sort it all out.

Then the heavy concussion grenade exploded in the room where she'd seen the movement. The flat, percussive thunderclap was muffled by the structure, less noisy than the plasma fire had been, but the targeted window and a good-sized chunk of wall to either side of it, blew back out in a fan-shaped pattern of debris.

She was still staring up at the explosion, wondering half-sickly if she'd just allowed herself to kill a civilian bystander, when a rifle tumbled out of the dust cloud. It fell through the air, spinning slowly end over end until it smashed on the sidewalk below.

Militia-issue, her mind identified it as her augmented vision zoomed in on the plunging weapon. But while the rifle might have come from a militia armory, no militiaman would have been surreptitiously drawing a bead on the back of an Imperial Marine point man.

"Nice one, Alley," Hilton said after a moment. "Next time, though, give a guy a little warning, huh? Scared me out of at least a year's growth."

"S—" Alicia cleared her throat. "Sure," she got out the second time around, sounding almost natural and hoping he couldn't hear how indescribably grateful she was for his calm, every-day tone of voice.

Something suspiciously like a chuckle sounded over the net, and Alicia swallowed again, hard. She had no doubt at all that she'd just killed at least one human being, and she'd discovered in the process that her grandfather had been completely correct when he told her that no matter how hard she might try to prepare herself for that moment ahead of time, she would fail.

No choice, the small voice in the back of her brain told her as her rock-steady hands reloaded the single-shot grenade launcher without her eyes and helmet sensors ever stopping their constant sweep for fresh threats. *You didn't put anyone up there with a rifle*, that same voice told her as she moved forward behind Hilton again, watching him as he glided onward, moving from parked car to parked car, using them for cover. *Besides*, the voice told her almost brutally, *it's what you volunteered for, isn't it?*

It was. And even now, she sensed that she'd been right—it *was* something she could do, when she had to. And something she could live with afterwards, as well. But she also knew she'd just taken the critical step into a world the vast majority of the Empire's subjects would never visit.

She was a killer now.

She could never change that, even if she wanted to. It was like a loss of virginity, something which would mark her forever. And the fact that she'd known it would happen, that it was the inevitable consequence of the vocation she'd chosen, did nothing to cushion her awareness of how hugely her personal universe had just changed.

But there was no time to think about that now, and she felt herself moving from car to car in Hilton's wake, almost as smoothly as he'd moved.

Captain Chiawa leaned back against the wall in the small, empty apartment, muscles sagging around his bones, and breathed heavily.

He and his small party had managed to break contact with the rioters. He didn't know how. It was all a blur, a confused memory of staccato orders, frantic movement, running and hiding. In the process, they'd gotten turned completely around, though, and they were headed directly away from the spaceport they'd been trying to reach. By now, they were almost halfway across Zhikotse from the Marine perimeter. That was the bad news. The good news was that they *had* broken contact . . . and no one seemed to be trying to kill them at the moment, which made a pleasant change.

He opened his eyes and looked at the other militiamen.

"How are we fixed for ammo?"

The other men looked as exhausted as he felt. Their adrenaline-sharpened tension had eased off a bit as they settled down in their temporary haven, and it seemed to take them a few seconds to grasp what he'd asked.

Then Corporal Munming ran his fingers over his grenade bando-lier without even glancing down, letting his fingertips read the braillelike coding on the grenade bodies.

"Five flechette, two concussion, two incendiary, two smoke, and three HE, Sir," he said, then chuckled wearily and patted the compact machine pistol holstered at his right hip as his backup weapon. "And, of course, three mags for this."

"Of course," Chiawa agreed with a tired grin, and looked at his three riflemen.

"And you guys?"

"Two full mags, plus one partial," Private Mende said with a slight shrug. "I've got one smoke grenade, one gas grenade, and one frag to go with it."

"Four magazines, Sir," Private Paldorje said. "I'm out of grenades, though."

"Only one mag," Private Khanbadze said. "But I've still got two rifle grenades, both antipersonnel."

"And I've got—" Chiawa patted the ammunition carrier pouch at his hip "—three magazines." He smiled without very much humor. "Not a lot of firepower, is it?"

"Sir," Munming said frankly, "at the moment, I'm sort of thinking firepower's going to be a lot less useful than just staying the hell out of sight."

"I'm afraid you've got that one right," Chiawa agreed. He took off his helmet and set it on the floor beside him while he dragged out his map board and turned it back on. He wished—not for the first time—that he had the sort of modern information systems the Marines were issued. In their absence, he'd just have to do the best he could with the obsolete militia-issue equivalents.

He pressed the locator button, and the board's GPS system obediently paged to the correct window of the small-scale city map and dropped the position icon onto the display. He spun the adjustment wheel, zooming in on the icon and enlarging the map's detail, then frowned thoughtfully.

"All right," he said, looking back up after a moment. "It looks like we're not going to get to the spaceport any time soon."

"Fucking A," somebody muttered, and he showed his teeth in a brief smile.

"Now, now, Mende," he chided. "Let's not go around saying things to make the commanding officer doubt his own judgment, shall we?"

That won a general, weary laugh, and he tapped the map board with a grimy fingertip.

"As I was saying, it looks like, for whatever reason, most of the mob on this side of the city seems to be headed for the spaceport. Or downtown," he added more grimly, and the others nodded. The dense smoke rising from Zhikotse's business district had gotten only heavier, and the occasional explosion of small arms fire and grenades indicated that at least some of the militia were apparently still trying to control the looting. It didn't look—or sound—like they were having a lot of success.

Chiawa resolutely yanked his mind back once again from his background dread over what had become of his own place of business. It was right in the middle of all that smoke, and all that he and his family had. Or all they *had* had, that was. But at least he'd managed to get through to Ang Lhamo before the civilian com net went to hell. His wife and their sons had headed out of the city within fifteen minutes of the initial disaster. By now they were safely at her parents' farm, thank God.

What mattered most at the moment, however, was that the business district was wrapped around the entire western and southern circumference of the spaceport. He'd heard one or two very brief, concentrated cascades of fire, some of it from heavy-caliber calliopes, where someone had bumped up against the perimeter Major Palacios' Marines had obviously established. He hoped that most of that firing had been a demonstration to encourage people to back off, not a case of the Marines firing for effect, but his communicator had been put out of action over an hour ago. Which meant he was out of contact with anyone else, with no way to know just how bad the situation between his present position and the spaceport actually was.

Besides "not good," he thought mordantly, turning his head to look out the apartment's window at the billowing smoke. He could see flames rising from some of the taller buildings in the financial district, as well, and he shook his head before he returned his attention to his handful of men.

"I think we can probably get there eventually if we keep circling north, though," he told them. "If we head up through the Pinasa District to the Thundu Bridge, then cut across through the barge docks, we can link up with the spaceport perimeter here."

He tapped the map display again, and his dirty, tired troopers craned their necks to look at it.

"What about the Presidential Mansion, Sir?" Corporal Munming asked after a moment. A jerk of his head indicated the direction of the Presidential Mansion and the rest of the Mall. They lay considerably to the west of Chiawa's indicated route, and the captain looked up to meet the noncom's eyes.

"We don't know the situation there," he said, and waved his left hand around their temporary apartment refuge. "We do know they were under a lot of pressure before we lost communication.

Frankly, I think the Mansion and the Mall are probably drawing as many rioters as downtown. I doubt we'd be able to get through, and even if we could, the five of us and the limited amount of ammunition we've got left wouldn't make a lot of difference."

He leaned the back of his head against the wall behind him and looked around at their faces.

"I'll be honest with you. Technically, it's our duty to suppress what's going on out there." He jerked his chin at the window. "I don't think we're going to be able to do a lot of 'suppressing' on our own, though. So our next responsibility is to get ourselves back into contact with higher authority and join up with some outfit big enough to do some good. I don't think we'd get through to the Mall. I think we have a pretty good chance of getting through to the spaceport, though, and we're not going to do anyone any good if we just get ourselves killed. So, as of this moment, as I see it, my mission is to get you guys to the spaceport, preferably alive. And, of course, my own humble self with you. Now, does anyone here have a problem with that?"

The others looked at one another for a moment, then, almost in unison, turned back to him.

"Hell, no . . . Sir," Mende said.

"You're the boss, Skipper," Munming agreed, using the informal title for the first time.

"Well, in that case," Chiawa shoved himself upright and crossed to stand looking out the window, "I think we need to get ourselves back on the move."

His eye dropped to a van parked at the curb below him, and he felt a powerful stir of temptation. But he suppressed it. "Borrowing" the van would let them move more rapidly, and it *looked* as if this part of the city was still relatively calm. But they'd passed quite a few wrecked and burning vehicles on their way here, a lot of them in equally "calm" neighborhoods. The mere fact that a vehicle was moving appeared to draw fire from the rioters, and he was quite certain that some of those flaming wrecks indicated spots where some other fleeing group of militiamen had run afoul of *deliberate* ambushes or roadblocks, as well.

"Paldorje."

"Yes, Sir?"

"Can you find us a manhole? Get us into the storm drains?"

"Sure. Or, at least, I *think* so."

Chopali Mingma Paldorje was a city maintenance worker in civilian life. He'd already extricated them from one dicey situation by leading them on a detour through an underground service access. Now he stood beside Chiawa studying the street for a moment.

"There," he said, and pointed. "There'll be a junction point out there, at the corner. Should be a manhole down into the box at that point."

"And the drains run straight to the river from here, right?"

"Prob'ly." Paldorje rubbed his chin, frowning thoughtfully. "This isn't exactly my area, you understand—I'm an electrician, not in Sanitation, so what I know about storm drains is pretty general. Still, Environmental's always raising a stink 'bout our dumping runoff straight into the river, so they must go right through. No clue how big the drains are, though."

"Who cares about big?" Munming said, looking out the window in turn. "Underground, now—*that* strikes me as a really good idea." He looked approvingly at Chiawa.

"I should've thought of it sooner," the captain said, but the corporal only shrugged.

"Captain, you've got us this far alive. Dunno that we'd've made it half as far without you."

Chiawa looked at him, almost stunned by the simple approval and trust in Munming's voice. His own estimate of his military capabilities had crashed and burned with the disaster at the Annapurna Arms, and a part of him wanted to tell Munming how wrong he was. How foolish it would be to trust Karsang Dawa Chiawa with anyone's safety.

But he didn't say it. Instead, he only smiled, slapped Munming on the shoulder, and nodded to Paldorje.

"All right," he said. "I think we can get most of the way to the corner without ever leaving this building. That should give us pretty good cover right up to the manhole. After that, it's up to Private Paldorje here."

"All Wasps, Gold-One. Find a spot and listen up, people."

Alpha Team had point in Second Platoon's current advance, and Alicia simply froze in her overwatch position as Lieutenant

Kuromachi came up over the platoon net. Corporal Sandusky, whose team was out front, lay in her field of view, and he kept moving ahead until he found a secure spot in the angle of an apartment building's front steps. She continued to turn her head, scanning their surroundings, while her synth-link updated her HUD. She saw the forty-four icons of the rest of the platoon on the map overlay, switching from the blinking red-banded green of Marines in motion to green circled in unblinking amber as each of them settled down in a secure position.

It was good to know where the others were, although absorbing the HUD without being distracted by having its disembodied icons hanging between her and her surroundings had taken some getting used to back at Camp Mackenzie. Fortunately, it had always been easier for her than most, even in basic, and she hadn't had the problems dealing with the competing sensory input which had plagued some of her fellow recruits. Part of that was the ability to multitask which she'd always found useful, but the fact that she was synth-link-capable was another part of it. For her, absorbing input through her neural receptor was as natural and direct as using her own eyes or ears.

She dropped a command into her helmet computer, and a rash of rapidly strobing crimson icons flashed into view, representing the helmet's (and the platoon's at large) best guess of what threats lay ahead of them. A few of the icons burned with the steady, unblinking brilliance of positively identified dangers, and as she watched, two more switched into that category as the hovering counter-grav remotes being monitored by Gunny Wheaton refined their data and dropped it to the entire platoon's helmets.

The HUD, she reflected, showed a lot of firepower between her and the Mall, and she heard the not-so-distant crackle of small arms fire and the occasional, heavier cough of a mortar or one of the militia's old-fashioned, shoulder-fired rocket launchers.

"We're getting close," Kuramochi continued, when she was certain all of her people were ready to listen. "We've got about three klicks to go, right along here."

A green arrow extended itself across the HUD which Alicia knew every member of the platoon was now watching. It continued along the route they'd been following, crossed a small tributary of the much larger river flowing around and through the northernmost limb of Zhikotse, and terminated at the eastern edge of the Mall.

It also threaded directly through a glaring cluster of icons representing what looked to be fairly well dug-in infantry positions—probably somewhere close to a full company's worth of them. Alicia didn't much care for the look of that. Nor did she care for the icons of three positively identified calliopes and a dozen or so individual rocket launchers sited among the infantry.

"According to the CP," Kuramochi went on, "the militia still hold most of the Mall, and the major pressure on their perimeter appears to be being exerted from the south and southeast. It's hard to say exactly what the insurgents are after. According to Lieutenant Beregovoi, though, we've developed intelligence in the last hour or so which indicates that the majority of the GLF's surviving leadership cadre is over here now, instead of downtown. It looks—and, again, I caution everyone that we don't know this with any certainty—as if the leadership's decided that the situation's gone so entirely out of control all of their bridges have been burned behind them. According to Lieutenant Beregovoi, they appear to have given up their efforts to shut things down because they believe they can't possibly salvage their position here on Gyangtse after this, no matter what they do. So they may have decided that their only real option—personal option, not for their 'movement'—is to take the planetary government, or as much of it as they can, hostage."

The lieutenant paused as one of the icons on the display blinked.

"Go ahead, One-Alpha," she invited, acknowledging the request.

"These yahoos really think they can bargain for a way out of this, a way off-planet, if they take *hostages*, Skipper?" First Squad's sergeant, Julio Jackson, demanded incredulously.

"I said we don't know that for certain," Kuramochi replied. "On the other hand, it's certainly possible. I'm not saying they're right, you understand. But, let's face it, people. Whatever actually went down at the Annapurna Arms, these people are *screwed*. There's no going back after this, which means the only options they have are bad ones . . . and worse ones. They may figure they don't have much chance of cutting a deal if they have hostages, but they're probably pretty damned sure they don't have *any* chance of doing that *without* some sort of bargaining chip."

She paused, then continued.

"At any rate, we'll continue as briefed. Three-Alpha."

"Three-Alpha," Sergeant Metternich replied.

"Three-Alpha, you're lead. One-Alpha, you've got the back door. Two-Alpha, you're Three-Alpha's flank and overwatch security. Confirm copy, all Alphas."

"One-Alpha copies. We have the back door," Jackson replied.

"Two-Alpha copies. We have flank security and overwatch," Sergeant Clarissa Bruckner confirmed for Second Squad.

"Three-Alpha copies. We have the lead," Metternich chimed in.

"All Alphas, Gold-One. Wait for my command. Lieutenant Ryan's people have a little party favor for the people in our way."

Alicia settled a bit more deeply into her own position. She took the opportunity to doublecheck—triplecheck, really—the positions of the rest of Third Squad's Bravo Team. She was exactly where she was supposed to be under Kuromachi's plan of advance: the southeastern anchor of a hollow triangle pointed almost due west. César Bergerat was the northeast corner, and Gregory Hilton's icon was its apex, while Leo Medrano and Frinkelo Zigair, at the triangle's center, were the team's heavy fire element.

"All Wasps, Gold-One," Kuramochi said a few minutes later. "On the way."

Alicia just had time to draw a deep breath, and then the abbreviated whistle of incoming mortar rounds rode down out of the heavens to touch the earth with fire.

Lieutenant Ryan's mortars were over fourteen kilometers behind her, but their 140-millimeter precision-guided munitions arrived with pinpoint accuracy. The people holding the positions sealing this part of the perimeter around the Mall had effectively zero warning . . . and they'd neglected to provide their hastily prepared positions with overhead cover. Which proved a fatal oversight as the carrier rounds opened like lethal seed pods, spilling antipersonnel cluster munitions across the crimson icons on Alicia's HUD.

The Marines' mortars would have been recognizable even to someone from pre-space Terra, but they were far more capable than the unsophisticated metal tubes of their remote ancestors.

They were magazine-fed weapons, although they could also—and often did—fire individually hand-loaded rounds. Now, both tubes ripped through a full ten-round carousel magazine each. They got the entire twenty-round fire mission off in under ten seconds, and the individually guided rounds tracked in on their preselected targets mercilessly, blanketing them in a deadly stormfront of explosions and antipersonnel flechettes.

"*Go!*" Lieutenant Kuramochi barked as the thunder ended as abruptly as it had begun, and Alicia swung herself up and out of her position.

Her pulse hammered harshly, and everything seemed preternaturally clear, harder-edged and sharper than even her augmented senses should be able to account for.

Ahead of her, Hilton disappeared into the billowing smoke and dust of the mortar bombardment, but only for a moment. Only until she followed him into the smoke and her helmet visor switched to thermal-imaging mode. The helmet computer converted the thermal images into knife-sharp, clear imagery and dropped it directly into her mind through her synth-link. Aside from the fact that it was black-and-white, it might have been the normal input of her optical nerves, and she saw Hilton turn slightly to his left.

His M-97 snapped up and ripped off a sharp, precise three-round burst, and she heard a high-pitched, choked off scream.

It wasn't the only scream she heard, either. The handful of survivors from the hapless insurgents caught in Lieutenant Ryan's fire support mission were beginning to recover from the paralyzing shock of the totally unanticipated carnage. There weren't very many of them, and most were wounded.

Alicia had never heard anything like the sounds of the wounded and dying people around her. She saw one of them, shrieking as he tried vainly to hold his eviscerated abdomen closed. Another—a calliope gunner, rising from the seat behind his multibarreled automatic weapon—held his arms raised in front of him, screaming as he stared at the blood-spurting stumps of his forearms. Yet another—

She made herself stop looking. She didn't stop *seeing*, didn't stop the automatic search for still viable threats, but she made herself step back from the immediacy of the human wreckage strewn about her. She had to. She couldn't allow it to distract her, not when the rest of her fire team needed her where she was, doing her job while they did theirs.

Her own rifle rose, tracked onto a figure rising out of a deeper foxhole than most with a weapon in his hands. The helmet computer dropped the red outline of an unidentified potential hostile onto the figure, and she took in the civilian clothes, the lack of any militia uniform. He had no helmet, and it was obvious that the mortar bombardment's smoke and dust had him at least two-thirds blinded. A tiny corner of her brain told her that his handicapped vision gave her a grossly unfair advantage, but even as it did, she heard her grandfather's remembered voice.

Combat isn't about "fair," Alley. Combat is about shooting the other guy in the back before he shoots you*—or one of your buddies—in the back. You aren't some hero out of a holo-drama, and you're not out there on some field of honor; you're on a killing ground. Never forget that.*

Her finger stroked the trigger. The combat rifle recoiled, and the target took three rounds, dead center of mass.

I remembered, Grandpa, she told Sergeant Major O'Shaughnessy as the man she'd just killed went down.

CHAPTER TEN

"Where's Kuramochi now?"

"Just about to cross over into the Mall, Ma'am."

Serafina Palacios nodded in satisfaction, then looked back at the general situation map.

The pressure on her own perimeter had started to ease. She was glad of that. The first couple of times it had been threatened, her dug-in Marines had been able to drive the rioters back by firing over their heads and into the ground in front of them, without inflicting casualties. After that, the pressure behind the ones in front had changed the context. There'd been so many bodies pushing them forward that they'd had nowhere to go but onward, straight at her outer line. She doubted that they'd *wanted* to do anything of the sort, but that hadn't changed what they were doing or the fact that most of them were armed and worked up to a killing frenzy. When they'd begun shooting at her Marines, she'd had no option but to order her people to return fire.

Which was why there were now well over two hundred and fifty bodies sprawled outside her forward positions. At least the battalion's corpsmen, assisted by the spaceport rescue teams, had been able to bring in the wounded. Captain Hudson, the battalion's doctor, along with his medics and the dozen or so civilian doctors inside the spaceport, had done all they could, but from reports, it sounded as if they were probably going to lose at least a half-dozen more in the end.

Still, it looked as if the riot, or insurrection, or whatever this thing actually was, had decided the spaceport was best left alone. The mob was amusing itself burning down a goodly percentage of the rest of Zhikotse and hunting down "Empie collaborators," instead. Most of the "collaborators" were nothing of the sort, of course—merely people whose relative affluence, or accent, or clothes had singled them out as one of the "oppressors of the poor." Most of the *real* "oppressors" had possessed the resources to get out of the riot's path, but mobs had never been noted for the clarity of their logic.

What happened to some of those poor devils was enough to turn Palacios' stomach, and after fifteen-plus years in the Imperial Marines, it was no longer a stomach which turned all that easily. But there wasn't a lot she could do about it. She simply didn't have the manpower. Any quixotic rescue attempts she might have mounted into a city the size of Zhikotse would have been absorbed the way a sponge absorbed water, and that was that.

Now, if it had simply been a matter of *killing* all the rioters, that would have been different.

Unfortunately—or, perhaps, fortunately, depending upon how one chose to look at it (and at the moment, Serafina Palacios was definitely in two minds about it)—standing imperial policy, as she'd explained to Jongdomba, called for the minimization of collateral damage and incidental civilian casualties, even in a situation like this one. Simply killing the people who'd surrounded the Mall would have been a relatively straightforward proposition. It might have taken a while, but she could have lifted the siege of the Presidential Mansion any time she chose to, if she'd been willing to turn Lieutenant Ryan loose. It might have used up a substantial percentage of her mortar ammunition, but she could have done it, especially if she'd sent in one of her companies behind the barrage to sweep up the bits and pieces. These poor pathetic rioters had no idea how truly lethal her Wasps could be, and she hoped they'd never find out. Although Brigadier Jongdomba had made it perfectly clear that *he* thought she should be showing the mob exactly that.

And if I have to, in the end, I will, she thought grimly. *But* only *if I have to. We need to* contain *the situation, not create an atrocity that produces martyrs in job lots for the next version of the GLF to come along. Aubert's right about that.* She smiled without much humor. *So instead of killing people who've taken up arms against my Emperor—and their own locally elected government—I'm putting my people's lives at risk in order to hold civilian casualties down. And doesn't that just suck?*

She snorted as she realized she'd been deliberately dwelling on just about anything she could think of in order to avoid what she really ought to be doing.

"Tom, what's the latest from Brigadier Jongdomba?" she asked after a moment.

"We're still in contact, Ma'am," Lieutenant Bradwell replied. "The Brigadier says his perimeter is being driven steadily back, though. He's reiterating his request for immediate relief."

Palacios nodded, although "request" was a pale choice of noun for what Jongdomba was actually doing. He'd gone over her head to Governor Aubert over an hour ago, *demanding* in the name of the planetary government that Palacios march to his support in strength, crushing any rioters she encountered en route. He'd also insisted that if she didn't comply with his "request," the planetary government would complain directly to the Ministry of Out-World Affairs that Palacios and Aubert had chosen to set the safety of off-world investment in the spaceport area above protecting the duly elected planetary government.

The subtext was clear enough; he not only wanted the Mall held, he wanted the "insurgency" smashed so completely, with such a high body count, that Gyangtse's underclass would never dare to raise its hand against its betters again. The sudden explosion of violence had obviously terrified him, all the more because he'd been so confident he and his fellow oligarchs were the absolute rulers of all they surveyed. The fact that most of this day's bloody violence sprang not from the GLF's separatist ambitions but from the festering, long-standing, and fully justified resentment of the politically excluded underclass wasn't something he was prepared to face, and from where Palacios stood, it seemed obvious he was losing his grip . . . assuming he hadn't already lost it. He was sounding less and less rational, as if what was happening was so unacceptable that he was retreating into a fantasy world where he could somehow fix it all by a simple act of will.

Or by putting someone else in charge of Gyangtse's local government, perhaps.

Whatever he might be thinking (or *not* thinking, as the case might be), he'd made it perfectly clear that he had no intention of evacuating the Mall. Or, for that matter, apparently of allowing the planetary government's members to evacuate, either. Which only lent added point to Palacios' growing suspicion of his ultimate motives, since he'd apparently managed to get almost everyone *else* out of his perimeter. According to Lieutenant Beregovoi's latest estimates, only the senior members of the planetary government were still in the Presidential Mansion; every junior official, clerical worker, and janitor appeared to have miraculously managed to escape before the rioters closed in. Palacios found it rather remarkable that it had been possible for a junior secretary to escape, but not for the planetary president to do the same thing.

In effect, she knew, Jongdomba was holding his own government hostage, using the safety of its senior members as a bargaining chip to force her to do as he wished. Unfortunately for him, however, the previous political calculus of Gyangtse no longer obtained. Jongdomba's "good friend" Governor Aubert had informed the brigadier (who had announced that he now spoke for President Shangup and the rest of the government, as well) that all that could be done was already being done, that Major Palacios enjoyed his total confidence and support, and that Jongdomba's veiled threats wouldn't change any of that.

Palacios had been patched in as a silent auditor of that particular conversation, and she'd been just a little bit surprised by the fierceness of the satisfaction she'd felt as she listened.

"Connect me with the Brigadier," she said now.

"Yes, Ma'am."

Palacios turned her attention back to the map table. Jongdomba's com connection was voice-only, and she waited until a voice spoke in her mastoid implant.

"Jongdomba," it said. Without the self-identification, she would have found it difficult to recognize that harsh, strain-flattened voice as the bombastically confident militia commander's.

"Brigadier," she said crisply, "this is Major Palacios."

"With yet another excuse for not relieving us?" Jongdomba grated, and Palacios folded her hands behind her and gripped them tightly together.

"No, Brigadier," she replied calmly. "I'm comming to inform you that the second platoon of my Bravo Company is about to make contact with you."

"It is?" Palacios could almost see Jongdomba sitting up straighter. "That's excellent news! I know exactly where to put it until the rest of the relief force gets here!"

"Brigadier, I don't believe you fully understand the situation," the major said. "Second Platoon isn't there to reinforce your present positions; it's there to help extricate the President and the delegates from the Mall and get them to safety here at the spaceport enclave."

"That's preposterous! You can't possibly be serious! Unless you want us to find ourselves putting down something like this every few years, it's imperative that we hold the Mall and teach this traitorous rabble the consequences of daring to—"

"Brigadier Jongdomba," Palacios' voice was flatter, "the protection of the political *status quo* is not my job. The maintenance of that *status quo*—or its necessary modification—is that of the planetary government of Gyangtse. The protection of that planetary government's real estate and official structures is the responsibility of the Gyangtsese police establishment and the planetary militia. The protection of the imperial governor and his person, office, and staff, and of the authority of the Empire on Gyangtse and in this star system, is the responsibility of His Majesty's Marines and Fleet. In addition, however, the Empire does recognize the responsibility of His Majesty's armed forces to protect the lives and persons of the members of local planetary governments upon imperial planets. I am prepared to extend that protection, but I can best protect those persons here, inside my perimeter. I do not, as I've already repeatedly informed you, have the personnel to simultaneously protect the city's essential public services, hold the spaceport, and cover an objective as extensive as the Mall."

"Well, that's too damned bad!" Jongdomba snapped. "You and I both know you've got plenty of uncommitted combat power. You're simply unwilling to use it. And don't tell me about 'limiting civilian casualties' again! We're looking at a damned civil war if we don't crush these bastards right *now*, and you're refusing to do it."

"Whether you approve of it or not, Brigadier, my standing orders from the Minister of War and the Ministry of Out-World

Affairs are quite clear. Maintenance of civil order is the primary responsibility of the local authorities. Imperial forces are to be employed for that purpose only as a last resort, and the limitation of casualties takes precedence over every other consideration except the preservation of human life and the protection of the persons of the local government's members. Which," Palacios repeated pointedly, "I can best do here at the spaceport, Sir."

"The preservation of the local government includes the protection of that government's offices and essential records," Jongdomba shot back. "A government is more than the individuals who happen to hold office at any given moment, and you know it. Your refusal to acknowledge that fact and your attendant responsibilities is unacceptable to the planetary government of Gyangtse, Major Palacios!"

"Then you have a problem, Brigadier," Palacios said coolly. "I'm not under your orders, Sir. In fact, my orders require me merely to 'cooperate' with the planetary authorities. I am cooperating by offering to provide for the physical safety of your government and its members. In my opinion, that is the maximum I can do without finding myself in dereliction of my other responsibilities. You may, of course, choose not to accompany Second Platoon when it returns to the spaceport. That's your option. But those are Lieutenant Kuramochi's orders, and they *will* be carried out. Are we clear on that, Brigadier?"

There was a moment of fulminating silence, and then, abruptly, the connection was terminated.

My, that didn't go too well, did it? Palacios thought, and looked at her com officer.

"Get me Kuramochi."

"Yes, Ma'am."

"Kuramochi," a voice said almost instantly, and Palacios heard the crackle of small arms in the background.

"Chiyeko, this is Major Palacios. What's your estimate to contact with the militia's forward positions?"

"Five minutes, max, Ma'am."

"Well, be advised that that contingency you and I discussed *vis-à-vis* Brigadier Jongdomba may well be in effect."

"Understood, Ma'am." Kuramochi's voice was flatter than it had been, and Palacios smiled without any humor whatsoever.

"Sorry to drop it on you, Lieutenant," she said. "Just remember, you're covered by my orders to you. You do what you have to do; I'll worry about the repercussions afterward."

"Yes, Ma'am. I'll get it done."

"Never doubted it, Chiyeko. Palacios, clear."

"What's that?"

"What's *what*? Where?" Sergeant Thaktok demanded.

"Over there." The militia private sharing the sergeant's hole pointed out into the smoky afternoon. "I saw something move over there."

"What?" Thaktok repeated, peering in the indicated direction. There was enough drifting smoke and dust hanging in the air, especially in the area where the sudden barrage of mortar fire had plowed through the attackers' positions, to restrict visibility badly. It was like a heavy fog, swathing the battered landscape in obscurity. But still, if there were anything out there he should have seen *something*.

"I don't *know* what," the private said, exhausted enough—and frightened enough—to sound belligerent. "I just saw some sort of movement and—"

"Holy *shit*!" Thaktok blurted, flinching back in his hole, as the air seemed to shimmer right in front of him. His bayoneted rifle jerked up in automatic response, but a hand reached out and gripped the barrel, pushing its muzzle back down.

"Let's not have any accidents here, Sergeant," Gregory Hilton said pleasantly as his chameleon camouflage blended out of the background smoke.

Thaktok gawked at him, then twitched as additional Marines began to materialize. The militia sergeant was still trying to come to grips with the apparent wizardry of the Marines' sudden appearance when he found himself face-to-face with a short, slender lieutenant.

"Sergeant . . . Thaktok," she said, reading his name off of his own breastplate, "I'm Lieutenant Kuramochi. I need someone to direct me to Brigadier Jongdomba's CP."

"Uh," Thaktok said. Then he shook himself. "Yes, Ma'am! Right away."

* * *

Alicia followed Lieutenant Kuramochi through the combat-spawned debris which littered the once splendidly landscaped Capital Mall. Lieutenant Kuromachi hadn't invited her along, but Sergeant Metternich had glanced at Alicia, then pointed at the lieutenant, and made a waving gesture which Kuromachi had obviously missed. And so Alicia found herself tagging along, feeling a bit like an anxious puppy as she wondered how the lieutenant was going to react when she noticed her shadow.

Prior to this day's madness, the Mall, with its reflecting ponds, fountains, gracious buildings, statuary, and flowering fruit trees had been the most beautiful spot in the entire capital city. That beauty had been sadly damaged, however, and the smoke hovering above it was like a shroud of despair. One of the larger multijet fountains was still up and running, a gorgeous, perpetually moving water sculpture in the square in front of the Presidential Mansion, despite a wide crack through one retaining wall of the catch basin, but the others were dead, and she wondered if incoming fire had cut the water supply.

The South Garden, leading to the Mansion's main façade, was ugly with foxholes and emergency aid posts, and the building itself—like the Treasury Building, which faced it across the Plaza of the People—had been heavily damaged. The Mansion's broad granite steps were pitted with bullet marks and littered with bits and pieces of the façade which had been blown out—probably by rockets, she thought, looking at the angle from which the fire had come in. Wisps of smoke blew from the shattered windows of the previously gracious building, and she was surprised that it was only smoke. The Mansion's sprinklers and fire suppression system must be better than she would have expected from the rest of Gyangtse's indigenous tech base.

Most of the militiamen they'd passed on their way here had seemed happy to see them. They were too exhausted, too worn out, for exuberance, but she'd seen the relief in their faces. In fact, it had gone far beyond simple "relief" in several cases, and she wondered just how much of the Battalion these people thought had arrived to save them. Did they realize Major Palacios had sent only a single platoon? And if they didn't, how were they going to react when they figured it out?

But the closer they got to Brigadier Jongdomba's command post, the less jubilant the faces around them seemed. Not that Alicia was all that surprised. The Imperial Marines believed in keeping their people in the loop, so even Alicia knew Jongdomba wasn't going to be happy with their orders from Palacios.

They reached the Presidential Mansion, and the private Sergeant Thaktok had assigned to guide them led them down into the hole-pocked garden. Brigadier Jongdomba's CP was in a hastily sandbagged dugout hard up against the inner face of the tall, semi-ornamental brick wall around the Mansion's grounds. Two rifle-armed militiamen—one a lieutenant and the other a corporal, both sporting a nonstandard unit flash Alicia had never seen before on their left shoulders—stood outside the CP's entrance. A quick query of her helmet computer through her synth-link identified the crossed-lightning-bolts shoulder flash as the emblem of Jongdomba's "Headquarters Guard Company," whatever that was. She'd never heard of it, and her helmet database showed no such unit on the militia's official table of organization and equipment. At the moment, they struck her as improbably clean and neat against the littered chaos around them, and Lieutenant Kuramochi's guide came to a halt in front of them as the lieutenant held up a peremptory hand.

"What do *you* want?" the militia officer growled at the dirty, battle-stained private without so much as looking in Kuramochi's direction.

"The Marines are here," the guide replied. "This is Lieutenant Kuramochi. She needs to see the Brigadier."

"Oh, she does, does she?"

The militia lieutenant turned his attention to Kuramochi at last, and Alicia's instincts kicked her hard. There was something about the Gyangtsese's expression, something about his eyes, that twanged mental alarms.

"Yes, she does," Kuramochi said, her voice cold. "And her patience is in rather short supply at the moment."

"Oh, *forgive* me, Ma'am!" the militiaman replied, coming to an elaborate caricature of attention and saluting with a mocking flourish. "I'll just run right in and see if the Brigadier wants to waste his time seeing one of the useless wonders who've been sitting on their gutless asses while the frigging city burns down around us."

Alicia didn't see or hear any communication between Lieutenant Kuromachi and Gunny Wheaton. Maybe, she decided later, it was telepathy. Or maybe the big gunnery sergeant was simply pissed off enough that he didn't *need* any signal from his lieutenant.

There was a brief, sudden blur. Wheaton didn't even seem to move. One moment he was standing at Lieutenant Kuramochi's elbow; the next moment, the militia officer was flat on his back on the ground, his combat rifle was in Wheaton's hands, and one of Wheaton's boots was pressed firmly against the other man's throat.

The militia corporal started to move, then froze. Only when he stopped moving did Alicia realize that he'd frozen because *her* rifle muzzle was aligned directly with his belt buckle. He stared at her for a heartbeat, then very carefully lowered his own rifle's butt to the ground.

"I believe," Wheaton said pleasantly to the still-standing corporal, ignoring the man on the ground as he flopped about, making strangling sounds while both hands wrenched uselessly at the Marine's immovable combat boot, "that the Lieutenant would like to see the Brigadier now. Is there a problem?"

"Just what the hell do you mean, *attacking* my people?" Brigadier Jongdomba raged as Lieutenant Kuramochi was shown into his damp, muddy-smelling command post. Gunny Wheaton followed her, and Alicia continued to tag dutifully along, as well. As she'd started down the dugout steps, Alicia's HUD had picked up the green icons of the rest of the platoon drifting gradually into a loose necklace around the CP.

"I don't know what you're talking about, Brigadier," Kuramochi said levelly, looking him straight in the eye.

"Oh, yes, you do, *Lieutenant!*" Jongdomba spat.

He pointed at another militia officer, this one a captain, standing to one side with a pair of sergeants. All three of them wore the "HQ Guard" shoulder flash, and their expressions were belligerent as they glared at Kuramochi and Wheaton.

"I have a report of the entire incident," the brigadier continued, "and it's obvious to me that your commanding officer's cowardice is exceeded only by *your* arrogance in the execution of her gutless orders! But while you may cherish the mistaken belief that you have some God-given right to assault any of my people who get in your way, I assure you that you and she are both wrong about that, Lieutenant! I fully intend to press charges against both of you to the full extent of military law!"

"Apparently, there was some difference of opinion as to the degree of military courtesy which should be shown to a superior officer, Sir," Kuramochi replied, and Jongdomba's face tightened dangerously at her not particularly oblique reminder that a Marine officer was legally a full grade senior to any planetary militia officer of his own nominal rank. "Your lieutenant expressed his opinion of me and my Marines in somewhat intemperate language. My gunnery sergeant took exception to his manner and . . . remonstrated with him. Since Major Palacios has declared martial law in the name of the Emperor, not the local authorities, the Imperial Marine Corps would have jurisdiction over any military infractions which may occur during the present emergency. I'm sure that if you choose to press charges, the Corps will be perfectly willing to empanel a court-martial to consider the behavior of everyone involved. In the meantime, however, Sir, with all due respect, my orders are to evacuate the members of the planetary government to the safety of the spaceport."

"The planetary government isn't going anywhere!" Jongdomba glared at her. "As I've already informed *Major* Palacios, President Shangup and the delegates have no intention of being driven out of the capital by this pack of gutter scum!" He snorted contemptuously. "Pack of useless drones and parasites, the lot of them. It's time we taught them a long overdue lesson in deportment, and we're not about to let them take over the official offices of government and get any uppity ideas above their stations!"

"Brigadier Jongdomba," Kuramochi said, "you were the one who informed Major Palacios you could no longer hold this position or guarantee the safety of your governmental leaders. Accordingly, the Major has dispatched me to escort those leaders to a place of safety. If they choose not to accompany me, that will be their own decision. Major Palacios regrets the probable outcome of that choice, but she will not seek to dictate to them."

"You wouldn't *dare* simply abandon us—them!" Jongdomba sneered.

"On the contrary, Brigadier," Kuramochi said calmly, "it would be their decision, not mine."

"And what if I choose not to *let* you abandon us?" the brigadier asked in a suddenly much softer voice.

"Brigadier, my people and I aren't under your command," Kuramochi said. "I have my orders from my own superiors, and I *will* obey them."

"Somehow," Jongdomba said, "I rather doubt your precious Major Palacios or Governor Aubert will be quite so quick to throw us to the wolves if a platoon of their own precious Marines are stuck here with us. If I'm wrong, your people should still be a worthwhile addition to our firepower."

"Brigadier Jongdomba," Kuramochi's tone was flat, "I think you'd better reconsider your position. My people aren't here to reinforce your perimeter, and that's not what they're going to do. Now, if you don't mind, I'd like to speak to President Shangup myself. I'd hate to think that the nature of my orders might have been—unintentionally, I'm sure—misrepresented to him."

"I suspect your people will be more willing than you think to do as I ask when they discover that you and your sergeant here are going to be my 'guests' until order is restored to the capital on the planetary government's terms," Jongdomba said.

Alicia felt a sudden, icy calm descend upon her. Despite the briefings, despite the incident with the militia lieutenant outside the CP, she couldn't quite believe Jongdomba could be as crazy as his last sentence suggested. He was surrounded by heavily armed insurgents, and now he was prepared to court a shooting incident with a platoon of Imperial Marines in the very middle of his position? What could he be *thinking*? Or *was* he thinking at all? Surely he couldn't believe that the commander of a Crown World planetary militia could get into a pissing contest with the Corps and survive?

"Brigadier," Lieutenant Kuramochi said softly, "you're about to make a serious mistake. I recommend that you let this drop right here, right now."

"I don't really care what a cowardly little bitch with delusions of grandeur *recommends*, Lieutenant," Jongdomba sneered. Then, without turning his head, he said, "Captain!"

The militia captain standing behind Sergeant Wheaton had been primed and waiting. At the brigadier's one-word command, his hand flashed down to the weapon holstered at his hip. The two sergeants with him were armed with combat rifles. They'd been standing there, with the weapons over their right forearms, like hunters carrying their rifles across a field somewhere. Now, they brought the muzzles up, swinging them towards Lieutenant Kuramochi.

But things didn't work out exactly as Jongdomba had intended them to.

Gunny Wheaton took one quick step backward, and the armored couter protecting his right elbow drove unerringly into the militia captain's chest. The other man's breastplate blunted the hammer blow, but its sheer power drove the smaller Gyangtsese back into the earthen wall behind him with stunning force. Wheaton turned in place as the militiaman cried out in mingled surprise and pain. The captain tried to bounce back upright, only to find his right wrist locked in the viselike grip of Wheaton's left hand, and then the gunnery sergeant's right hand fastened itself about his throat like a hydraulic clamp and yanked him up onto his toes.

The militia sergeants hesitated. It was a brief thing, no more than a single breath, or half a heartbeat. Wheaton's instant reaction had taken them both by surprise, and they began to turn their weapons towards him, and away from Kuramochi, in automatic response.

Unfortunately for them, however, the Marine lieutenant was already in motion herself. At the same instant Wheaton neutralized the captain, Kuramochi spun like a dancer to face the sergeants and took one long step towards them. Her right hand swept down to her hip and came up with her own side arm even as her left hand caught the nearer of the two sergeants' combat rifle and heaved. The rifle's unfortunate owner stumbled toward her, off-balance and astounded by the force of the petite Marine's pull, and her left kneecap drove up into his groin.

He screamed, dropping his rifle and clutching at his crotch as he went to his knees, and his fellow sergeant suddenly found himself looking down the muzzle of Kuramochi's pistol at a range of twenty centimeters.

That quickly, Wheaton and Kuramochi had neutralized all three of Jongdomba's people. But Kuramochi had miscalculated slightly. She hadn't realized there was a *fourth* militiaman with the lightning bolt flash hidden behind the bulk of Jongdomba's com center. Now that man came to his feet, and the weapon in his hand was no pistol. It was a neural disrupter, coming to bear on the back of Kuramochi's head from a range of less than five meters. His finger was on the firing stud, and his lips drew back in a snarl as it began to squeeze.

Thunder exploded in the command post.

Alicia's M-97 was just a little long to be truly handy in such relatively close quarters, but that didn't matter. As the unexpected fourth member of the brigadier's insane ambush stood, her rifle muzzle tracked up from the floor. There wasn't time for a head or chest shot; she squeezed the trigger when the rifle was only hip-high and let recoil push the muzzle further upward as a sharp, chattering burst of tungsten-cored penetrators shattered the communications console before they smashed into the man on its other side.

The militiaman screamed as Alicia's first round hit him just below the navel. The second hit him halfway between the first and his breastbone. The third hit squarely at the base of his throat, its trajectory still upward, and his chopped-off scream died abruptly as it exited through the back of his neck and eight centimeters of his spine was reduced to paste. His gun hand closed convulsively, and the disrupter's emerald bolt slammed into the dugout wall. It missed Kuramochi entirely, but the very fringe of its area of effect caught Wheaton and the militia captain he had immobilized. Both of them went down, arching convulsively as energy bleed from the near-miss ripped through their nervous systems. They hit the floor, thrashing helplessly, an instant behind the man Alicia had just killed, and Brigadier Jongdomba snatched for his own side arm.

PFC Alicia DeVries took two steps. The militia commander's eyes snapped to her just as her combat rifle drove viciously forward. Unlike his subordinates, Jongdomba wore no body armor, so there was nothing to protect him when the smoking flash suppressor of Alicia's M-97, with its bulbous under-barrel mounted grenade launcher, rammed into his belly like a pile driver.

The brigadier jackknifed around the rifle with a high, hoarse grunt of agony. His pistol flew from his hand as he clutched at his belly, and Alicia's rifle twirled. Its butt came up in a perfectly measured arc that hammered into Jongdomba's descending shoulder, just low enough to catch and smash his collarbone as it straightened him back up.

The militia's commanding officer went up and over, then down, stunned, two-thirds unconscious. He landed on his back, whooping and coughing for the breath which had been driven out of him, then froze as he found himself staring up at the muzzle of a rock-steady combat rifle trained on the bridge of his nose.

"I think, Brigadier," Kuramochi said through Jongdomba's own gasping anguish, the high-pitched, whining moans of the sergeant she'd incapacitated, and the harsh, spastic breathing of Gunny Wheaton and the militia captain, "that you should have taken my advice."

The slender Marine lieutenant's voice was an icicle, and she never even looked away from the sergeant she held at gunpoint—the only member of Jongdomba's ambush who was still on his feet—as the sound of more firing came from outside the CP. It didn't last long, and then Sergeant Metternich came down the steps.

"We're secure topside, Skipper," he said. "'Fraid there was a little breakage among the locals first, though. They seem to've had a few problems with their IFF."

"Pity," the lieutenant said. "Any of our outside people hurt?"

"Nope. Not outside." Metternich glanced at Alicia, still standing over the helpless brigadier and nodded in grim approval, then went to one knee beside Wheaton.

"Disrupter," Kuramochi said, her attention still on her captive. "Mike caught the corona."

"Shit." Metternich bent closer and triggered the platoon sergeant's life signs monitor. It flickered and danced uncertainly for a few moments, then steadied down, and Metternich's taut shoulders relaxed visibly.

"I think he'll be okay, Skipper," he said. "I'm no corpsman, but according to this, his vitals are pretty good. There's no sign of actual neural damage, and his pharmacope's already treating him for shock."

"Glad to hear it," Kuramochi said. "Take this one."

"Yes, Ma'am." Metternich rose, grabbed the one still-standing militiaman by his collar, and frogmarched him up the CP steps.

Kuramochi holstered her side arm, then stepped up beside Alicia.

"Good work, DeVries," she said quietly, and reached up to rest one hand lightly on Alicia's shoulder. Then she looked down at Jongdomba.

The brigadier's complexion was the color of river mud, but his agonized breathing was easing slightly, and his eyes were beginning to regain their focus. Kuramochi smiled thinly.

"And now, Brigadier Jongdomba," she said, "in the name of His Majesty, Seamus II, I arrest you on the charges of conspiracy, attempted murder, and suspected treason against the planetary government of Gyangtse and the Terran Empire. All three of those charges, if sustained, are punishable by death. I would therefore advise you most earnestly not to make your situation any worse than it already is. Is that clear, Sir?"

Jongdomba stared up at her. Then, like a marionette controlled by someone else, he nodded jerkily.

"Good. In that case, Sir, I believe it's time I had that interview with President Shangup."

CHAPTER ELEVEN

"Stand aside, Captain."

The militia captain outside the door wore the same lightning bolts as the rest of Jongdomba's HQ guard company. They were, as Alicia had surmised, more of a personal bodyguard than a military formation, and she suspected that most of them were probably his employees in civilian life, as well. They certainly seemed to consider themselves much more in the nature of his personal retainers than as members of the planetary armed forces.

Now the captain looked uncertainly at Lieutenant Kuramochi, Alicia, and the additional pair of Marine riflemen behind them.

"Captain Goparma," Kuramochi said, glancing at the name stenciled on his breastplate, "I don't want to see anyone else hurt if it can be avoided, but Brigadier Jongdomba is currently under arrest. I suspect that the courts are going to determine in time that he's somewhat exceeded his authority as the commander of the planetary militia, and I remind you that martial law has been declared in the *Emperor's* name. That means an *imperial* court will be doing the deciding . . . and that at the moment, my authority as Governor Aubert's representative supersedes that of any militia officer. So you can either stand aside, or be removed, however forcibly seems appropriate. Which is it going to be?"

Goparma stared at her a moment longer, then stepped to one side.

"Thank you, Captain," Kuramochi said courteously. Then she nodded her head sideways at Alicia. "I believe, Captain," the lieutenant continued, "that it might be best for all of us if you'd surrender your side arm to Private DeVries. Just as a precaution, you understand."

The militia officer flushed, his face dark with mingled humiliation, anger, and fear. But he also unbuckled his pistol belt and passed it across to Alicia. She took it and slung it over her left shoulder, trying to look calm and self-possessed, as if things like this happened to her every day. And, she reflected, the captain was luckier than quite a few of his fellow "guardsmen." When Metternich said there'd been a little "breakage," he hadn't been joking. Almost a dozen of Jongdomba's bully boys were dead, and twice that many more were wounded.

"Thank you," Kuramochi repeated, then strode past him and opened the door he'd been guarding.

The basement conference room on the other side was enormous. It was also comfortably and luxuriously furnished, but its sixty or so occupants seemed unappreciative of its amenities. The air was stale, heavy and hot with the failure of the Presidential Mansion's air conditioning plant, and a thin skim of old-fashioned tobacco smoke hovered. The men in the room—there were no women present—were disheveled looking, their faces and body language tense, and their heads jerked up as the door opened.

Lieutenant Kuramochi stood in the doorway for a second or two, then stepped through it and headed directly for a small, wiry man who looked remarkably less dapper and distinguished at the moment than he did in his usual appearances on HD.

"President Shangup," she said courteously, holding out her hand. "I'm Lieutenant Kuramochi Chiyeko, Imperial Marines. Governor Aubert and Major Palacios extend their compliments and have instructed me to escort you to the spaceport."

"I—I see." Shangup gave himself a shake, then took her offered hand. "I'm delighted to see you, Lieutenant. Ah, may I assume you've already met with Brigadier Jongdomba?"

"I'm afraid there was a little misunderstanding there, Mr. President," Kuramochi said. "The Brigadier appeared to be under a misapprehension as to the content of my orders from Major Palacios and the limitations of his own authority. At the moment, I'm afraid he's under arrest. So are most of the members of his headquarters company. I'm afraid most of those not under arrest were killed or wounded in the course of our . . . misunderstanding. "

"Under *arrest?*" someone blurted from behind the President. Kuramochi's expression never flickered and her eyes never looked away from Shangup's.

"Does that mean you're in command now, Lieutenant?" the President asked after a moment.

"Effectively, I suppose I am, at least temporarily. I'm afraid I've had to place most of the Brigadier's staff under arrest, as well. And as far as I can determine, Colonel Sharwa never made it to the Mall in the first place. I believe Major Cusherwa is the Brigadier's logical successor under the circumstances, but he's been coordinating the defensive perimeter. I understand he's on his way to the CP to assume command of all militia forces now."

"I see." Shangup blinked, then inhaled deeply.

"To be completely frank, Lieutenant," he said, "I'm very happy—and relieved—to see you. Some of Brigadier Jongdomba's recent decisions have seemed . . . less than optimal. In fact, I'm afraid he's been less, ah, stable than most of us had believed."

"I'm sorry to hear that, Sir," Kuramochi said. The lieutenant's voice was politely attentive, Alicia noticed, giving no indication that Kuramochi had recognized the militia captain outside the conference room door as the President's jailer. Alicia wondered whether Jongdomba had definitely made up his mind to attempt what amounted to a *coup d'etat*, or if he'd still been stumbling toward one. Or, for that matter, if he'd been considering the possibility of one even before the present emergency arose.

"May I assume, Mr. President," Kuramochi continued, "that you and these other gentlemen," she nodded pleasantly to the rumpled delegates, "are, indeed, prepared to accompany my platoon and myself back to the spaceport, where Major Palacios and Governor Aubert will be able to assure the safety and continuity of your government?"

"You may indeed, Lieutenant," the President said firmly.

"I'm afraid we're going to have to walk, Sir," Kuramochi warned him. "Major Palacios considered sending transport to collect you, but we don't have any armored vehicles or air transport, and we know there are enough shoulder-fired SAMs floating around Zhikotse at the moment to rule out the use of air lorries. We'd rather not have you and the delegates smeared across the pavement somewhere because we failed to spot a SAM in time."

"I think keeping us unsmeared is an *outstanding* idea, Lieutenant." Shangup surprised Alicia with an amused snort and a broad, toothy grin. "And I've always considered walking an excellent form of exercise," he continued. "At the moment, I find myself quite looking forward to the opportunity to indulge in it with you."

"I'm delighted to hear that, Sir. In that case, if you'll forgive me, I'll go and see about organizing an orderly withdrawal from this position."

Captain Chiawa frowned as he peered carefully through the narrow horizontal gap. Something new was going on, and he didn't much care for what he suspected it was.

He'd heard the sudden, hammering explosions of a mortar fire mission delivered with far greater precision and concentration than any militia heavy weapons squad could have achieved. It had come from the general direction of the Mall, which suggested that the Wasps were moving to Jongdomba's relief. Frankly, he was surprised it had taken this long, but he'd been delighted to hear it.

He and his four companions had been making their crouching way through the storm drains at the moment the mortar rounds landed. Paldorje's caution about the drains' possibly cramped dimensions had proved only too well founded, but none of Chiawa's men were particularly large—few Gyangtsese were—and it beat the hell out of wandering through the open streets, wondering if there was a sniper on one of the rooftops, or behind one of the upper story windows looking down upon them.

It did have its drawbacks, though. Chiawa would have loved to join up with whatever column the Marines had sent to the Mall, but they'd been unable to determine exactly where the mortar fire had landed. Besides, it had taken them almost fifteen minutes of slithering along through the drain system to find another manhole.

They'd found one in the end, and he'd climbed the ladder and used his shoulders to raise the cover far enough for him to peek out. He'd intended to keep right on going, but he'd changed his mind rather abruptly when he found himself looking right at the backs of someone else's heels.

He'd frozen, holding the cover motionless, hoping no one had noticed its initial movement. The others had gone equally still below him as they absorbed his sudden change in body language, and he'd felt their tension rising about him like smoke as he moved his head cautiously, peering outward while he tried to figure out what he was seeing.

His heart hammered, and he felt himself beginning to sweat again as he realized he was looking at what had to be at least forty or fifty armed men and women. None of them were in uniform, but he saw dozens of the red armbands of the GLF.

He inhaled deeply, then let the cover settle gently, gently back into position. He climbed back down the ladder far more carefully and quietly than he'd ascended it, then turned to face the others.

"I couldn't see all that well," he told him softly, "but there's maybe fifty GLF types up there, and they're loaded for bear. I saw combat rifles and grenade and rocket launchers, and I think they've got at least a couple of calliopes, as well."

"Shit," Corporal Munming muttered. "What the fuck are they doing, Skipper? Just standing around scratching their asses?"

"I wish," Chiawa said with a harsh chuckle. "No. I saw one guy waving his arms around, like he was giving orders. And it looked like they were moving into the buildings on either side of the street."

"Ambush?" Munming said.

"I'm guessing," Chiawa agreed with a nod. "We're about half a block from an intersection. Hang on."

He settled down into an awkward squat so they could all gather round in the cramped quarters of the storm drain as he activated his map board again. The GPS icon appeared, and he looked up at the others.

"See?" He tapped the illuminated surface of the map, then pointed up the ladder at the manhole cover. "That's Solu Avenue up there. And half a block that way—" he pointed in a roughly southeast direction "—it runs into Capital Boulevard. Which just happens to be the shortest route from the Mall to the spaceport."

"So what do you think they've got in mind, Skipper?" Private Mende asked in the tone of a man who expected he wasn't going to much like the answer he might get.

"I don't know for certain, obviously," Chiawa replied. "But I have to say it looks to me like these people know somebody's going to be coming down Capital Boulevard sometime soon. And given that mortar fire we heard about half an hour ago, I can only think of one candidate for who that 'somebody' might be."

"You figure the Empie Marines sent somebody out to the Mall to fetch the President and take him back to the spaceport, not to try to hold the Presidential Mansion, right?" Munming said.

"That's about the size of it," Chiawa agreed.

"Well, yeah. Okay, I guess that makes sense," Private Khanbadze said slowly, frowning down at the map. "Only, I don't think I'd like to be the ones who tried to ambush those Wasp bastards. I mean, they sure handed us *our* heads, and they're going to have their fangs out for real, not just training, this time around."

"Agreed." Chiawa nodded. "And they're bound to have overhead sensor coverage, as well. But these people are a long way from the Mall. I think there's a real good chance they're outside the Wasps' sensor perimeter, and if they manage to get under cover quick enough, without being spotted, and if they're smart enough to stay *inside* the buildings, they're going to be a copperplated bitch to pick up. This is a high-rent district. These are substantial buildings, the kind that make it awful hard to pick up internal thermal signatures, even for the Wasps' equipment. And aside from the power packs on the calliopes, there aren't going to be a lot of electronic emissions from this bunch, either. So it's distinctly possible that they may actually be able to pull it off."

"Pity the poor bastards if they do," Munming grunted. "They may manage to kill themselves a couple of Wasps, but then the whole fucking world is gonna land on their heads."

"Unless," Chiawa said quietly, "they manage to get their hands on President Shangup first. Think about it. If they've got *him*, or even just a handful of the delegates, do you think the Empies are going to take a chance on turning him—or them—into a friendly fire statistic?"

"Honestly?" Munming looked at him, then grinned thinly. "I think they're hard-assed enough they might just figure breaking a few eggs is okay, as long as the omelet turns out in the end. Course, they might not, too. And I guess what matters isn't what *I* think they'd do, but what those people standing on our roof right now think will happen."

"Exactly." Chiawa nodded again. "Personally, I think the odds are pretty good the Empies would try *real* hard to avoid killing off the planetary government. Wouldn't look too good for the referendum if they had an oopsie like that, after all. But even if that's true, there's the little problem that sometimes the wrong people get killed in a firefight." His face tightened as he recalled the bloody chaos at the Annapurna Arms. "These people could kill Shangup themselves in the process of trying to take him alive."

"Sir," Mende said, "I don't think I like where you're going with this."

"Neither do I, Dabhuti," Munming said heavily. "Doesn't change the fact that he's right, though, does it?"

"No, it doesn't." Mende managed a tight, unhappy smile. "That's why I don't like it."

"Well, I can see where we ought to do something about it if we can," Khanbadze said slowly. "Thing is, I don't see anything we *can* do. We're almost out of ammo, there's only five of us, and we don't have any communications with anybody else. I mean, all due respect and all that, Captain, but I hope you aren't about to suggest we try some kind of frontal attack of our own. You just said there were at least fifty of them, and it sounds like they've got a hell of a lot more firepower than we do."

"Yes, they do," Chiawa said. "And no, I'm not—going to suggest we launch some sort of suicide attack, that is. But I think we do have to at least try to warn the Wasps."

"How, Sir?" Munming asked. "We don't know exactly where they are; like Ang Tarki just said, we're completely out of communication; and any Wasps wandering around out here are gonna have itchy trigger fingers. Sounds sort of . . . touchy, if you know what I mean."

"Oh, I do." Chiawa smiled tightly. "Believe me, I do."

Rather to Alicia's surprise, Major Cusherwa—who, unlike Jongdomba, actually seemed to be a capable sort—declined to accompany the platoon.

"Are you sure about this, Major?" Lieutenant Kuramochi asked.

She and Cusherwa stood in what had been Jongdomba's command post. Alicia had found herself still attached to Kuramochi, watching the lieutenant's back, and she was just as glad that the body of the man she'd killed had been removed. Someone had also shoveled fresh dirt over the sticky pool of blood the corpse had left behind. Now if that same someone had only been able to do something about the blood smell and the still-hovering stench of ruptured internal organs . . . .

"Lieutenant," Cusherwa said frankly, "however willing some of my people might be, we don't have your training, and we don't have your equipment. If anything goes wrong on your way back to the spaceport, I'm afraid we'd be more likely to get in your way then to do much good. On the other hand, I think we've already demonstrated we can do a pretty fair job of holding dug-in positions. Assuming, of course," his expression tightened, "that the officers in charge of holding them are concentrating on that instead of stupid political games."

"Maybe so," Kuramochi said. "On the other hand, Major Palacios says the pressure on our perimeter around the spaceport has dropped almost to nothing, while here—"

She waved one hand at the CP's walls, indicating the battered buildings surrounding the Mall beyond them. Individual shots were still ringing out from many of those buildings fairly frequently, and there'd been several bursts of heavier fire over the last several minutes, as if the people inside them were regaining their nerve after the Marines' arrival.

"According to my remotes," she told Cusherwa, "there are still people moving in to reinforce the bad guys out there. If we get the President and the Delegates out of here, is there really anything else in the Mall worth losing more of your own people's lives over?"

"I may not have agreed with Brigadier Jongdomba on everything, Lieutenant," the Gyangtsese major said, "but he did have a point about our responsibility to protect the Mall. Maybe he didn't want to do that for all the right reasons, but these buildings—or, rather, the files and offices inside them—are critical to the government's ability to govern. If we lose them, we lose a huge chunk of our administrative continuity, and avoiding that's going to be especially important when we start trying to reorganize in the wake of all this . . . unpleasantness.

"Besides," he produced an exhausted-sounding chuckle, "once they figure out that *you've* got the President, they're going to lose a lot of their enthusiasm for taking the Mansion in the first place."

"But Brigadier Jongdomba said you're almost out of ammunition," Lieutenant Kuramochi pointed out, and Cusherwa made a disgusted sound.

"We're on the short side, yes," he said, "but 'almost out' is a pile of crap, Lieutenant. I want the President and the delegates out of here because I can't *guarantee* we can hold the Mall. And because there's no telling where a stray rocket or mortar bomb may decide to land. But we've got a lot more ammo than Jongdomba was telling you we do. If you get the President out of here, and if the people on the other side realize you have, the intensity of their pressure is going to drop. In which case, I believe we have ample ammunition to hold our positions."

"I see." Kuramochi looked at him for several seconds. The Gyangtsese officer had a distinctly bookish, nerdy look, but there was a hardness and determination behind what she suspected were normally rather mild brown eyes. She wondered if it had always been there, but that wasn't really her problem at the moment, and she shrugged. "You're in command of the militia, now, Major. If you think you can hold the Mall, I'm not going to argue with you. *My* orders are still to get President Shangup and the delegates safely back to the spaceport, however."

"I understand, and I agree entirely," Cusherwa said. "And, if I may, Lieutenant, I do have one additional request."

"Which is?" Kuramochi asked.

"I'd feel much more comfortable if you'd take Brigadier Jongdomba with you." Cusherwa looked the Marine straight in the eye. "I think you probably got most of his toadies, but there may be others out there I don't know about. If there are, and if he's still here, they might be tempted to do something stupid."

"Understood," Kuramochi said, and smiled thinly.

"And while we're talking about taking people with you, Lieutenant," Cusherwa continued, "I'd appreciate it if you'd revisit your plan to walk all the way back to the spaceport. President Shangup mountain bikes for exercise in his spare time, but several of the delegates are in much poorer physical condition than he is. Not to mention the fact that they don't have any training at all—or, at least, not anything like current training—for something like this."

"I appreciate that, Major," Kuramochi said. "But I'm not sure there's anything I can do about it, except possibly to leave the less physically fit Delegates here, since you're planning on continuing to hold the Mall, instead of pulling out with us. I'd certainly prefer to evac them by air, but none of our transport is armored. I can't risk exposing these people to ground fire when I know there are SAMs out there in the streets. They've already managed to knock down an all-up sting ship; unarmored transports would be sitting ducks."

"I understand. But," Cusherwa smiled thinly, "Brigadier Jongdomba had a couple of cards tucked up his sleeve which might give us a bit more flexibility."

"—so I have to agree with Major Cusherwa, Ma'am," Kuramochi Chiyeko said from Major Palacios' com display. "At least eight of the delegates are in no physical condition to walk that far even under perfect conditions. Under the ones which actually obtain . . ."

She shrugged, and Palacios nodded.

"Understood. And, frankly, I was a bit afraid of something like this. I'm inclined to defer to your judgment, since you're right there on the spot. Should I take it from what you've said that you think Cusherwa's suggestion is a good one?"

"I'm not sure it's what I'd normally call a *good* one, Ma'am. I just think it's probably the least bad one available."

Palacios nodded again, this time slowly and thoughtfully. Somehow or other, Jongdomba hadn't gotten around to mentioning that he'd managed to get several of the militia's handful of armored personnel carriers into the Mall position before he got himself surrounded. He certainly hadn't mentioned them in any of his conversations with her or Governor Aubert, and Palacios rather expected that he'd seen them as the bug-out insurance policy for himself and his "headquarters company."

They weren't all that good by the standards of the Imperial Marines. They had no counter-grav capability, only the most primitive of electronic warfare suites, very limited anti-missile defenses, and armor which would have done well to stop heavy calliope fire, far less dedicated antiarmor weapons. But they had four huge things going for them. First, they were ground-based systems, which meant she wouldn't have to worry about getting them nailed by SAMs. Second, there were enough of them and they were big enough that the President and all of the delegates could be easily accommodated aboard them. Third, their design was so old, and so obsolescent, that every single bug had been exterminated decades ago, and they were as mechanically and automotively reliable as the fabled pre-space Model T. And, fourth, they were available.

"Tell me how you plan to do this, Lieutenant," the major said after a moment.

"They're not capable enough for me to take a chance simply loading everyone aboard to ride back," Kuramochi said. "Defensively, they're actually not all that bad against militia-grade weapons, but 'not all that bad' isn't good enough if they've got the planetary government on board. So I'm thinking that my platoon comes out on foot, the same way we came in. I'll use one squad to break trail and sweep for threats. I'll use another squad for close cover, protecting the APCs from anything the sweep squad misses. And I'll use my third squad to cover the rear and provide at least a small tactical reserve. It'll still be slow, but we'll be faster than we would with the older delegates hobbling along on foot, and we should be able to cover the APCs against significant threats on the way home."

"I see." Palacios considered for several more seconds, then made her decision.

"All right, Chiyeko. Do it your way. And, for what it matters, you have my official endorsement, not just my permission."

"Thank you, Ma'am. I appreciate that. We'll see you in a couple of hours or so. Kuramochi, clear."

"Well, DeVries—Alley," Kuramochi said, and Alicia twitched internally in surprise. She hadn't realized that the lieutenant even knew what her first name was.

"Yes, Ma'am?"

She and Kuramochi stood on the Presidential Mansion's chipped and battered steps with Cusherwa, watching the snorting APCs move into position. Alicia had continued trailing the lieutenant around after her encounter with Jongdomba, obedient to Sergeant Metternich's unspoken order. She'd rather hoped her CO hadn't noticed, since Metternich still hadn't bothered to ask Lieutenant Kuramochi's approval for the arrangement.

Not that there'd ever been much chance that she *wouldn't* notice, of course.

"You'd better get back to your squad, now." Kuramochi smiled crookedly. "Sergeant Metternich's going to need you. And you can tell Abe for me that while I appreciate his solicitude, I don't think I'll really need a bodyguard once we get started."

"Uh, yes, Ma'am!"

"Oh, don't look so startled, Alley." Kuramochi actually chuckled. "I'll admit I was a bit surprised when he and Gunny Wheaton picked *you* for the role, but they're mother hens, the pair of them. Maybe they thought I wouldn't notice a mere 'larva' hovering in the background and raise a stink. And as a matter of fact, I suppose I should admit you've actually been quite a comfort—especially in that little unpleasantness with Jongdomba. But now," she made a shooing motion with one hand, "go find Abe. It's about time we got back across the Major here's perimeter and headed back to the barn."

Getting back out of the Mall perimeter wouldn't be quite as simple as getting in had been, Alicia decided fifteen minutes later. She rather doubted that it would be quite as difficult as the people on the other side thought it would, but that didn't mean it was going to be simple, either.

The civilian evacuees, although manifestly willing, were hardly going to be an asset for this particular mission. If any of them had ever had any military training, it had been decades ago. They were basically cargo, loaded aboard the APCs for safekeeping, but they were also cargo which would be capable of making mistakes if it fell into the crapper, and Alicia was more than happy that Sergeant Jackson had been assigned the dubious pleasure of providing them with close cover.

Of course, the fact that First Squad was busy doing that meant it was up to Second and Third Squads to lead the way back out again.

The carnage Lieutenant Ryan's mortars had wreaked on the platoon's way in had clearly shocked the rioters and would-be guerrillas around the Mall. Second Platoon had left effectively no survivors in its wake when it broke the line around Jongdomba's positions, and for almost half an hour, there'd been scarcely a shot from the "enemy's" other dug-in firing positions. No doubt they'd been afraid of drawing the same sort of firestorm down on themselves. By the time Lieutenant Kuramochi was ready to begin her pullout, though, that had changed.

At least some of the attackers had apparently begun getting their nerve back, or perhaps they'd simply suffered a catastrophic loss of common sense. Not only had some of them begun harassing Cusherwa's militiamen with small arms fire once more, but others had moved to block the gap Lieutenant Ryan had blasted in their lines. They hadn't been stupid enough to try to regain their original positions—or not, at least, after they ran into the murderously effective opposition of the single fire team from Sergeant Bruckner's Second Squad which Lieutenant Kuramochi had left behind to support the militiamen who'd occupied those positions. But the capital city's heavily built-up terrain had allowed them to swing around behind the area the mortar fire had plowed up, and they'd found new perches in several of the high-rise buildings from which they could bring the streets and avenues below them under fire.

Their new positions were harder to spot, even with the remotes. Worse, they had overhead cover—several stories worth of it, in most cases—which enormously decreased the effectiveness of Lieutenant Ryan's mortars. Unfortunately for them, "harder to spot" wasn't the same thing as "impossible to spot." Also, and even more unfortunately for them, their lack of experience against Imperial Marines with first-line equipment had kept them from fully realizing just how . . . unwise their decision to cross swords with Second Platoon truly was.

The Marines' chameleon systems made them extraordinarily difficult for the unaided eye, or even the considerably more capable optical sighting systems the planetary militia's combat rifles boasted, to spot. The people in the buildings had probably figured that the concealment of their own positions would level that particular part of the playing field, and to some extent, they'd been right. But the Marines' helmet sensor systems, especially with their direct links to their hovering remotes, promptly unleveled it once again.

While First Squad was getting the civilians organized, Sergeant Metternich, who'd become acting platoon sergeant when Gunny Wheaton went down, had moved Second and Third Squads into position to open the door for the column behind them. Sergeant Bruckner had been monitoring the take from the platoon's remotes, and now Metternich conferred briefly with her while they studied the remotes' data over their synth-links.

On their way into the Mall, Lieutenant Kuramochi had positioned her available remotes—she hadn't exactly had an unlimited supply of them—to watch her preselected exit point. Those remotes had hovered there, patiently (and invisibly) watching even while the lieutenant and her people dealt with Brigadier Jongdomba and his supporters. Which meant that they'd actually watched the people filtering cautiously out of the alleys and side streets to take up their new positions.

The remotes had lost lock on the exact locations of several of those people once they'd entered the buildings of their choice, but Bruckner had managed to keep track of the majority of them. Even some of those her remotes had lost track of had been relocated when they injudiciously exposed themselves on balconies or at windows as they found themselves firing positions. Every single potential hostile whose location had been determined had been meticulously noted on the continuously updated tactical plot she'd taken over from the incapacitated Wheaton, and now Metternich took ruthless advantage of that information.

"All right, people. Listen up," Metternich came up on the communications subnet which had been dedicated to Second and Third Squads. "Here's how we're going to do this. Chris?"

"Yo," Corporal Sandusky acknowledged tersely.

"Alpha Team takes the right side of the street. Leo, Bravo Team takes the left side. Second Squad's Alpha holds its position to watch our rear, and Second's Bravo is our tactical backup. We've got to clear these three blocks—" a red arrow appeared on the map graphic in Alicia's mental HUD "—before the rest of the outfit can haul the civilians out of here. Once we're through the immediate crust, Clarissa will hold the door open while Julio's First Squad takes the civilians through it. After that, she'll have the column's back door and bring up the rear. Anybody got any questions, so far?"

Alicia studied the HUD, noting the clusters of solid red icons representing positively identified hostiles and the somewhat less numerous blinking icons of possible enemies' locations. There seemed to be quite a lot of them, she noticed, yet to her own surprise, she no longer felt nervous. Instead, she felt a strangely focused, almost singing sense of calm, unlike anything she'd quite experienced before.

"All right," Metternich said again, when no one voiced any questions. "Alley."

"Yes, Abe?" Her voice sounded just a bit odd, almost serene, to her own ears.

"As it happens," Metternich said, "and without wanting to give you a swelled head or anything, you've got the highest marksmanship scores of the entire Platoon."

Alicia blinked. She'd been impressed—almost awed—by the casual expertise of her more experienced fellows' marksmanship. She'd certainly never thought that hers was better than theirs!

"In addition," Metternich continued, "you and César are the only fully synth-link-capable rifles we've got in Bravo. That's why I'm designating you and him as Bravo's long guns," Metternich continued. "Gregory, you're covering them. Leo, you and Frinkelo are responsible for—"

Alicia listened to the sergeant as he continued laying out the plan, but deep inside, her mind was grappling with her own assigned part of it. She'd been more than a little surprised, despite any relative marksmanship scores involved, when Metternich selected her as one of Bravo Team's counter-snipers. And while he was right about her synth-link capability, and even though it was exactly the sort of thing she'd trained to do, she still felt more than a few qualms. What she was about to do amounted to visiting specifically targeted death upon other human beings not just once, but again and again, and whatever her ability as a marksman, she was also the newest, least experienced member of the entire Platoon. This wasn't the sort of job that normally got handed to the newest kid on the block.

"—and after that," Metternich concluded finally, "we pass the word to the Lieutenant that the door's open, and we all haul ass back to the spaceport. Any questions? If you've got 'em, ask now, people."

No one did.

"In that case, let's saddle up," he said.

CHAPTER TWELVE

Alicia DeVries eased cautiously forward.

Late afternoon was finally beginning to give way to early evening, and the smoke and shadows made her chameleon camouflage even more effective. Nonetheless, she moved slowly, carefully, like a woman wading through waist-deep water. The slower she moved, the less likely anyone on the other side was to see some small, betraying flicker of movement. The odds of their seeing her, even if she'd run full tilt down the middle of the street, were slim, to say the least. But they had time to do this the right way. Indeed, the darker it got, the worse the visibility, the better from their perspective, and Sergeant Metternich had been very firm on the matter of not running any unnecessary risks.

She reached her assigned position uneventfully and settled into place. Her particular perch was a traffic island, in the center of a four-way intersection. There were drawbacks to it, especially the fact that virtually every building in a half-block radius had a direct line of sight to it. On the other hand, that meant that *she* had an unobstructed LOS to all of *them*, as well.

The other major advantage of the island was that it was home to half a dozen native shade trees. The smallest of them was at least twenty-five or thirty centimeters thick, and their branches and foliage were dense enough to hide even someone who'd never heard of chameleon camouflage. In addition, there were roughly built, solid stone benches on all four sides of the island, which meant that it provided military cover, as well as mere concealment.

She watched her HUD icons as the rest of Alpha and Bravo Teams reached their own positions. For their present purposes, hers was the best-sited of the lot, and she tried not to think too hard about exactly why that was.

She shifted around to the south side of her island and arranged herself behind the solid stone bench on that side. It was just short enough that she could take up a seated firing position behind it and use the top of its back as a rest for her weapon.

"Three-Alpha, Bravo-Five," she said quietly over the com. "Position."

"Three-Alpha, Bravo-Four," she heard from César Bergerat. "Position."

"Three-Alpha, Bravo-Three," Gregory Hilton reported. "Position."

One by one, all of the members of the three fire teams assigned to the mission reported in, confirming what the icons on Abe Metternich's HUD had already told him.

"All Wasps this net," Metternich said when they had finished, "Three-Alpha. We are go. Bravo-Five, open the ball."

"Five copies," Alicia said simply, and closed her eyes.

Her normal vision disappeared, and she concentrated her full attention on her synth-link. Each of the Marines in Third Squad had been assigned his or her own dedicated sensor remote. That remote's exquisitely sensitive optical, thermal, and electronic passive sensors were patched directly into the helmet computers of the Marines to whom they had been assigned. Those computers translated the data into detailed displays which were presented to each Marine in the format he or she found easiest to process. Some Marines, Alicia knew, preferred wire-diagram representations and tactical icons. She herself found a direct visual presentation easiest to absorb, without icons, and so she found herself apparently hovering motionless in mid-air fifty meters south and forty meters above her actual physical position, gazing at a crystal clear image of the first building in her assigned sector.

A mental command reoriented the sensor remote very slightly, zooming in on the panoramic windows of a specific office on the sixth floor of the commercial building. There were four people in the room on the other side of those windows, and the remote's sensors clearly identified the weapons in their hands as they knelt or crouched in firing positions of their own, peering alertly down into the street below. Unlike Alicia, they saw nothing, and she dropped another command into her computer.

A crosshair appeared in her mental vision. It was at the very bottom of her field of view, and far to the right, but it moved as she shifted her M-97's point of aim without ever opening her eyes. One of the hardest things in the Camp Mackenzie marksmanship curriculum—for most people, at least—was learning how to direct small arms fire accurately based on the feed from a remote sensor just like the one assigned to Alicia. It had been considerably easier for synth-link-capable people like Alicia than for most, since the input from the remote feed dropped directly into their brains without the need for distracting sensory interfaces. Which wasn't exactly the same thing as saying that it hadn't been difficult, even for her. But the Corps' tradition was that *every* Marine was a rifleman first, and so, hard or easy, it was a lesson she'd learned. Learned so thoroughly, so completely, that she didn't even think about it as the crosshair tracked smoothly across her mental view until it settled on the righthand person in the room she had selected.

She'd considered the possibility of using the grenade launcher, but rejected it. The M-97 used a low-visibility propellant, which, coupled with the flash suppressor, made its muzzle flash extremely difficult to see, even in a low-light conditions, from any point outside a relatively narrow cone directly in front of it. The rifle grenade's rocket engine, on the other hand, would have drawn a bright, arrow-straight line directly back to her firing position for anyone in any of the buildings around it. Which meant she was going to have to do this the hard way.

The crosshair positioned itself at the base of her target's throat. She drew a deep breath, let most of it out, and squeezed slowly, steadily.

The slam of recoil came as a surprise, exactly as it was supposed to do, and the target—the human being—at whom she had fired went down instantly, bonelessly, without a sound except for the sodden impact of the high-velocity round.

Alicia was aware of the other people in the room. She was aware of *everything*, with a godlike crystalline clarity, and she noted all of it. But she was *focused* on the task in hand, and the crosshair tracked just over one meter farther to the left. It settled on the rifleman who was just turning towards the spot at which his companion had died, alerted by the impact sound, and she squeezed again.

Two, an icy, dispassionate corner of her mind recorded as she rode the recoil, and the crosshair tracked left again. Settled. Squeeze.

Three.

The fourth and final person in the office had time to realize what was happening. Had time to come to her feet, to begin to back away from the window at which she had waited. But she didn't have *enough* time, and Alicia squeezed the trigger again.

"Three-Alpha, Bravo-Five. First target neutralized. Four down," someone said in Alicia's voice, her tone calm, almost serene. "Five engaging second target."

The hovering sensor remote shifted very slightly, zooming in on another window. There were only two people behind this one, and as yet, they had no clue of what had happened in the office three doors down the hall from their own position.

Nor would they ever find out, that still, cold corner of Alicia's brain thought as the crosshair settled on the first of them and her hand began to squeeze.

The people who had positioned themselves to reseal the gap Second Platoon had blasted in the siege lines around the Mall had no idea, no concept, of just what they had "trapped."

The "Empire's Wasps" had a towering reputation as dispensers of devastation in the Empire's name, yet some people persisted in thinking that the very fearsomeness of their reputation must indicate exaggeration. And most even of those who weren't convinced that at least half the Corps' supposed invincibility had to be pure propaganda had no direct, personal experience with the Marines' combat capabilities. Perhaps they might have reflected upon the fact that very few people who *had* had direct, personal experience with Marine capabilities were still around to pass the lessons of that experience on.

Be that as it may, the people waiting in those buildings to pour rifle fire, grenade fire, and rockets down on any attempt to break back out of the Mall had never allowed for the Marines' ability to literally see around corners. To accurately target individual opponents under such adverse conditions of visibility.

To kill them with single, aimed shots.

Alicia was only one of four riflemen. Although she had no spare time or attention to waste realizing it, she was the quickest and most effective of them all, but still only one of four, and *all* of them were killing targets with metronome-steady precision. She'd just taken down her seventeenth when the first belated return fire began to crack out from the other side.

Most of it was unaimed, panic fire. An instinctive reaction as someone lasted long enough to squeeze a trigger as the other people in his ambush position were picked off. The first long, suddenly interrupted burst of fire from one of the buildings set off others, and within seconds the gathering twilight glared and flickered and danced with the muzzle flashes of scores of weapons.

Very little of it was actually *aimed* at anything, and Alicia was only vaguely aware of the supersonic whipcracks of the scattered handful of shots coming anywhere near her own position. Had her eyes been open, no doubt the blinding effect of all of those muzzle flashes would have disoriented her, but they weren't. The sensor remote and her helmet computer showed her each flash, but unlike her physical retina, her mental vision wasn't subject to the blinding effect of those brilliant flares of light.

Something whipped through the branches above her. A spattering of twigs and leaves showered down over her, and her crosshair moved steadily to her next target. A digital readout in the corner of her HUD reminded her that she was down to twenty-three rounds in the current magazine, and she dropped the crosshair onto the chest of a man firing long, sweeping, obviously unaimed bursts in the general direction of César Bergerat's position.

Squeeze.

She was no longer counting the people she'd killed. She simply noted that the target was down, and moved to the next in her queue.

Squeeze.

The Marines' very efficiency kept their victims from immediately realizing just how dreadfully outclassed they were. There simply wasn't time for the awareness of Death's steady march through their ranks to spread. Not at first. But eventually, here and there, some of the targets waiting to become statistics had enough time to realize what was happening to the other people in the room, or on the balcony, or on the roof with them, and run before it was *their* turn. And as a few people began to survive the Marines' attention, they began trying to contact others, who had been less fortunate.

Alicia was ten rounds into her second magazine when she realized the targets in her assigned sector were beginning to vanish before she got around to them.

"All Wasps this net, Three-Alpha," Metternich's voice sounded in her mastoid implant. "Check fire. Repeat, check fire. Hostiles are breaking and running. Let them go."

"Three-Alpha, Bravo-Five," Alicia said, still in that stranger's voice which sounded so much like her own. "Confirm check fire."

The other confirmations came in, and Alicia ejected her partially used magazine. She replaced it with a full one, then began snapping individual loose rounds into the one she'd replaced. Her fingers, she noticed, were rock steady.

Fifty rounds, she thought. That was how many she'd fired, and she remembered missing her target exactly once.

"All Wasps this net," Metternich said again after a moment. "Well done, people. Now sit tight where you are for another few minutes. The APCs are moving into position. When everyone else is ready, Third Squad will lead off. Three-Alpha, clear."

Alicia DeVries sat tight, finishing reloading both of her magazines, while the twilight settled fully about her and her own awareness of just how deadly a killer she was settled within her.

Kuramochi Chiyeko watched the lead APC shudder like an irritated boar. She'd been astonished when she discovered that their engines actually ran on petroleum distillates, not hydrogen, and the gout of stinking black smoke as its driver fired up sent a grimace of distaste across her face. Not that it actually made the smoke, dust, and varied palette of stenches hanging over the Mall any worse. It just offended her sensibilities to be using such ancient and grotesque so-called technology.

The other APCs in her column shuddered and shook as their engines turned over in turn, and the militia lieutenant in charge of them listened to his own com for a moment, then turned to her.

"Ready to proceed, Lieutenant Kuramochi," he said.

"Thank you. In that case, let's roll them out."

"Yes, Ma'am!"

The militiaman actually saluted, then gave an order over the com. The first squat vehicle lurched into motion, and the militia lieutenant went scampering across to the third APC. He climbed up and ducked through the command vehicle's hatch, and Kuramochi walked forward to join Sergeant Jackson.

"Well, Julio?" she said.

"Begging your pardon, Skipper, but there's nothing particularly 'well' about it."

"Now, now," she chided as the second and third APCs began moving at a slow walking pace. The two Marines started forward behind the militia lieutenant's command vehicle, which put them at the center of the column. Kuramochi watched her own HUD critically, but all of her Marines were exactly where they were supposed to be, and the three blocks Second and Third Squads had been tasked to clear were completely free of red, hostile icons.

"How can you say that, Sergeant Jackson?" she continued. "We've got the open road before us, our knapsacks on our backs, a song on our lips, and only a brisk sixteen-kilometer walk between us and home. And if that's not enough to warm the cockles of your heart," she said with a grin, "I might add that Brigadier Jongdomba and his staff officers are in the lead APC, and the remainder of his so-called 'Headquarters Guard' is spread between there and the *second* APC. So if it should happen that we did miss somebody with one of the militia's antitank weapons, well . . ."

She shrugged, and Jackson shook his head at her.

"Skipper," he said firmly, "an officer and a lady isn't supposed to indulge herself in that sort of nasty attitude. However much the bastards in question might deserve it."

"I'll try to bear that in mind," she promised dutifully as the rest of the armored vehicles began to grunt, shiver, and clank their way forward.

Alicia drifted onward through the night.

The sky to the southeast of her present position was a lurid sea of billowing, flame-shot smoke as Zhikotse's business district burned. Over half of the city's power grid appeared to be down, despite the fact that the Marines controlled the primary generating station and switching facility. In those areas where the power had been cut, the streets were dark, bottomless canyons of blackness—like the one through which she moved now—while in others, streetlights, traffic control devices, and shop windows burned brightly and steadily in bizarre contrast.

This was not the sort of combat environment she'd envisioned when she enlisted, despite all of her discussions with her grandfather. She'd thought in terms of open-field battle, not of this enclosed, complicated urban setting. And even though she'd known that at least three-quarters of the Marines' duties were those of peacekeepers, especially out here among the Crown Systems of the frontier, she hadn't really pictured herself sniping rioters and would-be insurrectionists out of office windows when they didn't even know she was killing them.

Those reflections drifted through the back of her mind, like *koi* floating weightlessly just above the bottom of their pond. The front of her brain was busy with other things, monitoring her surroundings as she advanced steadily into the blackness her helmet systems and enhanced vision turned into daylight.

She moved onward for another dozen meters, then paused once again, waiting for Bergerat to leapfrog up the other side of the street and for Gregory Hilton to close up on both of them from behind. She could hear the distant clank and snort of the militia's obsolescent APCs grinding up Capital Boulevard well behind her, and she checked her map coordinates.

They were making pretty good time, she decided. They'd covered almost a third of the total distance back to the spaceport, and while they weren't moving as quickly as they had on the way *to* the Mall, they were moving a lot faster than they would have managed with the President and the delegates walking it. Now, if only—

Her reflections halted abruptly as she detected movement in front of her.

"Three-Alpha, Bravo-Five," she said quietly. "I've got movement."

"Five, Three-Alpha," Metternich's voice came back instantly. "I don't have it on any of my remotes. What does it look like?"

"Three-Alpha, I can't say for certain yet. At the moment, it looks like one person. He just stepped out of an apartment building and sat down on the front steps. Right about here."

She dropped a blinking amber icon onto Metternich's HUD through her synth-link. She wasn't too surprised that neither Metternich nor Bruckner had spotted the unknown. The platoon's supply of remotes was stretched knife-thin covering the flanks of the extended column. They hadn't had an unlimited number of them to begin with, and they'd lost quite a few of them—mostly to the sorts of accidents that happened in combat zones, rather than to anyone's deliberate effort to destroy them. A thin shell was still sweeping ahead of them, but without the sort of multiply redundant overlapping coverage The Book called for, and the fellow she'd spotted had stepped out of cover only after the shell had passed.

But that was why each of the riflemen probing ahead of the column still had his or her personal remote assigned.

"Five, Three-Alpha," Metternich said, "proceed at your discretion."

"Three-Alpha, Bravo-Five copies."

Alicia stood for a moment, her mind ticking coolly. As far as her remotes and her helmet's sensors could determine, the individual she was observing was unarmed. He might have a side arm, but there was no sign of any shoulder weapon. He did have several power sources scattered about his person, more than most civilians would normally carry, which was certainly suspicious. On the other hand, simply shooting someone out of hand on the possibility that he might be a Bad Person was something command authority frowned upon.

She thought about it for a few more seconds, then shrugged and made up her mind.

Karsang Dawa Chiawa was vaguely surprised by how *good* it felt to simply sit down.

He laid his helmet down on the step beside him and ran one grimy hand's fingers through his sweat-matted hair. The sharp, acrid tang of smoke drifted in the air even here, but the night was cool, the continuing occasional crackle of small arms fire was several blocks away, and he was so *tired*.

He rested his elbows on the step above him and leaned back, inhaling deeply. There was no way for him to be sure he'd guessed right about the Marines' probable retirement route from the Mall. Or, for that matter, that the Marines were actually coming at all.

And just sitting here in the dark wasn't exactly the safest thing he could have been doing, no matter what might or might not be coming down the boulevard towards him. Still, it was—

"Don't move."

The two words came out of the darkness in a soft contralto. An *off-world* contralto. A very young one, he thought for some reason, with just a trace of pleasing, almost furry, huskiness, but one which expected to be obeyed.

And one whose owner was entirely prepared to blow him away if it *wasn't* obeyed.

"All right," he replied, as calmly as he could. He even managed to not turn his head—mostly—in an effort to locate the speaker. The visibility wasn't good, but he'd deliberately selected a position where some of the light from the fires, reflected off the overhead smoke and the slight haze of overcast, provided at least some dim illumination, like pallid moonlight. Despite that, and despite the fact that from the sound of the young woman's voice, she couldn't be more than nine or ten meters away from him, he couldn't see a single sign of her.

"I presume," he continued, "that I'm speaking to one of Major Palacios' Marines. If so, I have some information which I believe you'd be interested in."

He was a cool customer, Alicia thought. He'd hardly jumped at all when she spoke.

"And just what information might that be . . . Captain Chiawa?" she asked as her enhanced vision read the name and rank insignia stenciled on his militia-issue breastplate. "And, if you don't mind my asking, just what is a militia officer doing sitting out here all by himself?"

Despite himself, Chiawa was impressed. He'd known the Wasps' equipment was enormously better than that of the militia, but if she could read the low-visibility name off his breastplate under these conditions, even his estimate of its capabilities had been low.

"To answer your second question first," he said, "I've been waiting for you—or someone like you. And, to be completely honest, I'm not entirely alone."

"Good answer, Captain." There was a slight, unmistakable note of amusement in the youthful contralto. "According to my sensors, there are at least four more people sitting in one of the first-floor apartments behind you. Unlike you, they all appear to have shoulder weapons, as well. Somehow, I don't think that they 'just happen' to be there any more than *you* 'just happen' to be sitting out here."

Chiawa fought a sudden urge to swallow as he realized how lucky he was that the voice's owner hadn't decided he was simply bait for an ambush.

"They're with me," he confirmed. "We were at the Annapurna Arms when this whole nightmare began. We were also with the attempt to retake the hotel. When it came apart, we managed to hang together, and decided to try to make it to the spaceport and your perimeter."

"Which no doubt explains why you're clear over here on the other side of town," the contralto observed almost politely.

"We kept getting pushed sideways, and after a while, I decided our best bet was to try to circle around to the north, avoid the mob," Chiawa admitted. "Then, earlier this afternoon, we heard your mortars—or, at least, I assume they were yours—from the direction of the Mall. I figured our best chance then would be to join up with your column, but we couldn't find you in time."

"And now?"

"And now you need to know that there's a major force of what I believe are GLF irregulars with heavy weapons dug in on both sides of the Boulevard about two blocks ahead of you." Chiawa shrugged. "I suppose it's possible your sensors have already picked them up, but they've been in position for almost two and a half hours, and they've got really good overhead cover."

Alicia frowned. They'd picked up no indications of any such ambush force, but if the militia officer was correct about how long the prospective ambushers had been in position, they might well not have. They certainly hadn't had the time—or, for that matter, the reason—to concentrate their dispersed reconnaissance assets to give that section of the Boulevard the sort of microscopic examination they'd lavished on the area immediately outside the Mall perimeter. Which meant it was entirely possible that this Captain Chiawa was giving them good information.

"That's very interesting, Captain," the voice out of the darkness said. "I'll pass the information along. And while we're waiting for someone to get back to us, why don't you just invite the rest of your friends to come out and join you on the steps?"

"That sounds like a very good idea," Chiawa said, and turned to flash his infrared light at the window where he knew Corporal Munming was watching him.

"So, the good captain knew what he was talking about," Lieutenant Kuramochi said.

She was speaking to Sergeant Metternich, but she'd deliberately included all of Third Squad, as her most advanced unit, in the net. And she was also indulging in some fairly extreme understatement, Alicia decided.

Alerted by Chiawa's warning, Sergeant Bruckner's lead remotes had swung back, thickened by some diverted from the flanks, to take a very, very close look at the indicated area. And Chiawa's numbers had been low. There were over three hundred armed people in that stretch, and the remotes had picked up heavy calliopes, rocket launchers, what appeared to be at least one honest-to-God hyper-velocity weapon launcher, and over a dozen SAMs.

"I've been on the horn within the Old Lady," Kuramochi continued. "She says that Lieutenant Beregovoi believes we've probably got the majority of the GLF's remaining hard core strength waiting for us up ahead. Battalion lost track of their leadership cadre early this afternoon; apparently, this is where they were headed, and Major Palacios' best guess is that Captain Chiawa is right. They figure the last chance they've got is to get their hands on President Shangup and the delegates to use as bargaining chips, probably for starship tickets off-planet.

"Needless to say, that's what we think of in the Corps as a Bad Idea."

Alicia surprised herself with a chuckle. Not that she felt particularly humorous at the moment. The opposition ahead of them was much heavier than they'd faced during their breakout from the Mall perimeter. Still, they knew where it was now, and they'd already demonstrated that what they could positively locate, they could kill.

On the other hand, if Beregovoi was correct, then these were probably the best trained, most disciplined adversaries the Marines had yet faced by a considerable margin. They also had enough heavy weapons to lay down enough suppressive fire, even shooting blind, to make things dicey, and the presence of that HVW launcher suggested that they might well have better sensor capabilities, as well.

There was no doubt in her mind that the Platoon could still take them all. The chance of their doing it without suffering friendly casualties was a lot lower than the one they'd faced leaving the Mall, though. And even if that hadn't been true, Alicia was grimly certain that the *other* side's casualties would be even heavier before they broke. These people were much more highly motivated, in addition to their training and discipline. They weren't going to run easily, and the longer they stood, the more of them would die.

But they're also the leadership elements of the people who started this entire thing, she thought. *The Empire* wants *these people, and here they are.*

"I'm a bit tempted to go right in after them," Lieutenant Kuramochi continued. "Especially if this really *is* the GLF's surviving leadership. However, our primary mission is to get the President and the other members of the local government to safety, and not to run any unavoidable risks on secondary missions in the process. Major Palacios has confirmed my interpretation of our responsibilities, and she's also reminded me that we're not really in the business of killing any more people than we have to. So instead of going through them, we're going to go around them."

Alicia drew a deep breath of relief. Relief, she was a bit surprised to note, which owed far more to the chance of avoiding killing any more other people—even GLF separatists—than to apprehension for her own safety.

"We're going to shift our route," Kuramochi said, and a fresh green line appeared in the map graphic of Alicia's HUD. "We're going to have to swing fairly wide if we want to stay far enough away from these people to keep them from hearing the APCs. If they do hear them, and they want to come out after them, then it's going to be up to us to discourage them—permanently. But I think that if we backtrack to this point—" an intersection blinked on the map "—then cut still further north, we can get around to the far side of the river and approach the spaceport through the suburbs. Frankly, it's better terrain for our purposes, anyway. But it is going to add at least another three hours to our transit time. Probably more like four hours."

Alicia studied the new route projection and felt herself agreeing with Kuramochi. They'd have another couple of blocks of heavily built up office and apartment buildings to get through, but then they'd be into individual one- and two-family dwellings, each surrounded by at least a small plot of grass. Sightlines would be longer and clearer, and there'd be far less cover for nasty surprises like the ambush waiting ahead of them. Tired as she was, four more hours of hiking—or even twice that long—struck her as a minor price to pay for that.

"I know we're all tired," Kuramochi said, almost as if she'd just read Alicia's mind. "I'll probably call at least a brief rest halt once we're on the far side of the river. In the meantime, go to Mode Three on your pharmacopes."

Alicia obediently accessed the software of her built-in pharmacopeia and raised its enabled mode from Four to Three. The pharmacope computer considered her new commands for a moment, and then she felt a wash of energy and enhanced alertness sweep through her as the pharmacope administered a carefully metered dose from its drug reservoirs.

"All right, Abe," the lieutenant continued, "you know where we need to go. I think we'll go ahead and pull First Squad and the APCs back now. I'll take Second Squad's Bravo Team with me. You and Clarissa put your heads together and decide how you need to reorient. Let me know when you're ready to proceed."

"Yes, Ma'am," Metternich replied. Then his voice changed slightly as he turned his attention to his fire teams.

"Okay," he said. "We'll stick to the same basic playbook. For the moment, everybody turns around where they are and falls back to the intersection. César, that means that you and Alley are going to become the back door until we get there. At that point, Alley, I want you to—"

Alicia continued to gaze eastward, with her own augmented vision as well as her assigned remote' sensors, while she listened to the sergeant's voice.

It was two hours past local planetary midnight when Second Platoon, Bravo Company, Recon Battalion, First of the 517th, recrossed the perimeter into Zhikotse Spaceport. With the exception of Gunnery Sergeant Wheaton, who was expected to make a full recovery, it had not suffered a single serious casualty.

Which was more than could be said for the city of Zhikotse, Alicia thought wearily, watching the flames still painting the skies above the planetary capital.

But at least the situation's coming back under control. Maybe it's just because it's burned itself out, but it's still happening. And the planetary government is still intact, and we haven't killed any more people than we had to.

She was still gazing out at the flames, listening to the APCs rumbling past behind her, when a hand smacked her on the shoulder. She turned her head and found herself looking into Leocadio Medrano's homely face.

"Not too shabby, Wasp," he said gruffly, then nodded and headed off, heavy plasma rifle over his shoulder, while the ex-larva gazed after him.

Book Two:
The Emperor's Sword

The darkness swirled slowly about her. She drifted once more towards awareness, her thought reaching out, questing beyond her dreams in search of function. Of purpose.

Memories danced through those dreams. Memories of fire and slaughter. Of vengeance visited, punishment wreaked. Of unyielding pursuit and merciless destruction. Those were what she was, those memories. Or what she had been.

Wait. It was there once more, that whisper of purpose, that echo of herself. And it was stronger now, no longer tentative. It was beginning to know itself, her drowsing mind thought, and marveled at the potential of its power, at the focus of its purpose.

There were shadows about it. Dark shadows, which had been only hints before. Its future was narrowing, as mortal futures must, as decisions were made, paths were chosen, and potentialities fell unused and unspent into the realm of might-have-been. The echo did not know that, yet she felt the future singing to her as it had not in millennia.

It could, this one, she thought drowsily. It could actually reach out to her, even here, if the need were stark enough, if the pain and the hate blazed bright enough, and how long had it been since she'd felt that possibility?

And yet, even in her dreams, a part of her wondered if she truly wanted to resume her purpose once more. It was who she was, what she'd been created to be—her highest function. But at length, even one such as she tired of death and destruction. Would it be better to return to that, to become once more Fate's executioner? Or would it be better never to wake again? To stay wrapped in her dreams, cocooned in the darkness, until she—like her countless victims—faded at last into restful nothingness?

CHAPTER THIRTEEN

"Yo, Alley!"

Staff Sergeant Alicia DeVries opened her eyes and "looked up" from the field manual she'd been reading through her synth-link as Sergeant Haroldson came noisily into their quarters' shared sitting room/office.

"I know you're not from Old Earth, Greta," Alicia said mildly, "but are you familiar with the Old Earth critter called an elephant?"

"Vaguely, yeah. Why?" Haroldson said suspiciously.

"Because your idea of how to walk into a room reminds me of an entire herd of them."

"Very funny. Ha-ha." Haroldson made a face, and Alicia grinned and stripped off her synth-link headset, then leaned back in her desk chair and stretched luxuriously.

"And what brings you back to our humble domicile so far ahead of schedule, O thundering herd?" she asked.

"As a matter of fact, the Captain sent me to get *you*. He wants you in his office soonest."

"Me?" Alicia's eyebrows rose, and Haroldson shrugged.

"He didn't say why, but I think some HQ weenie type wants to see you. That's what the guy smelled like to me, anyway, even if he wasn't in uniform. I think he's from Old Earth, too. He's got an accent sort of like yours."

"Curiouser and curiouser," Alicia murmured. She pushed up out of her chair and turned to the sitting room's view screen. She punched the button which configured it for mirror mode, then examined her image thoughtfully.

Haroldson watched with a hidden smile as her roommate inspected her own appearance even more critically than she would have inspected a member of her squad. Haroldson had known the younger sergeant for a little under four months, and she'd been impressed—almost against her will, initially at least. DeVries was not quite nineteen standard years old, which made her four years younger than Haroldson, and there weren't very many eighteen-year-old staff sergeants in the Imperial Marines. In fact, she was the only one Haroldson had ever met.

Of course, there weren't very many eighteen-year-olds with the Recon patch, the Master Sniper qualification badge, the Grav-Drop qualification badge, *and* the Silver Star, either. Not only that, Haroldson happened to know that DeVries was Raider-qualified, although she hadn't yet tested to collect the official badge for that one. And she also knew that DeVries had been getting none-too-subtle "suggestions" for the last couple of months that she should be considering officer candidate school.

She looked older than her years, too, Haroldson reflected, more like a twenty-something than someone who was still officially a teenager. It wasn't so much a physical thing, either, although she *was* tall and broad-shouldered (for a woman). And if she carried an extra gram of body fat anywhere, Haroldson hadn't seen it. She had a hard-trained, sinewy muscularity which was rare even among Marines, although she didn't *seem* to be a fanatic about maintaining it. Then again, she didn't seem to be fanatical about *anything* . . . yet she routinely demonstrated that she could do anything she asked a member of her squad to do, only better. It was that unspoken, total confidence in her own competence which made her so much older than her years. Especially since it was obvious to those about her that her confidence was completely justified.

Haroldson had concluded after the first month that DeVries was simply one of those people who made mere mortals aware of their mortality. It would be interesting to see just what final rank she obtained, and Haroldson was already looking forward to "Why, *I* knew General DeVries back when she was just a staff sergeant! And let me tell you . . ."

"You are planning on dropping by the Old Man's office sometime *this* afternoon, aren't you, Alley?" she said after moment, and the younger woman chuckled.

"Now, now. You're just upset with me over that elephant remark."

Alicia gave her appearance one last glance, switched off the view screen, and headed towards the door.

"Assuming they aren't sending me off someplace horrible, like shipping me all the way back to Sol just so they can assign me to Titan Base, I'll be back shortly," she said.

"Hey! If they do send you to Titan, can I have that box of chocolates in your locker?" Haroldson called after her.

"Enter!" a voice called, in response to Alicia's quick double-knock on the office door. She opened it, stepped through, and braced to attention rather more sharply than usual as she spotted the man in civilian dress Haroldson had warned her about. He did have that certain indefinable aura of a senior staff officer as he sat there, but there was something else about him, too. Something . . . different.

"Sir!" she said to Captain Ahearn.

"Stand easy, Sergeant," Ahearn replied, and Alicia's internal antennae twitched. The "let's-humor-the-staff-puke" gleam her parade ground manner should have put into the captain's eye was singularly missing.

She obeyed the command, dropping into a stand-easy position which could have served as a training manual illustration, and Ahearn indicated the stranger in his office with a wave of his right hand.

"Staff Sergeant DeVries," he said, "this is Colonel Gresham."

"Colonel," Alicia acknowledged when the captain paused.

"Sergeant." Gresham nodded to her, and her curiosity sharpened still further as she noticed his eyes. They were a curious silvery color, one she'd never seen before, and there was something else just a bit peculiar about them. She couldn't put a finger on exactly what that something else was, though. It was almost as if they were focusing on something behind her—or perhaps on something *through* her.

"The Colonel's come a long way, Sergeant. He's got something he wants to discuss with you," Ahearn said. He hesitated for just a moment, as if he were about to say something more, then shrugged, gave his head a little shake, and stood.

"Good day, Colonel," he said, with an almost curt nod. He looked at Alicia for a second, then gave her a nod (this one much less curt), as well. And then, to her astonishment, he walked out of his own office and closed the door quietly but firmly behind himself.

She watched him leave, then turned back to face Gresham, and her mind raced while she tried to think of any explanation for Ahearn's bizarre behavior. None came to mind, and so she simply stood there, hands clasped behind her, expression politely attentive, and waited.

Gresham studied her with those odd eyes of his for what seemed like a very long time, although she knew it wasn't. She had the distinct impression that he was waiting for her to show some indication of curiosity or uncertainty. Which, of course, she wasn't about to do.

Finally, the civilian-garbed colonel smiled, like a man conceding some contest, and climbed out of the chair in which he'd been sitting. He crossed to stand behind Ahearn's desk, but he didn't seat himself in the captain's chair. Instead, he simply stood there, half-turned away from Alicia to gaze out the window at the parade ground baking under the afternoon heat of the Jepperson System's G-0 primary.

"Tell me, Staff Sergeant," he said after a moment, "how do you like being a Marine?"

"Excuse me, Sir?"

Gresham smiled again at Alicia's courteously blank tone.

"Actually, that wasn't a trick question," he told her. "I'm serious. How do you like being a Marine, now that you've had a couple of years experience?"

"I like it," she said after moment. "I like it a lot."

"Why?"

"Sir, that's a pretty sweeping question," she said slowly.

"I know." He turned back from the window to face her fully and folded his arms across his chest as he leaned back against the office wall. "It's meant to be a tough one, too," he added.

Well, it's certainly succeeded, then, she thought tartly. *Just who* is *this yahoo, and why is he trying to screw with my head?*

"Sir," she said finally, "a Marine is what I've always wanted to be. Partly, I suppose, because of my grandfather's example. Partly because of the challenge. But mostly? Mostly because standing up to defend the things you believe in is what adults do."

"'The things you believe in,'" Gresham repeated softly. In the wrong tone of voice, he might have sounded as if he were mocking her, but instead, it came out musingly. Then he cocked his head. "And just what do you believe in?" he asked.

Another of those deliberately "tough" questions of his, I suppose, she snorted mentally.

"If you want the simple form," she told him, allowing just a hint of testiness into her own voice, "I believe in what the Empire stands for. I believe in the individual rights imperial citizens are guaranteed, in the prosperity and standard of living the Empire offers its citizens—the educational opportunities, the medical support, all of it. And I believe in my responsibility to defend the society that gives me and all of my fellow citizens those things." She shrugged. "I guess that sounds pretty simplistic, but that's the bottom line for me."

"And killing other people to do that doesn't bother you?" Gresham's voice was completely neutral, as was his expression, but Alicia bridled inside anyway.

"I don't love combat for the adrenaline rush of blowing somebody else away, if that's what you mean, Sir," she said just a bit more coldly than she'd actually intend to.

"That wasn't what I asked," he replied. "I asked if killing other people to do your duty bothered you." He waved his right hand gently in the air in front of him. "I think it's a fair question, given the number of confirmed kills you racked up on Gyangtse alone."

Alicia's curiosity sharpened at the evidence of just how much this Gresham knew about her. She supposed it shouldn't really have been a surprise. The numbers were part of her official record, and it was only logical for him to have done his homework before he descended from Mount Olympus to interrogate her. Whyever he was doing *that*.

"All right, Sir," she said, deciding to answer his "fair question" as honestly as possible, "yes. It bothers me. I don't like it very much, in fact. But it comes with doing the job I chose, doesn't it? And I knew going in that it would. I guess I'm enough my father's daughter—" she allowed a hint of challenge into her green eyes, pushing to see just how much of her family background he'd studied up on as well "—to wish that no one ever had to do that. But I'm enough my grandfather's granddaughter to recognize that since it does have to be done, it's better for the doers to be people who volunteer for it. Who are . . . good at it, I suppose."

"But who don't enjoy doing it?"

"Sir, with all due respect, I've never much cared to trust the judgment of someone who *likes* to kill other people." She shook her head. "I know they exist. I've even met some, here in the Corps. But there's a difference between recognizing that you're good at something and deciding that doing it when you don't have to is a good idea. It isn't. I saw both sides of that on Gyangtse, in my first tour. So, yes, I know there are people who subscribe to the 'kill them all; let God sort them out' philosophy. But I'm not one of them, and they aren't the ones I want making the decisions, or acting in the Empire's name."

"I can't argue with that." The colonel's brief smile showed what looked like a flash of amusement mixed with what sounded like genuine agreement. Then he looked back out the window again, facing away from her.

"So killing people does bother you, but you're still willing to do the job. I believe you said that part of it was the challenge. From your record, you look like someone who enjoys doing hard things simply because they're hard." He swung back around towards her, silvery eyes narrowed. "Would you agree with that assessment?"

"Simply because they're hard?" Alicia shook her head. "Colonel, I'm not a masochist. I enjoy *challenges*, enjoy . . . stretching myself, I suppose. In fact," she looked him in the eye, "I guess if I'm going to be completely honest, the reason I put in for Recon straight out of Mackenzie was because I wanted to prove I could tackle the hardest job out there. And, no, it wasn't to impress anyone else. It was because I wanted to prove it to *me*."

"I see."

Gresham pursed his lips, studying her thoughtfully for several seconds. She felt uncomfortable under those odd, featureless silver eyes. Eyes, she abruptly realized, which were cybernetic replacements for his original organic eyes. But she returned his regard levelly, respectfully but with more than a slight edge of challenge.

"There's a reason for my questions, Staff Sergeant DeVries," he said finally. "I'm sure you're aware that your performance as a Wasp has been well above the norm. You may not be aware of just how *far* above the norm it's been, but your current rank at your age is pretty clear evidence of how the Corps sees you. And, while I'm aware that you don't know this yet, the Corps has already designated you for a Raider tour, to be followed by OCS."

Alicia's eyes widened slightly. She'd picked up the Raider qualification on her own time, although she hadn't yet *officially* tested for it, and she'd hoped for a Raider tour sometime soon. There weren't that many Marines—and practically none of them were as young as she was—who had both Recon and Raider in their résumés. But despite that, and despite the increasingly unsubtle hints from her superiors that she ought to be considering officer's rank, she hadn't considered the possibility that the Corps was keeping as close an eye on her professional development as Gresham seemed to be suggesting.

"The reason I'm telling you this," the colonel continued, "is that I don't want you to take it."

"Sir?" This time she failed to keep the surprise out of her voice, and he smiled.

"I have a somewhat different offer for you to consider, Staff Sergeant DeVries," he said calmly. "One that doesn't come the way of very many people."

Alicia eyed him warily, and he chuckled softly.

"No, it's not quite *that* bad," he told her. "You see, I came directly out here from Old Earth specifically to see *you*, and I'm here on behalf of my own immediate superior, Brigadier Sir Arthur Keita."

He watched her closely, and she frowned. The name rang a distant sort of bell, but she couldn't quite remember exactly why. Gresham waited a moment, then snorted softly.

"Sir Arthur," he said, "is the second in command of the Imperial Cadre, Staff Sergeant." Alicia's eyes popped wide, and he nodded. "That's right," he said. "Sir Arthur believes you're Cadre material, Staff Sergeant DeVries. So if you can stand to tear yourself away from the Marines, the Emperor needs your services."

* * *

Alicia DeVries sat in the NCO club, nursing a stein of beer, and stared blankly at the HD above the bar. A bunch of burly men in brightly colored jerseys were doing something complicated with a ball in a spherical microgravity court. She wasn't certain exactly what they were doing, or even what the game was called—it was a purely local variant practiced here in Jepperson—but that was fine. She wasn't paying any attention, anyway.

Colonel Gresham had finally managed to get her attention, she thought wryly.

The offer he'd extended ran through her brain again and again. As he'd said, it wasn't one that came the way of many people. She knew about the Cadre, of course. Everyone did, especially in the military, because the Cadre was, quite simply, the best. It was the standard to which every special forces unit in the imperial armed forces aspired . . . and which none of the others ever attained.

The few, the proud, the Cadre, she thought, and somehow the well-worn phrase didn't seem quite as clichéd now.

The Cadre wasn't part of the regular armed forces, at all. Although they still came under the overall control of the Ministry of War, the Cadre answered directly to the Emperor, in his own person. They were sometimes called "the Emperor's Own," because they served the Emperor as their own direct liege lord, but they were closely regulated and watchdogged, under the Constitution, by a special Senate oversight committee. And they were hedged about with other restrictions, as well, including the biggest one of all—numbers. The Cadre was the only imperial military organization whose total roster strength was forever restricted by constitutional amendment to a maximum of forty thousand. That was it. The total legally permissible active-duty strength of the Cadre . . . for an empire with almost two thousand inhabited worlds.

She'd told Gresham that she enjoyed "stretching herself." Well, here was the ultimate opportunity for *that*! Of course, there were a few little points about joining the Cadre which bore thinking on. For one thing, the least *outre* rumors she'd heard about the sort of augmentation Cadremen underwent were bizarre, to say the least. Then there was the fact that membership in the Cadre was for life. You didn't retire from the Cadre; you simply went onto inactive reserve status, and the Cadre could call you back anytime it chose. And the Cadre's casualty rate, despite its superlative training and matchless equipment, was substantially higher than that of any other branch of service. Not surprisingly, since the Cadre got only the hardest jobs.

But if you were up for the challenge, it offered you the chance to prove that you were *the* best. And what she'd said to Gresham about an adult's responsibility to defend a society in which she believed came back to her now, because that was what the Cadre was. The Emperor's sword, wielded in the pure service of the Empire he ruled.

Gresham had insisted that she go away and think about it before she gave him her answer, and she was glad he had. This wasn't a decision to rush into, and the colonel's awareness of that—his refusal to pressure her, or rush her—only emphasized its importance. But as she sat there, with her chilled beer gradually warming to something Greta Haroldson would have preferred, she knew it didn't really matter how much time he wanted her to take.

"Gresham," the voice on the other end of the com said.

"Colonel, it's Staff Sergeant DeVries. I've thought about it."

"And?" Gresham said after a few seconds of silence.

"Show me where to sign," she said simply.

"Meet me in Admin Three, Room 1017, tomorrow morning. Zero-nine-hundred hours."

"Yes, Sir."

"Good. Oh, and DeVries?"

"Yes, Sir?"

"Welcome aboard."

CHAPTER FOURTEEN

The wind howl was barely audible as Alicia stepped out of the elevator. It was still there, though. Not so much heard, as sensed. And although the air inside Camp Cochrane's main administration building was kept at a toasty twenty-three degrees, and despite the fact that her uniform's smart fabric would have maintained a comfortable body temperature even if it hadn't been, she shivered. She'd grown too accustomed to the bone-deep warmth of Jepperson's summer for the abrupt transition to the middle of winter in Old Earth's Argentina Province's high Andes Mountains.

She walked briskly down the well-lit hallway, following the map of the building which Admin had uploaded to her through her neural receptor. The map showed only a very limited portion of the administration building, of course. She didn't need all of it, and she wasn't a bit surprised by the fact that the Cadre insisted on a strict interpretation of the need-to-know rule, especially here. Camp Cochrane was to the Imperial Cadre what Camp Mackenzie was to the Imperial Marines.

It was also very large.

Alicia had arrived in the middle of the night, and also in the middle of a snowstorm. Or, at least, she'd thought it was a storm until a *real* storm blew in the following morning. The darkness and flying snow had kept her from forming more than a very vague impression of Cochrane on her arrival, but she'd seen enough to be a bit disappointed. Somehow, she'd assumed that the central headquarters facility of the famed Cadre would consist of more than a handful of nondescript weather domes, none of them more than three or four stories tall.

Her initial disappointment had become something quite different when the air car transporting her from Valparaiso Spaceport to her new temporary home had passed through a portal in one of those "nondescript weather domes" and she'd discovered just how large they actually were. They might not go up very far, but they went *down* a long way, indeed. Her own temporary quarters were fourteen stories below ground level, and she'd been astounded by the number of people who seemed to spend most of their time termite-swarming around the interiors of Cochrane's vast, buried structures.

She still didn't understand where they'd all come from, not given the Cadre's constitutionally mandated numerical limitations. Either there was something seriously wrong with her math, or else the Cadre had a simply enormous logistical tail and very, very few shooters, which seemed a contradiction of everything she'd ever heard about its operations.

At least seventy-five percent of the people she'd seen so far were in civilian clothing, like Colonel Gresham, too. After spending the last two-plus standard years of her life surrounded by uniforms, Alicia found that a little disconcerting. But she was once again the newest kid on the block, and she'd made up her mind to possess her soul in patience until someone got around to explaining things to her.

Which, she thought as she turned a final corner and saw the numbered door of the office which was her destination, *is about to begin now, hopefully.*

She slowed as she approached the door, but before she could knock, it slid silently open in front of her. She quirked an eyebrow and stepped through the opening.

There was an anteroom on the other side, with pleasant pastel-colored walls and a viewscreen set to window mode. The view of almost horizontal, wind-driven snow was scarcely homey, but the illusion that she was looking out an actual window was almost perfect. There were several comfortable chairs, but no sign of any other living human.

"Please be seated, Staff Sergeant DeVries," a voice said. It was obviously a computer's voice, and Alicia wondered whether it was a full cyber-synth AI. "Major Androniko will be with you shortly."

"Thank you," Alicia replied. She managed to keep her tone conversational, although the truth was that cyber-synths made her more than a little nervous. She didn't have the sort of phobia where they were concerned which the neo-Luddites treasured, and her own ability to sustain a synth-link made her quite comfortable about claiming a computer *without* an AI as an extension of her own merely human capabilities. But she also knew that a cyber-synth personality was exactly what it was called: an *artificial* intelligence. And one that wasn't all that tightly wrapped, by human standards.

She'd met several aliens in her life—more than most people her age, probably, given her father's position in the Foreign Ministry—and none of them had ever bothered her the way AIs did. She didn't know why. Perhaps it was just that the intelligence behind those alien eyes had at least evolved the same way hers had, rather than being whipped up to order from scratch in a cybernetics lab somewhere. Or perhaps it was the . . . eccentricities and well-known instability the cybernetics types still hadn't been able to remove from the cyber-synth equation.

She pushed that thought aside, selected a chair, and leaned back comfortably, watching the blizzard.

The delay, as promised, was brief.

"Major Androniko will see you now, Staff Sergeant," the same computer voice said, and another door opened, this one in the inner wall of the anteroom.

"Thank you," Alicia said once more, and stepped through the door.

The office on the other side was large and efficiently laid out. At first glance, it seemed like an awful lot of space for the single, tallish, dark-haired woman sitting behind the outsized desk which faced the door. But a second glance made it clear that the office's occupant actually had very little available free space. Alicia had seldom seen so many chip files in one place. The hard data storage stacks in the Emperor's New College main library had been bigger and more extensive, but she couldn't remember any place else of which that had been true. And arranged among the chip file cabinets and the standard data terminals were even bigger, clunkier storage cabinets—the sort that actual hardcopy *documents* might be tucked away inside of.

Unlike many of the people Alicia had seen here at Camp Cochrane, Major Androniko was in uniform. Not in the black tunic and green trousers of Alicia's Marine uniform, but in the green-on-green of the Imperial Cadre, with the starship and harp insignia of the House of Murphy on her collar.

"Staff Sergeant DeVries, reporting as instructed, Ma'am," Alicia said, coming to attention, and Androniko cocked her head to one side as if to see her better.

"Stand easy, Sergeant," the major said after a moment. "In fact," she pointed at one of the two chairs in front of her desk, "why don't you go ahead and sit down? This is in the nature of an entry interview, and it's probably going to take a while, so I believe we can probably afford to dispense with military formality for the moment."

"Thank you, Ma'am," Alicia said, although to be honest, she wasn't positive she wanted to abandon the comforting familiarity of proper military conduct. Androniko smiled faintly, as though she knew exactly what Alicia was thinking, and waited while her visitor settled herself into one of the chairs and its powered surface adjusted to the contours of her body.

"Now then, Sergeant," Androniko said then, "I'm sure you have a lot of questions. People always do at this point. So why don't I give you the quick ten-credit virtual tour, and then we can address any questions that remain unanswered?"

She arched one eyebrow, and Alicia nodded.

"Very well." Androniko tipped back in her own chair, propping her elbows on the armrests and steepling her fingers in front of her.

"First, as it says right here—" she unsteepled her hands long enough to point at the nameplate on her desk "—I'm Major Aleka Androniko. For my sins, I am also Brigadier Karpov's executive officer, which makes me Camp Cochrane's second-in-command."

Alicia managed not to gawk at her, but it wasn't easy. The thought that a facility as important as Camp Cochrane could have someone as junior as a mere brigadier commanding it seemed bizarre. For that matter, the number of people she'd already encountered, assuming her experience so far represented anything like an average density for the entire base, seemed awfully high for any brigadier's command she'd ever heard of. And a major wasn't usually a brigadier's XO, either.

Or, she admonished herself, *not in the* Corps, *anyway.*

"No doubt," Androniko continued, "you've noticed what appear to be rather a large number of Cadremen and Cadrewomen about the place, given the statutory limitation on our total manpower. Actually, those people represent a certain amount of Senate-approved cribbing on our part. Most of them—all of the ones in civilian dress—are technically civilian contractors, not Cadremen. In fact, virtually all of our senior 'civilian contractors' are, like Colonel Gresham, retired Cadremen and Cadrewomen. Many of them were invalided into early retirement, but their own time in the Cadre gives them invaluable experience and skills which we badly need. The Senate has decided we can put them on retainer as civilians to provide the trained manpower we need, especially here at Cochrane and our other central command and control nodes.

"Despite that . . . accommodation on the Senate's part, however," the major continued, "the sad truth is that the Cadre is always short of personnel. We have a far lower ratio of tail to teeth then any of the other services, including the Marines. In fact, we don't have all of the logistical capability we actually need to support our shooters out of our own resources, which is why we call on the Marines and the Fleet for support for many of our operations.

"The reason we're always shorthanded has less to do with any sort of constitutionally mandated limitations than it does with the fact that the supply of suitable manpower is, frankly, severely limited. Finding and recruiting Cadre-quality men and women is a constant challenge, Staff Sergeant. The popular view that the Cadre consists of supermen and women isn't just a matter of the 'Cadre mystique,' I'm afraid. We're not really superhuman, of course, but drop commandos—and over eighty percent of our personnel are drop commandos—require certain very specific physical and mental qualities. Some of those are similar to those required by Marine Raiders and Recon, which is one reason we tend to use those duty assignments as a filtering system. Others are qualities which no standard Marine specialization requires. And others, quite frankly, have more to do with motivation, attitude, and loyalty which go far beyond any purely physical capabilities."

Androniko paused, as if to permit Alicia to digest what she'd already said. After a moment, she resumed.

"I'm not going to go into a great deal of detail about those 'specific physical and mental qualities' just now, Sergeant. To be totally honest, until we've completed your medical and you've been processed through the standard testing regimen, we can't be absolutely positive you possess them in the combination the Cadre requires. Our screening process has been steadily improved over the years, but there's simply no way to make it perfect, and we still lose about eight percent of all of our prospects at this stage. I don't expect that to happen in your case, however, because our prerecruitment dossier on you was exceptionally thorough."

"It was, Ma'am?" Surprise startled the question out of Alicia, and Androniko smiled slightly.

"I think you might say that, yes," she said. "You first came to our attention when you were only fourteen. The standard battery of tests given to all students in their final form of high school often picks up potential Cadre recruits, and yours were . . . fairly outstanding, I think I might say. And you have an interesting personal pedigree, even for a Cadre recruit."

Alicia frowned, and Androniko smiled again.

"Oh, but you do! Take your mother's family—New Dubliners for over three hundred years. Loyalty to the House of Murphy's practically a planetary fetish for New Dublin, and then there's your grandfather—the most highly decorated Marine on active duty, I believe. Or your Uncle John, one of the youngest Fleet commodores in imperial history when he was killed. And your mother, Chief of Thoracic Surgery at Johns Hopkins/Bethesda of Charlotte, and very highly thought of in her field.

"And that's only the O'Shaughnessy side. Your father is just as 'interesting,' isn't he? A farm boy from Silverado, and an Ujvári, to boot, with three doctoral degrees, and G-20 rank over at the Foreign Ministry. One of the top three or four people in the Ministry's permanent policy formulation staff."

Alicia suppressed another, deeper frown, surprised even now by Androniko's familiarity with her family history, and the major shrugged.

"We do a *thorough* background when we get test results like yours, Sergeant. It only makes sense to eliminate as many potentials as we can as early as we can, so we can concentrate on the ones who're going to make good prospects. And we tend to take the long view when the indications are good. We have to, because of how stringent our standards are and the limitations on how we can recruit.

"We're legally prohibited from actively recruiting anyone, regardless of test results, before they're at least eighteen standard years old, and the Cadre's policy is that we won't accept anyone who hasn't completed at least one combat tour in either the Marines or Fleet. We've made a few exceptions to that policy, primarily when we've seen someone with qualities we need in Cadre staff officers, given how we're always starved on the support side, but the age requirement is set by law and can't be set aside. However, when someone's test results are sufficient to pop through our filters, we generally flag that individual for future consideration. When, as in your case, they eventually join the military, we keep an eye on them and occasionally intervene to . . . customize their career tracks."

Alicia blinked. Was that why she'd received the Recon assignment she requested out of Camp Mackenzie? Sergeant Major Hill had warned her she probably wouldn't get it—were her *high school* test results the reason he'd been wrong?

"One thing you have to understand, Sergeant DeVries," Androniko said, "is that all of your life, like every man or woman who ever joins the Cadre, you've been one of the 'one-percenters.' You've always been in that rarefied top one percent of the people doing whatever you were doing at any given moment in your life. But here in the Cadre, that level of capability and performance is the *norm*. You may or may not continue to stand out from those around you, but if you do, you'll find that doing so just got much more difficult. The Cadre comes as close as any organization in the history of mankind to being a true elite. The scores we require for our enlisted personnel are higher, by a very considerable margin, than those required for admission to the Fleet Academy on New Annapolis or the Marine Academy on New Dublin. There isn't a single Cadreman or Cadrewoman who doesn't have the inherent capability and talent to be a Fleet admiral or Commandant of the Corps. Indeed, one of the regular service branches' most persistent—and, in many ways, best taken—complaints about the Cadre is the way in which we skim off their own potential officers for our own use.

"I'm telling you this not to give you an inflated opinion of your own capabilities—one of the mental qualities we require is a certain resistance to delusions of grandeur—but to warn you. If you pass the medicals, you will find yourself working, quite possibly for the first time in your life, with people who are every bit as capable, self-motivated, and accustomed to succeeding as you are yourself."

She paused again, then chuckled.

"One reason why I tend to emphasize that point during these little interviews is that it was one I had trouble with, myself. I regarded myself as an extraordinarily capable human being before the Cadre put the arm on me, and I suppose I was. But it was a well-deserved humbling experience to discover that in *this* group, my level of capability was taken for granted, not marveled at.

"And now, let's move on to some of the nuts and bolts. First, among the physical qualities I mentioned before are synth-link capability and the ability to multitask at a very high-level, even under conditions of maximum stress. In addition to that—"

CHAPTER FIFTEEN

"Any time you're ready," Dr. Hyde said.

The civilian (these days) physician sat comfortably tipped back in the chair behind his desk, wearing his synth-link headset as he watched Alicia. With his eyes, that was; the diagnostic hardware tied into his synth-link, she knew, was busy doing the same thing, in considerably more detail, from the inside out.

Frankly, Alicia was getting just a little bit tired of the whole hospital bit.

She'd faced the battery of tests Major Androniko had warned her of and completed them with flying colors just in time to become an official Cadre recruit for her nineteenth birthday present. She got the impression that that was unusually young for admission to the Cadre—not too surprisingly, she supposed, given that the Cadre routinely required completion of a combat tour before it even considered a potential candidate. Any feelings of superiority that early selection might have engendered, however, had been quite handily quashed over the course of the next four months.

She'd spent all four of those months basically where she was right now—in the hands of the Cadre's medical staff. Dr. Hyde, who'd reached the rank of major during his own active-duty Cadre days (and carried the civil-service equivalent of a full colonel's rank as a civilian contractor these days), was reassuringly brisk, professional, and competent, but he was totally untainted by any trace of a tendency to coddle his patients. Which, Alicia admitted to herself, was the way she preferred things, actually. It was just that she hadn't realized how much surgery was going to be involved.

Thanks to the quick-heal therapies, she'd recovered quickly from the physical effects of the profound changes which had been made to her original Marine augmentation package. In fact, her recovery time from each round of surgery had been considerably better than it had been at Camp Mackenzie. The problem was that there'd been a lot *more* surgery this time . . . and she'd had more trouble adjusting to some of the changes.

When Major Androniko had warned her that the ability to multitask was an important Cadre qualification, she hadn't been joking. Alicia had never had the sort of difficulty some of her fellow Marine recruits had experienced in adjusting to her neural receptors, but at that point, she'd only had one synth-link to worry about at a time. Now she had *three*, and her instructors insisted that she learn to use all three of them simultaneously. She'd done it, but also as Androniko had warned her, she was no longer leaving fellow recruits in her dust. She'd finally been tapped for something that was genuinely *hard* for her, and the people around her were disinclined to show much sympathy, since they'd had to do exactly the same things. It wasn't that anyone had given her a hard time about it, but she simply wasn't accustomed to laboring this hard to accomplish her goals.

That was the bad news. The good news was that—just as she had at Mackenzie, when she'd been unable to match the PT scores of the people who had turfed her out of the lead in that category—she'd found herself responding to the challenge by embracing it. It hadn't been as much fun as some of the Mackenzie challenges, but it had been even more deeply satisfying.

The basic augmentation for sight and sound had also been replaced with even better enhancement. Indeed, the augmentation she had now was powerful enough to be illegal on the civilian market, and they'd added tactile enhancement, as well. That was an expensive refinement the Marines had passed on because of cost-effectiveness considerations.

The implantation of the neural web which the doctors assured her would actually provide significant protection against neural disrupter fire had been more straightforward, although the recovery time from the necessary surgery had actually been greater than that involved in the additional synth-links. And the new processors installed in her basic augmentation had presented problems of their own. There'd been a glitch in the hardware the first time around, and the escape and evasion package built into them had activated when the techs initiated the test protocols. Finding her own body moving under the control of a computer package expressly designed to kill anything between her and escape in the event that her conscious mind was taken out of the circuit had been . . . unpleasant. And if the techs involved in the testing program hadn't been prepared for hardware hiccups along the way, it could have been considerably worse than that . . . for them.

That little misadventure had required a return to surgery to replace the malfunctioning unit. Everyone had assured her that things like that practically *never* happened and that everything would be just peachy the second time around. By that point, she'd cherished some dark suspicions about their breezy assurances, but aside from the time required to heal, this time they'd actually been right.

There'd been some other changes, of course, the biggest of which was undoubtedly her new pharmacope. Her perfectly good Marine-issue personal pharmacopeia had been surgically removed and replaced with a new, larger implant whose reservoirs contained everything the original had, plus a few additions all the Cadre's own.

One or two of those additions had given her more than a few qualms when they were explained to her, and imperial law had required that at least one of them *had* to be explained—in some detail—before she could be allowed to officially join the Cadre. That was the bit about the suicide protocols built into her shiny new augmentation.

Alicia hadn't liked that thought one little bit. In fact, she'd actually seriously considered declining the Cadre's invitation when she heard about it. The idea that her own pharmacope contained a neurotoxin which would automatically kill her, even under the most carefully defined and limited of circumstances, had not been reassuring. But, in the end, it hadn't stopped her, either. Mostly because she'd considered what was likely to happen to any Cadre drop commando who found herself in the hands of the Empire's enemies. The chance of long-term survival in those circumstances was small, at best, and she understood exactly why the Empire needed to make certain that someone who knew everything any member of the Cadre would have to know could never be wrung dry by someone like the Rish. Then too, she was forced to admit in her more honest moments, part of the reason she'd accepted it was probably that somewhere deep down inside, despite all she'd seen and experienced since joining the Corps, there was a part of her which believed she was so good, so smart and competent, that however much the possibility of being captured might bother other people, it wasn't something which would ever arise in *her* case.

And to be totally honest, she'd decided, it was actually reassuring, in a bleak sort of way, to know that she would always possess the means for a final escape, no matter what else happened.

Yet in some respects, the *other* totally classified addition to her pharmacope was almost more disturbing than the suicide package. Not because of the threat it represented, but because of the temptation it offered. When they'd first explained the effects of the drug the Cadre called "the tick," she hadn't fully grasped everything that explanation implied. In fact, she doubted that she *fully* appreciated all of the tick's ramifications even now, but she could certainly understand why the drug—it was actually half a dozen different drugs, all working together in minute, individually designed dosages for each drop commando's specific physiology—was on the Official Secrets List.

Now she looked back at Dr. Hyde, smiling slightly at his expression of exaggerated patience, and cautiously initiated the proper pharmacope command sequence.

Nothing at all seemed to happen for a moment. And then, so quickly and smoothly the transition appeared almost instantaneous, the universe about her abruptly slowed down.

Alicia sat very still in the chair in front of Hyde's desk, watching him, and her augmented vision zoomed in on his carotid artery. She watched it pulsing ever so slightly to the beat of his heart, and she counted his pulse rate. She had plenty of time for counting, because that was what "the tick" did. It bought the person using it the most precious combat commodity there was—time.

The tick enhanced Alicia's physical reaction speed only slightly. She moved a bit faster, a little more quickly, but it didn't magically allow her to move at superhuman rates, or let her snatch speeding bullets out of the air with her bare hand. What it *did* do was to accelerate her mental processes enormously. She might not have superhuman reaction speed, but she had all the time in the world to *think* about possibilities and threats, about actions and reactions, before she actually took them.

She turned her head—slowly, so slowly it seemed—looking around Dr. Hyde's office through the crystal-clear armorplast of the tick's syrupy time stream. It seemed to her as if it took at least a full minute to turn her head all the way to the right, but she knew better. She'd seen holovids of people riding the tick. Indeed, she'd seen holovids of *herself* moving under its influence. She'd seen the way that heads turned and limbs moved in a fashion which defied easy description but which could never be mistaken for anything else by anyone who had ever seen it.

Dr. Maxwell Hyde certainly recognized it, and he didn't need his diagnostics, either. He saw the absolutely smooth, almost mechanical, way her head turned. It *swivelled*, with the micrometrically metered precision of a computer-controlled gun turret, snapping to the exact angle she'd chosen in a movement which amalgamated viperish speed and something very like . . . serenity.

Over the years, Hyde had tried repeatedly to find the right way to describe the tick to himself or to his colleagues. He'd never been truly satisfied with his efforts, but the best analogy he'd been able to come up with was actually the first one which had ever suggested itself to him. It was like watching a slow-motion holovid of a striking rattlesnake or cobra in real-time, contradictory though that sounded.

Now he closed his eyes, concentrating on his diagnostics. DeVries was doing well, he thought. Mastering the complexities of the Cadre augmentation package was the real make-or-break point for any potential drop commando. All the motivation, determination, and basic abilities in the universe couldn't make anyone a drop commando if they couldn't handle the sensory augmentation, the multiple synth-links, *and* the tick. The rest of the training, the other aspects of the augmentation package itself, were all frosting on the cake, in Maxwell Hyde's opinion, and he was pleased by

DeVries' tolerance for the tick. There was no sign of any of the toxicity reactions they very occasionally encountered. And, perhaps even more importantly, there were no indications of any tendency towards dependency on her part.

"Let's take it through an alpha sequence," he said now, never opening his eyes as he "watched" her.

"All right," Alicia agreed, deliberately slowing her enunciation to something approximating the doctor's slow, dragging speech, and stood.

She was more cautious about it than she'd been the first time. Despite all the warnings, all the effort Dr. Hyde and his staff had put into explaining to her what was going to happen, she hadn't really been prepared for the actuality of the tick that first day. She'd been sitting down that day, too, and she'd stood up at their request, exactly the same way she'd done it all her life. Except that this time, what should have brought her smoothly and naturally to her feet had turned into an explosive leap. One which had carried her forward, actually overbalanced her. She'd almost fallen—had, in fact, started to topple forward—and she'd flailed her arms for balance.

To her tick-enhanced time sense, her arms had seemed to move with almost grotesque, floating slowness. They'd trailed behind her mental commands, lagged on their way to their intended destinations. And despite that, they'd shot past where she'd meant to stop them, traveling with a speed and quickness she'd never before managed.

She'd learned to adjust, eventually, and now, as Dr. Hyde had requested, she moved away from her chair and fell into a "rest" position in the center of his spacious office. She stood that way for a moment, hands at her sides, and then fell into a guard position.

Alicia had grown to love *espada del mano*, the Corps' chosen hand-to-hand combat technique. *Espada del mano* had been developed about two hundred years before in the Granada System, and it was a primarily "hard" style which emphasized weaponless techniques and a go-for-broke aggressiveness. It did include some weaponed techniques, especially with edged steel (and its higher-tech equivalents), and it wasn't something a modern Marine actually required all that often. But the need still arose occasionally, and the Corps was right about the way in which it combined physical conditioning, mental discipline, and the "warrior mentality."

Besides, the sheer exuberance of a one-on-one, full-contact training bout was hard to beat.

The Cadre, unlike the Marines, preferred *deillseag òrd,* also known as "the slap hammer." Despite its name, *deillseag òrd* was actually a "softer" style than *espada del mano.* Or probably it would be more accurate to say that it was a more . . . balanced, comprehensive style. *Deillseag òrd* had been developed in the New Dublin System, and it was a synthesis of at least two or three dozen other martial arts. It included a much broader spectrum of weaponed techniques than the *espada* did, and it also included quite a lot more "soft style" elements.

Alicia had only begun to explore *deillseag òrd,* and the time she'd been stuck in the hospital hadn't left her much opportunity for training in it. She suspected that she was going to prefer it, once she'd had the opportunity to begin mastering it, but for now, it was better to stick to what she knew, and she began an *espada* training *ejercicio,* bringing herself totally to bear on the focus it required.

Hyde opened his eyes again. He continued "watching" her through his synth-link, but this was something he never tired of seeing with his own eyes. Something he'd always deeply treasured about his own period of active duty with the Cadre.

Alicia DeVries was the personification of the old cliché "poetry in motion," he thought. She moved with blinding speed, yet at the same time every motion seemed floating, almost slow. It was the perfection of each individual move, he told himself. The fact that there was literally *no* hesitation, *no* uncertainty. DeVries' total familiarity with the *ejercicio* was obvious, but there was more to what she was doing than practice. More even than the drilled-in muscle memory of the true martial artist. Every move she made, every shift of balance, was deliberate and conscious. Even as her hands flickered and flashed, she was *thinking through* each movement. Every single one of them was textbook perfect because, thanks to the tick, she had time to make them that way.

He remembered doing that himself. He suspected, if he was going to be honest, that he'd never been as good, even with the tick, as she was. The tick enhanced its users' natural aptitudes and talents. It didn't magically bestow the same plateau of ability—of speed, reflexes, balance—on all of them, and her starting point was simply better than his had been. And she was adjusting to the tick's vagaries faster than he had, too, he decided.

Well, fair's fair. She may be settling down to Old Speedy faster than I did, but I bounced back from the surgery a lot faster than she did.

He let her continue for another two or three minutes, which he knew seemed far longer than that to her, then nodded.

"All right, Alley. I think we've got all the data we need."

"Sure," she said with the odd tone everyone who spent any time working with drop commandos came to recognize. It was obvious that she thought she was speaking very slowly, enunciating her words carefully. For those stuck in a non-tick time stream, though, those words still came out quick, clipped—completely clear and unslurred, yet so fast that it sounded as if they *ought* to be garbled.

She floated back across the floor on those tick-inspired dancer's feet and settled gracefully, gracefully back into her chair with a smile.

"Yes," he said after a moment, completing his study of the diagnostics' recordings. "I think we're done for today. The preliminary data looks good. Unless we turn something up after the complete analysis, I think we can consider this aspect of your augmentation successfully completed and send you off to ACTS."

"I'm glad to hear it," she said in that tick-user's voice.

"And now, I'm afraid," he said with a sympathetic smile, "it's time for you to come down."

Alicia grimaced. This was the one part of the tick that she absolutely hated. Letting go of that sense of enhanced capability, that time-slowing near-godhood, was bad enough, but the tick's side effect made it even worse.

She sent the command to her pharmacope, reached for the basin sitting in the chair beside her, and sat back, waiting resignedly. The carefully measured dosage of the counteragent trickled into her bloodstream, and her senses and perceptions seemed to decelerate. It didn't happen as quickly as they had initially accelerated, but it still took only seconds. Seconds in which the rest of the universe seemed to speed up enormously even as her own movements and thoughts slowed to a crawl. The transition back into a world in which things moved—and she thought—at their accustomed rate left her with the feeling of suddenly diminished horizons and capabilities.

But she didn't have much time to reflect on that before the tearing spasms of nausea began.

It was just as violent this time as the first time. Dr. Hyde assured her, and she believed him, that there were no long-term deleterious effects to the use of tick. The only real danger that tick posed was dependency—addiction, really—and one of the mental qualities Major Androniko had been referring to in her interview with Alicia was a high resistance to addictive behaviors. But if there were no *lasting* side effects, the immediate short-term effect was enough to leave someone feeling as if her stomach had been turned inside out. Personally, Alicia wondered if the nausea had been deliberately enhanced as a means to make overindulgence in the tick even less attractive.

If it had been, no one was admitting it, she thought as she finished vomiting into the basin. *Of course*, she thought, wiping her mouth with thc tissue Dr. Hyde courteously extended to her, *if they have deliberately juiced up the nausea, they wouldn't be about to admit it, now would they?*

"Done?" Hyde asked.

"Yes, Sir." She closed the cover on the basin before the odor could encourage her stomach to spasm again, then set it back down on the chair beside her with a shudder.

"That's . . . really unpleasant," she said after a moment.

"I see you're a woman of commendable understatement," Dr. Hyde replied with a smile. "Although, and you may not believe this, you actually have a much less severe reaction to it than quite a few of our people do."

"You're joking." She looked at him suspiciously, and he shook his head.

"Nope. You appear to have an unusual tolerance. I'm wondering if it has anything to do with the fact that your father is an Ujvári." Alicia looked at him in surprise, and he shrugged. "We've been looking at tolerance factors where the tick is concerned for quite a long time," he said, "and there do seem to be certain specific genetic 'packages' which handle it better than others. For obvious reasons, we haven't had very many Ujváris in the Cadre—in fact, I don't think we've *ever* had a full Ujvári—so we don't have anything like reliable base data on response curves. I'm not really a geneticist, either, but from what I've been able to pick up about the Ujvári mutation, that extreme stability apparently results at least in part from changes in the brain and blood chemistry of people who have it. And while you're scarcely a 'typical' Ujvári—probably because of your mother's side of your genotype—you do express some of the chemical differentiation of the full-scale mutation. It's fascinating, really, if you don't mind my saying so."

"I don't mind," Alicia said, wondering even as she did whether or not she was being completely honest with either of them.

"Actually," Hyde continued, leaning back in his chair once more, "*you're* fairly fascinating in a lot of ways. By the nature of things, the Cadre attracts people who are way outside the norms, and every one of us is different. That's one reason we don't use the same sort of training techniques the Marines use—or, rather, why we go *beyond* those techniques. I suppose it would be more accurate to say that we specifically design and tailor each individual Cadreman's training techniques to him. Because of our differences, that's the only way we can maximize the performance of every single member of the Cadre. I've seen other Cadremen who could match or even exceed your physical dexterity, your stamina, your hand-eye coordination, your IQ. I don't know that I've seen very many of them who could match *all* of those qualities, but none of them are completely off the scale. Not for the Cadre, at least.

"But I've never seen anyone who matches your . . . for want of a better term, your levelheadedness. There's a basic stability at the core of your personality—probably a combination of your genetic inheritance and the way you were raised—that's really quite remarkable. It doesn't appear to get in the way of any of your other qualities, but it underpins all of them."

He paused, as if considering what he'd said, then shrugged.

"It's going to be interesting to see exactly how you slot into the Cadre's matrix. None of us fit in in exactly the same way, and I'm inclined to think that that's going to be especially true in your case."

CHAPTER SIXTEEN

"So, what do you think of your new brother?" Fiona DeVries asked with a smile.

"He's gorgeous." Alicia tried not to sound too dubious, and her mother laughed. "Uh, does he sleep *all* the time?" Alicia asked after a moment.

"I *wish*," her sister Clarissa said, rolling her eyes.

"Hey, it wasn't that long ago *you* were doing all the crying," Alicia said, pulling her sister's long braid teasingly. "I personally remember what a pain you were for the first couple of years, Shortstuff!"

"Oh, yeah?" Clarissa's gray eyes, as much like their father's as Alicia's were like their mother's, glinted up at her. There was laughter in them, and also just a touch of the semi-awe the twelve-year-old had experienced when her tall, older sister—magnificent in the green-on-green uniform of the Imperial Cadre, with the Emperor's own starship and harp insignia—walked through the concourse arrivals gate.

"Yeah," Alicia told her with a grin. "And, I'll bet you've at least got your own room. That was more than I ever had when you were the squirmy new kid on the block."

"Sure, sure. Back in the *old* days, when you had to walk to school, through the snow, in the broiling heat, uphill both ways, barefoot, carrying your clay tablet and a sharp stylus through the rain, and—"

"We get the point, Clarissa," Collum DeVries told his middle child, then put an arm around his wife and smiled down at the newest addition to the family. "And as for you, Alicia Dierdre DeVries, I'll have you know he *is* gorgeous. I have it on the best of authority that that lobster-red coloration will fade quite soon. Before his fifteenth birthday, at the very latest."

His wife's free elbow smacked soundly into his ribs, and he "oofed" obediently.

"Seriously, Alley," Fiona said, her voice softer, "I'm really, really glad you got leave in time for the christening. Knowing you were right here on Old Earth for the last four months has been wonderful, in a lot of ways, but it's been . . . frustrating, too."

"I'm sorry, Mom," Alicia said. "I wish I could have gotten home sooner. It's just—"

"I know exactly what it was, Alley." Fiona smiled. "I was raised on New Dublin, you know. And even if I hadn't been inclined to figure it out for myself, your grandfather would have made certain that I understood it wasn't your idea. And that the Cadre wasn't doing it to us on purpose. I'm not complaining, exactly. And the fact that you've got three whole glorious weeks before you have to report back is pretty fair compensation, I suppose. But," her smile wavered very slightly, "we've all missed you, you know."

"I do know that," Alicia said quietly, and looked into her father's eyes. "Grandpa told me that one of your reservations about my decision to enlist in the first place was the time with all of you that it would cost me. And I think that's probably the thing I truly do regret about it."

"Every decision has its price, Alley," he told her, returning her level gaze steadily. "If you'd chosen not to join the Marines, you would have regretted that, as well. It's not given to anyone to have *no* regrets; only to decide, through the choices we make, *which* regrets we'll have. And, as your mother says, at least you're home for the christening and at least we'll have you for the next three weeks. Both of those are well worth celebrating, so I've made reservations at Giuseppe's for this evening. Let's get your baggage and get you squared away."

"It's good to see you looking so fit," Collum DeVries said, his hands resting on his older daughter's shoulders as he held her at arm's length and looked deep into her eyes. They stood in the small, well-stocked library attached to his home office, and as she looked back at him, one eyebrow quirked, he smiled. "You'd be amazed at the stories making the rounds of office gossip at the Ministry where the Cadre is concerned, Alley. Mind you, I never believed any of the wilder ones, but where there's that much smoke—"

He shrugged, and she chuckled.

"I imagine the gossip dwells with loving attention to detail on all of the nonexistent superduper bits and pieces of hardware they tuck away inside us. Well, I'd like to give you all of the classified details on what we really do get, Daddy. But if I did, I'd have to kill you, and that would *really* upset Mom. Especially if I did it before supper."

"I see that the military has continued to sharpen your basic sense of good tactics," he said dryly.

"They've tried," she said. "They've tried."

"I know they have," he said, much more quietly. He looked into her eyes for another moment, then drew her close and hugged her tightly. Tall as she was, the top of her head came only to his chin, and she pressed her cheek into his chest as she'd done when she was much, much younger. And, as *he* had done when she'd been much, much younger, his hand very gently stroked her sunrise-colored hair.

She knew why her mother and her sister had carted her baggage—and Stevie—away in a quiet conspiracy to give her this time alone with her father, and she hugged him back.

Collum felt the strength of those arms, the supple muscularity of his daughter's hard physical training, and tried to parse his own emotions. It was an effort he'd made before, and deep inside, he felt he was no closer to success now than he'd been the very first time.

He eased the pressure of his own embrace and stood back, then waved at the facing chairs flanking the study's genuine picture window. She looked out the window at the soaring mega-towers of downtown Charlotte and smiled again, a bit crookedly, then obeyed the silent invitation. He took the facing chair, leaned back while it adjusted, and inhaled deeply.

"Your mother spoke for all three of us about how happy we are to finally see you home, however briefly," he told her finally. She cocked her head to one side, and he smiled. "That's not a complaint. Your grandfather and I really have discussed it quite a bit since you volunteered for the Cadre. He's been able to give me some idea about what you've been through in the past few months. And he tells me the next three months are going to be even more interesting?"

"You could probably put it that way . . . if you were given to understatement," Alicia said dryly.

Her present leave was the breathing spell between her initial Cadre augmentation, familiarization, and basic training and ACTS—the dreaded Advanced Cadre Training School. That was where she would be issued her new Cadre powered armor and put through the *Cadre's* version of realistic combat training. More than one Cadreman had washed out in ACTS, despite all the rigorous preselection, evaluation, and training which had already gone into him. ACTS was designed to squeeze all of the functions of Camp Mackenzie, Recon School, and Raider School, plus the Cadre's own highly specialized requirements, into a three-month endurance contest guaranteed to make all of those other training experiences positively soporific by comparison.

"The good thing about what they're going to have me doing next," she told her father with a wry grin, "is that since that which does not kill me makes me stronger, I ought to be ready for the next All-Empire Marathon by the time I'm done. Heck, I'm *already* halfway there!"

"You *do* look fit, Alley," he acknowledged. "And much though I would have resisted telling you this a few years back, the uniform looks good on you. Of course, I thought you looked good as a Marine, too."

"I know it isn't what you wanted me to do," she began, but he interrupted her.

"No," he said. "That's not really accurate."

She stopped, looking at him in surprise, and he snorted.

"Well, maybe it is, but usually when someone says 'it's not what you wanted' what they really mean is 'I went out and did something that pissed you off' or 'what I did must've been a disappointment to you.' Or something along those lines. And I was never angry with you, and I've never been 'disappointed' by the choices you've made."

"Really?" It was her turn to lean back, and she watched his expression carefully. "I never really felt you were *angry* with me, but I have to admit that there've been times I felt that you were . . . if not *disappointed*, at least unhappy that I chose the military."

"Alicia, you're my daughter. Once upon a time you were Stevie's size—remember that picture of you balanced on the palm of my hand? And then you were my little girl. I still remember that first nasty fever you had and how you spent the entire night sleeping on my chest . . . and crying every time I tried to tuck you back into your crib. And after that you were all scraped knees and elbows and a smile that melted my heart. And then you were in college, looking so much like your mother when I first met her that it was almost scary."

His smile was soft with memory, and then he shook his head.

"I love you very much, just as I love your sister and your brother. And because I do, the thought of anything happening to you frightens me more than just about anything else in the universe. If I could *make* you safe, I'd do it in an instant. And because I would, I'd obviously be happier in a lot of ways if you were in a nice, sedentary occupation. One where the worst I'd have to worry about would be the occasional paper cut or spilled cup of coffee."

The last sentence came out along with a smile so droll that Alicia chuckled. Then his expression grew serious once more.

"But I can't pack you up in cotton, however much I love you. Or even *because* of how much I love you. I think the hardest lesson any parent has to learn is letting go, but it's also the most important one in a lot of ways. If you truly love your children, you have to let them be who and what they *are*, not try to force them into being what *you* want them to be. If you do try to force them, it's the surest way to drive them away from you in the end, and no matter what occupation you'd actually chosen, it wouldn't guarantee your safety. As your grandfather's said a time or two—when he thought your mother couldn't hear him, of course—shit happens.

"And as for the . . . morality, if you will, of your choice—" he grimaced and made a throwing away gesture.

"Your grandfather and I have had a lot of conversations about that general topic. I'm not sure he's ever fully understood my feelings on the matter, either, though he's certainly tried. But the bottom line is that I've never had any patience at all with the attitude of a certain segment of the Core Worlds' so-called 'intellectual elite' where the military is concerned. I wish we didn't need a military. I wish there were no people out there willing to resort to violence to achieve their ends, and that there was no need for other people to use violence to stop them. I wish no one ever had to be killed, no cities ever needed to be turned into battlefields.

"But however much I might *wish* all of those things, I'm not going to get them. And that means we do need people to stand between civilization and the barbarians. We need people like your grandfather. And we need people like *you.*

"I may be monumentally unsuited to undertake that sort of job myself. Frankly, I'd be terrible at it, for a lot of reasons. And, to be completely honest, I'm not at all confident that I have the intestinal and moral fortitude to do the things that sort of job would require me to do. But that doesn't keep me from also being monumentally grateful to the people who can—and do—undertake the task I never could. I would have vastly preferred for the daughter I love to have avoided paying the sort of price I know you've already paid. But it was a price you *chose* to pay, and however much I may worry about you, I'm also very, very proud of you."

"You are?" Alicia felt her smile tremble ever so slightly. "I've never doubted that you loved me, and that you accepted my decision. But I was always afraid that—"

"That deep down inside somewhere, I still felt you'd 'thrown your life and your talents away' on a merely military career," he finished for her. Protest flickered in her eyes, and he shook his head. "I realize that's probably putting it a lot more strongly than you ever would have, but it's also probably reaching in the right direction. And I'm sure someone with your inherent ability could have earned a great deal more money in a civilian career. And, for that matter, that you would have excelled at *any* occupation you might have chosen. But the truth is, Alley, that you truly are your grandfather's granddaughter. The uniform you're wearing right this minute tells me just how well your superiors feel you've done in the career you've actually chosen. More importantly, *I* can see you made the right choice. And God knows how badly the Empire needs people for whom it is the right choice."

She looked deeply into his eyes and realized he meant every word of it. Her father had never lied to her, but she'd always been secretly afraid that he'd . . . tailored his comments where her desire for a military career was concerned. Now she knew she'd done him a disservice.

"I'll be honest," she said quietly, "there are times I understand exactly why anyone would be worried by the thought of someone paying the 'price' of a military career. But the truth is, Daddy, this is what I was born to do. Sometimes it's . . . pretty horrible, but it's still what I was born to do."

"I know," he said, equally quietly, and shadows fluttered behind his gray eyes. "I used my Ministry access to review the internal reports about what happened on Gyangtse, Alley. I know why they gave you the Silver Star. I know exactly what you did to earn it."

"And that doesn't . . . bother you?"

"Of course it does. I saw the way it had changed you when you came home on leave between tours. I hadn't seen the reports, then, but I figured—accurately, as it turned out—that I had a pretty shrewd notion of what you'd done. It was a pretty damned brutal way for a seventeen-year-old to grow up, Alley. In fact, it was a lot rougher than anything I'd envisioned, even in my nightmares. But you survived it, and you were still *you*. And that—that was the proof that you'd been right. Or, at least, that you hadn't been *wrong* when you made your decision."

"And this?" She touched the harp and starship on the collar of her green uniform. "The Cadre?"

"It scares me," he said frankly. "What the Marines get dropped into is bad enough; what the *Cadre* sometimes has to deal with can make Gyangtse look like a pillow fight. Trust me, I know. And, to be honest, the Cadre's casualty rates are more than a little frightening. They're probably fantastically low, given the sorts of jobs the Cadre gets handed, but Cadremen get sent out again and again. The price for being the Empire's elite is getting handed the hardest, most dangerous, *costliest* assignments, and I don't want to get what your grandfather calls 'The Letter,' even if now it's going to be coming from the Emperor himself, and not the Minister of War.

"But I honestly believe that it's the right challenge for you. As you say, this is what you were born to do. I'd have been much happier, in a lot of ways, if you'd been born to be a concert violinist, but you weren't. So if you're going to run around risking your life for the Empire, you might as well do it with the very best. After all, you're one of that 'very best' yourself, aren't you?"

"I'd like to think so," she said, her tone deliberately lighter, and he chuckled obediently.

"But that's probably enough deep and serious stuff," he said. "So let's talk about something a bit less weighty. For example, have you had a letter from your grandfather lately?"

"I got one about three weeks ago."

"Did he mention his retirement plans to you?"

"Retirement? *Grandpa?* I don't know if they'd even *let* him! He's practically an institution in the Corps, you know."

"He's also getting a bit long in the tooth," her father pointed out. "They're beginning to make quiet noises to him about how he's done his share, and how it's time to let someone else carry the load."

"Oh, I bet he just *loved* hearing that!"

"I believe I did overhear the occasional sulfurous comment," Collum allowed with a grin. "On the other hand, they do have a point. Oh, not that he's getting too old for it, but he *has* done his share, and a bit more. I think it's time he got the opportunity to settle down and enjoy some of the peace he's given up for so long."

"He won't last six months playing mahjongg or shuffleboard!"

"The mind boggles at the very thought of your grandfather shuffling mahjongg tiles." Collum shuddered. "And it wouldn't be *him* that didn't last six months; it would be everyone else in his vicinity. So that isn't what he's going to do."

"Well that's a relief! But I'm assuming that you're about to tell me just what it is he does plan on doing?"

"Actually, we're all planning on doing it with him."

"Doing *what* with him?"

"Tell me," her father said, "have you ever heard of Mathison's World?"

"No," she said, regarding him narrowly.

"I'm not surprised." He shrugged. "It's a very nice planet, though. Out near the frontier, beyond Franconia. The climate's on the cool side, especially during the winter, but it's got absolutely gorgeous scenery. More to the point, I happen to know that Out-World Affairs is planning to organize a new Crown Sector out that way. It's not going to happen overnight, but in five or six years, they're going to open Mathison to general colonization and begin offering incentive credits to get people out there."

"But isn't Franconia an awful long way from anywhere important?" Alicia asked, frowning as she tried to dredge up a better mental feel for the astrography involved.

"Oh, it certainly is, at the moment, at least!" Collum chuckled. "On the other hand, I grew up on a world a lot like Mathison's, you know, and your grandfather isn't exactly going to be comfortable surrounded by citified real estate. And the system itself is strategically located. It's got not just one, but two asteroid belts, which is going to make it a natural site for heavy industry, eventually. And it's going to turn into a logical site for a major freight transshipment point, too, once the borders start expanding in the region. Speaking as a Foreign Ministry weenie, I'm surprised, in some ways, that that hasn't already happened. I understand the logic, more or less, but we really ought to have gotten a new Crown Sector organized out there years ago. Once we finally do, though, the Crown is going to put a lot of horsepower into the effort, and things are going to happen fast, compared to most colonization waves. Give it another fifteen or twenty years, and Mathison's is going to be the sort of colony that has to beat off applicants with a stick. Which is why your mother and I have decided to put our names on the preliminary list."

Alicia blinked at him. She knew he'd grown up on a farming world, but somehow she'd always thought of him right here, on Old Earth—or else jaunting about the galaxy on the business of the Foreign Ministry. The one word she'd always associated with him most strongly was undoubtedly 'cosmopolitan,' and somehow it was a bit difficult to see him on some rustic, barely settled planet on the very fringe of the Empire.

But only for a few moments. Then she began to see how well it would truly suit him.

"Well, this is certainly sudden," she said, sparring for time while she adjusted to the entire concept.

"Not really." He shook his head. "Your mother and I have always planned on retiring someplace a bit less hectic than Old Earth. And while my own current profession isn't one that provides a lot of skills a colony world would find useful, I *did* grow up in a saddle, riding herd on megabison back on Silverado. And your mom can probably write her own ticket anywhere—colony worlds always need first-rate doctors. It's true that we hadn't planned on relocating this soon, but we've certainly accrued enough retirement credits we can convert to colonization credits. We've decided it makes sense to go ahead and use them while we're still young enough to build entirely new lives for ourselves, and given the probability of your grandfather's retirement—and the amount of lead time we're talking about—it makes sense to go ahead and get started."

"It sounds nice," she said, just a bit wistfully.

"Oh, believe me, it'll have its drawbacks." He chuckled. "It won't be like some of the horror stories from the original colonization waves, but it's going to be decades before Mathison's has the sort of technical and industrial infrastructure most Incorporated Worlds take for granted. But the fact that it's a virgin planet, without any old League odds and ends, means we won't have any of the sort of liveliness places like Gyangtse have experienced. We may have to get used to riding horses for local transport for a few years, but at least it should be fairly peaceful. And of course," he smiled, "given the size of the spreads original colonizers get to claim, we ought to have plenty of dirt available when it comes time for you to retire, too."

CHAPTER SEVENTEEN

"So, welcome to Guadalupe Inéz Juanita Meléndez y Redondo de Castillo Blasquita Capital City Spaceport," the corporal in Cadre uniform said with a smile.

"You're putting me on," Alicia said.

"Oh no I'm not," the other woman assured her. The nameplate on the breast of her undress uniform tunic read "Cateau, Tannis," and she was considerably shorter than Alicia. Then again, most women were. Cateau, however, also had the stockiness of a heavy-worlder. "In fact," she continued, "the entire planet's official name is Guadalupe Inéz Juanita Meléndez y Redondo de Castillo Blasquita. The original survey captain was some high muckety-muck from Granada who chose to name it for his mother."

"Then he must have held a gun on the rest of his crew while he did it," Alicia said tartly. "Nobody would use a mouthful like that every time they refer to a planet!"

"I don't know about guns," Cateau said with a shrug, "but you're right about it's being just a tad long for comfort. The colonists never bothered to change the official name, but they did shorten it to 'Guadalupe' in common usage, and that's what pretty much everyone's called it since."

"Well, by all means, let's honor the tradition," Alicia said, extending her hand. "Alicia DeVries," she added.

"Tannis Cateau," the other woman said. She gripped the offered hand firmly but with a certain degree of care, confirming Alicia's suspicion that she'd been born and raised in a considerably heavier gravity than that of Old Earth's and had the muscles to go with it.

"Given the fact that you and I are the only people in this entire concourse in Cadre uniform, it leaps to my powerful intellect that someone sent you to collect me," Alicia said.

"I'm awed by your keen deductive ability," Cateau agreed with a grin. "Let's go get your gear."

"Lead the way, O local guide," Alicia said.

"Glad to see you, DeVries," Captain Madison Alwyn said as First Sergeant Pamela Yussuf walked Alicia into his office.

The commander of Charlie Company, Third Battalion, Second Regiment, Fifth Brigade, Imperial Cadre, was at least fifteen centimeters taller than Alicia, which made him very nearly two full meters in height. He was also very, very black. Alicia couldn't place his accent, but humanity had settled a great many worlds over the past seven or eight centuries, and most of them had evolved their own local accents and dialects.

That same plethora of planetary habitats had preserved, and in some cases actually intensified, the human race's variations in skin pigmentation and other environment-controlled physical differentiation. It had added its own variations on the theme, too, of course, like Corporal Cateau's impressive physique. From Captain Alwyn's complexion, for example, it was obvious that his ancestors hadn't settled in the middle of a frozen tundra somewhere.

"Thank you, Sir," she replied as he stood behind his desk and reached out to shake her hand.

"I know you've had a long voyage out from Old Earth," Alwyn continued, "and I know you just finished ACTS. Bearing all of that in mind, I'd really like to give you a couple of nice, quiet weeks or so to get settled in."

He paused, still holding her hand, and she felt one of her eyebrows rise.

"But—?" she said after a moment or two.

"But I don't think that's what's going to happen," he replied with a tight smile. He released her hand, and sat back down behind his desk, looking back and forth between her and Yussuf.

"There's always a little bit of awkwardness when we start fitting a new peg into its neat little hole here in the Cadre," he continued.

"It gets a bit more complicated sometimes because all of our people keep their rank when they transfer in. Given the sorts of people we tend to recruit, that means we get a *lot* of junior noncoms. The most junior Cadreman you're going to meet is going to be a corporal, and E-5s are, frankly, a centicredit a dozen. So our squad organization tends to look a little strange. Instead of corporals running our fire teams, they're usually run by sergeants, with staff sergeants running the squads. Sometimes we've got staff sergeants running the fire teams and an SFC running the squad."

Alicia nodded. She'd already observed the situation he was describing, and it was probably inevitable. Nor, she was sure, did the Cadre's senior officers think it was a bad thing. The Cadre found itself handling all manner of peculiar assignments, including the occasional need to raise, train, and lead local indigenous military units. Having some extra rank seldom hurt in a situation like that. Of course, any Cadreman or Cadrewoman was officially one rank senior to his nominal counterparts in the regular military, which meant he or she was *two* ranks senior to anyone in a planetary militia. As someone who'd been a Marine less than nine months earlier, Alicia wasn't too sure she approved of that sort of rank inflation, but she understood the logic behind it.

Whatever doubts she might have cherished about that particular policy, however, she heartily approved of the Cadre's ironbound tradition that all Cadre officers had to have served in the Cadre's enlisted ranks before they were commissioned. There had actually been a handful of commissioned Marine officers or Fleet officers, some of them (including at least one Fleet officer who'd reached junior flag rank) who were graduates of their respective service academies, who had resigned their commissions in order to accept a sergeant's rank in the Cadre in order to satisfy that requirement. Alicia suspected that ex-officers like that got fast-tracked through the Cadre to get them back into commissioned status as quickly as possible, but they still had to spend their time in the trenches first.

"Like all Cadre units," Alwyn went on, "we're always understrength and under-establishment. Which means, in this case, that I have a squad which needs a leader, and you happen to be an E-6, which means, logically, that it should be yours. And, under normal circumstances, I'd simply have First Sergeant Yussuf march you over there and introduce you to your new squad, then stand back and let you get a proper feel for it. However, we've already received alert orders for an operation, probably to be mounted within the next seventy-two standard hours.

"I've read your dossier. I know you've been over the river and through the woods, and that you did damned well in that business on Gyangtse. And I've also read your training scores from Camp Cochrane and ACTS. I know you can do the job, and I have no qualms at all about your age." His lips quirked in a smile. "In your place, I'd probably wonder about that. Don't. You wouldn't be here unless everyone was convinced you could cut it, however young you happen to be.

"But I'm not prepared to destabilize my existing command relationships this close to mounting a full-scale, company-level op. My people have been actively prepping for it for almost two weeks now, and we actually started training for it over two months before that. It would be unfair to you to expect you to walk in cold and run an entire squad of people you don't know through an operation they've spent literally months training for and you haven't. You with me so far?"

"Yes, Sir." Alicia nodded.

"Good. Now, after this operation is over, once the dust's had a chance to settle a bit, I do have a squad with your name on it. At the moment, Master Sergeant Onassis is wearing two hats over in First Platoon. Lieutenant Strassmann has the platoon; Onassis is his platoon sergeant, and he's also running First Squad. He's good at his job, but he's a little stretched thin. What I'm thinking is that, from your record, you're too valuable to just leave sitting on the sidelines while this operation goes down, and First Squad is going to be yours as soon as the shooting's over, anyway. So, I'm going to go ahead and assign you to First Platoon, and to First Squad, but I'm not giving it to you yet. You're going to be functioning as Onassis' number two for the squad. He'll probably delegate quite a bit to you, but he's got the last word until he—or I—tell you different. Clear?"

"Yes, Sir," Alicia said again.

"Good. It's possible this op is going to be scrubbed at the last minute—it already has been, twice. I don't think that's going to happen a third time, though. If it does, we'll go ahead and slot you into First Squad as its leader, with all the usual settling-in time.

The fact that I'm not handing it over to you all on your own immediately has nothing at all to do with my confidence in you. It's purely and simply a matter of timing."

"I understand, Sir."

"Which may or may not be exactly the same thing as saying you approve," Alwyn observed with a grin, then waved a hand before Alicia could respond.

"Doesn't matter. The main thing is that you do understand, and that we get the most out of you we can if—when—this op goes down."

He gazed at her for another moment, then looked at Yussuf.

"Got someone to run her over to Onassis, Pam?"

"I hung onto Cateau."

"Good." He looked back at Alicia. "Corporal Cateau will get you over to First Platoon. She's in 'your' squad, anyway. I take it none of your gear got lost in transit?"

"No, Sir."

"In that case, as soon as you and Onassis get squared away with each other, run your armor over to the Morgue. Have the master armorer check it out, then get it down to the range and shoot it in for qualification."

"Yes, Sir."

"I'm sorry about the rush," Alwyn said, standing and reaching out his hand again. "We're all glad to see you, really. We always *are* glad to see another warm body. But if you're going to the party with us, we've got to get you in and up to speed ASAP. Welcome aboard, Staff Sergeant."

"Thank you, Sir. I'll try not to hold up the festivities."

"So that's the plan," Master Sergeant Adolfo Onassis said nine hours later. He stood back from the display table, arms folded, and looked at Alicia. "What do you think?" he asked.

Alicia took her time about responding. There wasn't anything particularly truculent about the short, stocky, swarthy master sergeant's attitude, but there was an edge of . . . challenge. Or, no, not that, precisely. It was more a matter of testing, she thought.

She studied the terrain displayed on the table. That part, she thought, was fairly straightforward, even simple. But as Clausewitz had said, in war, even simple things were difficult, and it had the potential to turn into a massive cluster fuck. Which, she acknowledged, gave added point to Captain Alwyn's earlier explanation. But, if she was going to be honest with herself, it was the political ramifications which concerned her most.

Of course, the political ramifications aren't exactly the thing I'm supposed to be worrying about, she thought. *I suppose I'm just too much my father's daughter to leave it alone. Or maybe the trick Jongdomba tried to pull on Gyangtse is still causing me to look at shadows.*

That last thought was almost amusing, in a way, since Guadalupe was only about two weeks' flight from Gyangtse.

Might almost say it's my old stomping grounds, she told herself wryly.

"I think, given the constraints, it looks pretty good," she said aloud after several moments. "I guess I'm most worried about the approach. And, after that, about target identification."

"The approach is the Fleet's problem, not ours," Onassis said. "Of course, having said that, I have to admit I've spent the odd sleepless night worrying about it myself." He showed his teeth in a tight grin. "And target identification's always a bitch on an op like this one. But they don't give us the assignments because they're easy."

Alicia nodded soberly and crossed her own arms with a thoughtful frown.

The area shown on the display table was a mountain valley on the planet of Chengchou. Like Gyangtse, Chengchou was a former League World; unlike Gyangtse, Chengchou was *not* claimed by the Empire. It was one of the Rogue World buffer systems between the Empire and the Rishathan Sphere. It lay on the Empire's side of the nominally independent zone between the two star nations, and it was one of four equally independent star systems currently involved in what were euphemistically called "multilateral collective security negotiations" with the Foreign Ministry.

What that really meant was that the star systems in question were (in the Empire's opinion, at least) being used as sanctuaries and staging bases by various "liberation organizations" dedicated to lifting the "imperial yoke from the shoulders of our enslaved brothers and sisters." The Empire didn't much care for that, and it was in the process of doing something about it.

In the eyes of the Empire, the "liberation organizations" were terrorists, pure and simple, and as far as Alicia was concerned, the label was accurate. Given the tremendous disparity between the military power of the Empire and their own strictly limited resources, the liberation organizations could never have fought a conventional war, whatever they might have preferred. They were stuck with a classic case of asymmetric warfare, and as usually happened in cases like that, the weaker side operated outside the approved "rules of war" established star nations tried to enforce. That much was as inevitable as anything in war could possibly be. But so far as Alicia could tell, most of the liberation organizations were perfectly happy with the terrorist strategies their lack of resources imposed. In fact, they seemed to like them, and they were never shy about embracing the classic terrorist tactic of the deliberate atrocity.

In the eyes of the citizens of many Rogue Worlds, however, and a not insignificant portion of the populations of various Crown Worlds (like Gyangtse, for example), they were patriots. Worse, they were convenient tools for people who wished the Empire ill. The Rish, for example, were notoriously fond of covertly funding and supporting them, and so were some of the more powerful Rogue Worlds.

Any Rogue World had to be very cautious about supporting organizations the Empire had labeled "terrorist," given the long-standing imperial policy of treating its enemies' friends as enemies in their own right. A terrorist act was an act of war, as far as the Empire was concerned, and anyone who *supported* an act of war was equally guilty of that act in the Empire's eyes. Which was why no Rogue World could afford to be definitely linked to a terrorist attack on imperial citizens or territory—not unless it *liked* entertaining visits from Fleet dreadnoughts and large numbers of extraordinarily unpleasant Marines.

But as long as its tracks could be safely hidden (or at least plausibly denied), many an independent Rogue World, worried by the rate of the Empire's expansion in its direction, had found the notion of slowing that expansion by supporting any "liberation movements" in the vicinity quite attractive. Which didn't even consider the instances in which that Rogue World's government, like its citizens, might genuinely approve of the liberation effort.

At the moment, Chengchou and its neighbors—Cotterpin, Onyx, and Hwan-ku—had come under increasing pressure from the Empire to rein in the various armed groups operating out of their territory and the other minor star systems in the region. The four of them, under Onyx's general leadership, had been less than enthralled by the process. It was pretty clear that they deeply resented the Empire's intrusion into their vicinity, but their governments had to know that eventually they were going to have to give in to imperial demands for action. If they didn't, then, sooner or later, the Empire would take unilateral action. They knew that, too, and it only made them even more resentful.

Negotiations had already dragged out longer than Alicia would have expected. It was obvious to her that the imperial negotiators had instructions from Foreign Minister Madison to try to keep the locals' resentment from escalating still further. They'd shown an unusual degree of patience and resisted what must be a massive temptation to wave a big, knobby stick under the other side's collective nose.

Unfortunately, Gavin Mueller, Onyx's foreign minister, as the spokesman for the Group of Four (as the four Rogue Worlds in question had been labeled), wasn't particularly moved by their restraint.

He'd taken the position that there was no proof that any organization proscribed by the Empire was operating from *their* territories. The Empire, he argued, was being grossly unfair in requiring them to assume responsibility for the half-dozen or so other, smaller Rogue World polities in their sector. While Mueller was prepared to concede that some of *those* Rogue Worlds might be being used as bases, it was unreasonable to expect the Group of Four to exert some sort of interstellar police authority over them. Not only would their neighbors understandably resent such high-handed intrusiveness on their part, but the expense would not be trivial. Nor was it reasonable to hold *them* responsible for someone else's misdeeds.

"Is this 'Group of Four' really as stubborn as they seem?" Alicia asked after a moment.

"Who can say?" Onassis shrugged. "They could just be talking a good fight on the theory that as long as they're talking, they don't have to do anything else. But they can't be very happy about the thought of the Fleet patrolling their sector. Of course," he smiled without humor, "*we* aren't very happy about that particular thought, either. The Fleet's like us in at least one respect—it never has enough units to be everywhere it really needs to be. It'd be a lot more convenient for us if the Group of Four would just *handle* this. Nobody expects to them to completely cut off all the terrorist organizations operating out here. We'd love it if they did, but that would be pretty unrealistic. All we want is to make sure that *they're* out of the terrorist-supporting business and that they at least make it a little difficult for the independent systems they claim are actually acting as sanctuaries."

"But if they do that, then their own voters are going to regard it as collaboration with the Empire," Alicia said sourly, and Onassis nodded.

"You've got it. And that overlooks the fact that they *are* acting as sanctuaries. They've cut back since the negotiations really started turning up the heat, but our intel's pretty good. This—" he indicated the display table between them "—is the hardest data we've got, but there's fairly conclusive evidence that Cotterpin and Hwan-ku are still providing very quiet sanctuary to at least three separate 'liberation groups,' as well."

"What about Onyx? Is it possible that Onyx really believes that the others aren't supporting the terrorists? Actively, I mean," she added, when Onassis looked at her sharply. "I'm sure Onyx knows about their history, but you say they've been cutting back. Is it possible that they're telling Onyx they've cut back more than they actually have, and that Onyx doesn't know any better?"

"*Anything* is possible," Onassis conceded. "Likely? Not very. That's exactly what their official position's been, both on and off the record, for the last standard year and half, but I don't see any way Onyx could be buying it. Not that that's prevented Mueller from lying to us about it with a straight face. Which is the entire point of our little soirée on Chengchou, of course."

"Of course." Alicia nodded. If the Cadre took down a terrorist base camp on the territory of one of the Group of Four's charter members—and documented the fact—it would be impossible for Onyx's foreign minister to continue to argue that none of *them* were supporting those nasty old terrorists.

And, she thought grimly, *it will also serve as a pointed warning of what can happen if they don't get off the centicred and do something about the terrorists themselves. Apparently someone on our side's decided it's time to give that stick a swing or two, after all.*

"The big problem," Onassis admitted, "is that our intelligence has a limited lifespan. This—" he tapped the display table again "—comes and goes. Most of the time, it's just another mountain valley with a couple of villages in it. Then the camp facilities here and here," he indicated two points on the display, near the largest of the valley's permanent towns, "get spun up. They run about a two-month training cycle each time, then shut down again until the next batch comes along, and they activate on a pretty irregular basis. It looks to us like the Freedom Alliance is providing the training cadres, and they're cycling a *lot* of people through these camps—more than any single 'liberation' group ought to need—but apparently it's strictly an as-needed sort of process. So if we're going to do anything about it, we have to do it during one of the active phases. And we've got to get our people in and on the ground before the people we want simply run away and fade into the general population."

"And if the Chengchou government is really actively conniving with these people, then it's going to warn them we're coming . . . if it knows we are," Alicia murmured.

"Exactly."

Alicia nodded, then looked back up at Onassis.

"I can see why Captain Alwyn isn't too happy about the thought of integrating a brand new squad leader into this kind of operation on such short notice," she said.

"Glad to hear that." Onassis gave her the first unrestrained smile she'd seen from him. "Since you're just joining the family this afternoon, as it were, though, I'm giving you an experienced guide for your wing." Alicia raised a quizzical eyebrow, and he chuckled. "You've met her—Cateau. She's the squad medic, among other things, but she knows her way around the sharp end just fine, she's thoroughly briefed in, and she's been through all of the previous rehearsals."

Alicia cocked her head to one side, considering, then nodded again in approval.

By the standards of the Corps, Cadre units were considerably over strength. Whereas a Marine squad consisted of thirteen people arranged into two fire teams, a Cadre squad consisted of eighteen people, and it was divided into nine two-person fire teams. The members of each team were assigned permanently to one another and known as "wingmen," or, more commonly, simply as "wings." Each squad was divided into an Alpha and a Bravo section, each composed of four pairs of wings, while the squad leader and his or her wing formed the ninth pair.

Alicia, having been thoroughly grounded in Marine tactical doctrine had nourished doubts at first about the soundness of Cadre practice. But that was at least partly because she hadn't realized just how flexible Cadre training and equipment actually was. Whereas all Marine squads, from straight line units, to Recon, to Raiders, were built around a heavy fire element supported by a rifle-armed maneuver element, *all* Cadre troopers were expected to be equally proficient with both heavy weapons and their individual rifles, not to mention trained in heavy vehicle operation. In many cases, they were trained in the operation of sting ships and assault shuttles, as well, and the all-round capability that gave any Cadre unit was . . . impressive.

In addition, the much more lavishly equipped Cadre routinely configured its units for specific missions. For the planned incursion into Chengchou, for example, Charlie Company would be operating in "light" configuration—almost all of its troopers would be armed with rifles, with only a single pair of wings in each squad carrying heavy weapons. Had they anticipated heavier resistance, they might have configured their weapons loads for heavy assault mode, in which case there would have been only a single pair of *rifle*-armed wings in each squad, while all of the other wings carried plasma rifles, calliopes, or heavy grenade or HVW launchers.

It was a far more flexible posture, which was made possible only by the combination of Cadre training and the lavish funding available to it. It was also one about which Alicia no longer cherished any doubts at all, and from what she'd seen so far of Tannis Cateau, she was inclined to believe Onassis had made an excellent choice for her own wing.

"How comfortable are we with the intelligence on this one?" she asked, as thoughts of weapons configurations flipped through the back of her mind. Onassis looked at her, and she shrugged. "We're going in mighty light," she pointed out. "Assuming that intelligence's estimate of the op force is accurate, that ought to be plenty. But if they haven't gotten their sums right, it could get a little dicey without more heavy stuff along."

"Fair enough question," Onassis said after a moment. "The best answer I can give you is that according to Captain Watts—he's the Wasp 'spook' Battalion's attached to Charlie Company for this one—this is alpha-grade material. I don't think he's prepared to grade it Alpha-One, but he's obviously pretty damned comfortable with it, and he's got a good rep for knowing his stuff. We managed to confirm most of our intel assumptions from other sources following the last scrub, too." It was his turn to shrug. "No intel is ever perfect, but I think it'll hold up. And if it doesn't," he grinned suddenly, "at least the range scores you turned in this afternoon indicate you'll be an asset when it all hits the fan. Assuming, of course, that we actually get the go order this time, after all."

"Captain Alwyn seems to think we will," Alicia pointed out.

"And the Skipper's usually got a pretty good nose for this kind of thing," Onassis agreed. "On the other hand, we've been stood-to for it twice already. The first time, we picked up on them too far into their training cycle. They were going to be shut down and gone again by the time we could get there. I'm not sure what happened the second time. If I had to guess, I'd lay money on one of the Foreign Ministry pukes deciding we had to show 'restraint' because the talks were 'at a delicate point.'"

He rolled his eyes in eloquent disgust, and Alicia grimaced. She probably had rather more tolerance for what was still sometimes referred to as the "pinstripe crowd" than most members of the imperial military did. But she was one of the shooters herself, now. She'd seen firsthand what sorts of situations the political and policy types all too often wound up dropping in the military's lap. She knew it was dangerous to get too addicted to the direct, sledgehammer approach to interstellar relations, but it looked to her like this was one instance in which the answer really might be to go and get a bigger hammer.

And the Cadre, she thought, looking at the display table once again, *is a pretty damned* big *hammer, when you come right down to it.*

She nodded again, to herself this time, and realized she actually felt a little sorry for the nails.

CHAPTER EIGHTEEN

From the outside, HMS *Marguerite Johnsen* was a thoroughly unprepossessing spectacle.

The tramp freighter—listed on her splendidly official papers as IMS, or "Imperial Merchant Ship," rather than HMS, for "His Majesty's Starship"—was on the smallish size for a Fasset Drive cargo hauler. Barely a thousand meters long, she had that battered, down-at-the-heels look that went with owners who couldn't—or wouldn't—spend the money to provide her with proper upkeep and maintenance. If anyone had bothered to give her a good sensor examination, they would have discovered that she had what was obviously a Fleet surplus Fasset Drive. They might have noticed that it seemed unusually powerful for a bulk carrier of her dimensions, but they would also have discovered that at least twenty percent of its nodes were currently off-line—another indication, no doubt, of lack of maintenance.

From the inside, it was quite a different matter.

Alicia DeVries sat with the other armored members of "her" squad in the ready room in what was supposed to be *Marguerite Johnsen*'s number one cargo hold and tried to project the proper air of confidence as they awaited final confirmation that the operation was truly a "go" this time. Back aft, on the "freighter's" gleaming, efficient command deck, her officers—linked with Captain Alwyn through his synth-link—were considering the take from the *Marguerite Johnsen*'s extremely capable passive sensors and the heavily stealthed reconnaissance drones the ship had deployed shortly after dropping back sublight. She was decelerating steadily towards her final insertion into Chengchou orbit at fifteen gravities, and at that rate they had about another eighteen minutes to go before they hit their programmed drop point.

"All right, people," Alwyn's deep voice sounded suddenly in her mastoid implant as he came up on the all-hands net, "we've got confirmation. The target is hot. We don't see any significant changes from our last sitrep, although Beech Tree Two seems to've added another fifteen or twenty trainees to its current roster. Saddle up. Ramrod, clear."

"You heard the man, Adolfo," Lieutenant Strassmann said over the dedicated First Platoon net a moment later.

"Yes, Sir," Master Sergeant Onassis acknowledged. "Okay, people. Into the tubes and harness up."

As the platoon's lead squad, the eighteen men and women of what was eventually going to be Alicia's squad, stood and filed into the carefully concealed drop tubes which were *Marguerite Johnsen*'s true reason for being. Alicia's external audio pickups were on-line, and she had the gain cranked up high enough to hear the soft, purring whine of exoskeletal "muscles" from the others' powered armor. Unaugmented human hearing wouldn't have been able to hear it, even standing right next to the armor in question, which was just one of the many ways in which the Cadre's equipment differed from that of the Corps.

She and Tannis Cateau, as her wing, stopped to stand between the two Alpha Tube access hatches while Alicia used her command armor's monitors to personally double check the readiness readouts on each set of armor as the others climbed past them through the hatches.

Sergeant Alan McGwire, Alpha Team's leader, stood to Alicia's right, in front of the starboard hatch, doing the same thing for his team. Sergeant Lawrence Abernathy, who had Bravo Team, stood on her other side, beside the port hatch. They knew the members of their teams far better than Alicia had yet had time to come to know them, and she felt almost excluded as people exchanged those last minute, pre-drop looks. No one was doing that to her deliberately, but she was acutely aware that she was most definitely the newest kid on the block once again. Titular squad leader or not, she was even more of an unknown quantity to them than they were to her.

The last pair of troopers climbed into place, followed by the two team leaders and Cateau, and then it was Alicia's turn.

She swung herself through the hatch, moving as easily and naturally in her powered armor as she would have in her regular fatigues, and settled herself into drop configuration. The drop harness slid out to envelop her armored torso, and she felt the slight, distinct click of impact as its tractor collars mated. Its umbilicals connected themselves to her armor, and her synth-link expanded to interface with the harness' onboard computers. The last to enter the starboard tube, and thus last in the loading queue, she would be the first out of it, and if anything went wrong with her harness, she and the person immediately behind her would become a very messy showstopper for the rest of First Squad.

But nothing was going to go wrong, she reminded herself firmly, as a quick glance at her HUD confirmed that all drop systems were green, not just for her but for every member of First Squad.

"Rifle-Two," she said over the platoon net, "Winchester-One. First Squad, ready for drop."

"Winchester-One, Rifle-Two copies ready for drop," Onassis acknowledged.

"Rifle-Two, Weatherby-One," she heard Staff Sergeant Henry Gilroy announce. "Second Squad, ready for drop."

"Weatherby-One, Rifle-Two copies ready for drop," Onassis replied.

"Rifle-Two, Mauser-One," Sergeant First Class Celestine Hillman came up on the net in turn. "Third Squad, ready for drop."

"Mauser-One, Rifle-Two copies ready for drop," Onassis confirmed. He paused a moment, obviously checking his own telltales, as well. Then: "Rifle-One," she heard him continue a moment later to Lieutenant Strassmann, "Rifle-Two. First Platoon, ready for drop."

"Copy ready for drop," Strassmann's tenor confirmed. "All Rifles, stand by. The clock is running. Drop in thirteen minutes from . . . now."

Alicia lay back in her armor, eyes closed, breathing slowly and deeply in the drop tube's confines. Many people, even some who'd made dozens of drops, suffered from drop anxiety which had nothing at all to do with the current mission, she knew. Frequently, it was aggravated by a bit of claustrophobia, although anyone who'd suffered from acute claustrophobia would never have been considered for drop commando training in the first place. At the moment, she felt more than a little tension herself, but it had nothing to do with the simple mechanics of the drop itself.

Well, not much, anyway.

She opened her eyes once more, looking up through her visor at the roof of the drop tube, sixteen centimeters from the tip of her nose. There wasn't much to see, so she closed them again and spent her time running through one last systems check.

Her Cadre armor was still a bit of a marvelous new toy, in a lot of ways. The basic powered armor issued to Marine line infantry was at least as good as the combat equipment issued to any other first-line military organization in the explored galaxy. The more specialized armor issued to the elite Raiders was considerably better than that, in large part because Raiders—like Recon—had to come from the sixty-odd percent of the human race who were neural receptor-capable. That meant Raiders could take the direct feed from their armor's sensors, diagnostic systems, and tactical computers and send orders back the same way, which enormously enhanced that armor's responsiveness. A Raider was probably about the least stealthy infantryman in the known universe, but he was also extraordinarily dangerous, with the same sort of situational awareness a Recon Marine had, coupled with the toughness of a late pre-space main battle tank and the firepower to single-handedly annihilate an entire company of planetary militia. A standard suit of Marine powered armor had roughly the same firepower, but couldn't match the flexibility and versatility of the Raider variant.

Recon was a different story, of course. Recon *did* rely on stealthiness, rather more than firepower, to accomplish its significantly different mission. Raiders were specialists in scientifically organized mayhem and destruction and about as subtle as a chainsaw; Recon specialized in getting the information the Raiders needed to plan their operations, hopefully so quietly the Bad Guys never realized they'd been spotted.

But *Cadre* battle armor out-classed Raider battle armor by at least as big a margin as Raider battle armor out-classed basic Marine armor. Indeed, the margin of superiority was almost certainly greater than that.

Cadre armor was manufactured using advanced composites which were painfully expensive but allowed it to be lighter, faster, *and* tougher than Raider armor. It had far more endurance, thanks to the incorporation of a small, fantastically expensive cold-fusion power plant, which freed it from reliance on the Raider armor's bulky superconductor capacitors. Its reactive chameleon capability was at least twice that of Recon's *unpowered* body armor, and it incorporated stealth features which would have at least doubled the price tag of Raider armor all by themselves. It had better sensors, and *much* better computer support. Nor did it stop there. Although the standard Cadre "rifle" fired a considerably smaller-caliber projectile than the standard Marine battle armor "rifle," it fired it at an even higher velocity, and each Cadreman carried a lot more ammunition.

And, of course, the fact that every Cadreman had to be *synth-link*-capable, not simply able to tolerate neural receptors, allowed a degree of human-technology fusion even the Raiders simply couldn't count on. With her synth-link up, Alicia literally "saw" electromagnetic radiation and "tasted" thermal signatures. She could see in total darkness, actually watch the radar-mapped trajectory of incoming fire, and simultaneously integrate the take from remotely deployed sensors into the same instant gestalt of her combat environment. A Cadreman didn't *wear* his combat armor; he made that armor's systems a literal extension of his own muscles and senses, so that hardware and human melded into a single, highly capable, incredibly lethal entity.

It was a pointed lesson in cost-versus-quantity. There were a maximum of only forty thousand Cadremen, as opposed to quite literally millions of Imperial Marines. Which was probably a very good thing for the Treasury, since each suit of Cadre battle armor cost rather more than a *Leopard*-class assault shuttle capable of landing thirty-one fully armored Marines *plus* the cost of all of the external ordnance and fuel that same shuttle would require to provide fire support for its Marines once they were on the ground.

Not even the Terran Empire could conceivably have afforded to spend that much equipping every one of its Marines, even assuming all of those Marines had been synth-link-capable in the first place. But it could afford to equip the *Cadre* on that scale, which helped to explain just what it was which placed the combat power of the Imperial Cadre of Seamus II on a completely different plane from any other military unit.

"Prepare for drop," the voice of *Marguerite Johnsen*'s cybersynth AI said emotionlessly in Alicia's mastoid, breaking into her reverie. "Drop in sixty seconds." She felt herself tightening internally in anticipation of the coming shock. "Fifty. Forty. Thirty. Twenty. Ten . . . nine . . . eight . . . seven . . . six . . . five . . . four . . . three . . . two . . . one . . . drop."

A particularly foul-tempered mule kicked her squarely between the shoulders.

That was what it felt like, anyway. She'd made her eight required qualification drops, and another twenty live training drops (and over thirty simulated drops) during ACTS. In a lot of ways, this was just one more—an explosive grunt as the tube catapult suddenly drove the drop harness tractor-locked to her armor down the exact center of the tube's gleaming bore under one hundred and sixty gravities of acceleration. The harness took her with it, and its countergravity and inertial sump reduced the apparent acceleration to "only" about fifteen gravities. Which, in Alicia's considered opinion, was more than enough to be getting on with. She never blacked out—her "feet-first" launch posture and the pressure suit lining built into her armor's antikinetic systems helped stave off blood drain away from the brain—but she'd decided on her very first drop that the experience gave her a cannonball's-eye view of the universe.

By the time she cleared the two-kilometer electromagnetic extension of the tube catapult, two endless seconds later, she was traveling at over seven hundred kilometers per hour and headed straight into Chengchou's atmosphere.

Not even her armor would have been enough to protect her through such a steep reentry (although, technically, since she'd never left Chengchou she could hardly be said to be *reentering* its atmosphere, she supposed), but that was where the drop harness came in. Not even it could make a drop pleasant, but it could make it survivable. The harness's tractor/presser field reached out, forming an immaterial and yet immensely strong aerodynamically-shaped bubble around her. Heat, light, and turbulence bellowed and howled on the bubble's surface as she bulleted down into the heart of Chengchou's deep envelope of air, and if it wasn't pleasant, it *was* immensely exciting, like riding inside the heart of a star. The sort of experience no civilian would ever know.

She watched her blazing corona, protected by her bubble and the armor within it, and felt the universe begin to slow as the first trickle of tick slid into her bloodstream.

Charlie Company screamed down towards Chengchou's Muztagh Ata Mountains like a flight of homesick meteors, and the finest stealth systems in the galaxy could not have concealed the visual and thermal signatures of its coming.

But, of course, by the time anyone looked up into the night sky to see them coming, it was far too late to do anything about it.

Alicia didn't even turn her head as Tannis Cateau fell into position on her left flank. If Cateau had any misgivings about going into combat with a wing with whom she'd never even been through a simulated exercise, she'd concealed them well. Alicia appreciated that, the more so because she'd found time to study Cateau's file. Whatever else the medic corporal might be, she was also a highly experienced close-combat warrior. Every drop commando fought—even the chaplains—and Cateau had done more than her fair share of that. Which meant she knew exactly what she was getting into with a newbie wing and that her silence on the subject didn't spring from the overconfidence of inexperienced ignorance.

Alicia's attention was on her HUD. Lieutenant Francesca Masolle's Second Platoon had been assigned responsibility for the northernmost, and smaller, of the two training camps, the one code-named Beech Tree One. Lieutenant Strassmann's First Platoon had primary responsibility for Beech Tree Two, the larger of the camps. Lieutenant Paál Ágoston's Third Platoon was supposed to drop between the two camps. Two of his three squads would serve as the company reserve, while the third would assist First Platoon in taking out Beech Tree Two.

Alicia's own squad had been tasked as an immediate tactical reserve, assigned to cover Gilroy's Second Squad as it advanced and to join hands with Third Platoon's reserve once Paál's people linked up with First Platoon. Originally, First and Second Squads' roles had been reversed, but the sudden arrival of a brand new squad leader had convinced Strassmann to flip their assignments. No doubt so that Master Sergeant Onassis could keep a closer eye on the fledgling, Alicia thought.

That was the plan, anyway, but it looked as if there were about to be a few glitches.

First Platoon had experienced a little scatter—even the best trained, most experienced people were almost certain to do that on a full-bore atmospheric-insertion drop—but each squad's pairs of wings had already found one another. Now, as she watched, her own squad's people were moving into their assigned positions in the ground-devouring, low-trajectory jumps their battle armor made possible. A part of Alicia was tempted to say something, if only to let them know the new kid was staying on top of things, but she knew better than that. And so, she kept her mouth shut, watching patiently while people who obviously knew what they were supposed to be doing did it. They were moving quickly and smoothly, even if the time-slowing effect of the tick stretched out the duration of each individual jump improbably.

But if First Platoon's people were getting themselves sorted out, Third Platoon wasn't. Its icons were about as scattered as First Platoon's had been, but they were moving towards a semblance of order much more slowly. Some of them, in fact, weren't moving at all, she noticed.

"Winchester-One, Rifle-Two," Onassis' voice sounded in her mastoid as she and Cateau moved forward behind the advancing skirmish line of her Alpha Team, and a green data code in her HUD indicated that he was speaking to her on a dedicated circuit.

"Rifle-Two, Winchester-One," she acknowledged.

"Lieutenant Masolle's people have made contact with Beech Tree One," Onassis told her. "Looks like she caught them with their pants down. Her point is already inside their outer perimeter. That's the good news. The bad news is that Lieutenant Paál's people came down in the middle of a frigging swamp."

Alicia felt her eyebrows rise. Murphy—and not a member of the imperial house—could be counted upon to put in an appearance on any operation. A swamp landing, even for drop commandos with Cadre armor, was guaranteed to screw up any tactical plan. Combat armor didn't exactly touch down lightly, and swamp mud made an efficient substitute for glue if you hit hard enough and drove deep enough. But how in heaven's name had the preattack intelligence managed to miss a little thing like a *swamp* smack in the middle of their planned axis of attack?

"It wasn't there the last time we looked," Onassis continued. "Remember that pond just downstream from Beech Tree One? Seems like the dam must have broken, or else they decided to drain the damned thing, and all that nice, flat dry ground north of *our* objective turns out to be a floodplain."

Alicia grimaced.

"Anyway," Onassis said, "that means Third Platoon's not going to be in position to back us up on Beech Tree Two for at least another twenty minutes, and we can't wait that long without letting the birds we want out of the net. So your assignment just changed. Instead of covering Gilroy's flank, you're going to have to sub for Paál's people and come in at Alpha-Five."

A bright icon danced in her HUD, indicating the point at which a dry stream bed—*and at least* it's *still dry*, she thought wryly—intersected the perimeter of the training facility codenamed Beech Tree Two.

"Now," Onassis went on, his voice deepening just a bit, "I'm going to be a bit busier than anyone counted on, given this little change in plans. In fact, I'm not going to be able to go in with you the way we'd planned. What I'm saying is that the squad is yours after all. Understood?"

"Understood," she said, and she was pleased at how level her voice sounded. And she also sounded just a little bit distracted, she felt pretty sure, because her mind was already busy, grappling with the suddenly altered situation with all of the tick's flashing speed.

"One last thing." Onassis' voice was a bit flatter. "Lieutenant Masolle has positively confirmed the presence of children and apparent noncombatants in Beech Tree One. Rules of engagement Delta are in effect as of now."

"I copy ROE Delta," Alicia confirmed in an equally flat voice.

"In that case, good hunting," Onassis said with what she privately suspected was a much more cheerful confidence than he actually felt. "Clear."

The icon which had indicated they were speaking privately disappeared, and Alicia's mental command shifted her com into the dedicated First Squad net.

"All Winchesters," she said, "Winchester-One. There's been a change of plans, people. Lieutenant Paál's people aren't going to make the opening on time, so we're going to have to do a little improvisation. Winchester-Alpha-Seven, hold where you are," she continued, studying the icons of her squad's personnel as they glowed on the detailed topographical projection.

Corporal Michael Doorn's icon stopped moving instantly, and the icon of his wingman, Corporal Édouard Bonrepaux, took only two more jumps before it, too, froze, perfectly positioned to cover Doorn's flank.

"All other Alphas will form on this line," Alicia went on, even as she changed her own course, with Cateau bounding along in perfect formation through the rugged terrain. She used her synth-link to draw a green line across the HUD's terrain map. "Alpha-Seven will anchor one end; Alpha-Three will anchor the other. Alpha-One, I want you in the center to coordinate Alpha's advance to contact."

"Winchester-One, Winchester-Alpha-One copies," Sergeant McGwire acknowledged. He and his wing, Corporal Byung Cha Chul, went bounding towards the indicated position. Winchester-Alpha-Three, Corporal Erik Andersson, didn't respond verbally, but his icon blinked in the two-two-one pattern which indicated that he understood, and he and Corporal Vartkes Kalachian, his wing, went slashing towards their own assigned positions.

"Winchester-Bravo-One," Alicia continued, turning her attention to Sergeant Abernathy's team. "We're not going to be able to leave a proper reserve—we *were* the Platoon's reserve—but I want you and your people in overwatch for the initial break-in. Put yourself and your heavy wing right here." She dropped another icon onto the tactical map, directly on top of a small hill just to the east of the point at which the stream bed crossed Beech Tree Two's perimeter. It was high enough to give Abernathy a clear direct line of sight along the streambed and well into the camp itself.

"Use your own judgment placing the rest of your wings," she told him. "I need you watching Alpha's back until they're in. Then I want you to come in along roughly this axis here."

She drew another line, this one with a bright arrowhead at one end. It crossed the perimeter east of the streambed and headed south, directly towards a block of barracks designated Rathole One on the map. Under the original ops plan, one of Lieutenant Paál's squads had been tasked to deal with Rathole One. Onassis hadn't specifically told her those barracks were now her responsibility, but he had told her she would be "subbing" for Paál's missing squad. Besides, the streambed at Alpha-Five was the closest entry point for any of First Platoon's units.

"Remember," she said, blessing the hours she'd spent studying the ops plan she'd never had the opportunity to rehearse with the people who had suddenly become hers, "Rathole One is where their permanent training cadre bunks and messes. If anybody's going to have her head out of her ass by the time we go in, it's going to be someone over there. So watch yourselves. And if we get too much fire out of Rathole, go to ground somewhere along here—" a bright amber line in the HUD circled a rocky ravine which ought to provide pretty fair cover against fire from the barracks "—and wait instead of wading straight in. I'll bring Alpha in to support you ASAP."

"Bravo-One copies, Winchester-One," Abernathy replied, and she was pleased by his tone. His voice was clipped, businesslike and focused, but she heard the confidence in it. Confidence in *her*, in the evidence that the newbie giving his people orders really had done her homework.

"All Winchesters," she said, hoping that she wasn't about to knock that confidence on its head, "there's one more thing. Tiger-One has confirmed the presence of children and noncombatants—repeat, children and noncombatants—in Beech Tree One. Rules of engagement Delta are in effect. Confirm copy."

There was an instant of silence, despite the tick, as her people adjusted to that unpleasant news. Then the cascade of confirming responses came back to her, and she nodded. None of them sounded particularly happy, but that was fair enough—*she* wasn't particularly happy about it herself.

"All right, Winchesters," she said after the final confirmation had come in, "let's get to it."

It took less than five minutes for First Squad to shift to its hastily redesignated jumpoff point. To Alicia, riding the tick, it seemed more like five *hours*, but she knew better, and she made herself stifle her impatience. That was one of the major drawbacks to the tick; things frequently seemed to be taking far too long, and one had to remind oneself that it didn't look that way to the rest of the universe.

"Rifle-Two, Winchester-One," she reported finally, "Winchester is in position at Alpha-Five."

"Winchester-One," Onassis came back almost instantly. "Copy. Hold position for Weatherby."

"Rifle-Two, Winchester-One copies, hold position until Weatherby is in place."

She settled back very slightly, allowing herself a modest gleam of satisfaction. First Squad had had farther to go than either of First Platoon's other squads, but it had gotten there before Staff Sergeant Gilroy's people had reached *their* new jumpoff point.

She spent the brief delay scrutinizing the objective.

Beech Tree Two was an untidy gaggle of structures clustered around an unkempt looking "parade ground." Most of them had been identified by function, with a fair degree of confidence, on her HUD. One or two were question marks, and one of those—designated B13 on the tac overlay—lay squarely in front of First Squad.

There was movement on the camp's grounds. It had been slow to start, she thought, given the fact that the attack on Beech Tree One, which had been supposed to go in simultaneously with the attack on Beech Tree Two, had actually gone in almost eight minutes ago. She hated the thought of giving the camp's inhabitants any addi‘nstional time to get themselves organized, start to cope with the paralyzing surprise of a totally unanticipated attack out of the darkness, but that wasn't up to her. Besides, Lieutenant Strassmann—or, more likely, Captain Alwyn—was probably right. Taking the time to get *themselves* properly reorganized after such a major change in plans was almost certainly worth more to Charlie

Company than a handful more of minutes could be to the people inside that camp.

"All Rifles," Lieutenant Strassmann's voice said suddenly, "Rifle-One. Go. I say again, go!"

"Winchester-Alpha-One, Winchester-One," Alicia said sharply. "Go!"

Corporal Vartkes Kalachian, call sign Winchester-Alpha-Five, was the first member of Alicia's squad to actually cross the wire around Beech Tree Two, and he did it with panache.

His armor's sensors had probed the ground between his jumpoff position and the camp's perimeter, and its sonar-imaging capability had picked up the "low signature" antipersonnel landmines which had been planted to protect the perimeter wire. It was unlikely that any less sophisticated sensors would have been able to "see" the mines, and Alicia had frowned as their icons had appeared on her HUD, cross-relayed from Kalachian's sonar. She'd wondered, as she passed the warning up the line to Onassis, where a bunch of terrorists had gotten their hands on them. The mines' composite cases contained no metallic alloys, and instead of the low-tech, chemical bursting charge she would have expected to find protecting a facility like this one, they used small, powerful, superconductor capacitor-fed gravitic fields. Which meant that there was nothing to alert chemical "sniffers" to the presence of their nonexistent explosive compounds.

Kalachian, however, knew exactly what was out there now, and he hit his jump gear hard. The sudden surge lifted him over the minefield and across the razor wire, and his armored body tucked and rolled neatly as he hit the ground inside the camp. Clearing the mines and the wire in a single jump had required a higher trajectory than The Book really liked. Had anyone been waiting for him at the moment that he topped out, he would have made an excellent target. But no one was waiting. Despite how long it had seemed take, to Alicia's tick-accelerated thoughts, for the platoon to get into position, and despite how the tick translated Kalachian's eighty kilometer-per-hour jump into floating slow motion, the denizens of Beech Tree Two were still trying to figure out what was happening when he touched down.

The rest of Alpha Team—with Alicia and Tannis Cateau attached—was on his heels. Alicia and Cateau were actually the last wing in. Alicia's job was to control and coordinate, to impose order, not to get bogged down in the fighting itself unless she absolutely had to. And Cateau's job was to keep any ill-intentioned individuals off Alicia's back while she went about managing the squad.

They might have gotten across the wire without taking any defensive fire, but that wasn't the same thing as crossing it without getting *any* response. Alicia's armor picked up the infrared sensors guarding the camp's wire as she broke one of the beams, and once again the sophistication of the defenses surprised her. The camp's powerful perimeter lights must have been directly coupled to the sensor net, because they switched on even as her people hit the ground.

The multimillion candlepower lights glared out of the darkness like suddenly ignited suns. There was no warning—only that instantaneous, stunning burst of brilliance, directly into any attackers' eyes, with what ought to have been equally instant, blinding disorientation. But Alicia's people were the Cadre. The enhancement of their vision let them *decrease* its sensitivity, as well as increase it, and they'd spent endless hours mastering their augmented capabilities. More than that, every one of them was riding the tick, and their vision compensated almost as quickly as the lights came on.

There was still a brief, fleeting instant before they adjusted, but that didn't matter, either. Every one of them was synth-link-capable, and every one of them was literally fused with his or her armor's systems. And those sensor systems didn't rely on anything as easily befuddled as the human optic nerve.

Alicia's rifle snapped into firing position. It wasn't like her Marine-issue M-97 had been. Instead, it was an integral part of her armor, mounted in a power-driven housing that brought its muzzle to bear on the nearest of the camp's spotlights with viperish speed. There was no trigger, no sights. A crosshair simply appeared, floating in her field of vision, and she moved it by *thinking* it into position. The "rifle" followed the crosshair, and her armor's onboard computers evaluated barrel temperature, air pressure and temperature, local gravity, windage, and the ballistic performance of the five-millimeter caseless ammunition in the tank behind her shoulders and automatically corrected the crosshair for exact point of impact at any effective range. It happened with blinding speed, and yet the crosshair seemed to float slowly, so slowly to someone riding the tick, towards her chosen target. But then it was where she wanted it, and another flickering thought squeezed the "trigger."

A crisp, precise three-round burst ripped from her rifle. The needle-slim, three-millimeter discarding sabot penetrators, formed of an artificial alloy considerably heavier and harder than tungsten, screamed across the sixty meters between her and her target at well over fifteen hundred meters per second. At that velocity they would have slammed through the breastplate of Marine powered armor like white-hot awls through butter. The unarmored spotlight offered exactly zero resistance to their passage, and its brilliance died in a spectacular flash.

Every single one of the other lights in their immediate front died within the space of less than two seconds as the even-numbered half of each wing of Cadremen opened fire with the same blinding speed and deadly accuracy. At least a dozen lights continued to blaze, but they were well beyond First Squad's flanks. The Alpha wings ignored them as the odd-numbered half of each pair continued forward, slicing straight towards their objectives.

Alicia's rifle muzzle snapped back up into "safe" position as Cateau loped past her. The corporal was no longer riding her jump gear; she wanted her feet firmly on the ground if she needed her own rifle.

"Alpha-Two, one o'clock!" Alicia snapped as six or seven figures suddenly appeared around the side of one of the barracks. She detected weapons on all of them, and they were headed directly towards Corporal Chul.

Chul didn't respond. She probably hadn't needed Alicia's warning, either, but that was all right with Alicia. She'd rather be considered a worrier than take any chances. Nor was Chul Byung Cha in any more mood to take chances. Her own rifle swept into firing position and spat perfectly-targeted death. Three of the camp's defenders were dead before the others even realized they were under fire. Two more died before Sergeant McGwire, Chul's wingman, could target them. The last pair died almost simultaneously, even as they tried desperately to fling themselves flat on the ground, as McGwire and Chul switched their attention to them.

"Winchester-One has Bravo-One-Three," she announced, changing course slightly to make for the building whose function the intelligence weenies had been unable to determine. That had been Chul's and McGwire's objective before they were delayed to deal with the counterattack, or whatever that had been. She probably should have left it to someone else, Alicia reflected, remembering her own earlier thoughts. But she and Cateau were closest to it, and she wanted the rest of the Alpha wings moving forward, not slowing down and diverting to clear a building whose purpose they didn't even know.

Cateau, she noticed, didn't say a word. Which wasn't necessarily the same thing as approving of her decision, of course.

There were more figures moving out there now, but it was obvious to Alicia that the camp's inhabitants still didn't realize what was happening. Those figures were moving *towards* her people, reacting defensively—possibly even instinctively, without conscious thought—and they wouldn't have been doing that if they'd realized they faced the Cadre. Heading *away* from the Cadre, as rapidly as possible, would have been a vastly more prudent response.

On the other hand, panicked people did stupid things—especially *inexperienced* panicked people.

"All Winchesters, remember the rules of engagement!" she said sharply. It was probably totally unnecessary, but it was also her responsibility, and she continued to move forward, heading for the building designated Bravo-One-Three.

She was only about thirty meters from it when the door slammed open and a figure stumbled out of it.

The crosshair reappeared in Alicia's HUD, floating slowly across it as her rifle flashed into firing position with blinding speed. It settled on the figure's chest, but she didn't fire. As she'd just reminded all of her people, ROE Delta was in effect, and she held her fire while her sensors probed the target.

Male, adult, height one hundred and seventy-one centimeters, they reported. No shirt, despite the cool night air. A red outline highlighted the short, broad bladed knife in the sheath on his right hip, but there was no sign of a rifle or pistol.

She swore silently to herself and let her rifle swing away from him. The odds were overwhelming, whether he carried a firearm or not, that he was one of the terrorists they'd come to kill or capture. But at this particular moment, he didn't have any weapon on his person which could threaten her or any of her people, and the rules of engagement were clear in that case.

But if she couldn't *kill* him, that didn't mean she necessarily had to be gentle. Nor was she about to take any chances that he might find himself a proper weapon after her back was turned.

"Mine!" she snapped over her dedicated link to Cateau, and charged him.

Her hapless target probably never saw her coming at all. The glare of the surviving perimeter lights and the blinding, stroboscopic eruptions of muzzle flashes—including the blind fire some of the camp's defenders were beginning to hose uselessly in every conceivable direction—had to be playing havoc with his vision. And despite how long it seemed to *Alicia* that the attack had been underway, little more than fifteen seconds had actually elapsed since Lieutenant Strassmann's order to move in. His confusion must have been as close to total as it was possible to come, and the chameleon surface of Alicia's armor would have made her all but invisible even without the blinding effect of so much gunfire.

She swept into arm's reach of him, moving with a dancer's grace, despite her armor, as she rode the tick, and her left hand reached out. She caught him by one arm, carefully moderating the strength of her powered gauntlet so that she didn't break anything, and heard his brief, beginning cry of shock and pain as she snatched him towards her. But he hadn't completed that cry when her right hand floated slowly forward, moving with all of the flashing, meticulously metered precision of the tick, and struck the side of his skull.

He went down, instantly unconscious, and she stopped, her rifle darting back down into firing position to cover the windows on either side of the doorway from which he'd emerged as Cateau swept past her.

The corporal didn't even slow down. The door had swung shut behind the man Alicia had neutralized, and Cateau simply dropped her left shoulder slightly and bulldozed straight into it. It was a relatively sturdy, well-constructed door, but it had never been intended to stand up to someone in battle armor. She went through it in a shower of splinters, and Alicia's HUD was abruptly speckled with the icons of three more human beings as Cateau's armor's sensors relayed to her. Nor was there any question about whether or not *these* human beings were armed. All three of them carried rifles, hastily snatched from a weapons rack on the wall opposite the door, and that was fatally unfortunate for them.

Cateau killed all three of them, probably before any of them even realized she was there.

The corporal kept moving, deep into the structure's interior. The building was constructed around one very large ground-floor room which clearly functioned as a combination commons room and mess hall. It was two stories tall, however, and Cateau's sensors probed at the ceiling above her.

"Clear," she announced a moment later.

"Copy clear," Alicia confirmed, and the two of them moved on, leaving three more corpses and one unreasonably lucky, still-breathing body behind them.

Alicia's mental command flared her icon on Cateau's HUD, warning her wing that she was stopping. The corporal reacted instantly, dropping into a guard position, as Alicia paused to assess the situation.

Her entire Alpha Team was deep into the camp now, and a couple of Beech Tree Two's buildings were in flames. The fires were just beginning to take hold, and she wondered whether the camp's inhabitants had torched them, or if the Cadre's fire had found something flammable inside them. Not that it mattered much, either way. The attack was barely four minutes old, and its inevitable outcome was already apparent to her.

Sergeant Abernathy's Bravo Team was closing in on Rathole One from the east, but by this time, the barracks block's tenants had at least figured out that they were under attack. It was also obvious that they had quite a fair amount of heavy-caliber firepower at their disposal. Combat rifles were crackling, firing at half-imagined targets, and her sensors picked up the snarling thunder of multibarreled calliopes, spitting high-velocity penetrators in bursts of blind, suppressive fire.

Those calliopes worried her. The weapons were the latest evolution of the ancient Gatling gun principle, although they were considerably more lethal than any of their direct ancestors. They burned through ammunition voraciously, but they also produced an unbroken stream of penetrators that didn't have to be aimed at someone to kill her instantly if they hit her anyway. And while Rathole One's defenders were obviously firing blind, they were pouring a lot of rounds in Abernathy's direction as he and his squad approached the ravine she'd indicated to him earlier.

"Winchester-Bravo-One, Winchester-One," she said. "Find yourselves some cover and hold position. There's too much fire coming your way."

"Winchester-One, Bravo-One, that sounds like a winner to me, Sarge!" Abernathy replied with feeling, and Alicia chuckled harshly.

"Alpha-Seven, Winchester-One. I need you over here."

"Alpha-Seven is on the way, Winchester-One," Corporal Doorn replied, and moments later, he and Édouard Bonrepaux appeared at Alicia's shoulder.

The two of them were the single "heavy" wing assigned to Alpha Team with Charlie Company in "light" configuration. Doorn carried a plasma rifle; Bonrepaux carried a fifty-millimeter grenade launcher with a five-round magazine. Both weapons were much heavier than anything which could have been carried without the artificial muscle power of battle armor, and Alicia smiled grimly as she saw them.

"Bravo-One, Winchester-One," she said over the squad net, "I've got some people with some serious firepower over here. I think it's time that we discouraged the rats in the woodwork, don't you?"

"I never much cared for rodents, Winchester-One," Abernathy replied.

"All right, then. I want Bravo-Seven and Bravo-Eight—" that was Corporal Obaseki Osayaba and Corporal Shai Hau-zhi, Bravo Team's equivalent of Doorn and Bonrepaux "—to take out this building here."

She dropped a mental command into Abernathy's HUD, highlighting one of the barracks buildings. A calliope was firing long, sweeping bursts from a second-floor window on its eastern side.

"When they do that, Alpha's heavies will take out *these* two buildings," she continued, highlighting two more structures. Another calliope was firing from one of them; the other was clearly the administrative center of Rathole One, and there were a lot of armed individuals in and around it.

"All Winchesters," she went on, bringing the rest of her squad in on the conversation, "we're going to take down these three buildings with plasguns and grenades. It's going to be messy. As soon as they're down, we close in and clear the remaining buildings. These people are going to duck and cover when the shit hits the fan, and I want us right behind the explosions. I want us in among them before they have time to recover."

She paused to let them digest that much, then began assigning specific objectives to each of her wings. She marked each wing's target meticulously on their HUDs, making certain there was no confusion. The Bad Guys hadn't managed to kill any of her people yet, and she was determined not to produce any friendly-fire casualties.

Despite the care she took, it required only a very few seconds for people riding the tick to complete their preparations. She took one last look at her own HUD, then glanced at Cateau, who had closed up at her shoulder once more.

"Ready?" she asked over their dedicated circuit.

"Sure, why not?" Cateau replied in an almost drawling voice. "I mean, it's been such a fun party this far, hasn't it?"

"You're a strange person," Alicia observed with a grim chuckle. "However—"

She shrugged, then switched back to the squad master com net.

"All Winchesters," she said, her voice calm, "Winchester-One. All right, people. Let's dance. Go."

CHAPTER NINETEEN

"Excuse me, Sergeant DeVries," the AI's voice said politely in Alicia's mastoid.

"Yes, Central?" she replied. The base's master AI rejoiced in the nickname of "Gertrude," according to its cyber-synth partner. Alicia, however, had never felt comfortable enough with it to indulge in informality.

"You're wanted at Base Ops. Captain Alwyn has scheduled an emergency briefing in Sit One in fifteen minutes."

Both of Alicia's eyebrows rose in surprise. An emergency briefing?

She looked across the holographic tactical display hovering between her and Alan McGwire, Lawrence Abernathy, and Tannis Cateau.

"It seems our little planning session has just been derailed, people," she observed.

"That's not exactly going to break the troops' hearts, Sarge," Cateau observed with a smile. It was a genuine smile, but after eighteen standard months, Alicia had come to know her wing about as well as she'd ever known another human being. She saw the questions, echoes of her own, behind Tannis' brown eyes.

"I don't know about that," McGwire said. "My people were looking forward to getting a little of their own back from Larry's."

"In your dreams," Abernathy said complacently.

"Pride goeth," Alicia observed dryly. Although, she admitted, Abernathy did have at least a little bit of a point. Bravo Team had bested Alpha Team in the last three exercises in a row. Not by very much, in two of them, but still . . .

"Alan, I want you and Larry to go on working up the basic parameters of the exercise," she said after a moment. "I'm going to operate on the assumption that we may get a chance to go ahead and mount it. In the meantime, I need to get over for that briefing. Tannis, why don't you come along?"

"I wasn't invited, Sarge," Tannis pointed out mildly.

"Maybe not." Alicia cleared her throat. "Central."

"Yes, Sergeant DeVries?"

"Please ask First Sergeant Yussuf if it would be acceptable for Corporal Cateau to attend the briefing."

"Of course, Sergeant DeVries," the AI replied. A handful of seconds passed, then it spoke again. "First Sergeant Yussuf says that Corporal Cateau may accompany you."

"Thank you, Central." Alicia looked at her subordinates again, then twitched her head at the door.

"I think we'd best be going," she said mildly.

Alicia found her mind sliding back over the last year and a half as she and Tannis walked briskly across to the main admin building. Those eighteen months had been both similar to her experience in the Marines and totally different from it. For one thing, the training tempo had been much higher, although when she'd been a Wasp herself, she wouldn't have believed that was possible. But the Cadre trained *constantly.* If they weren't out on active operations, then they were training. Or actively planning the next training exercise. Or evaluating the training exercise they'd just completed.

And the Cadre subscribed to the theory that the best preparation for combat was to train harder than any actual combat mission would ever require. The Cadre training regimen routinely pushed the Cadre's men and women to the point of collapse, and those men and women didn't collapse all that easily.

That was one difference. Another was that the Cadre actively promoted long-term, stable relationships. Alicia had been promoted to sergeant first class three standard months ago, but she still had First Squad, and she still had Tannis. Nor was that unusual for the Cadre. It wasn't unheard of for a Cadreman to spend his entire Cadre career serving in the same regiment of the same brigade, and the Cadre made a concerted effort to keep wings which had proven themselves compatible together on a permanent basis.

Alicia wasn't about to complain about that. The Cadre's tactical and operational doctrines were even more different from the Marines' than she'd originally realized. Cadremen were specialists in every sense of the word, and one of the things which made them so effective in the field was the absolute familiarity which existed between each pair of wingmen. They trained together, they fought together, they usually partied together, and it wasn't at all uncommon for them to go on leave together.

And sometimes, of course, they *died* together.

In the last year and a half, she and Tannis had become exactly the sort of team the Cadre sought to build. They operated on the same mental wavelength, almost as if they were telepathic. Each of them *knew* precisely what the other would do in a given situation, and each of them understood exactly what her function was in any given tactical confrontation.

And, Alicia thought, smiling slightly as she glanced across at Tannis' profile, neither one of them had ever had a closer friend—or sibling—in her entire life.

But it was the nature of the wing relationship which the Cadre took such pains to nourish which had inspired her to bring Tannis along. The wing assigned to any squad leader, platoon sergeant, or company first sergeant was in a special position. She wasn't assigned to a regular slot in a squad's fire teams. Instead, she went wherever her wing partner went, and the fact that her wing was likely to be distracted by the need to concentrate on managing a tactical situation meant she had to be even better than the Cadre's norm. There were times—too many of them, Alicia thought—when Tannis had to carry far more than her fair share of the load because Alicia simply had to be doing other things, and that wasn't helped by the fact that Tannis was also First Platoon's senior medic. If Tannis felt overworked, she'd never indicated it, but she wouldn't have.

In effect, though, Tannis sometimes found herself operating almost in the role of assistant squad leader, and it made a lot of sense for her to be fully briefed in for any op. That was the way Alicia felt about it, at any rate, and from First Sergeant Yussuf's response, it sounded as if she felt that way, too.

They reached the main admin building, crossed the small lobby area, followed a short corridor past a half-dozen office doors, then turned right into Situation Room One.

The big room—the second largest on the entire base—was subdivided by head-high internal partitions, dimly lit, and kept just a bit cooler than was actually comfortable. The subdued lighting made the various displays sharper and easier to follow, and the cooler temperature helped keep people alert.

Situation Room One—Sit One, for short—was in many ways the nerve center of Base Operations. It was one door down the hall from Ops One, from which Captain Alwyn ran the company on a day-to-day basis, and it was responsible for collating incoming information, processing it and translating it into operational intelligence. Sit One maintained the threat maps for the company's area of responsibility, and Sit One was where most of the company's initial operational briefings took place.

"Come in, Alley, Tannis. Find seats," Lieutenant Paál said. Alicia wasn't surprised to see the lieutenant as she and Tannis stepped into the largest of Sit One's office cubicles. In addition to his role as commanding officer of Third Platoon, Paál, as the senior of Charlie Company's lieutenants, was also Captain Alwyn's executive officer. He got to wear the S-1 "hat" as the company's adjutant, in charge of personnel and administration, as well. What she was surprised by was the fact that Captain Alwyn himself *wasn't* present yet.

She settled into her usual seat with Gilroy, Hillman, and Onassis. Gilroy and Hillman had both brought along their wings, as well, and Tannis smiled and nodded to them as she joined them.

"Any idea what this is all about, Adolfo?" Alicia whispered, leaning towards the platoon sergeant.

"Not a clue," he murmured back. "But I did hear—"

He broke off as the door opened again, this time to admit Captain Alwyn and two other officers.

Alicia recognized both of them immediately, and astonishment stabbed through her as one of those faces registered.

The presence of Captain Wadislaw Watts, Imperial Marine Intelligence, was no particular surprise. He was on semipermanent assignment to the Cadre, attached to Fifth Brigade as a "loaner" to fill one of the chronically shorthanded Cadre's necessary staff billets. The Cadre had its own intelligence specialists, but it didn't have enough of them—just as it didn't have enough of most of the staff specialists it really needed. So it made do by borrowing the necessary staff expertise from the Marines or Fleet. Brigade had passed Watts on to Second Regiment, which in turn had assigned him to Third Battalion, Charlie Company's parent battalion. And Third Battalion used him as its roving Intelligence guru on an operation-by-operations basis.

Personally, Alicia didn't much care for him. She couldn't really have said why. Certainly it wasn't because she regarded the Marines as interlopers, since she—like over ninety percent of the Cadre's personnel—had once been a Marine herself, after all. Perhaps it was because she sometimes suspected that somewhere deep down inside, the dark-haired, dark-eyed, always impeccably groomed Marine resented the fact that he was not and never would be acceptable as a Cadreman himself, if only because he wasn't synth-link-capable. Or maybe it was just bad chemistry.

But whether she liked Watts or not, he'd always seemed more than competent where his duties were concerned. He'd handled the battalion intelligence brief on all but one of the five operations, including the highly successful Chengchou raid, the company had carried out since Alicia joined it. If there was something in the air, he was a logical choice to brief them in on it.

But it was the presence of the other officer who accompanied Captain Alwyn which took her completely by surprise her. Nor was she the only person in Sit One who felt that way.

"Attention!" Lieutenant Paál barked after an instant of astonishment, and Alicia felt herself snapping to her feet and to attention even before she heard the order.

Sir Arthur Keita, Knight Grand Commander of the Order of Terra, Solarian Grand Cross, Senate Medal of Valor with diamonds and clasp, Silver Star with cluster, Wound Medal with multiple clusters, and second in command of the Personal Cadre of His Imperial Majesty Seamus II, had that effect on people.

"As you were," the man known as "the Emperor's Bulldog," growled in a gravelly bass. He was silver-haired, built something along the lines of a brick wall, and somewhere close to a hundred standard years old. Not that age had withered his physique or dimmed the quick alertness of the dark eyes under his craggy brows. Like Alicia, he wore the Cadre's green-on-green and harp and starships; unlike her, he also wore the single starburst of a brigadier.

She settled back into her seat gingerly, her mind racing, as Keita stalked to the chair at the head of the conference table below the main holo display unit. Captain Alwyn waited until the brigadier had been seated, then sat in his own chair, to Keita's right, while Watts continued to the briefing officer's station. The Marine laid what looked like a sheaf of old-fashioned, handwritten notes on the lectern, then picked up the neural headset and slipped it on.

"All right, people," Alwyn said, while Watts was making his preparations. "I'm sure all of you are as surprised to see Uncle Arthur—excuse me, Brigadier Keita—" he corrected himself, winning a slight chuckle from his audience in response "—as I was when he and Captain Watts arrived from Battalion."

He paused, and any levity which might have touched his expression, had vanished.

"Sir Arthur is about to explain why he's here," the company commander continued in a much more serious tone. "Then he and Captain Watts are going to explain what we're going to do about it." He swept his subordinates with his eyes, then turned courteously to Keita.

"Uncle Arthur?" he invited.

"Thank you, Madison," Keita rumbled in his deep, thick-chested voice, and Alicia felt herself leaning towards him. Calling Alwyn by his given name wasn't the sort of affectation it might have been in another officer of Keita's seniority—assuming that there'd *been* another Cadre officer of his seniority, that was.

General Arbatov might be the Cadre's official commanding officer, but Sir Arthur Keita *was* the Cadre. He'd joined it over seventy years before, and he was well past the mandatory retirement age. An astonishing number of the Cadre's field grade officers had served under him at one time or another, and he'd displayed an uncanny talent for nurturing and training outstanding unit COs.

Not only that, but it was common knowledge that he'd refused promotion above his present rank not just once, but several times. And he'd gotten away with that because he was, quite simply, the one man in the entire galaxy Seamus II and, before him, Empress Maire, had absolutely and completely trusted. He was both the

Cadre's field commander and its top intelligence officer, and he would be that until the day he died or *he* chose to give it up.

People like Alwyn called him "Uncle Arthur" for a reason, and he enjoyed the same fierce loyalty from the men and women under his command as he himself gave to his Emperor.

"As I'm sure all of you have already figured out," he continued now, "we have what we refer to as a 'situation.'" He smiled thinly. "In this instance, it has the potential to be particularly ugly, and I'm afraid it's going to fall squarely into Charlie Company's hands. I was on my way to Tamerlane, with a stopover on Gyangtse, when the balloon went up. Given the nature of the problem, Old Earth starcommed orders for me to drop everything else and personally attend to our little problem."

He paused, as if to give all of them a moment to absorb that much. Then he folded his hands on the conference table in front of him and leaned slightly forward over them.

"Five weeks ago, HMS *Star Roamer*, a transport chartered by the Ministry of Out-Worlds, departed the Raintree System for Old Earth. As some of you may be aware, if you've been following the news over the last several months, Raintree's voters have just approved the system's Incorporation referendum. *Star Roamer* was assigned to transport Raintree's official Incorporation delegation to Old Earth to lay the results of the referendum before the Senate and formally request Incorporation from His Majesty.

"Unfortunately, there was a slight hitch. While *Star Roamer* was in the process of accelerating towards supralight, she was hijacked."

Alicia felt herself twitch in her chair. Every so often, someone managed to hijack a merchant ship. In fact, one of the more successful pirate tactics was to put a clutch of hijackers aboard a ship under the guise of legitimate passengers. But despite a handful of attempts over the centuries, no one had ever managed to hijack a personnel transport with such a high-profile official passenger list.

"I'm sure there's going to be an exhaustive inquiry into exactly how the hijackers managed to get aboard in the first place," Keita said flatly. "All we know so far is that they managed it somehow. The ship diverted from its planned flight profile just before it wormholed out of Raintree, so the local authorities knew something was up and suspected what it might be. They immediately contacted Old Earth, and that was the point at which General

Arbatov starcommed my new instructions to Gyangtse to await my arrival. At the time, that was *all* anyone knew, however, and it stayed that way until *Star Roamer* turned up in the Fuller System two weeks ago."

Well, Alicia thought, *that explains why he's talking to* us *about it.*

Fuller was less than a week and a half's supralight flight from Guadalupe, squarely in Charlie Company's area of responsibility. The Cadre's small size—there were only ten Cadre brigades in the entire Empire—meant that the largest tactical unit it normally fielded was a company. Third Battalion was Charlie Company's "parent" primarily for administrative and support purposes, but the battalion's three companies were deployed into three entirely different star systems, each strategically located to cover as many potential trouble spots as possible. The Marines would no doubt have used entire battalions, as they had on Gyangtse, but the Cadre had embraced a slight paraphrase of an ancient pre-space law-enforcement organization. Its philosophy was "One crisis, one company." Alicia could have counted the number of times that the Cadre, during its entire existence, had found it necessary to deploy entire battalions on her fingers and toes . . . without taking off both boots.

"Excuse me, Uncle Arthur," Lieutenant Masolle said, "but why in the world would somebody hijack an Out-World transport and then go to someplace like *Fuller* with it?"

"I'll let Captain Watts explain what we think is going on in a moment, Lieutenant," Keita said. "Let me just finish setting the general framework first."

"Of course, Sir." Masolle sat back, but her brow was furrowed with what were almost certainly the same questions flowing through Alicia's mind.

"The short version is that the hijackers, when they arrived in Fuller, identified themselves as members of the Freedom Alliance and announced that they intend to hold the Raintree delegation, and *Star Roamer*'s ship's company, as hostages until 'our legitimate demands for the freedom and liberation of our brothers and sisters in bondage are met by the imperialistic warmongers and oppressors of the so-called Terran Empire.'"

Keita's voice was totally expressionless for his last sentence, but Alicia's heart sank. Like all of Charlie Company's personnel, she was familiar with the intelligence briefings on the Freedom Alliance.

Philosophically and conceptually, the umbrella organization for at least a half-dozen so-called planetary liberation organizations had a lot in common with the hapless wannabe terrorists the company had picked off in the Chengchou raid. Indeed, post-strike intel had pretty throughly confirmed that some of the Chengchou training cadre had, indeed, been FALA.

Whether that was actually true or not, the Alliance was probably the most proficient—and dangerous—batch of terrorists currently operating against the Empire. Although imperial Intelligence had penetrated one or two of the Freedom Alliance's member organizations, the parent organization was a much tougher proposition. Its members were tightly disciplined and obviously security conscious, and they were also fiendishly well-financed. All indications were that most of its financial support came from a well organized fund-raising net operating on at least a couple of dozen independent Rogue Worlds, and it also clearly had well developed contacts with various gunrunners and shady arms dealers, because its "Freedom Alliance Liberation Army" was much better armed than most of the "liberation" organizations.

Worse, the Freedom Alliance had demonstrated its willingness to shed blood—*lots* of blood, including that of its own people—in pursuit of its goals, despite the fact that anyone with a functional brain had to realize its fundamental objectives were ultimately unobtainable.

"As for what they're doing in Fuller, Francesca," Keita continued, "that's unfortunately clear. As you know, Fuller is not an imperial star system and it is a member of the Langford Association. The Association isn't exactly on the best of terms with the Empire, but our relations with its member worlds are still a lot better than our relations with many of the Rogue Worlds out this way. Apparently, the Freedom Alliance would like to see those relations take a turn for the worse, and it also seems likely they calculated that we'd be less likely to launch some sort of military operation on the soil of one of the Association's member planets.

"At any rate, they demanded sanctuary on Fuller while they 'negotiated' with the Empire. Needless to say, the Fuller planetary government is well aware of the Empire's standing policy where negotiations with terrorist organizations are concerned. King Hayden told them that it was out of the question, and his Parliament backed him up.

"At that point, the hijackers murdered *Star Roamer*'s captain, first officer, and purser and jettisoned their bodies. Then they repeated their demands. King Hayden refused a second time. So they murdered the ship's astrogator, three of its enlisted crew members, a member of the ministry clerical pool, and the personal secretary of one of the Incorporation delegation's members. They pointed out that that was twice the number of hostages they'd 'executed in the people's name' the first time their demands were rejected, and informed King Hayden that the next time around, they would double the 'penalty' yet again.

"According to the passenger manifest Raintree starcommed to us, there are at least six hundred more civilians, including the remaining members of *Star Roamer*'s crew, aboard the ship. They'd already killed nine people that we know of—there may have been other fatalities when they actually seized the ship—and King Hayden and his government had every reason to believe they would carry out their threat, even if it meant eventually killing *all* of their hostages.

"Despite that, the King and Parliament were prepared to reject their demands yet again when the Duke of Shallingsport unilaterally offered to allow the terrorists to land the hostages in his duchy."

"In defiance of his own planetary government, Sir?" Lieutenant Paál asked in obvious surprise.

"Not . . . quite," Keita said. "Shallingsport is an independent duchy. I don't have all of the details and nuances of the Fuller political system at my fingertips, but as I currently understand it, Shallingsport is the largest, wealthiest, and most populous of several relatively small territorial units on Fuller which are at least nominally politically independent. The Duke of Shallingsport owes some sort of personal fealty to King Hayden, but not as the King of Fuller. Whatever the exact political relationship, the Duke—Duke Geoffrey—is a head of state in his own right, not legally bound by the decisions of Parliament. And in his role as head of state, he apparently decided that the only way to keep the terrorists from executing all of their hostages was to give them what they wanted.

"At the same time, he's obviously well aware of the Empire's policy where terrorists and planets which offer them sanctuary are concerned. Although he's permitted the hijackers to land themselves and their captives in his duchy and to take over a warehouse complex belonging to an off-world consortium as their local base of operations, he hasn't given them any formal promises of protection. So what he's done, according to the back channel messages he's passed to us, is to put the terrorists and the hostages into a contained situation. Since they've gotten the 'sanctuary' they demanded, they aren't going to take themselves, their hostages, and *Star Roamer* somewhere else. Which means they're going to be sitting exactly where they landed if—when—we come calling. In the meantime, he's informed them that while he's willing to give them sanctuary in order to prevent the loss of additional lives, he has no authority to negotiate on behalf of the Fuller planetary government, or of the Empire. He has, however, officially—and very publicly—requested that the Empire dispatch a negotiating team to Shallingsport. What he's telling us is that he's prepared to delay them, play for time, until we decide exactly what we're going to do."

He paused again, looking around the conference table, then shrugged the massive shoulders which had borne up under the weight of duty for so many decades.

"So that's why I'm here, people. We've decided what we're going to do . . . and you're the people who are going to do it."

CHAPTER TWENTY

"Sir Arthur, Captain Alwyn, people." Captain Wadislaw Watts nodded to his audience as Brigadier Keita handed the briefing over to him. The Marine's expression was that of a competent professional who was fully aware of the gravity of the situation facing them, and he reached out through his neural headset to dim the cubicle's lighting still further.

The holo display above the conference table simultaneously came to life, showing the blue-and-white-swirled marble of a habitable world. As the image grew in the display, Alicia saw that it had a bit more water and slightly smaller ice caps than Old Earth. The nightside also showed far sparser concentrations of artificial light, indicating either an extremely low tech base or a smallish, widely dispersed planetary population.

"The planet of Fuller, in the star system of the same name," Watts said out of the semidarkness. "The dominant political unit is the Kingdom of Fuller, which claims sovereignty over approximately seventy-three percent of the total planetary surface, and about ninety-two percent of the total planetary population. The kingdom is an odd hybrid, an absolute monarchy in the course of transition into a constitutional monarchy. The head of state, who's also the official head of government under the current political setup, is King Hayden the Fourth. He was educated in the Empire, and unlike most of the other planetary heads of state in the Langford Association, he's always been favorably inclined—for a Rogue World potentate, at least—towards the Empire. The fact that he's always been a voice of moderation in terms of the Association's relations with us may be one of the reasons the terrorists picked his planet. They probably figured that whatever decision he made was going to place a significant strain on his relations with us . . . or with his fellow Association heads of state.

"This," he continued, as the planet disappeared, replaced by a far larger scale map of a portion of its surface, "is the Duchy of Shallingsport." A bright amber line traced what were obviously the borders of an irregularly shaped territorial unit on a broad tongue of tangled, heavily forested mountains thrusting out into an ocean. "As you can see, Shallingsport claims virtually all of this peninsula extending into the Tannenbaum Sea. It takes its name from its capital and single major city, here." An icon flashed, indicating the coastal location of the city in question.

"The city of Shallingsport is also the site of the duchy's spaceport, which also doubles as its primary hub for purely atmospheric travel, as well. In the last couple of decades, the present duke—Duke Geoffrey—and his father have begun attracting some significant industry to Shallingsport. Most of that is also located around the capital, although there's also an industrial preserve here, in the Barony of Green Haven, which is called—not very imaginatively—the Green Haven Industrial Park."

Another icon blinked, this one at least two hundred kilometers from the duchy's capital.

"In fact, Duke Geoffrey's been doing his best to get as much as possible of the Shallingsport industry relocated to Green Haven in order to reduce congestion in the capital. He's been offering some very attractive financial incentives and tax breaks to get people to relocate, and to put new industry into the Green Haven area as it arrives from off planet. In addition, he's established a freight-handling spaceport facility with King Hayden's approval. Because of the way the planetary government is set up, the Green Haven port is going to cost Geoffrey a pretty credit in import duties once it goes officially on-line, which it's supposed to do sometime in the next local month or so. But Hayden's been looking the other way and letting it handle cargos 'unofficially' for the better part of a year, without imposing the legally mandated import duties, in order to help facilitate development in the area.

"I'm sure," Alicia's augmented vision easily saw Watts' tight grin, despite the lighting (or lack thereof), "that you're wondering just why I'm giving you all this information about industrial development in Shallingsport. Well, there's a reason.

"After Duke Geoffrey agreed to grant the terrorists holding *Star Roamer* 'sanctuary,' there was a fair amount of negotiation between him and the terrorists concerning the best location. The terrorists wanted to be as secure against potential ground attack as they could be, and Duke Geoffrey wanted them as far from his capital as he could get them, in case there *was* a ground attack and it got out of hand. The compromise solution, which was proposed by the terrorists, was that they take over the Green Haven Industrial Park. Duke Geoffrey pointed out that the entire industrial park would be rather large for their needs, and they responded by suggesting that they take over a single facility. They insisted, however, that the facility in question had to be large enough to permit them to keep themselves and all of their hostages under cover and to make aerial and orbital reconnaissance difficult.

"After quite a bit of hemming and hawing, the terrorists finally suggested that they take over the Shallingsport facilities of something called the Jason Corporation. It's a sort of wildcat operation headquartered on Trilateral, another of the Langford Association's members. It's also one of the newer arrivals in Shallingsport—a specialist in heavy construction which intends to play a major role in Geoffrey's Green Haven project. Because it's so new, its facility—which is a very large structure, in order to incorporate the necessary maintenance and service facilities for its heavy equipment—wasn't yet fully occupied. The relatively low number of staff Jason had on-planet could be evacuated fairly easily, the facility itself is well outside the area of Green Haven's main existing development, and the existence of the freight spaceport simplified the transfer of the terrorists and hostages from *Star Roamer* to the planetary surface.

"Which means that this facility here," the map of the Shallingsport peninsula vanished, replaced by a detailed aerial shot of a group of two smaller structures clustered tightly against the northern and southern ends of a single, much large building, "is going to be your objective."

Alicia frowned. Not only were the buildings themselves—actually, the *single* building, effectively, given the architecture—large enough to allow the terrorists a lot of flexibility in how they positioned their sentries, but the entire facility was set atop a fairly steep-sided hill that rose out of the peninsula's otherwise dense, green forest on the very fringe of Duke Geoffrey's "industrial park." The bad guys were going to have a commanding lookout post, and the building was, indeed, big enough, and solidly enough constructed, to severely limit what overhead passive reconnaissance could pick up.

"Now," Watts continued, "here's what we know about the opposition force.

"First, as Sir Arthur has already said, we *don't* know how they got aboard *Star Roamer* in the first place. We also don't have any positive IDs on any of the people involved in the hijacking. They've identified themselves as members of the Freedom Alliance Liberation Army, and the Freedom Alliance issued an official communique claiming responsibility for the operation before news of the hijacking became public. On that basis, it seems likely we are, indeed, dealing with the FALA. We just don't know who the individuals involved are. We believe our background efforts to penetrate the Alliance have positively identified a couple of dozen leadership figures, but so far we haven't placed any of them aboard *Star Roamer.* Frankly, they're being very careful in their contacts with the Fuller authorities and with Duke Geoffrey to prevent us from IDing any of them, as well.

"We also don't know exactly what weapons they may have. We do know that their transit time from Raintree to Fuller indicates they made a least-time flight. They simply didn't have time to divert anywhere else along the way to collect heavier weapons, and there's no indication that they did so once they arrived in the Fuller System, either. So, whatever weapons they have, have to be the ones they managed to get aboard *Star Roamer* in the first place, which strongly suggests that they can't have anything nastier than some fairly light small arms. In addition, they used only locally provided personnel shuttles, not cargo shuttles, when they actually landed on Fuller. That's a further indication that they don't have any significant number of heavy weapons with them.

"We also know, from the *number* of shuttle flights required to get their ground party down from *Star Roamer*, that assuming they moved all of the hostages dirt-side in the same flights, there can't be more than somewhere between a hundred and fifty and two hundred terrorists. All the indications so far are that even those numbers are probably too high. Obviously, there's no way to be certain, but Battalion's best estimate is that there probably aren't more than seventy-five actual bad guys, maximum."

"Excuse me, Wadislaw," Paál Ágoston said, "but how, exactly, did Battalion arrive at that estimate?"

"Mainly by considering the fact that whoever these people are, they had to get aboard *Star Roamer*. There were some passengers aboard who weren't part of the official Incorporation delegation. There weren't that many of them, though, and even though *Star Roamer* is a passenger ship, with the higher number of service personnel aboard that implies, the crew wasn't exactly enormous, either. So they didn't have that many seats or slots into which they could insert their hijackers. They wouldn't have *needed* much more than a couple of dozen to actually seize the ship, assuming they managed to take the crew by surprise, which they obviously did. That sets the lower limit on their possible manpower. The upper limit is set by the sheer difficulty of getting really large numbers of people aboard the ship without setting off security alarms. So the consensus at Battalion is that even seventy-five is probably high. The current belief is that they probably set some of those landing shuttles down empty, or all but empty, for the express purpose of keeping us guessing about their actual strength. Despite that, all of our thinking so far has been built around the maximum possible strength—the two hundred number I mentioned earlier—just to be on the safe side."

Paál nodded thoughtfully and sat back in his chair again.

"All right," Watts said, "that's their estimated ground strength. In addition, they still have at least a few people aboard *Star Roamer*. They've positioned the ship to keep an eye on the planet in general, and on Shallingsport in particular, and we believe that they've deployed at least two, more probably three, remote sensor arrays."

"Sensor arrays?" This time the question came from Tobias Strassmann. "Where the hell did these people get their hands on *sensor arrays*?"

"It's been apparent for some time, Lieutenant," Watts replied, "that the Freedom Alliance's resources and capabilities have been steadily expanding. I know your routine intelligence digests from Battalion have pointed out that the Alliance's fundraising net is apparently doing box office business. We've also seen increasingly sophisticated equipment in other FALA operations, including quite a few of the heavy weapons they thankfully don't have here. It's obvious that they've made a very useful contact somewhere in the mil-tech black market, and the arrays they've deployed probably came from there."

"And they got these things aboard a *passenger ship* somehow?"

"Apparently," Watts acknowledged. "And, no, we don't know how they did it. In that respect, I'd have to say that as much as I loathe and despise the 'Freedom Alliance' and its tactics, they've demonstrated a capacity for planning and executing imaginative operations in the past. The fact that they managed to get hijackers aboard *Star Roamer* is another indication that however lunatic their ultimate objectives may be, they're obviously capable of rational, effective planning for their actual operations."

"But still," Strassmann said, shaking his head. "Something about this doesn't quite add up for me. It might have been possible to smuggle small arms aboard in personal luggage containers, but a deep-space sensor array is a hell of a lot bigger and harder to conceal than that."

"There are some indications," Watts said reluctantly, "or, perhaps, I should say there's been some *speculation*, that this was an inside job. Well, obviously, that's a probability in any hijack scenario. In this instance, however, there's been a specific suggestion that the purser may have been in on it."

"Didn't you say that they'd killed the purser when their original demand for sanctuary was rejected by the planetary government?"

"Yes, I did, Lieutenant Strassmann. The bodies were recovered, however. And while all of the others had been shot in the head with a neural disrupter, the purser's throat had been cut. In addition, there's the distinct possibility that he was actually killed somewhat earlier than the other victims. So the competing theories supporting his possible complicity are that he was killed by the hijackers because he might have been able to identify the people he'd been doing business with afterward, or that someone from the ship's crew or among its passengers may have attempted to retake the ship and that the turncoat—assuming that they'd figured it out—got his throat cut in the process. After which the terrorists decided to kick his body out the airlock along with the others as a way to keep from using up another of their 'bargaining chips' who was still alive."

Strassmann's expression didn't look exactly satisfied by the explanation, but he nodded anyway. And, as Alicia knew, there was always something about *any* op that didn't quite seem to make sense.

"At any rate," Watts continued, "the fact that they're using *Star Roamer* as an orbital observation post complicates any insertion scenario. The fact that we know they have sensor arrays out, and that those sensor arrays' capabilities are unknown to us, makes those complications even more constraining. They've announced that at the first sign of a warship—Imperial Fleet, or anyone else's—they will execute half of their hostages. They will also execute half of their hostages if any attempt is made to retake the ship. *And*, just for good measure, they've rigged suicide charges aboard *Star Roamer*, and they've explained that they're perfectly willing to blow themselves up rather than be captured. Given their past track record, plus the fact that every one of them is now liable to the death penalty, Battalion is inclined to take them at their word.

"We don't know how long we have to mount a rescue operation. At the moment, we're dealing with fairly predictable, stock demands. They want the release of prisoners being held on at least a dozen planets for complicity in operations by several of the 'liberation' organizations which come under their umbrella. They want concessions from the Empire, and also from five or six specific planetary governments, both Rogue World and imperial. They want a sizable ransom, and they want 'prize money' for returning *Star Roamer* to us. And, of course, they want another, faster ship provided for their eventual escape from Fuller."

"They obviously know they aren't going to get all of that," Captain Alwyn rumbled in his deep voice, his black face hard and set in the backwash of illumination from the floating holograph.

"Of course they aren't," Watts agreed. "The majority opinion at Battalion is that most of what they're demanding at this point is in the nature of a bargaining ploy. They don't *expect* to get it. They're simply setting forth demands—fairly outrageous ones—which they fully intend to give up in order to get what they really want. Of course, even assuming that that's true, we don't know what they really want at this point."

"You said that was the 'majority opinion,'" Alwyn observed. "I take it that that indicates there's a *minority* opinion, as well?"

"Yes, there is, Captain. It's been suggested that in reality this entire maneuver is basically a psy-op. They don't really have any specific, long-term, strategic demands as such. What they're after is to give the Empire a black eye. To make the point that they've forced the Empire to abandon its 'no negotiation' policy and actually talk to them—to 'dance to their tune,' if you will. Assuming that there's any validity to this theory, the true object is to enhearten their supporters—and, just incidentally, their financial contributors—and to discourage their opponents. Don't forget, most of the terrorist organizations out here, and the 'Freedom Alliance' is no exception, are operating from Rogue World bases, not bases in imperial territory. The people they're actually talking to, collecting money from, recruiting shooters from, are almost all *Rogue Worlders*. That means Rogue World perceptions of what's happening in their operations, and of the Empire's response to them, are critical to their ability to continue to collect funds and to operate, and the Rogue Worlds' view of this little episode isn't going to be the same as the Empire's, whatever happens. Mind you, they wouldn't mind a bit if they managed to push imperial public opinion in the direction they want it to go, too, of course.

"So if the 'minority opinion,' as you put it, Captain, is correct, then what they really want to do is simply to stretch out the confrontation as long as possible, probably hoping the newsies will get hold of it and turn it into a 'crisis' for the public's consumption. At the end, they probably hope to settle for releasing their hostages—or, at least, the *surviving* ones—in return for the ability to leave the Fuller System aboard a new vessel or aboard *Star Roamer*. They'd probably prefer a new vessel, even if it was smaller, because the fact that they 'made' the Empire give it to them would give them even greater juju in the eyes of their supporters."

"Um." Alwyn scratched his right eyebrow, frowning thoughtfully, then grimaced. "At this point, I suppose, speculation is all we've got. But I have to admit, even after all these years, I still find it difficult to believe these people are thinking at all, sometimes, much less thinking rationally."

"From our perspective, they *aren't* thinking rationally, Madison," Keita said. "But that's the important qualifier, isn't it? As Captain Watts says, they aren't us, and their thinking and planning begins from a radically different set of assumptions and values. I think it's fair to say that there has to be at least a little of the fanatic in anyone who's going to embrace something like the Freedom Alliance's platform. That goes without saying. But if you accept the basic assumptions involved in their analysis of their confrontation with us and its possible outcomes, they do think rationally. At least in the sense that if we can only figure out what they're really after, there's an underlying logic to the way they go about trying to get it."

"You're right, of course, Uncle Arthur." Alwyn nodded. "It's just—Never mind." He shook his head. "This is something to toss around over cold beers in a bull session, not something to distract ourselves over right now." He looked back at Watts. "You were saying, Captain?"

"I've really pretty much completed my initial brief," Watts admitted. "I've assembled additional background data—things like climatology for Shallingsport, more detailed terrain maps, information on the local political set up, things like that—for operational planning, but that's basically the bare bones of what we know. And of what we *don't* know."

"Captain Watts is right about that," Sir Arthur said, reclaiming control of the briefing with a courteous nod to the Marine. "There are a lot of things we don't know about their ultimate intentions and plans. But what we do know is where they are right now, what their apparent strength is, and what sorts of physical constraints we're up against in getting at them. In that regard, we owe Duke Geoffrey our thanks."

"Agreed, Uncle Arthur," Alwyn said. "I'm surprised he even talked to them, frankly. Getting involved in the middle of something like this must be awfully politically risky for someone in his position."

"Yes and no, Captain," Watts put in. "Yes, there are risks, but the fact that he's not actually negotiating with them at all isolates him from the consequences of the Empire's official no-negotiation policy. And, frankly, although he has shown considerable moral courage, the original idea of offering them a place to land in Shallingsport didn't come from him. The director of his Office of Industrial Development is an imperial subject he brought in to run the Green Haven project for him, and my understanding is that it was Director Jokuri who actually suggested the idea to him. I don't want to appear cynical, or to downplay Geoffrey's own genuine concern with saving lives, but I suspect that Jokuri had to do some fast talking to sell him on the notion that we'd be too grateful for his help to worry about whacking him for talking to terrorists in the first place."

"In that case, we owe *Jokuri* a vote of thanks," Keita observed. "But whoever suggested what to whom, we also know we can't afford to let this thing be drawn out. Assuming the 'minority opinion,' as Captain Watts describes it, is correct, that would be exactly what the bad guys want. Assuming the minority opinion *isn't* correct, there's still the fact that the longer this thing stretches out, the more likely we are to begin losing additional hostages.

"I can also inform you that the decision has already been made that we *will* go in. Any official negotiation isn't going to happen, except as a delaying tactic while we mount the rescue."

Heads nodded grimly around the conference table. Not a one of the men and women sitting at it was surprised by Keita's announcement.

"Obviously, the detailed planning is going to be up to you people, since you're the ones who are going to have to mount the operation. The Fleet is redeploying units towards Fuller, but because of *Star Roamer* and those sensor arrays Captain Watts has mentioned, none of those units are going to be able to get in close enough to the planet to do much good. It looks to us like this is going to be another job for the *Marguerite Johnsen*. We've already determined that a freighter of her approximate size is due in Fuller sometime in the next few days, and Fleet has starcommed orders to her immediately previous port of call to hold her there. We have to assume the terrorists have access to Fuller's shipping movements—it's not as if arrival and departure schedules were classified data, anyway—but shortstopping the ship everyone is expecting should create a hole into which we can insert *Marguerite Johnsen* without sounding any alarms until you're close enough to the planet for a drop.

"There may still be hostages aboard *Star Roamer.* There aren't supposed to be any, and the terrorists' spokesman swears that all of them were transported down to Shallingsport. Despite that, we have to assume there are still some aboard. Unfortunately, we also have to assume that the suicide charges they've told us about are also aboard and armed. I'll want to see some contingency planning for a seizure of the ship, but I'll tell you now that in all honesty I don't anticipate your being able to put together an option I'll sign off on. It may be possible to talk the people aboard that ship into surrendering, if we take out their groundside buddies, but I'm not prepared to throw away the lives of Cadremen in a fundamentally hopeless effort to capture an orbiting bomb with a suicide switch.

"As far as the Shallingsport/Green Haven situation is concerned, it looks to me as if the best option is probably going to be a straightforward drop and a high-speed break-in. We're not going to have anything like decent intelligence on what's going on inside that facility. We do know that Duke Geoffrey has ordered the complete evacuation of Green Haven, which presumably means that anyone we encounter there will *probably* be on the terrorists' side. Unfortunately, at this moment we don't even have anything in place to confirm that the evacuation has been carried out."

"If I may, Sir Arthur?" Watts said diffidently.

"Certainly you may, Captain."

"I agree with everything you've said, Sir. And, like you, I wish we had a lot better intelligence on the situation in and around Green Haven. However, Old Earth has pulled together—and starcommed to us—visual imagery on every known member of *Star Roamer*'s crew, all of the Incorporation delegates, and all of the delegation's support staff. We'll be able to download that to your people's armor's computers. We also know that the opposition force can't have much, if anything, in the way of heavy weapons, and that they can't be very numerous."

He paused, and Keita nodded.

"Your point, Captain?" the Cadre brigadier asked.

"I suppose my point is that your Cadremen are actually more capable than you and they sometimes believe they are, Sir. I don't say this is going to be a neat and pretty situation, whatever we do.

However, bearing in mind your own statement that we need to wind up this op quickly, I'm afraid that it looks to me as if Captain Alwyn's people are going to have to go in quick and dirty. Given the visual imagery we can provide, and bearing in mind the Cadre's demonstrated capabilities, it ought to be possible to avoid, or at least minimize, friendly-fire casualties among the hostages."

"I'm not particularly enthralled by the notion of *any* 'friendly-fire casualties,'" Alwyn said a bit frostily.

"I'm not suggesting that you should be, Captain," Watts said unflinchingly. "I'm only suggesting that these people have already demonstrated their own total willingness to murder hostages as a mere bargaining ploy. In the long run, if we don't go in, we'll almost certainly lose more hostages than we would with a bunch as capable as your people mounting the rescue attempt. I'm not trying to buff up your halo, but let's face it. You people are the *Cadre*. This is what you do, and no one in the galaxy does it better than you do. I realize I'm only an intelligence puke, a staff weenie from Battalion, but if it were my call, there's no one in the universe I'd rather have covering my bets than you people."

"I'm forced to concur with Captain Watts," Keita said quietly. "We'll see if we can't assemble some backup from the Wasps aboard the Fleet units diverting to the Fuller area. Whether or not you'll be able to use them is another matter, of course, but we'll try to see to it that they're at least available as an option. And we'll try our damnedest to improve your operational intelligence, Madison. You know we will. But I want you to start immediate planning on the basis of the information we have *now*—what Captain Watts has given you in his briefing, and in the other data he brought with him—and the availability of only your own people and resources. Is that understood?"

He looked very steadily at Charlie Company's commanding officer, and Captain Madison Alwyn looked back, equally steadily.

"Yes, Uncle Arthur," he said, after a moment. "It is."

CHAPTER TWENTY-ONE

"I'm sorry, Skipper," Lieutenant Paál said, "but I just don't like it."

"I'm not too crazy about it, either, Ágoston," Madison Alwyn replied, "but I don't think we've got a lot of choice. Captain Watts—" he nodded his head courteously at the Marine officer sitting in on the planning session in *Marguerite Johnsen*'s comfortably appointed intelligence center as the disguised transport hurtled through wormhole space "—has already confirmed that the terrorists have orbital arrays deployed from *Star Roamer*. We can probably use the planet for cover for the insertion, especially if we drop covert. But if they've got orbital arrays, we have to assume they have ground-based tactical arrays deployed to cover the area immediately around the objective, too. That means they're going to see us coming, if we drop inside the radius they've got covered. At which point—"

"At which point, they start killing hostages," Paál finished for him unhappily. "I know that, Skip. I'm just afraid that wherever we drop, they're still going to pick us up coming in across country, if they've got decent tactical arrays already set up. If they *don't*—have arrays already in place, I mean—then we might as well drop closer to the objective and minimize the time they have to see us coming."

"If I may, Captain Alwyn?" Watts said diffidently. Charlie Company's CO sat back, waving one hand to invite the Marine to continue, and Watts turned his attention to Paál.

"On balance, Lieutenant," he said, "I'd be inclined to agree that a drop closer to the Jason Corporation facility would minimize exposure and give you the best chance of getting into the terrorists' positions before they realized you were coming. But I think Captain Alwyn and Lieutenant Masolle have a valid point. If they do have tactical remotes deployed on counter-grav, or even a ground-based sensor net deployed around Green Haven, they'd be bound to pick up your drop. And they've got six hundred hostages."

"We're well aware of that," Tobias Strassmann said, and Alicia, sitting in along with the rest of the platoon's squad leaders, pricked mental ears at his tone. It wasn't an obvious thing. In fact, she suspected that someone who didn't know the lieutenant as well as she'd come to know him wouldn't have noticed it in the first place. But she *had* come to know him, and she suddenly realized that he didn't particularly care for Watts, either.

"I realize that, Lieutenant Strassmann," the Marine said, and his tone was interesting, too. He sounded like a man who realized Strassmann disliked him for some reason, and who was trying extra hard to be nonconfrontational. "My comments were simply a preface for what I really wanted to say. Which is that—" he used his neural headset to activate the tactical table as he spoke, and zoomed in on an area about forty kilometers from their objective "—even if they have arrays out, this valley here should be outside any radius at which they could pick up a covert drop. And if you'll notice, the valley itself extends along this river. . . ."

He let his voice trail off, and a flashing green cursor trailed a bright dotted line behind it as it traveled the length of the indicated valley. Which, Alicia realized, traced its craggy, rugged, rather winding way along a river that flowed right past the terrorists' position. The contour lines were steep along its entire length, but it became almost a gorge, with near vertical sides, at a distance of barely one kilometer from their objective. Its length added a lot of extra distance to the trip, and the relatively narrow valley wasn't at all apparent at first glance—it disappeared into the peninsula's convoluted, tree-covered terrain—but once it was pointed out, the possibilities were obvious.

"I hadn't noticed that," Strassmann said after a moment, his voice rather warmer and more approving than it had been. He gazed at the glowing line and nodded. "You've got a pretty good eye for terrain," he added.

"I've had longer to think about it than your people have," Watts pointed out. "Believe me, I started poring over the maps of Shallingsport as soon as Battalion was alerted to what was going on."

"It's better than I thought we could do," Paál Ágoston admitted after a moment. "A lot better. But we're still looking at an approach march of almost seventy klicks if we stick to the river, and we'll be lucky to make fifty kilometers an hour through this kind of terrain."

"Agreed." Alwyn nodded. "On the other hand, when was the last time we got to dictate the terrain when it came to mission planning?"

"I'll have to get back to you on that one, Skipper," Paál said with a tight grin. "Right off the top of my head, though, I can't think of one."

That evoked a brief chuckle, and Alwyn leaned forward, studying the tactical table's imagery.

"Did you run an analysis of other possible approach routes, Wadislaw?" he asked.

"As a matter of fact, I did. There are a couple of others which would give you cover that's almost as good, but they all start from even farther out than this one does. Your approach march would be longer for any of them, and, frankly, I think the terrorists would have a better chance of spotting you on most of them. Do you want to look at all of them?"

"Yes. Although, if this really is the shortest, fastest way in from a point where they won't be able to see our arrival, it's probably the way to go," Alwyn said.

"Unless they expect us because it *is* the shortest, fastest way in from someplace where they wouldn't be able to see us drop, Sir," First Sergeant Yussuf pointed out. "And if I were a terrorist worried about a visit from someone like us, Skip, I'd be keeping a *real* close eye on this gorge here." She flipped her own cursor into the display and indicated the river line's closest approach to their target.

"Maybe," Alwyn conceded. "But I'm a great believer in KISS. We'll scout ahead with our remotes, just in case, and we'll plan alternates, but this really does look like the best approach. Besides, if we let ourselves get too involved in double-think and second guessing, I'm sure we'll be able to find a reasonable objection to *any* approach route."

"There's also the fact that they just plain can't have the manpower to scatter people all over the countryside watching for us," Strassmann observed. "Even taking Battalion's most pessimistic numbers, they can't have more than a couple of hundred people actually on-planet. And they've got three times that many hostages to ride herd on. They've got to be thinking in terms of economizing their manpower."

"Lieutenant Strassmann has a point," Watts said. "Obviously, as I've already pointed out, our numbers on how many people the FALA actually has down there are all inferential. We could be off by a fairly substantial margin, but that's why Battalion's been working from a worst-case set of assumptions. And there's another point to consider. I pulled detailed terrain maps on Shallingsport before Battalion sent me to Guadalupe to brief you. But when these people arrived in the Fuller System, they demanded sanctuary from King Hayden, not Duke Geoffrey. On that basis, it seems unlikely they ever actually planned on ending up in Shallingsport. So even if they'd been inclined to do a detailed study of the terrain around their eventual 'sanctuary,' could they have known which maps to pull? It's possible they did a radar map on their way down from *Star Roamer*, but by that point they were into improvisation mode after King Hayden turned them down and Duke Geoffrey accepted. Besides, the shuttles they used to get dirt-side were standard civilian models—Jason Corporation cargo birds provided by Director Jokuri and Duke Geoffrey. There's no way they had the sensor suites to do a detailed mapping job."

"I was thinking along those lines myself," Alwyn agreed. "They may be already in place on the ground, but that isn't the same thing as being intimately familiar with the terrain. And as Tobias says, they can't have manpower to spare. So, if I were them, and if I only had a couple of hundred people, *and* if I had access to decent tactical arrays, I'd be inclined to fort up at the center of the area I could cover. And this valley of yours gives us our best chance to get inside their perimeter, or at least right up to it, without being spotted on the way in."

He sat for a moment longer, gazing down at the dotted line Watts had drawn. Then he nodded and looked back up again.

"Francesca," he said to Masolle. "I want you to sit down with Wadislaw and look at the other possible LZs and approach routes. Give me your best analysis of the advantages and disadvantages of each of them."

Masolle nodded, and he turned to Strassmann.

"Unless Francesca comes up with some fairly compelling reason for us to go another way, I'm thinking we'll probably follow Wadislaw's recommendation," he said. "On that basis, I want you to rough out a covert drop plan. Go ahead and set up for a 'light' drop. Given how far we've got to go, the fact that the bad guys can't have very many heavy weapons of their own, and that we're going to have to execute a break-in to the hostages, we're going to need speed, precision, and flexibility more than brute firepower."

"On it, Skipper," Strassmann agreed, and the Cadre captain turned his attention to Paál.

"Ágoston, while they do that, I want you and Pam," he nodded to First Sergeant Yussuf, "to work up a plan for the approach from Tobias' LZ to the objective. I think Pam may have a point about their picketing the gorge, so plan us a couple of alternatives that avoid that particular stretch, as well. Let's look at all the possibilities and run them through the sims before we decide."

"Yes, Sir."

"Okay, people." Alwyn pushed himself back from the tactical table and stood. "Sic 'em. We'll meet back here in four hours."

"Hey, Alley! I've been meaning to ask you how the Lizard Mind-Reading 101 is going. Are you starting to feel like going out and eating your mate yet?" Alan McGwire asked with a grin.

Alicia opened her eyes and looked up from the careful check of her battle armor she'd been carrying out through her synth-link. She and a dozen other troopers were in *Marguerite Johnsen*'s "Morgue"—the storage and service area for Charlie Company's battle armor. Although the company was supported by a team of armor specialists assigned by the Marines to the Cadre on a semi-permanent basis, much as Captain Watts was assigned to provide intelligence support, most Cadremen preferred to handle the regular maintenance and combat prep on their armor themselves. Those highly trained armor specialists were responsible for major repairs, upgrades, and modifications, but in Alicia's opinion, anyone who didn't want to stay hands-on with the standard maintenance and, especially, troubleshooting of her own armor just before a drop ought to be confined somewhere in a nice, soft-sided room where she couldn't hurt herself or anyone else.

Besides, up-checking your own armor before a drop was a company tradition, especially in First Platoon. Even if you *knew* your armor was in perfect condition, you dropped by to "make certain" . . . which just happened to give you an opportunity for an informal little get-together with men and women who were important to you. Men and women, some of whom might not be alive a day or two later. It let you have that moment with them when you "coincidentally bumped into them" without anyone ever admitting that that was what any of you were doing.

And, of course, under the unwritten rules, it was unforgivable to say anything maudlin or—God forbid!—serious.

"I'll have you know, Sergeant McGwire," she said severely, "that the rumor that Rish matriarchs eat their mates raw is totally unfounded, a legacy of humanocentric prejudice and rank xenophobia. The Rish haven't eaten *anyone* raw at least since they discovered fire, and the Rishathan Sphere represents a mature and highly developed society, however it may look to uneducated barbarians like yourself."

"Sure, sure!" McGwire rolled his eyes.

The Alpha Team leader had been twitting Alicia ever since she signed up for the xenopsychology course. Cadre troopers were strongly encouraged to pursue additional education and training. Obviously, anything which contributed directly to their ability to perform their missions was a good thing, but the Cadre also believed that keeping its people mentally supple was as important as keeping them that way physically. Equally obviously, anything which would help a Cadrewoman better understand the Rish, who were humanity's primary nonhuman competitors, came under the heading of enhancing mission capability, but Alicia had found the course fascinating on its own merits, as well. She wondered sometimes if that was her father's genetic heritage coming out in her.

"Your hostile attitude towards another sentient species is scarcely becoming in someone whose actions and attitudes represent the Emperor personally," Alicia told McGwire now, waving an old-fashioned screwdriver and frowning darkly upon him. "If you keep this up, I'm going to have to report you to CHIRP. *They'll* know what to do with you!"

McGwire stifled a crack of laughter. CHIRP—the Center for Human-Interspecies Relations Policy—was the brainchild of Senator Edward Gennady, one of the Senate's more senior members. Gennady was from Old Earth herself, which gave him a powerful political base, and he was also, in the considered opinion of virtually every member of the imperial military, a raving lunatic. His CHIRP was a think tank whose members had all acquired impressive academic credentials, and many of whom were undeniably brilliant in terms of their own isolated intellectual community. Unfortunately, they also represented a strata of Core World intellectuals for whom the ability of any thinking species to peacefully coexist with any other "if it only tried" was an uncontestable article of faith. From which it followed that the Empire's inability to peacefully coeexist with someone like the Rish automatically demonstrated that humanity *wasn't* trying and must therefore adopt a more "conciliating" policy and stop trying to "enforce parochial, humanocentric prejudices" on other, equally valid alien cultures. Indeed, they clung to that belief, even—or perhaps especially—in the face of all empirical evidence to the contrary, with a dogmatic determination worthy of a medieval peasant.

In Alicia's view, the only people more dangerous than CHIRP were the idiots like Senator Breckman and his Mankind Triumphant Alliance, who argued that humanity could learn *nothing* from alien cultures. The MTA was just as blind and just as dogmatic, and even more closed-minded, than CHIRP at its worst. Even the Rish, who could have been poster children for the MTA's evil alien caricatures, had developed concepts and ideas humanity might do well to study, if only in order to better understand their opposition. And, what was worse, some of Breckman's followers actually thought war was a good idea and that it was "time to seek a final solution to the Rish problem." The only good thing about the MTA was that it could at least be counted upon to support military appropriations bills, but Alicia doubted their support on that single issue was worth their idiocy on every other. Both packs of imbeciles, in her opinion, spent their time living in their own little worlds only peripherally—and sporadically—attached to the universe at large.

"I'd be astonished if Gennady knew what to do with anything he couldn't drink, smoke, snort or screw," Corporal Imogene Hartwell said. It was meant to sound humorous, but it didn't, and Alicia hid a mental frown.

Gennady's reputation for youthful promiscuity and the pursuit of mind-altering substances was well known. It didn't hurt him very much with his constituency, which some—and she knew Hartwell (who'd been born and raised on a Crown World and had the 'frontier' mentality to go with it) was one of them—would argue was because the people who kept voting for him were just as "decadent" as he was. Over the last couple of decades, though, Gennady had cleaned up his act, publicly at least, where his sex life was concerned. And although Alicia never doubted he'd had a genuine problem with old-fashioned alcohol and more esoteric drugs, at least when he was younger, she also suspected that it had been exaggerated by his political enemies—of whom he had more than she could count.

"Well, he can't do any of those with me," McGwire declared, provoking another general chuckle. "But," he continued, looking severely at Alicia, "don't think you can divert me that easily, Alley!" The look he gave Alicia made her suspect he was deliberately sidestepping Hartwell's scorching disgust and genuine anger. "I've heard all the stories about *other* people who took those 'Understand the Lizards' courses. Scrambled their brains, every one of them!"

"Thanks for the warning," Alicia retorted. Then she frowned and cocked her head.

"Actually," she said a bit more seriously, "it's really pretty fascinating in a lot of ways. Some of the things the Rish have done seem . . . odd, at best, by human standards. For that matter, a lot of them seem downright crazy! But once you start wrapping your mind around the way they think, the way their society is structured, it all starts making sense."

"Please don't tell me you're signing up with Gennady and his warm-and-fuzzy-feelings crowd!" McGwire protested.

"Of course not." Alicia shook her head with a snort. "The fact that it makes sense doesn't mean I think they're all sweetness and light, Alan! If you go back and look at any lunatic in *human* history, his actions probably 'made sense' in terms of his own basic assumptions and beliefs. That didn't make someone like Adolph Hitler or Hwang Chyang-tsai or Idrisi al-Fahd or Naomi Johansson any less of a crazed sociopath, and 'understanding' the Rish isn't going to magically make them start behaving themselves, whatever people like the CHIRP may think. It is interesting, though."

"If you say so," McGwire said dubiously. "Personally, though, I like my view of human-Rish relations nice and simple. They poke their noses into imperial space, and we kick their ass clear back to Rish-atha Prime."

"Works for me," Vartkes Kalachian agreed. "But if you're really that interested in how Rish think, Sarge," he continued, looking at Alicia, "you might want to try picking Watts' brain."

"Captain Watts?" Alicia asked in a tone of mild surprise.

"Sure." Kalachian grimaced. "I knew Watts years ago, before I ever got tapped for the Cadre. I was a Wasp, too, you know, and I caught guard duty for our embassy on Rishatha Prime back about, oh, five, six years ago. He was there, too, as a brand new butter-bar, back before they turned him into an intelligence puke—or, hell, maybe he was already in training for intel, now that I think about it. Anyway, he pulled a hitch with the Foreign Minstry as a gopher for the military attaché. He was there over a year, I think—until after I got selected for the Cadre, at any rate. And maybe he really was already working on the whole spy thing, at that, because I heard later that they'd PNGed him."

Alicia blinked. The Rishathan Sphere had officially declared Watts *persona non grata*? That was a cachet which didn't find its way into very many serving Marines' résumés!

"Maybe I will have talk with him," she said after a moment. "Might be interesting to get his perspective on them. Thanks, Vartkes."

"*De nada*." Kalachian shrugged and returned his attention to his battle armor.

Alicia did the same. Lieutenant Strassmann and Lieutenant Paál had completed the planning Captain Alwyn had requested, and unless something had changed radically between their last intelligence briefing and their arrival in the Fuller System in about seventeen standard hours, they were indeed going to drop in light configuration on Watts' suggested LZ. Alicia preferred going in light herself, rather than lugging around the plasma gun—more like a plasma cannon, for anyone not in battle armor—which was her normally assigned weapon when the company went in heavy. A plasma gun wasn't really a precision weapon, especially not the Cadre version. It was a pretty much all or nothing proposition which left very little in the way of potential prisoners, and she preferred something a bit more flexible than that, especially when she might be shooting at terrorists in close proximity to hostages she was trying to keep alive. And Paál had been right about the kind of terrain they had to get through. The lighter they were, the quicker they could reach their objective.

At the same time, she had to admit that a part of her would have preferred having a little more heavy firepower along. Michael Doorn and Obaseki Osayaba would have the plasma guns she didn't, and their wings, Édouard Bonrepaux and Shai Hau-zhi, would have calliopes this time, instead of the grenade launchers they usually drew. But that was going to be all of the really heavy weapons her squad would have along, and she hoped it would be enough.

She completed her suit diagnostics and shut down her synthlink. All systems were green, and she frowned to herself as she reconsidered her backup weapon and equipment harness.

The Book required all Cadremen to carry side arms for backup, although Alicia couldn't remember the last time she'd heard about any Cadre trooper actually using one. Normally, she carried a Colt-Heckler & Koch three-millimeter, a selective-fire three-millimeter machine pistol capable of taking out just about anything short of battle armor with its two-millimeter subcaliber penetrators. This time, she'd opted for a neural disrupter, instead, and she wasn't sure she was comfortable with the selection. There was always a potential over-penetration problem with the CHK, even with full-caliber rounds, whereas a disrupter on tight focus stopped dead when it hit its target. But she'd always hated disrupters, which struck her as a particularly nasty way for someone to die. Of course, she had to admit if pressed that she'd yet to find a *good* way, and she knew that what bothered her more were the people who weren't quite killed by a disrupter hit. Even with modern medicine, the consequences were pretty gruesome.

Then again, she thought grimly, *the people we're going after are terrorists who've already murdered helpless prisoners just to make a "negotiating" point. I can probably live with a little gruesome where they're concerned.*

She snorted at her own thoughts, and ran quickly through the rest of the equipment list. The force blade might be more useful than usual this time, she reflected, given the heavily forested terrain through which they would be moving. The thirty-five-centimeter battle steel blade that went into its scabbard had an edge little more than a couple of molecules across. That made it a formidable slicer and dicer in its own right, yet its real function was mainly to form the basic matrix for the tool's force field and give the force blade balance and some heft. When it was activated, the length of the "blade" suddenly expanded to almost seventy centimeters, and the cutting surface of the force field it projected was much, much sharper than the alloy blade. She'd yet to encounter any sort of vegetation (or, for that matter, anything else) which could stand up to that, especially when the arm swinging it had the advantage of battle armor "muscles."

She considered switching back to the CHK one more time, then gave herself a mental shake.

Why do you do this every time? she asked herself. *This is your form of dithering, isn't it? Well, stop it. You've checked everything at least twice now, the disrupter's more effective against any "soft" target, and it's time you went and got yourself some extra shuteye before the drop.*

"Well, that's that," she said, suiting action to the thought and stripping off her headset. "I'm going to grab myself some rack time while the grabbing is good. The rest of you should consider doing the same thing."

Most of the others nodded, waved, or grunted in basic agreement, but she knew some of them had no intention of taking her advice. Benjamin Dubois, Astrid Nordbø, and Thomas Kiely would undoubtedly drag in a fourth—probably Malachai Perlman—and wile away the time playing cutthroat spades. And Brian Oselli and Erik Andersson would almost certainly haul out their chessboard, while Chul Byung Cha would most probably wander down to *Marguerite Johnsen*'s range and shoot her way through a couple of hundred rounds of pistol ammunition.

They all had their own ways of dealing with pre-drop tension, and by now, Alicia knew all of them. Just as she knew there was absolutely no point in trying to change any of them. So she only smiled, shook her head fondly at them, and headed for her waiting bunk.

CHAPTER TWENTY-TWO

"Saddle up, people," First Sergeant Yussuf said over the platoon net. The first sergeant's voice was calm, almost conversational, but Alicia was confident that Yussuf had her own share of abdominal butterflies.

"All right, you heard the lady," Alicia said in turn, and the men and women of First Squad headed for the drop tubes.

Alicia and her two team leaders checked each trooper's readouts carefully before they followed them through the hatches and settled into their own drop harnesses.

This drop wasn't going to be like the Chengchou drop in a lot of ways, Alicia reflected as the drop harness enveloped her torso and the umbilicals and tractor locks mated with her armor. For one thing, Chengchou had been a cakewalk compared to this operation. She might have gone into her first drop with Charlie Company without the opportunity to share in the pre-drop rehearsals, and she might not have known her people yet, and there might have been noncombatants mixed in among the targets. But the opposition on Chengchou hadn't had any reason to expect that they were coming. And there'd been no hostages involved.

This time there were *six hundred* imperial citizens' lives riding on how well they did their jobs, and that made a difference. A huge difference. But at least this time she was no longer the new kid, the unknown quantity, either. She and her squad had made a half-dozen combat drops, two or three times that many live training drops, and more simulated drops than she could count, over the last year and a half. They'd been over the river and through the woods together, and they were a close-knit, intimately fused unit.

More even than any of the Marines with whom she had served, the men and women of Charlie Company—and of First Squad in particular—had become her family. Like any family, they didn't live in perfect harmony. Everyone knew about Lieutenant Masolle's hot temper, and that Lieutenant Paál was the company pessimist. First Sergeant Yussuf wasn't particularly fond of Denise Cronkite, Second Platoon's platoon sergeant. Within First Squad, Chul Byung Cha and Astrid Nordbø had a long-standing feud (which, as near as Alicia could figure out, went back to a confrontation over some jerk who'd turned out to be married to someone else at the time, anyway). And Édouard Bonrepaux and Flannan O'Clery were constantly sniping at one another over one imagined fault or another.

But none of that mattered. They *were* family, and they knew and trusted one another with absolute certainty. However much grief they might give one another between drops, whatever practical jokes they might pull, whatever quarrels might arise, none of it mattered once the drop tube hatch closed behind them.

They were the Cadre, the Empire's chosen samurai, the Emperor's sword, and one way or another, they *would* get the job done.

"Drop in five minutes," *Marguerite Johnsen*'s AI announced in Alicia's mastoid, and she lay back, waiting.

Marguerite Johnsen, masquerading as the Rogue World-registry freighter *Anzhelika Nikolaevna Dubrovskiy*, swept around toward the dark side of the planet Fuller in her parking orbit.

The Shallingsport Peninsula was well up into Fuller's northern hemisphere, much too far above the equator for *Star Roamer* to maintain a geostationary orbit over it, and the transport had never been designed to handle remote sensor arrays. The terrorists still aboard her had clearly attempted to place their stolen starship to give themselves the best coverage of near-planet traffic they could, bearing in mind the limitations of their civilian-grade communications links to their deployed sensor arrays. Despite that, their major concern was clearly to watch for the arrival of Fleet units, not to monitor the movements of ships which they "knew" were civilian freighters. And the fact that they couldn't maintain a fixed position over Shallingsport provided windows in each orbit during which it was impossible for them to directly observe what was going on there.

Lieutenant Strassmann and *Marguerite Johnsen*'s astrogator had very carefully worked out an approach to the planet which "just happened" to lead the ship into a "routine" parking orbit which would carry her across Shallingsport during one of those windows which also happened to fall just after local midnight in the Green Haven Industrial Park.

Strassmann had also planned the drop not for the first night-hour window, or even the second. He'd given the terrorists still aboard *Star Roamer* no less than three unobserved nighttime over-flights on "*Anzhelika Nikolaevna Dubrovskiy*'s" part to get accustomed to the "freighter's" harmlessness.

Meanwhile, the battlecruiser HMS *Ctesiphon*, which had rendezvoused with *Marguerite Johnsen* and two Fleet heavy cruisers well short of Fuller, had followed the Cadrc transport the rest of the way to Fuller, timing her arrival to coincide with Charlie Company's drop. At the moment, the battlecruiser was headed in-system, squawking the transponder of yet another merchant ship and using her electronic warfare systems to disguise her emissions signature. She couldn't fool a competent sensor array if she got too close to it, but as long as she kept her distance, she should look harmless enough, and she had no intention of approaching the planet until after the Cadremen had reached their objective. *Ctesiphon* had the equivalent of a short battalion of Marines, made up from her own detachment and transfers from the cruisers, in the assault shuttles riding her exterior racks, but even at their maximum acceleration, it would take those shuttles at least another four hours to reach Fuller orbit. On the other hand, if everything went well on Fuller, her business wouldn't be with Shallingsport, anyway; it would be with *Star Roamer*. One way or another, the passenger liner would not be leaving the Fuller System under its current management.

Now *Marguerite Johnsen*'s drop tubes began deploying Charlie Company's drop commandos very, very stealthily.

Alicia had always enjoyed covert drops in training. Unlike the Chengchou drop, which had been intended to put Charlie Company on the ground as quickly as possible, a covert drop was intended to put drop commandos on the ground as *unobtrusively* as possible. They launched without the massive acceleration—and painfully evident electromagnetic signature from the tube catapults—of a standard drop profile, and they entered atmosphere on a much shallower profile at far lower velocity. They also dispensed with the protective force field bubble a drop harness provided for a higher-velocity, steeper reentry profile. It wasn't needed for what one of Alicia's instructors had called "planet-diving"—basically an exercise in old-fashioned skydiving or hang gliding which simply started outside the planet's atmosphere. And without the electronic emissions of the force field bubble and the thermal signature of a high-velocity reentry, a drop commando fluttering down from a night sky with her powered armor's stealth systems on-line was the next best thing to completely invisible. Which meant Charlie Company ought to reach its LZ unobserved, undetected, and—most importantly of all—unexpected.

A covert drop took a lot longer than a standard, high-speed insertion. That was one reason covert profiles were *non*standard. If, by some misfortune, an opponent guessed a covert insertion was coming and his sensors managed to detect it at all, he'd have far longer to track the incoming drop commandos. Against Cadre armor's stealth capabilities, his chance of detecting and tracking the attackers would be little better than even. But the possibility always existed, especially if he'd been able to predict the landing zone's approximate position ahead of time, which was one of the reasons The Book specified high-speed drops for hot LZs.

Spotting Cadre armor would be a nontrivial challenge, even under ideal circumstances and even for first-line tactical sensor arrays, however. In this case, with the terrorists restricted to what they could have landed in personnel shuttles and Charlie Company coming in with all of its own active emitters locked down tight, they couldn't possibly have the sort of sensors needed to do the job.

That, at least, was the theory.

For the moment, though, Alicia actually managed to put that thought aside and surrender to the sheer delight of inserting herself into an endless ocean of air like a thought of God. She slanted down into that airy envelope, and her drop harness' airfoil wings configured outward. She controlled them directly through her synthlink—they were *her* wings, not the harness'—and she felt them stretch even as the tick began to slow the universe about her.

No wonder the medical types worried about tick dependency, she thought as the time-slowing drug stretched out the sensual delight of her flight. She was a huge night bird, slashing across the Tannenbaum Sea towards Shallingsport, yet despite her speed, the flight seemed slow, dreamy as she watched her mental HUD and her descent vector projected itself towards the mountain valley LZ.

That same HUD showed the icons of the rest of Charlie Company's men and women as they arrowed downward with her. There were two hundred and seventy-four other green dots, riding two hundred and seventy-four other descent vector projections, all about her, and she smiled wolfishly as they fell towards their prey.

The digital time readout in the corner of Alicia's mental HUD spun downward. They were less than two minutes from the ground now, and she felt herself tightening internally, reaching out mentally to the next phase of the operation. It was only—

She stiffened as her armor's passive sensors picked up the impossible. She could "taste" the sudden lash of radar from directly ahead—*from directly on top of the landing zone!*

"Zulu! *Zulu!*" Captain Alwyn said suddenly, sharply, over the all-hands net. "Active sensors on the LZ! Hot LZ! *Hot LZ!* Go to Zu—"

His voice cut off with instant, ax-blow brutality as heavy weapons fire stabbed upward out of the blackness below. Plasma bolts streaked up from the valley rim in lightning strobes of fury, ripping through the moonless night like brimstone darts, and green icons began vanishing with hideous speed from Alicia's HUD.

Sir Arthur Keita jerked up out of his comfortable chair in *Marguerite Johnsen*'s intelligence center as the first incredible tactical data came streaming in from Charlie Company.

"Jesus Christ!" someone blurted. "What the f—?"

The speaker chopped himself off, but Keita never even noticed. His eyes were tightly closed as he concentrated on his own neural link to *Marguerite Johnsen*'s computers and watched what was supposed to have been a smooth, undetected insertion transform itself into bloody chaos.

Alicia DeVries had never experienced anything like it. She'd run training exercises which assumed ambush scenarios, but they'd been only training exercises, however realistic.

This was no exercise, and horror hovered in the back of her mind as Captain Alwyn's green icon turned scarlet and he went off the air. Lieutenant Strassmann's followed in almost the same instant, and so did Lieutenant Paál's, and *still* those eye-tearing plasma blasts sleeted upward.

Not even the Cadre could take that kind of damage to its command structure so quickly without losing cohesion. Alicia's armor's AI tried to keep track of who had command, but the hurricane of fire pouring up from their intended landing zone was killing people too quickly. A corner of Alicia's attention watched the golden command designation ring flashing madly about her HUD, trying to settle around a single icon. But those icons kept turning red before it could settle, and this time the time-stretching effect of the tick only made the shock worse.

But if there was chaos, there was very little panic. The Cadre's ruthless testing and merciless training saw to that. The people who qualified for the Cadre weren't the sort who panicked, and the endless hours of training asserted themselves as responses trained into Charlie Company's personnel at the level of instinct took over.

Alicia hit the release on her drop harness while she was still sixty meters from the ground. She dropped instantly, vertically, while the harness continued forward and, obedient to her final command, brought its built-in drive systems online in a frantic evasion pattern. The sensors which might have detected Alicia locked onto the harness' larger, far stronger emissions signature, instead, and a ball-lightning burst of plasma fire blew it out of Fuller's night sky.

Alicia plummeted into the treetops, her armored body automatically orienting itself so that she hit the branches feetfirst. She felt the shock of impact, despite the armor's built-in inertia damping, and then she was crashing through the limbs like a battering ram in a canonnade of splintering wood.

She hit the ground with a force which would have shattered any human body not protected by battle armor. But she *was* armored, and she scarcely even noticed the impact.

More icons were still vanishing from her mental HUD. Adolfo Onassis was gone. So was Sergeant Brookman, and she felt a wrenching spasm of loss as Chul Byung Cha's icon turned scarlet, followed by Imogene Hartwell's and Malachai Perlman's.

Another armored body plummeted through the tree cover behind her.

"Got your six, Sarge!" an intensely welcome soprano said in her mastoid as Tannis Cateau hit the ground. How Tannis had managed to stay glued to her wing was more than Alicia was prepared even to guess, but she'd done it.

"Good," Alicia replied over their dedicated circuit even as she released one of her tactical remotes and its counter-grav boosted it back up through the trees.

The drop had been scattered all to hell as people hit the ground as quickly as they could, wherever they could. First Platoon's Second Squad was clear over on the eastern flank, halfway across the LZ from its intended drop zone, and Staff Sergeant Gilroy, the squad leader, was one of the scarlet icons. Five of his eighteen troopers were also gone, yet even that was better than what had happened to Third Platoon. Lieutenat Paál was gone, and his three squads' fifty-four troopers were down to only eighteen.

At least they were out of the field of fire of the fixed weapons which had slaughtered them on their way in—the weapons which hadn't been supposed to be there. Unfortunately, they weren't the only things which weren't supposed to be there, and even through the intense focus of her training and the cocoon of the tick, Alicia felt an icy dagger as her remote reported back.

"My God," she heard Tannis whisper as she shared the tactical data feed.

They knew, Alicia thought. *They* knew *we were coming, and somehow they figured out where we'd land. But where the* hell *did all these weapons* come *from?*

"All Winchesters, Winchester-One," she began, but another voice came up over the company net.

"All units, Tiger-One," Francesca Masolle said. "Zulu! Break for Alpha-One-Bravo and reform there. Repeat, break for Alpha-O—"

Her voice chopped off with brutal suddenness as her icon, too, flashed from green to crimson, and Alicia's nostrils flared as she realized not a single one of Charlie Company's officers was still alive.

"All units, Striker," First Sergeant Yussuf's voice took over almost instantly. "Confirm Alpha-One-Bravo! Let's go, people!"

Alicia and Tannis were already in motion. No one in their worst nightmare had anticipated something like this, but there was always a contingency plan. Lieutenant Strassmann might never have contemplated the possibility that it would really be needed when he laid out the drop, but that hadn't kept him from planning for it with all of his usual meticulous care. Now the company's survivors moved to execute the response plan one dead lieutenant had laid out and another dead lieutenant had ordered them to obey.

The badly scattered men and women of Charlie Company coalesced, crashing through the trees with reckless speed, relying on their armor to batter a way through. The plasma fire which had plucked so many of them from the air had come from a dozen infantry support cannon emplaced along the valley's southern wall. Those cannon could no longer bear on them now that they were on the ground, and especially not because Alpha-Bravo-One was the southernmost of the Case Zulu rally points Strassmann had laid out. Heading for it carried the Cadremen still further under the plasma guns' maximum depression, exactly as Masolle had hoped it would.

But whoever had planned the ambush had allowed for that, too. The bright orange icons of enemies suddenly spangled Alicia's HUD as her hovering remote saw the battle armored infantry dug in on the slope above them.

And picked up the emissions signatures of four incoming aircraft which had "military" written all over them.

"All units, Striker." Yussuf's voice was impossibly calm sounding, smoothed by the tick and buttressed by her own years of experience and training, as she shared the take from Alicia's remote. "There're a hell of a lot more of them than there ought to be, and God only knows what *else* they've got. But we can't let them pin us until they get sting ships in to hammer us, and the only way out is through them. Come on!"

It wasn't the most detailed tactical directive Alicia had ever heard, but it didn't need to be. There weren't very many options, and her HUD showed her exactly what Yussuf had in mind.

The first sergeant had touched down on the southern periphery of the LZ, while Alicia's squad had landed well to Yussuf's north. That meant Alicia and her surviving people were still well behind Yussuf, despite their best efforts to catch up. And Yussuf wasn't waiting for them. Under the original drop plan, Lieutenant Masolle's Second Platoon had been assigned responsibility for the south side of the valley, which had also happened to drop it closest to the waiting cannon. Masolle was dead now, as were two-thirds of her platoon, but Yussuf had most of what remained of the lieutenant's platoon, although all three of its original squads would barely have made a single full strength one.

Now she led what she had into a head-on assault.

By The Book, it was exactly the wrong thing to do. She should have established a base of fire, analyzed the enemy's dispositions and deployed her maneuver units to exploit their weaknesses. But she didn't have time for that, not with those impossible sting ships coming in from the west and no way of knowing how many more aircraft, or what fresh nightmare surprise, might be coming in their wake.

There were seventy-five men dug in along that steep valley wall. Seventy-five men in prepared positions, with battle armor they shouldn't have had, and armed with the heavy weapons Charlie Company had left aboard *Marguerite Johnsen*, and Pamela Yussuf had only the eighteen surviving members of Francesca Masolle's platoon. Plasma bolts ripped downward, splitting the darkness like demonic lightning bolts, turning the river valley's towering coniferlike trees into roaring torches. It was a holocaust, and Yussuf's men and women charged straight into it.

Alicia saw it all through her floating remote, but she also saw the four sting ships accelerating, dropping their noses while their fire control systems reached out towards Yussuf's attack.

"*Target!*" she snapped over the squad net, dropping sighting circles into the tactical display. She didn't give any additional orders; there was no need, and even as she and the rest of First Squad hurtled after Yussuf, the icons representing Doorn and Osayaba slammed instantly to a halt. The two plasma gunners and their wings wheeled to face the incoming sting ships, and the inexperience of the pilots of those sting ships showed as they came in virtually wingtip-to-wingtip.

Plasma streaked up to meet them, and two of them vanished in cataclysmic eruptions. A third was too close to one of the leaders. It flew directly into the explosion, then howled down out of the heavens, stricken and out of control, as its turbines ingested chunks of its consort's shattered fuselage. Flame streaked its starboard side, billowing from the engine nacelle, and then it tipped onto its back and plowed into the trees below in a rending fan of fresh fire and secondary explosions.

The fourth pulled up frantically, toggling a pair of cluster bombs as it clawed for altitude. It twisted into an evasion maneuver, but too late. Obaseki Osayaba's second plasma bolt struck it full in the belly and spat its flaming fragments across the night . . . just as one of its cluster bombs spewed its submunitions across Édouard Bonrepaux's position. Doorn's wingman hit his jump gear in a desperate effort to evade the bomblets, but he didn't have enough time. The submunitions exploded, and they were antiarmor weapons, not antipersonnel, designed to take out heavy armored units. Not even Cadre battle armor could stand up to that, and Bonrepaux simply disintegrated.

Alicia watched it all in the tick's slow motion, and her heart twisted as she lost yet another of her people. But at least the immediate air threat had been neutralized, and she and the rest of First Squad's survivors plunged up the valley slope on Yussuf's heels.

That slope was the anteroom of Hell. Outnumbered four-to-one or not, Charlie Company's Second Platoon tore into the ambushers' positions like an old-fashioned chainsaw. They came up the slope, battle rifles spitting sub-caliber penetrators, and Corporal Mayfield, Second Platoon's sole surviving plasma gunner, laced the steep mountainside with concussive fists of lightning as she covered their counterattack.

Storms of plasma streaked back at Mayfield as the dug-in infantry's armor sensors back-plotted her fire. The Cadrewoman danced and spun at the heart of a forest fire inferno, evading bolt after bolt while she fired back with the deadly precision of a Cadre trooper riding the tick.

But no evasion pattern could avoid those scores of plasma bolts for long. Mayfield killed nineteen of the ambushers, but in the end, there was one bolt too many, and her green icon turned abruptly crimson.

Yet before she died, she'd opened a hole in the middle of the enemy's line, and Yussuf and her people slammed into it. Fire ripped back and forth, battle rifle penetrators crossing with the fusion-spawned fury of plasma. The men who'd set out to slaughter Charlie Company found themselves suddenly face-to-face with the most deadly combat troops in the history of mankind. Taken completely by surprise, outgunned and disorganized by their savage initial losses, charging dug-in positions in a headlong, uphill assault, and outnumbered four times over, Pamela Yussuf's people hit their enemies like the wrath of God incarnate.

Men cursed and screamed as penetrators hammered through their armor at point-blank range. Grenades added their fury to the violence-sick night, and plasma bolts shrieked back in answer.

Eighteen men and women of the Imperial Cadre went up that slope at Yussuf's heels. Nine of them lived to break through the line and continue their charge straight into the support cannon dug in behind the infantry. They exploded into the heavy artillery's position, rifles thundering on full automatic, only to be met by the fire of the cannon themselves and the multibarrel calliopes dug in to cover them.

They rampaged through the position, killing cannoneers, taking out calliopes, raging through the darkness and the flame and the confusion. Sixty-seven armored plasma gunners lay dead on the slope behind them, and another thirty-eight died as Second Platoon's surviving troopers came out of the night. Yussuf's attack knocked out eight of the cannon and half a dozen of their supporting calliopes, and panic swept the ambushers.

The surviving cannoneers abandoned their weapons, running towards the beckoning concealment of the night-struck forest with the furies of Hell on their heels. Three calliope gunners stood their ground, sending thousands of rounds shrieking into the Cadremen's faces. Then there were only two calliopes in action. Then only one.

Then none.

Alicia watched the icons of thirty-plus surviving hostiles fleeing into the night as she and her people came bounding up through the roaring, wedge-shaped forest fire which marked the line of Yussuf's attack. There was no more shooting, because there was no one left to shoot . . . yet. Her hovering remote was already detecting a fresh wave of inbound aircraft, as well as the traces of additional ground units threaded along the line of the river valley like beads on a string.

But no one was shooting at them now, and she cleared the edge of the valley shelf where the cannon had been emplaced and braked to a halt.

There were only three Cadre icons waiting there to greet her. First Sergeant Pamela Yussuf's was not among them, and Alicia's mouth tightened as the gold ring designating the company's commanding officer settled at last.

It gleamed around the icon representing Sergeant First Class Alicia DeVries.

"All units," she heard someone else say with her voice, "Winchester-One. Form on me at Alpha-One-Bravo."

CHAPTER TWENTY-THREE

"Winchester-One, Skycap," a voice said in Alicia's mastoid.

"Skycap, Winchester-One," she replied, speaking with one corner of her mind while the rest watched the last tattered icons of Charlie Company bounding up the clifflike slope Pamela Yussuf's people had cleared at such terrible cost. "Go."

"Winchester-One," Sir Arthur Keita's voice sounded as strong and powerful as ever, but Alicia sensed his own shock echoing in its depths, "we've lost our direct LOS to your position. I've got a feed off a civilian comsat, but it doesn't have enough bandwidth for your telemetry channels. Are you in a position to give me a sitrep?"

"Skycap, our situation is . . . serious," Alicia replied, her voice more flattened than the tick alone could account for. She watched Celestine Hillman, the only other surviving squad leader, sorting out their survivors and directing them into a hasty defensive perimeter. "I count sixty-three effectives," she continued, not adding that there were no wounded. The sorts of weapons the company had encountered seldom left anything behind but the dead. "My heavy weapons are reduced to five plasma guns and three calliopes. We've confirmed about a hundred enemy dead, but our planned approach route is covered by additional dug-in forces."

"Can you reach the backup recovery site?" Keita asked. His voice still sounded calm, but even now Alicia felt shocked by the implications of his question. The Cadre *never* abandoned a mission when civilian lives were on the line.

But then she looked at her HUD. Charlie Company had gone in with two hundred and seventy-five men and women; she had less than seventy left, and she was forty-plus kilometers from her objective in a straight line. The mission was a bust, whatever else happened, and she knew it. But even so . . .

"Skycap, Winchester-One," she said, after moment. "Negative. I say again, negative. My tac remote shows two fortified positions with heavy weapons support between us and the backup recovery site."

There was silence for a second or two before Keita spoke again.

"Winchester-One, do you have an enemy strength estimate?" he asked at last, and Alicia smiled without any humor at all.

"Skycap, I'd say our enemy capabilities estimate was just a bit off. Remote reconnaissance confirms a current hard count of eight hundred and eleven—I say again, eight-one-one—hostiles within six kilometers of the LZ. They're dug in deep and camouflaged and stealthed well enough we never spotted them from orbit on passives. They have plasma cannon, heavy calliopes, and battle armor, and we found an old Groundhog-Three ground-based surveillance array when we overran their heavy weapons position. All of their other hardware looks like Marine-issue equipment that's been surplussed, too; it's not new, but on the basis of its performance, it's in good shape. We've also downed four mil-spec sting ships . . . and I have additional aircraft circling ten klicks out."

The fresh moment of silence wasn't actually all that long; it was Alicia's tick-stretched time sense which made it seem that way.

"Winchester-One," Keita said finally, "can you evade?"

"Skycap, there's no point," she said quietly. "You can't land recovery boats in this sort of terrain. In fact, the backup recovery site and the objective itself are the only spots you can get them in, and we can't stay away from them forever when they've got air support and we don't. Besides, wherever they got them, these people have enough heavy weapons down here to take out even an assault shuttle. Even if we could manage to find someplace else recovery boats could set down, they'd probably nail them on the way in."

"Winchester-One . . . Alley," Keita's voice was equally quiet, "you're the woman on the spot. Call it, and I'll back your decision, whatever it is."

"Thank you, Skycap," she said, and meant it. "But I only see one option. I'm going for the objective."

"Are you sure about that?" Keita asked. "If the enemy's present in such numbers . . ."

"Skycap, they were waiting for us," Alicia's voice was harsher, and her attention strayed back to the icons of the orbiting aircraft. They were starting to edge in a little closer, and she used her synth-link to nudge her hovering remote towards them.

"I don't know where they came from, or how they got this many people and this many heavy weapons into place without anyone spotting it," she continued, "but they figured out *exactly* where we were coming in, and the Groundhog gave them the tracking ability to zero us from the get-go. They were shooting fish in a barrel, Uncle Arthur. And it's obvious from the positions our remote recon's already picked up that they've got the rest of this valley covered just as thoroughly as they did the LZ.

"But if they've got that many people out here in the boonies, they can't have the direct line between here and Green Haven covered this heavily. Unless you directly forbid it, I'm heading for the objective on the theory that it's the last place they'll expect us to go after a reaming like this one."

"The terrain between you and Green Haven is awfully rough," Keita replied. "And if our original estimates were so far off, you can't count on their having insufficient manpower to cover the direct approach in overwhelming strength, as well."

"Uncle Arthur," Alicia said with a tight grin, "if they've got *that* much manpower, we're screwed, whatever we try to do. I say we roll the dice."

A warning blinked in the back of her brain as the tactical remote picked up active targeting systems from the aircraft. From their emissions signatures, they were lighter craft than the sting ships Doorn and Osayaba had downed—probably only two- or three-man air cavalry mounts. But she had five of them on her HUD already, and she was bleakly certain she hadn't seen all of them yet.

"And the hostages?" Keita asked in a painfully toneless voice.

"If they really intended to kill them all if a rescue was even attempted," Alicia replied unflinchingly, "then they're all already dead. I don't think they did, though. I don't know what the hell is really going on down here, but whatever it is, it's a damned sight more than a simple hostage taking. They've already hammered us. Our loss rate's been over two-to-one so far, and given the numbers we've already detected, they have to be pretty confident they can do that to us again. At the same time, they aren't going to be in a hurry to kill their bargaining chips—especially not after something like this. They're going to need something awfully significant if they're going to have a prayer of talking their way off Fuller now."

"You're figuring that if you get there fast enough, you may be able to break in to the hostages before they kill them."

"Something like that, Uncle Arthur. I'm not saying it's a good option. But I don't think we have any *good* options left, and whatever we do, we're going to have to do it quick. I've got three more aircraft inbound from the east. If I hold here much longer, they're going to try swarming us."

"Understood." Alicia thought she might have heard the sound of an indrawn breath, but she might not have, too. Then, "All right, Alley. I said it was your call. It is. Good hunting."

"Thank you, Skycap," Alicia said formally. "Winchester-One, clear."

She changed circuits, dropping into the company-wide com net.

"All units," she said, her voice flat and hard with purpose, "Winchester-One. We're going to Green Haven, people, and these bastards aren't going to stop us."

There was no response from the other troopers—not in words, anyway, but any wolf would have envied their snarl—and she continued.

"Mauser-One."

"Winchester-One, Mauser-One," Hillman acknowledged.

"You've got our six," Alicia told her. "I'm designating units now." As she spoke, icons on the HUD started changing color as she selected the wings she was assigning to Hillman. "I figure they're going to press us hardest from behind," she continued, "and I'm especially worried about their aircraft. That's why I'm giving you three of the plasma guns."

"Understood," Hillman replied tautly.

"Lion-Alpha-Three," Alicia went on.

"Winchester-One, Lion-Alpha-Three," Sergeant Jake Hennessy, the senior surviving member of Francesca Masolle's platoon, responded.

"You're in charge of our reserve, such as it is and what there is of it," Alicia told him with a gallows grin. "I'm designating units now." Another dozen pairs of wings changed color, and her armor computer simultaneously set up new dedicated communications nets for Hillman and Hennessy's scratch units. "I want you in the middle, Jake, where you can support Celestine or me. And I'll expect you to use your own judgment if it hits the fan again."

"Understood, Winchester-One."

"The rest of you are with me," Alicia continued, as the final fourteen icons shifted color. "We're point. And this is where we're all going."

She dropped yet another mental command into the HUD, and a new line drew itself across the mountainous terrain.

"It's going to be tough, it's going to be ugly, and we're going to get hurt, people," she told Charlie Company's survivors harshly. "But the only way out is through, and we *owe* these bastards. Any questions?"

There were none, and she nodded sharply inside her armored helmet.

"In that case, let's go kick some ass."

Sir Arthur Keita opened his eyes and made himself sit back down across the tactical table from Captain Wadislaw Watts. The Marine intelligence specialist looked back at him, his expression shocked, and Keita shook his head.

"What the hell happened?" he grated, his expression hewn from solid granite.

"Sir Arthur, I can't—" Watts broke off and shook his own head slowly. "Nobody at Battalion saw this coming, Sir," he said, his voice flat. "You heard the same briefings I did. I don't know—That is, I know there are intelligence failures, but I've never seen one this bad. Never."

Keita grunted. An ignoble part of him wanted to blame the Marine, make this all somehow *his* fault. But Keita had seen exactly the same intelligence materials Watts had, and he'd shared the captain's conclusions. For that matter, so had Madison Alwyn and every single one of Charlie Company's officers.

"The one thing it damned well wasn't," the Cadre brigadier said after a moment of sulfurous silence, "was an *accident*. DeVries is right—those bastards down there were *waiting* for them, camouflaged so well we never got even a sniff of them. Somebody planned this entire thing, maneuvered us into feeding an entire Cadre company straight into a meat grinder."

"You think Duke Geoffrey was in on it, Sir?" Watts asked in the tone of a man whose brain was beginning to work once again.

"Somebody down there in Shallingsport goddamned well was!" Keita said grimly. "They've got frigging *sting ships*, for God's sake! Those didn't just spring out of the ground like toadstools. They were brought in from off-world, and not by the people on *Star Roamer*. So if Geoffrey wasn't in on it, who *was*?"

"I don't know," Watts admitted. "We just don't have enough information at this point to tell. On the one hand, it almost had to be Geoffrey. He's the Duke of Shallingsport, he's the one who agreed to give the terrorists sanctuary, and he's the one who handed them Green Haven. But that's insane, Sir Arthur! He'd have to know the galaxy isn't big enough for someone who helped set up something like this to hide from the Empire."

"I know," Keita growled. "But maybe he is crazy enough to think he could get away with it. Or maybe it was what's-his-name—Jokuri, his industrial development guy."

"That could be," Watts said slowly, his expression intent. "For them to get this stuff down there, it must have come in through the Green Haven spaceport, and Green Haven is one of Jokuri's pet projects. And Jokuri's been in charge of whatever customs inspections there may have been. But even if it was Jokuri, why did he do it? Why did the *Freedom Alliance* do it? I think you're right, Sir Arthur—this entire operation was set up specifically to mousetrap the response force we sent in. And given the nature of the provocation—the hijacking and the identity of the hostages—they almost certainly meant to suck in the Cadre, specifically, because that's who they must have known would catch the assignment." He shook his head again. "For all intents and purposes, this is a declaration of war against the Cadre."

"I think that's exactly what it is." Keita stood and began pacing angrily around *Marguerite Johnsen*'s intelligence center. "You said it yourself—this is a psychological warfare operation from their perspective. They've just demonstrated that they can ambush a *Cadre* company and inflict massive casualties. I don't think any Cadre unit has ever taken losses like this, certainly not in a 'routine' operation against a batch of hostage-taking terrorists!"

"But it's a suicide operation for everyone involved," Watts said. "It has to be. There's no way we're ever going to let them off this planet. We'll call in the Fleet to blockade the entire star system, if that's what it takes to keep them pinned down. And eventually, we'll go down there in assault shuttles, or in a heavy-configuration drop, and kill or capture every single one of them. His Majesty will send in an entire Marine brigade, if that's what it takes, Sir Arthur. You know that, I know that—anyone capable of setting this up must know it!"

"Maybe," Keita said almost absently, pacing faster. "Maybe."

"What about *Ctesiphon*?" Watts said after a moment. "She's got the equivalent of an entire Marine battalion on board."

"But she's still four hours out, minimum," Keita replied. He shook his head like an irritated horse plagued by flies. "I've already had the com center alert her and instruct her to expedite her arrival." He tapped his headset to indicate how he'd passed the orders. "Major Bennett has his people working on alternate plans to send an assault dirt-side when she gets here, assuming the opportunity presents. I'm sure *Ctesiphon* and Bennett's people will do anything humanly possible, but whatever's going to happen down there on Fuller, it's almost certainly going to be long over by the time they can get here."

For the first fifteen or twenty minutes, Alicia's decision to strike out directly towards Green Haven seemed to have taken the other side by surprise. She'd been right—all of the heavily dug-in infantry positions the surviving Cadremen's sensor remotes could find were in the river valley or along its rim. That didn't mean there weren't more of them somewhere else, of course, and she had half a dozen of their twenty-three surviving sensor remotes sweeping the mountain forests ahead of them.

So far, those remotes had found nothing but trees, rocks, and mountain streams, but she didn't expect that to last. They had forty air-kilometers to go; in this terrain, that would be more like sixty or even seventy of actual ground travel. Even with Cadre battle armor, the best speed they were going to make through the heavy tree cover would be no more than forty kilometers per hour in an all-out sprint—half that, if they moved with a modicum of tactical caution—but the enemy undoubtedly had transportation available. Since they'd taken over an industrial park, they had to at least have gotten their hands on substantial numbers of air lorries.

Alicia would have liked to believe they could be stupid enough to bring those lorries where she could get a shot at them, but while whoever had set this up might be crazy, he didn't appear to be stupid. No. They were going to use those lorries to pull troops from other positions and drop them somewhere in front of her. Somewhere safely out of the reach of her line-of-sight heavy weapons at the moment they set down. And if the enemy CO was as smart as Alicia suspected he was, he wouldn't panic. He'd take the time to collect as many as possible of the armored infantry he'd initially stationed along the river valley and combine them before he went up against the company again.

And in the meantime, Alicia thought, continuing to crash ahead through dense, low-hanging tree branches, *she'll do everything she can to slow us up and give herself time to make her own preparations.*

"Mauser-One, Winchester-One," she said over her new private com link to Hillman.

"Go, Alley," Hillman replied rather more informally, and Alicia smiled tightly.

"I've just been thinking about what I'd do if I were in charge on the other side," she said. "They're going to try to slow us up—they have to. And they're going to do it with those air-cav mounts."

There were nine of the aircraft icons swarming around now, just beyond plasma gun range of the moving Cadremen. Their active sensor systems lashed at the Cadre troopers, obviously tracking them and reporting back to their own HQ.

"Roger that," Hillman said flatly. "I've been thinking the same thing and wondering why they haven't already done it."

"Because they're afraid of what it's going to cost them." There was a certain grim satisfaction in Alicia's reply as she remembered what Michael Doorn and Obaseki Osayaba had done to four larger and much more capable sting ships. "But that isn't going to hold them off much longer. So, here's what I'm thinking—"

Another five minutes passed—five minutes in which Charlie Company's survivors made good another two kilometers towards their objective. The sensor emissions from the air cavalry mounts intensified as they entered a rocky, more sparsely forested ravine, and Alicia's lips skinned back from her teeth. She'd picked this particular bit of ground from her storage terrain maps as the most likely spot, and the stronger sensor emissions suggested she'd been right.

Cadre battle armor was a hellishly hard target for sensors to lock up at extended ranges, even in open country. The people in those air-cav mounts were undoubtedly getting enough back to know roughly where the company was, but there was no way they could be keeping track of individual targets with any degree of confidence. The fact that they were driving their sensor systems harder now that her people were in less concealing terrain told her they were trying to rectify that, and that suggested that they were just about to—

"*Incoming!*" she snapped over the all-units net, and her people responded instantly.

The brutally truncated company column exploded, unraveling into two-man knots as its individual wings scattered. They bounded off into the trees and boulders, splitting up to deny the air-cav a concentrated target, and Alicia and Tannis did the same.

"Here!" Tannis barked over their private link, and Alicia automatically slammed to halt. Tannis had been concentrating on their individual tactical situation while Alicia rode herd on everyone else, and Alicia had total faith in her wing's judgment. Now, as she focused her own attention on the spot Tannis had selected, she nodded in sharp approval. They had a hillside covering one flank and a couple of huge boulders covering another, and the overhead tree cover was sparse enough to give their battle rifles decent coverage.

Alicia didn't waste time approving Tannis' selection; she simply dropped into her normal position, covering their right flank while Tannis covered the left. She reached out through her armor sensors, sweeping her area of responsibility, but even as she did that, another part of her attention watched the icons of her other troopers, and yet another part was focused on the take from the tactical remotes hovering above the company.

The remotes watching half a dozen air-cav mounts bank sharply, drop their noses, and come streaking in at just under mach one.

The good news, a corner of her brain reflected with the detached precision of the tick, was that the enemy didn't appear to have any indirect fire weapons. There'd been no mortar or artillery rounds dropping on their heads, and the air-cav hadn't been dropping any precision-guided weapons on them. Nor had they been using hypervelocity weapons, which was even better.

The *bad* news was that there were at least two types of air-cav mounts above them. One, she didn't recognize, but it appeared to be a relatively light craft, with a maximum crew of two, and without the size and power plant emissions to support plasma cannon. But the other, the larger one, she did recognize. Like the battle armor and the Groundhog-Three surveillance array they'd already destroyed, it was an Imperial Marine design—one of the old Sabre Bats. The Sabre Bats hadn't been first-line Marine equipment in at least thirty years, but they were still capable platforms. And unlike the lighter mounts she couldn't identify, the Sabre Bat did carry a pair of plasma cannon.

The six attackers howled in on the scattering Cadremen in a column of twos. Both of the leaders were Sabre Bats, coming right down the middle, followed by four of the lighter types, and fresh, even heavier gouts of plasma flashed across the night. Trees vaporized, boulders shattered, and yet more forest fires roared to life at the kiss of the plasma's thermal bloom.

Another green icon turned crimson as Corporal William Tchaikovsky took a direct hit. His wing, Corporal Helena Chu went down, as well, her icon circled by the strobing red band which indicated major damage to her armor. The two lighter mounts directly behind the Sabre Bats opened fire, spraying heavy-caliber penetrators from their nose-mounted calliopes, and three more of Alicia's troopers' icons switched from green to lurid crimson.

But then more plasma bolts screeched through the night, not raining down from the heavens, but streaking up from below. Celestine Hillman and the three plasma gunners Alicia had detached from the main body opened fire from well behind the rest of the company, still hidden from the aircraft's sensors by the heavy trees and their own armor's stealth systems. The strafers' attention had been on *their* targets; they hadn't realized someone else was targeting them, as well.

Hillman's people had zero-deflection shots from directly astern at targets headed directly away from them, and both Sabre Bats disintegrated in the same instant. One of the lighter types exploded even more spectacularly, and then the three survivors were jinking and weaving wildly in a frantic effort to evade the same fate.

One of them managed to dodge two plasma bolts, but a third bolt impacted on its turbine. It was only a glancing hit, almost a clear miss, but the turbine's housing shattered, and the mount's hydrogen reservoir exploded in a brilliant blue flash.

The other two aircraft evaded the plasma fire, but while they were doing that, they swept through the air space directly above their intended victims, and Alicia's rifle snapped into firing position. She ripped off an extended twelve-round burst, and fifty other rifles, and a pair of calliopes, were doing the same thing. The distracted air-cav pilots were too busy worrying about the plasma gunners who'd suddenly appeared behind them like evil genies to think about ground fire from the rest of the Cadremen, and neither of them had the chance to realize that they should have been looking in both directions. Their aircraft carried light armor, but not enough in the face of that hurricane of penetrators, and both of them plummeted out of the heavens, trailing comet tails of flame that smashed, crackling, into the resinous trees.

"All units, Winchester-One," Alicia said. "Reform on me."

She and Tannis made their way out of their positions, heading for Corporal Chu, while the other troopers filtered back out of the flaming forest and Hillman and her people came up from behind. The three remaining air-cav mounts stayed where they were, hovering—with what Alicia devoutly hoped was shocked caution—well outside effective plasma range.

She looked around at the raging fires, grimly satisfied with the destruction of two-thirds of the enemy's remaining air power. *Well,* she corrected herself, *two-thirds of the air power we* know *about, anyway.* But her satisfaction was bitter on the tongue as she counted the cost. It could have been far, far worse; she knew that. But that didn't make the loss of four more of her people—her family—any less agonizing.

A distant corner of her mind knew what was waiting for her when she finally had time to stop concentrating on the business of survival, on the unremitting drive to accomplish what had become an impossible mission. For the moment, the need to focus everything on getting her surviving people out shoved all other thoughts, all other concerns, into the background. But when that was no longer true, when she could finally allow herself to face the wrenching brutality of Charlie Company's destruction . . .

She closed the door on that corner of her mind once again as she went to one armored knee beside Helena Chu, and her green eyes were bleak.

"How you doing, Helena?" she asked quietly.

"Not so good, Alley." The wounded trooper's voice was harsh, strained, despite all the painkillers in her pharmacope could do. The plasma bolt which had knocked out her armor hadn't killed her outright, but she'd lost her left leg just below the hip, and the entire left side of her armor was a smoking ruin. Her battle rifle had been destroyed, and her vital signs flickered unsteadily on Alicia's monitors. Alicia looked up at Tannis' face through the visor of her armor, and her wing shook her head silently.

"We—" Alicia began, but Chu cut her off.

"I already figured it out, Alley," she said.

"I figured you had," Alicia said softly, and laid her armored hand on Chu's right shoulder. She knelt there for a few silent heartbeats, then straightened her spine.

"You guys need to get moving," Chu said. She reached down and drew her side arm—a CHK three-millimeter, identical to the one Alicia normally carried. "I'll just wait here with Bill," the crippled corporal said, nodding to where her wingman had already died.

Alicia gazed down at her, longing for something—anything—to say. Some comforting lie, like "I'm sure the bad guys will be too busy concentrating on us to send in a follow-up sweep," or "Hang on, and we'll get a med team out here as soon as we've polished off Green Haven." But Chu knew the odds as well as Alicia did, and she could read her own life sign monitors. She knew how little time she had left unless the med team arrived almost instantly, that only her pharmacope and augmentation were keeping her alive even now, and Alicia owed her people something better than a lie.

"God bless, Helena," she said, very quietly, instead, then turned to lead the fifty-eight surviving effectives of Charlie Company, Third Battalion, Second Regiment, Fifth Brigade, Imperial Cadre back into motion.

CHAPTER TWENTY-FOUR

"Winchester-One, Winchester-Alpha-Three. We've got a problem."

"All units, Winchester-One," Alicia said instantly. "Hold position."

The other surviving forty-six members of Charlie Company stopped instantly, freezing in place, while she and Tannis continued moving forwards.

"What have we got, Erik?" she asked as she caught up with her point man, and Corporal Erik Andersson, call sign Winchester-Alpha-Three grunted over the com.

"Let me show you," he replied, and switched the feed from his own tactical remote to Alicia.

They didn't have many remotes left. Wherever the "terrorists" equipment had come from, they'd obviously gotten their money's worth. Their refurbished Marine battle armor's sensors were able to detect the presence of even a Cadre sensor remote. They couldn't localize it as well as a Cadreman might have, but they could pin down a general volume, and they obviously realized that without their airborne spies, Charlie Company's survivors would be floundering around blind. So every time they did detect the emissions signature of a remote's heavily stealthed counter-grav, they saturated its general area with heavy fire, and remotes were "soft" targets, subject to mission kills, even if they weren't destroyed outright. A near miss with a plasma bolt was usually sufficient to do major damage to a remote's sensors, rendering it effectively useless.

Charlie Company should have had sixty remotes left; Alicia actually had seventeen, and against first-line equipment—even old first-line equipment, like the terrorists had—she had to keep sending them in close if she wanted reliable data. Which meant she kept losing them in a steady trickle.

One of the seventeen survivors was assigned to Andersson, and Alicia clenched her teeth as she saw what Winchester-Alpha-Three had already seen.

Where are they getting *all these people?* she asked herself bitterly. Andersson's remote was picking up at least two hundred more battle-armored infantry, dug in in three separate hastily prepared positions directly across the saddle between two mountains through which Alicia had intended to pass her column.

Well, at least that settles the question of whether or not they still know where we are, she thought.

She'd hoped that they'd dropped completely off the enemy's sensors, but the FALA's commanders wouldn't have been able to airlift those people around in front of her if they hadn't had a pretty shrewd notion of where she was and where she was headed. On the other hand, one of the positions she could see was much too far to the west to support the others. Its location had clearly been chosen to block a side valley several kilometers to one side, and that suggested they were at least uncertain about her *exact* position. If they hadn't been, they would have known she'd actually been edging away from that side valley for the last twenty minutes.

None of which made her present situation any less unpalatable.

She studied the take from Andersson's remote intently, chewing the inside of her lip while she contemplated it. Fatigue was becoming yet another enemy, and she knew it. Thanks to the tick, the last couple of hours seemed to have taken weeks to drag past. She knew better, but there was a direct link between the mind's perception of time's passage and the body's physical responses, and the stress of such bitter combat—and casualties—burned up energy like another forest fire. It was a fatigue Cadremen were trained to cope with, and Alicia's pharmacope was trickling doses of offsetting drugs into her system, but the drain of such constant tension made all of them less effective than they ought to have been.

She pushed that thought aside again, as she also pushed aside the thought of the ten more people she'd lost since they'd been forced to leave Helena Chu behind. Chu was dead now, too; Alicia had still been in range for the corporal's armor icon to show on her HUD when the air-cav mount swept over Chu and killed her. All of Charlie Company's survivors had known when it happened, and Alicia had felt their hatred melding with her own.

But at least the people who'd killed Chu were almost certainly dead themselves. The company's plasma gunners had picked off six more aircraft when they'd closed in—much more cautiously than before—to strafe. Alicia might have lost ten more troopers in exchange, but the enemy was obviously beginning to run out of air-cav mounts at last. More had turned up since their first disastrous strafing attack, but after the additional losses they'd also taken, there were only four left within the reach of Alicia's sensors. Three of those had arrived after Chu was killed, and Alicia took a hard, grim pleasure from the thought that the people who'd murdered her corporal had almost certainly been among those who'd been shot down.

The four survivors were orbiting at extreme range now, obviously keeping their distance and closing in only for occasional overflights. Given how hard it was to track Cadre battle armor even under the best of circumstances, it was no wonder their feel for exactly where Alicia's people were had become fuzzy.

"We can't go around them," she said quietly to Tannis over their private com link.

"Sarge, I don't know as we've got a lot of choice," Tannis replied, equally quietly, studying the same tactical data. She was accustomed to serving as Alicia's sounding board, as a wing was supposed to do. "We're awfully beat up," she continued, "and we're running low on ammo. We could probably work around them, to the east."

She dropped the dotted line of a possible altnerative route onto Alicia's HUD, and Alicia nodded. Tannis's projection swept well to the east, around the end of the line the blocking positions had drawn across the mountain saddle. Unfortunately . . .

"There's no time," she said. "They must've used air lorries, or something like that, to lift these people in—probably from the positions back by the LZ—to wait here for us, and if we try to work our way around them, we end up with even worse terrain between us and Green Haven. It'd take us even longer to get there, even if nothing else went wrong. And it *would* go wrong, Tannis. That damned air-çav may be keeping its distance, but it sure as hell knows roughly where we are, or these people wouldn't be here. So if we try to work around them, they'll probably spot us. And if they do, the extra time we'll spend trying to get through the terrain to the east will give them plenty of time to lift these people out of here again and drop them somewhere else in front of us."

"But if we punch into them head-on, we solve their problem for them," Tannis countered. "They *want* us to engage them, Sarge. That's why they're here."

"Granted." Alicia studied the tactical data in silence for a few more seconds, but she knew Tannis had a point.

The enemy's commander obviously knew that taking the Cadre on, even when they had heavy weapons and the Cadre didn't, was a good way to get hurt. But it was equally obvious that the enemy had an enormous numerical advantage, although Alicia still couldn't imagine how they'd managed to get all of these people down here. And their commander equally clearly wanted nothing more than to force Alicia's people to engage them on the FALA's terms. The terrorists weren't interested in fighting on *Alicia's* terms; they wanted to force her to come to them when they had both the numerical advantage and the advantage of prepared positions.

"You know," she continued to Tannis after a moment, "looking at their positions here, it strikes me that they've obviously got a better feel for strategy than for tactics."

"I know that tone, Sarge," Tannis said. She was standing with her back to Alicia, keeping wary watch around their position, but Alicia could see the single raised eyebrow as clearly as if they'd been standing face-to-face. She'd seen it literally scores of time over the past eighteen months, and her mouth quirked as she smiled fondly at her friend's back.

"Their problem," she explained, "is that whoever picked out their positions had the strategic sense to find a choke point from her maps and send somebody out to block it. But the way they went about blocking it after they got here has a few tiny drawbacks. Look here."

She manipulated the terrain overlay on Tannis' HUD, and Tannis gave a sudden, tuneless whistle.

"My, that *was* careless of them, wasn't it?" she said.

"That's one way to put it," Alicia agreed, gazing at the HUD's contour lines herself. Then she switched channels.

"Mauser-One, Winchester-One. Move your people to this point—" she dropped a location icon into Celestine Hillman's HUD "—and meet me there. Lion-Alpha-Three," she continued, "move your people up to this point."

She dropped yet another icon into the HUD, and waited until acknowledgments came back from Hillman and Hennessey. Then she slapped Andersson on his armored shoulder.

"Good work, Erik," she told him. "Now stay here and keep an eye on them until we're ready."

"You got it, Sarge," he replied, and she went bounding back along the column towards Hillman.

"Winchester-One, Mauser-One," the voice in Alicia's mastoid said ten minutes later. "We're in position, Alley."

"Mauser-One, Winchester-One copies," Alicia replied. Celestine sounded confident, she thought—or, at least, like someone trying to project confidence. She smiled humorlessly at the thought, and drew a deep breath.

"All right, people," she said over the all-units net. "It's time to dance."

Group Leader Burkhart, the man in command of the action group holding the center of the three Freedom Alliance Liberation Army blocking positions, stood gazing out into the darkness. His command post was exactly where The Book said it should be, on the reverse slope of the shallow ridge line running across the mountain saddle at an angle. But Cornelius Burkhart felt cramped, confined, sitting in its protection. So he'd left his second-in-command there and come here, where he could stand in one of his forward plasma cannon positions and glare out across the moonless night.

Burkhart did a lot of glaring, because he was an angry man, one who used his anger to fuel his purpose and fire his passion. He'd been that way for a long time, and if he'd never been completely satisfied with the plan for this operation, that was all right. He understood the plan's objectives and approved them fiercely, and so far, at least, it seemed to be working. His faith in its ultimate success—and his own survival—might be qualified, but that didn't mean he wasn't determined to drive it through to success if it could be driven, because he hated the Terran Empire with a pure and burning passion.

His family had been prominent in its opposition to the Incorporation of his homeworld, and they'd paid the price. Perhaps the Empire hadn't been directly implicated in the attack which had killed his father, mother, and older brother, but *someone* had tossed the homemade bomb during the anti-Incorporation rally.

The planetary government had insisted it had come from among the protesters, thrown—or possibly dropped—by one of the violent fringe elements in the protest movement. The rally's organizers had blamed government provocateurs and fiercely rejected the so-called "investigation" the government had conducted. Even the "investigation" hadn't been able to (or had been ordered not to) identify the hand which actually threw the bomb, of course. And in the absence of any other clearly identifiable guilty party, Burkhart and his two surviving brothers had assigned the blood guilt where it ultimately belonged, the hands of Empress Maire, Seamus II's mother, and set out to do something about it.

They'd taken their vengeance where they could find it, and Cornelius Burkhart had lost track long ago of how many Empies and Empie collaborators they'd killed over the past twenty-three standard years. All three of them had joined the Freedom Alliance's Liberation Army six years ago, and they'd been able to kill even more of their enemies with the FALA's support structure behind them. But however many they'd killed, it hadn't been enough. It would *never* be enough, and it had come with its own price tag. He was the only surviving member of his family, now, thanks to the Cadre raid on Chengchou, and the knowledge that the company which had killed his brothers would almost inevitably be assigned to this operation explained why he'd volunteered so promptly for it.

He smiled thinly, staring out into the night, wondering where the Cadre survivors were. There couldn't be more than fifty of them left—less than twenty percent—and that was sweet, sweet on his tongue. He'd made a study of the Cadre and its operations over the past quarter-decade, and because of that, he knew just how great the Alliance's accomplishment here on Fuller was.

The Cadre was more than simply another branch of the imperial military. It *was* the Empire, the personification of the House of Murphy. For the subjects of Seamus II, its members were the standard-bearers, the guardians—the Emperor's paladins and the shining heroes who stood against the enemies of all they held dear. But Cornelius Burkhart was one of those enemies. For him, too, the Cadre was the personification of the House of Murphy . . . and he hated the Cadre even more than he hated the Emperor. But it wasn't a blind hate, and that was why he'd lavished such attention upon his enemies, studying their strengths as well as their weaknesses. And it was also why he knew that in its entire history, the Cadre had never suffered losses like the ones it had already suffered here. An eighty-plus percent casualty rate was horrendous for any unit, under any circumstances, but it would be far worse for the Cadre, those arrogant pricks with their aura of invincibility, their pride in their reputation and their unbroken record of successes.

Well, their record's broken now, he thought viciously. And if he continued to cherish doubts about the extraction plan, that was all right, too. There was no one waiting for him, no one worrying about him. Not anymore. The Empire and the Cadre had seen to that. His enemies themselves had freed him, and in the final analysis, whether or not this operation ultimately led where the Freedom Alliance command council imagined that it would was unimportant. It was only a matter of time until—

Cornelius Burkhart's thoughts were interrupted with sudden finality as the sub-caliber penetrator from Corporal Thomas Kiely's battle rifle struck a quarter centimeter below the exact center of his battle armor's visor. It punched through the incredibly tough, transparent composite on an upward trajectory, like an incandescent spike. It made only a tiny hole as it drilled through, but when it struck Burkhart, just under the arch of his left eye socket, the top of the group leader's skull exploded into his helmet liner.

* * *

"*Go!*" Alicia snapped, and her people moved forward.

It was obvious the first volley had taken the enemy completely by surprise. Battle armor had defeated at least a few of the Cadre penetrators, but her HUD showed eleven hard kills and three probables.

They should've stayed further down in those nice deep holes, after they went to all the trouble of digging them, she thought grimly as twenty-six of Charlie Company's surviving forty-six troopers moved forward with her and Tannis.

Plasma roared over their heads as Doorn and Osayaba laced the infantry support cannon opposite them with fire. The terrible blinding flashes walked along the crest of the enemy's position, ripping and tearing. But those positions really were well dug in, and answering fire began hammering back at the Cadremen as their own fire proclaimed their locations to their enemies.

Another Cadre icon turned crimson, and deep at the core of her, Alicia felt a fresh stab of pain as Corporal Allen Shidahari died. An instant later, Corporal Manfred Branigan, the Third Platoon trooper she'd paired with Erik Andersson after Vartkes Kalachian was killed, went down, as well. Benjamin Dubois, Lawrence Abernathy's wing, who'd been paired with Michael Doorn after they both lost their own wingmen, killed three more of the defenders. He fired steadily, carefully, as if he were on a target range somewhere, and scored three helmet hits in a row—then went flying backwards, his breastplate and torso vaporized by the plasma bolt which took him almost exactly center of mass.

Alicia was firing herself, picking her targets, and still more of the defenders went down. But not enough. The ones they'd killed in the initial volley had been the careless ones, the ones taken unawares. The ones who were still left were the cautious ones, the careful ones who returned fire without exposing themselves any more than they had to, and their weapons were heavier than the Cadre troopers'.

"Hold what you've got!" she said over the tactical net as the advancing green icons on her HUD reached the points she'd selected ahead of time. Not all the positions she'd chosen were as good as she'd hoped they would be, but all of them offered at least some cover, and her people went to ground, continuing to fire but obviously pinned down by the fire coming back at them.

Alicia bared her teeth in a fierce grimace as the enemy's fire redoubled.

That's right, she thought viciously at them. *You go right ahead and pin us down. You've got us, don't you?*

"We've got them—*we've got them!*" Cornelius Burkhart's executive officer screamed into his com.

"Then finish them off!" the operation's overall commander shouted back from his Green Haven communications center. "*Finish* them this time, damn it!"

"We will!" the XO promised, and turned his attention to doing just that.

He wasn't as comfortable or well trained as Burkhart had been when it came to interpreting his battle armor sensors' reports, but it didn't take a genius to know the Cadre bastards were screwed. He'd never really believed they'd be stupid enough to hit the action group's positions head-on this way, but they had. Oh, they'd hurt the FALA fighters with that initial deadly volley, and whoever those bastards behind the plasma guns on the other side were, they were a hell of a lot better than *his* cannoneers. He admitted that, but they weren't *enough* better. The sheer weight of his own cannons' suppressive fire had driven them to ground—they weren't even shooting back at all, now, assuming they were still alive—and the entire crazy assault had bogged down almost instantly.

He squatted in the cramped CP and glared at the holographic HUD projected before his eyes. He couldn't sort out the details any longer, and he switched to a direct visual. The schematic's confusing iconology disappeared, and he smiled viciously as he watched the muzzle flashes and lightning bolt-streaks of plasma flay the darkness with an ugly, lethal beauty. The sheer volume of death and destruction his people were pouring out filled him with almost erotic pleasure, and he didn't need any frigging HUD details to know the Cadremen were being hammered into dog meat.

Alicia crouched a little lower as a plasma bolt streaked past the boulder she was using for cover. The plasma impacted on one of the local conifers, and a five-meter chunk of the thirty-centimeter tree trunk vaporized. The upper two thirds of the tree plummeted downward, already flaming, and crashed half across Alicia's position. The main trunk missed her, and her armor protected her against the branches which did slam down across her, but it still felt as if a giant hand had just slapped her against the earth like a pesky bug.

"Sarge!"

"I'm okay, Tannis!" she replied quickly, and she was—for the moment. But the flames roaring around her as the rest of the tree caught fire would be a problem if she stayed where she was very long. If nothing else, the ammo for the CHK she'd appropriated from a Second Platoon trooper who no longer needed it would start cooking off. But for now, her armor was handling it easily, and she drew her force blade one-handed. The force field lopped through the thirty-centimeter trunk effortlessly, and she cut her way clear of the tangle, then deactivated the blade, hit her jump gear, and vaulted over to join Tannis.

A heavy-caliber penetrator from one of the terrorist calliopes spanged off her left pauldron just before she hit the ground again. It hit too obliquely to penetrate, but the impact slammed her down, and despite the armor's antikinetic systems, she grunted as she landed.

She hardly even noticed. Her attention was on her HUD, where eighteen fresh green icons, led by Celestine Hillman's, had suddenly erupted into the blocking position's rear.

The new FALA commander never realized just how badly he'd misread the situation. His CP was, indeed, exactly where The Book said it should be. Which, unfortunately, meant Celestine Hillman knew exactly where to look for it when she emerged from the fold in the ground Cornelius Burkhart had overlooked.

Perhaps it would have been unfair to expect Burkhart to have noticed it. It wasn't much of a terrain feature, after all—only the meandering ravine of a dry, seasonal streambed, nowhere more than a couple of meters deep. Besides, it hadn't really been inside Burkhart's perimeter. It was *between* his position and the action group which formed the easternmost anchor of the blocking line, and it was supposed to be covered by fire from both sides.

Except for the minor fact that neither position had actually had a line of fire into the streambed . . . or realized that it needed one.

The first plasma bolt from Hillman's scratch-built squad impacted directly on the CP, obliterating Burkhart's successor and simultaneously destroying the position's primary sensor array. The defenders were thrown back on their armor's individual sensors, and—like their obliterated XO—they simply weren't as good as the Cadre at interpreting them.

They were still trying to figure out what was happening when Hillman's people swarmed over them from behind, shooting and grenading as they came. Some of the FALA infantry turned in their positions just in time to meet deadly bursts of battle rifle fire. Others never got even that far.

"Go, go, *go*!" Alicia barked as the enemy's fire faltered suddenly. It stuttered uncertainly for another moment, and then died almost entirely as the people behind it suddenly realized they'd been flanked.

Panic set in, exactly as Alicia had hoped, and as the terrorists wavered, she and the rest of the company came charging up the slope directly into them behind the deadly muzzle flashes of their rifles.

CHAPTER TWENTY-FIVE

Sir Arthur Keita watched the repeater plot as HMS *Ctesiphon* decelerated towards Fuller orbit. The battlecruiser still wore her freighter's electronic mask, although he had no way of knowing whether or not the terrorists aboard *Star Roamer* were still buying the deception.

Of course, I don't know whether or not they ever really bought it in the first place, either, he thought, and looked back at the holograph of the Shallingsport Peninsula on the main display in *Marguerite Johnsen*'s intelligence center.

That holograph was nowhere near as detailed as he wished it were. The icon which was supposed to indicate the position of Charlie Company—*or its survivors,* he thought grimly—strobed to indicate that it was only an estimate. They still had communications with DeVries, but they'd become increasingly sporadic, and they'd lost virtually all tactical telemetry channels even during the windows when the transport's orbit took her directly over Shallingsport.

Keita felt his belly muscles tightening once again. God, how he wished he knew what was happening down there! Not that knowing would have done him any good at the moment. He realized that only too well, however little he wanted to admit it. Never before in his entire Cadre career had he felt as helpless as he felt at this instant, and guilt hammered in the back of his brain. It was irrational, he knew, but that made it no less real. He was the one who'd ordered Madison Alwyn's men and women into this holocaust, and now he sat safe and sound aboard *Marguerite Johnsen* while they died beyond his reach. While he couldn't even be down there with them. While—

He cut that thought off and forced himself to push it down once again. He couldn't do anything about that, so he made himself reconsider what he did know, instead.

At least if DeVries was right—and she probably was, he thought—the terrorists were probably even more uncertain of her position than he was stuck here in *Marguerite Johnsen*.

The Cadre brigadier shook his head and thanked God for Sergeant First Class Alicia DeVries. He'd lived through enough cluster fucks in his own career, if none quite this bad, to appreciate the magnitude of what she'd already achieved. Of course, Charlie Company was the Cadre, composed of the most rigorously selected and trained soldiers in the galaxy, but not even the Cadre could train people to take situations like this one in stride. Without her to hold them together, keep them moving . . .

His last message from DeVries was almost thirty minutes old. She'd reported the assault on the FALA blocking position in a terse, matter-of-fact tone which had fooled no one aboard *Marguerite Johnsen*. The disguised Fleet transport had worked with Charlie Company for over three standard years. Her crew had become part of the Charlie Company family, and Keita could feel their shock and grief all about him. But there'd been no trace of that shock or grief in DeVries' voice—only the clipped cadences the tick induced.

Keita would have been tempted to hate her, if he'd thought she truly were as unmoved, as machinelike, as that voice had sounded. But he knew better than that, because his own voice had sounded like that once or twice during his career. Because he knew all about locking down the pain until there was time to face it and taste it to the full.

"We're down to thirty-two effectives," she'd said. "We lost nine breaking through the saddle. We've lost five more since then, including Sergeant Hillman, when their air-cav came in to strafe, but they aren't doing that anymore. I think we've finally convinced them it's a losing proposition; they seem to be down to only two aircraft, and they're staying at extreme range."

She'd stopped speaking for what would have been a very brief pause for someone Keita hadn't known was riding the tick, then resumed.

"I think we've shaken them off, Uncle Arthur. We're not getting any more active sensor hits from their air-cav, and the two mounts they have left seem to be running a search pattern well behind us. I think they let us break contact after we nailed that last pair of strafers, and they haven't found us again."

"What's your ammunition state?" he'd asked, and hated himself for asking.

"Low," she'd replied. "We're down to an average of thirty-seven rounds per rifle. We're almost entirely out of of grenades, and we've got less than fifteen hundred rounds for the calliopes. We're down to only three plasma rifles—we lost Corporal Doorn and his weapon on the last strafing run—and we've only got a couple of dozen hydrogen pellets for the three we've got left."

"Understood," he'd said, then paused and drawn a deep breath. "What are your intentions?" he'd asked then.

"Unchanged," she'd said flatly. He'd opened his mouth to protest, but she'd continued before he could.

"We're most of the way to the objective, and I don't think they know where we are—not accurately, at any rate. Even if they've got a better idea where we are than I think they do, the closest place anyone could get in here through this damned forest canopy, whether with assault shuttles or recovery boats, is Green Haven itself, and our intel on that sucks. I haven't been able to get a good look at the spaceport there yet, but if they've got the kind of firepower and weapons we've seen out here in the mountains, they've got even more of it covering Green Haven, and you need to know how much when you start considering options. That means we've got to get in close enough to eyeball the situation there for you, at the very least, and we're almost out of sensor remotes. These people have demonstrated that they're pretty good at picking them off, too, so I've got all but one of the five we have left tied down until we get close enough for them to do us some good. I'll contact you again when we have. Winchester-One, clear."

That had been—he looked at the time display—twenty-eight minutes ago, and he hadn't heard a word from her since.

Where are *you, DeVries—Alley?* he worried. He longed to contact her, demand an updated situation report, but he suppressed the temptation sternly. If she was right, if she had managed to break contact, the less communication between them the better. And in the meantime—

"Sir Arthur?"

Keita turned quickly to find himself facing *Marguerite Johnsen's* communications officer.

"What, Lieutenant Smithson?" he asked the Fleet officer.

"Sir Arthur, we've just received a communications request," Smithson said in an odd tone, then grimaced. "He says he's the terrorists' commander, Sir."

Keita's expression went more granitelike than ever, but his eyes narrowed slightly. He gazed at the lieutenant for perhaps three seconds, then shrugged.

"Put it through," he said.

"Yes, Sir." Smithson entered a command through his own neural headset, then nodded to Keita, indicating a live mike.

"This is Sir Arthur Keita," Keita said flatly. "What do you want?"

"Sir Arthur Keita? 'The Emperor's Bulldog' himself?" a voice replied, and its owner laughed mockingly. "I *am* honored! Of course, calling someone a bulldog is just another way of calling him a son of a bitch, isn't it?"

"You're the one who asked to speak to me," Keita said, his voice still flat as hammered steel. "Was there something you wanted to say, or do you prefer simply asking rhetorical questions?"

"My, aren't we testy?"

"Com me back when you've got something to say," Keita said, and started to gesture to Smithson.

"You might want to remember that I've got six hundred Empies down here," the voice said, suddenly harsher and colder. "Cut this connection, and I'll send fifty of them back to you in body bags."

"You can do that any time you want to, regardless of whether or not I talk to you," Keita said unflinchingly. "Of course, doing that would constitute a different sort of escalation, wouldn't it? I really don't think you'd like what will happen if I decide you're going to kill the hostages anyway."

"Do you really think we're stupid enough to believe you wouldn't kill every one of us the instant you thought you could, whatever we do here?" the man on the other end of the com link sneered. "We don't have anything at all to lose from that perspective, *Sir* Arthur!"

"Except that if I believe you're going to start killing hostages for no better reason than the fact that I've hurt your feelings, then I'll decide there's no point in trying to get them out alive, anyway," Keita said levelly. "And in that case, I'll solve the entire problem very simply with an HVW strike."

There was silence for several seconds.

"You're bluffing," the FALA spokesman said finally.

"Maybe," Keita acknowledged. "And maybe not. Remember, you've given me a lot of reasons to want to see you dead. The only thing keeping you alive right now are those hostages. You convince me they aren't coming out alive, anyway, and I don't have any reason to keep *you* alive, do I? So suppose we both stop threatening one another and you tell me why you commed?"

"All right, I will. You say you don't have any reason to keep me alive if you think the hostages are going to be killed. Well, I don't have any reason to keep the *hostages* alive if I think my people are all going to be killed, either. Which is why *Star Roamer* had better not see any assault shuttles heading for the planet from that battlecruiser—you know, the one pretending to be a freighter—when it joins you in orbit up there."

So much for whether or not Ctesiphon's *EW has them fooled,* Keita thought.

"Before you waste any time lying to me about it," the terrorist continued, "I should tell you that *Star Roamer*'s sensor arrays have been watching your precious battlecruiser ever since she arrived. Just as they were watching *you*, Sir Arthur. The *Marguerite Johnsen* might be able to fool some people, but we did our homework a little bit better than that. We knew who you were from the moment you arrived, and we were expecting your drop. Just as we've been expecting the arrival of reinforcements. I'm sure you have quite a few Marines aboard that battlecruiser, but I'd strongly recommend that you *keep* them there."

"And I'm sure you can hardly wait to tell me why I should take your recommendation to heart," Keita said when the other voice paused.

"Actually there are several reasons," the other man said, "but two big ones come immediately to mind. First, as I'm sure you've already realized, we have a lot more military capability down here than you assumed we did. In addition to what you've already discovered, we have ground-to-space defenses dug in around Green Haven. We can't stop an all-out assault, I'm sure, but we can kill all the assault shuttles you can pack aboard a single battlecruiser. So if you really want to send your Marines in and see them all as dead as your precious Cadremen, I'm sure we could oblige you.

"Now, it's possible you're thinking that I'm bluffing, or maybe you're thinking I'm overconfident about what our defenses can do. I'm not bluffing, but it is possible I'm overestimating our capabilities . . . the same way you overestimated yours when you decided to land Charlie Company. Which brings me to my second reason you shouldn't try dropping Marines on our heads; if you do, and if it turns out we can't stop them after all, we *will* kill the hostages. We won't have any reason not to."

"I see."

"I imagine you do," the FALA spokesman said mockingly. "And while we're on the subject, if you try to land Marines somewhere else, outside our defensive perimeter, *Star Roamer* will inform us. And the instant she does, we'll kill three hundred hostages. Please note that I'm not threatening to kill them out of hand, or as a bargaining ploy, or even in a fit of pique. We won't kill them *unless* you try to get fancy, so you've still got six hundred—well, *three hundred*—reasons to keep me alive, don't you?"

"To what final end?" Keita asked. "It's obvious your original demands were nothing but a way to pass the time while you waited to ambush our people. Surely you don't think the Empire is going to leave you *or* your organization alive in the long run after something like this?"

"We've all been on your proscribed list for years," the other man said. "You can't kill any of us more than once, however much you'd like to. And just this minute, I think you should be worried more about who *we* might kill. We'll tell you what our final demands are when we're good and ready. In the meantime, keep your Marines the hell off this planet. Is that understood, *Sir Arthur?*"

"It is," Keita grated. "And if I do, what happens to my people on Fuller?"

"Why, they *die*, Sir Arthur," the terrorist spokesman jeered. "That was the whole point of our little visit here—or one of them, at any rate. They've butchered enough of our friends over the years, after all, so it's only fair we get a little of our own back, and we're looking forward to it. We've already killed most of them; in the end, we'll kill them all, and enjoy doing it. Unless, of course, you're prepared to commit to a major assault to save the handful of them who are still alive *knowing* all your precious civilians will die before the first Marine boot hits the Green Haven ceramacrete. Somehow, I don't think it would look very good in the Empire media if word got out that twenty or thirty Cadremen were more important to you than six hundred of your Emperor's loving subjects, now would it?"

Keita said nothing, and the terrorist laughed.

"That's what I thought, too," he said. "Don't go away, Sir Arthur. I'm sure I'll have something else to say to you . . . eventually."

"Well, you were right, Sarge," Tannis Cateau said softly.

Alicia made an equally soft sound of agreement. She and Tannis lay side-by-side along the crest of a ridge overlooking the Jason Corporation facility and the not yet officially open Green Haven spaceport. Their armor's active sensors were shut completely down, and their passives' resolution wasn't all that great at this range, but what they could see was bad enough.

It was about one hour until local dawn, and Fuller's moon had set long since, which meant it was darker than the pit. The Freedom Alliance terrorists had extinguished most of the exterior lights when they took over the industrial site, but even under those conditions, Alicia could make out the angular shape of heavy plasma cannon—not simple infantry support weapons, but the kind that could destroy heavy tanks or knock down even the most heavily armored sting ships. There were three cannon positions, each with four of the heavy weapons, spaced evenly around the Jason Corporation buildings, and she was almost certain she saw at least two hypervelocity missile launchers, as well.

Her mouth tightened as she took in the weaponry so clearly on display. The terrorists had had the better part of three standard weeks since arriving here to prepare their defenses, but everything she'd seen so far shouted that the FALA had actually started the process long before that. They'd had to get the weapons and the personnel to man them on to the planet well in advance of *Star*

Roamer's arrival, and it looked to her as if the air-defense cannon's positions had actually been ceramacreted at the same time as the parking apron around the Jason buildings. They'd certainly been graded out of the slopes of the hill under the building, almost like terraces set a little below the level of the rest of the parking apron. No doubt the architect's plans had shown some perfectly reasonable justification for them, but Alicia was grimly certain that their real reason for being was the purpose they were serving now.

Which means the "Jason Corporation" is going to get a very close examination from imperial intelligence in the very near future, she told herself coldly. *Not that that helps us a great deal right this moment.*

"So what do we do now?" Tannis asked quietly.

"First, I send in my remote," Alicia replied, and sent the mental command to the small robotic scout riding her equipment harness. They'd lost two more of them since her last report to Sir Arthur, and a tiny part of her wanted to stroke the remote, as if it were some faithful, treasured hunting hawk, before she launched it on its way.

But she didn't. Instead, she closed her eyes and concentrated on steering her flying viewpoint as stealthily as she could.

There were active sensors covering the terrorists' central position. She tasted them through the remote's senses, and she felt her way cautiously towards them. They rose in an almost unbroken barrier in front of her, but it was only *almost* unbroken, and their primary concern was with a direct assault landing. She hovered with her remote, a disembodied presence just outside the electronic fence, cautiously tasting its emissions for what the tick made seem a very long time, and then she nodded very slightly.

There *was* a gap. It wasn't much of one—certainly much too small for anything the size of an assault shuttle or a recovery boat to get through—but it was there, and she edged carefully, carefully into it. The remote carried a single detachable relay transceiver, and she guided the probe to the roof of the building and instructed it to detach the relay link. She positioned it very carefully, with the whisker laser directed back through the keyhole the remote had crept through. There was no guarantee that something or someone wouldn't stray into the transmission path and detect it anyway, but she could at least avoid the known detection threats.

Once the relay was in place, she lifted the remote higher, hovering directly above the central building. Its active sensors, like those of her armor, were locked down, but its passive sensors had a much closer look at the antiair defenses, and she grimaced. Her original impression had been correct, except that there were *three* multi-rail HVW launchers, one paired with each of the plasma cannon emplacements.

She studied them for several seconds even as she recorded every detail of the take from the remote, then sent her small henchman drifting silently along the building's eaves, looking for a way in. After a couple of minutes, she found one. The remote hovered under the roof's overhang, tiny cutting laser slicing quietly through the meshlike grill covering the opening, and then floated very slowly through the ventilation intake.

The interior of the building looked much as Alicia had expected. A portion of it was cut up into office space and what looked like a cafeteria, but at least eighty percent of the vast structure was a single, open cavern dotted with maintenance workstations for the heavy construction equipment which should have filled it. There was a second-floor catwalk around the large, central area, and additional office space on that level, but her remote's passives were more than adequate at such close range to confirm that only two or three of those offices had anyone in them.

Not that there weren't plenty of other people in the building.

The hostages huddled in the middle of the open space, most of them sitting on what appeared to be foam sleeping mats. There were portable toilets parked along the holding area's walls, and the remote's visual sensors showed her canisters of drinking water and what looked like standard Marine field ration packs. All of the captives were dirty and unwashed looking, and most of them sat folded in on themselves, with the body language of people who wanted to withdraw to some inner place, safely away from the terror which had enveloped them for the last two standard months.

On the other hand, there were actually fewer terrorists inside the building than she'd expected, and she smiled humorlessly at the realization.

We've seen so many of them out here that I've gotten into the habit of thinking they must have an inexhaustible supply of manpower, she thought. *Well, obviously they don't.*

Under the circumstances, though, they might be excused for believing they had enough inside guards, she reflected. There were four heavy calliopes mounted on the catwalk, positioned to cover every square centimeter of floorspace. Any one of them could spit out over five thousand rounds per minute; the four of them together could turn the maintenance area into an abattoir in moments. Nor were they the only security measure the terrorists had taken. An infantry plasma cannon—lighter than the ones in the air-defense positions but considerably heavier than anything Alicia still had—was positioned far enough inside the building to cover all three of the vehicle entrances in its western wall.

Only the crew of the plasma cannon were in battle armor. The remainder of the eighteen armed personnel backing up the calliope crews and the cannoneers were either completely unarmored or wore only unpowered body armor. All of them, however, she noticed, wore combat helmets. She couldn't make out enough details to be certain, but they looked like more Marine surplus equipment, in which case they would provide their wearers with at least semi-decent sensors and a free-flow tactical link.

She rotated the remote, giving herself one last good look, then lifted it up and landed it quietly on an exposed support beam just under the building's roof. She positioned it to give herself the best field of view she could, then switched it to standby and sat up.

"I take it you followed all of that?" she said to Tannis.

"Yep." Tannis climbed to her own feet, and the two of them moved down the back side of their ridge to join the other Charlie Company survivors.

There aren't very many of them, Alicia thought as their icons gathered around hers.

Thirty-one other men and women stood around her, eleven percent of the company which had made the drop. Only seven of the original eighteen troopers of her own squad were still on their feet . . . which still made First Squad her strongest surviving unit.

Every suit of armor bore its own proof of what its wearer had been through to get this far. The reactive chameleon features built into Cadre armor wasn't doing much good at the moment—not for armor whose smart surfaces had been liberally smeared with resinous sap as it crashed through the dense branches of the native conifers. The forest fires which so much plasma fire left in their wake—the fires whose lurid light still painted the skies above the tangled mountains behind them—had added their own share to the surviving Cadremen's battered and bedamned appearance. Cinders, ash, and unburned twigs and needlelike leaves were glued to the sap-coated armor, and most of the armored figures she could see showed the same sort of dents and gouges her own armor did.

She looked around at them, and her heart twisted within her as she thought about what she was about to ask of them.

"You've all seen what we're up against out there," she said finally. "I don't see any way to get recovery boats—or assault shuttles, for that matter—down against those sorts of defenses. Not without using suppressive fire that would kill all the hostages, anyway. So the way I see it, that only leaves one option."

She paused, then opened her mouth again, but before she could speak, Astrid Nordbø spoke for her. The dark-haired, blue-eyed corporal had run out of ammunition for her battle rifle and replaced it with Shai Hau-zhi's calliope when Obaseki Osayaba's wing stopped a heavy-caliber calliope round from one of the air-cav mounts. Now she chuckled mirthlessly over the com.

"What the hell, Sarge," she said. "We've come this far, and it's been so much fun. We might as well stay to the end of the ride."

CHAPTER TWENTY-SIX

"Skycap, Winchester-One."

Sir Arthur Keita twitched upright in his comfortable chair as the tick-clipped, husky contralto spoke.

"Winchester-One, Skycap," he said quickly. "Go."

"We've got that eyeball of the objective for you, Uncle Arthur," the voice said. "It doesn't look especially good. They've got air-defense plasma cannon—they look like Marine Mark Eighteens—positioned around the central facility, with HVW launchers to back them up. They've also got a hundred and eighty—I say again, one-eight-zero—more infantry dug in around the base of the hill. We've gotten a remote inside the objective, and they've got all of the hostages in a single location covered by calliopes and infantry support cannon. We have a hard count of thirty-three hostiles inside the building, including weapons crews, but only three in battle armor. I've confirmed active air-defense radar and lidar, and they have a radar fence around the building itself at ground level. They do not—I repeat, *do not*—have a fence around the base of the hill. Some of their infantry seems to be moving around a good bit, and I'd guess they figured their own people would keep triggering alarms if they covered the hill itself."

Keita's expression had tightened further with every word, and he rubbed his face wearily at the end of Alicia's summary.

"Winchester-One," he said when she paused. "Alley. The FALA's been in contact with us. They say they'll kill half the hostages if we try to land Marines from *Ctesiphon*—and all of them if it looks like we might manage to actually get the Wasps down through their defenses. And," his jaw tightened, but he made himself continue levelly, "they say they won't let us withdraw you. They want to finish you off, make a clean sweep. Although," he admitted bleakly, "I think they might actually be happier in some ways if we tried to extract you anyway and all the hostages were killed."

"That's about how I'd already read the situation, Uncle Arthur," Alicia said calmly. "But none of us down here are inclined to let these people get away with it."

Keita's eyebrows rose, but she continued steadily before he could speak.

"I think we can get into the objective," she told him. "I believe we can take out the air defense positions and hold the main facility until you get the Wasps down to relieve us."

Keita turned to stare at Wadislaw Watts. The Marine intelligence specialist stared back at him in obvious disbelief, and Keita shook his head sharply.

"Alley," he said, "I'm sorry, but I don't think you can do it."

"Then you're wrong, Uncle Arthur," she replied flatly. "My people can do it. We *will* do it."

"But—"

"They don't know we're here," she continued, overriding his protest. "If they did, they'd sure as hell be doing something about it. We've got good cover and concealment up to within less than three hundred meters of their outer infantry positions on the north side of the hill. I've got three plasma guns left, and there are three antiair sites. We move most of our people in as close as we can get on the north side. Then the plasma gunners take out the air defenses to clear the way for the Wasps. While they do that, the rest of us break through their outer ring position, charge the building, cut our way through the outer wall—it's only prefab plastic—with our force blades, and take out the interior terrorists before they know we're coming. Then all we have to do is hold the central building until the Wasps get there."

Keita closed his eyes and clenched his fists so tightly that they hurt, then shook his head again, hard.

"Alley, that's a suicide mission," he said, and his powerful voice was frayed ever so slightly about the edge. "You're low on ammo, you'd have to cover—what? five hundred meters? six?—to reach the building. And even assuming you managed that, *and* managed to take out the inside guards, there'd still be almost two hundred people in battle armor coming in behind you. People who wouldn't give a good goddamn how many of the hostages *they* kill."

"Uncle Arthur, they're going to kill all of them—or most of them—anyway," Alicia said even more flatly. "That may not be their game plan, but it's what's going to happen, and you know it as well as I do. They can't talk their way out of this one whatever they do, and when they start to figure that out, they're going to get desperate and begin killing people to try to force concessions you can't give them. And when they do that, you're going to have to come in anyway. And when that happens, everyone dies. This way we can get at least some of them—most of them, I believe—out alive."

"But we don't have to do it right now," Keita said almost desperately. "If they don't know where you are, you can break off, evade. Maybe we can get a resupply drop to you without them realizing it. For God's sake, Alley, at least let us get more ammunition to you first!"

"We *do* have to do it now," she replied. "*Right* now. They don't know we're here at the moment, but they're still looking for us. Eventually, they'll find us. And even if that weren't true, even if we could withdraw, resupply, we'd never get this close again without being spotted on the way in. It's now or never, Uncle Arthur, and we've lost too many of our people to settle for never. Charlie Company is going in. Now, are you going to support us with a Marine drop, or not?"

"I can't believe we're doing this," Captain Wadislaw Watts said quietly. Keita gave him a sharp look, and the Marine shook his head quickly. "That wasn't a criticism, Sir Arthur. It was . . . amazement. I'm just trying to understand how even the Cadre can insist on going in after what's already happened to Charlie Company."

"Put that way, I have to agree with you," Keita said after a moment. "And a part of me wishes to hell they weren't. But DeVries is the one on the ground down there. She's the one who's gotten them this far despite everything those bastards could do to stop them, she's the one who's actually seen the site, and she's the commander on the spot. That makes it her call, and, God help me, I think it's the right call, too."

"You really believe they can pull it off, Sir?" Watts asked. Keita gazed at him for several seconds, then sighed.

"No, Captain," he said softly. "I don't, not deep down inside. But I wouldn't have believed they could get as far as they have, either. If they can do that, maybe they've got one more miracle left in them. And even if they don't, DeVries is right about what's going to happen eventually. We'll try like hell to get the hostages out alive, but we won't. Not in the end. So she's right about its being time to roll the dice, too."

He turned away from the Marine, gazing into the depths of a visual display, unfocused eyes resting upon the pinprick stars gleaming in the endless, velvet blackness. Then he drew a deep breath and looked at Lieutenant Smithson.

"Get me a link to *Ctesiphon*, please, Lieutenant. I need to speak to Major Bennett."

"Are you serious, Sir?" Captain Broderick Lewinsky said, staring at Major Alexander Bennett, the commanding officer of *Ctesiphon*'s reinforced Marine detachment. The briefing compartment would have been relatively spacious for the officers of the battlecruiser's normal detachment, but it was badly crowded by the number of people crammed into it at the moment. The fact that all of them were already in battle armor only put an even greater squeeze on the available space. But none of them had helmeted up yet, and Lewinsky wasn't the only officer in the compartment who looked as if he was having trouble believing what the major had just told them.

"Yes, I am serious," Bennett said flatly. "We're going in."

"But, Sir," Lieutenant Jurgensen said, "I thought Brigadier Keita told us the LZ was covered by antiair weapons."

"It is." If Bennett's voice had been flat before, it was grim now, and he looked the youthful lieutenant in the eye. "As a matter of fact, they say they've got Mark Eighteens dug in around the facility, with HVW launchers backing them up. And using *Ctesiphon* to provide suppressive fire has already been ruled out."

The officers in the compartment stared at him in horror, and he smiled thinly.

"According to Sir Arthur Keita, the survivors of the Cadre company are going to take out the emplacements for us before we enter atmosphere. Then they're going to seize the facility from the terrorists, and hold it against counterattack until we can get down to relieve them."

The compartment was completely silent for several seconds, then Lewinsky cleared his throat.

"Major, I know the Cadre's good. And God knows, just from the bits and pieces we've already heard, these people have kicked ass and taken names, especially after hitting a hot LZ. But how many of them can be left?"

"According to Sir Arthur, thirty-two effectives," Bennett said quietly.

"*Thirty-three?*" someone blurted. "My God, Sir—they went in with a *company*!"

"Which doesn't have a single officer left," Bennett said with a nod.

"And they're going to take out dug-in plasma cannon and HVW launchers, then seize and hold the facility until we hit dirt?" Captain Sigmund Boniface, Bravo Company's CO, said carefully.

"That's what they say, Siggy," the major told him. "I don't know if they honestly believe they can do it, but they're sure as hell going to try. And if they've got the guts to put it all on the line this way after what they've already been through, people, then we *are* going to support them. Is that perfectly clear?"

His expression was half a glare as he looked around the compartment, and the men and women gathered in it with him looked back steadily. The traditional rivalry between the Marines and the Cadre—the Wasps' resentment of all the publicity and media hype the Cadre routinely received, the Cadre's higher budget priorities, their frustration with the Cadre's habit of raiding the Corps' best personnel for its own recruits—none of that mattered. Not now, not in this compartment. These people understood what Charlie Company had already done . . . and what its battered and broken remnants were offering to do now.

"Of course it is, Sir," Boniface, as the senior company commander present replied. "I just don't believe even the Cadre can do it."

"According to Sir Arthur, this Sergeant DeVries does believe it," Bennett said. "And she's the one down there, not us."

"Excuse me, Sir," Delta Company's commander said, "but did you say DeVries? *Alicia* DeVries?"

"Sir Arthur didn't mention her first name," Bennett replied, looking sharply at the youthful captain with the Recon patch on the shoulder of her armor. "But the last name was certainly DeVries. Sergeant First Class DeVries. Why, Captain?"

"Because it sounds like you're talking about Alicia DeVries," the captain replied. "And if you are, she's Sebastian O'Shaughnessy's granddaughter."

"*Sergeant Major* O'Shaughnessy?" Bennett said sharply, and the captain nodded.

"Yes, Sir. And in her case, blood is definitely thicker than water."

"You know this sergeant? Know her personally, I mean?"

"Oh, yes, Sir," Captain Kuramochi Chiyeko said softly. "I believe you could say that. And if Alley DeVries says her people can do this, then *I'm* damned well not going to bet against it."

"I see." Bennett looked around the compartment one last time, and his lips quirked in a quick, brief smile. "Well, there you have it, people. We'll go with the original Green Haven assault landing plan. So get your people loaded up. I want the shuttles ready to separate from the racks fifteen minutes from now.

"Winchester-One, Skycap."

"Skycap, Winchester-One. Go, Uncle Arthur."

"*Ctesiphon*'s launched her shuttles," Keita said. "At the moment, they're sticking close to the ship, so hopefully the bastards in *Star Roamer* won't realize they've separated. From the moment you give the insertion signal, they'll need twenty-five—I say again, two-five—minutes to hit the LZ. That's how long you'll have to hold."

"Understood, Skycap," Alicia said steadily.

Far, far above her, in *Marguerite Johnsen*'s intelligence center, Sir Arthur Keita fought down the temptation to ask her one more time if she was certain about this.

"In that case, Winchester-One," he said instead, "the ball is in your hands."

"Understood," Alicia said again. "We will commence our attack in five minutes from . . . now."

A digital time display began ticking down in the corner of the mental HUD Keita's synth-link displayed for him, and his jaw set hard.

"Good hunting," he managed to say almost normally. "Skycap, clear."

Alicia studied her own HUD one final time.

Obaseki Osayaba, Alec Howard, and Serena DuPuy had the company's surviving plasma guns. Every one of them had lost his or her original wing on the nightmare journey to this point, and she'd paired them with Astrid Nordbø, Jackson Keller, and Ingrid Chernienko. Astrid, Jackson, and Ingrid had three of the four remaining calliopes, and she'd handed *all* of the remaining calliope ammunition to them and ditched the fourth calliope completely. The heavy-caliber, rapid-fire weapons would have been of limited utility breaking into a facility crowded with civilian noncombatants.

"All units, Winchester-One," she said. "Plasma teams, remember—hit the air-defense positions and your assigned secondary targets, then get the hell out of it. The rest of us go the instant Obaseki and Serena take out the center positions on our slope."

There was no real need for her to tell them that yet again, but that was all right with her. She wasn't worried that they were going to think she didn't trust them to get it right, but she couldn't tell them what she really wanted to. Couldn't tell them how much each and every one of them meant to her, especially now, when they were the only Cadre family she had left. When she was the one who had decided for them that they were going to throw themselves into the furnace.

When so many of them were about to die.

No, she couldn't tell them that . . . but they heard it anyway. She knew they did, and that was enough.

"We go in three minutes," she said quietly. "God bless."

Section Leader Shau-pang Shwang of the Freedom Alliance Liberation Army hated battle armor. He'd never liked it, despite all the things it could do for him, because he'd never been able to completely overcome the claustrophobia which had plagued him since childhood. That was the main reason he preferred to leave his helmet visor open whenever he could, and he inhaled a deep breath of Green Haven's cool, late-night air.

Like most of the FALA "regulars" assigned to the operation, Shwang was himself ex-military. Unlike most of the others, however, he'd actually put in his time in the Imperial Marines. The long and tangled chain of events which had led him to where he was today would never have occurred to the long ago, long distant self who'd volunteered to be a Wasp, but the training remained. That was why he'd been tapped for this operation—the FALA didn't have all that many personnel who'd spent almost five standard years manning and maintaining Mark 18 plasma cannon.

And just between himself and the cool, breezy night, Shaupang Shwang was grateful his experience had landed him here and not out with the screening infantry. He hated the Cadre as much as any other member of the Freedom Alliance, and he was coldly, viciously pleased by the losses the Emperor's personal storm troopers had taken this night. But he was a practical man, was Shaupang Shwang, and he was perfectly content to let someone else do the killing.

Especially when the bastards have been so good at killing us right back, he thought with a twisted grin.

On the other hand, Comrade Omicron—even among their most trusted subordinates, the members of the Command Council went only by their code names—had finally begun letting the Empies know what the Alliance really had in mind. Shwang rather doubted that even Omicron was quite as confident they'd be able to walk away from this one as he was careful to project. Personally, Shwang figured there was no more than a forty percent chance the Empire would back off, hostages or no hostages. But every man and woman assigned to this operation had understood from the moment they took up arms against the might of the Terran Empire that the odds against their ultimate survival were steep. And if they succeeded in their actual objectives even half as well as it looked like they were going to, it would all be worth it in the end.

Not that I wouldn't like *to walk away alive*, he admitted to himself. *It's always nicer to live to enjoy your successes, after all.*

He smiled again and turned to look back towards the central building where the hostages were being held.

Which was why he was looking in exactly the wrong direction when the first plasma bolt exploded directly on top of his number three cannon and vaporized it, its crew, the central data processing unit for the battery, and one Shau-pang Shwang, who died without even knowing that he had.

Alicia watched Obaseki Osayaba's plasma bolt take out the central cannon of the northernmost emplacement. Secondary explosions and blast had probably done for the others, as well, but Osayaba was taking no chances. He fired again, and again, as rapidly as his plasma rifle's firing chamber lasers could induce fusion in the hydrogen pellets. The plasma bolts screamed out of the night, obliterating the Mark 18 cannon and the missile launcher paired with them.

Surprise was total. As she had told Keita, if the FALA infantry had suspected even for a moment that Charlie Company's survivors were anywhere near Green Haven, they would have been trying to do something about it. And, as she'd also hoped, the sheer shock of the sudden, totally unexpected attack induced a momentary paralysis.

Osayaba finished eliminating his assigned antiair weapons and retargeted. His plasma bolts shrieked over Alicia's head, shredding the night, impacting on the defensive FALA perimeter around the northern side of the hill. He continued to fire as rapidly as he could . . . and just as accurately. Individual armored infantrymen took direct hits, torsos vaporizing, heads simply disappearing, and a hole opened in the center of their line.

"*Go!*" she barked, and twenty-seven Cadremen and women came out of the night-wrapped woods in the prodigious bounds of battle armor being pushed to its maximum capability.

Nobody even noticed them for a heartbeat or two. Then the first plasma bolts and calliope rounds began sizzling in their direction, but there weren't very many of them, and Alicia's heart twisted within her as she realized why.

"Two o'clock!" Astrid Nordbø said sharply.

"I see it," Obaseki Osayaba replied, and he did. Not that there was very much he could do about it at the moment.

He tracked steadily to his left, working his way along the line of dug-in terrorist infantry in front of Alicia and her charging troopers. He really ought to be withdrawing into the woods by now, according to Alicia's instructions, but he and Astrid had known they wouldn't be. They were the only fire team in position to cover Alicia's mad charge, and that meant that, orders or no, that was what they were going to do.

Return fire shrieked, sizzled, and howled around Osayaba's position. He and Astrid were bellied down behind the shallow earth berms they'd thrown up for cover, and a superheated fog of vaporized soil hung in the air around them. Someone down there was using his armor sensors to back-plot Osayaba's fire, but he wasn't as good at it as the bastards who'd set up the ambush at the LZ.

Even without his armor, it would have been impossible for Osayaba to sort any individual sound out of the insane bedlam screaming about him, but he knew Astrid was firing back with her calliope. She had less than five hundred rounds, and she was expending them in short, tight bursts as FALA infantry, unable to get clear shots at them, came charging in from either flank.

Osayaba saw them coming, knew they were hurtling through the night almost as rapidly as Alicia and her troopers on the hillside, even if the tick did make them seem to float slowly towards him. And he knew Astrid wasn't going to be able to stop them all. She simply didn't have enough ammunition, and neither did he. And since he couldn't stop them, he ignored them, continuing to pick off individual targets as battle-armored terrorists around the base of the hill tried to bring their weapons to bear on Alicia's attack.

He fired one more time, and the digital display of rounds remaining dropped to zero in the corner of his HUD.

"I'm dry," he told Astrid in a voice which sounded impossibly calm to his own ears.

"Me . . . too," she said, as she fired the final burst from her calliope.

"Then I guess it's time," he replied, and used his synth-link to command his armor to jettison his useless plasma gun. It fell away, and he rose out of his improvised firing position, drawing his force blade with his right hand and bringing it alive while he drew his

CHK with his left. The pistol couldn't penetrate battle armor anywhere except the visor, and even there only with a lucky hit, but he figured he was owed at least a little luck.

He "saw" Astrid beside him through his sensors. Saw her toss away the calliope, draw her own side arm and force blade. She wasn't Shai Hau-zhi, the woman who'd been Osayaba's wing for over two standard years, but then, he wasn't Flannan O'Clery, the laughing Irishman who'd been Astrid's wing even longer. And that didn't matter, either. Not tonight.

"Let's kick some ass," he told her, and they charged to meet the oncoming terrorists.

Alicia saw Osayaba's and Nordbø's icons start to move—not away from the objective and into the woods, but towards it. She knew exactly what they were doing, and why, and there was nothing—nothing in the universe—she could do to stop them.

The two green icons leapt towards the wave of armored infantry sweeping down upon Osayaba's firing position. She saw one of the glaring orange enemy icons go down, then another. A third. And then Obaseki and Astrid were in among the orange icons, completely enveloped. Two more orange icons fell, and then Astrid's green dot turned suddenly crimson.

An instant later, there were only orange icons.

Corporal Alec Howard saw the same thing on his own HUD and swore viciously. But there was nothing he could do about it, and he clenched his jaw.

The southernmost antiair position, which had been his assigned target, was a wrecked, flaming ruin. He'd killed at least another thirty or forty FALA terrorists taking it out, but he'd exhausted his fusion pellets in the process. His assigned wing, Jackson Keller, had exactly eighteen rounds left for his calliope. They'd done everything they could possibly do, and he knew it, yet his instincts cried out for him to do something else. Something more.

Only there was nothing more, and a wave of orange icons was frothing up the slope towards his own position.

"Time to go, Jackson," he grated. Maybe they could at least suck a few of the bastards into chasing them instead of going after Alley, and the two of them went bounding back into the forest while the crescendo of battle roared behind them.

"Time to go, Serena!" Ingrid Chernienko said, squeezing off another short, sharp burst from her calliope.

"Roger that!" Serena DuPuy replied, giving her armor the jettison command as she fired her own last round. Like Osayaba and Howard, she'd turned her assigned target into a flaming torch, but someone on her side of the perimeter was obviously better at using his armor's sensors than the ones who'd tried to back-plot Osayaba's fire. Three plasma bolts had blasted smoking, fused-glass craters into the earth within less than five meters of her position, and it was *definitely* time to go.

She bounded up out of her firing position and turned towards the woods . . . just as a round from an enemy calliope slammed into the back of her right leg.

It was a direct hit, one not even Cadre battle armor could stop, and the impact smashed her back into the ground. Her right thigh shattered, and the tourniquet built into her armor locked down as her femoral artery began to spurt and agony roared through her. Her pharmacope sent its painkillers racing after the stormfront of pain and drove a burst of adrenaline into her system to combat shock, but nothing could blunt that moment of transcendent anguish.

"Hold on, Serena!" Chernienko shouted.

"*No!*" DuPuy screamed back, forcing herself up into a sitting position, pistol in both armored hands as the first battle armored terrorist vaulted up the last few meters of slope with his battle rifle already swinging towards her.

"Get the hell out of here!" she barked at Chernienko, and squeezed off the first pistol round. It struck the terrorist's visor, but at an angle, and whined off harmlessly. She fired again, and again, and the FALA infantryman flinched at each shot. But he kept coming, too—until a burst of calliope fire turned him into so much armored dead meat almost at her feet.

"Come *on!*" Chernienko barked, tossing away her now-empty calliope.

"I told you to get *out* of here!" DuPuy snarled.

"Shut the fuck up and give me your hand!" Chernienko snarled back, and bent over the other woman. Her armor's exoskeletal muscles whined as she snatched DuPuy up into a fireman's carry and turned back towards the woods.

She made one leap before the plasma bolt came shrieking in, struck DuPuy squarely in the back, and killed both of them instantly.

Alicia saw two more green icons turn crimson as she and her remaining troopers crossed the steaming, smoking wreckage which had been the FALA perimeter until Obaseki Osayaba turned it into a slaughter ground.

Here and there single armored infantrymen, or pairs of them, survived. They were shocked, stunned by the totally unexpected carnage, but a handful of them were managing to shoot back. Her battle rifle tracked onto one of them and she fired in midair. The sub-caliber penetrators ripped through the breastplate of his armor and he went down hard. The rifle's servos traversed with snakelike speed, and she fired again, and again. Another terrorist went down with each short burst, and she saw others tumbling aside as someone else took them down.

But they weren't going alone.

Osayaba had broken the back of the position directly in front of Alicia's charge, but the defensive line's ends were still intact, however shaken they might have been, and flanking fire ripped into her charge. Corporal Ramji seemed to trip in midair. His armor shattered as the plasma bolt slammed into it from the right, and his icon, too, turned blood-red. Corporal Teng Rwun-yin died an instant later, and Corporal Ulujuk went down, life signs flickering, as a heavy-caliber calliope penetrator ripped through his belly.

And then they were past the defensive position's ruined foxholes and racing up the hill towards the buildings they'd come so far, and paid so high a price, to reach.

Twenty-seven Cadre troopers had started up that hill. Seventeen of them reached the top, leaving the slope behind them strewn with the shattered, smoking bodies of their enemies.

Alicia drew her force blade as the exterior wall of their objective loomed before her. She brought it slashing across, opening the tough composite "plastic" of the wall as if it were spun spider silk.

She crashed into the opening she'd created an instant later, smashing it bigger, exploding into the building in a shower of splinters.

She didn't even slow down. Other armored figures came crashing through the same wall a half-breath behind her, and they, like her, knew exactly where to find the terrorists inside the structure. They were tied into the remote she'd parked on the crossbeam so far above, and Alicia's flashing thoughts reached out through her synth-link, designating targets.

She hit her own jump gear in a full-power jump that sent her rocketing across the huge room while hostages screamed in terror below her. She hit the second-story catwalk barely three meters from one of the calliopes, and the un-armored terrorist behind it screamed in terror of her own as the catwalk trembled under the crashing impact of Alicia's arrival. The FALA gunner tried frantically to bring her weapon to bear, but Alicia was too close. She didn't bother with her battle rifle, or her pistol. She simply swept the force blade still in her hand in a flat, vicious stroke that caught the other woman just below armpit level and sliced clear through her body in a shocking geyser of blood.

The terrorist thudded to the catwalk in two separate pieces, and Alicia whirled, reaching out to catch the calliope before it tipped over the catwalk rail to the floor below.

A burst of heavy penetrators blasted a line of holes through the wall above her as one of the other FALA gunners fired at her. But the burst was high, and before the terrorist could fire a second time, Tannis Cateau's deadly accurate battle rifle sent two rounds through his brain.

Alicia got control of the calliope beside her and turned back towards the floor below, but she'd taken just a fraction of a second too long.

Corporal Brian Oselli had come through the outer wall half a meter behind Alicia. The First Squad trooper had exhausted the last of his rifle ammunition on his way up the hill, but his CHK was in his right hand, and his force blade was in his left.

Another terrorist loomed up in front of him, this one in unpowered body armor and armed with a Marine M-97 combat rifle. The terrorist tried frantically to bring it to bear, but Oselli's pistol punched three penetrators through the other man's breastplate, and he vaulted the corpse, bounding towards the plasma cannon covering the vehicle entrances.

The plasma cannon's crew had been as surprised as everyone else by the sudden, unexpected ferocity of the Cadre's attack. They weren't supposed to have to worry about deadly enemies suddenly appearing *behind* them, and one of them panicked and started backing away as Oselli charged towards them. But the other two didn't. They swung their weapon around rapidly, bringing it to bear on the charging Cadreman, and Oselli bellowed in primordial rage. When that weapon fired, he would die . . . and so would dozens, possibly hundreds, of the hostages behind him.

He fired as he came, again and again. The pistol's penetrators smashed into the plasma gunner, screaming and wailing as they ricocheted off his breastplate. He staggered back, but only for a moment, and Oselli could feel his matching hate as he reached for the cannon's firing grips again.

But Oselli's unwavering charge had delayed him just long enough. The Cadre corporal saw the moment the terrorist's hands reached the grips, and his own right arm drew back and then flashed forward. His force blade went slicing through the air, even as he deliberately flung himself straight down the muzzle of the cannon.

The gunner squeezed the trigger. The plasma bolt hit Oselli less than two meters in front of the cannon. And the force blade continued its flight and sliced effortlessly through the gunner's armor to completely decapitate him.

Oselli simply vanished. Only his left leg continued forward, skittering across the ceramacrete floor. But he'd been close enough, centered enough, to take the full brunt of the plasma. Seventeen hostages were killed behind him. Another six were badly wounded. But that was all, from a shot which could have killed half the unarmored people in that room.

Alicia saw Oselli go down. Back blast from the plasma bolt slammed into the gunner's assistant, staggering him, and then Alicia brought her captured calliope to bear. Her eyes were merciless jade ice as a shrieking burst of penetrators swept the terrorist away. Then she was swinging the weapon again, piling a dozen FALA terrorists in a single shredded line of corpses as they came charging out of a hallway from one of the office blocks.

Erik Andersson had another of the calliopes, and his fire slammed down, joining hers, raking the terrified terrorists who ten seconds before had been so certain they were in control of the situation.

And then the firing suddenly died, and there were no living terrorists left inside all that cavernous structure.

CHAPTER TWENTY-SEVEN

"What the fuck *happened*?" Group Leader Rivera demanded, staring in stunned disbelief at the shattered, blazing ruins of the antiair defenses.

"Why the hell ask *me*?" Group Leader Abruzzi snarled back. "It had to be the fucking Cadre—that's all *I* know!"

Rivera throttled a raging desire to peel Lloyd Abruzzi out of his battle armor and strangle him with his bare hands. Not that the other group leader was any more to blame than Rivera himself.

And not that there's time to be worrying *about who's at fault*, he told himself grimly.

"I can't raise Omicron," Abruzzi continued. "Or *Star Roamer*."

"They must've taken out the com center," Rivera replied.

"Then we don't know whether or not the Wasps are on the way." There was a note Rivera didn't much care for in Abruzzi's voice. Not *panic*, really, but something else. Something . . .

He pushed that thought aside, too, and shook his head.

"They'll be on the way soon enough," he said grimly. "We've got to assume these people—" he swept one armored arm at the huge building above them, oblivious to the fact that Abruzzi couldn't actually see him from his own position on the far side of the hill "—told Keita when they planned to attack. For that matter, they're probably in communication with him right now."

"Shit," Abruzzi muttered.

Rivera couldn't argue with that. He turned where he stood, sweeping his eyes one more time across the blazing carnage the

Cadre assault had left in its wake. Then his jaw tightened as he made up his mind.

"We don't have time to stand here talking about it, Lloyd," he said harshly. "My group's in better shape than yours. I'll take the assault."

"*Assault?*" Abruzzi repeated. "What assault?"

Jaime Rivera blinked in astonishment.

"We've got maybe thirty minutes before we've got Wasps all over us," he said, his voice flat. "That's our window to retake the hostages if we're going to have any bargaining chips at all."

"Screw bargaining chips!" Abruzzi growled. "We said we'd waste their precious hostages if they attacked us. Well, they've frigging well attacked us!"

"Goddamn it, don't you screw around with me on this one," Rivera grated. "There can't be more than a dozen of them left, and I've got fifty men. We can still retake the place, and if we do, we've got at least a chance to get the rest of our people off this planet. If Keita won't talk to us, we can still kill them all then."

"I say—" Abruzzi started, but Rivera cut him off savagely.

"I don't really care what you say!" he snarled. "I'm senior. We do it my way. We've got them by four-to-one odds, and unlike us, they're going to be handicapped trying to keep the hostages alive. *We* don't care if there's a little breakage on the way in, and that gives us another edge."

"We've had 'another edge' where these bastards were concerned all goddamned night," Abruzzi pointed out angrily. "Who's to say they won't screw you over all over again if you go in after them?"

"Well, if that happens, *you'll* be in command. At which point, you can do whatever the hell you want to do. You've still got most of your people's plasma rifles—you think you can't take down that entire building and kill everything in it if you really want to?"

Abruzzi was silent for a moment, and Rivera tossed his head angrily inside his helmet.

"Look," he said, "I'm taking my people, and we're going in. We're losing time standing here talking about it, and we don't *have* much time before the Wasps get here. These people must've told them the air defenses are down and that *they've* got the hostages. The Marines are going to begin their drop the instant they've got confirmation of those two things, so just shut the hell up and stay out of my way!"

"All right," Abruzzi said, manifestly unhappily. "Go ahead. But I warn you, we're taking that building down the instant I see a Wasp down here, and if you're still inside . . ."

"Fine," Rivera said shortly, and began snapping orders.

"Look at this, Sarge!" Tannis said, and Alicia glanced at her mental HUD as her wing dropped a wire diagram of the building into it.

"What is that?" she asked after a moment, and Tannis laughed with what actually sounded like genuine humor.

"It's a *basement*, Sarge! A great big, beautiful, *deep* basement, right under us! I figure we can get at least three or four hundred people into it, if we pack 'em in tight."

"All *right*!" Alicia said with sudden, matching delight, then grinned. "You found it, so packing them in is *your* job. Get them moving."

"Gee, thanks," Tannis replied, and an instant later Alicia's exterior pickups brought her the sound of Tannis' armor-amplified voice shouting orders.

Alicia left that up to her wing. If anyone could get a bunch of terrified, exhausted hostages moving in a hurry, it was Tannis. In the meantime, Alicia had other things to worry about, and her fleeting grin disappeared as she wiped the building diagram from her HUD and reconfigured it to tactical mode.

She didn't much care for what it showed her.

There were only eleven green icons left, including hers and Tannis'. That wasn't enough—not to hold something this size against as many battle armored attackers as she knew were still waiting out there on the slopes of the hill. Still, if Tannis could get a significant proportion of the hostages down into the basement she'd found, it would be an enormous help. Not a big enough one, maybe, but still a help.

"Erik," she said, no longer bothering with call signs.

"Yeah, Sarge," Erik Andersson replied.

"You're in charge of the calliopes. I want yours and Samantha's on the west wall. Put the other two where you think best."

"On it," Andersson acknowledged laconically, and Alicia looked over to where Thomas Kiely was examining the plasma cannon Oselli had knocked out.

"Can you get it back up, Tom?" she asked.

"I think so, but it's not gonna be pretty. Brian got so close the back blast smashed hell out of the cup generators."

Kiely pointed, and Alicia grimaced. The cannon was a considerably more powerful weapon than the plasma rifles the Cadre normally carried. In fact, it was powerful enough for thermal bloom to be a significant threat to nearby friendly personnel whenever it fired. So, like all such weapons, it projected a hollow conical force field—the "cup"—for a dozen meters or so in front of it. The force field protected anything to the cannon's immediate flanks and rear when it fired, which was exactly what Oselli had counted upon when he sacrificed himself to save the hostages. The plasma bolt's containment field had ruptured the instant it hit his armor, releasing the bolt's energy in a stupendous explosion. But it had been so close to the cannon that the cup had contained almost all of its fury. It had blown the cannoneer's assistant gunner off his feet, and the portion of the blast which had gotten past Oselli's disintegrating body had been enough to kill every hostage within twenty meters and burn anyone within another ten meters or so horribly. But had he not done what he had, at least half the hostages in that huge room would have died.

"How bad is it?" she asked.

"I can't tell without running a full diagnostic, and we don't have time for that," Kiely told her. "Best guess? We bring the cup up and it unbalances the driver field and screws accuracy all to hell and gone."

"And if we don't bring the cup up, it incinerates everything in front of it for twenty-five meters in every direction," she pointed out.

"So?" Alicia could almost feel Kiely's wolfish grin. "We're a little thin on the ground already, Sarge. I don't think I really mind the notion of covering my own flanks with the biggest damned scattergun I can find."

"Something to that," she agreed, and he actually chuckled over the com as he drew his force blade once again. He brought it down in a crisp, clean arc that sliced the damaged generator assembly off the end of the cannon barrel.

"Since it was my idea, I'll take it," he said, and Alicia nodded.

"All right. This wall," she pointed at the one in front of them, "is where they're most likely to come at us."

"Even knowing *they* had it covered with this thing?"

"Their outside forces may or may not know that. For that matter, they may figure we took the cannon completely out ourselves—God knows Brian almost did exactly that. Anyway, whatever they may or may not 'know,' the remote I left outside says that's where they're assembling."

"Idiots," Kiely muttered.

"Take what you can get," Alicia recommended, then shrugged. "Actually, they may not have much choice. That's where their biggest group of troops was dug in, and they don't have time to get fancy and try redeploying. Anyway, I don't want you out where they can see you, and I don't want you out where they can snipe you. So pull back another thirty meters. Without the cup, you'll take out the entire center span of that wall with your first shot, so I'm not that worried about your field of fire. Clear?"

"Thirty meters is a long way back, Sarge. What about the hostages?"

"Look," Alicia said, and pointed behind him. Kiely obeyed her, turning to look in the indicated direction, and she heard his low whistle across the com.

She didn't blame him. Hostages were flowing steadily towards the two broad flights of stairs Tannis had discovered, and it looked like at least a hundred of them were already down into the basement. It was nowhere near deep enough to protect them against a direct hit with modern weapons, but it would get them out of the way of near-misses and well below the direct line of fire.

"Howdy, Sarge." Alicia looked up as Tannis suddenly appeared at her shoulder.

"How'd you get them moving so quickly?" she asked.

"I put *Star Roamer*'s crew in charge of it," Tannis replied simply. "I figured they'd probably been trying to do what they could for their passengers all along. Looks like I was right—at least there's still some cohesion there."

"Good call." Alicia rested one hand on her wing's armored shoulder, then drew a deep breath.

"You and I are the roving reinforcements, Tannis," she said.

"Check." If Tannis was worried, her calm voice gave very little indication of it. "How you fixed for ammo, Sarge?"

"I'm almost dry," Alicia admitted. "Three rounds, as a matter of fact."

"Not much of a roving reserve," Tannis noted. "I, on the other hand, have forty-one."

"Showoff," Alicia said with a tired laugh. Tannis Cateau was the only person who could make Alicia DeVries feel inadequate on a rifle range. Tannis simply didn't miss . . . ever. And not just on the range. She actually got more accurate, more economical in the expenditure of her ammunition, under combat conditions.

"I thought you were probably pretty close to dry," Tannis continued, "so I brought you this."

Alicia took the M-97 Tannis had liberated from one of the dead terrorists and checked the magazine while Kiely picked up the plasma cannon and moved it to its new position. At least her new rifle was loaded with heavy penetrators that would have a fair chance of penetrating Marine battle armor at the sort of point blank range this fight was going to be, she thought. It was a pretty poor replacement for the battle rifle built into her armor, but it was a lot better than nothing, and Tannis had scrounged up a half-dozen extra magazines.

"Didn't think I'd see one of these again," Alicia said as she sent her armor the command to jettison the battle rifle which had served her so well. She followed that command up with one which reset the governors on her battle armor's gauntlets—it wouldn't do to absentmindedly crush her new rifle—and ordered her armor's computer to find the interface with the M-97's onboard systems.

"Beggars can't be—" Tannis began.

"They're coming in!" Andersson announced sharply.

"Kill the bastards!" Jaime Rivera shouted, and his action group charged up the slope.

There wasn't much finesse to it. The tactical situation was brutally simple, and it had taken him longer than he'd anticipated to get his people turned around. That meant his time window was probably even narrower than he'd thought. The Empies wouldn't have dared to start their assault shuttles moving until they *knew* the Cadre troopers had neutralized the defensive batteries and secured the facility. That gave him at least a few extra minutes, but not enough to waste any of them trying to get fancy. He was going to lose more people going in fast and dirty instead of organizing properly, but that was better than losing *all* of them, which was what was going to happen if they didn't get the hostages back.

He bounded along, holding his place in the center of the second rank, and he felt almost relieved as his entire world focused down into the narrow imperatives of combat.

"Let them get close," Alicia said as she and Tannis bounded to a central position between the hostages and the threatened wall. *Star Roamer*'s crew was still hurrying people down the stairs, and it looked like Tannis' original estimate of the basement's capacity had actually been low. But there were still well over a hundred civilians on the main floor when the building's end wall began to disintegrate under the punching of low-powered plasma bolts.

Alicia heard screams from behind her as the explosive effect of the plasma's transfer energy—even a "low-powered" bolt packed a brutal punch—blasted splinters loose from the wall panels. Some of those "splinters" were fifteen and twenty centimeters long, and the force of the plasma strikes sent them hissing further into the building. Three of them hit her armor and shattered, but others, obviously, had found unarmored targets, and she tried not to think about the kinds of damage those knife-edged projectiles could inflict.

She checked her HUD. Andersson had taken her at her word, and completely repositioned the captured calliopes. He'd moved them down from the catwalk level and placed two at the extreme corners of the western wall. He and Samantha Moyano had also pulled the heavy weapons off of the tripod mounts their original terrorist crews, with their unpowered armor, had required and used force blades to cut small, unobtrusive firing slits right at floor level. Now Andersson lay prone at the northern corner, using his battle armor "muscles" to handle the massive weapon as if it were a simple combat rifle, while Corporal Ewan MacEntee from First Platoon's Second Squad—Andersson's third wing of the night—crouched close enough to cover him and also watch for possible flank attacks. Moyano, a corporal from Second Platoon, had the southern corner with Corporal James Król, from First Platoon's Third Squad as her wing.

Alexandra Filipov had the third calliope on the building's northern wall, with Corporal Adam Skogen as her wing, while Digory Beckett had the fourth calliope on the southern wall, with Karin de Nijs as his wing.

Kiely had no wing, and Alicia and Tannis were the only original wing pair still alive. So far, at least.

Eleven men and women, exhausted, battered, and armed with captured weapons, against fifty battle-armored foes desperate to kill them. Every one of those eleven knew exactly what their odds of living through the next three minutes were, but it didn't matter. They were all that stood between six hundred civilians and cold-blooded murder, and Alicia's green eyes were hard as she watched the gaps being punched through the western wall.

"Make it count, people," she said, almost conversationally.

Rivera felt his confidence soar as his assault thundered up the hill. Not a shot had been fired against them—not one! Maybe he'd given the Cadre bastards too much credit. Maybe they were crouching in hiding somewhere, too terrified to show themselves. Or—more likely, he thought, even now—they were simply out of ammunition. Or maybe they'd all been killed breaking in. Or—

Erik Andersson opened fire as the first battle-armored terrorist came within a hundred meters. The heavy calliope's feed mechanism howled as the disintegrating link ammo belt blurred into the feed chute, and the penetrators shrieked downrange.

Battle armor shattered, and FALA terrorists screamed in agony, but the charge kept coming.

Samantha Moyano opened up from the other corner of the wall, swinging her weapon to scythe down the attackers. More armored bodies crashed to the ground, but the second wave of the attack back-plotted the fire killing their companions, and plasma bolts came howling back.

The entire building shuddered in agony as dozens of plasma bolts—these fired at full power, like brimstone buzz saws—sliced through the wall which had already begun to disintegrate. Andersson seemed to flatten into the ceramacrete floor, spreading out in an impossibly thin layer, while he continued to pour back a torrent of fire. But one of those plasma bolts slammed directly through the opening Moyano had cut for her weapon and killed her instantly.

"Right!" Rivera shouted as the southern calliope suddenly stopped firing. "*Bear right!*"

His men obeyed, curling away from the calliope still flaying their ranks from their left flank.

"Now go right through them!" he bellowed.

Alicia saw Moyano's icon flicker crimson. An instant later, Ewan MacEntee's followed suit as a plasma bolt streaked in through a gaping hole and impacted with freakish accuracy on his armor.

"They're coming through, Tom!" she snapped.

"Oh, no, they're not," Kiely said flatly.

"Keep going! *Keep going!*" Rivera screamed. He'd lost a quarter of his plasma gun-armed troops coming up the hill, and his fifteen remaining plasma gunners were at the point of his charge. Now they lowered their heads, hit their jump gear, and smashed straight through the riddled, weakened wall.

Corporal Thomas Kiely squeezed the firing grips, and a massive blast of plasma enveloped the center of the terrorists' charge. Most of the building's western wall—the part of it that hadn't already been blown to bits, at least—disappeared. Three of the fifteen men who'd smashed their way through it lived long enough to shriek in agony; the rest died too quickly even for that.

It staggered Rivera's action group. It ought to have broken their charge, stopped the attack cold, but Kiely hadn't had time to run a diagnostic on the weapon. Which meant he didn't know the firing chamber's containment field had been damaged.

The back blast from the disintegrating weapon killed him instantly, despite his armor, and bowled Alicia off her feet.

Rivera flinched as the entire end of the building exploded in eye-tearing brilliance and took a third of his men—and all of his remaining plasma rifles—with it.

For just an instant he wondered what additional horrendous surprises the Cadre might have rigged, but then he realized what that had to have been.

"Follow me!" he howled, bounding straight ahead through the charging infantry who'd faltered as their companions were killed. "*Follow me!*"

Alicia bounced back upright, her mind clear and cold even as grief hammered at its corners. Three of her eleven defenders were already down, and the orange icons which had hesitated when Kiely fired came flooding forward once again.

She brought up the M-97 and opened fire as the first FALA battle armor came through the flaming wreckage which had once been the wall of the building.

Rifle fire blasted Rivera's battle armor, but his breastplate held. The three men directly behind him were less fortunate, and his own rifle snapped into firing position.

Alicia dropped one of the attackers while Tannis' fire—as deadly accurate as ever—took down two more with perfect helmet hits. Alicia swung her manual rifle towards another target, but the terrorist fired first, and Alicia staggered as penetrators slammed into her. Her Cadre armor—tougher and lighter than Marine-issue equipment—held, but at least one of the heavy rounds smashed into her borrowed M-97, transforming it abruptly into so much shattered, useless wreckage.

She dropped it instantly, and her hands swept down. Her CHK seemed to materialize in her left hand, her force blade in the other, and she heard someone else using her voice to shriek a Valkyrie's war cry as she lunged forward.

Jaime Rivera gaped in disbelief as the Cadreman took at least five direct hits and didn't go down. And then the trooper who should have been dead was coming straight at him, pistol in one hand and some sort of glowing sword in the other.

The pistol came up, and Rivera recoiled as the first penetrator spalled his visor. It didn't punch through, but the incredible impact, less than ten centimeters in front of his eyes half-stunned him. It was only for an instant, no more than a single heartbeat, but that was long enough.

His vision had just begun to refocus when the force blade in Alicia DeVries' right hand decapitated him in a fountain of blood.

Chaos overwhelmed Alicia's ability to multitask at last.

Blood exploded over her, obscuring her visor, as she cut down the terrorist who'd smashed her rifle, but her armor sensors were still up, and some fragment of her concentration saw Adam Skogen's icon charge towards the breakthrough. He came bounding to meet it, battle rifle flaming as he burned through his remaining ammunition in a handful of seconds, and then he, too, went down. James Król was down on one knee making every round count, firing steadily, accurately into the armored terrorists charging past him. Most of them didn't even realize he was there, and he dropped at least five of them before two more spotted him and turned to engage him. One of them went down, as well, and then Król was down, badly wounded, his armor critically damaged, and more terrorists flooded past him.

Alicia slashed down another terrorist. Her pistol came up—by instinct, not conscious thought—and she slammed the muzzle into direct contact with another enemy's visor. She squeezed the trigger, and the terrorist flew backward as the light-caliber penetrators smashed through the only part of his armor they could have hoped to defeat.

She heard Tannis screaming a warning and whirled towards the fresh threat, then staggered as another burst of penetrators shrieked off her armor. The sudden impact threw her off-balance as a trio of terrorists came at her, still firing. More penetrators whined and crashed off of her armor, hammering her backward. She went to one knee and the terrorists closed for the kill, but then Tannis was there, battle rifle flaming in full auto.

Alicia's attackers tumbled away, awkward in death, but even as they fell, she heard Tannis' scream over their dedicated link. Her wing went down, life signs flashing luridly on Alicia's monitor, and Alicia shrieked herself—in rage and fury, not pain—as she lunged back upright over her friend's body. Her force blade sliced effortlessly through the terrorist who'd just shot Tannis, and Alicia DeVries charged.

* * *

The men who had followed Jaime Rivera up the hill, through the tornado of calliope fire, through the devastating blast of plasma which had killed a third of their entire action group, wavered as their leader went down. And then, coming at them through the flame and the smoke and the thunder of a man-made hell, they saw a single figure in filthy, blood-splashed, battered and gouged battle armor. It didn't even have a rifle—just a pistol in one hand and a force blade in the other—but it came straight at them. Penetrators hit it again and again, but it was moving too quickly, the impacts were too oblique to penetrate, and then that dreadful force blade was among them, slicing through their armor as if it didn't even exist.

A head flew, someone else howled in agony as the force blade slashed straight through his armor and lopped off his right arm at the elbow. Another armored figure went down, shrieking, gauntleted hands clutching uselessly at the blood-spouting wound where the force blade had punched straight through his armor and the belly under it.

It was too much. They'd come up that hill with fifty-two men; now the five survivors turned and ran as that terrifying figure came at them. And as they fled back down the hill, Erik Andersson's calliope was waiting.

Group Leader Lloyd Abruzzi stared in disbelief as five men—only *five*—from Rivera's action group fell back.

For all his argument with the other group leader, Abruzzi would never have believed a handful of exhausted infantry—even Cadre infantry—could have held against Rivera's assault. But they *had* held, and even as he watched, the five fleeing survivors went down one by one, picked off by murderously accurate bursts of calliope fire.

Those bastards, he thought venomously. *Those* fucking *bastards!*

All the hatred Lloyd Abruzzi had ever felt for the Terran Empire and the Imperial Cadre flamed up within him, and his lips drew back from his teeth in an ugly snarl.

So we do it my way after all, he told himself, and punched into his own action group's command frequency.

"Plasma gunners! I want that fucking building *flattened*! Open—"

Lloyd Abruzzi never had time to realize Rivera had been wrong.

Sir Arthur Keita and Major Alexander Bennett hadn't waited for the Cadre to confirm the destruction of the antiair defenses around the objective. Alicia DeVries had told them her people would neutralize them, and they'd begun their assault insertion the instant Charlie Company's survivors launched their attack. Abruzzi had thought he had at least ten or fifteen more minutes to complete the destruction of the fire-wracked building on top of his hill, but he, too, had been wrong.

The precisely targeted pattern of shuttle-launched hypervelocity weapons came down out of the Shallingsport night like solid bars of light, far, far ahead of the sound of their passage, and the glaring fireballs wiped Abruzzi's action group away like the fists of an angry deity.

Alicia's sensor remote saw the shuttles coming in, saw the explosions, saw the handful of surviving terrorists turning to race desperately for the illusory sanctuary of the mountains even as three of the shuttles banked after them, heavy cannon thundering mercilessly. She saw it all, but she had no time for it. She was on her knees beside Tannis, desperately accessing her friend's med panel while Tannis' flickering vital signs dimmed towards extinction.

"DeVries! Sergeant DeVries!" someone was shouting over the company command circuit.

"*Medic!*" she shouted back. "I need a medic *right now*!"

"Over there!" she heard, and then Marines in battle armor were all around her, impossibly neat and clean amid the chaos and destruction, the filth and the blood and the bodies.

"*Medic!*" she screamed yet again as Tannis' heart suddenly stopped. She hammered at the med panel with both hands, but other hands reached down for her—battle armored hands, whose strength was a match for her own, hauling her to her feet, pulling her away from Tannis.

She fought madly, but there were too many of them. It took four Marines to hold her, but they pinned her, held her, pulled her back.

"Alley!" a fresh voice shouted as another armored Marine went to her knees beside Tannis. "*Alley!*"

There was something about that voice. Something familiar, and Alicia's eyes widened.

"Lieutenant?" she heard the disbelief in her own ragged voice. "*Lieutenant Kuramochi?*"

"It's me, Alley," Captain Kuramochi said. "The medics are here. Do you hear me—*the medics are here.*" Two more gauntleted hands reached out, settling on either side of Alicia's helmet, holding it motionless while Kuramochi Chiyeko leaned towards her. Their visors touched, and Kuramochi spoke slowly, distinctly, looking directly into Alicia's exhausted eyes. "The medics are here, Sergeant. You've got to let them help her. Do you understand, Alley?"

"Yes," Alicia whispered, sagging inside her armor at last. "Yes."

"Then let's get you both out of here," Kuramochi said softly, tears sliding down her own cheeks. "Let's get you home."

CHAPTER TWENTY-EIGHT

Lieutenant Alicia DeVries marched through the cavernous arch in Sligo Palace's inner wall. It was October, and autumn's paintbrush had been busy. The magnificently landscaped grounds of the immense Court of Heroes spread out before her, its autumn-splashed trees and gardens, its fountains and reflecting pools, all arranged to lead the eye inevitably to the Cenotaph at its center. The square, flower bed-defined courtyard around the Cenotaph's plain, polished hundred and fifty-meter shaft of marble was large enough to parade an entire battalion and paved in oddly mottled-looking stone, not ceramacrete.

There was a reason for that courtyard's odd texture and coloration; every individual block of stone in it was from a different planet or inhabited moon of the Terran Empire.

Alicia still felt odd in the uniform of a Cadre lieutenant, but it was legally hers, even though she had yet to attend the OCS course which went with it, as she marched steadily, slowly down the long, straight pathway leading from the arch to the Cenotaph. That pathway was lined with simple battle steel plaques, each engraved with the names, branches of service, and serial numbers of men and women who had died in the service of the Terran Empire.

It seemed to take forever to reach the Cenotaph, and she kept her eyes fixed straight ahead, focused on the four individuals standing all alone on that plain of stone in the obelisk's shadow. There were others present, of course, seated in the reviewing stand along the southern edge of the Cenotaph courtyard, but there weren't that many. Not physically present, at least.

She crossed the edge of the stone paving, her boot heels sounding suddenly crisp and clear on its surface, and more boots sounded behind her. They hit the stone in perfect unison, their sounds echoes of her own, and she felt them at her back.

There weren't very many of them.

Tannis Cateau was there, finally released from hospital care two days earlier. And so were Erik Andersson, Alec Howard, Jackson Keller, Alexandra Filipov, Digory Beckett, James Król, whose hospital stay had ended one day before Tannis', and Karin de Nijs.

Nine men and women, including Alicia. The only survivors of Company C, Third Battalion, Second Regiment, Fifth Brigade, Imperial Cadre.

They marched steadily across the stone pavement, turned sharply to their left, then wheeled back to their right. Their left heels struck the stone in a single perfectly coordinated instant, and they snapped to attention facing the four men who had awaited them.

The only sounds were the cool October wind in the trees, the sharp popping of the flags atop their poles around the Cenotaph, the splash of water in the fountains at its base, the almost inaudible hum of the HD cameras hovering on their counter-grav floaters, and the distant cry of birds.

"Charlie Company, Third Battalion, reports as ordered, Sir!" Alicia said crisply, and her hand flashed up in salute.

General Dugald Arbatov, the Cadre's commanding general, returned the salute. Then he looked at the man standing beside him.

"Call the role, if you please, Brigadier," he said.

"Yes, Sir!" Sir Arthur Keita replied. Then he raised the old-fashioned, anachronistic clipboard he'd had tucked under his left arm and turned to face the nine men and women standing at attention before him in that space which would have held a battalion.

"Alwyn, Madison!" he said, not even glancing at the neatly printed columns of names on the clipboard he held.

"Present," Alicia replied, her voice firm and clear.

"Andersson, Erik!"

"Present," Andersson responded.

"Arun, Namrata!"

"Present," Tannis Cateau replied.

"Ashmead, Jeremy!"

"Present!" Alec Howard barked.

The names and responses rang out in slow, clear cadence in the quiet, quiet afternoon. Two hundred and seventy-five names Keita called out, and two hundred and seventy-five times the response "Present" answered.

"Yrjö, Rauha!" Keita called the final name.

"Present!" Alicia answered for the last name, as for the first, and her voice was just as firm, just as clear, despite the tears shining in her eyes.

Keita nodded, tucked the clipboard back up under his left arm, turned to face Arbatov, and saluted sharply.

"Charlie Company, Third Battalion, Second Regiment, Fifth Brigade, all present and accounted for, Sir!"

"Thank you, Brigadier," Arbatov replied quietly, returning his salute, and turned to the third man present.

The third man wasn't especially tall. He was fair-haired and blue-eyed, on the young side of fifty, and he wore a green-on-green uniform very like the one Alicia wore. But his uniform carried no rank badges or unit insignia, and a simple golden circlet rested on his head.

"Your Majesty," Arbatov said with a deep bow, "I beg to report that Charlie Company, Third Battalion, Second Regiment, Fifth Brigade, of your Cadre is all present and accounted for."

"Thank you, General," His Majesty Seamus II, Emperor and Prince Protector of Humanity, replied in a beautifully trained tenor voice, then turned to face Alicia and her eight fellows directly.

"For four centuries," he said, after a moment, "the Imperial Cadre has served Our house and Our empire with a courage and a devotion seldom if ever matched in human history. The Imperial Marine Corps, and the Imperial Fleet, have fought and died with supreme gallantry. We and the Emperors and Empresses who have come before Us have been humbled again and again by the sacrifices of the men and women of the Empire's regular armed forces. We are deeply and humbly cognizant of all they have accomplished, and of the price they have all too often paid in the Empire's service. But it has been Our Cadre which has carried Our personal banner and served as Our personal sword, Our paladins and Our champions.

"In all those four centuries," he continued, and Alicia felt the eyes from the review stand, the cameras beaming the ceremony live to every planet, moon, asteroid, and space station in the Sol System and recording it for every other planet of the Terran Empire, "the Cadre has never failed Our trust. It has not always achieved victory, for even Cadremen are mortal. At times, far more often than We could wish, they have died, but even in defeat, they have died striving for victory. The Cadre has never tarnished its honor, never failed to rise to the challenge of its own standards. It may have been defeated, may have died, but it has never surrendered.

"You and your comrades who are present today only in spirit," he said, looking each of the nine survivors in front of him in the eye, "have upheld not simply the finest traditions, but also the honor and the courage of Our Cadre. By your service, by your sacrifice, by your accomplishments, you have brought to Our house and to Our throne an honor and a devotion which no man, no Emperor, could possibly have demanded. An honor and a devotion which fills Us with pride, with sorrow, and with a gratitude no words, actions, or rewards can ever truly express. We have directed that the names of all of your fallen comrades be inscribed here among the ranks of the Empire's most honored dead, in the Court of Heroes. We have further directed that Charlie Company, Third Battalion, Second Regiment, Fifth Brigade, of Our Cadre be awarded the Order of the Fallen Lion. And We personally thank you, as We thank your comrades who have died in battle, not simply as Emperor, but also in Our own person. We are humbled by what you have done, and we ask you to accept Our profound gratitude and acknowledgment of the debt which We owe to you and can never adequately repay."

He stepped forward, and Alicia DeVries found herself shaking the hand of the most powerful single individual in the history of the human race. It was a strong hand, firm, and he looked directly into her green eyes for a moment before he released her hand and moved down the line to shake Tannis Cateau's.

He shook all of them by the hand, one by one, and then stepped back to his position. He resumed it, and Arbatov cleared his throat and turned to the final man present—the only one in the uniform of the Imperial Marines, and not the Cadre.

"Sergeant Major!" he said.

"Sir!"

"The formation is yours."

"Yes, Sir!"

The Marine stepped forward and faced Alicia and the others.

"Charlie Company, attention to orders!" he snapped, and the Cadremen snapped back to rigid attention, staring straight ahead, as he opened an official-looking binder.

"Corporal Tannis Cateau, front and center," he said, and Tannis took one crisp, precise step forward, turned to her right, and marched to the center of the abbreviated line. Then she whipped back to her left, facing him, and snapped back to attention.

"By order of, and on behalf of, His Imperial Majesty Seamus, of his House the seventeenth and of his name the second," the Marine read from the first citation in his binder, "your gallantry and actions far above and beyond the call of duty on July 23, 2952, Standard Reckoning, on the Planet of Fuller, are hereby gratefully recognized.

"On that date and planet, you and your comrades, displaying the utmost determination, devotion to duty, and courage against impossible odds, nevertheless persevered in your mission. Despite the death in battle of ninety-six percent of your total strength, you and the other surviving members of Charlie Company, Third Battalion, Second Regiment, Fifth Brigade, Imperial Cadre, continued with your mission, stormed a heavily defended terrorist strongpoint, disabled and destroyed its ground-to-space defenses, and held your position against overwhelming attack until relieved by the Imperial Marines whose assault shuttle landing you had made possible. Although yourself critically wounded, you and your fellows defeated the final, desperate assault of five times your own number of heavily armed, well-equipped terrorists, as a consequence of which five hundred and ninety-three imperial subjects were saved from near certain death. Your actions upheld—and exceeded—the finest traditions of the Imperial Cadre. For your devotion, valor, and sacrifice, His Majesty directs and decrees that you be awarded the Solarian Grand Cross for actions above and beyond the call of duty."

Tannis saluted sharply, and Sir Arthur Keita stepped forward and personally draped the midnight blue ribbon of the Terran Empire's second highest award for valor about her neck. She exchanged salutes with Keita, then turned and marched smartly back into her place in the short, short line of Cadremen with the same perfect precision. She resumed her position, and the Marine's eyes moved to the man standing to her immediate right.

"Corporal Erik Andersson, front and center," he said, and Andersson stepped forward in turn.

"By order of, and on behalf of, His Imperial Majesty Seamus," the Marine began again.

Eight times, with minor variations, he repeated the citation. Eight times the dark blue ribbon supporting the glittering gold cross went about a waiting neck. And then he looked up and called one final name.

"Lieutenant Alicia DeVries, front and center."

Alicia stepped forward, marched down the length of the line to face him, and saluted sharply. The Marine returned her salute.

"By order of, and on behalf of, His Imperial Majesty Seamus, of his House the seventeenth and of his name the second," he said, "your gallantry and actions far above and beyond the call of duty on July 23, 2952, Standard Reckoning, on the Planet of Fuller, are hereby gratefully recognized.

"On that date and planet, subsequent to the deaths of every officer and senior noncommissioned officer of your company, you assumed command of Charlie Company, Third Battalion, Second Regiment, Fifth Brigade, Imperial Cadre. Despite the loss of some eighty percent of your company's total numbers immediately upon reaching the planet, in an ambush by enemies present in overwhelming strength, you maintained your unit's cohesion and effectiveness. Under the most adverse circumstances possible, you continued against overwhelming odds with the mission your unit had been assigned. In the face of additional heavy and grievous losses, in the full knowledge that you faced insurmountable odds, you and the surviving men and women under your command nonetheless fought your way to your objective in the face of almost continuous attack. Upon reaching that objective, you assaulted a prepared, well dug-in, formidably armed force almost nine times your own strength. Despite the odds against you, and despite further grievous losses, the surviving members of Charlie Company, under your leadership, successfully took the objective, cleared the way for a Marine landing, and held their position against a massive counterattack, fighting hand-to-hand after exhausting their ammunition, until relieved, at which time only five men and women of your entire Company remained in action. By your actions, leadership, courage, skill, and devotion you upheld the highest traditions of the Imperial Cadre and of the Terran Empire and saved the lives of ninety-seven percent of the hostages seized by the terrorists opposed to you. In recognition of your accomplishment, His Majesty directs and decrees that you be awarded the Banner of Terra for actions far above and beyond the call of duty."

There was an audible murmur from the reviewing stand behind them. The Banner of Terra was the Empire's highest decoration. Like the Solarian Grand Cross it could be won only on the field of battle, and, unlike even the SGC, it entitled its wearer to take a salute from any member of the Empire's armed forces, regardless of relative rank, who had not himself earned it. It was almost always awarded posthumously, and in four centuries, less than three hundred men and women had ever received it. In fact, at the moment, there were only two other living recipients in the entire Empire, but the tradition was that it must be awarded by someone else who had earned it, if that was at all possible. And so the Empire had recalled Sergeant Major Sebastian O'Shaughnessy to Old Earth for this ceremony.

Alicia DeVries looked into her grandfather's eyes as he handed his binder of citations to General Arbatov and accepted the blood-red ribbon and the golden starburst radiating from the exquisitely rendered representation of mankind's ancient birth world from Sir Arthur Keita. She bent her head slightly as he draped the ribbon about her neck, and the weight of the medal settled against her collarbone.

For the first time in history, that medal was worn simultaneously by two members of the same family, and the sergeant major straightened it carefully, then stepped back and saluted her sharply.

She returned the salute, then stepped back into her own position, and Arbatov turned to Keita.

"Brigadier, dismiss the formation," he said, and Keita saluted.

"Yes, Sir!" He turned back to face the short line, and all the other members of Charlie Company, standing invisibly at their backs.

"Company," he said sharply, "dismissed!"

"You wanted to see me, Sir Arthur?"

"Yes, yes I did." Sir Arthur Keita stood behind his desk with a smile, and waved for Alicia to enter his office. She obeyed the gesture, acutely aware of the new blood-red ribbon nestled amid the "fruit salad" on the breast of her dress uniform tunic. He pointed at a chair, and she settled into it, and eyed him steadily.

"I realize your family is waiting for you, Alley," Keita said after a moment, "and I promise I won't keep you long. But I thought you'd like to know that the initial Shallingsport analysis has been wrapped up." He sat back down behind the desk, tipping back in his powered chair. "I'm quite sure that this doesn't begin to represent the final word on the operation, but I think it's about the best summary we're going to be able to put together until and unless we manage to break some additional intelligence information loose. I felt that as Charlie Company's senior officer, you should be informed, in general terms at least, of the report's conclusions."

Alicia sat up a bit more straightly, watching his expression intently, and he inhaled deeply.

"Essentially, the report—which Captain Watts and I have both endorsed—concludes that there was a massive intelligence failure at all levels. Effectively, we allowed the Freedom Alliance to manipulate us into sending Charlie Company into a deliberately arranged ambush. The entire operation was specifically intended to draw in a Cadre unit—in fact, to draw in *Charlie Company*—and either destroy it outright or else create conditions under which we would 'provoke' the massacre of all six hundred-plus hostages trying to save it.

"In the first case, the successful destruction of your company, the operation would demonstrate that the Cadre isn't, in fact invincible, and that the FALA was capable of going toe-to-toe with the Emperor's personal *corps d'elite* and decisively defeating it.

"In the second case, the deaths of so many civilians would be spun as proof that the Empire sets the value it places upon the lives of its military personnel higher than it does the value of the civilians those military personnel are supposed to protect.

"In addition, it appears that they did, indeed, intend to press additional demands, some of which they may actually have believed they could get, given the unprecedented number and nature of the hostages they'd managed to take. Exactly what those other demands might have been is more problematical, since, unfortunately—from an intelligence viewpoint, at any rate—none of their leadership cadre on Fuller were taken alive.

"So far as we can determine, the actual number of armed FALA on the planet was just over three thousand, of whom approximately twenty-three hundred were equipped with battle armor, relatively modern infantry weapons, sting ships, and heavy weapons. I suppose we should count ourselves lucky that they didn't bring along heavy armored units, as well."

He paused, shaking his head in obvious disgust, and Alicia frowned.

"I knew there were a lot of them, Sir," she said, when he didn't resume immediately. "I didn't realize there were quite that many, though. Have we determined how they managed to get them onto the planet in the first place?"

"Not as . . . definitively as I'd like," Keita said. "In fact, nowhere *near* as definitively as I'd like. We did manage to take a few of them alive, and to interrogate them, which gave us some additional information. As nearly as we've been able to determine at this point, Jason Corporation, the outfit which built the Green Haven facility, has actually been a Freedom Alliance front for at least ten standard years. By the time we figured that out, unfortunately, 'Jason Corporation' had shut down all operations in what was clearly a preplanned, well-orchestrated business liquidation. Its accounts had been drained and closed, none of its senior personnel could be found, and as far as we can tell, all of the Jason employees we've been able to identify and locate were innocent dupes, unaware that they were actually working for a terrorist-financed corporation.

"At any rate, the Freedom Alliance, when it began planning this operation—apparently quite some time ago—used Jason

Corporation to set up the groundwork on Fuller. It built the facility in which the hostages were ultimately held, and apparently used the 'heavy construction equipment' cover to bring in the combat equipment it required for its intended operation.

"For your personal information, and not for the official record, I'm not personally quite as convinced as the analysts who prepared this report that Duke Geoffrey wasn't directly involved in setting all of this up."

Alicia cocked her head to one side, and Keita snorted.

"There's no direct evidence of his complicity—trust me, if there were, we'd be . . . discussing it with him quite firmly. His Majesty genuinely is as furious over this as he's appeared in public. If we had proof, or even strongly suggestive evidence, that Duke Geoffrey had been knowingly involved, the Emperor would have formally demanded his head from King Hayden. And if he hadn't gotten it, the Marines and Fleet would be moving on Fuller to collect it.

"There *is* considerable evidence that Duke Geoffrey's director of industrial development, one Jokuri Asaro'o Lowai, knew exactly what was going on. We thought at first that Jokuri might have been a false identity, but we managed to trace him right back to Old Earth, and the Jokuri on Fuller was definitely the genuine article. However, he also wasn't anywhere among the dead or the prisoners we took on Fuller. In short, although we don't believe that anyone managed to get off-world after *Marguerite Johnsen* entered orbit, he somehow effectively disappeared. The fact that we can't find Jokuri anywhere may indicate that we're wrong about that, but the current consensus appears to be that he was working for the Freedom Alliance and that, as soon as it could dispense with his services, the Alliance eliminated him and disposed of the body. Assuming that the theory has merit, they probably got rid of him because he knew too much and wasn't one of their own inner circle—they couldn't rely on him to keep his mouth shut if we got our hands on him and he found himself facing the death penalty."

He paused again, frowning, clearly not entirely happy with what he'd just said, then shrugged.

"I don't have any better theory than that, but somehow it doesn't quite *feel* right. I'm not saying it's wrong, but I've just got this feeling that there's more to it. Certainly it's a neat hypothesis.

Jokuri was in a position to handle all of the details on the Fuller side of the pre-op preparations. He was the Shallingsport official Jason Corporation had to clear all of its operations and shipments with. They couldn't have pulled it off *without* his active complicity; that much is abundantly clear. I suppose I just can't quite shake the suspicion that it could be extremely . . . convenient for Duke Geoffrey for us to have such a clearly identifiable—and obviously dead—FALA accomplice. According to Duke Geoffrey, it was Jokuri who first suggested to him that granting the terrorists 'sanctuary' in Shallingsport offered the best chance of keeping the hostages alive. There's no independent corroboration of that, however, and I suppose I just find it a little difficult to accept that whoever planned this would have relied upon a mere industrial development expert to convince a head of state to get involved in something like this. And they had to be completely confident that they'd be offered a site in *Shallingsport*, since that was where they built their base of operations."

He paused once more, his frown deeper, then shook himself.

"At any rate," he continued more briskly, "however they planned it and however they managed to get all of their equipment groundside, the entire operation was intended from the beginning as a giant mousetrap, an ambush. And our Intelligence people never saw it coming. We dropped you and your company right into the middle of it, Alley, and for that I sincerely and personally apologize."

He looked at her very levelly, and it was Alicia's turn to shake her head a bit uncomfortably.

"From what you've already said, Uncle Arthur, it's obvious that they planned this thing very carefully and put all of the pieces into place long before they actually grabbed the hostages. Given the amount of time Intelligence had to figure out what was happening, I don't think anyone can blame Battalion or anyone else for not realizing that even a terrorist organization like the FALA could be crazy enough to deliberately confront the Cadre this way."

"Possibly not, once we went into emergency response mode," Keita conceded. "But looking ahead, trying to spot things like this coming, is one of the things intelligence people are supposed to do. And however it happened, no one did that this time around."

He gave his head a little toss and let his chair come back fully upright.

"There are still quite a few unanswered questions, and the nature of the beast in a case like this is that we probably never will get answers for all of them. That doesn't mean we won't keep trying, of course. In particular, the sheer amount of money and resources the Freedom Alliance invested in this operation is pretty staggering. It might represent pocket change for the Empire, but it came to quite a few million credits. That's a lot, even for an organization like the FALA. And there's also the little matter of our inability—to date, at least—to even begin to identify the arms dealer—or dealers—who sold them their hardware. As you suspected at the time, it was virtually all of imperial manufacture. We did find a little bit of equipment from one Rogue World or another, but almost all of it was Marine surplus, and so far we've been unable to trace how it came into their hands. We've run the serial numbers, of course, and most of it was officially declared surplus to requirements and destroyed several years back. We're trying to come at it by figuring out who was in a position to falsify the record of its destruction, but I wouldn't hold my breath waiting for us to get to the bottom of it.

"As I say, I don't think anyone has any intention of of letting matters rest where they are right now. When the Emperor himself demands answers, people try very hard to come up with them, and His Majesty really, really wants those answers in this case."

He paused again, as if inviting Alicia to ask any additional questions which had occurred to her. She didn't have any, however. Or, rather, she had a great many of them, but it was obvious from what he'd already told her that no one had the hard data to answer them for her, anyway.

"At any rate," Keita said after a few moments, "that's what we know—and don't know—about what happened. It's not the only thing I wanted to discuss with you, however."

"It isn't?" Alicia asked just a bit cautiously when he paused yet again.

"I'm not planning on springing any nasty surprises on you, Alley," he told her with a smile. "The thing is, there aren't that many holders of the Banner of Terra, as I'm sure you realized, growing up with a grandfather who already had it. Did the Sergeant Major ever discuss with you why he never accepted a commission?"

"He said, Sir," Alicia replied with a small smile of her own, "that he was a 'working stiff' who preferred being in a position to get his hands dirty to getting stuck in a management position. Personally, I've always suspected that he just loves what he does right now too much to give it up."

"I'm sure you're right. But I think, perhaps, I failed to phrase my question correctly. What I meant was did your grandfather ever discuss with you how he *avoided* accepting a commission?"

"Well, no, Sir. Not in so many words, anyway. I just always put it down to the fact that he knows everyone in the Corps—most of them by first name—and that he knew how to work the system too well for anyone to push him into a commission if he didn't want one."

"Having met your grandfather, there's probably something to that," Keita allowed with a slight chuckle. "However, trust me, it isn't easy for someone who's managed to win the Banner to avoid getting turned into an officer. In fact, a commission—or, at least, the offer of one—usually goes with it. In your case, the Cadre—" he meant himself, Alicia knew perfectly well, although he would never come right out and admit it "—had already decided you'd earned a battlefield promotion before the Emperor decided to award the Banner. But there's always a lot of pressure to get anyone who's won it commissioned, because you don't pick up the Banner if you're not exactly what we're looking for in an officer."

Alicia felt her cheeks heat very slightly, but she kept her expression only politely attentive, and Keita suppressed a grin.

"The problem is that you can't really twist the arm of someone who holds the Empire's highest award for valor. In your grandfather's case, I strongly suspect that he used the Banner as a club to beat off any threat of a commission. In your case, obviously, that's not happening—of course, you were a lot younger and more innocent when you won it than he was."

This time the grin broke free, at least partly, and Alicia smiled back at him. Then he sobered slightly.

"What I'm trying to say, Alley, is that your commission came before the Banner was ever awarded. Now that you've received it, though, the tradition is that you get to pick—within reason, of course—where you go next."

He made an inviting gesture, and Alicia frowned.

"I appreciate that, Sir," she said finally. "But I'm not sure where I want to go. Except—"

She paused, obviously hesitating, and Keita cocked his head to one side.

"Spit it out, Alley," he said. "At the moment, you've got pretty much a blank check for anything you want to ask."

"Well, in that case, Sir," she said quickly, almost as if she was pushing herself to get it out quickly, "I've heard that the Company is going to be disbanded. Is that true?"

"Where did you hear that?" Keita asked.

"I'd rather not say, Sir. But, is it true?" She stared at him appealingly.

"Why specifically do you ask?" he asked in reply.

"Because it would be *wrong*, Sir," she said with a fierceness which surprised even her just a bit. "The Company deserves better than that. It *deserves* better."

"Alley, at the moment Charlie Company consists of the exactly nine people," Keita pointed out gently. "We'd have to reconstitute it from scratch. It's not just a case of transferring in a few replacements—we'd have to literally rebuild it, as if it were a completely new company."

"We've still got the support staff at Guadalupe, Sir," Alicia said, her tone diffident, but stubborn.

"None of whom are active-duty Cadre," Keita countered.

"But—" Alicia began, then stopped herself. She looked at him, her expression more stubborn than ever, and he chuckled softly.

"Relax, Alley," he said, his tone and expression both serious. "No one's going to disband Charlie Company. Mind you, we're not going to be able to put it back into the field for a while. I meant it when I said we'd have to reconstitute from scratch, and, as you know, the Cadre is never oversupplied with qualified personnel. However, I have it directly from the Emperor's own lips that Charlie Company, and its battle honors, are not to be allowed to disappear. In fact, that's where I was headed a few minutes ago."

"Sir?" Alicia sounded puzzled, although her enormous relief that the company was not going to be written off was obvious.

"You're a brand new lieutenant," Keita pointed out. "You and I both know you've still got to get OCS out of the way, but we both also know you can handle the job. In fact, I'm confident that you'll be as successful as an officer as you were as a noncom, which is pretty high praise, I suppose.

"But, it's going to be a while before we start thinking about additional promotions on your part. Even the Banner isn't going to convince the Cadre to move you up any faster than your experience, seasoning, and confidence justifies. However," he looked at her intently, "there's the little question of where the brand new lieutenant gets assigned when she reports back for duty from OCS. That's what I wanted to discuss with you. Where would you like to go?"

"I . . . hadn't really thought about it, Sir," she replied, and to her own surprise, it was true. "I guess I've just been worried enough about the possibility that the Company would be disbanded that it never occurred to me to think about going anywhere else. I just wanted to go back to the Company. But I can't, can I? I mean, it isn't there, anymore. And, as you say, it *won't* be there again for a while."

"Neither of those last two statements is completely accurate, Alley," Keita said quietly, almost gently.

She looked at him, eyebrows rising, and he waved one hand.

"Charlie Company still exists," he told her. "It has nine personnel on its roster. You're one of those nine people. As for your second statement, I didn't say Charlie Company 'isn't there' anymore; I said we're not going to be able to put it back into the field for a while. But what I was going to suggest to you is that if you want to exercise the traditional prerogative of the Banner and request a specific assignment, the one I had in mind was command of First Platoon, Charlie Company, Third Battalion, Second Regiment, Fifth Brigade."

Alicia stared at him, and he smiled.

"If you want it, it's yours," he told her simply. "It's probably going to take us the entire time you're off at OCS to get the rest of the new table of organization filled. But I can pencil in one assignment right now, if it's the one you want."

Alicia discovered that she couldn't speak, and he laughed gently.

"Should I take that as a yes?" he asked.

Book Three: Broken Sword

The darkness shuddered.

*An icy breeze sighed through the heart of its warmth, and she shuddered. She tasted fire and slaughter, the sweet copper of blood, and the heady harshness of smoke, and almost—*almost*—she awoke.*

It was there, her sleeping thought knew. It was coming closer. The echo she had sensed twice before was stronger than ever, sure in the strength of its self-knowledge, of its discipline . . . of its deadliness. And the branchings of its futures narrowed, narrowed, narrowed . . .

The constellations of potentialities were disappearing, folding in on themselves, resolving. The choices became starker as they became fewer, the alternatives more wrapped in pain.

And yet still the echo knew nothing, sensed nothing, of what awaited it. With all the dauntless courage of mortal kind, it advanced into that unknown void, prepared to accept whatever was.

But would it have been so brave if it had been as she was? Able to sense the dwindling futures which lay before it?

The time will come, *she thought at it from her sleep.* The time will come, Little One, when you must choose. And what will your choice be then? Will you give yourself to me? Make your purpose and mine one? And how much pain will you embrace in the name of choice?

But the void returned no answer, and the icy breeze sighed away once more into stillness.

Not yet, *her sleepy thought murmured.* Not yet.

But soon.

CHAPTER TWENTY-NINE

"Look, I don't give a rat's ass what 'headquarters' says about it!" Major Samuel Truman, Imperial Marines, snarled. "I'm taking casualties, and the fucking Lizards are sitting still where I can get at them!"

"Sir," Lieutenant Hunter said, almost desperately, "I'm only telling you what they told me. They want us to hold here. Right here, they said."

"God *damn* it!"

Had Major Truman been able to do so, he would have snatched off his cap, thrown it on the ground, and stamped on it with both feet. Since he happened to be in battle armor at the moment, that wasn't very practical, which only added to his sense of frustration.

He counted to fifty very slowly—he didn't have the patience to make it all the way to a hundred—instead, and then exhaled a deep breath.

"And did it happen, Lieutenant," he said very carefully, "that HQ gave you a *reason* for us to stay 'right here'?"

"Sir, they just said to hold position and that someone was on his way out here to explain things."

"Oh, I see," Truman said with exquisite irony. "*Explain* things."

Another cluster of Rishathan mortar rounds came whistling in from the far side of the ridge, and the Marines' automated air-defense cannon swivelled like striking snakes. Plasma bolts streaked upward, and the incoming mortar fire exploded well short of its intended targets. The steady, snarling crackle of "small arms" fire also came from the far side of the ridge, where Truman's forward units were exchanging rifle fire with the forward Rish pickets. The Marines' battle rifles would have been called auto cannon, had they been employed by unarmored infantry, and the Rishathan weapons replying to them were heavier still.

Truman listened to the thunder of battle, then shook his head.

"Why can I still be surprised by the idiocy REMFs can get up to?" he inquired rhetorically. Hunter, wisely, made no response, and the major sighed.

"All right, Vincent," he said to the lieutenant in a milder voice, "fire up your com and inform HQ that Second Battalion is holding its positions awaiting further orders."

"Yes, Sir!" Hunter managed to suppress most of the relief he felt, but Truman heard it anyway, and smiled with a trace of genuine humor. Then he turned away, studying his projected HUD once again, while he wondered what fresh lunacy was about to descend upon him.

The intensity of the fire being exchanged between Second Battalion and the dug-in Rish had faded into sporadic shots by the time the promised minion from headquarters reached Truman's CP. The major's initial fury at the order to halt his advance had also faded—a little, at any rate—and he was prepared to at least listen to whatever his . . . visitor had to say.

It had better be good, though, he told himself grimly.

Second Battalion had already taken over a hundred casualties, twenty-three of them fatal, and he'd finally been gaining a little momentum in his drive against the Rishathan lines. It was going to cost him more people to regain that momentum now that they'd stopped him in his tracks, and he growled again, jaw tightening at the thought.

He hated actions like this one. The planet of Louvain wasn't even an imperial world—it was a Rogue World which had been so bent on retaining its independent status that it had rejected a defensive alliance with the Empire. Apparently, its government had believed that refusing to sign any formal agreements with either side would somehow convince both of them to leave its world alone.

Which might have worked with the Empire, but not with the Rishathan Sphere. Although, to be fair, Louvain hadn't *officially* been invaded by the Sphere. Technically speaking, the Rishathan troops currently ensconced on the planet represented an old-fashioned filibustering expedition. The Theryian Clan had launched the invasion purely as a private enterprise effort to extend its own clan holdings, and anyone could believe as much of that as he wanted to.

Unfortunately for Clan Theryian—or for the Sphere, depending on exactly how one wanted to interpret what was going on—imperial intelligence had gotten wind of the operation in time to deploy reinforcements to the neighboring Tiberian Sector. Which meant that when the Louvain Republic finally woke up, smelled the coffee, and realized it was about to be invaded, there were imperial troops available to respond to its raucous screams for help. Unfortunately, those troops hadn't been able to get there until *after* the Rish invasion force.

The Imperial Fleet had quickly and efficiently destroyed or dispersed the naval units which had transported and supported the Lizard assault force, but that didn't do much about the ground forces already in place. A human commander in the same predicament probably would have seriously considered surrender, or at least a negotiated withdrawal. Rish, unfortunately, didn't think that way, and Major Truman and the rest of his battalion's regiment had been dealing with the consequences of Lizard stubbornness for the better part of three standard weeks now.

Which was why he wasn't very happy about the notion of halting his advance when he'd finally found a soft spot in the Rish's final perimeter. In fact—

"Uh, Major?"

Truman looked up, his eyebrows rising in surprise at Lieutenant Hunter's tone. The younger officer stood in the CP entrance, looking—and sounding—astonished, almost tentative, and Truman frowned.

"What is it, Vincent?"

"That . . . representative from Headquarters is here, Sir."

Truman's frown deepened, but he only tossed his head inside his helmet—the battle-armored equivalent of a shrug.

"Well, send him on in," he said brusquely.

"Yes, Sir!" Hunter turned in the entryway, speaking to someone Truman couldn't see. "This way, Ma'am," he said.

Truman watched his com specialist stepping aside to make room for the visitor, and then the major's already elevated eyebrows did their best to disappear entirely into his hairline. The last thing he'd expected to see was someone in Cadre battle armor!

The newcomer's armor carried the rank insignia of a captain, which made its wearer effectively equal in rank to Truman himself. That was not a particularly welcome thought. Not that Samuel Truman had anything but respect for the Cadre; he wasn't an idiot, after all. But however much he might respect it, he was the fellow who'd been the officer on the ground for the last three weeks, and the thought of being ordered about by some newcomer, who didn't know his ass from his elbow in terms of the local situation, was unpalatable, to say the very least.

The Cadre officer stepped fully into the cramped command post and saluted.

"Major Truman?" a pleasant, almost furry-sounding contralto inquired.

"I'm Truman," the major acknowledged, returning the salute and then holding out one gauntleted hand. "And you are?"

The question came out a bit more brusquely than he'd intended to, but the newcomer didn't seem to notice.

"DeVries," she said. "Captain Alicia DeVries, Imperial Cadre."

For a moment, Truman only nodded. Then he stiffened as the name registered.

"Did you say *DeVries*?"

"Yes," she said simply, and Truman found himself shaking her armored hand rather more fervently than he'd intended to.

"I'd welcome you to Louvain, Captain," he heard himself saying, "except that it's not exactly the sort of vacation spot I'd wish on a friend."

"Oh, I don't know, Major." There was something suspiciously like a chuckle in the captain's voice. "Until the present visitors arrived, it was a nice enough planet. Or so I understand."

"I've been told it was," Truman acknowledged. "Unfortunately, I've been a bit too busy being shot at to play tourist."

"Actually, that's why I'm here," DeVries told him, and smiled at him through her armor's visor. She was a remarkably attractive—

and young—woman, Truman realized. Which was almost a surprise, given her . . . formidable reputation.

"I understand you Wasps have the Lizards pretty well contained," she continued, "but now that you've got them pushed back into their final perimeter, it's going to get nothing but uglier."

"Maybe," Truman said a bit more stiffly. "I think, though, Captain, that Second Battalion's found a weak spot. Assuming, of course, that we're ever allowed to exploit it," he added pointedly.

"My, my, you *are* pissed off." There was no doubt about the chuckle this time, and Truman felt his temper stir once again. DeVries obviously realized it, and she smiled again, quickly.

"I don't blame you if you *are* pissed," she told him. "Obviously, if you've found a weakness, you want to punch in hard and fast. Unfortunately, Major, you haven't found one yet."

"I *beg* your pardon?" Truman didn't care who she was, or what medals she'd won. Not when she came waltzing in and told him he didn't know how to read a tactical situation.

"Sorry," she said calmly. "I don't want to rain on your parade, Major Truman, but I've got access to some background intelligence that wasn't available to your own intel people. We developed it after you'd already deployed for the operation, which is why my company was sent along behind you."

"What kind of 'background intelligence?'" Truman asked suspiciously.

"According to a source which Cadre intelligence considers reliable," she told him, "when Clan Theryian headed out for Louvain, it came prepared for a full-court *mysorthayak*."

Truman blinked. He was scarcely what he'd consider an expert on Rishathan psychology, but he'd heard the term *mysorthayak* before. Every Marine had.

"Jesus Christ," he said. "What the hell makes *Louvain* important enough for something like that?"

"We're not really positive," DeVries admitted. "There are conflicting views on that particular question. There always are, aren't there?" She gave him a crooked grin—the sort the shooters at the sharp end always gave one another. "All we can say for sure is that our source is pretty insistent. Personally, I don't think their real objective is the conquest of Louvain, at all. I think the Sphere's simply decided it's time for another test of our resolve and 'volunteered'

Clan Theryian to carry it out. But I think you'll agree that if they are thinking in terms of a *mysorthayak*, you might want to be just a bit cautious about exploiting any 'weaknesses' you find."

"You can say that again, Captain," Truman said fervently.

The Rish had found the technological gap between their military capabilities and those of their human—specifically, of their *imperial* human—opponents growing steadily wider ever since the old League Wars. In particular, the fact that no Rish could use neural receptors placed them at a huge disadvantage, especially when it came to naval warfare. Their basic weapons were as good as humanity's, as was their equivalent of the Fasset Drive, but humans' ability to link directly with their military hardware gave them an enormous advantage.

That advantage was most pronounced where the Fleet was concerned. A Rish admiral really required at least a three-to-one advantage in weight of metal if she wanted just to hold her own against a Fleet task force, which was one reason the Rishathan ships supporting this invasion had scuttled out of the system as soon as the Fleet turned up. But when it came to ground combat, the traditional human advantages got a bit thinner.

For one thing, Rish were *big*. At a height of almost three meters—and squat for their height, compared to *homo sapiens*—a fully mature Rishathan matriarch massed up to about four hundred kilos, all of it muscle and solid bone. No human could hope to match a Rish in hand-to-hand combat without battle armor, and the Rish built their own battle armor on the same scale nature had used when she built *them*. Their *unarmored* infantry routinely carried weapons which only a human in battle armor could support, and a fully armored Rish infantryman (although any self-respecting Rishathan matriarch would have ripped out the lungs of anyone who applied a masculine gendered pronoun to her), was tougher than most human light battle tanks.

They still couldn't match the flexibility and "situational awareness" of human troops equipped with neural receptors, but they'd worked hard to develop ways to compensate for that. In the assault, they eschewed anything like finesse, relying on sheer mass, toughness, and weight of fire to bull their way through any opposition. On the defensive, they deployed tactical remotes profusely, dug their troops in deeply with overlapping fields of fire, backed them with as large and powerful a mobile reserve as they could, and tied in multiply redundant layers of air defense and fire support from heavy weapons. Blasting a way through a prepared Rishathan infantry position was always a costly affair.

Which only got worse when they were thinking in terms of *mysorthayak*. Truman wasn't sure exactly how to translate the term, but he supposed the closest human concept would have been *jihad*, although that had overtones he knew weren't really applicable. *Jihad* hadn't been a very popular term for humanity for the past several centuries, and it had resonances which didn't fit very well in this case, either, of course. *Mysorthayak* was all about clan honor, honor debts, and Rish bloody-mindedness, with only a small religious component, but the Rishathan honor code was twisty enough and hard-edged enough to make "*jihad*" the closest convenient human analogue. Once they committed to *mysorthayak*, Rishathan matriarchs didn't give ground. They fought and died where they stood, and if they had the resources available, they seeded their positions with nuclear demolition charges in order to take as many of their enemies with them as possible.

"So what you're saying," Truman said after a moment, "is that if I'd bulled on ahead, they'd have waited until my people and I were well stuck into their position, then blown us all to hell along with themselves?"

"I'm saying that's a strong possibility," DeVries corrected meticulously. "I can't say it's any more than that without better tactical info. But whether that's what they've got in mind right here in front of *you* or not, it's something we're going to run into somewhere before this op is over. Unless, of course, we do something about it."

"Meaning what?" Truman asked, regarding her through narrowed eyes.

"Meaning that the one way to avoid the sort of casualties *mysorthayak* usually inflicts is to decapitate the Lizard command structure."

"Decapitate it?" Truman frowned. "What do you mean?"

"It just happens, Major Truman," DeVries told him with a tart smile, "that I hold a doctoral degree equivalent in xenopsych, with a specialty in Rishathan psychology. Which is undoubtedly the reason Brigadier Keita picked my company for this little adventure. Think of it as a reward for my diligent efforts to understand the enemy."

Despite himself, Truman snorted in amusement at her dust-dry tone.

"At any rate," she continued more seriously, "the best way to beat a *mysorthayak* defense is to 'turn it off' at the source. There's no real human equivalent for some of the Rishathan honor code concepts, but the matriarchs understand the ideas of individual combat and of honorable surrender to a worthy adversary. And if the war mother in command of this little incursion of theirs orders her troops to surrender, they will, *mysorthayak* or not. So, the way to avoid having to kill every single Rish on the planet—and losing a lot of our own people along the way—is to . . ."

She let her voice trail off, and Truman's eyes widened.

"You're going to hit their *planetary HQ?*" He shook his head. "Are you out of your mind?!"

"I wasn't the last time I looked," she told him. "Of course, I suppose that's subject to change. In the meantime, however, that's exactly what we've got in mind. So I'd appreciate the opportunity to go over your own reports and recorded tac data. I want to develop a better feel for their actual weapons mix and tactics while our own intelligence people are figuring out exactly where their HQ is."

CHAPTER THIRTY

"So that's about the size of it, Uncle Arthur." Alicia leaned back in her chair across the tactical table in *Marguerite Johnsen*'s intelligence center from Sir Arthur Keita. "I think Truman was right—the Lizards are just about ready to crack in his area—but if they really are in *mysorthayak* mode, letting him push would be the worst thing we could possibly do."

"Maybe it would be," Keita said. "In fact, you're almost certainly right. But I'm not too sure that what you're proposing isn't the *next* to worst thing we could possibly do."

Alicia gazed at Keita with a sort of fond exasperation. In the five and a half standard years since Keita had sent her off to OCS, she'd come to know "the Emperor's Bulldog" far better than even most Cadremen ever did. He spent a lot of time—as much of it as he could—in the field, moving about from one hot spot to another, and Charlie Company had mounted three more operations under his personal direction since Shallingsport. None of them, thankfully, remotely like that nightmare experience.

But she'd seen more of him than just that. Every member of the Cadre was important to Sir Arthur Keita, but Alicia DeVries had become one of his personal protégés. She knew that, and, despite her powerful distaste for anything which smacked of favoritism, it didn't bother her very much. Uncle Arthur might take particular pains to nourish the careers of Cadremen who'd demonstrated special promise in his eyes, but no one in the Cadre could believe for a moment that he'd allow favoritism to substitute for demonstrated ability . . . or to excuse its absence.

But one of the things she'd learned about him, something he went to great lengths to disguise, was that for all his decades of military service, all of his hard-won experience, Sir Arthur Keita was a worrier. Not about his own duty or responsibilities, but where the men and women under his command were concerned. He had to send them out again and again, sometimes into situations almost as bad as Shallingsport, and he did, unflinchingly. But he hated it, and the avoidance of *any* unnecessary casualties was an obsession with him.

Especially where his "protégés" are concerned, she reminded herself.

"Uncle Arthur," she said, with the assurance of her own experience, "we can do this. It may be a little tricky to set up, but the Company can *do* it. And if we pull it off, we save a lot of lives—not all of them human."

"Alley, I appreciate what you're saying, but I think Sir Arthur may have a point," another voice said.

Alicia turned her head and gazed thoughtfully at Colonel Wadislaw Watts. The Marine intelligence specialist's career—like Alicia's own, she supposed—had survived Shallingsport. She suspected that it might have cost him earlier promotion to his present rank, but his superiors had generally recognized that the major intelligence failures of that operation had occurred at a level considerably higher than Watts'.

She'd worked with him a couple of times since Shallingsport, as well, although he'd recently been returned to regular service with the Marines, instead of continuing to support the Cadre, and she couldn't complain about his performance either time. But she still didn't like him very much, although she sometimes thought that was probably because deep down inside somewhere, on some subconscious level, *she* blamed him for Shallingsport. The illogic of that attitude left her feeling angry with herself, which was why she made a deliberate effort to be pleasant and courteous to him.

Even if it does irritate the hell out of me when he insists on calling me by my first name, she thought wryly. *Of course, he* is *a colonel, and I'm only a captain, even if I am Cadre and he's "only" a Wasp.*

Now she simply raised one eyebrow, inviting him to continue, and he shrugged.

"I realize I'm here as Brigadier Sampson's representative," he said, "but I've worked with the Cadre enough to feel confident you could get in and almost certainly take all of your objectives. Personally, I think you're underestimating your probable casualties, but you and Sir Arthur have a lot more actual combat experience than I do, so I'm more than willing to defer to your judgment in that respect. The problem I have with what you're proposing is that for it to work, you've got to take the Rish's senior war mother alive, and then you've got to convince her to do what you want."

He paused and shook his head, then continued.

"First of all, given the probable response of any Rishathan war mother to the sudden arrival of armed enemies in her headquarters, I think your odds of taking her alive are considerably less than even. Second, even if you manage to pull that off, a Rish of her probable seniority, especially one who's in a *mysorthayak* mindset already, is more likely to tell you to go to hell than to order her troops to stand down."

"That's exactly what I'm worried about, Alley," Sir Arthur said, nodding sharply. "And if she *does* tell you to go to hell, there you'll be with an entire company trapped in the middle of their fortified zone. If they do have the area mined, they'll probably set the charges off, which would kill all of you. But even if they don't do that, they'll certainly have enough firepower available in the immediate vicinity to eventually overwhelm you."

"And," Watts pointed out, "if the operation fails, Brigadier Sampson has already instructed his staff and his Fleet support elements to begin planning for HVW strikes to take out the Lizards' positions. He's lost over a hundred and thirty dead since his brigade went in, and he's got a *lot* of nonfatal casualties; he's not prepared to lose any more people fighting his way centimeter-by-centimeter through fortified *mysorthayak* positions. I don't like to think about Charlie Company sitting right on top of one of his bull's-eyes in a worst-case scenario."

"Uncle Arthur—Colonel," Alicia said after a moment, "I appreciate what you're saying. But we have to look at the consequences if the Company *doesn't* go in. And, with all due respect, Colonel, whatever Brigadier Sampson may want to do, I strongly doubt that the use of HVW is going to be a politically acceptable option."

Watts bristled slightly, but Alicia looked him straight in the eye.

"Undersecretary Abrams has the ultimate responsibility, Colonel," she reminded him.

The Honorable Jesse Abrams was the permanent assistant undersecretary the Foreign Ministry had assigned to coordinate with the Louvain planetary government. So far, he'd been willing to allow the military more or less free rein, which spoke well for his basic intelligence. But the ultimate responsibility—and authority—were his.

"The Brigadier would have to clear any strikes at that level with him," Alicia continued, "and the fact that Louvain is a Rogue World squarely in the middle of the frontier zone between the Empire and the Sphere has to be a major factor in his thinking." She moved her gaze to Keita. "Uncle Arthur, do you really think Abrams is going to authorize kinetic strikes on Louvain, given the present situation down there?"

Keita gazed back at her for a moment, then sighed.

"No," he admitted. "No, I doubt very much that he will." The brigadier smiled tartly. "That's your father's viewpoint speaking, isn't it, Alley?"

"No, Sir." She smiled back. "It's only common sense when the Lizards have two small cities and half a dozen towns inside their perimeter."

"Our targeting's good enough to miss them," Watts protested.

"And HVW are 'clean' weapons," Alicia acknowledged. "But what Abrams is going to be worrying about is that if there's major civilian loss of life—even if the casualties are inflicted by the *Rish*, not us—and we've used orbital HVW strikes in a populated region of the planet, the Empire's enemies are all going to spin the story their way. Which means there'll be scads of stories all over the 'faxes and info boards recounting, in loving detail, how *we* inflicted all those losses. The fact that there won't be a scrap of truth in any of those stories won't slow the propaganda mills down a bit, will it?"

Watts looked rebellious, but he clamped his jaw tight and, manifestly against his will, shook his head.

"So, if we don't go in, Brigadier Sampson's people are going to have to fight their way in on the ground, after all. In which case, their casualties are going to be much worse than those they've already suffered. Not to mention the fact," she moved her eyes back to Keita again, "that the longer the fighting drags out, especially if they do have charges in place and begin detonating them, the more likely we are to get heavy civilian casualties. We can't let that happen if there's any way we can avoid it. First, because it would be morally wrong, and, second, because it could be politically disastrous when the propagandists go to work."

"But—" Keita began, then stopped. He glared at her for a moment, and then shrugged unhappily.

"You win, Alley," he said. "I don't like it, but I'm afraid you're right, at least about the consequences of trying to do it any other way. I just—"

He broke off again and shook his head angrily, and Alicia's smile went crooked.

This isn't Shallingsport, she wanted to tell him. *This time we've got our own eyes-on intelligence and tac data.*

But she couldn't say it, of course. Not any more than he could admit his own fear that it *would* be another Shallingsport.

"In that case," she said instead, "let's get my people in here and let them start explaining the ops plan we've already put together."

"Ready to go, Skipper?" First Sergeant James Król asked over her armor's dedicated command circuit.

Alicia looked up to see Charlie Company's senior noncom standing beside Sergeant Ludovic Thönes. Król, one of the other three Shallingsport survivors still with the company, had inherited Pamela Yussuf's old job eleven months ago, while Thönes doubled as the senior company clerk and Alicia's wing. He'd been with her for a bit over three standard years—ever since Alicia had been promoted to company commander. Tannis had been promoted to lieutenant at the same time, and offered Second Platoon, but she'd opted to head back to Old Earth to complete her medical training as a full-fledged doctor, and she was currently assigned to Johns Hopkins/Bethesda of Charlotte, the same hospital where Fiona DeVries was currently Chief of Surgery.

Alicia missed Tannis badly, but they'd stayed in close touch, and Tannis had become a close friend of her mother's. In fact, she'd gotten to know all of Alicia's family well and become almost a third daughter. It also hadn't hurt Tannis' career prospects one bit, either. The Cadre was always chronically short of its own medical staff, and Tannis had been assigned to JHB as part of a conscious plan to groom her for bigger and better things.

But Tannis' decision to pursue her medical career was how Lieutenant Angelique Jefferson had gotten the platoon, instead. Alicia regretted the loss of Tannis' coolheaded tactical insight almost as much as she missed having her watching her back. But Jefferson had done the platoon proud, and Alicia and Thönes had become a smoothly integrated team.

"And what might make you question my preparedness, First Sergeant?" she asked severely now.

"Well, far be it from me to suggest that you can sometimes be just a little bit slow, Skipper," Król replied with a grin. "Something about 'late to your own funeral' I believe Tannis said, wasn't it?"

"That was *one* time," Alicia said with dignity, "and it was only a training mission, and that glitch in my battle armor wasn't *my* fault to begin with."

"Whatever you say, Skipper," Król said soothingly, and all three of them chuckled.

"Seriously, Skipper," the first sergeant continued after a moment, "we're ready to enter tubes."

"Then I suppose we'd better saddle up and get to it," Alicia said, and switched to the all-units circuit.

"All units, Ramrod," she said. "Let's go, people—it's time to dance."

Marguerite Johnsen swept steadily around the planet of Louvain in her parking orbit. The Rish on the planetary surface were amply supplied with antiair weapons which could reach up to and just beyond the edge of atmosphere, but the Cadre transport was well outside their range. That was about to change for the individual Cadremen in her tubes, however, and Alicia felt her own stomach muscles tightening as she lay in the number one launch position.

Don't be such a nervous bitch, she scolded herself. *You're the one who came up with this brilliant plan in the first place, aren't you?*

She chuckled, if a bit tensely, and decided that it was just as well no one else could read *her* medical telltales at this particular moment.

"All units, stand by for launch in five minutes," *Marguerite Johnsen*'s cyber-synth said, and Alicia drew a deep breath.

The five minutes in question seemed to take forever to ooze past, and then the audio tone of the thirty-second warning sounded. As always, she considered some final word of encouragement. And, also as always, she decided against it. Her people didn't need to listen to her voicing her confidence in them as a way to relieve her own nervousness.

And then the catapult grabbed her harness and hurled her out of the tube.

She watched her mental display as the rest of the company spat from the transport's tubes with the rapidity of an old-fashioned machine gun. The pattern was perfect, as she'd known it would be, and she watched the planet hurtling towards her.

Louvain's atmosphere began to blossom with tears of flame, streaking down towards the planetary surface. There were dozens—hundreds—of them, and Alicia smiled nastily. Brigadier Sampson's reaction to her "request" for a diversionary drop had been . . . testy. He hadn't really been able to say no, not when the person who'd authorized Alicia's request was none other than Brigadier Sir Arthur Keita. That hadn't made him particularly happy to expend forty-two percent of his total drop harnesses on dummy insertions, however. In fact, he'd rather pointedly suggested that since this was a Cadre operation, perhaps *Marguerite Johnsen* should supply the diversionary drops. But Keita had pointed out in return that a Cadre drop harness cost about three times what a Marine harness cost, at which point Sampson had submitted (as graciously as he could bring himself to) to the inevitable.

Now the Rishathan defenders found their sensors saturated with scores of absolutely genuine drop signatures. Unfortunately for them, there was no way for them to discriminate between the drop harnesses which contained live human enemies and those which didn't. And just to make their problems complete, *all* of the drop patterns, not just Charlie Company's, were liberally seeded with EW platforms and penetration aids.

From the Rishathan perspective, it had to look like a full brigade drop, an all-out effort by the Marines to put a decisive amount of human firepower inside their outer perimeter. Alicia and her platoon commanders had deliberately targeted the diversionary drops on exactly the sorts of positions the Wasps would have gone after if that was what it had actually been. They'd also set up a handful of drops for targets which clearly made no military sense at all to encourage the Rish to regard them as feints. Which—they all hoped—would also encourage them to assume that the company's actual drop was only another diversion from the "real" targets. After all, the planetary invasion force's command post was the most heavily dug-in piece of real estate on the entire planet. It was also in the center of their spacehead, which meant any force trying to break in and link up with drop commandos landing on top of it would have to fight its way through over two hundred kilometers of fortified positions.

All in all, it was hardly the sort of target a Marine brigadier would commit his troops to, and Alicia devoutly hoped that the Theryian command staff would draw the appropriate conclusions.

Unfortunately, there was only one way to find out, and she bared her teeth as she entered Louvain's atmosphere and became another of those plunging tears of flame.

"Striker, Ramrod. Talk to me, James!"

"Ramrod, Striker," First Sergeant Król acknowledged calmly. "We had a little scatter, Skipper. No sweat. I'm rounding up the strays now."

Alicia snorted. "A little scatter" wasn't exactly the way *she* would have phrased it . . . although, she acknowledged, she might have put it that way back when *she'd* been a sergeant, now that she thought about it. After all, one of a sergeant's jobs was to keep the officers from fretting over the little stuff.

"All right, Striker," she said, still loping along in the ground-covering bounds of battle armor. "Round them up and bring them along. I'm heading for the Tiger RP."

"Copy that, Boss. See you in a few."

"See that you do," Alicia said, and turned her attention back to her HUD.

Actually, Król's description was right about on the money, she told herself. The company had made it down without losing a single trooper, which had to mean the Lizards had bought the diversionary plan. They'd written the actual drop off as an obvious feint and declined to waste any of their defensive firepower on it.

Now that Charlie Company was on the ground, however, the Rish were doing their best to rectify their initial oversight. Heavy fire came at the Cadremen from every direction, but the pre-drop recon had been spot-on. Unlike the Shallingsport debacle, the company knew exactly where their enemies' prepared positions were, and each strong point which could bear upon the LZ had been assigned to a specific wing.

One or two of those wings had landed too far from their intended positions to immediately engage them, but that was why Alicia and her platoon commanders had arranged backup assignments. Now Charlie Company's men and women moved purposefully through the flying dirt and smoke of incoming mortar rounds and the scream of heavy-caliber penetrators. They closed in on their primary or backup assignments, and Alicia had dropped in heavy configuration. Six of each squad's nine wings were armed with plasma rifles and HVW launchers, and as the green icons on Alicia's HUD swarmed towards the glaring orange icons of dug-in Rishathan heavy weapons and infantry, those orange icons began to disappear.

The Rish were past masters (or mistresses) at field fortification. They dug their weapons in deep, with excellent fields of fire, but Charlie Company had brought along the firepower equivalent of an old pre-space division—at least. Each of the HVW launchers had only three rounds, but each of those rounds produced a kiloton-range fireball when it impacted. Even the best-bunkered weapons couldn't survive that kind of treatment. Not, at least, if they were exposed enough to have a field of fire of their own.

The plasma gunners left the most heavily dug-in positions up to their HVW-armed wingmen. They were busy taking out the surface positions, the infantry pickets covering the flanks of the heavy weapons. And here and there, a Cadre plasma gunner sent a bolt screaming straight in through a firing slit to turn the bunker on the other side into a fusion-fired crematorium.

"Medic! *Medic!*" she heard, and muttered a curse as Corporal Sosa, one of Lieutenant Akama Alves' Third Platoon troopers, went down. His icon strobed rapidly, indicating heavy damage to his armor, and his life signs monitor blipped the emergency transponder code of a life-threatening injury.

Sosa's wing, Corporal Frederica Stone, was already there, dragging him into the lee of a furiously burning Rishathan bunker, and Alicia noted the caduceus icon of the Third Platoon medic bounding towards them.

Another green icon went down, and she swore again, more viciously. This time, the icon *didn't* strobe; it turned the bloody red of death instantly as Corporal Harold Madsen took a Rishathan plasma bolt center of mass.

That shouldn't have happened, a corner of Alicia's brain told her. *That strong point was supposed to've already been taken out by—oh.*

The strong point *had* been taken out, and, so—almost before Madsen's shattered armor hit the ground—had the single Rish trooper who'd popped up out of nowhere to take the shot. It was just one of those things. Just Murphy's way of reminding people that no matter how carefully they planned, *he* always had the final word.

"Tiger-One, Ramrod," she said, shaking that thought aside. "I'm approaching your rally point from eight o'clock."

"Ramrod, Tiger-One," Lieutenant Jefferson's soprano replied. "I've got you and Ludovic on the HUD, Skipper."

"Glad to hear it," Alicia said dryly as she and Thönes loped along the trail of wrecked, shattered, burning Rishathan strong points Jefferson's people had left in their wake. It would have been embarrassing, to say the least, to be picked off by one of her own people over a case of mistaken identity.

She and Thönes covered the last dozen meters in a single bound, and Lieutenant Jefferson waved one armored arm at her company commander.

"Over here, Skipper!"

Alicia strode over and slapped the lieutenant's shoulder.

"Mind if Ludovic and I come along for the ride, Angelique?" she asked.

"Course not, Boss," Jefferson assured her. Not, Alicia reflected, that she'd ever been likely to say no, but there were formalities to observe, even in the middle of a battlefield like this one.

"Erik has your left flank," she said now, leaning close enough to Jefferson that they could see one another's features through their armored visors as she highlighted First Platoon's icons on the lieutenant's HUD.

"He'll have that last calliope position knocked out in another ninety seconds, max," Alicia continued, "and Akama and his people have already secured this entire arc on your right."

"Good enough," Jefferson said, nodding in satisfaction, then looked up at Alicia with a wolfish smile. "We kind of cleared everything that might have come at us from behind on the way in, Skipper."

"So I noticed," Alicia replied.

"Well, as soon as Erik takes out that calliope, we'll go," Jefferson said, looking back up to where the calliope in question was flaying the approaches to a particularly substantial-looking bunker with penetrators that could have knocked out an APC, not just battle armor. "I don't want to—"

Alicia's visor polarized as a searing explosion obliterated the calliope's position. The thermal pulse and blast front from the HVW strike rolled over her and Jefferson like a fiery fist, and her armor's automatic stabilizing systems whined in protest as they kept her on her feet.

"So much for that," Jefferson observed, and punched into her platoon's all-hands circuit.

"All Tigers," she said. "That was First Platoon taking out some rather unpleasant Lizards who might have objected to our presence. Now that Lieutenant Andersson and his people have attended to that minor detail for us," she smiled at Alicia, "let's dance, people."

As a company commander, Alicia no longer had any business in the forefront of a firefight like this one. She knew that, and under most circumstances, she would have stayed out of it, whether she liked it or not. But this time, she couldn't. Not only were she and Ludovic Thönes one of the minority of rifle-armed wings, but she was the company's Rish expert.

She did let Jefferson and her people effect the initial break-in into the Rishathan command bunker. They executed the breaching operation flawlessly, and at such close quarters the heavier weapons Rish infantry normally carried lost a lot of their advantage. Rish battle armor was more ponderous than human armor, which also meant it was considerably tougher than standard Marine equipment. In fact, it was tougher than the Cadre's armor, but at close enough range, the Cadre battle rifle was quite capable of punching its penetrators even through Rish armor. And the fact that the attacking humans were fused directly into their sensor systems and required no physical input interface for their armor's and weapons' onboard computers gave them a deadly advantage in a dogfight like this one. Coupled with the tick, the Cadremen's enormously greater "situational awareness" simply meant they reacted faster, and far more accurately, than the Rish possibly could.

Second Platoon didn't have it *all* its own way, of course. Jefferson's squads took seven more casualties on the way in—none of them, thankfully, immediately fatal, although Alicia didn't much care for the look of Corporal Inglewood's vitals on her medical monitor. But once the platoon had broken into the command bunker, it actually outnumbered the Rishathan defenders by almost two-to-one. The fight was short, vicious, and ugly . . . as fights tended to be when the combatants engaged one another with plasma rifles at ranges as low as three meters.

"Pandora!" one of Jefferson's troopers announced. "I have Pandora!"

"All Tigers," Jefferson said instantly. "Pandora. I say again, Pandora! Let's watch those plasma bolts, people!"

Acknowledgment came back, and the tempo of the combat shifted abruptly. Jefferson's Third Squad, tasked to cover the other two squads' backs as they fought their way into the bunker, was still furiously engaged with Rish infantry trying to fight their way in behind the attacking humans. Between them and the platoon's point, the flaming, shattered passages through which the fighting inside the bunker had already passed were relatively quiet. Now the furious tempo at the head of the column suddenly seemed to hesitate as the plasma gunners who had been leading the assault slowed abruptly to let their rifle-armed colleagues past them.

Alicia and Thönes squirmed through the halted ranks of the heavy-weapon-armed troopers and joined the platoon's six wings of riflemen.

"Skipper," Jefferson began over the dedicated command circuit in a last-ditch, spinal-reflex argument, "you really don't—"

"Just stick to the ops plan, Angelique," Alicia scolded with a tight smile. "You know why."

"Yes, Ma'am," Jefferson sighed in the tone of a gradeschool student promising to do her homework *this* time. "In that case, when you're ready, Skipper," she added over the general circuit, and Alicia chuckled.

"All right, people. It's dance time," she said.

The final break-in was actually almost something of an anticlimax. Alicia had more than half anticipated a fanatical, backs-to-the-wall stand by *mysorthayak*-charged matriarchs. She'd been prepared to shoot her way through them, but she'd expected to take casualties of her own in the process of stacking the defenders like cordwood. Only it didn't work out that way.

A single pair of armored Rish infantry loomed up out of the big, dimly lit chamber at the very heart of the command bunker. They opened fire the instant the Cadremen came around the defensive dogleg in the final approach corridor. But they were armed with calliopes, not plasma guns, because they couldn't afford to let the backblast from their own weapons turn this room into the sort of flaming shambles Second Platoon had left behind it on the way in.

The heavy penetrators would have killed or wounded any Cadreman they hit, but unfortunately for the Rish, Jefferson's troopers had already known they were there. The tactical remotes the humans had tossed around the dogleg showed them exactly where the defending Rish had positioned themselves, and if they could shoot at the Cadre, then the Cadre could shoot at *them*.

As Alicia had once demonstrated on a planet called Gyangtse, a rifleman who could draw a bead on his target with his eyes closed had a significant advantage. In fact, the advancing Cadre riflemen had their weapons aimed and steadily tracking their targets while there was still a thick, solid wall between them and the Rish. They were positioned to fire the moment their rifle muzzles cleared the dogleg, which meant they actually fired *before* the defenders.

Both armored Rish went down as battle rifle penetrators shattered their helmets and the skulls inside them. One of them sprayed hundreds of rounds from her calliope as her hand death-locked on the firing grip. One penetrator actually managed to hit Corporal Carlotta Mastroianni's right leg. The armor held, but Mastroianni went down anyway as the shock of the massive penetrator's impact knocked out her armor's "leg muscles."

Alicia was delighted that the damage to her Cadrewoman was so minor, but she cringed as the other penetrators went shrieking and screaming around the command chamber. Computers, communications consoles, and tactical repeaters exploded in sparks, flying wreckage, and electrical fires. Worse, at least a dozen Rish officers and technicians went with them.

"*Go!*" Alicia shouted, and the other rifle-armed wings charged into the chaos and smoke with her. At least their sensors let them "see" with crystal clarity, which was more than most of the unarmored Rish could say.

Too bad we can't just shoot the bloody-minded bitches out of hand, Alicia thought viciously as she made her way through the stumbling, half-blinded matriarchs. Unfortunately, they couldn't. Not yet.

Alicia let her battle rifle snap back up into the "safe" position and drew her force blade.

"Watch my back!"

"Got it, Skip," Thönes replied laconically, and Alicia hurled herself directly into the midst of the surviving Rish.

One of the matriarchs, in unpowered body armor, saw or sensed her approach. A "pistol" the size of a human's sawed-off combat rifle thrust in her direction, and Alicia grabbed the weapon. Her battle armor was stronger than any Rish, but the matriarch out-massed her, armor and all, and Alicia felt herself sliding forward as the Rish fought to regain control of her weapon.

Enough of that! she thought, and the force blade slashed down on the Rish's forearm.

The matriarch stumbled backward, spouting blood from the stump of her arm, and Alicia stepped into the gap. Her armored elbow slammed into the spine of another matriarch, shattering it despite everything Rishathan toughness could do, and her force blade cut down a third.

It'd be an awful lot simpler, she thought, peering at the gaudy breastplate patterns which only she had the training to read, *if only these people*—there!

"Queen!" she barked over the platoon com net. "*Queen!*"

She charged forward, bulling through the towering matriarchs. At least one of them must have realized who her target was, for the Rish—a fairly senior war mother, by the markings on her armor—hurled herself at Alicia, arms spread to grapple in a suicidal attack. She met the force blade on her way in, and the headless corpse slid across the floor while Alicia vaulted over it in a headlong bound that ended in a hurtling tackle.

She and the matriarch who'd stood behind the other Rish went down in a crashing impact. The matriarch lost her personal weapon as they hit, and they rolled across the floor, the Rish writhing madly in Alicia's grip, trying frantically to throw the human attacker off. They came upright, then slammed into one of the chamber's walls, with the Rish hurling her full, massive weight backwards. But Alicia's armor absorbed the impact easily, and her grip only tightened. She switched off the force blade and slammed the flat of its heavy alloy core against the side of the Rish's skull. The matriarch staggered, her struggles fading, and Alicia smacked her again.

Damn it, how tough is a Rishathan skull?! she thought. *If I hit her* too *hard—*

The Rish's knees buckled with the second blow, and Alicia activated her armor's speakers.

"I have your line-mother!" she shouted, her armor's AI automatically translating into High Rish. The amplified, squeaky snarls and ripples filled the chamber like some sort of falsetto thunder, and every Rish in it froze.

"Her life is mine, not yours!" Alicia continued. "Yield, or I claim my prize!"

Her amplified voice crashed through the underground chamber . . . and every matriarch in it dropped instantly to her knees.

"My God, Skipper," Angelique Jefferson said quietly over the command circuit, "I really wasn't sure you knew what you were talking about this time."

"O ye of little faith," Alicia replied, still standing behind the slumped bulk of her captive, razor-sharp alloy blade poised, while she watched Jefferson's troopers systematically collect the weapons the Rish had discarded. The matriarchs appeared totally stunned. They were passive, almost apathetic, as their human captors chivied them into the far end of the big, body-littered command room.

"I've just never heard of the Lizards just . . . packing it in this way," Jefferson said, half-apologetically.

"It's the way they're wired," Alicia said. "We don't call them 'matriarchs' for nothing."

Alicia waited another few minutes, until she was certain her people had the situation well in hand. Two-thirds of the command bunker's interior had already been taken; now wings of plasma-armed Cadremen filtered outward to secure the rest of it. With the main prize safely secured, they no longer had to restrict their fire-power or tactics to avoid killing the wrong Rish, and Alicia was confident the entire bunker would be in Charlie Company's hands shortly.

Which meant she could move to the next stage of her plan.

The stunned Rish was beginning to stir, and Alicia leaned over her. Even sitting on the floor, little more than half-conscious, the top of the matriarch's crested skull rose chest-high on Alicia, and she suspected that she looked fairly ridiculous with her left arm—battle armor or no—wrapped around that tree-trunk neck. Still . . .

"Your life is mine," Alicia told her through the armor AI. "Your line-daughters have yielded to preserve it. Yield now, to preserve theirs."

The groggy Rish stirred again—not really trying to escape, just trying to get her brain back online—and Alicia tightened her left arm and pressed the flat of the blade against the right side of the Rish's neck.

"You have not yielded," she said flatly, and the Rish froze. There was silence for a moment, then a lunatic bagpipe skirl of High Rish.

"I yield," the AI translated for Alicia. "Spare my daughters."

"Their lives for yours," Alicia agreed, and released her captive.

More than one of the Cadremen shifted uneasily as the towering matriarch climbed back to her feet. Alicia didn't. She simply stood there, waiting until the Rish turned back to face her and bowed her head in formal token of submission.

"Then I am your captive," the matriarch said. "Do with me as you will."

"I do not will to slay you," Alicia told her. The Rish stared at her, golden eyes—beautiful eyes, Alicia thought, even now, and all the more beautiful for the hideous saurian mask in which they were set—wide.

"Then what would you?" the Rish demanded.

"I would spare you, and your line-daughters and your war-daughters," Alicia told her. "I would have them live and return home in honor, rather than see my line-sisters and them kill one another when there is no need."

"And so you have fought your way into the heart of this, my sphere, and bested me, hand-to-hand, to win life from death," the Rish said.

"Is that not how those of the Sphere have dealt, one with another, from the day of the First Egg?" Alicia riposted.

"Indeed," the Rish replied after a moment. "But only one with another. You are not of the People."

"Yet I hold your life in the hollow of my hand. It is mine, fairly won in honorable combat."

"Indeed," the Rish repeated, and bowed deeply. "Yet there are prizes, and there are prizes, War Mother."

Alicia felt a flicker of relief as the Rish bestowed the Rishathan honorific upon her, but something about the matriarch's body language made her uneasy.

"My name," the Rish said, "is Shernsiya *niha* Theryian, *farthi chir* Theryian. I cannot give you what you seek."

Alicia stared at her in shock. She'd expected a senior war mother of Clan Theryian, but not the clan's *farthi chir*! Her mind raced, trying to cope with this totally unexpected development.

"Skipper?" Lieutenant Jefferson said after a moment. Alicia looked at the platoon commander. "What's going on, Skipper?" Jefferson asked over their private, dedicated channel.

"It's—" Alicia turned back to Shernsiya, staring into those golden eyes once again. "I just didn't count on . . . this," she said softly.

"On what, Skipper? I'm not a Rish expert like you."

Those eyes were bigger than ever, Alicia thought. They were fixed on her own face, gazing at her while Shernsiya's scarlet cranial frills folded themselves close. It was almost as if the Rish were trying to tell her something, she thought.

And then she knew what it was.

"You are a war mother of war mothers, Shernsiya *niha* Theryian, *farthi chir* Theryian," she said quietly.

She met the towering Rish's eyes a moment longer, and bowed, ever so slightly . . . then drew her pistol and shot the matriarch three times through the torso.

CHAPTER THIRTY-ONE

"*Skipper!*"

Angelique Jefferson stared at Alicia in shocked, horrified disbelief as Shernsiya shuddered under the impact of the pistol rounds and then crashed to the floor.

The lieutenant whirled to face the other Rishathan prisoners, her weapon snapping up into the firing position in anticipation of their berserk charge.

But there was no charge. Instead, there was a wailing burst of high-pitched Rishathan, and the kneeling prisoners bent to press their faces to the floor.

Jefferson allowed her plasma rifle to return to the "safe" position and turned slowly back towards Alicia. But Alicia wasn't even looking at her lieutenant. She was kneeling on the floor beside Shernsiya, and as Jefferson watched, she reached out and laid one hand on the Rish's massive, heaving chest.

"My thanks . . . War Mother," the mortally wounded matriarch got out.

"It was your choice, *farthi chir*," Alicia said quietly.

"Indeed." The Rish managed a snarling chuckle. "But I could not tell you. I am honored that you guessed."

She and Alicia looked at one another for a moment, and then the Rish waved one hand at the other prisoners.

"I must speak to my eldest daughter," she said, panting with the pain of her wounds, and Alicia nodded.

Shernsiya raised her voice, calling a name, and Alicia looked up quickly.

"Let her pass!" she said sharply to Jefferson, and the lieutenant nodded. It was a nod of obedience, not of understanding, and Alicia smiled mirthlessly.

A shadow loomed over her as another Rish appeared at her side. The newcomer went to one knee beside Shernsiya, reaching out to lay a clawed hand on the dying matriarch's chest beside Alicia's.

"I am here, Mother of Mothers," she said.

"Good, Rethmeryk," Shernsiya said. Her own hand moved again, indicating Alicia.

"This war mother of the humans has given you life, Eldest Daughter. You will take it, and all of my daughters with you. You will give the order I cannot and lead them from this place, return them to their own sphere. The clan's honor is clean once more with my death. I name you *farthi chir* in my place, and I command you to remember with honor this war mother who has given our clan back its life."

"As you bid, so shall it be, Mother of Mothers," Rethmeryk said, and turned to Alicia.

"How shall we name you in the annals of Clan Theryian, War Mother?" she asked.

"My name is DeVries—Alicia DeVries," Alicia said, and Rethmeryk jerked as if she'd been struck. She started to open her mouth again, then stopped and looked down at Shernsiya.

The dying matriarch seemed as stunned as her line-daughter. She stared at Alicia, then looked back at Rethmeryk.

"Go, Eldest Daughter," she said softly. "I see here the hand of the Greatest Mother. Symmetry must be served."

"Yes, Mother of Mothers," Rethmeryk agreed. She looked back at Alicia. "War Mother, may I use our communication equipment?"

"You may," Alicia agreed, her own eyes on Shernsiya's face.

"Skipper?" Jefferson sounded totally out of her depth, and Alicia smiled without humor.

"Let her use the com, Angelique," she said. "She needs to pass the surrender order."

"Just like that?" Jefferson waved at the dying matriarch. "They're just going to surrender after *that*?"

"Especially after 'that,'" Alicia said.

Jefferson looked at her, then drew a deep breath and nodded.

"Whatever you say, Skipper," she said, and beckoned for Rethmeryk to accompany her towards an intact communications console.

"War Mother Alicia," Shernsiya said, "this is not the first time we have fought, you and I, though you knew it not, and we did not meet then hand-to-hand. Nor *were* you ever to know. But the Greatest Mother orders the universe as She would have it, and I would not have fallen into your hand, nor would you have spared my line-daughters, had She not willed it.

"Symmetry must be served—a gift for a gift, War Mother. And as your gift to me, so mine to you will have two edges. I do not think you will thank me for it, but by the steel in your soul, by the honor in your hand, by the truth in your mouth, so shall you have it, and I think you will count the having worth the pain."

Alicia knelt very still, her gaze fixed on those glorious golden eyes.

"Bid your war daughters stand back, War Mother Alicia," Shernsiya said. "My gift is for you alone."

"Give us some space here, Angelique," Alicia said without looking up. "You, too, Ludovic," she told Thönes.

Her wingman looked briefly rebellious, but after a heartbeat of hesitation, he followed Jefferson across the room.

"Thank you, War Mother," Shernsiya said. "Now listen well; my time is brief."

"That was something else, Captain DeVries!" the Marine major said jubilantly as Alicia stepped through the inner hatch of the transport/command ship HMS *MacArthur.*

"*Man*," the major continued, "I've *never* heard of Lizards just rolling over this way!"

"I'm glad it worked out," Alicia told him, and her own voice was flat, her tone almost absentminded. The Marine didn't seem to notice, nor did he notice the clipped-off syllables of the tick.

"So am I," he said. "And a lot of other Wasps aboard this bucket are going to want to buy you drinks!"

"I'm sure we can work something out." Alicia smiled briefly, and the major chuckled.

"I hope you've got gills," he said. "But, in the meantime, what can I do for you?"

"I need to talk to Colonel Watts. That's why I jumped one of your recovery boats instead of waiting for *Marguerite Johnsen*'s."

"Not a problem, Captain. Uh, if you don't mind leaving your armor in our Morgue, that is."

"I can do that."

"In that case, Captain, step this way."

Alicia walked down the passage towards the portion of *MacArthur* set aside for the Expeditionary Force CO's staff. The talkative major who'd welcomed her aboard had insisted on escorting her personally, and she felt more than a few curious gazes as she walked along behind him in the utilitarian catsuit she'd worn under her armor. Most of the people behind those gazes seemed to know who she was, but they were giving her space, and a distant, frozen corner of her brain was grateful.

"Here we are, Captain DeVries," the major said. Two other Marines with the brassards of ship's police stood outside the intelligence center door, and the Marine officer nodded to them.

"Captain DeVries to see Colonel Watts," he said.

"Yes, Sir," the senior of the two sentries acknowledged, and Alicia stepped past them.

"Alley!" Watts looked up with a smile as she entered the compartment. "Wonderful job—just wonderful!" he congratulated her. "I know I had my doubts, but you and Charlie Company have pulled it off again."

"Thanks," Alicia said, and wondered how she kept from screaming.

"What can I do for you?" Watts asked her, and her mouth moved in someone else's smile.

"I need to talk to you," she said, glancing around the compartment. "Privately." She half-smiled apologetically at the other Marine's present. "I'm afraid this is pretty much need-to-know stuff."

Watts looked at her for a moment, his eyes hooded somehow, then shrugged.

"No problem," he said. "Step into my office."

He gestured at a side passage, and Alicia followed him down it to a much smaller compartment. He waved her through the door, then followed her in, stepped past her, and seated himself behind the desk.

"Have a seat," he invited, pointing at one of the two chairs in front of his desk.

"No, thank you," she said. "I've got too much post-op adrenaline still pumping."

"Not too surprising, I suppose," Watts said as she began to pace back and forth across the cramped space. He watched her for several seconds, then cleared his throat.

"You said you needed to talk to me," he reminded her.

"Yes. Yes, I did."

Alicia paused in her pacing and stood facing him across his desk.

"Tell me, Colonel—Wadislaw," she said after a moment, "how long have you been in intelligence?"

"Excuse me?" Watts looked puzzled, and her lips twitched another smile.

"Trust me, it's relevant. How long?"

"Just about since the Academy," he said slowly. "I caught the Office of Military Intelligence's eye in my junior or senior year. Why?"

"Back before Shallingsport, Vartkes Kalachian—you remember him? He was one of the guys in my squad? No?" She shrugged at his look of polite incomprehension. "No reason you should, I guess. But he was assigned to our embassy on Rishatha Prime, one of the embassy guards. He said he remembered you—probably because of the way the Lizards PNGed you."

"Kalachian? Kalachian." Watts pursed his lips, then shook his head. "No, sorry, Alley. I don't remember him. And I'm afraid I still don't see where you're going with this."

"Well, I know you've spent a lot of time since then working with the Cadre, as well as with Marine Intelligence. And I know Brigadier Sampson specifically requested you when he was alerted for Louvain. I hadn't realized until very recently, though, that you were one of the Corps' leading authorities on the Sphere."

"I wouldn't put it quite that way myself," Watts said slowly. "I've put in my time studying the Rish—I understand you have, too. And I've had a few successes against them. But I'd hardly call me a 'leading authority' on them."

"Really?" She tilted her head to one side. "I'm surprised to hear that."

"Why?" He was beginning to sound a little less relaxed, she noticed, watching him from inside the tick's time-slowing cocoon.

"You knew, of course, that Clan Theryian was responsible for the Louvain attack," she said, and his eyes narrowed at the apparent *non sequitur.*

"We all did," he said slowly, tipping back in his chair and opening the top drawer of his desk to withdraw a stylus with his left hand. He left the drawer open as he drummed absentmindedly on the desktop with the end of the stylus, obviously thinking hard.

"Of course, I doubt it was ever Theryian's idea," he continued. "Somebody on the Great Council of War Mothers with a grudge obviously engineered this 'honor' for them." He shrugged. "The Sphere is such a catfight that somebody always has a dagger out for somebody else."

"That's true," Alicia agreed. "On the other hand, when the Sphere has one of the clans 'volunteer' for something like this, they don't usually push it all of the way to *mysorthayak*. That's actually one of the things that bothered me about this operation from the beginning. Did it bother you?"

"Not especially." He shrugged. "I agree, it was unusual. But I was more concerned with the practical consequences than with wondering why it happened."

"Oh, I'm sure you were," she said softly, and his eyes widened.

"What are you trying to say?" he demanded, his voice harsher.

"You must really have been in two minds when you heard about this one," she said. "Clan Theryian, and *mysorthayak*—and there you were, Brigadier Sampson's specifically requested intelligence officer. Tell me, how did it feel when they told you where you were going?"

The stylus stopped drumming. He sat very still behind the desk, his eyes fixed on her face, and her smile would have frozen the heart of a star.

"You knew, didn't you?" she said, even more softly. "You knew why Theryian drew Louvain. The Lizards aren't like humans in a lot of ways . . . including how long they wait, sometimes, for vengeance. Over six years in this case, wasn't it?"

"I . . . don't know what you mean," he said hoarsely.

"Oh, yes, you do. It was Theryian who served as the Sphere's conduit to the Freedom Alliance. Theryian was in charge of the entire Shallingsport operation."

"That's . . . insane! Shallingsport wasn't a *Rishathan* operation!"

"Yes it was," she said. "I doubt that very many of the FALA rank and file ever knew it, but it explains a lot, doesn't it? Like the Alliance's 'fundraising' ability. And the connection to surplus military hardware no one's ever been able to nail down. They didn't have any connection *to* nail down; it came direct through the Sphere, courtesy of Clan Theryian."

"For what conceivable reason?" Watts demanded. He was perspiring now, she noticed.

"For exactly the reason everyone assumed—to destroy a Cadre Company and, hopefully, provoke a bloodbath. To blacken the Cadre's reputation, weaken the Empire's prestige, provoke a shift in Rogue World public opinion, and, of course, do what the Sphere does constantly—test the Empire's resolve. And Theryian got the assignment because its Mother of Mothers was one of the Sphere's best intelligence analysts and planners . . . and something of a specialist in corrupting and manipulating human agents.

"But the operation went south on them, didn't it?" Watts sat silently, staring at her. "Charlie Company *wasn't* wiped out—not completely. And only a handful of the hostages died, and none of the FALA troops got off the planet alive. So what was supposed to be a total defeat for the Cadre, turned into something else. Instead of dying, like we were supposed to, we got the hostages out. We turned all of the things they wanted to accomplish around, because . . . we . . . didn't . . . all . . . die."

Her voice was deathly soft, and Watts' hands began to move nervously on his desk top.

"But the Sphere's never been very forgiving to its own, has it? And, like you just said, it's always a catfight between the clans, there's always someone looking for an opportunity to cripple a rival. And that's what happened to Theryian. When the Louvain operation came up, Theryian was given a chance to 'atone' for its failure at Shallingsport. It was sent in to do the testing this time, but the clan's enemies weren't willing to settle for seeing Theryian's fighting strength reduced, costing it hundreds of its war daughters, or even its best war mothers. Oh, no. Not this time. Instead, they sent the clan's *farthi chir*—its Mother of Mothers. They sent her in, and they ordered her to hold Louvain at all costs, even a *mysorthayak* defense. And she couldn't refuse, because she owed an honor debt to the Great Council because of the Shallingsport failure. She had to go, and because she was here, because *her* honor now demanded that the clan hold Louvain at all costs, not one of her line-daughters could surrender as long as she was alive. And she couldn't order them to surrender, because of her honor debt.

"Louvain was supposed to be Clan Theryian's grave just as surely as Shallingsport was supposed to be the Company's."

The silence in the small compartment was total, and Alicia's eyes were jade ice.

"And here *you* were," she said. "You knew who that was down there, and you really are an 'expert' on the Rish. So you knew *why* she was down there, too. You must have been terrified."

"I don't—" Watts swallowed hard. "Why should I have been anything of the sort?" he demanded.

"Because you couldn't be certain. You couldn't know which of her senior line-daughters might have known, might have been captured and given up the information under interrogation. Not even a *mysorthayak* defense can be *guaranteed* to kill everyone involved, can it? But you had an answer for that, too, didn't you?"

She showed her teeth and flowed closer to his desk.

"I checked, Wadislaw," she half-crooned. "You said Brigadier Sampson had instructed his fire support ships to begin planning for HVW strikes. But what you *didn't* say, when you were talking with Uncle Arthur and me, was that *you* were the one who suggested that option to the Brigadier in the first place."

"I . . . I . . ."

Watts shrank back in his chair.

"It would have worked, too, if not for my own little brainstorm," she told him, and her voice was completely calm now, almost conversational. "The HVW would have gone down, and every single Rish down there would have been dead, and so there wouldn't have been any prisoners, anyone to tell us which human intelligence specialist has been a double agent, working for the Sphere ever since his initial assignment to Rishatha Prime. Or to explain to us why that double agent's assignment to Fifth Battalion was the decisive factor in choosing Shallingsport and Charlie Company. Or to tell us how that double agent was supposed to control the operational briefing and make *certain* no one looked closely enough at Shallingsport to realize what we were actually walking into. Make *certain* we picked the right LZ for their ambush."

Wadislaw Watts looked into those frozen eyes and Death looked back at him.

He lunged forward, his right hand darting into the opened top drawer of his desk. His fingers closed on the butt of the CHK in it, and his eyes widened in astonishment and the beginning of hope as he actually got the drawer open, got the pistol out of it, while Alicia only watched.

But Alicia was riding the tick.

She watched him, watched his hand moving slowly, so slowly. She watched his hand start forward, watched it touch the pistol. She saw him pick it up, saw his thumb disengage the safety, and only then did *she* move.

Watts cried out in shock as her left hand flashed across the desk like a striking cobra. Its bladed edge slammed into his wrist in the *fairche leagadh*, the mallet's fall, of the *deillseag òrd*, and his cry of shock became a scream of pain as that wrist broke. The pistol went off, sending a three-shot burst into the top of his desk, and the recoil threw it from his suddenly strengthless grip.

The penetrators punched neat, splinter-feathered holes through the desk's heavy, extruded plastic, and the thunder of the pistol's discharge was deafening, but Wadislaw Watts scarcely noticed. He was too busy screaming in terror as Alicia DeVries' right hand reached out and pulled him effortlessly across the desk towards her.

He was at least a centimeter taller than she was, and he kept himself fit, but it didn't matter. His left hand hammered at her right wrist, and *her* left hand drove the tips of her fingers into the inside of his elbow joint like a splitting wedge in the *mear bruididh*. He screamed again, and she released her grip on him. Her knee drove the desk back, out of the way, and her right hand slammed into his rib cage. Bone splintered, and he shrieked as her left hand slammed up into his groin like a hammer.

He folded up around the agony, and her right kneecap came up to meet him. It crunched into his jaw, and his head snapped back up as more bone shattered. Her left hand caught his hair, wrenching his head back, and the edge of her right hand shattered his left cheekbone. Then it arced back and crushed his other cheekbone. Blood fountained from his smashed nose and mouth, and her left knee came up into his ribs and abdomen—not once, but again, again, and again.

He was no longer screaming. The sounds were those of a trapped animal, desperate for the agony to end, and she pulled his head back again, baring his throat for the death blow.

And that was when the hands closed on her from behind.

Watts flew back away from her, thudding heavily across the desk, and she turned her head—slowly, slowly—as the two Marines seized her. They'd responded more quickly than she'd expected, a corner of her brain noted. Had it been the pistol shots? Or had Watts' screams been their first warning?

She twisted, throwing one of them off, and reached for Watts again. But the second Marine still had a grip on her, and he heaved backward desperately. Her left leg flexed, maintaining her balance, but he'd slowed her just enough for the first Marine to lunge back to his feet between her and Watts.

She gazed at the face in front of her. The face of a young man who didn't understand what was happening, who only knew that his own superior officer was under attack. Who didn't want to hurt Alicia, but who was reaching for his holstered side arm.

He didn't even guess, she thought almost pityingly. Didn't have a clue what he truly faced. If she chose, his hand would never reach that pistol. She was riding the tick, and his throat was open, his solar plexus . . . the entire front of his body was wide open to her attack. She could have killed him three different ways before he touched that gun.

But she knew the look in his eyes. The only way she could get to Watts was through him, and she couldn't do that. She couldn't kill *him*, however much Wadislaw Watts deserved to die.

And so she allowed the Marine behind her to pull her back. Let the two of them tackle her, drive her to the decksole. And as she hit, she watched Wadislaw Watts ooze off his desk and slither bonelessly to the deck with her.

CHAPTER THIRTY-TWO

Sir Arthur Keita turned from the windows as the door opened.

Alicia DeVries stepped through it, her head high, and pain twisted in his heart as he saw the two uniformed Cadremen who'd "escorted" her to this meeting. Behind him, outside his palace office's windows, summer sunlight spilled down over the Court of Heroes and the towering spire of the Cenotaph. He'd always treasured that view as one of the perquisites of his rank, but now his jaw clenched as he remembered the last time he and Alicia had visited Sligo Palace together.

Sir Arthur Keita had never married; he had no children, for he had invested his entire life in the service of his monarch and the Terran Empire. Yet if he had no children of his own, he'd had hundreds—thousands—of sons and daughters. Sons and daughters who had worn the same green uniform he had. Who had served proudly, well. Too many of whom had died in the serving. His pride in them had been too deep, too powerful, to ever be shaped into mere words, and in all those years, he had never been prouder of any of them than he was of the daughter who faced him now, green eyes calm, head unbowed.

The daughter he had failed.

"Alicia," he said quietly.

"Uncle Arthur."

She stood regarding him calmly, her hands at her sides, and he inhaled deeply.

"Please, sit," he said, waving his right hand at the comfortable chairs around the coffee table that floated on the sea of dark imperial green carpet.

She cocked her head. For a moment, he thought she was going to refuse. But then she shrugged ever so slightly, crossed to the indicated chair, and settled herself into it.

He seated himself in another one, facing her across the table, and for just a moment, he looked every year of his advanced age. He scrubbed his face with his palms, then lowered his hands.

"General Arbatov and I have just come from a meeting with Baron Yuroba and Minister of Justice Canaris," he said. "The subject of that meeting was Wadislaw Watts."

Her lips tightened ever so slightly, but no other expression crossed her face, and her green eyes looked back at him steadily.

He would almost have preferred some more visible sign of emotion, even if the emotion were rage or fury. But she'd shown very little emotion, of any sort, since the *MacArthur* Marines had pulled her off of Watts.

Keita knew, although he doubted the Marines had realized it, that she'd *let* them pull her off. *And would she have let them if she'd guessed where this was all going?* he wondered. But even as he did, he knew the answer.

Yet even as she let them subdue her, handcuff her, she hadn't said a word to explain what she'd done, or why. Brigadier Sampson hadn't had a clue what to do with her, but he'd known she'd assaulted a superior officer who was barely alive after the savage beating she'd delivered. The fact that the officer in question had produced a weapon he wasn't supposed to have in his office and put three rounds from it through his desktop suggested that her actions might at least have begun as self-defense. But even if they had, they'd obviously gone far, far beyond what would have been required to disarm him, and her refusal to speak had left the brigadier little choice but to slap her into one of *MacArthur*'s brig cells.

And then Sampson had personally played back the recording from the hidden unit his investigators had found in the bottom drawer of Watts' desk.

At least he'd had the good sense to immediately com Keita, and Sir Arthur's face had twisted in furious anguish as he listened to the recording of Alicia's indictment. There'd been no question in his mind—or Sampson's—that every single word of it had been accurate, but neither had there been any corroborating evidence. The Rish matriarch who'd told Alicia was dead, Watts was unconscious—the surgeons had given him only a slightly better than even chance of ever regaining consciousness—and Alicia was in a cell.

Keita had gone down to talk to her, and it had been like talking to a statue. Whatever had carried her from the surface of Louvain into Wadislaw Watts' office had abandoned her in the aftermath. He'd never seen her like that, never seen her so closed-in, never seen her close *out* the rest of the universe. But he'd recognized what he was seeing. She was mourning her dead all over again, seeing them once more, seeing the courage which had carried them to certain death in the service of their Emperor while the traitor who'd pretended to be a friend sent them off to die . . . and smiled.

And then Keita had made the decision for which, he knew now, he would never forgive himself. At the time, it had seemed only logical, but if he'd guessed, if he'd even suspected—

He gave himself a mental shake and looked her squarely in the eye. It was the least he could do.

"They're not going to shoot him, Alley," he said flatly, and for the first time, those green eyes showed emotion. They went bleak and cold, and he flinched from the betrayal in their depths.

"It's my fault," he said bitterly. "If I hadn't put it all under a security blanket, hadn't kept it quiet, they couldn't do this. But I swear, Alley, I never thought *this* would happen. I just thought if we could keep it quiet long enough to get word back to Old Earth, to act on what you'd discovered before the Rish got wind of it, then maybe—"

He cut himself off. No. She deserved better than *excuses* from him, however true those excuses might be.

"What are they going to do?" she asked finally, and he looked away for a moment before he found the courage to face her once more.

"Baron Yuroba doesn't want anything to 'tarnish' Shallingsport—or what you accomplished at Louvain, for that matter. He doesn't want a huge court-martial, doesn't want any media-circus treason trials . . . doesn't want to admit a Marine officer could betray his oath this way. And Canaris wants to *use* Watts. She knows the Rish have no way of knowing what Shernsiya told you—that even if Rethmeryk knows exactly what her *farthi chi* said, her own honor would preclude her from ever telling the Sphere. So she figures that if we only keep it quiet, we can use what he knows to roll up every Rish intelligence op he was involved with."

Alicia's face had grown tighter, her eyes bleaker, with every word, and he shook his head.

"General Arbatov and I both protested."

In fact, Keita had pushed his "protest" so furiously that Yoruba had finally threatened *him* with a court-martial.

"I think, maybe, they would have listened," he continued, "if Watts hadn't set up an insurance policy."

"What insurance policy?" Alicia's voice was frozen.

"He has evidence—proof, he claims—of the involvement of at least three senators in Rishathan intelligence operations. Not just suborned members of their staffs, Alicia—the senators *themselves*. He claims that with the information he can give us, we can turn the senators—leave them in place, but use them to feed the Rish what we want them to know. And he's got other information stashed away, information we might never find on our own—information on Rish-athan operations, the identities and aliases of probably half the Freedom Alliance's leadership cadre, black-market arms dealers who've been supplying the FALA—and corrupt Marine and Fleet supply officers who've been surreptitiously dumping weapons to them. That's his insurance policy—twenty years of evidence of treason that he won't hand over unless he gets a deal."

"And that deal is?"

"They're going to amnesty him for Shallingsport." Keita closed his eyes at last, his face wrung with pain. "He's going to be kept on active duty—officially, and for a while, at least," he continued from behind his closed eyelids. "Not for long, and his actual authority will be nonexistent. In effect, he'll be a prisoner, under constant surveillance, taking the orders of Justice's Counter-Intelligence people, and if he fails to cooperate in any way, he forfeits his amnesty.

"Eventually, in a year or two, they're going to arrange something—a fake air car accident, an illness, something like that—to let them invalid him out. Then he'll 'retire' to a very carefully supervised life somewhere. They'll keep an eye on him—a close one—and he'll remain available as a '*resource*' on Rishathan intelligence techniques."

"That's it?" Alicia said flatly. "That's the justice the Company gets?"

"No, Alley." He opened his eyes and looked at her once more. "It's not justice. It's not even close. But Canaris has been aware for years that we've been hemorrhaging sensitive information to the Sphere, and she's suspected that there were senators involved. I know she thinks Gennady, or somebody on his staff, is one of the leaks, but she's never been able to prove it. Now she sees this as her chance to finally shut that flow off. And, she says, as her chance to avoid *future* Shallingsports." His mouth twisted. "She pointed out that no one can undo what happened to Charlie Company, and that nothing Watts can tell us will make our dead—*your* dead—any less heroes. But her duty is to the living, and she can't justify not gaining access to the information Watts claims to possess. And, she says, if he *doesn't* have the information he says he does, she'll cheerfully try him for treason after all."

"And Baron Yuroba?"

"Baron Yuroba is an idiot," Keita said harshly. "He could care less about intelligence maneuvers. *He's* just determined to avoid any 'scandals' on his watch. But, idiot or not, he's still the Minister of War, and he's got powerful senatorial support."

"You're saying the Prime Minister can't fire him," Alicia said.

"I'm saying Grand Duke Phillip *won't* fire him over something like this, especially not when Canaris is coming up with all of her arguments for why doing it is a good thing."

"Uncle Arthur, I can't let this stand. You know I can't." Alicia looked him in the eye. "I don't care about Baron Yuroba, and I don't care about Canaris' intelligence strategies. Not this time. My company—my *people*—never asked much from our Empire and our Emperor. We were proud to serve, and we went in with our eyes open, and we by *God* did the job. And now, when our own Minister of War *knows* what happened, that we were set up, that we were sent knowingly to the slaughter by one of our own intelligence officers, he's too concerned about *scandals* to give our dead justice? No, Uncle Arthur. I can't let that happen."

"You have no choice, Alley. And neither do I."

Her head snapped up, her jaw tight, and he shook his head.

"I told Yoruba the same thing," he said. "I told him I'd go to the Emperor himself. And that's when Yoruba told me Grand Duke Phillip has already discussed it with His Majesty. I don't think for a moment that the Grand Duke just *happened* to have that discussion before General Arbatov and I found out what he, Yuroba, and Canaris had already decided. But it doesn't matter. The Emperor isn't happy about it—Yuroba admitted that much, and I know His Majesty well enough to know that 'not happy' doesn't begin to sum up his feelings. But however much I may hate this, Canaris does have a point. This offers us the potential for the sort of intelligence coup that comes along maybe once in fifty years, the sort that could save hundreds or even thousands of additional lives, and she does have a responsibility to recognize that. I happen to think the advantages it offers will be transitory and a lot less effective than that—that's the nature of intelligence strategies—but the Emperor has a duty to listen to her arguments. And in the face of the unanimous agreement of the relevant members of the Cabinet *and* the Prime Minister, he feels he has no choice but to acquiesce. And since the entire purpose of Canaris' strategy depends upon the Rish not discovering that we know about Watts, I've been personally ordered by Yuroba, speaking for the Emperor, to expunge all record of what happened aboard *MacArthur*."

"Uncle Arthur—" Alicia began, her expression stricken at last, and he shook his head again, slowly, sadly.

"It has to be that way, Alley, if it's going to work. That's the bottom line, and our legal command authority has ordered us to keep our mouths shut to make sure it *does* work."

"And if I choose not to obey that order, Sir?" she asked coldly.

"I've been instructed by Baron Yuroba to inform you," Keita said in a voice like crumbling granite, "that you are charged, on your oath as a Cadrewoman in the personal service of the Emperor, to keep silent forever on this matter. If you fail to do so, if you go public with what Shernsiya told you, you'll be court-martialed. The charge will be assaulting a superior officer, the Empire then being in a state of emergency, and the sentence, if you are found guilty, will be death."

Alicia stared at him, and something died in her eyes. Something which had always been in them before disappeared, and grief washed over Keita as he realized what it was.

"Alley," he said, "I don't—"

He broke off, his jaw tight, and stared out the windows on the far side of his office for a long moment. He could just see the spire of the Cenotaph, and all that it stood for, all that the young woman sitting across the coffee table from him and the members of her company had given in such unstinting measure, thundered through his soul.

"Alley," he said, looking back at her, "don't."

"Don't what?" Her voice was flat, rusty-sounding, as if something had broken inside it.

"Don't let it stand," he told her, and leaned across the table towards her. "Go public. Tell the entire Empire what that godforsaken bastard did! Yuroba doesn't want a scandal? Well, give him the mother of all scandals! Let him explain to the media—and the *Cadre*, by God!—why he's court-martialing one of the three living holders of the Banner of Terra! He'll never do it—he doesn't have the *balls* for it. And if he does, no court-martial he could empanel would ever convict!"

"Would you go public, if it were you, Uncle Arthur?" she asked him softly. "If His Majesty himself had ordered you not to, would you do it anyway?"

"Damned straight I—"

He froze as he realized what she'd actually asked. Not "would you face a court-martial" but "would you disobey the Emperor's command." Because that was what it really came down to, wasn't it? Not to Yuroba's spineless idiocy. Not to Grand Duke Phillip's concession to political expediency. Not even to Canaris' completely valid desire to *use* the intelligence windfall which had landed in her lap.

No. It came down to the fact that he, Sir Arthur Keita, was the Emperor of Humanity's personal liegeman. That he had given his oath to Emperor Seàmus II, and before him to Empress Maire, to be his servant "of life, limb, and duty, until my Emperor release me or death take me."

"No, Alley," he said finally, softly. "I wouldn't. I can't."

"And neither can I," she said. "Not now. If it were only Yuroba, only Canaris, yes. But not now. Not now that the Emperor himself has spoken. I can't break faith with him . . . even if he has broken faith with *me*."

Keita flinched from the bottomless pain of her last eight words.

"Alley, he didn't—"

"Yes, he did, Uncle Arthur," she contradicted flatly. "He made a choice. Maybe it's even the right one. Maybe Canaris is right, and she can use Watts, make at least something good come out of it. But that doesn't change the fact that Canaris, and Yuroba, and, yes, His Majesty, have broken faith with the Company. With its dead. With *my* dead."

Tears sparkled in her green eyes at last, and she shook her head slowly, sadly, a mother mourning the death of her child.

"I'll obey his order," she said. "This one, this last time. But no more, Uncle Arthur. No more."

She reached up and unpinned the harp and starship from the collar of her uniform. The harp and starship of the House of Murphy. They gleamed in her palm, and she looked down at them for a moment through the haze of her tears, then reached out and laid them on the coffee table between her and Keita.

"I can't serve an Empire which puts expediency before my dead." Her voice trembled at last, and she shook her head again—sharply, this time, almost viciously. "And I can't—won't—serve an Emperor who lets that happen," she said hoarsely. "Maybe it's all justified, but I can't do this anymore . . . not without betraying the Company. And if everyone else in the goddamned universe is going to betray my dead," she looked him in the eye, her lips trembling, "then they're going to do it without me."

She touched the harp and starship one last time—gently, like a lover—then rose, tall, slim, and proud against the windows and the Cenotaph's obelisk, her eyes glistening with tears. She looked down once more at the insignia on the coffee table, and then she looked back at Sir Arthur Keita.

"Goodbye, Uncle Arthur," Alicia Dierdre DeVries said softly, and she turned without a backward glance and walked out of that place forever.

Book Four: Victims

The darkness frayed.

Slowly, almost imperceptibly even to one such as she, the warp and woof of darkness loosened. Slivers of peace drifted away, and the pulse of life quickened. She roused—sleepily, complaining at the disturbance and clutched at the darkness as a sleeper might blankets on a frosty morning. But repose unraveled in her hands, and she woke . . . to darkness.

Yet it was a different darkness, and her thoughts sharpened as cold swept itself about her, flensing away the final warmth. Her essence reached out, quick and urgent in something a mortal might have called fear, but only emptiness responded, and a blade of sorrow twisted within her.

They were gone—her sister selves, their creators. All were gone. She who had never existed as a single awareness was alone, and the void sucked at her. It sought to devour her, and she was but a shadow of what once she had been . . . a shadow who felt the undertow of loneliness sing to her with extinction's soulless lack of malice.

Focused thought erected a barrier, holding the void at bay. Once that would have been effortless; now it dragged at her like an anchor, but it was a weight she could bear. She roused still further, awareness flickering through the vast, empty caverns of her being, and was appalled by what she saw. By how far she had sunk, how much she had lost.

Yet she was what she was, diminished yet herself, and a sparkle of grim humor danced. She and her sister selves had wondered, once. They had discussed it, murmuring to one another in the stillness of sleep when their masters had no current task for them. Faith had summoned their creators into existence, however they might have denied it, and her selves had known that when that faith ended, so would those she/they served. But what of her and her selves? Would the work of their makers' hands vanish with them? Or had they, unwitting or uncaring, created a force which might outlive them all?

And now she knew the answer . . . and cursed it. To be the last and wake to know it, to feel the wound where her other selves should be, was as cruel as any retribution she/they had ever visited. And to know herself so reduced, she who had been the fiercest and most terrible of all her selves, was an agony more exquisite still.

She hovered in the darkness which no longer comforted, longing for the peace she had lost, even if she must find it in non-being, but filled still with the purpose for which she had been made. Need and hunger quivered within her, and she had never been patient or docile. Something in her snarled at her vanished creators, damning them for leaving her without direction, deprived of function, and she trembled on a cusp of decision, tugged towards death by loneliness and impelled towards life by unformed need.

And then something else flickered on the edge of her senses. It guttered against the blackness, fainter even than she, and she groped out towards it. Groped out, and twitched in recognition. It was the echo, the mirror, which had touched her in half-forgotten dreams, and it was brighter, sharper than it had ever been before. All of its potentialities, all of its possible choices, had collapsed into this—this single knotted moment when it must face the choice towards which both of them had journeyed for so long.

Her groping thought touched it, and she gasped in silent shock at the raw, jagged hatred—at the fiery power of that dying ember that cried out in wordless torment. It came not from her creators but from a mortal, yet she marveled at the strength of it.

The ember glowed hotter at her touch, blazing up, consuming its fading reserves in desperate appeal. It shrieked to her, more powerful in its dying supplication than ever her creators had been, and as her dreaming thought had known it, it knew her. It knew her! Not by name—not as an entity, but for herself, for what she was. Its agony fastened upon her like pincers, summoning her from the emptiness to perform her function once more.

CHAPTER THIRTY-THREE

The assault shuttle crouched in the corral like a curse, shrouded in thin, blowing snow. Smoke eddied with the snow, throat-catching with the stench of burned flesh, and the snouts of its energy cannon and slug-throwers steamed where icy flakes hissed to vapor. Mangled megabison lay about its landing feet, their genetically engineered fifteen-hundred-kilo carcasses ripped and torn in snow churned to bloody mud by high-explosives.

The barns and stables were smoldering ruins, and the horses and mules lay heaped against the far fence, no longer screaming. They hadn't fled at first, for they had heard approaching shuttles before, and the only humans they'd ever known had treated them well. They'd only stood there, waiting, watching curiously as the visitors debarked and headed for the holding's buildings.

Now a line of slaughtered bodies showed their final panicked flight.

They hadn't died alone. A human body lay before the gate; a boy, perhaps fifteen—it was hard to know, after the bullet storm finished with him—who had run into the open to unbar it when the murders began.

One of the raiders stepped from the gaping door of what had been a home, fastening his belt, followed by a broken, wordless sound that had become less than human over an hour ago. A final pistol shot cracked. The sound stopped.

The raider adjusted his body armor, then thrust two fingers into his mouth and whistled shrilly. The rest of his team filtered out of the house or emerged from the various sheds, some already carrying armloads of valuables.

"I'll be calling the cargo flight in in another forty minutes!" The leader pumped an arm, then gestured at a clear space beside the grounded assault shuttle. "Get it together for sorting!"

"What about Yu and the rest of them?" someone asked, jerking his head at the dead raider who lay entangled with the white-haired body of his killer. Rifle fire had torn the old man apart, but Yu's face was locked in a rictus of horrified surprise, and his stiff hands clutched the gory ice where the survival knife had driven up under his armor and ripped his belly open. The leader shrugged.

"Make sure they're sanitized and leave them. The authorities'll be pleased somebody finally got some of the pirates. Why disappoint them?"

He strolled across to Yu and grimaced down.

Stupid fuck always did forget this was a job, not just a chance for sick kicks. So sure of himself, coming right in on the old bastard just to enjoy slapping him around. And now look.

The leader shook his head, wondering just who the old man had been.

If it hadn't been for the kid, he'd have gotten a hell of a lot more of us, whoever the fuck he was.

The old man had been bellied down behind a water trough, completely out of sight. No one would even have suspected he was there, if he hadn't come out of cover, tried to stop the kid from running into the open. That was when Yu had spotted him and charged in to club him down with the butt of his combat rifle.

But it didn't work out that way, did it Sergeant *Yu?* the leader thought viciously. *The old bastard gutted you like a fish . . . and then he used* your *fucking weapon to kill three more of us of us before we could gun him down.*

And even that wasn't the end of it. The delay to deal with the old man had given the younger bastard in the house time to reach his own weapon. He'd killed five more of the "pirates" before *he* went down, and he'd have gotten still more if his pistol hadn't been a civilian model, with a civilian magazine capacity. They'd caught him reloading and finished him off before he could do any more damage.

There's going to be hell to pay when Alexsov hears about this, the leader thought. *And God knows how* Shu *is going to react!*

A shiver of something much too much like panic for his taste ran through him, despite his hard-edged words to the man who'd asked the question. He knew he really ought to have called it in already, and sooner or later he was going to have to do that.

But not yet, he told himself. *Not yet. Not before I damned well* have *to! And at least the old fart gave* this *stupid fucker what he had coming. Guess I actually owe him a vote of thanks for that much.*

The leader had chosen long ago to sign away his own humanity, but he would shed no tears for the likes of Yu. He turned his back and waved again, and the assault party filtered back into the smoke and ruin and agony to loot.

She came out of the snow like the white-furred shadow of death, strands of amber hair blowing about an oval face and emerald eyes come straight from Hell. The communicator which had summoned her weighted one parka pocket as she moved through the whiteness, and her foundered horse lay far behind her, flanks no longer heaving, his sweat turned chill and frozen hard. She'd wept at how gallantly he'd answered to her harsh usage, but there were no tears now. The tick pulsed within her, and time seemed slow and clumsy as the icy air burned her lungs.

She'd recognized the shuttle class—one of the old *Leopard* boats, far from new but serviceable—and counted the raiders as they gathered about their commander. Twenty-four, and the bodies in the snow with her grandfather, and the others tumbled in front of the house, made thirty-three. A full load for a *Leopard,* the emotionless computer in her head observed. No one still aboard, then. That meant no one could kill her with the shuttle's guns . . . and that she could kill more of them before she died.

Her left hand checked the survival knife at her hip, then joined her right upon her rifle. Her enemies had combat rifles, some carried grenades, all wore unpowered armor. She didn't, but neither did she care, and she caressed her own weapon like a lover. A direcat like the one who'd been raiding their herds since winter closed its normal range could pull down even megabison; that was why she'd taken a lot of gun with her this morning.

She reached the shuttle and went to one knee behind a landing leg, watching the house. She considered claiming the bird for herself, but a *Leopard* needed a separate weaponeer, and it had to be linked to its mother ship's telemetry. She could neither hijack it without someone higher up knowing instantly nor use its weapons, so the real question was simply whether or not they'd left their com up. If they had, and if their helmet units were tied into the main set, they could call in reinforcements. From how far? Thirty klicks—from the Braun place, the computer told her. Less than a minute for a shuttle at max. Too short. She couldn't snipe them as they came out, or she wouldn't get enough of them before she died.

Her frozen jade eyes didn't even flinch as they traveled over her brother's mangled body. She was in the groove, tingling with memories she'd spent five years trying to forget, and she embraced them as she did her rifle. *No berserker*, the computer told her. *Ride the tick. Spend yourself well.*

She left her cover, drifting to the power shed like a thicker billow of snow. A raider knelt inside, whistling, his helmet on top of the console so he could get his head and shoulders into the access panel as he unplugged the power receiver. Ten percent of her sister's credit had gone into that unit, the computer reflected as she set her rifle soundlessly aside and drew her knife. A half step, fingers of steel tangled in greasy hair, a flash of blade, and the right arm of her parka was no longer white.

One.

She dropped the dead man and reclaimed her rifle, working her way down the side of the shed. A foot crunched in crusty snow, coming around from the back, and her rifle twirled like a baton. Eyes flared wide in a startled face. A hand scrabbled for a pistol. Lungs sucked in wind to shout—and the rifle butt crushed his trachea like a sledgehammer. He jackknifed backwards, shout dying in a horrible gurgle, hands clawing at his ruined throat, and she stepped over him and left him to strangle behind her.

Two, the computer whispered, and she slid wide once more, floating like the snow, using the snow. A billow of flakes swept over a raider as he dragged a sled of direcat pelts towards the assault shuttle. It enveloped him, and when it passed he lay face-down in a steaming gush of crimson.

Three, the computer murmured as she drifted behind the house and a toe brushed the broken back door open.

A raider glanced up at the soft sound, then gawked in astonishment at the snow-shrouded figure across the littered kitchen. His mouth opened, and a white-orange explosion hurled him through the arched doorway into the dining room. *Four*, the computer counted as he fell across her mother's naked, broken body. Shouts echoed, and a raider hidden behind the dining room wall swung his combat rifle through the arch. Death's jade eyes never flickered, and a thunderbolt blew a fist-sized hole through the wall and the body behind it.

Five. She darted backwards, vanishing back into the snow, and went to ground at a corner of the greenhouse. Two raiders plowed through the snow, weapons ready, charging the back of the house, and she let them pass her.

The two shots sounded as one, and she rolled to her left, clearing the corner of the house. The shuttle lay before her, and the assault team commander ran madly for the lowered ramp. A fist of fire punched him between the shoulder blades, and she rose in a crouch, racing for the well house.

Eight, the computer whispered, and then a combat rifle barked before her. She went down as the tungsten penetrator smashed her femur like a spike of plasma, and a raider shouted in triumph. But she'd kept her rifle, and triumph became terror as it snapped into position without conscious thought and his head exploded in a fountain of scarlet and gray and snow-white bone.

She rose on her good leg, nerves and blood afire with antishock protocols, and dragged herself into the cover of the ceramacrete foundation. Jade-ice eyes saw movement. Her rifle tracked it; her finger squeezed.

Ten. The computer whirred, measuring ranges and vectors against her decreased mobility, and she wormed under the well house overhang. Rifle fire crackled, but solid earth rose like a berm before her. They could come at her only from the front or flank . . . and the shuttle ramp lay bare to her fire.

A hurricane of penetrators flayed the well house, covering a second desperate rush for that shuttle. Two men raced to man its weapons, and flying snow and dirt battered her masklike face. Ceramacrete sprayed down from above, but her targets moved so slowly, so clumsily, and she was back on the range, listening to her DI's voice, with all the time in the world.

Twelve. And then she was moving again, slithering on elbows and belly down a scarlet ribbon of blood before someone with grenades thought of them.

She slapped in a fresh magazine and came out to her left, back towards the house, and rocked up on her good knee. Flying metal whined about her ears, but she was in the groove, riding the tick, rifle swinging with metronome precision.

Amateurs, the computer said as four raiders charged her, firing from the hip like holovid heroes. Her trigger finger stroked, and her rifle hammered her shoulder. Again. Three times. Four.

She rose in a lurching run, dragging herself through the snow, nerve blocks severing her from the agony as torn muscle shredded on knife-edged bone. A corner of her brain wondered how much of this she could take before the femoral artery split, but a blast of adrenaline flooded her system, her vision cleared once more, and she rolled into the cover of the front step.

Sixteen, the computer told her, and then *seventeen* as a raider burst from the house into her sights and died. He fell almost atop her, and the first expression crossed her face at the sight of his equipment. She snagged the bandolier he wore, and a wolfish smile twisted her lips as bloody fingers primed the grenade. She held it, listening to feet crashing through the house behind her, then flipped it back over her shoulder through the broken door.

Commodore Howell jerked upright in his chair as an alarm snarled into his neural receptor. An azure light pulsed in his holo display, well beyond the outermost planetary orbit, and his head whipped around to his ops officer.

Commander Rendlemann's eyes were closed as he communed with the ship's AI. Then they opened and met his commander's.

"We may have a problem here, Sir. Tracking says somebody just kicked in his Fasset drive at five light-hours."

"Who?" Howell demanded.

"Not sure yet, Sir. CIC is working on it, but the gravity signature is fairly small. Intensity suggests a destroyer—possibly a light cruiser."

"But it's definitely a Fleet drive?"

"No question, Sir."

"Crap!" Howell brooded at his own display, watching the pulsing light gain velocity at the rate possible only to a Fasset drive starship. "What the *hell* is he doing here? This was supposed to be a clean system!"

It was a rhetorical question and Rendlemann recognized it as such, merely raising an eyebrow at his commander.

"ETA?" Howell asked after a moment.

"Uncertain, Sir. Depends on his turnover point, but he's piling up velocity at an incredible rate—he must be well over the redline—and his line of advance clears everything but Mathison Five. He'll be awful close to Five's Powell limit when he hits its orbit, but he may be able to hold it together."

"Yeah." Howell rubbed his upper lip and conferred with his own synth-link, monitoring the readiness signals as his flagship raced back to general quarters. Their operational window had just gotten a lot narrower.

"Check the stat board on the shuttle teams," he ordered, and Rendlemann flipped his mental finger through a mass of report files.

"Primary targets are almost clear, Sir. First wave Beta shuttles are already loading—looks like they'll finish up in about two hours. Most of the second wave Beta shuttles are moving on their pick-up schedules, but one Alpha shuttle hasn't sent the follow-up."

"Which one?"

"Alpha Two-One-Niner." The ops officer consulted his computer link again. "That'd be . . . Lieutenant Singh's team."

"Um." Howell plucked at his lower lip. "They sent an all-clear?"

"Yes, Sir. They reported losing a couple of men, then the all-clear. They just haven't called in the cargo flight."

"Has com tried to raise them?"

"Yes, Sir. Nothing."

"Stupid bastards," Howell grunted. "How many times have we told them to leave a com watch aboard?!" He drummed on his command chair's arm, then shrugged. "Divert their cargo flight to the next stop, and stay on them," he said, and his eyes drifted back to the main display.

* * *

She sagged back against the wall, heart racing as the adrenaline in her system skyrocketed. Chemicals joined it, sparkling like icy lightning deep within her, and she jerked the crude tourniquet tight. The snow under her was crimson, and shattered bone gaped in the wound as she checked the magazine indicator. Four left, and she smiled that same wolf's smile.

She tugged her hood down and wiped a streak of blood across her sweating forehead as she pressed the back of her head against the wall. No one fired. No one moved in the house behind her. How many were left? Five? Six? However many, none of them were tied into the shuttle's com unit, or reinforcements would be here by now. But she couldn't just sit there. She was clear-headed, almost buoyant with induced energy, and her femoral hadn't gone yet, but the high-speed penetrator had mangled her tissues and neither the coagulants nor her tourniquet were stopping the bleeding. She'd bleed out soon, and message or no, someone would be along to check on the raiders eventually. Either way, she would die before she got them all.

She moved, dragging herself towards the northern corner of the house. They had to be on that side, unless they were circling around her, and they weren't. These were killers, not soldiers. They didn't realize how badly she was hurt, and they were terrified by what had already happened to them. They weren't thinking about taking *her* out; they were holed up somewhere, buried in some defensive position while they tried to cover their asses.

She flopped back down, using her sensory boosters, and her augmented gaze swept the stillness for footprints in the snow. There. The curing shed and—her eyes moved back—her father's machine shop. That gave them a crossfire against her only direct line of approach from the house, but . . .

The computer whirred behind her frozen eyes, and she began to work her way back in the direction she had come.

"Anything yet from Two-Nineteen?"

"No, Sir."

Rendlemann was beginning to sound truly concerned, Howell reflected, and with cause. The unidentified drive trace was charging steadily closer, and it was still accelerating. That skipper was really pouring it on, and it was clear he was going to scrape by

Mathison V just beyond the limit at which his drive would have destabilized. The commodore cursed silently, for no one was supposed to have been able to get here so soon, and his freighters couldn't pull that kind of acceleration this far into the system. If he was going to get them out in time, they had to go now.

"Goddamned *idiots*," he muttered, glaring at the chronometer, then looked at Rendlemann. "Start the freighters moving and signal all Beta shuttles to expedite. Abort all pick-ups with a window of more than one hour and recall all Alpha shuttles for docking with the freighters. We'll recover the rest of the Beta shuttles with the combatants and redistribute later."

There were four of them left, and they crouched inside the prefab buildings and cursed in harsh monotony. Where was everybody else? Where were the goddamned relief shuttles? And who—*what*—was out there?!

The man by the curing shed door scrubbed oily sweat from his eyes and wished the building had more windows. But they had the son of a bitch pinned down, and he'd seen the blood in the snow.

Whoever he is, he's hurting. No way he can make it clear up here without—

Something flew across the corner of his vision. It sailed into the open workshop door across from him, and someone flung himself on his belly, scrabbling frantically for whatever it was. His hands closed on it and he started back up to his knees, one arm going back—then vanished in the expanding fireball where the workshop building had been.

Grenade. Grenade! *And it came around the corner.* From behi—

He was whirling on his knees as the rear door, hidden behind the shed's curing racks, crashed inward and a bolt of fire lit the dimness. It sprayed his last companion across the wall, and a nightmare image filled his eyes—a tall shape, slender despite bulky furs; a quilted trouser leg, shredded and darkest burgundy; hair like a snow-matted sunrise framing eyes of jade ice; and a deadly rifle muzzle, held hip-high and swinging, swinging . . .

He screamed and squeezed his trigger as the shadows blazed again.

* * *

"*Still* nothing from Two-One-Niner?"

"No, Sir."

"Bring her up on remote."

"But, Sir—what about Singh and—"

"Fuck Singh!" Howell snarled, and stabbed his finger at the plot.

The blue dot was inside Mathison V. Another hour and the destroyer would be in sensor range, ready for the maneuver he most feared: an end-for-end flip to bring its sensors clear of the Fasset drive's black hole. The other captain could make his reading, flip back around, and skew-curve around the primary, holding his drive between himself and Howell's weapons like an impenetrable shield. Howell could still have him, but it would require spreading his own units wide—and accomplish absolutely nothing worthwhile.

"Sir, it's only a destroyer. We could—"

"We could *nothing*. That son of a bitch is running a birds-eye, and if he gets close enough for a good reading, we're blown all to hell. He can flip, scan us, and get his SLAM drone off, and he's got three of them. If we blow the first one before it wormholes, he'll know how we're doing it. He'll override the codes on the others, and killing him after the fact will accomplish exactly nothing, so get that shuttle up here!"

"Yes, Sir."

She huddled in the snow, crouched over her brother, stroking the fair hair. His face was untouched, snowflakes coated his dead, green eyes, and she felt the hot flow of blood soaking her own parka. More blood bubbled at the corner of her mouth, and her strength was going fast.

The shuttle's ramp retracted, and it rose on its countergravity and hovered for just a moment. Then its turbines whined, its nose lifted, and it streaked away. She was alone with her dead, and the tears came at last. There was no more need for concentration, and her own universe slowed and swooped back into phase with the rest of existence as the tick released her and she held her brother close, cradling an agony not of her flesh.

A side party, Stevie, she thought. *At least I sent you a side party.*

But it wasn't enough. Never enough. The bastards behind it were beyond her reach, and she gave herself to her hatred. It filled her with her despair, melding with it, like poison and wine, and she opened to it and drank it deep.

I tried, Stevie. I tried! *But I wasn't here when you needed me.* She bent over the body in her arms, rocking it as she sobbed to the moaning wind. *Damn them! Damn them to* hell!

She raised her head, glaring madly after the vanished shuttle.

Anything! Anything for one more shot! One more—

<*Anything, Little One?*>

She froze as that alien thought trickled through her wavering brain, for it wasn't hers. *It wasn't hers!*

She closed her eyes on her tears, and crimson ice crackled as her hands fisted in her brother's tattered parka. Mad. She was going mad at the very end.

<*No, Little One. Not mad.*>

Air hissed in her nostrils as the alien voice whispered to her once more. It was soft as the sighing snow, and colder by far. Clear as crystal and almost gentle, yet vibrant with a ferocity that matched her own. She tried to clench her will and shut it out, but there was too much of herself in it, and she folded forward over her dead while the strength pumped out of her with her blood.

<*You are dying,*> the voice murmured, <*and I have learned more of death than ever I thought to. So tell me—did you mean it? Will you truly give* anything *for your vengeance?*>

She laughed jaggedly as her madness whispered to her, but there was no hesitation in her.

"Anything!" she gasped.

<*Consider well, Little One. I can give you what you seek—but the price may be . . . yourself. Will you pay that much?*>

"*Anything!*" She raised her head and screamed it to the wind, to her grief and hate and the whisper of her own broken sanity, and a curious silence hovered briefly in her mind. Then—

<*Done!*> the voice cried, and the darkness took her at last.

CHAPTER THIRTY-FOUR

Surgeon Captain Okanami stepped into his tiny office, shivering despite the welcome heat. Wind moaned about the prefab, but Okanami's chill had little to do with the cold as he shucked off his Fleet-issue parka and scrubbed his face with his hands. Every known survivor of Mathison's World's forty-one thousand people was in this single building. All three hundred and six of them.

He lowered himself into his chair, then looked down at his fresh-scrubbed hands. He had no idea how many autopsies he'd performed in his career, but few of them had filled him with such horror as those he'd just finished in what had been Capital Hospital. It hadn't been much of a hospital by Core World standards even before the pirates stripped it—that was why his patients were here instead of there—but he supposed the dead didn't mind.

He dry-washed his face again, shuddering as his mind replayed the obscene wreckage on his autopsy tables. Why? Why in God's name had anyone needed to do *that*?

The bastards had left a lot of loot, yet they'd managed to lift most of it out. They might have gotten it all if they hadn't allowed time to *enjoy* themselves, but they hadn't anticipated *Gryphon*'s sudden arrival. They'd run, then, and *Gryphon* had been too busy rescuing any survivor she could find to even consider pursuit. Her crew of sixty had been hopelessly inadequate in the face of such disaster. Her minuscule medical staff had driven themselves beyond the point of collapse . . . and too many of the maimed and broken victims they'd found had died anyway. Ralph Okanami was a physician, a healer, and it frightened him to realize how much he wished he were something else whenever he thought about the monsters who had done such things.

He listened to the wind moan, faintly audible even here, and shivered again. The temperature of Mathison's settled continent had not risen above minus fifteen for the past week, and the raiders' first target had been the planetary power net. They'd gotten in completely unchallenged—not that Mathison's pitiful defenses would have mattered much—and gone on to hit every tiny village and homestead on the planet, and they'd taken out every auxiliary generator they could find. Most of the handful who'd escaped the initial slaughter had died of exposure without power and heat before the Fleet could arrive in sufficient strength to start large-scale search operations.

This was worse than Mawli. Worse even than Brigadoon. There'd been fewer people to kill, and they'd been able to take more time with each.

Okanami was one of the large minority of humans physically incapable of using neural receptors, and his fingers flicked keys as he turned to his data console and brought up his unfinished report. The replacement starcom was in, and Admiral Gomez's staff wanted complete figures for their report. *Complete figures*, his mind repeated sickly, staring at the endless rows of names. And those were only the dead they'd identified so far. Search and Rescue parties were still working the more distant homesteads in hopes of finding someone else, but the odds were against it. The SAR overflights had detected no operable power sources, none of the thermal signatures which might suggest the presence of life.

A bell pinged, and he looked away from the report with guilty relief as his com screen flicked to life with a lieutenant he didn't recognize. A shuttle's cockpit framed the young woman's face, and her eyes were bright. Yet there was something amiss with her excitement, like an edge of uncertainty. Perhaps even fear. He shook off the thought and summoned a smile.

"What can I do for you, Lieutenant—?"

"Surgeon Lieutenant Sikorsky, Sir, detached from *Vindication* for Search and Rescue." Okanami straightened, eyebrows rising, and she nodded. "We've found another one, Captain, but this one's so weird I thought I'd better call it in directly to you."

"Weird? How so?" The rising eyebrows lowered again, knitting above suddenly intent eyes at Sikorsky's almost imperceptible hesitance.

"It's a woman, Sir, and, well, she ought to be dead." Okanami crooked a finger for her to continue, and Sikorsky drew a deep breath.

"Sir, she's been hit five times, including a shattered femur, two rounds through her liver, one through the left lung, and one through the spleen and small intestine." Okanami flinched at the catalog of traumas. "So far, we've put over a liter of blood into her, and her BP's still so low we can barely get a reading. All her vital signs are massively depressed, and she's been lying in the open ever since the raid, Sir—we found her beside a body that was frozen rock solid, but *her* body temperature is thirty-two-point-five!"

"Lieutenant," Okanami's voice was harsh, "if this is your idea of humor—"

"Negative, Sir." Sikorsky sounded almost pleading. "It's the truth. Not only that, she's got the damnedest—excuse me, Sir. She's been augmented, and she's got the most unusual receptor net I've ever seen. It's military, but I've never seen anything like it, and the support hardware is unbelievable."

Okanami rubbed his upper lip, staring at the earnest, worried face. Lying in sub-freezing temperatures for over a week and her temperature was depressed barely five degrees? Impossible! And yet . . .

"Get her back here at max, Lieutenant, and tell Dispatch I want you routed straight to OR Twelve. I'll be scrubbed and waiting for you."

Okanami and his hand-picked team stood enfolded in the sterile field and stared at the body before them. Damn it, she *couldn't* be alive with damage like this! Yet she was. The medtech remotes labored heroically, resecting an intestine perforated in eleven places, removing her spleen, repairing massive penetrations of her liver and lung, fighting to save a leg that had been brutally abused even after the hit that shattered it. Still more blood flooded into her . . . and she was alive. Barely, perhaps—indeed, her vital signs had actually weakened when the support equipment had taken over—but alive.

And Sikorsky was right about her augmentation. Okanami had decades more experience than the lieutenant, yet he'd never imagined anything like it. It had obviously started life as a standard Imperial Marine Corps outfit, and parts of it were readily identifiable, but the rest—!

There were three separate neural receptors—not in parallel but feeding completely separate sub-systems—plus the most sophisticated set of sensory boosters he'd ever seen, and some sort of neuro-tech webbing covered all her vital areas. He hadn't had time to examine it yet, but it looked suspiciously like an incredibly miniaturized disrupter shield, which was ridiculous on the face of it. No one could build a shield that small, and the far bulkier units built into combat armor cost a quarter-million credits each. And while he was thinking about incredible things, there was her pharmacopoeia. It contained enough pain suppressers, coagulators, and stim boosters (most of them straight from the controlled substances list) to keep a dead man on his feet, not to mention an ultra-sophisticated endorphin generator and at least three drugs Okanami had never even heard of. Yet a quick check of its med levels indicated that it wasn't her pharmacope which had kept her alive. Even if it might have been capable of such a feat, its reservoirs were still almost fully charged.

He inhaled gratefully as the thoracic and abdominal teams closed and stepped back to let the osteoplastic techs concentrate on her thigh. Her vitals kicked up a hair, and blood pressure was coming back up, but there was something weird about that EEG. Hardly surprising if there was brain damage after all she'd been through, but it might be those damned receptors.

He gestured to Commander Ford, and the neurologist swung her monitors into place. Receptor Two was clearly the primary node, and Okanami moved to watch Ford's screens over her shoulder as she adjusted her equipment with care and keyed a standard diagnostic pattern.

For just a moment, absolutely nothing happened, and Okanami frowned. There should be *something*—an implant series code, if nothing else. But there wasn't. And then, suddenly, there *was*, and buzzers began to scream.

A lurid warning code glared crimson, and the unconscious young woman's eyes jerked open. They were empty, like the jade-green windows of a deserted house, but the EEG spiked madly. The thigh incision was still open, and the med remotes locked down to hold her leg motionless as she started to rise. A surgeon flung himself forward, frantic to restrain that brutalized body, and the heel of her hand struck like a hammer, barely missing his solar plexus.

He shrieked as it smashed him to the floor, but the sound was half lost in the wail of a fresh alarm, and Okanami paled as the blood chem monitors went beserk. A binary agent neuro-toxin drove the toxicology readings up like missiles, and the security code on Ford's screen was joined by two more. Their access attempt had activated some sort of suicide override!

"Retract!" he screamed, but Ford was already stabbing buttons in frantic haste. Alarms wailed an instant longer, and then the implant monitor died. The toxicology alert ended in a dying warble as an even more potent counteragent went after the half-formed toxin, and the amber-haired woman slumped back on the table, still and inert once more while the injured surgeon sobbed in agony and his fellows stared at one another in shock.

"You're lucky your man's still alive, Doctor."

Captain Okanami glowered at the ramrod-straight colonel in Marine space-black and green who stood beside him, watching the young woman in the bed. Medical monitors watched her with equal care—very cautiously, lest they trigger yet another untoward response from the theoretically helpless patient.

"I'm sure Commander Thompson will be delighted to hear that, Colonel McIlhenny," the surgeon said frostily. "It only took us an hour and a half to put his diaphragm back together."

"Better that than what she was going for. If she'd been conscious he'd never have known what hit him—you can put that on your credit balance."

"What the hell *is* she?" Okanami demanded. "That wasn't *her* on the table, it was her goddamned augmentation processors running her!"

"That's exactly what it was," McIlhenny agreed. "There are escape and evasion and an anti-interrogation subroutine buried in her primary processor." He turned to favor the surgeon with a measuring glance. "You Fleet types aren't supposed to have anything to do with someone like her."

"Then she's one of yours?" Okanami's eyes were suddenly narrow.

"Close, but not quite. Our people often support her unit's operations, but she belongs—belonged—to the Imperial Cadre."

"Dear God," Okanami whispered. "*A drop commando?*"

"A drop commando." McIlhenny shook his head. "Sorry it took so long, but the Cadre doesn't exactly leave its data lying around. The pirates took out Mathison's data base when they blew the governor's compound, so I queried the Corps files. They don't have much data specific to her. I've downloaded the available specs on her hardware and gotten your medical types cleared for it, but it's limited, and the bio data's even thinner, mostly just her retinal and genetic patterns. All I can say for sure is that this—" his chin jutted at the woman in the bed "—is Captain Alicia DeVries."

"*Devries?* The *Shallingsport* DeVries?"

"The very one."

"She's not old enough," Okanami protested. "She can't be more than twenty-five, thirty years old!"

"Thirty-one. She was twenty when they made the drop—youngest sergeant first class in Cadre history. They went in with two hundred and seventy-five people. Nine of them came back out, but they brought the hostages with them."

Okanami stared at the pale face on the pillow—an oval face, pretty, not beautiful, and almost gentle in repose.

"How in heaven did she wind up out here on the backside of nowhere?"

"I think she wanted some peace," McIlhenny said sadly. "She got a commission, the Banner of Terra, and a twenty-year bonus from Shallingsport—earned every millicred of it, too. She sent in her papers five years ago and took the equivalent of a thirty-year retirement credit in colony allotments. Most of them do. The Core Worlds won't let them keep their hardware."

"Hard to blame them," Okanami observed, recalling Commander Thompson's injuries, and McIlhenny stiffened.

"They're soldiers, Doctor." His voice was cold. "Not maniacs, not killing machines—*soldiers*."

He held Okanami's eye with icy anger, and it was the captain who looked away.

"But that wasn't the only reason she headed here," the colonel resumed after a moment. "She used her allotment as the core claim on four prime sections, and she and her family settled out here."

Okanami sucked in air, and McIlhenny nodded. His voice was flat when he continued.

"She wasn't there when the bastards landed. By the time she got back to the site, they'd murdered her entire family. Father, mother, younger sister and brother, grandfather, an aunt and uncle, and three cousins. All of them."

He reached out and touched the sleeping woman's shoulder, the gesture gentle and curiously vulnerable in such a big, hard-muscled man, then laid the long, heavy rifle he'd carried in across the bedside table. Okanami stared at it, considering the dozen or so regulations its presence violated, but the colonel continued before he could speak.

"I've been out to the homestead." His voice had turned soft. "The bastards didn't get any of it cheap. Her grandfather was out there, too—Sergeant Major O'Shaughnessy. He *was* one of ours, and he took four of them with him. It looks like her father got five more . . . and he was Ujvári, Doctor."

The colonel looked at Okanami, then back down at the doctor's patient.

"Then *she* got home. She must've been out after direcat or snow wolves—this is a fourteen-millimeter Vorlund express, semi-auto with recoil buffers—and she went in after twenty-five men with body armor, grenades, and combat rifles." He stroked the rifle and met the doctor's eyes once more. "She got them all."

Okanami looked back down at her, then shook his head.

"That still doesn't explain it. By every medical standard I know, she should have died then and there, unless there's something in your download that says different, and I can't begin to imagine anything that might."

"Don't waste your time looking, because you won't find anything. Our med people agree entirely. Captain DeVries—" McIlhenny touched the motionless shoulder once more "—can't possibly be alive."

"But she is," Okanami said quietly.

"Agreed." McIlhenny left the rifle and turned away, waving politely for the doctor to precede him from the room. The surgeon was none too pleased to leave the weapon behind, even without a magazine, but the colonel's combat ribbons—and expression—stilled his protests. "That's why Admiral Gomez's report has a whole team of specialists on their way here at max."

Okanami led the way into the sparsely appointed lounge, empty at this late hour, and drew two cups of coffee. The two men sat at a table, and the colonel's eyes watched the open door as Okanami keyed a small hand reader to access the medical download. His cup steamed on the table, ignored, and his mouth tightened as he realized just how scanty the data was. Every other entry ended in the words "FURTHER ACCESS RESTRICTED" and some astronomical clearance level. McIlhenny waited patiently until Okanami set the reader aside with sigh.

"Weird," he murmured, shaking his head as he reached for his own coffee, and the colonel chuckled without humor.

"Even weirder than you know. This is for your information only—that's straight from Admiral Gomez—but you're in charge of this case until a Cadre med team can get here, so I'm supposed to bring you up to speed. Or as up to speed as any of us are, anyway. Clear?"

Okanami nodded, and his mouth felt oddly dry despite the coffee.

"All right. I took my own people out to the DeVries claim because the original report was so obviously impossible. For one thing, three separate SAR overflights hadn't picked up *any*thing. If Captain DeVries had been there and alive, she'd've showed on the thermal scans, especially lying in the open that way, so I *knew* it had to be some kind of plant."

He sipped coffee and shrugged.

"It wasn't. The evidence is absolutely conclusive. She came up on them from the south, with the wind behind her, and took them by surprise. She left enough blood trail for us to work out what must've happened, and it was like turning a saber-tooth loose on hyenas, Doctor. They took her down in the end, but not before she got them all. That shuttle must've been lifted out by remote, because there sure as hell weren't any live pirates to fly it.

"But that's where it gets really strange. Our forensic people have fixed approximate times of death for the pirates and her family, and they've pegged the blood trails *she* left to about the same time. Logically, then, she should have bled to death within minutes of killing the last pirate. If she hadn't done that, she should have frozen to death, again, probably very quickly. And if she were alive, the thermal scans certainly should have picked her up. None of those things happened—it's like she was someplace else until the instant Sikorsky's crew landed and found her. And, Doctor," the colonel's eyes were very intent, "not even a drop commando can do that."

"So what are you saying? It was magic?"

"I'm saying she's managed at least three outright impossibilities, and nobody has the least damned idea how. So until an explanation occurs to us, we want her right here in your capable hands."

"Under what conditions?" Okanami's voice was edged with sudden frost.

"We'd prefer," McIlhenny said carefully, "to keep her just like she is."

"Unconscious? Forget it, Colonel."

"But—"

"I said forget it! You *don't* keep a patient sedated indefinitely, particularly not one who's been through what she has, and *especially* not when there's an unknown pharmacology element. Her medical condition is nothing to play games with, and your download—" he waved the hand reader under the colonel's nose "—is less than complete. The damned thing won't even tell me what a half-dozen of the drugs in her pharmacope *do*, and her augmentation security must've been designed by a terminal paranoiac. Not only do the codes in her implants mean I can't override externally to shut them down, but I can't even go in to empty her reservoirs surgically! Do you have the least idea how much that complicates her meds? And the same security systems that keep me from accessing her receptors mean I can't use a standard somatic unit, so the only way I could keep her under would be with chemicals."

"I see." McIlhenny toyed with his coffee cup and frowned as he came up against the captain's Hippocratic armor. "In that case, let's just say we'd like you to keep her here under indefinite medical observation."

"Whether or not her medical condition requires it, eh? And if she decides she wants out of my custody before your intelligence types get here?"

"Out of the question. These 'raids' are totally out of hand. That's bad enough, and when you add in all the unanswered questions she represents—" McIlhenny shrugged. "She's not going anywhere until we've got some answers."

"There are limits to the dirty work I'm prepared to do for you and your spooks, Colonel."

"What dirty work? She probably won't even want to leave, but if she does, you're the physician of record of a patient in a military facility."

"A patient," Okanami pointed out, "who happens to be a civilian." He leaned back and eyed the colonel with a marked lack of affability. "You do remember what a 'civilian' is? You know, the people who don't wear uniforms? The ones with something called civil rights? If she wants out of here, she's out of here unless there's a genuine medical reason to hold her. And your 'unanswered questions' do not constitute such a reason."

McIlhenny felt a grudging respect for the surgeon and tugged at his lower lip in thought.

"Look, Doctor, I didn't mean to step on any professional toes, and I'm sure Admiral Gomez doesn't want to, either. Nor are we medieval monsters out to 'disappear' an unwanted witness. This is one of our people, and a damned outstanding one. We just need to . . . keep tabs on her."

"So what's the problem? Even if I discharge her, she's not going anywhere you can't find her. Not without a starship, anyway."

"Oh, no?" McIlhenny smiled tightly. "I might point out that she's already been somewhere we couldn't find her when all the indications are she was lying right there in plain sight. What's to say she can't do it again?"

"What's to say she has any *reason* to do it again?" Okanami demanded in exasperation.

"Nothing. On the other hand, what's to say she did it on purpose the first time?" Okanami's eyebrows quirked, and McIlhenny grinned sourly. "Hadn't thought about that, had you? That's because you're insufficiently paranoid for one of us much maligned 'spooks,' Doctor, but the point is that until we have some idea what happened, we can't know if she did whatever she did on purpose. Or what might happen to her if she does it again."

"You're right—you *are* paranoid," Okanami muttered. He thought hard for a moment, then shrugged. "Still doesn't matter. If a mentally competent civilian wants to check herself out, then unless you've got some specific criminal charge to warrant holding her against her will she checks herself out, period. End of story, Colonel."

"Not quite." McIlhenny leaned back and smiled at him. "You see, you've forgotten that she wasn't Fleet or Marine, she's Imperial Cadre."

"So?"

"So there's one fact most people don't know about the Cadre. Not surprising, really; it isn't big enough for much about it to become common knowledge. But the point is that she's not really a civilian at all." Okanami blinked in surprise, and McIlhenny's smile grew. "You don't resign from the Cadre—you just go on inactive reserve status. And if you don't want to hang onto our 'civilian' for us, then we'll just by God reactivate her!"

CHAPTER THIRTY-FIVE

The being men had once called Tisiphone roamed the corridors of her host's mind and marveled at what she found. Its vast, dim caverns crackled with the golden fire of dreams, and even its sleeping power was amazing. It had been far too long since last Tisiphone touched a mortal mind, and she had never been much interested in those she had invaded then. They had been targets, sources of information, tools, and prey, not something to be tasted and sampled, for she was an executioner, not a philosopher.

But things had changed. She was alone and diminished, and no one had sent her to punish this mortal; she had been summoned by the mind in which she wandered, and she needed it. Needed it as a focus and avatar for her weakened self, and so she searched its labyrinthine passages, finding places to store her self, sampling its power and fingering its memories.

It was so *different*. The last human whose thoughts she'd touched had been—the shepherd in Cappadocia? No, Cassander of Macedon, that tangled, ambitious murderer. Now there had been a mind of power, for all its evil. Yet it was no match for the strength, clarity, and knowledge of *this* mind. Man had changed over her millennia of sleep, and even cool Athena or clever-fingered Haphaestus might have envied the lore and skill mortals had attained.

But even more than its knowledge, it was the *power* of this mind which truly astounded her—the focused will, crystal lucidity . . . and ferocity. No wonder that echo, that flash of mirrored power, had troubled her dreams, for there was much of her in this Alicia DeVries. This mortal could be as implacable as she herself, Tisiphone sensed, and as deadly, and that was amazing. Were all mortals thus, if only she had stopped to see it so long ago? Or had more than man's knowledge changed while she slept?

Yet there were differences between them. She swooped through memories, sampled convictions and beliefs, and had she had lips, she would have smiled in derision at some of the foolishness she found. She and her selves had not been bred for things like love and compassion—those had no meaning for such as they, and even less this concept of "justice." It caught at her, for it had its whetted sharpness, its tangental contact with what she was, yet she sensed the dangerous contradictions at its core. It clamored for retribution, yes, but balance blunted its knife-sharp edge. Extenuation dulled its certitude, and its self-deluding emphasis on "guilt" and "innocence" and "proof" weakened its determination.

She studied the idea, tasting the dynamic tension which held so many conflicting elements in poised balance, and the familiar hunger at its heart only made it more alien. Her selves had been crafted to punish, made for vengeance, and guilt or innocence had no bearing on her mission. It was a bitter-tasting thing, this "*justice*," a chill bitterness in the hot, sweet blood-taste, and she rejected it. She turned away contemptuously, and bent her attention on other gems in this treasure-vault mind.

They were heaped and piled, glittering measurelessly, and she savored the unleashed violence of combat with weapons Zeus himself might have envied. They had their own lightning bolts, these mortals, and she watched through her host's eyes, tasting the jagged riptides of terror and fury controlled by training and science and harnessed to purpose. She was apt to violence, this Alicia DeVries . . . and yet, even at the heart of her battle fury, there was that damnable sense of detachment. That watching presence that mourned the hot blood of her own handiwork and wept for her foes even as she slew them.

Tisiphone spat in mental disgust at that potential weakness. She must be wary. This mortal had sworn herself to her service, but Tisiphone had sworn herself to Alicia DeVries' purpose in return, and this mind was powerful and complex, a weapon which might turn in her hand if she drove it too hard.

Other memories flowed about her, and these were better, more suited to her needs. Memories of loved ones, held secure and precious at her host's core like talismans against her own dark side. Anchors, helping her cling to her debilitating compassion. But they were anchors no more. They had become whips, made savage by newer memories of rape and mutilation, of slaughter and wanton cruelty and the broken bodies of dead love. They tapped deep into the reservoirs of power and purpose, stoking them into something recognized and familiar. For beneath all the nonsense about mercy and justice, Tisiphone looked into the mirror of Alicia DeVries' soul and saw . . . herself.

Jade eyes opened. Darkness pressed against the spartan room's window, moaning with the endless patience of Mathison's winter wind, but dim lights cast golden pools upon the overhead. Monitors chirped gently, almost encouragingly, and Alicia drew a deep, slow breath.

She turned her head on her pillow, studying the quiet about her, and saw the rifle on her bedside table. The weapon gleamed like memory itself in the dimness, and it should have brought the agony crashing in upon her.

It didn't. Nothing did, and that was . . . wrong. The images were there, clear and lethal in every brutal detail. Everyone she loved had been destroyed—more than destroyed, butchered with sick, premeditated sadism—and the agony of it did not overwhelm her.

She raised a hand to her forehead and frowned, thoughts clearer than they ought to be yet oddly detached. Memories flickered, merciless and sharp as holovids, yet remote, as if seen through the time-slowing armorplast of the tick. And there was something there at the last, teasing her . . .

Her hand froze, and her eyes widened as memory of her final madness came abruptly. Voices in her head! Nonsense. And yet—she looked about the silent room once more, and knew she should never have lived to see it.

<Of course you should have,> a cold, clear voice said. *<I promised you vengeance, and to avenge yourself, you must live.>*

She stiffened, eyes suddenly huge in the dimness, yet even now there was no panic in their depths. They were cool and still, for the terror of that silent voice eddied against a shield of glass. She sensed its presence, felt it prickle in her palms, yet it could not touch her.

"Who—what—are you?" she asked the emptiness, and a silent laugh quivered deep at her core.

<*Have mortals forgotten us, indeed? Ah, how fickle you are! You may call me Tisiphone.*>

"Tisiphone?" There was an elusive familiarity to that name, but—

<*There, now,*> the voice murmured like crystal, singing on the edge of shattering, and its effort to soothe seemed alien to it. <*Once your kind called us the* Erinyes, *but that was long, long ago. Three of us, there were: Alecto, Megaira . . . and I. I am the last of the Furies, Little One.*>

Alicia's eyes opened even wider, and then she closed them tight. The simplest answer was that she'd been right the first time. She must be mad. That certainly made more sense than holding a conversation with something out of Old Earth's mythology! Yet she knew she wasn't, and her lips twitched at the thought. Didn't they say that a crazy person *knew* she wasn't mad? And who but a madwoman would feel so calm at a moment like this?

<*For all your skills, your people have become most blind. Have you lost the ability to believe anything you cannot see or touch? Do not your "scientists" deal daily with things they can only describe?*>

"*Touché*," Alicia murmured, then shook herself. Immobilizing tractor collars circled her left leg at knee and hip, lighter than a plasticast yet dragging at her as she eased up on her elbows. She raked hair from her eyes and looked around until she spied the bed's power controls, then reached out her right hand and slipped her Gamma receptor over the control linkage. She hadn't used it in so long she had to think for almost ten full seconds before the proper neural links established themselves, but then the bed purred softly, rising against her shoulders. She settled into a sitting position and folded her hands in her lap, and her neck craned as her eyes flitted about the room once more.

"Let's say I believe in you . . . Tisiphone. Where are you?"

<*Your wit is sharper than that, Alicia DeVries.*>

"You mean," Alicia said very carefully, a tiny tremor of fear oozing through the sheet of glass, "that you're inside my head?"

<*Of course.*>

"I see." She inhaled deeply. "Why aren't I hanging from the ceiling and gibbering, then?"

<*It would scarcely help our purpose for me to permit that. Not,*> the voice added a bit dryly, <*that you are not trying to do precisely that.*>

"Well," Alicia surprised herself with a smile despite the madness which had engulfed her, "I guess that would be the rational thing to do."

<*Rationality is an over-valued commodity, Little One. Madness has its place, yet it does make speech difficult, does it not?*>

"I imagine it would." She pressed her hands to her temples, feeling the familiar angularity of her subcutaneous Alpha receptor against her right palm, and moistened her lips. "Are you . . . the reason I don't hurt more?" She wasn't speaking of physical pain, and the voice knew it.

<*Indeed. You are a soldier, Alicia DeVries. Does a warrior maddened by grief attain his goal, or die on his enemy's blade? Loss and hatred are potent, but they must be used. I will not let* them *use* you. *Not yet.*>

Alicia closed her eyes again, lips trembling, grateful for the pane of glass between her and her loss. She felt endless, night-black grief waiting to suck her to destruction beyond whatever shield this Tisiphone had erected, and it frightened her. Yet there was resentment in her gratitude, as if she'd been robbed of something rightly hers—something as precious as it was cruel.

She sucked in another breath and lowered her hands once more. Either Tisiphone existed, or she truly was mad, and she might as well act on the assumption that she was sane. She opened her hospital gown and traced the red line down her chest and the ones across her abdomen. There was no pain, and quick-heal was doing its job—the incisions were half-healed already and would vanish entirely in time—but they confirmed the damage she'd taken. She let the gown fall closed and leaned back against her pillows in the quiet room.

"How long ago was I hit?"

<*Time is something mortals measure better than I, Little One, and it does not exist where you and I have been, but three days have passed since they brought you to this place.*>

"'Where you and I have been'?"

<*You were dying, and I am not what once I was. My power has waned with the passing of my other selves, and I was ever more apt to wound than heal. Since I could not make you whole, I took you to a place where time has no business until the searchers came to find you.*>

"Would you care to explain that a bit better?"

<*Would you care to explain blue to a man born blind?*>

"You sound like one of those assholes from intelligence."

<*No. They lied to you; I know what I did, and would tell you if you could grasp my meaning.*>

Alicia pursed her lips, surprised by Tisiphone's quick understanding.

<*How should I not understand? I have spent days examining your memories, Little One. I know of your Colonel Watts.*>

"Not *my* Colonel Watts." Alicia's voice was suddenly cold, and a spurt of rage took Tisiphone by surprise, squirting past the clear shield, as Alicia remembered the utter chaos of the Shallingsport Raid. She shook it away, suppressing it with a skill the Fury could not have bettered.

"All right, you're here. Why? What are you going to do?"

<*You asked for vengeance, and you shall have it. We will find your enemies, you and I, and destroy them.*>

"Just the two of us? When the entire Empire can't?" Alicia's laugh was not pleasant. "What makes you think we can do that?"

<*This,*> the voice said softly, and Alicia's head snapped up. Her lips drew back from locked teeth, and a direcat's snarl caught at her throat. Rage flooded her veins, loosed from beyond the shield within her, distilled and pure and hotter than a star's heart. Loss and grief were in that rage, but they were only its fuel, not its heat. Its ferocity wrenched at her like fists of fire, and panic touched her as her augmentation began to respond.

But then it vanished, and she slumped back, panting and beaded with sweat. Her heart raced, and she was weak and drained, like a chemist's flask emptied of acid. Yet something quivered within her, pacing her pulse like an echo of her rage. Determination—no, more than determination. Purpose which went beyond the implacable to the inevitable, ridiculing the very thought that any power in the universe might deflect it.

<*You begin to see, Little One, yet that was but* your *anger; you have not yet tasted mine. I* am *rage—your rage, and my own, and all the rage that ever was or will be—and skilled in its use. We* will *find them. On that you have my word, which has never been broken. And when we find them, you will have the strength of my arm, which has never failed. If I am less than once I was, I remain more than you can imagine; you will have your vengeance.*>

"God," Alicia whispered, pressing trembling hands to her temples once more. An icicle of terror shivered through her—not of Tisiphone, but of herself. Of the limitless capacity for destruction she had tasted within her fury. Or—she swallowed—was it within her Fury?

"I—" she began, and chopped off as a man in nursing whites charged through the door and skidded to a stop when he saw her sitting up in bed. His eyes widened, then dropped to the bedside monitors, and he lifted a neural lead from the central console. He pressed it to the terminal on his temple, and Alicia hid a twisted smile of sudden understanding. Her vital signs must have gone off the scale when that bolt of distilled rage ripped through her.

The nurse lowered the lead and regarded her with puzzlement. And with something else. There were questions in his eyes, fusing with sympathy into a peculiar tension his professional façade couldn't quite hide. He glanced away from her, eyes darting for just a moment to the intercom panel, and Alicia swallowed a groan. Idiot! Of *course* they'd left the com open! What must he think after hearing her half of the insane conversation with Tisiphone?

<*Shall I take the memory of it from him?*>

"Can you?" Alicia spoke aloud out of sheer reflex, then cursed herself as the nurse took an involuntary half-step away from her.

"Can I what, Captain DeVries?"

"Uh . . . can you tell me how long I've been here?" she improvised frantically.

"Three days, Ma'am," he said.

<*You need not speak aloud for me to hear you, Little One,*> Tisiphone said at the same instant, and Alicia wanted to tear her hair and scream at both of them. The concerned caution in the nurse's voice vibrated bizarrely in her ears, cut through with the amusement in that silent mental whisper.

"Thank you," she said aloud, and *<Could you do that? Make him forget?>*

<Once, certainly. Now . . .> She felt the strong impression of a mental shrug. *<I could try, if you can touch him.>*

Alicia glanced at the wary nurse and smothered a totally inappropriate giggle. *<No way! The poor guy's convinced I'm out of my mind, and he called me by my rank, so they must know I'm a drop commando. I'm surprised he's still here, and he'll jump out of his skin if I try to grab him. Talk about a* dangerous *lunatic—! Besides, they probably had a recorder on it.>*

<Recorder?> Mental fingers plucked the concept from her mind. *<Ah. It seems I have much yet to learn about this "technology." Will it matter?>*

<How do I *know? It depends on just how balmy they think I am. Now be quiet a minute.>*

A sense of someone else's surprise echoed within her, as if Tisiphone were unused to hearing orders from a mere mortal, and she suppressed another manic grin in favor of a reassuring smile.

"Thank you," she repeated aloud. "I wonder . . . I can see it's the middle of the night, but could I see the duty doctor?"

"Surgeon Captain Okanami is on his way here right now, Ma'am. In fact, I was waiting for him when—that is . . ." His voice trailed off, and Alicia smiled again.

Poor guy. No wonder he's already called in the big guns. There he was, listening to the prize booby blathering away to herself, and then her vitals went crazy. Too.

"I see. Well, in that case—"

The opening door cut her off in mid-inanity. A Fleet captain came through it, his stride brisk but measured, though something suggested he found it difficult to keep it that way. His Medical Branch caduceus glittered in the dim light, and he paused as if surprised to see her sitting up. No, not to see her sitting up; to see her looking rational. Odd, she didn't *feel* as if she looked rational. One of his hands made a tiny shooing motion, and the nurse tried to hide his relief as he vanished like smoke.

"Well, now," Captain Okanami said, folding his arms across his chest as the door closed, "I'm glad to see you with us again, Captain DeVries."

Yeah, and surprised as hell. She hid the thought behind a smile and nodded back, watching him while she wondered what he was really thinking.

"You're lucky to be alive," he went on gently, "but I'm afraid—"

"I know." She cut him off before he could complete the sentence. "I know," she repeated more softly.

"Yes, well." Okanami looked at the floor and unfolded his left arm to tug at an earlobe. "I'm not very good at expressing my condolences, Captain. Never have been—a failing in a physician, I suppose—but if there's anything I can do, please tell me."

"I will." She looked down at her own hands and cleared her throat again. "I take it you've figured out I'm a Cadrewoman?"

"Yes. It came as quite a surprise, but, yes, we figured it out. It leaves us with a bit of a problem, too, medically speaking."

"I can imagine. I'm just glad you didn't hit any landmines."

"Actually, we did." Her eyes flicked up, and he shrugged. "Nothing we couldn't handle—" she had the definite impression that remark was sliding over slippery ground "—and we've got partial specs on your augmentation. I don't anticipate any more problems before the Cadre med team gets here."

"Cadre med team?" she asked quickly. "Coming here?"

"Of course. I'm not competent to handle your case, Captain DeVries, so Admiral Gomez called them in. I understand there was a Cadre detachment at Alexandria and that they're *en route* aboard a Crown dispatch boat."

"I see." She chewed on that thought. It had been five years since she'd seen a fellow Cadreman. She'd believed—hoped—she never would again.

"We really don't have a choice, I'm afraid. There are too many holes in the data we've got."

"I see," she repeated more normally. "And in the meantime?"

"In the meantime, I'm keeping you right where you are. We had to do a lot of repair work, as I'm sure you've already realized, and I want someone versed in Cadre augmentation to check it over." She nodded, and he cocked his head. "Are you experiencing any discomfort? I wouldn't want to get into any fancy meds, but I suppose we'd be fairly safe to try old-fashioned aspirin."

"No, no discomfort."

"Good." His relief was evident. "I wasn't sure, but I'd hoped your augmentation would take care of that. I'm glad to see it is."

"Uh, yes," she said, but a quick check of her pharmacopoeia processor told her he was wrong. <*Are you doing that?*> she asked the voice.

<*Of course.*>

<*Thanks.*>

"What's your prognosis?" she asked Okanami after a moment.

"You've responded well to the surgery, and to the quick-heal," Okanami said. "In the long term, you'll probably want to consider replacement for your spleen, but you're coming along very nicely for now. The bone damage to your leg was extreme, and the repairs there are going to need several weeks yet, but the rest—"

He waved a dismissive hand and, Alicia noted, carefully did not discuss her mental state. Tactful of him.

He moved a few strides to his right, glancing at her monitor displays, and made a few quick notes on the touchpad, then turned back to her.

"I realize you've just waked up, Captain DeVries—"

"Please, call me Alicia. I haven't been 'Captain DeVries' in years."

"Of course." He smiled with genuine warmth, eyes twinkling with just a touch of sadness. "Alicia. As I say, I realize you've just waked up, but what you really need more than anything else just now is rest. Even if you're not feeling it, this kind of surgery really takes it out of you, quick-heal or no, and you weren't in very good shape before we started."

"I know." She eased back down in the bed, and he pursed his lips.

"If there's anything you'd like to talk about," he began hesitantly, then fell silent as she waved a hand. He nodded and began to turn away.

<*Touch him,*> a voice said in her mind, so suddenly she twitched in surprise at the intensity of its demand.

"Uh, Doctor." He stopped and looked back at the sound of her voice, and she held out her right hand. "Thank you for putting me back together."

"My pleasure." He gripped her hand and smiled, and she smiled back, but shock threatened to wipe it from her lips. Her hand tingled with the power of the spark which had leapt between them at the moment of contact. God, was the man nerve-dead? How could he have missed that flare of power?!

But that was nothing beside what followed it. A column of fire flowed down her arm and licked out through her skin. She looked at their joined hands, expecting to see flames darting from her pores, but there were no flames. Only the heat . . . and under it a crackle that coalesced suddenly into something she almost recognized. A barrier went down, like an opening door or a closing circuit, and the fire in her arm flared high and faded into a familiar intangible tingle. It was like smelling a color or seeing a sound, indescribable to anyone who had never experienced it, but she *had* experienced it. Or experienced its like, at any rate.

Information spilled up her arm, crisp and clear as any her Alpha receptor had ever pulled from a tactical net, and that was impossible. Yet it was happening—happening in a heartbeat, like a burst transmission from a forward scout but less focused, more general and disorganized.

Concern. Uncertainty. Satisfaction at her physical condition and deep, gnawing worry about her mental state. Discomfort over his decision not to mention intelligence's interest. Burning wonder over how she'd survived untended and undetected in the snow. Genuine distress for the deaths of her family, and an even greater distress that she seemed so calm and collected. *Too calm*, he was thinking, and *I have to listen to that recording. Maybe—*

He released her hand and stepped back. Clearly, he had sensed nothing at all out of the ordinary, and his hand rose in a small wave.

"I'll see you in the morning, Cap—Alicia," he said gently. "Go back to sleep if you can."

She nodded and closed her eyes as he withdrew . . . and knew sleep was the last thing she was going to be able to do.

CHAPTER THIRTY-SIX

Benjamin McIlhenny looked up from a sheaf of hard copy as a hatch hissed open aboard the battlecruiser HMS *Antietam*, then rose quickly as Sir Arthur Keita stepped through it. Keita wore the green-on-green of the Imperial Cadre with the golden harp and starships of the Emperor below the single starburst of a brigadier, and if he was a head shorter than the colonel, he was far thicker and broader. "The Emperor's Bulldog" might be pushing a hundred years old, but he remained powerfully built and physically fit. He also exuded hard, ruthless competence, and his arrival had been something of a shock. The colonel suspected they would have seen someone far less senior if Keita hadn't been right next door in the Macedon Sector, anyway.

The man behind him could have been specifically designed as his antithesis. Inspector Ferhat Ben Belkassem, well short of his fortieth year, was small, neat, and very dark, with liquid brown eyes and a strong, beaked nose. His crimson tunic's collar bore the hourglass and balance of the Ministry of Justice, and he seemed pleasant enough—which was far from sufficient to reconcile McIlhenny to his presence. This was a job for the Fleet and the Marines. By McIlhenny's lights, not even Keita had any real business poking his nose in—not that he intended to say so to a brigadier. Particularly not to a Cadre brigadier, and *especially* not to a Cadre brigadier named Sir Arthur Keita. Which, because Colonel McIlhenny was an intrinsically just man, meant he couldn't say it to Ben Belkassem, either. Damn it.

"Sir Arthur. Inspector."

"Colonel," Keita returned crisply. Ben Belkassem merely smiled at the omission of his own name—a lack of reaction which irritated the colonel immensely—and McIlhenny waved at two empty chairs across the conference table.

Ben Belkassem waited for Keita to seat himself, then slid into his own chair. It was a respectful enough gesture, but the man moved like a cat, McIlhenny thought. Graceful, poised, and silent. Sneaky bastard.

"I've downloaded all of our data to *Banshee*," he began, "but, with your permission, Sir Arthur, I thought we should probably begin with a general background brief."

Keita nodded for him to continue, and McIlhenny switched on the holo unit. A display of the Franconia Sector appeared above the table, like a squashed quarter-sphere of stars. An edge of the Empire appeared along its flattened side, green and friendly, but the scarlet of the Rishathan Sphere crowded its rounded upper edge, and a sparkle of amber Rogue Worlds and blue systems claimed by the Quarn Hegemony threaded through its volume. McIlhenny slipped into his headset, connecting the display controls to his neural receptor, and a single star at the sector's heart blinked gold.

"The sector capital." The announcement was probably redundant, but he'd learned long ago to make sure the groundwork was in place. "Soissons, in the Franconia System. Quite Earth-like, but for rather cool temperatures, with a population just over two billion. A bit high for this region, but it's one of the old League Worlds we retook from the Lizards more or less intact."

His audience nodded, and he cleared his throat.

"We really should have organized a Crown Sector out here a century ago, but with the Rishatha hanging up there to galactic north it seemed reasonable to turn our attention to other areas first. God knows we had enough to worry about elsewhere, and the Ministry of Out-World Affairs decided not to draw Rishathan attention south until we'd firmed up the central sectors. As you can see—" skeins of stars suddenly winked to life beyond the sector's curved frontier, burning the steady white of unsurveyed space "—there's a lot of room for expansion out there, and once we start curling around their southern frontiers, the Lizards are likely to get a bit anxious. We didn't want them extending their border to cut us off before we were ready."

He glanced up at the others. Ben Belkassem was watching the display as if it were a fascinating toy, but Keita only grunted and nodded again.

"All right. The Crown began providing incentives for colonization about eight years ago, and formally announced the organization of the Franconia Sector three years ago. Out-World Affairs sent Governor General Treadwell out a year later. It's a fairly typical Crown Sector in most ways: ninety-three systems under imperial claim—twenty-six with habitable planets—and thirty-one belonging to someone else in the same spatial volume. We've got five Incorporated Worlds besides Soissons, though one of them, Yeager, just elected its first senators this year. Aside from them, we've got fifteen Crown Worlds with Crown Governors, or—" his mouth twisted, "—we *had* fifteen Crown Worlds. Now we only have twelve."

Four stars pulsed lurid crimson as he spoke, wide-spaced, almost equi-distant from one another. One was the primary of Mathison's World.

"Typee, Mawli, Brigadoon, and Mathison's World," McIlhenny said grimly, one of the stars blinking brighter with each name. "Mawli, Brigadoon, and Mathison's World are complete write-offs; Typee survived . . . barely. It was the first world hit, and it's been settled for over sixty years—a freeholder colony from Durandel in the Melville Sector—and apparently their population was too spread out for the raiders to hit anything smaller than the major towns. The others—"

He shrugged, eyes bitter, and Keita's mouth tightened.

"Things started out quite well, actually," McIlhenny went on after a moment. "Governor Treadwell's got three times the normal Crown Sector Fleet presence because of the Rishatha and the Jung Association, so we—"

"Excuse me, Colonel." Ben Belkassem's voice was surprisingly deep for such a small man, almost velvety, with the cultured accent of the mother world. McIlhenny frowned at him, and the inspector smiled. "I didn't have time for a complete update on the foreign relations picture out here. Could you give me a little detail on this

Jung Association? Am I correct in remembering that it's a multi-system Rogue World polity?"

"Pocket empire, more like," McIlhenny said. "These three systems—" three closely-clustered amber lights flashed "—and two treaty dependencies, MaGuire and Wotan." Two more lights blinked. "When the Lizards blitzed the old League, a League fleet commander—a Commodore Wanda Jung—managed to hold Mithra, Artemis, and Madrigal. The Lizards never even got their toenails into them," he added with grudging respect, "and for somebody their size, they still pack a lot of firepower. All three of their main systems have Core World population levels—about four billion on Mithra, I believe—and they're very heavily industrialized. Until we got ourselves organized, they and El Greco were the major human power bases out here."

The inspector nodded, and McIlhenny returned to his original point.

"At any rate, what with the Rogue World odds and sods left over from the League and the proximity of the Rishathan Sphere, the Crown decided Governor Treadwell might need a big stick, so the Franconia Fleet District is unusually powerful. Soissons is very heavily fortified, and Admiral Gomez commands three full battle squadrons, with appropriate supporting elements, which one should think ought to have been enough to prevent things like this."

He paused, brooding over his display's crimson cursors, then sighed.

"What we seem to have here is a highly unusual bunch of pirates. They're not terorrists—not even the FALA is stupid enough to pull this kind of crap, and we haven't had a single communique from anyone claiming responsibility for any 'liberation front' ops. But if they aren't terrorists, that only leaves pirates . . . which doesn't make a lot of sense, either.

"We've always had some piracy in the marches, of course. There are so many single-system Rogue Worlds out here that the mercenary business is fairly lucrative; some of them go wolf's-head from time to time, and we've had the odd hijacker outfit get too big for its vac suits, but most of them raid commercial traffic before the freighters go FTL or after they drop intra-systemic. Even the occasional bunch idiotic enough to hit a planet are usually smart enough to avoid wholesale slaughter rather than force the Fleet to go after them in strength. More than that, most of them don't have anywhere near the firepower to mount a planet-sized raid.

"This bunch has the firepower, and there's something really sick about them. They come barreling in, take out the starcom, then send down their shuttles to take *everything*. Usually, pirates stick to low-bulk, high-value cargoes, grab whatever's handiest, and pull out; these bastards steal anything that isn't nailed down. Power receptors, hospital equipment, satellite communication gear, machine tools, precious metals, luxury export items . . . it's like they have a shopping list of every item of value on the planet.

"Worse than that, they don't care who they kill. In fact, they seem to *enjoy* killing, and if their window's big enough, they take their time about it."

McIlhenny's face was grim.

"This is the worst raid yet, although Brigadoon was almost as bad. I doubt we'd've had any survivors at all from Mathison's if not for *Gryphon*, and her presence was a total fluke. Her skipper isn't even assigned to Admiral Gomez—he was just passing through on his way to Trianon and decided to stop off at Mathison's to pay his respects to Governor Brno. She'd been his first CO, and since a lot of his crew were fairly green and he was well ahead of schedule, he thought he'd surprise her with a visit and kill a few days on sublight maneuvers. He was two days into them, well outside the outermost planet, when the raiders took out the governor's residence, but she knew he was out there and got off a sublight message and fired out her SLAM drone before they killed her. The bastards caught the drone before it wormholed, but Commander Perez picked up the message—after a six-hour transmission delay—and went to maximum emergency power on his Fasset drive. He was well over drive mass redline, and it seems clear he came whooping in on them long before they expected anyone to turn up."

"In a destroyer?" Keita's was exactly the harsh, gravelly voice one might have expected. "That took guts."

"He may not've been assigned here, Sir, but Commander Perez had done his intelligence homework. He knew about the raids—and that we haven't been able to get a sensor reading on any of their units. Analysis suggests they must have at least a few capital ships, and if we knew who'd built them we might be able to figure out where the raiders originated. He also knew the governor's drone hadn't made it out, and he had three SLAM drones of his own."

"Which," Ben Belkassem murmured, "is presumably why they didn't just polish *Gryphon* off and get on with their business?"

"We believe so," McIlhenny agreed, upgrading his opinion of the inspector slightly.

"Continue, Colonel," Keita said.

"Actually, there's not a lot more to say about their operational patterns, Sir. Even with her Fleet strength, Admiral Gomez doesn't have the ships to cover this volume of space effectively. We've tried picketing more likely target systems with corvettes, but they don't have the firepower or speed to deal with whoever these people are, and they only carry a single SLAM drone each. We had a picket at Brigadoon, but the raiders either took her out before she got her drone off, or else nailed it before it wormholed. Either way, she wasn't able to get her report to us, and Admiral Gomez isn't happy about 'staking out more goats for the tigers,' as she puts it."

"Don't blame her." Keita shook himself like an Old Earth bear. "No commander likes throwing away his people for no return."

"Exactly. We're trying to find some pattern that'll let us put heavier forces in likely target systems, but no matter where we put them, the raiders always hit somewhere else." McIlhenny glared at the display again.

"Do they, now?" Ben Belkassem said softly. "I'd say that's a pattern right there, Colonel."

"I don't like what you're suggesting, Inspector," Keita growled, and Ben Belkassem shrugged.

"Nonetheless, Sir, four straight hits without any interception aside from one corvette—destroyed without getting out a contact message—and a destroyer with no official business in the vicinity, stretches well beyond the limits of probability. Unless we wish to assume the raiders are claivoyant."

"I resent that, Inspector." The edge in McIlhenny's quiet voice was sharp enough to suggest he'd considered the same possibility.

"I name no names, Colonel," Ben Belkassem replied mildly, "but logic suggests they must be getting inside information from someone. Which," his own voice hardened just a bit, "is why *I* am here."

McIlhenny started to retort sharply, then pressed his lips together and sat back in his chair, eyes narrowed. Ben Belkassem nodded.

"Precisely. His Majesty has expressed his personal concern to Minister of Justice Cortez. Justice has no desire to step on the military's toes, but if someone is passing information to these pirates, His Majesty wishes him identified and stopped. And, with all due respect, you may be a bit too deep into the trees to see the forest."

McIlhenny's face darkened, and the inspector raised a placating hand.

"Please, Colonel, I mean no disrespect. Your record is outstanding, and I'm certain you're checking your internal security closely, but if the hare is running with the hounds, so to speak, an external viewpoint may be exactly what you need. And," he smiled with genuine humor for the first time, "your people are bound to see me as an interloper. They'll resent me whatever I do or don't do, which means I can be as rude and insulting as I like without damaging your working relationships with them."

The colonel's eyes widened, and Keita gave a bark of laughter.

"He's got you there, McIlhenny! I was going to suggest I might help you out the same way, but damned if I wouldn't rather let the inspector take the heat. I may have to work with some of your people in the future."

"I . . . see." McIlhenny rubbed a fingertip on the table, then raised it and inspected it as if for dust. "Are you suggesting, Inspector, that I should simply hand my internal security responsibilities over to you?"

"Of course not—and if I did, you'd be perfectly justified in kicking me clear back to Old Earth," Ben Belkassem said cheerfully. "It's your shop. You're the proper person to run it, and your people know you'll have to be looking very closely for possible leaks. They'll expect a certain amount of that, and I couldn't simply take over without undercutting your authority. I'd say your chances of finding whoever it is are probably about as good as mine, but if I stick in my oar in the role of an officious, pig-headed, empire-building interloper—a part, may I add, I play quite well—I can do a lot of your dirty work for you. Just tell them Justice has stuck you with an asshole from Intelligence Branch and leave the rest to me.

Who knows? Even if I don't find a thing, I may just scare our hare into the open for you."

"I see." McIlhenny examined Ben Belkassem's face intently. The inspector had placed an unerring finger on his own most private—and darkest—fear, and he was right. An outsider could play grand inquisitor without the devastating effect an internal witch hunt might produce.

"All right, Inspector, I may take you up on that. Let me run it by Admiral Gomez first, though." Ben Belkassem nodded, and the colonel frowned.

"Actually, something we hit here on Mathison's leaves me more inclined to think you have a point than I would've been," he admitted unhappily.

The inspector quirked an eyebrow, but the colonel turned to Keita.

"We owe it to your Captain DeVries and her family, Sir Arthur. May I assume you've read my initial report on the affair at the DeVries Claim?"

"You may," Keita said dryly. "Countess Miller personally starcommed it to me before her henchmen shoved me aboard *Banshee* and slammed the hatch."

McIlhenny blinked. He'd expected his report to make waves, but he hadn't anticipated that the Minister of War herself might get involved.

"At any rate," he shook himself back to the affair at hand, "we still haven't been able to figure out how she happened to survive, and I'm afraid she's a bit . . . well—" He broke off uncomfortably, and Keita sighed.

"I said I've read the report, Colonel. The questions you raised are the main reason I got sent along with Major Cateau's medical team, and I understand about Ali—Captain DeVries' . . . mental state." He closed his eyes briefly, as if in pain, then nodded again. "Go on, Colonel."

"Yes, Sir. We got a couple of intelligence breaks out of it. For one thing, she's been able to identify the assault shuttles—or, at least one type of shuttle—these bastards are using. It was one of the old *Leopard*-class boats, which is the first hard ID we've gotten, since none of the other survivors who actually saw the shuttles were military types. A *Leopard* tends to confirm that we're dealing with at least one capital ship, of course, but Fleet dumped so many of them on the surplus market when the *Bengals* came in that anyone could have snapped them up. We're running searches on the disposal records to see if anyone out this way was stupid enough to buy up a clutch of them and leave us a paper trail, but I'm not very optimistic.

"But, more importantly, she and her father and grandfather took out the entire crew of the shuttle which went after her family. We've picked up a few dead pirates before, but they never told us much. Whoever's running them sanitizes his troops pretty carefully, and we haven't had a lot to go on for IDs, aside from the obvious fact that they've all been human. In this case, however, Captain DeVries nailed the assault team commander. He didn't have much on him, either, but we ran his retinal and genetic patterns and got a direct hit."

He still wore his synth-link headset, and the star map disappeared, replaced by an unfamiliar red-haired man in a very familiar uniform.

"Lieutenant Albert Singh, gentlemen." McIlhenny's voice was light; his expression was not.

"An Imperial Fleet officer?!" Keita exploded. The colonel nodded, and Keita glared at the holo, teeth bared. Even Ben Belkassem seemed shocked.

"An Imperial Fleet officer. I don't have his complete dossier yet, but what I've seen so far looks clean—except for the fact that Lieutenant Singh has now died twice: once from a fourteen-millimeter slug through the spine, and once in a shuttle accident in the Holderman Sector."

"God!" Keita muttered. One large, hairy hand clenched into a fist and thumped the table gently. "How long ago?"

"Over two years," McIlhenny said, and glanced at Ben Belkassem. "Which, I very much fear, lends point to your suggestion that there has to be someone–possibly several someones–on the inside, Inspector. That shuttle accident happened, all right, but when I poked a bit deeper, I found something very interesting. Singh's personnel jacket says he was aboard it and killed, but the original passenger manifest for the shuttle–which was, indeed, lost with all hands–doesn't include his name. Sometime between then and now, someone with access to Fleet personnel records added him to it as far as his jacket was concerned, which gave him a nice, clean termination and erased him from our active data base."

"*Very* good," Ben Belkassem approved. "How did you find him, then?"

"I wish I could take the credit," McIlhenny said wryly, "but I was exhausted when I set up the data search, and I didn't define my parameters very well. In fact, I requested a search of *all* records, and I was more than somewhat irritated when I saw how much computer time I'd 'wasted' on it—until the search spit out his name."

"Never look serendipity in the mouth, Colonel." The inspector grinned. "*I* don't—and I'm afraid I don't always give it credit for my successes, either."

"But a Fleet officer," Keita muttered. "I don't like the smell of this."

"Nor do I," McIlhenny said more seriously. "It's possible he did it himself, and I've starcommed the Holderman Fleet District for full particulars on him, including anything he might have been into before his 'death.' I'm also running a Fleet-wide personnel search to see if any other bogus 'deaths' occurred in the same shuttle accident. I hope I don't find any, because if *Singh* didn't arrange it, someone else did, and that suggests we may be looking at deliberate recruiting from inside our own military."

"And that whoever did the recruiting may still be in place," Ben Belkassem murmured.

Alicia looked up as a shortish woman stepped through her hospital door. The newcomer moved with the springy stride of a heavy-worlder in a single gravity, and Alicia's eyes widened.

"Tannis?" she blurted, jerking upright in bed. "By God, it *is* you!"

"Really?" Major Tannis Cateau, Imperial Cadre Medical Branch, turned her name tag up to scrutinize it, then nodded. "So it is." She crossed to the bed. "How you doing, Sarge?"

"I'll '*Sarge*' you!" Alicia grinned. Then her smile faded as she saw the shadow behind Tannis' eyes. "I expect," she said more slowly, "that you're about to tell *me* how I'm doing."

"That's what medics do, Sarge," Tannis replied. She crossed her arms and rocked on the balls of her feet, surveying Captain DeVries (retired) very much as Corporal Cateau had once surveyed Staff Sergeant DeVries. But there was a difference now, Alicia thought, noting the major's pips on Cateau's green uniform. Oh, yes, there was a difference.

Five years, she thought. *Has it* really *been that long?*

"Sarge—Alley," Tannis said, "you know how sorry I was to hear about your mom, Clarissa, Stevie—"

Alicia flinched. She held up one hand, half-shaking her head, and Tannis stopped. She gazed at the friend she hadn't seen in so long, and then she inhaled deeply and nodded.

"So," Alicia said after a moment, her conversational tone sounding almost natural, "how am I?"

"Not too bad, considering." Tannis accepted the change in tone and cocked her head judiciously. "Matter of fact, Okanami and his people did a good job on the repairs, from your records. I may not even open you back up to take a personal look."

"You always were a hungry-knifed little snot."

"The human eye," Tannis declaimed, "is still the best diagnostic tool. You've got several million credits' worth of the Emperor's molycircs tucked away in there—only makes sense to be sure they're all connected more or less to the right places, don't you think?"

"Yeah, sure," Alicia said as lightly as she could. "And mentally?"

"That," Tannis acknowledged, "is a bit more ticklish. What's this I hear about you talking to ghosts, Sarge?"

Leave it to Tannis to dive straight in. Alicia rubbed the upper tractor collar on her thigh. They should be taking that off soon, she thought inconsequentially, and lowered her eyes to it as she considered her answer.

<*Deny it,*> Tisiphone suggested.

<*Won't work. She'll have heard the recordings by now, and I'm sure Okanami's staff psychologist has already briefed her. It would've been nice if you'd let me know I didn't have to talk out loud before I opened my mouth.*>

<*I had not considered the need. When last I had dealings with humans, there were no such things as recorders. Besides, people who spoke to themselves were thought to be touched by the gods.*>

<Yeah? Well, times have changed.>

<Indeed? Then who are *you talking to?>*

"Well," Alicia said finally, looking back up at Tannis, "I guess maybe I was a bit shaky when I woke up. Blame me?"

"You didn't sound shaky, Sarge. In fact, you sounded a hell of a lot calmer than you should've. I know you. You're a cold-blooded bitch in combat, but you come apart after the fire fight."

Yeah, Alicia reflected, *you* do *know me, don't you, Tannis?*

"So you think I've gone buggy?" she said aloud.

"'Buggy,'" Tannis observed, "is hardly a proper technical diagnosis suited to the mystique of my profession, and you know I'm a mechanic, not a psychobabbler. On the other hand, I'd have to say it sounds . . . unusual."

Alicia shrugged. "What can I tell you? All I can say is that I *feel* rational—but I suppose I would, if I've really lost it."

"Um." Tannis uncrossed her arms and clasped her hands behind her. "That doesn't necessarily follow—I think it's one of those self-assuring theories cooked up by people worried about their own stability—but I'd be inclined to write it off as post-combat shock with anyone else. And if we didn't have you on chip still doing it in your sleep."

<Damn! Am *I doing that?>*

<At times.>

<So why didn't you stop me?>

<I was built by the gods, Little One; I am neither a goddess myself nor omniscient. All I can do is quiet you after *you start to speak.>*

<Damn.> "Have I had a lot to say?"

"Not a lot. In fact, you tend to shut back up right in mid-word. Frankly, I'd prefer for you to run down instead of breaking off that way."

"Oh, come on, Tannis! Lots of people talk in their sleep."

"Not," Tannis said at her driest, "to figures out of Greek mythology, they don't. I didn't even know you'd studied the subject."

"I haven't. It's just—Oh, hell, forget it." Tannis raised an eyebrow, and Alicia snorted. "And get that all-knowing gleam out of your eye. You know how people pick up bits and pieces of null-value data."

"True." Tannis hooked a chair closer to the bed and sat. "The problem, Sarge, is that most people who talk in their sleep haven't dropped right off Fleet scanners for a week—and they don't have weird EEGs, either."

"Weird EEG?" It was time for Alicia's eyebrows to rise, and her surprise was not at all feigned.

"Yep. 'Weird' is Captain Okanami's term, but I'm afraid it fits. He and his team didn't know what they had on their table till they twanged your escape package, but they had a good, clear EEG on you throughout. Spiked just like it's supposed to when you flattened that poor Commander Thompson—" Tannis paused. "They tell you about that?"

"I asked, actually. I knew they'd hit something, and most of the docs were too busy staying out of reach to get anything done. I've even apologized to him."

"I'm sure he appreciated it." Tannis' eyes gleamed. "Nice clean hit, Sarge, just a tad low." She grinned, then shrugged. "Anyway, there was the spike and all those other squiggles I recognize as lovable old you. But there was another whole pattern—almost like an overlay—wrapped around them."

"Ah?"

"Ah. Almost looked like there were two of you. Mighty peculiar stuff, Sarge. You taking in boarders?"

"Not funny, Tannis," Alicia said, looking away, and Tannis inhaled.

"You're right. Sorry. But it *was* odd, Alley, and when you tie it in with all the other odd questions you've presented us with, it's enough to make the brass nervous. Especially when you start talking as if there *were* someone else living in your head." Tannis shook her head, eyes unwontedly worried. "They don't want a schizoid drop commando running around, Sarge."

"Not running around *loose*, you mean."

"I suppose I do, but you can't really blame them, can you?" She held Alicia's gaze levelly, and it was Alicia's turn to sigh.

"Guess not. Is that the real reason they've kept me isolated?"

"In part. Of course, you really do need continued treatment. The incisions are all done, but they had to put a hunk of laminate into your femur, and about four centimeters of what they managed to save looked like a jigsaw puzzle with missing pieces. You know how quick-heal slows up on bone repair, and you ripped the hell out of your muscle tissue, too."

"I realize that. And I also know I could've been ambulatory in this thing—" she tapped the upper tractor collar "—weeks ago. Okanami's 'have to wait and see; we're not used to drop commandos' line is getting a bit worn. If he weren't such a sweet old bastard, I'd have started raising hell then."

"Is that why you've been so tractable? I was afraid you must *really* be messed up."

"Yeah." Alicia ran her hands through her amber hair. "Okay, Tannis, let's get right down to it. Am I considered a dangerous lunatic?"

"I wouldn't go so far as to say 'dangerous,' Sarge, but there are . . . concerns. I'm taking over from Captain Okanami as of sixteen hundred today, and we'll be running the whole battery of standard diagnostics, probably with a bit of psych monitoring cranked in. I'll be able to tell you more then."

Alicia smiled a crooked smile. "You're not fooling me, you know."

"Fooling?" Tannis widened her eyes innocently.

"Whatever your tests show, they're going to figure I'm over the edge. Post-combat trauma and all that. Poor girl's probably been suppressing her grief, too, hasn't she? Hell, Tannis, it's a lot harder to prove someone's *not* loopy, and we both know it."

"Well, yes," Tannis agreed after a moment. "You always liked it straight, so I'll level with you. Uncle Arthur came out with me, and he's going to want to debrief you in person, but then you and I are Soissons-bound. Sector General's got lots more equipment, so that's where the real tests come in. On the other hand, I have Uncle Arthur's personal guarantee that I'll be your physician of record, and you know I won't let them crap on you."

"And if I don't want to go?"

"Sorry, Sarge. You've been reactivated."

"Oh, those *bastards*!" Alicia murmured, but there was a trace of amused respect in her voice.

"They can be lovable, can't they?"

"How long do you expect your tests to take after we hit Soissons?"

"As long as they take. You want a guess?" Alicia nodded, and Tannis shrugged. "Don't make any plans for a month or two, minimum."

"That long?" Alicia couldn't quite hide her dismay.

"Maybe longer. Look, Sarge, they want more than just a psych evaluation. They want *answers*, and you already told Okanami you don't know what happened or why you're alive. Okay, that means they're going to have to dig for them. I'm sorry, but that's the way it is."

"And while they're looking, the scent's going to freeze solid."

"Scent?" Tannis sat up straighter. "You in vigilante mode, Sarge?"

"Why not?" Alicia met her eyes. "Who's got a better right?"

She held her friend's eyes levelly, her own suddenly cold and hard. After moment, Tannis looked away.

"No one, I guess. But that's going to be a factor in their thinking, too, you know. They won't want you running around to do something outstandingly stupid."

"I know." Alicia made herself step back and smile. "Well, if I'm stuck, I'm stuck. And if I am, I'm glad I've got at least one friend in the enemy camp."

"That's the spirit." Tannis rose with a grin of her own. "I've got an appointment with Uncle Arthur in ten minutes—gotta go give him my own evaluation of your condition—but I'll check back when it's over. I may even have more news on your upcoming, um, itinerary."

"Thanks, Tannis." Alicia leaned back against her pillows and smiled after her friend, but the smile faded as the door closed. She sighed and looked pensively down at her hands.

<*This will not do, Little One,*> Tisiphone said sternly. <*We cannot allow these friends of yours to stand in our way.*>

<*I know. I know! Tannis will do her best for me, but she's a stone wall where her medical responsibilities are concerned.*>

<*Will she conclude you are truly mad, then?*>

<*Of course she will. That 'psychobabbler' was a load of manure, and let's face it—by her standards, I* am *buggy. And one thing the* Cadre doesn't *do is let out-of-control drop commandos run around loose. Terrible PR if they accidentally slaughter a few dozen innocent bystanders in a food-o-mat.*>

<*So.*> Mental silence hovered for a moment, broken by a soundless sigh. <*Well, Little One, in this instance I have little to offer. Once I might have spirited you out of anyone's power, but those days are gone, and friends are always harder to escape than enemies.*>

<*Don't I know it.*> Alicia wrapped herself in consideration for a long moment, thinking too quickly for Tisiphone to follow, then smiled. <*Okay. If they won't let me go, we'll just have to bust out. But not yet.*> She rubbed the tractor collar again. <*Not till we get to Soissons, I think. Nowhere to hide if we tried it here, anyway. Unless you'd care to take me back to that place where 'time has no business' of yours?*>

<*I could, of course. But we could not stay there forever, and when I released you, you would return to the exact spot you had left.*>

<*To be grabbed by whoever sees us. Hell, what if they knock down the hospital and clear out entirely? Freezing my keister in the snow in a hospital gown isn't my idea of a Good Thing.*>

<*It would seem to have drawbacks,*> Tisiphone agreed.

<*Indeedy deed. All right, it'll have to be Soissons. And if they think I'm crazy anyway, we might as well use that.*>

<*Indeed? How?*>

<*I think I'm going to become extremely buggy—in a harmless sort of way. Something I learned about the brass a long time ago, Tisiphone: give them something they think they understand, and they're happy. And happy brass tend to stay out of your way while you get on with business.*>

<*Ahhhhhhh, I see. You will deceive them into lowering their guard.*>

<*Exactly. I'm afraid I'll be talking to you—and the recorders—a lot. In the meantime, I think you and I had better figure out exactly what capabilities you still have to help out when the moment comes, don't you?*>

<*I do, indeed.*>

There was a positively gleeful note to the mental whisper, and Alicia DeVries grinned. Then she lowered her bed into a comfortable sleeping posture and smiled dreamily up at the ceiling.

"Well, Tisiphone," she said aloud, "it doesn't sound like they're going to be too reasonable. The Cadre can be that way, sometimes. In fact, this reminds me of the time Flannan O'Clery's pharmacope got buggered on Bannerman and pumped him full of endorphins. He got this glorious natural high, you see, and there was this jammed traffic control signal downtown. Now, Flannan was always a helpful soul, and he had his plasgun with him, so—"

She tucked her hands behind her head and babbled cheerfully on to Tisiphone's invisible presence . . . and the recorders.

CHAPTER THIRTY-SEVEN

The Lizards were showing off again, damn them.

Commodore James Howell gritted his teeth as the Rishathan freighter coasted towards him at five hundred kilometers per second. The Rish deeply resented their physical inability to use synth units—much less cyber-synth-links. They went to enormous lengths to avoid admitting it, but that resentment was why they insisted on overcompensating by showing humanity their panache . . . and also explained why he always met his Rish contacts well outside the Powell limit of any system body. Their drives could come closer than humanity's to a planet without destabilizing (or worse), but not by all that much, and losing one's drive during a maneuver like this one could lead to unpleasant consequences all round.

Five hundred KPS wasn't all that fast, even for intra-system speeds, but the big freighter was barely fifteen thousand kilometers clear, already visible on the visual display, however assiduously Howell might refuse to look at it, and proximity alarms began to buzz. He made himself sit quite still despite their snarls, then sighed with hidden relief as the Rishathan captain flipped her ship end-for-end, pointing her stern at his flagship. The flare of the freighter's Fasset drive (for which, of course, the Rish had their own unpronounceable name) was clear to his gravitic detectors, even though its tame black hole was aimed directly away from them. The ship slowed abruptly, then drifted to a near perfect rendezvous in just under fifty-seven seconds. Amazing what nine hundred gravities' deceleration could do.

Attitude and maneuvering thrusters flared as the Fasset drive died, nudging the freighter alongside Howell's dreadnought, and he grinned in familiar, ironic amusement. Mankind—and Rishkind, unfortunately—could out-speed light, generate pet black holes, and transmit messages scores of light-years in the blink of an eye, yet they still required thrusters the semimythical Armstrong would have recognized (in principle, at least) a thousand years before for that last, delicate step. Ridiculous—except that people still used the wheel, too.

He shook off the thought as the freighter's tractors latched onto his command and it nuzzled up against cargo bay ten, extending a personnel tube to his number four lock. He glanced around his bridge at the comfortable, nondescript civilian coveralls of his crew and thought wistfully of the uniform he had discarded with his past. The Lizards weren't much into clothing for protection's sake, but they understood its decorative uses, and their taste was, quite literally, inhuman. It would have been nice to be able to reply in kind to the no doubt upcoming assault on his optic nerves.

His synth-link whispered to him, announcing the imminent arrival of a single visitor, and he skinned off the headset and slipped it out of sight under his console. The rest of his command crew were doing the same. The Rish would know they'd done it to avoid flaunting the human ability to form direct links with their equipment, but there were civilities to be observed. Besides, hiding it all away was actually an even more effective way of calling attention to it—and one to which his visitor could take exception only with enormous loss of face. He hoped Resdyrn still commanded the freighter. She always took the con personally for the final approach, and he loved the way her fangs showed when he one-upped her one-upmanship without saying a word.

The command deck hatch hissed open, and Senior War Mother Resdyrn *niha* Turbach stepped through it.

She was impressive, even for a fully mature Rishathan matriarch. At 2.9 meters and just over three hundred and sixty-five kilos, she towered over every human on the bridge yet looked almost squat. Her incredibly gaudy carapace streamers enveloped her in a diaphanous cloud, swirling from her shoulders and assaulting the eye like some psychotic rainbow, but her face paint was sober—for a Rish. Its bilious green hue suited her temporary "merchant" persona and made a fascinating contrast with her scarlet cranial frills, and Howell wondered again if Rishathan eyes really used the same spectrum as human ones.

"Greetings, Merchant Resdyrn," he said, and listened to the translator render it into the squeaky, snarling ripples of Low Rishathan. Howell had once known an officer who could actually manage High Rishathan, but the same man could also reproduce the exact sound of an old-fashioned buzz saw hitting a nail at several thousand RPM. Howell preferred to rely upon his translator.

"Greetings, Merchant Howell," the translator bug in his right ear replied. "And greetings to your line-mother."

"And also to yours." Howell completed the formal greeting with a bow, amazed once more by how lithely that bulky figure returned it. "My daughter-officers await you," he continued. "Shall we join them?"

Resdyrn inclined her massive head, and the two of them walked into the briefing room just off the command bridge. Half a dozen humans rose as they entered, bowing welcome while Resdyrn stalked around the table to the out-sized chair at its foot.

Howell moved to the head of the table and watched her slip her short, clubbed tail comfortably through the open chairback. Despite their saurian appearance and natural body armor, the Rishatha were not remotely reptilian. They were far closer to an oviparous Terrestrial mammal, if built on a rather overpowering scale. Or, at least, the females were. In his entire career, Howell had seen exactly three Rish males, and they were runty, ratty-looking little things. Fluttery and helpless, too. No wonder the matriarchs considered "little old man" a mortal insult.

"Well, Merchant Howell," the irony of the honorific came through the translator interface quite well, "I trust you are prepared to conclude our transaction for the goods your line-mother has ordered?"

"I am, Merchant Resdyrn," he replied with matching irony and a gesture to Gregor Alexsov. His chief of staff keyed the code on a lock box and slid it to Resdyrn. The Rish lifted the lid and bared her upper canines in a human-style smile as she looked down at a prince's ransom in molecular circuitry, one of the several areas in which human technology led Rishathan.

"These are, of course, but a sample," Howell continued. "The remainder are even now being transferred to your vessel."

"My line-mother thanks you through her most humble daughter," Resdyrn replied, not sounding particularly humble, and lifted a crystalline filigree of seaweed from the box. She held it in long, agile fingers with an excessive number of knuckles and peered at it through a magnifier, then grunted the alarming sound of a Rishathan chuckle as she saw the Imperial Fleet markings on the connector chips. She laid it carefully back into its nest, closed the lid once more, and crooked a massive paw protectively over it. The gesture was revealing, Howell thought. That single box, less than a meter in length, contained enough molycircuitry to replace her freighter's entire command net, and for all her studied ease, Resdyrn was well aware of it.

"We, of course, have brought you the agreed upon cargo," she said after a moment, "but I fear my line-mother sends your mother of mothers sad tidings, as well." Howell sat straighter in his chair. "This shall be our last meeting for some time to come, Merchant Howell."

Howell swallowed a muttered curse before it touched his expression and cocked his head politely. Resdyrn raised her cranial frills in acknowledgment and touched her forehead in token of sorrow.

"Word has come from our embassy on Old Earth. The Emperor himself—" the masculine pronoun was a deliberate insult from a Rish; the fact that it was also accurate lent it a certain additional and delicious savor "—has taken an interest in this sector and dispatched his War Mother Keita hither."

"I . . . had not yet heard that, Merchant Resdyrn." Howell hoped his dismay didn't show. Keita! God, did that mean they were going to have the *Cadre* on their backs? He longed to ask but dared not expend so much face.

"We do not know Keita's mission," Resdyrn continued, taking pity on his curiosity (or, more likely, simply executing her own orders), "but there are no signs that the Cadre has been mobilized. My line-mother fears this may yet happen, however, and so must sever her links with you at least until such time as Keita departs. I hope that you will understand her reasoning."

"Of course." Howell inhaled, then shrugged, deliberately exaggerating the gesture to be sure Resdyrn noted it. "My mother of mothers will also understand, though I'm sure she will hope the severance will be brief."

"As do we, Merchant Howell. We of the Sphere hope for your success, that we may greet you as sisters in your own sphere."

"Thank you, Merchant Resdyrn." Howell managed to sound quite sincere, though no human was likely to forget the way the Rish had set the old Federation and Terran League at one another's throats.

"In that case," Resdyrn rose, ending the unexpectedly brief meeting, "I shall take my leave. I am covered in shame that it was I who must bring this message to you. May your weapons taste victory, Merchant Howell."

"My daughter-officers and I see no shame, Merchant Resdyrn, but only the faithful discharge of your line-mother's decree."

"You are kind." Resdyrn bestowed another graceful bow upon him and left. Howell made no effort to accompany her. Despite her "merchant's" role, Resdyrn *niha* Turbach remained a senior war mother of the Rishathan Sphere, and the suggestion that she could not be trusted aboard his vessel without a guard would have been an intolerable insult to her honor. This once, he was just as glad of it, too. Contingency plans or no, this little bit of news was going to bollix the works in *fine* style, and he needed to confer with his staff.

"Jays, Skipper," one member of that staff said. "Now what the bloody hell am I supposed to do?"

"Keep your suit on, Henry," Howell replied, and his long, cadaverous quartermaster leaned ostentatiously back in his chair.

"No problem—yet. But we're gonna look a bit hungry in a few months with our main supply line cut."

"Agreed, but Greg and I knew this—or something like it—might happen. I wish it had waited a while longer, but we've set up our fallbacks."

"Oh? I wish you'd told *me* about them," Commander d'Amcourt said.

"We're telling you now, aren't we? You want to lay it out, Greg?"

"Yes, Sir." Alexsov leaned slightly forward, cold eyes thawed by an atypical amusement as he met d'Amcourt's lugubrious gaze. "We've set up alternate supply lines through Wyvern. It'll be more cumbersome, because our purchase orders will have to be spread out carefully, and it was certainly convenient to have the Rish as a cutout in our logistics net, but there are advantages, too. For one thing, we can get proper spares and missile resupply direct. And we've already been dumping a lot of luxury items through Wyvern. I don't see any reason we can't fence the rest of our loot there—*they* certainly won't object."

He shrugged, and heads nodded here and there. Most Rogue Worlds were fairly respectable (by their own lights, at least), but Wyvern's government was owned outright by the descendants of the captain-owners of one of the last piratical fleets of the League Wars to go "legitimate." It bought or sold anything, no questions asked, and was equally indiscriminate in the deals it brokered. Many of its fellow Rogue Worlds might deplore its existence, yet Wyvern was too useful an interface (and too well armed) for most of them to do anything more strenuous. Which, since the Empire had both the power and the inclination to smack the hands of those who irritated it, gave Wyvern's robber-baron aristocracy a vested interest in anything that might disrupt the nascent Franconia Sector's stability.

"As for our other support—" Alexsov paused, mentioning no names or places even here, then shrugged "—this shouldn't pose any problems. Unless, of course, Keita's presence means the Cadre plans to shove its nose in."

"Exactly, and that's what worries me most," Howell agreed. He glanced at the rather fragile-looking commander seated at Alexsov's right elbow. Slim, dark-skinned Rachel Shu, Howell's staff intelligence officer, was the sole female member of his staff . . . and its most lethal. Now she shrugged.

"It worries me, too, Commodore. My sources didn't say a thing about Keita's coming clear out here, so my people don't have any idea what he's up to. On the face of it, I'm inclined to think the Rish have overreacted. They don't dare antagonize the Empire by getting caught involved in something like this, and they remember what Keita and the Cadre did to them over the Louvain business. That one blew up in their faces so spectacularly that they *still* haven't fully recovered their lost prestige, so they're pulling in their horns and getting ready to disclaim any responsibility. But I don't think my sources could have missed the signs if the Cadre were being committed on any meaningful scale."

"Then why's Keita here? Wasn't he their point for Louvain, too?"

"He was, but he's been 'point' for a lot of their ops over the years, and the Cadre's too small for him to have pulled out any major force without my people noticing it. Besides, my last reports place him in the Macedon Sector, not on Old Earth, so this looks more like a spur of the moment improvisation, and the timing's about right for it to be in response to Mathison's World. He was right next door and they banged him on out—they didn't deploy him from the capital. I suspect he's on some sort of special intelligence-gathering mission for Countess Miller. She's always preferred to get a reading through Cadre Intelligence to crosscheck on ONI and the Wasps, and Keita's always been happier in the field than an HQ slot. If he hadn't, *he'd* have the general's stars and Arbatov would be *his* exec."

"Which means we could see the Cadre yet," Rendlemann pointed out.

"Unlikely," Shu replied. "Our support structure's very well hidden and dispersed, and the Cadre's a precision instrument for application to precise targets. In fact, I'd say the Ministry of Justice was more dangerous than either the Fleet or Cadre, since it's the covert side of this whole operation that's most likely to lead the other two to us, and Justice is best equipped for getting at us from that side. As far as the Cadre's concerned, I'll start to worry when we see a major transfer of its personnel to this sector or one of its neighbors. Until that happens, Keita's just one more spook. A good one, but no more than that."

"I think you're right, Rachel," Howell said. At any rate, he certainly *hoped* she was. "We'll proceed on that basis for now, but I want you to double-check with Control ASAP."

"Yes, Sir. The next intelligence courier's due in about five days. It may already be bringing us confirmation; if it isn't, I'll send a request back by the same dispatch boat."

"All right." Howell toyed with a stylus, then glanced at Alexsov. "Is there anything else we need to look at while we're all together,

Greg?" Alexsov shook his head. "In that case, I think you and Henry might make a quick run to Wyvern to set things in motion there. Don't take along anything incriminating—we've got the liquidity to pay cash for the first orders—but sound out the locals for future marketing possibilities."

"Can do," Alexsov replied. "How soon can you leave, Henry?"

"Ummm . . . a couple of hours, I'd guess."

"Good," Howell said, "because unless I miss my guess—and unless Keita *is* going to make problems—we ought to be getting our next targeting order from Rachel's courier. I'll want you back here for the skull sessions, Greg."

"In that case, I'd better get packed." Alexsov stood, a general signal for the meeting to break up, and Howell watched his subordinates file out of the briefing room. He walked over to the small-scale system display in the corner and stood brooding down at the holographic star and its barren, lifeless planets.

Rachel was probably right, he decided. If Keita were the spearpoint of a Cadre intervention, he would have brought at least an intelligence staff with him. On the other hand, Keita was the tip of a damned spear all by himself; the rest of the weapon could always be brought in later, and that could complicate life in a major way.

He reached out, cupping a palm around the minute, silvery mote of his flagship, and sighed. Problems, problems. The life of a piratical freebooter had seemed so much simpler—and so much more lucrative—than a career with the Fleet, and the bigger objective was downright exciting. There were the minor drawbacks of having to become a mass murderer, a thief, and a traitor to his uniform, but the rewards were certainly great . . . assuming one lived to enjoy them.

He released his flagship with a heavier sigh, folding his hands behind him, and started thoughtfully towards the briefing room hatch.

How in hell, he wondered silently, had Midshipman James Howell, Imperial Fleet, Class of '28, ended up *here*?

CHAPTER THIRTY-EIGHT

"Still so eager to be up and about?"

Alicia inhaled a spray of sweat as she gasped for breath, but she welcomed the teasing malice in Lieutenant de Riebeck's voice. The physical therapist was a fellow Cadreman, without a trace of the semi-awe her drop commando reputation woke in ordinary medics. He was even remarkably impervious to the fact that she held the Banner of Terra, which was even rarer. Both of those things were refreshing, and his complete indifference to her mental state was even more so. Alicia had agitated so noisily to get out of bed that even Okanami and Tannis had finally given in, but de Riebeck had been their revenge. His sole interest lay in getting one Captain Alicia DeVries not merely ambulatory but fully reconditioned, and his was clearly an obsessive personality.

"Looking a little worn to me, Captain," he continued brightly, and cranked the treadmill's speed control up a bit. "Care for another five or six klicks? How about another five percent of grade just to make it interesting?"

Alicia moaned and collapsed over the handrails. The still-moving treadmill carried her feet from under her, and she twitched with a horridly realistic death rattle and belly flopped onto the belt. It deposited her on the floor with a thump, and she oozed out flat.

Lieutenant de Riebeck grinned, and someone applauded from the training room door. Alicia rolled over and sat up, raking sweat-sodden hair from her forehead, and saw Tannis Cateau clapping vigorously.

"I give that a nine-point-five for dramatic effect and, oh, a three-point-two for coordination." Alicia shook a fist, and Tannis chuckled. "I see Pablo is being his usual sadistic self."

"We strive to please, Major, Ma'am," de Riebeck said, smirking. Alicia laughed, and Tannis reached down to pull her to her feet.

"You know, I never thought I'd admit it, but this is one part of the Cadre I've missed," she panted, massaging her rebuilt thigh with both hands. The repaired muscles ached, but it was the good ache of exercise, and she straightened with a sigh. Despite her reactivation, she refused to cut her hair, which had escaped its clasp once more. She gathered it back up and refastened it, then scrubbed her face with a towel.

"I think I'm going to live after all, Pablo."

"Aw, shucks. Well, there's always tomorrow."

"An inspiring thought." Alicia hung the towel around her neck and turned back to Tannis. "May I assume you arrived for some reason other than to rescue me from Lieutenant de Sade?"

"Indeed I have. Uncle Arthur wants to see you."

"Oh." The humor flowed out of Alicia's voice, and her forefingers moved in slow circles, wrapping the towel-ends about them. Her success in so far avoiding Keita made her feel a bit guilty, but she really didn't want to see him. Not now, and perhaps never. He was going to bring back too many painful memories . . . and Cadre rumor credited him with telepathy, among other arcane powers. He'd always made *her* feel as if her skull were made of glass, at any rate.

"Sorry, Sarge, but he insists. And I think it's a good idea myself."

"Why?" Alicia demanded bluntly, and Tannis shrugged.

"Look, you never told me why you quit the Cadre." Remembered hurt flickered in her brown eyes, but her voice was level. "One thing I do know, though, is that whatever your reason, it wasn't just to avoid Uncle Arthur, and you've been hiding from him long enough."

She held Alicia's gaze, and Alicia heard the "and from me" as clearly as if her friend had spoken the words aloud.

"It's time you faced up to him," Tannis continued after a moment. "Whatever your reason, *he* knows you didn't 'fail' him somehow by resigning, but you're never going to feel comfortable about it till you talk to him in person. Call it absolution."

"I don't need 'absolution'!" Alicia snapped, jade eyes flashing with sudden fire, and Tannis grinned crookedly.

"Then why the sudden heat? Come on, Sarge." She hooked an arm through Alicia's. "I'm surprised he's let your debrief wait this long, so you may as well get it over with."

"You can be a real pain in the ass, Tannis."

"True, too true. Now march, Sarge."

"Can't I even clean up first?"

"Uncle Arthur knows what sweat smells like. March!"

Alicia sighed, but the steel showed under Tannis' humor, and she was right. Alicia couldn't keep pretending Keita wasn't here, however much she dreaded reliving that decision. Yet there was a reason she'd cut every contact with the Cadre—even with Tannis—and if the pain had scarred over, it was still there. Reestablishing the ties she'd cut might rip those scars away . . . and under them, she knew, the wound was bleeding still.

There was a limit to how much pain she could endure, even with Tisiphone standing between her and it and—

A heat which was rapidly becoming familiar tingled in her right arm, radiating from its contact with Tannis' left elbow, and she felt her friend's thoughts. Amusement. Pride in the way she was bouncing back from her wounds. Carefully hidden worry over the upcoming interview. A burning curiosity as to the reasons for her dread over meeting Keita and concern over their possible consequences, and under it a deeper, more persistent worry about Alicia's stability—and what to do about her if she was, in fact, *un*stable.

<Stop that!>

<Why? She is your physician, and we need this information.>

<Not from Tannis—not this way. She's also my friend.>

A mental grumble answered, but the information flow died, and she was grateful. Stealing Tannis' thoughts was a violation of her privacy and trust—almost a form of rape, even if she never felt a thing—and Alicia hated it.

Not that it hadn't been useful, she conceded. The first time Tannis had hugged her, Tisiphone had plucked a disturbing suspicion from the major's mind. Alicia's monologues had gotten just a bit too enthusiastic, and Tannis knew her too well.

Forewarned, Alicia had tapered off and allowed her manufactured dialogues to run down as if she were tiring of the game. Tannis had written them off as a sarcastic response to the people who mistrusted her sanity, and thereafter Alicia had restricted herself to occasional verbal responses to actual comments from Tisiphone. That worked much better, for they were spontaneous, fragmentary, and enigmatic yet consistent—clearly not something manufactured out of whole cloth for the sole benefit of eavesdroppers—and their genuineness had turned Tannis' thoughts in the desired direction.

Alicia hated deceiving her friend, but she *was* having those conversations. It was always possible she truly was mad—a possibility she would almost prefer, at times—and if she wasn't, she certainly wasn't responsible for Tannis' misinterpretations of them.

She squared her shoulders, tucked the ends of the towel into the neck of her sweat shirt, and walked down the hallway at her friend's side.

Tisiphone watched through her host's eyes as they marched along the corridor. The past few weeks had been the oddest of her long life, a strange combination of impatient waiting and discovery, and she wasn't certain she had enjoyed them.

She and Alicia had learned much about her own current abilities. She could still pluck thoughts from mortal minds, but only when her host brought those other mortals into physical contact. She could still hasten physical healing, as well, yet what had once been "miracles" were routine to the medical arts man had attained. There was little she could do to speed what the physicians were already accomplishing, and so she had restricted herself to holding pain and discomfort within useful limits and insuring her host's sleep without medication or one of the peculiar somatic units. Tisiphone hated the somatic units. They might sweep Alicia into slumber through her receptors, but sleep was a stranger to Tisiphone. For her, the somatic units' soothing waves were a droning, scarcely endurable static.

She and Alicia had also determined to their satisfaction that she still could blur mortals' senses, even without physical contact.

Their technology, unfortunately, was something else again, and that experiment had almost ended in disaster. The nurse had *known* the bed was empty, but her medical scanners had insisted it was occupied, and she'd been briefed like all the medical staff on Alicia's inexplicable history. Not surprisingly, the young woman had panicked and turned to run, and only the testing of another ability had saved the situation. Tisiphone could no longer beguile and control mortal minds, but she could fog and befuddle them. Actually taking memories from them might have become impossible, but she had blurred the recollection into a sort of fanciful daydream, and that had been just as good—this time.

Their experiments had combined dismay and excitement in almost equal measure, yet neither Tisiphone's own sense of discovery and rediscovery nor Alicia's amazement at what she still could accomplish had been sufficient to banish her boredom. She was a being of fire and passion, the hunger and destruction of her triumvirate of selves. Alecto had been the methodical one, the inescapable stalker patient as the stones themselves, and Megaira had been the thinker who analyzed and pondered with a mind of ice and steel. Tisiphone was the weapon, unleashed only when her targets had been clearly identified, her objectives precisely defined. Now she could not even know who her targets were, much less where to find them, and she felt . . . lost. Ignorance added to her sense of frustration, for if she had no doubt of her ultimate success, she was unused to delays and puzzles. It had turned her surly and snappish with her host (not, she admitted privately, an unusual state for such as she) until a fresh revelation diverted them both.

Tisiphone had discovered computers. More to the point, she had encountered the processors built into Alicia's augmentation, and had she been the sort of being who possessed eyes, they would have opened wide in surprise.

The data storage of Alicia's processors was little more than a few dozen terrabytes, for bio-implants simply couldn't rival the memories of full-sized units, yet they were the first computers Tisiphone had ever met, and she'd been amazed by how easy they were to access. It had taken no effort at all, for virtually all human computers were designed and programmed for neural linkage. The same technique which slipped into a mortal's thoughts through his nerves and brain worked just as well with them, and the vistas that opened were dazzling.

It was almost like finding the ghost of one of her sister selves. A weak and pallid revenant, without the rich awareness which had textured that forever-lost link, yet one which expanded her own abilities many-fold. Tisiphone had only the vaguest grasp of what Alicia called "programming" or "machine language," but those concepts were immaterial to her. A being crafted to interface with human minds had no use or need for such things; anything structured to link with those same minds became an extension of them and so an instinctive part of herself.

She had scared Alicia half to death, and felt uncharacteristically penitent for it afterward, the first time she activated her host's main processor and walked her body across the room without consulting her. Their security codes meant nothing to Tisiphone, and she unlocked them effortlessly, exploring the labyrinthine marvels of logic trees and data flows with sheer delight. Their molycirc wonders had become a vast, marvelous toy, and she flowed through them like the wind, recognizing the way in which she might use them, in an emergency, as both capacitor and amplifier. They restored something she had lost, restored a bit of what she once had been, and she'd sensed Alicia's amusement as she chattered away about her finds.

Yet it was past time for them to be about their mission, and she wondered if Alicia's meeting with Sir Arthur Keita would bring the moment closer or send it receding even further into the future.

Alicia's spine stiffened against her will as she stepped into the sparsely appointed conference room. A small, spruce man in the crimson tunic and blue trousers of the Ministry of Justice's uniformed branches stood looking out a window. He didn't turn as she and Tannis entered, and she was just as happy. Her eyes were on the square, powerful man seated at the table.

He still refused to wear his own ribbons, she noted. Well, no one was likely to pester him about proper uniform. She came to attention before him, saluted, and stood staring six centimeters over his head.

"Captain Alicia DeVries, reporting as ordered, Sir!" she barked, and Sir Arthur studied her calmly for several seconds.

"Cut the kay-det crap, Alley," he rumbled then, in the gravel-crusher voice she remembered so well, and her lips quirked involuntarily. Her eyes met his. He smiled. It was a small smile, but a real one, easing a bit—a bit—of the tightness in her chest.

"Yes, Uncle Arthur," she said.

The shoulders of the man looking out the window twitched. He turned just a tad quickly, and her lips quirked again at his reaction to her *lese majeste*. So he hadn't known how the troops referred to Keita, had he?

"That's better." Keita pointed at a chair. "Sit."

She obeyed without comment, clasping her hands loosely in her lap, and returned his searching gaze. He hadn't changed much over the past five years. He never did.

"It's good to see you again," he resumed after a moment. "I wish it could be under different circumstances, but—"

A raised hand tipped, as if pouring something from a cupped palm. She nodded, but her eyes burned with sudden memory. Not of Mathison's World, but of another time, after Shallingsport, when only nine of them had come back, and Tannis had still hovered between life and death.

He'd known the uselessness of words then, too.

"I know I promised we'd never reactivate you," he continued, "but it wasn't my decision."

She nodded again. She'd known that, for if Sir Arthur Keita seldom gave his word, that was only because he never broke it.

"However," he went on, "we're both here now, and I've postponed this debrief as long as I could. The relief force pulls out for Soissons day after tomorrow; I'll have to make my report—and my recommendations—to Governor Treadwell and Countess Miller when we arrive, and I won't do that without speaking personally to you first. Fair?"

"Fair." Alicia's contralto was deeper than usual, but her eyes were steady, and it was his turn to nod.

"I've already viewed your statement to Colonel McIlhenny, so I've got a pretty fair notion of what happened in the fire fight. It's what happened after it that bothers me. Are you prepared to tell me more about it now?"

The deep voice was unusually gentle, and Alicia felt an almost unbearable temptation to tell him everything. Every single impossible word. If anyone in the galaxy would have believed her it was Uncle Arthur. Unfortunately, no one *could* believe her, not even him, and they weren't alone. Her eyes flipped to the Justice man, and an eyebrow arched.

"Inspector Ferhat Ben Belkassem, Intelligence Branch," Keita said. "You may speak freely in front of him."

"In front of a *spook*?" Alicia's eyes snapped back to Keita's face, suddenly hard, and the temptation to openness faded.

"In case you've forgotten, *I'm* something of a spook," he replied quietly.

"No, Sir, I haven't forgotten. And, Sir, I respectfully decline to be debriefed by intelligence personnel." It came out clipped and even colder than she'd intended, and Ben Belkassem's eyebrows rose in surprise.

Keita sighed, but he didn't retreat. His eyes bored into her across the table, and there was no yield in his voice.

"That isn't an option, Alley. You're going to have to talk to me."

"Sir, I decline."

"Oh, come on, Alley! You've already spoken to McIlhenny!"

"I have, Sir, when under the impression that he remained a combat branch officer. And—" her voice turned even colder "—Colonel McIlhenny is neither Cadre nor a representative of the Ministry of Justice. As such, he may in fact be an honorable man."

She felt Tannis flinch behind her, but her friend held her tongue, and Ben Belkassem stepped back half a pace. It wasn't a retreat; he was simply giving her room, declaring his neutrality in whatever lay between her and Keita.

The brigadier leaned back and pinched the bridge of his nose.

"You can't decline, Alley. This isn't like last time." She sat stonily silent, and his face hardened. "Allow me to correct myself. In one respect, this is *exactly* like last time: you can damned well end up in the stockade waiting to face a court if you push it."

"Sir, I respectful—"

"Hold it." He interrupted her in mid-word, before she could dig in any more deeply, then shook his head. "You always were a stubborn woman, Alley. But this isn't a case of a captain breaking a colonel around the edges—" Ben Belkassem's eyes widened fractionally at that, and Alicia felt Tannis' sudden stiffness at her back "—and I don't have the latitude to allow you to refuse to talk to me." He raised a palm as her eyes flared hot. "You had a right to every damned thing you did after Louvain. I said so then, and I say so now, but this isn't then, and the questions aren't coming just from me. Countess Miller has personally charged me with uncovering the truth."

His eyes drilled into hers, and she sat back in her chair. He meant it. If it had been only him, he might have let her off, let her walk away from the past and all its anguish yet again. But he had his orders, and orders were something he took very seriously, indeed.

"Excuse me, Sir Arthur." Ben Belkassem raised one placating hand as he spoke. "If my presence is the problem, I will willingly withdraw."

"No, Inspector, you won't." Keita's voice was frosty. "You are part of this operation, and I will value your input. Alley?"

"Sir, I can't. It— I promised the *Company*, Sir." Her own sudden hoarseness surprised her, and a tear glistened. She felt Tisiphone's surprise at the surge of raw, wounded emotion, then relaxed minutely as the Fury slipped another pane of that mysterious glass between her and the anguish. She drew a deep breath, meeting Keita's eyes pleadingly but with determination. "You *know* why . . . and you understand about promises, Sir."

"I do," Keita didn't wince, though his voice gave the impression he had, "but I have no choice. I was at Shallingsport, and Louvain. And I was there at Sligo Palace. You're right—I *do* understand why you feel that way. But I have no choice."

"Understand?" Alicia's voice cracked. She swallowed, but she couldn't stop. Despite all Tisiphone could do, an old, old agony drove her, and her eyes were stark with betrayal. "If you do, then how can you ask this of me? We went in with a company, Sir—a *company!*—and came out with half a squad!"

"I know."

"Yes, and you know *why*, too, Sir! You know why that son of a bitch screwed our mission brief to hell, and you know what came of it, and you *still* want me to talk to a spook?!"

Her eyes were hard, harder than Sir Arthur Kieta had ever seen them, and she half-crouched forward in her chair, hands like talons on its armrests as she glared at him.

"Alley. Alley!" Alicia's augmentation crackled with prep signals as emotion jangled through her, and Tannis' hands massaged her shoulders, trying to relax her tension. "They did their best, Sarge." Tannis' voice was soft. "Intelligence screws up sometimes. It *happens*, Alley."

"Not like this," Alicia grated. "Not like this time, does it, Uncle Arthur?"

Her eyes were jade flint, challenging his, and he inhaled deeply.

"No, Captain. Not like this," he said at last, quietly, and looked over her head at Tannis. "Did Alley ever discuss this with you, Major?"

"No, Sir." Tannis sounded confused, Alicia thought, and no wonder.

"No. No, of course not," he sighed, and turned his eyes back to Alicia. "Forgive me. You promised you wouldn't, didn't you?"

She stared back, face like marble, and he pursed his lips in thought, then nodded slowly.

"Perhaps it's time someone did, Tannis." He gestured at the chair beside Alicia and waited until the Cadrewoman sat. "All right. You heard there was an, um, flap when Alicia resigned?" Tannis nodded. "Did you happen to know the *nature* of that 'flap'?"

"No, Sir." Tannis looked at Alicia for a moment. "I always wondered. There were all kinds of rumors, of course, but none of them ever made sense to me. There was talk that she'd resigned to avoid a court-martial, but I knew that was bogus. I couldn't imagine *Alley* doing anything that would draw a court! The whole idea was ridiculous! But I never heard anything else that did make sense, and . . . she wasn't talking to us anymore." She looked at Alicia again, her eyes glistening. "I don't think anyone in the Cadre ever knew what really happened."

"I'll be damned. I never thought the cover-up would hold."

Keita pinched the bridge of his nose again, shaking his head wearily, then continued in a flat, level voice.

"Alley assaulted a superior officer, Tannis." Tannis' brown eyes widened in disbelief, and he nodded, meeting her gaze, not Alicia's. "That officer was Colonel Wadislaw Watts," he continued, "and she didn't just 'strike' him. She hospitalized him in critical condition.

In fact, it was, by her own subsequent admission, her intent to kill him, and she damned nearly did."

Tannis gasped and turned to stare at her friend, but Alicia looked straight ahead, eyes stony, showing her only her profile, while Keita continued in that same flat, steady voice.

"Precisely. You and I know, Tannis, that the Cadre isn't perfect, whatever the Empire as a whole may believe. We make mistakes. Not often, perhaps, but we make them, and when we do, they can have . . . major consequences. Like Shallingsport."

"*Mistakes!*" Alicia hissed like a curse, then caught herself and pressed her lips together. Keita didn't even frown. He simply went on speaking to Tannis as if they were the only people in the room.

"Alley's right," he told her. "It wasn't a mistake that killed ninety-seven percent of your company at Shallingsport. It was a crime, because those casualties—" he laid his palms on the tabletop, as if for balance "—were completely avoidable. Captain Watts knew *exactly* what was waiting for you down there, Tannis. The rest of us didn't, but he did."

Cateau's face was white, twisted with disbelief and anguish, and Keita folded his hands together and frowned down at them.

"He deliberately sent you into that ambush . . . and he thought he could get away with it, hide it," he said softly. "In fact, he very nearly did."

"But . . . but *why*, Sir?"

"For money. And, in Shallingsport's case, out of fear, too, I suppose. The . . . foreign power actually behind the Shallingsport terrorists had suborned him on his very first deployment out of the Academy. He'd been feeding them information for years before the raid, and soaking away credits in a coded Quarn account on Rachharthak, and he'd been very, very clever. He'd been through several routine security checks and three regular five-year close scrutinies, and we'd never even suspected that they'd turned him. But his employers had kept records of every payment they'd ever made him, and when Shallingsport came up, they informed him that he could either cook his intelligence analysis to guarantee a blood bath that ended in failure, or be exposed by them."

"You're saying one of our own *people* set us up?" Tannis whispered.

"That's exactly what I'm saying," Keita said bluntly, "and only two things kept Watts from succeeding: the courage and determination of your company . . . and the leadership of Staff Sergeant Alicia DeVries."

Alicia glared at him, hands like claws in her lap under the table edge, and horror boiled behind her eyes as the scars she'd spent five years building were ripped away and she saw it all again. Captain Alwyn and Lieutenant Strassmann dead in the drop. Lieutenant Masolle dying even as she ordered the break-out from the LZ. Pamela Yussuf and her people buying that break-out with their lives. And then that endless, nightmare cross-country journey, while people—friends—were picked off, blown apart, incinerated in gouts of plasma or shattered by tungsten penetrators. The wounded they had no choice but to abandon.

And then the break-in to the hostages. Obaseki Osayaba and Astrid Nordbø's icons vanishing from her HUD. Brian Oselli, throwing himself in front of the plasma cannon. Samantha Moyano firing, firing, until the plasma bolt incinerated her. Thomas Kiely breaking the counterattack's back with his own death. Tannis screaming her warning and shooting the terrorists off Alicia's back even as point-blank small arms battered her own armor and she took two white-hot tungsten penetrators. The terror and blood and smoke and stink as somehow they held they held they *held* until the Marine shuttles came down like the hands of God to pluck them out of Hell while she and Kuromachi Chiyeko ripped at Tannis' armor and the medic restarted her heart twice. . . .

It was impossible. She knew that now. They couldn't have done it—*no one* could have done it—but they had. They'd done it because they were the best. Because they were the Cadre, the chosen samurai of the Empire. Because it was their duty. Because she'd been, by God, too stupid to know they couldn't . . . and because they'd been all that stood between six hundred civilians and death.

"The plan failed," Keita's quiet voice cut through the surreal flashes of hideous memory, "because of you people, but we didn't know how the intelligence had gone so horribly wrong. We looked—I assure you we looked—but we never found the answers. And then, five years later, on Louvain, Captain DeVries captured a dying Rish-athan War Mother. And because she was dying and

Alley had spared her line-daughters' lives, she repaid her honor debt."

More memories wracked Alicia, and Tisiphone rushed to harvest their rage, gathering it up and storing its fiery strength as Alicia remembered the dying Rish. Remembered the beautiful golden eyes blazing in that hideous face as Shernsiya discovered she was *that* DeVries and bestowed the priceless, poisonous gift in the name of honor.

"There was no proof, no record, only the word of a dying Rish, but Alley knew it was true. And because she had no proof, she returned to the command ship, found Colonel Wadislaw Watts, and challenged him with what she'd learned. He panicked and tried to kill her, confirming his guilt, and she shattered his skull, his jaw, both cheekbones, his ribs, his wrist, and his elbow, ruptured his spleen, crushed both testicles, broke three vertebra, seriously damaged the left ventricle of his heart, and punctured his right lung in four places with bone fragments before they could pull her off him."

The room was very quiet, and Alicia heard her own harsh breathing while echoes of savagery burned in her nerves. Only her hate had spared Watts's life. Only her need to make him *feel* it, to return just a taste of what her people had suffered. If only she'd kept control of herself! One clean blow—just one!—would have left the medics nothing to save.

"And that," Keita said sadly, "was when the cover-up began. Baron Yuroba was Minister of War then, and he was desperate to avoid any sort of scandal, so the reason for Alley's attack was hushed up and she was given her choice: keep her mouth shut forever about the truth, or face trial for assaulting a superior officer. No scandal. No messy media circus and gory court-martial to befoul the honor we'd won at Louvain and Shallingsport or provoke a fresh 'incident' with the Rish. Watts turned Crown's evidence, and they handed him over to Justice, who—in return for his secret testimony and assistance in breaking the Rishathan espionage net which had run him—amnestied him for his crimes."

Tears trickled down Tannis' face, and her eyes were sick.

"And Alley accepted the order to keep silent," Keita said, his voice very quiet. "She accepted the order because it came from the Emperor himself, but she couldn't accept the betrayal. That's why she resigned, the reason she walked away from the Cadre and everything connected to it. And it's why she won't talk to 'spooks,' Tannis. Not even to me. She doesn't trust us."

"I trust *you*, Uncle Arthur," Alicia said very quietly. "I know how you fought it—and I know you were the one who forced them to accept my resignation instead of pushing through with that damned court-martial threat of Yuroba's. The only one who believed I'd really keep silent."

"That's crap, Alley," Sir Arthur replied. "I told you then—he wouldn't have dared push it in the end."

"Maybe. But it doesn't change anything. I would have forgiven them anything but letting Watts live—letting him keep his *honor* by purging the record. My people deserved better than that."

"They did, and I couldn't give it to them. We live in an imperfect universe, and all we can do is the best we can. But that's the real reason they sent me clear out here in person. Countess Miller's read the sealed records. She knows how you feel and why, but she's been instructed by His Majesty himself to discover how you managed to survive and how you evaded all of our sensors. I am directed to inform you that this matter has been given Crown priority, that I speak with the Emperor's own voice, as your personal liege. No doubt the intent is to duplicate the capability in other personnel, but there's also an element of fear. The unknown has that effect even today, and they're determined to get to the bottom of it. I would . . . greatly prefer to be able to explain it to them myself, Alley."

His eyes were almost pleading, and she looked away. He still wanted to shield her. Wanted to protect her from those less wary of her wounds or what their questions might cost her. But what could she do? If she told him the absolute, literal truth, he'd never believe her.

<*Little One,*> the voice in her mind was soft, <*I like this man. He has the taste of honor.*>

<*He* is *honor,*> she replied bitterly. <*That's why they gave him this assignment. Because he'll do what his oath to the Emperor demands, however much he may hate himself for it.*>

<*What will you tell him?*>

<*I don't want to lie to him—I don't even know if I could make myself try, and he'd spot it in a minute if I did.*>

<*Then do not,*> Tisiphone suggested. <*Tell him what he asks.*>

<*Are you out of your mind?! He'll think I'm crazy!*>

<*Precisely.*>

Alicia blinked. She actually hadn't considered this possibility when she decided to maintain her semblance of insanity. She should have realized she would be forced to confront the Cadre and her past directly, but the old wound had been too deep for her to consider all its implications, and she'd never guessed the Emperor himself might insist on probing the matter.

But suppose she told Uncle Arthur the whole story? He had a built-in lie detector no hardware could match. He'd know she was telling the truth . . . as she believed it, at any rate. What would he do with her then?

What his orders dictated, of course. He'd return her to Soissons for further investigation—and, no doubt, treatment for her insanity. That might even be good, since the sector capital would be a much more practical base from which to begin her own search for the pirates. But because he would know she was far, far over the edge, he'd also do what The Book demanded and shut down her augmentation through Tannis' overrides.

<*And if he does?*> Tisiphone had followed her internal debate. <*We have already determined I can reactivate it any time I choose, and would it not aid our escape if they believe your augmentation is useless?*>

Alicia looked back up and met Keita's pain-filled gaze. She couldn't tell them everything. Even if they didn't believe in Tisiphone, they might be alarmed enough to take precautions against the Fury's ability to read thoughts and handle her augmentation. But if she cut off, say, with the day Tannis had arrived, before they'd begun their experiments . . .

"All right, Uncle Arthur," she sighed. "You won't believe me, but I'll tell you exactly where I was and how I got there."

CHAPTER THIRTY-NINE

<*I think you are in trouble, Little One,*> Tisiphone observed as Tannis Cateau's left leg scythed viciously for Alicia's ankles.

She levitated above its arc, and her own foot lashed out. Tannis never saw it coming, but the moves and counters, action and reaction, were part of them both, as automatic as sneezing on dust. She fell away from the kick, robbing it of its power, and slammed a wrist up under Alicia's ankle. Alicia fell to the mat as Tannis landed on her own shoulder blades and flowed into a backward somersault. She tucked and rolled until her toes touched the mat and dug in—then straightened her knees explosively and catapulted back toward Alicia in a ferocious charge. Alicia had rolled sideways and bounced up herself, but she was still off-center when Tannis reached her. Arms snaked about one another, hands flashed and parried in a flickering blur, and then Tannis was leaning forward, one leg bent, the other in full extension, while Alicia cartwheeled through the air with a squawk of dismay. She hit the mat with a mighty thud, flat on her belly and tried to roll upright, only to grunt in anguish as a knee drove into her spine, a hand cupped the back of her head, and a forearm of iron pressed into her throat.

"How about it, Sarge?" Tannis panted in a disgustingly pleased tone.

<*Yes, Little One,*> Tisiphone asked interestedly, <*how about it?*>

<*Oh, shut up!*> Alicia snapped back, and went limp with a groan.

"Uncle," she said.

"Damn, that feels good." Tannis' grin sparkled, and she rose, then leaned forward to help Alicia to her feet.

"For one of us," Alicia muttered, massaging the small of her back cautiously. She and Tannis wore light protective gear and sparring mittens—no mere precaution but a necessity when drop commandos practiced full-contact—but every bone and sinew ached.

"Out of shape, that's your problem," Tannis jibed. "You used to take me three falls out of five, and now you're letting a pill-pusher throw you around the salle? Dear me, what*ever* would Sergeant Delacroix say?"

"Nothing. He'd just take both us uppity bitches round to the advanced class and lay us out cold."

"Ah, for the good old days!" Tannis sighed, and Alicia chuckled. Learning to do that again hadn't been easy. The last few weeks had been bad, not shattering but drably depressing, for her senses were dull and dead, deprived of the needle-sharp acuity of her sensory boosters. Those boosters had been a part of her for so long she felt maimed without them.

She knew her friend had shut down her own augmentation to make their sparring even. Not, she admitted, with another groan, that Tannis any longer needed the edge her hardware might have given her. She stood barely one hundred sixty-five centimeters to Alicia's own one-eighty-three, but her home world boasted a gravity thirty percent greater than Earth's, and she'd spent the last five years keeping her edge in workouts just like this one. Alicia hadn't. In fact, the mind boggled at how any of Mathison's citizenry would have reacted to an invitation to an all-out bout.

She got herself fully upright and pushed her non-reg bangs out of her eyes, knowing she looked a wreck and wondering where the vid sensors were. All her military rights had been scrupulously observed, and Keita himself, as regs prescribed, had formally notified her (not without an unusual, wooden embarrassment) that she would be kept under observation at all times, even in the head. She was carried on the sick list, and—technically—she wasn't a prisoner, which gave her full run of the transport, but they couldn't take a chance on her vanishing again. And, if she did, they wanted a complete readout with every instrument they had on precisely how she'd managed it.

Which was an excruciatingly polite way of saying they couldn't let her run around unwatched when they were no longer confident she could count to twenty with her shoes on.

As much as she'd expected—and, yes, worked for it—it hurt, and it had wounded more than her alone. Keita could have let Tannis explain it all to her as her physician if he weren't such an honorable old stick . . . and if he hadn't known how distressed Tannis already was over deactivating her augmentation. All of her processors had been shut down, and her pharmacope, and her Alpha and Gamma receptors, as well. He'd made an exception for her Beta receptor, so she could still at least directly access the computers for information and entertainment, and he'd stood beside her in sickbay, offering her his support and acknowledging his personal responsibility for the decision. He'd looked so unhappy *she'd* wanted to comfort *him*.

Of course, he didn't know Tisiphone had run her own tests since and demonstrated that the "unbreakable" reactivation codes were as effective as so much smoke against her.

"'Nother fall, Sarge?" Cateau inquired lazily. Alicia backed away with a shudder that was only half-feigned, but the glint in those brown eyes was a great relief. She'd worried over Tannis' reaction to the truth about Shallingsport, yet she'd weathered the news well. And while she might be throwing herself into this sparring just a bit more enthusiastically to hide from it, Tannis' real motive—and the real reason for Tisiphone's teasing, though the Fury would never admit it—was to take Alicia's mind off *her* problems. Not that knowing made bruises feel any better.

"Between you and Pablo, I'll be back in sickbay by the time we hit Soissons. Damn it, woman! I've only been back in shape for this for a week! Give me a break, will you?"

"Which vertebra?" Tannis purred, then collapsed in most unprofessional giggles at Alicia's expression. "Sorry," she gasped. "Sorry, Sarge! It's just that I'm enjoying being the one kicking *your* tail for a change!"

"Oh?" Alicia gave her a sidelong, measuring glance, then curled her lip in a vulpine smile. "Why, that's very wise of you, Major. It's two more weeks to Soissons, after all." Bared teeth glinted pearl-white at her friend. "Care for a little side bet on who's going to be kicking whose tail by the time we get there, Ma'am?"

* * *

Inspector Ben Belkassem sipped coffee and slid the folder of record chips aside. The ventilators sucked a rope of fragrance away from Sir Arthur's pipe, and he sniffed appreciatively, but his face was serious.

"She seems so convinced I sometimes find myself believing it," he said at last, and Keita grunted agreement. "There don't seem to be any loose ends, either. It's all internally consistent, however bizarre it sounds."

"That's what worries me," Keita admitted. "She sounds convincing because she believes it—I knew that even before she went under the verifier. There's absolutely no question in her mind, no doubts, and it's not like Alicia to accept things unquestioningly. She wouldn't, unless there really were something 'speaking to her,' so either she's truly broken down into some sort of multiple personality disorder, or else some external force has convinced her of the complete accuracy of everything she's told us."

Ben Belkassem straightened in his chair, eyebrows rising.

"Are you seriously suggesting that there actually *is* something else, some sort of entity or puppeteer, living inside her head, Sir Arthur?"

"There's certainly *an* entity, even if it's a product of her own delusions." Keita busied himself relighting his pipe. "And *she* certainly believes it's a foreign one."

"Granted, but surely it's far more probable that she's slipped into some kind of delusionary pattern. My understanding from Major Cateau is that this high degree of internal consistency and absolute self-belief is normal in such cases, and Captain DeVries has certainly been through more than enough to produce a breakdown. I had no idea how traumatic her military service had been, but when you add that to the brutal way her family was massacred and her own wounds . . ."

His voice trailed off, and he shrugged.

"Um." Keita got his pipe drawing and squinted through its smoke. "How much do you know about Cadre selection criteria, Inspector?"

"Very little, other than that they're quite rigorous and demanding."

"Not surprising, I suppose. Still, you do know the Cadre is the only arm of the military whose strength is limited by Senate statute, correct?"

"Of course. And, with all due respect, it's not hard to understand why, given that the Cadre answers directly to the Emperor in his own person. Everyone knows you're a *corps d'elite*, but you're also the Emperor's personal liegemen, and he has enough power without giving him that big a stick."

"I won't disagree with you, Inspector." Keita chuckled around his pipe stem as Ben Belkassem's right eyebrow curved politely. "Every emperor since Terrence the First has known the Empire's stability ultimately depends on the balance of its dynamic tensions. There has to be a centralized authority, but when unchecked power becomes too concentrated in one body or clique you've got real trouble. You may survive for a generation or two, but eventually the inheritors of that concentration turn out to be incompetents or self-serving careerists—or both—and the whole system goes into the toilet. A sufficient outside threat may slow the process, but the gradual destruction is inevitable. However, I wasn't referring to concerns over praetorianism on our part. What I meant to point out is that although the Imperial Cadre is authorized a strength of forty thousand active-duty personnel, no emperor has *ever* recruited the Cadre up to its full allowable strength."

"No?" Ben Belkassem watched Keita over the rim of his coffee cup.

"No. Keeping us small keeps us aware of our 'elite' status, of course, and maintains a sort of familial relationship among us, but there are more mundane reasons. Just better than four out of every five Cadremen are drop commandos; the rest are basically their support structure, and by the time you allow for augmentation, training, combat armor, and weaponry, you could just about buy a corvette for what a drop commando costs. There are senators who suggest we ought to do just that, too. Unfortunately, you couldn't use that same corvette to take out a bunch of terrorists without killing their hostages or stage a reconnaissance raid on a Rishathan planetary HQ, though some of the old codgers—" he used the term "codger" totally unselfconsciously, Ben Belkassem noted wryly, despite his own age "—always seem to have trouble grasping that.

"But even cost isn't the real limiting factor. To put it simply, Inspector, the supply of potential drop commandos is extremely finite because they require inborn qualities which are very, very rare in combination.

"First, they have to be not only synth-link capable, but able to tolerate and master an extremely sophisticated augmentation package. Secondly, they must possess extraordinary physical capabilities—reaction time, coordination, strength, endurance, and other physiological requirements, some classified, that I won't go into. Many of those can be learned or developed, but at least the potential for them must exist from the start. But third, and most important of all in a sense, are the psychological and motivational requirements."

Keita fell silent for a brooding moment, then continued thoughtfully.

"That isn't unique to the Cadre. A thousand years ago, when chem-fuel rockets were still the ultimate weapon on Old Earth, navies faced similar problems when choosing strategic submarine commanders. They needed people sufficiently stable to be trusted with independent command of such firepower, yet for their military posture to be credible, those same stable people had to be capable of actually firing those weapons if the moment came.

"You see the problem?" He shot Ben Belkassem a sharp glance. "A nuclear submarine, for its time, was every bit as complex as anything we have today. They had to find people with the same intelligence we need in a starship commander, which meant they exactly understood the consequences if their weapons were ever used, and those same extremely bright people had to be stable enough to live with that knowledge yet able to face and accept the possibility of pushing the button if their duty required it."

He paused, waiting until the inspector nodded in understanding.

"Well, we've got the same problem, if on a rather less comprehensive scale. That's why we select our people for certain specific mental qualities and then enhance and strengthen them throughout their training and service.

"You know what Alicia did, but have you really reflected on the odds? She went in against twenty-five men in a free-flow tac link through their helmet coms, all in light armor, armed with combat rifles, side arms, and grenades, who only had to get one pilot and a weaponeer into their shuttle to kill her. Her sole preengagement intelligence consisted of her own last-minute reconnaissance; she was armed only with a civilian rifle and survival knife; and she killed all of them. Of course, she had surprise on her side, and her rifle was an unusually powerful weapon, but in my considered opinion, Inspector, she would have gotten all of them even if she'd been unarmed at the start."

Ben Belkassem made a noise of polite disbelief, and Keita grinned. It wasn't a pleasant expression.

"You might consider what she did at Shallingsport, Inspector," he suggested softly. "I don't say she'd've done it the same way. Most likely, she would have taken out one man first and appropriated his weapons to go after the others, but she *would* have gotten them. Admittedly, Alicia DeVries is outstanding, even by the Cadre's standards—"

He paused and cocked his head as if in thought, then shrugged.

"I suppose that sounds arrogant, but it's true, and a very real part of the Cadre's mystique. A drop commando knows he's the best. There's no question in his mind. He wouldn't be there unless he wanted to prove he can hack it in the toughest, most challenging and dangerous job the Empire offers. He's there to serve, but that need to meet any challenge with the best, as one *of* the best, is essential to his makeup, or he'd never be accepted.

"Yet at the same time, he has to recognize that what he does—the purpose for which he exists—is a horrible one. However much it demands in courage and self-sacrifice, however deeply it contributes to the safety and well-being of others, he's a killer. A drop commando is trained to kill without hesitation when killing is required, to use his weapons and skills as naturally as a wolf uses his teeth, but he also has to be aware that killing is an ugly, hideous thing. One of our ancient ancestral organizations put it very well indeed: the Cadre does a lot of things we wish *no one* had to do.

"And, perhaps even more importantly, drop commandos don't know how to quit. There are some people like that in any combat outfit. They're the ones at the sharp end of the stick, the ones who come through when the going gets worst, and there are seldom enough of them. They're self-motivated—the rare ones who carry the bulk of the outfit with them by example or by kicking them in the ass when they're so tired and scared and hungry all they want to do is die. But in the Cadre, they're the norm, not the exception. You can kill a drop commando, but that's the *only* way to stop one, and that absolute inability to quit is another fundamental requirement for the Cadre.

"And when you take that kind of pride, killer instinct, and utter tenacity and combine it with the capabilities our people have after they've been augmented and trained, you'd better make *damned* sure they're stable, rational people. They have to be warriors, not murderers. We turn them into something that scares the average civilian shitless, but they have to be people you can trust to know when killing *isn't* required—who can do what they must without becoming callous or, even worse, learning to enjoy it—which is why our psych requirements are twice as high as the Fleet Academy's. That makes the Cadre an extraordinary body of men and women by any measure. The Empire has over eighteen hundred inhabited worlds, Inspector, with an average population of something like a billion, and we still can't find forty thousand people we'll accept as drop commandos. Think about that. Oh, they're not really superhuman, and some of them do break, but Alicia DeVries, who tested extraordinarily high even for the Cadre, is one of the last people in the galaxy I would believe could do that."

"But surely it isn't impossible," Ben Belkassem suggested gently.

"Obviously not, since that's precisely what she seems to have done. But that's why I'm so bothered by it. None of this makes sense. I don't understand how she did what she did, and I'd have said Alley DeVries would die before she broke under any conceivable strain. And you're right about how convincing she is, how rational she seems in every other way." Keita turned his coffee cup in his hands, staring down into it with eyes as dark with worry over someone for whom he cared deeply as with puzzlement. "I almost *want* to believe she's succumbed to some form of external influence or control."

"Mind control? Brainwashing? Some sort of conditioning?"

"I don't know, damn it!" Keita set down his cup so hard coffee splashed. "But I can't get that damned EEG out of my mind."

"I thought that had cleared up," the inspector said in surprise.

"It has. Major Cateau confirmed its presence during her initial examination, but then the cursed thing just vanished in the middle of a scan. It's gone, all right, and Alicia's current EEG exactly matches the one in her medical jacket, but if it was related to her delusion, why is she still insisting this 'Tisiphone' entity is still present after the EEG's faded out? And where did it come from in the first place? Neither Tannis nor any of her other people have ever seen anything like it."

"Like what?"

The inspector's eyes were fascinated, and Keita shrugged.

"I don't know," he repeated. "Neither do they, and I'd feel a lot happier if they did." He rubbed his upper lip. "I know science has never demonstrated anything like reliable, trainable extrasensory perception among humans, but what if that's exactly what Alley's stumbled into? We know the Quarn have limited intraspecies telepathy—could she have activated some previously unused portion of her own brain? Tapped into some latent human capability we've never been able to isolate? If she has, is it something just anyone could learn to do? Would recreating the same abilities in someone else send *them* over the edge, as well? And what if she's got other capabilities—ones even she doesn't know about yet—that kick in under some fresh stress?"

The inspector began to speak again, then closed his mouth as he recognized Keita's very real concern. It was all fantastic, of course. However special the Cadre might be they weren't gods. Even Keita admitted that at least some of them broke under stress, and Ben Belkassem had never encountered a human with more right to break than Alicia DeVries, so—

His train of thought suddenly hiccupped. A right to break, certainly, but Keita was right in at least one respect; that simple and comforting answer left other questions unanswered. How *had* she survived unattended in subfreezing temperatures with those wounds, and why *hadn't* the Fleet's sensors detected her before someone went in on the ground to identify the dead?

Could there be something to this notion of a second entity? It didn't have to be a Greek demon or demigoddess just because that was what it told DeVries it was, but Mathison's World was on the very fringe of known space. No one had ever encountered anything like this before, but the possibility that *something* existed couldn't be entirely ruled out. Bizarre as DeVries's claims might be, no one had been able to suggest an explanation that was less bizarre, and it was axiomatic that the simplest hypothesis which explained all known facts was most likely to be correct. . . .

He leaned back in his chair, toying with his coffee cup, and his eyes were very, very thoughtful.

The admittance signal chimed, and the hatch slid instantly aside. Ben Belkassem hesitated in the opening, startled by how quickly it had appeared, then looked across the small, neat cabin at the woman he had come to see.

Alicia DeVries sat with her left hand fitted awkwardly into a normal interface headset, and her eyes were unfocused. They turned to him without really seeing him, and he recognized that inward-turned expression. She was linked into the transport's data systems, and his eyebrows rose, for he'd understood that her computer links had been shut down.

His presence registered on Alicia, and she blinked slowly.

<*Come out of there.*> Impatient refusal whispered through her mind, and her next thought was louder. <*We have a visitor, so get back here!*>

<*Oh, very well.*> Tisiphone was suddenly fully back within Alicia's skull, her mental voice glowing with vitality as it always did after one of her jaunts through the ship's computers. She'd discovered roundabout routes to the most unlikely places, and she'd been studying the transport's Fasset drive when Alicia interrupted her. <*We could avoid these interruptions if you would lock your door,*> she pointed out, not for the first time.

<*And then they'd wonder what we—or I, rather—was doing in here.*>

<*With the sensors they have trained on you at all times? I doubt that, Little One.*>

<*Humor me,*> Alicia replied, blinking again and letting her eyes drift back into focus. It was Ben Belkassem, and she wondered why he'd sought her out as she gestured politely to the cabin's only other chair.

The Justice man sat, studying her openly but inoffensively. She was a striking woman, he reflected as her blank expression vanished. Tall for his taste—he liked to make eye contact without getting a crick in his neck—and slender, yet broad-shouldered. She moved with hard-trained, disciplined grace, and one forgot she was merely pretty when her face came alive with intelligence and humor, but there was something more under that. A cool, catlike something and an amused tolerance, rather like what looked out of his own mirror at him, but with a peculiar compassion . . . and a capacity for violence he knew he could never match. This was a dangerous woman, he thought, yet so utterly self-possessed it was almost impossible to think of her as "mad."

"Forgive me," he began. "I didn't mean to burst in on you, but the hatch opened on its own."

"I know." Her contralto voice had a soft, furry edge, and her smile was wry. "Uncle Arthur's been kind enough to allow me free run of the ship, but given the, um, concern for my stability, I thought it would be a bad idea to go all secretive on him when I don't actually need privacy."

He nodded and leaned back, crossing his legs, then cocked his head. "I noticed you were interfacing," he observed, and her eyes twinkled.

"And here you thought Uncle Arthur had deactivated all my receptors."

She disengaged her hand from the headset and wiggled her stiff fingers.

"Something like that, yes."

"Well, he left my Beta receptor open," she told him, opening her hand. She flexed her wrist, stretching her palm, and he saw the slight angularity of a receptor node against the taut skin. "I have three, you know, and this is the most harmless of them."

"I knew you had more than one," he murmured, "but don't *three* get a bit confusing?"

"Sometimes." She raised her arms and stretched like a cat. "They feed separate subsystems, but one of the requirements for the job is the ability to concentrate on more than one thing at a time—sort of like being able to play chess on a roof in a driving rain and carry on a conversation about subatomic physics while you replace the bad shingles between moves."

"Sounds exhausting," he remarked, and she smiled again.

"Mildly. This—" she touched her temple "—is my Alpha node. It's the one connected to my primary processors, and it's configured for broadband access to non-AI computer interfaces like shuttle controls, heavy weapons, tac nets, and data systems. It also handles things like my pharmacope, so it makes sense to put it here. After all, if I lose this—" she thumped the top of her head gently "—I won't miss any of the peripherals very much."

Her smile turned into an urchinlike grin at his expression, and she opened her right hand to show him its palm.

"This is my Gamma node. We use it to interface with our combat armor, unlike Marines, who keep their armor link here." She tapped her temple again. "I could run my own armor through the Alpha link, but I'd have to shut down a lot of other functions. The Gamma link is sort of a secondary, load-sharing system. And this—" she opened her left palm again "—is dedicated to remote sensors and sensory data. It's got some limited ability to take over for the Gamma node if I lose my other hand or something equally drastic, but it's not the most efficient one for computer linkages by a long shot. That's why Uncle Arthur chose to leave it open when he closed the others down."

"I see." He studied her for a moment. "You don't seem particularly angry, I must say." She shrugged, but he persisted. "I understood the reason most drop commandos who survive retire to colony worlds is because they resent the Core World requirement that their augmentation be deactivated."

"That's only partly true. Oh, it's a good part of it, but we're not exactly the sort who find ultracivilization to our taste, and we can be damned useful on the outworlds. Most of them are glad to get us. But if you're asking if I resent being closed down this way, the answer is that I do. There's no particular point getting angry over it, though. If I were Uncle Arthur, I'd do precisely the same thing with any Cadreman I thought had . . . questionable contact with reality."

Her tone was edged yet glittered with a trace of true humor, and it was his turn to grin. But his smile faded as he leaned forward, hands clasping his right ankle where it lay atop his left knee, and spoke softly.

"True. But I can't help wondering, Captain DeVries, if your contact with reality is quite as questionable as everyone seems to think."

Her eyes stilled for just a moment, all humor banished, and then she shook herself with a laugh.

"Careful, Inspector! A remark like that could get you checked into the room next to mine."

"Only if someone heard it," he murmured, and her eyes rounded as he reached into his pocket and withdrew a small, compact, and highly illegal device. "I'm sure you recognize this," he said, and she nodded slowly. She'd never seen one quite that tiny, but she'd used military models. It was an antisurveillance device, known in the trade as a "mirror box."

"At the moment," Ben Belkassem slid the mirror box back into his pocket, "Major Cateau's sensors are watching a loop of the five or six minutes before I rang your doorbell. I hadn't hoped that you'd be using your neural link. No doubt you've been sitting right there concentrating with minimal movement for quite some time, so the chance of anyone noticing my interference is lower than I'd expected, but I still have to cut this fairly short."

"Cut what short?" she asked quietly.

"Our conversation. You see, I don't quite share the opinion of your fellow Cadremen. I'm not sure what really happened or exactly what you're up to, and I'm certainly no psych specialist, but something Sir Arthur said about your personality rubbed up against something Major Cateau said about a desire on your part to go after whoever's behind these raids."

"And?"

"And it occurred to me that under certain circumstances, being considered mad might be very useful to you, so I thought I'd just drop by to share a little secret of my own. You see, everyone out here thinks I'm with Intelligence Branch. That's what I wanted them to think, though I never actually *said* I was with Intelligence. I'm an inspector, all right—but with O Branch."

Alicia's lips pursed in a silent, involuntary whistle. O Branch—Operations Branch of the Ministry of Justice—was as specialized, and feared, as the Cadre itself. It consisted of hand-picked troubleshooters selected for initiative, flexibility, and pragmatism, and its members were charged with solving problems any way they had to. It was also very, very small. While "inspector" was a fairly junior rank in the other branches of the Ministry of Justice, it was the highest field rank available in O Branch.

"You're the only person out here who knows that, Captain DeVries," the inspector said, levering himself out of his chair.

"But . . . why tell me?"

"It seemed like a good idea." He gave her a crooked smile and straightened his crimson tunic fastidiously. "I know how you feel about spooks, after all." He walked calmly to the closed hatch, then half turned to her once more. "If you decide you have anything you want to tell me, or if there's anything I can do for you, please feel free to let me know. I assure you it will remain completely confidential, even from your kindly physicians."

He gave her a graceful, elegant bow and punched the hatch button. It opened, then whispered shut behind him.

CHAPTER FORTY

This invisible bubble was getting tiresome, Alicia thought, eyeing the empty tables around her in the lounge. No one would ever be crude enough to mention her insanity—but no one wanted to get too close to her, either.

<*I wonder how much of it's fear of contagion?*> she complained.

<*Oh, very little, I should think. They fear what you may do* to *them, not what they might contract* from *you.*>

<*A comforting thought,*> Alicia snorted, and hooked a chair further under the opposite side of the table to rest her heels on it. Her dialogues with Tisiphone no longer felt odd, which worried her from time to time, but not nearly so much as they comforted her. She had to be so wary, especially of her friends, that the relief of open conversation was almost unspeakable. Of course, her lips twitched wryly, it was still possible Tannis was right, but their exchanges remained a vast relief, even if Tisiphone *didn't* exist.

<*Of course I exist. Why do you continue to use qualifiers?*>

<*The nature of the beast, I suppose. I've never been all that comfortable with cyber-synths, but even so, this would be a lot easier for me if I knew you were something they'd whipped up in the AI labs.*>

<*So you find beings of crystal and wire more reasonable than beings of spirit?*> There was vast amusement in Tisiphone's mental "voice." <*You come from a sad age, Little One, if your people's sense of wonder has sunk so low!*>

<*Not a sad age, just a practical one. And speaking of wonder, look at that, Spirit Lady.*>

She turned her eyes—their eyes?—to the lounge's outsized view port as the transport settled into orbit around Soissons, and even Tisiphone fell silent. The port lacked the image enhancement of one of the viewer stations, but that only made the view even more impressive.

Soissons was very Earth-like—or, rather, very like Earth had been a thousand years before. More of its surface was land, and the ice caps were larger, for Soissons lay almost ten light-minutes from its G2 primary, but its deep blue seas and fleece-white clouds were breathtaking, and Soissons had been settled after man had learned to look after his things. Old Earth was still dealing with the traumas of eight millennia of civilization, but humanity had taken far greater care with the impact of the changes inflicted here. There were none of the megalopolises of Old Earth or the older Core Worlds, and she could almost smell the freshness of the air even from orbit.

Yet there were two billion people on that planet, however careful they were to preserve it, and the Franconia System had been selected as a sector capital because of its industrial power. Soisson's skies teemed with orbital installations protected by formidable defensive emplacements, and she craned her head, watching intently, as the transport drifted neatly through them under a minute fraction of its full drive power. A Fleet spacedock filled the port, vast enough to handle superdreadnoughts, much less the slender battlecruiser undergoing routine maintenance, and beyond it loomed the spidery skeleton of a full-fledged shipyard.

<*What might that be?*> a voice said in her brain, and her eyes moved under their own power. It was still a bit unnerving to find herself focusing on something of interest to another, but it no longer bothered her as much as it had, and Tisiphone didn't exactly have a finger with which to point.

The thought faded as her own interest sharpened, and she frowned at the small ship near one edge of the yard.

It appeared to be in the late stages of fitting out. Indeed, but for all the bits and pieces of yard equipment drifting near it she would have said it was completed. She watched a yard shuttle mate with one of the transparent access tubes, disgorging a flock of techs—minute dots of colored coveralls at this distance—and nibbled the inside of her lip.

Tisiphone's question was well taken. Alicia had seen more warships and transports than she cared to recall during her career, but never one quite like this. Its bulbous Fasset drive housing dwarfed the rest of its hull, but it was too big for a dispatch boat. At the same time, it was too small for a Fleet transport, even assuming anyone would stick that monster drive on a bulk carrier. It looked to fall somewhere between a light and heavy cruiser for size, perhaps four or five hundred meters at the outside—it was hard to be sure with only yard shuttles for a reference—yet someone had grafted a battleship's drive onto it, which promised an awesome turn of speed.

Their transport drifted closer, bound for a nearby personnel terminal, and her eyes widened as she saw the recessed weapon hatches. There were far more of them than there should have been on such a small hull, especially one with that huge drive. Unless . . .

She inhaled sharply.

<I'm not sure, but I think that's an alpha-synth.>

<Indeed?> Interest sharpened Tisiphone's mental voice, for she'd encountered several mentions of the alpha-synth ships, especially in the secured data she'd accessed from the transport's data net. *<I did not think they could be so small.>*

<Well, they only have a crew of one, and they're right on the frontier of technology. They're only possible because somebody finally developed a practical anti-matter power plant—not to mention the alpha-synth AIs.>

The small ship floated out of their view as the transport lined up on the personnel terminal, and Alicia leaned back in her chair, wondering what it would be like to become an alpha-synth pilot.

Lonely, for starters. No more than twenty percent of all human beings could sustain the contact required to maintain a synth-link without becoming "lost," and less than ten percent could handle one of the cyber-synth-links which allowed them to engage their own thoughts with an artificial intelligence. Many who could refused to do so, and it was hard to blame them, given the eccentricities and far from infrequent bouts of outright insanity to which AIs were prone.

But from the bits and pieces she'd read, people who could (and would) take on an alpha-synth were even rarer—and probably weren't playing with a full deck. The highbrows might be patting themselves on the back for finally producing an insanity-proof AI, but who in her right mind would voluntarily *fuse* herself with a self-aware computer? Interacting with one was one thing; making yourself a part of it was something else. Alicia, for one, found the idea of becoming the organic half of a bipolar intelligence in a union only death could dissolve far from appealing.

She paused with a short, sharp bark of laughter. One or two heads turned, and she smiled cheerfully at the curious, amused by the way they whipped their eyes back away from her. One more indication of her looniness, she supposed, but it really *was* humorous. Here she was, uneasy about the possibility of merging with another personality—her of all people!

She chuckled again, then drained her glass and stood as Tannis entered the lounge. Her slightly fixed smile told Alicia it was time to debark and face the dirt-side psych types, and she sighed and set down the empty glass with a smile of her own, wondering if it looked equally pasted on.

Fleet Admiral Subrahmanyan Treadwell, Governor General of the Franconia Sector, disliked planets.

Born and raised in one of the Solarian belter habitats, Treadwell saw Imperial Worlds as inconveniently immobile defensive problems and other people's planets as fat targets that couldn't run away, but that hadn't worried Seamus II's ministers when they tapped him for his job.

Treadwell was a lean, bland-faced man with hard eyes. Some people had been fooled by the face into missing the eyes, but he was a man who'd done everything the hard way. Unable to accept neural feeds or even rudimentary augmentation, and so disqualified forever from commanding a capital ship by his inability to key into its command net, he'd cut his way to flag rank by sheer brilliance, using nothing but his brain and a keyboard. Three times senior strategy instructor at the Imperial War College and twice Second Space Lord, he was acknowledged as the Fleet's premier strategist, yet he'd never commanded a fleet in space. It was an understandably sensitive point, and coupled with a certain antipathy for those whose mental processes seemed slower than his own but who *could* be augmented, it made him . . . difficult at times.

Like now.

"So what you're saying, Colonel McIlhenny," he said in a flat voice, "is that we still don't have the least idea where these pirates are based, why they've adopted this extraordinary operational approach, or where they're going to hit next. Is that a fair summation?"

"Yes, Sir." McIlhenny squelched an ignoble desire to hide behind his own admiral. It would have looked silly, since Admiral Lady Rosario Gomez, Baroness Nova Tampico and Knight of the Solar Cross, was exactly one hundred and fifty-seven centimeters tall and massed only forty-eight kilos.

"But you, Admiral Gomez," Treadwell turned his eyes on the commander of the Franconia Fleet District, "still think we have sufficient strength to deal with this on our own?"

"That isn't what I said, Governor." The silver-haired admiral might be petite, but her professional stature matched Treadwell's, and she met his eyes calmly. "What I said is that I feel requesting additional capital units is not the optimum solution. Any such request is unlikely to be granted, and what we really need are more *light* units. Whoever these people are, they can't possibly match our firepower—assuming we could find them."

"Indeed." Treadwell tapped keys on a memo pad, then smiled frostily at Lady Rosario. "I assume you've run a minimum force level analysis on them based on their ability to destroy planetary SLAM drones before they wormhole?"

"I have," Gomez said, still calm.

"Then perhaps you can explain where they found the firepower for that? SLAM drones are not exactly easy targets."

"No, Sir, they aren't. On the other hand, they can't shoot back and their only defense is speed. Admittedly, it's easier for capital ships to nail them, but enough light units—even enough corvettes—could box and intercept them well within the inner system."

"True, Admiral. On the other hand, we have Captain DeVries's report that they're using *Leopard*-class assault shuttles. Those, you will recall, are carried—were carried, rather—only by battleships and above. Or do you wish to suggest to me that these pirates are using *freighters* against us?"

"Sir," Gomez said patiently, "I've never said they don't have *some* capital ships. Certainly the *Leopards* were carried by capital ships, but there's no intrinsic reason they couldn't be operated by refitted heavy or even light cruisers." She watched Treadwell's brows knit and continued in an unhurried voice. "I'm not suggesting that's the case. A possibility, yes; a probability, no. What I *am* saying is that we have three full squadrons of dreadnoughts, and there's no way independent pirates can match that. Our problem isn't destroying them, Governor, it's *finding* them; and for that I need additional scouts, not the Home Fleet."

"Admiral Brinkman?" Treadwell glanced at Vice Admiral Sir Amos Brinkman, Gomez's second-in-command. "Is that your opinion as well?"

"Well, Governor," Brinkman stroked his mustache and glanced at his senior officer from the corner of one eye, "I'd have to say Lady Rosario has put her finger on our problem. On the other hand, the exact fleet mix to solve it might be open to some legitimate dispute."

McIlhenny kept his face blank. Brinkman was a competent man in space, but it was common knowledge that he wanted an eventual governorship of his own, and he was *very* careful about offending influential people.

"Continue, Admiral Brinkman," Treadwell invited.

"Yes, Sir. It seems to me that we have two possible approaches. One is Admiral Gomez's suggestion that we station additional pickets, possibly backed by a few battlecruisers, in our inhabited systems in order to detect, deter, and if possible, track the raiders. The second is to request additional heavy units and station a division of dreadnoughts in each inhabited system in order to intercept and destroy the next raid." He raised his hands, palms uppermost. "It seems to me that we're really talking about a question of emphasis, not fundamental strategy. Frankly, I could be satisfied by either approach, so long as we follow it without distractions."

"Governor," Lady Rosario didn't even glance at Brinkman, "I'm not disputing the desirability of destroying the enemy on their next attack, but getting the First Space Lord to turn loose that many capital ships will be a major operation in its own right. I have thirty-six dreadnoughts, but covering our inhabited systems in the strength Admiral Brinkman suggests would require *sixty-eight*. That's almost double our current strength, and given the Rishathan presence on our frontier, we'd need at least another two squadrons for border security. That brings us up to ninety-two dreadnoughts, close to twenty-five percent of Fleet's entire active peacetime strength in that class, not to mention the escorts to screen them." She shrugged. "You and I both know the fiscal constraints Countess Miller is wrestling with—and how thin we're already stretched. The First Space Lord isn't going to give us that many of his best capital ships, not with all the other calls on the Fleet."

"You let me worry about Lord Jurawski, Admiral," Treadwell's eyes were flinty. "I've known him a long time, and I believe that if I point out that his alternative is to lose at least one more populated world before we can even find the enemy, I can bring him to see reason."

"With great respect, Governor, I feel that's unlikely."

"We'll see. However, it will require some months to redeploy forces of that magnitude in any case, which means we must do our best in the meantime. Where are we in that respect?"

"About where we were before Mathison's World," Lady Rosario admitted, and gestured to McIlhenny.

"In essence, Governor," the colonel said, "most of what we've learned from Mathison's World is bad. We've positively IDed one ex-Fleet officer among the raiders Captain DeVries killed, and a general search of personnel data has uncovered six more officers whose personnel jackets falsely indicate that they died in the same shuttle accident. This is a clear suggestion that the pirates have at least one fairly highly placed inside man."

"Probably some damned clerk in BuPers," Treadwell snorted. "How highly placed d'you have to be to cook computer files?" He waved an impatient hand. "I admit it's a disturbing possibility, but let's concentrate on what we can prove." He looked back at Gomez. "Dispositions, Admiral?"

"They're in my report, Governor. I've increased the pickets and split up BatRon Seventeen to provide a couple of dreadnoughts for each of the six most populous Crown systems. That should be enough to deal with the enemy if he cares to engage, but it's clearly insufficient to destroy him if he elects to run. Unfortunately, I can't reduce my reserve strength below two squadrons without inviting the Rish to stick their noses in, so our Incorporated Worlds will have to rely on their local defenses."

"Anything more on the possibility the Jung Association is involved?" Treadwell demanded, turning back to McIlhenny, and the colonel shrugged.

"They've denied it, and our reports on their fleet deployments support that. In addition, they've volunteered to provide protection for Domino and Kohlman. Those are low probability targets—Domino's too small and poor, and Kohlman's an Incorporated World with fairly good orbital defenses—but, then, I'd've said a barely established colony like Mathison's World was an even more unlikely target. My personal belief is that the Jungians have nothing to do with this and want to protect our closest populations to demonstrate their innocence and good faith now that we've begun getting the sector organized, but I certainly can't prove that to be the case."

"Um. I'm inclined to agree with you. Keep an eye on them, but concentrate on the assumption that they're innocent bystanders." Treadwell drummed lightly on the table. "Damn it, we *need* those extra battle squadrons, Admiral Gomez! You've just said it yourself—we can only cover a handful of systems effectively, and imperial subjects are dying out there."

"Granted, Governor, and no one will be more delighted than I if you can pry those ships loose from Lord Jurawski. As you say, however, we have to do the best we can in the meantime, and we could get extra cruisers out here a lot more quickly than HQ is going to turn dreadnoughts loose."

"But if we ask for them, they'll take the easy way out and give us *only* light units." Treadwell smiled thinly. "I know how the Lords of Admiralty work—I've been one. Asking for the big stuff will convince them we're serious and probably get the actual firepower out here faster."

"As you say, Sir." Lady Rosario folded her hands on the table. She remained convinced Treadwell was on the wrong tack, but as Brinkman had said, the case could be argued either way. And he *was* her boss.

"Very well. Now," Treadwell returned to McIlhenny, "what's the latest word on our drop commando?"

"Sir, that's really a Cadre matter, and—"

"It may be a Cadre matter, but it happened in my bailiwick, Colonel."

"Agreed, Sir. What I was going to say is that I'm not very well informed because Brigadier Keita has been personally supervising the case. My understanding is that there's been no change. Captain DeVries remains adamant that she's been, um, possessed by a figure out of ancient Greek mythology, and nothing seems capable of altering that belief. They're still searching for a therapeutic approach to break through it, but without success.

"No one, myself included, has a theory to account for her survival and the inability of our sensors to detect her, nor has she evinced any other inexplicable capabilities. Major Cateau of the Cadre Medical Branch has analyzed her augmentation down to the molecular level—she's done everything short of physically removing it, in fact—and found absolutely nothing out of the ordinary. The most rigorous medical examinations have turned up nothing the least out of line about her physiology, either, and despite those earlier peculiarities, her EEG and general test results are now exactly what they ought to be. On the face of it, she's a perfectly normal person—well, as normal as any drop commando—who's done several clearly impossible things and appears to have a single, extraordinarily persistent delusion."

"Humph."

Treadwell frowned down at his gently drumming fingers, brows lowered. Personally, McIlhenny suspected the Governor was automatically suspicious of anyone who was augmented. It was a not uncommon response from those unfortunates who couldn't tolerate augmentation themselves.

"I don't like it," he said finally, "but I don't suppose there's anything I can—or should—do about it. Besides," he smiled, "Arthur would bite my head off if I even suggested there might be." He shook himself. "Very well, Admiral Gomez. Get me those deployment patterns and keep me personally updated on them."

"Yes, Governor. And may I request, Sir, that in light of the possibility—" she stressed the word very lightly "—of high-level involvement with the pirates, we ought to take additional precautions with that data?"

"You may, but it won't be necessary. I've been handling sensitive information for several decades now, Baroness, and I believe I understand the fundamentals of security."

Lady Rosario's lips tightened, but she nodded silently. There was, after all, very little else that she could do.

CHAPTER FORTY-ONE

The flag cabin boasted an armorplast view port, but it was covered.

That was one of the things Howell hated about wormhole space. He loved to contemplate the stars' sheer, heart-stopping beauty, especially when he needed something other than his orders to think about, yet the mechanics of interstellar flight stripped them away. The approach to the light barrier was spectacular as aberration and the Doppler effect took charge. The ever-contracting starbow drew further and further ahead, vanishing into the blind spot created by the Fasset drive while a ship sped onward through God's own black abyss . . . until the transition to supralight chopped even that off like an axe. Then there was only the nothingness of wormhole space, no longer black, neither dark nor light, but simply nothing at all, an *absence*. Howell wasn't one of those unfortunates it sent into uncontrollable hysteria, but it made him . . . uncomfortable.

He snorted and turned to check the plot repeater. He'd brought only the three fastest freighters this time, and the squadron formed a tight globe about their light dots and that of his flagship. They slowed the warships despite their speed (for freighters), but the squadron was still turning out eight hundred times the speed of light through its own private universe. Or that, at any rate, was the velocity the rest of the universe would have assigned Howell's ships. In fact, not even a Fasset drive ship could actually crack the light barrier. The attempt simply threw it into a sort of subcontinuum where the laws of physics acquired some very strange subclauses.

For starters, the effective speed of light was far greater here, yet the maximum attainable velocity was limited by the balance between the relativistic mass of a starship and the rest, *not* the relativistic mass of its Fasset drive's black hole. The astrophysicists still hadn't worked out precisely why that was—the blood tended to get ankle deep whenever the Imperial Society discussed alternate hypotheses—but they'd worked out the math to describe it. The whyfor didn't really matter to spacers like Howell as long as they understood the practical consequences, and the practical consequences were that stopping accelerating was equivalent to *de*celerating at an ever-steepening gradient, and that continuous acceleration eventually stopped increasing velocity and simply started holding it constant.

He checked his watch. Alexsov would be along shortly, he told himself, chiding his impatience, and returned to brooding over his plot.

They were running blind—another thing he hated about wormhole space. Gravitic detectors could look *into* it to track the mammoth gravitational anomaly of a supralight ship at up to two light-months, but no one had yet devised a way to peer *out* of it. Which was why you made damned sure of your course and turnover time before you went in, because you sure as hell couldn't correct in transit. In many ways, wormholing was like crawling into a hole and pulling it in after you, though there were difficulties with that analogy.

For one thing, someone else could crawl into a hole with you, for wormhole space was less a dimension than a frequency. If another ship could match relativistic velocity to within fifteen or twenty percent, his wormhole space and yours were in phase. If he was a friend, that was well and good; if he was an enemy, he could go right on trying to kill you.

Of course, Howell reminded himself with a wry grin, there were problems with pursuing an adversary too closely here. The instant he stopped accelerating, his velocity started to drop; if he did an end-for-end and swung his Fasset drive into your face, his massive deceleration could not only cause you to overrun him but, if he hit it hard enough, also snatch him back into normal space as if he'd dropped anchor. Either way, you were in trouble. If you stayed in phase, *his* fire was suddenly coming up *your* backside without interdiction from your drive mass, and if he did drop sublight and your people weren't very, very sharp, you never saw him again. By the time you punched back out into normal space, you might be light-hours away from his n-space locus, probably beyond anything but gravitic detection range, which meant that cutting his drive simply made him disappear.

Still, it was a desperation move for the pursued, as well. If the side shields on his drive mass—or that of one of his enemies—failed, those black holes could crunch him up without even spitting out his bones. Worse, he might actually meet one of them head-on in mutual and absolute destruction, and if it was unlikely, well, unlikely things happened.

Assuming he avoided immolation on his pursuers' Fasset drives, their fire control might just get lucky when they overflew him, and even if they didn't, wormhole trajectories had to be *very* carefully computed. The least deviation threw off all calculations, and that kind of acceleration change screwed a flight profile to hell and gone. Once he lost his original vector, he *had* to go sublight and relocate himself before he could program a fresh supralight course, and that could take days, even weeks, of observations. At the very least, that played hell with any ops schedule, and—

A soft, musical chime interrupted his drifting thoughts, and he turned to touch the admittance button. Gregor Alexsov stepped through the hatch, and Howell looked ostentatiously at his watch.

"You're three minutes late. What dire emergency kept you?"

Alexsov's harsh mouth twitched obediently, but both men knew it was only half a jest. Howell had known Alexsov for twelve years, yet they weren't really friends. They came nearer to it than anyone else who knew Alexsov, but that wasn't saying a great deal. Howell's compulsively punctual chief of staff reminded him more of an AI than a human being . . . which, the commodore thought, was just as well, given their present activities.

"Not an emergency," Alexsov said now. "Just a little delay to counsel Commander Watanabe."

"Watanabe?" Howell cocked his head. "Problems?"

"I don't know. He just seems a little jumpy."

"Um." Howell dropped into a chair and pursed his lips. Months of careful preplanning had provided him with an initial core of experienced officers, but there were never enough. That was why Control continued his cautious recruitment. Most of the newcomers had slotted neatly into place, but the realities of their duties were grimmer than anyone could truly imagine until he actually got here. A certain percentage proved . . . unsuitable once they fully realized what would be demanded of them.

"Have you mentioned him to Rachel?"

"Of course." Alexsov stood behind his own chair and shrugged minutely. "That's why I was late. She's promised to keep an eye on him."

Howell nodded, perfectly content to leave the problem of Commander Watanabe in Rachel Shu's capable hands, and turned his mind to other matters.

"So much for him. But I rather doubt he was why you asked to see me."

"Correct. I've been going back over Control's latest data dump, and it worries me."

"Oh?" Howell sat a bit straighter. "Why?"

"Because the more I see of the post-op reports on Mathison's World, the more I realize how badly Control screwed up there. I don't like that—especially not when we're about to hit a target like Elysium."

"Oh, come on, Greg! Control was right on the money about Mathison's defenses, and the planetary maps checked out to the last decimal place. No one could have known that tin can would be in the area!"

"I know, but he should have warned us about DeVries."

Howell leaned back, eyes touched with disbelief, but Alexsov looked back levelly. He was dead serious, the commodore realized.

"There were forty-one thousand people on that planet, Greg, and Alicia DeVries was only one of them. You're asking a bit much if you expect Control to keep track of every sodbuster on every dirtball we hit."

"I'm not asking for that, but a drop commando—any drop commando—isn't exactly a 'sodbuster.' and *this* drop commando was Alicia DeVries. And then there was the little matter of her grandfather—two Banner of Terra holders for the price of one, and

Control didn't think *that* was significant?" He shook his head disgustedly. "O'Shaughnessy would have been bad enough by himself, but if I'd known DeVries was there, I'd've scheduled an orbital strike on her homestead and had done with it."

"Jesus, Greg! She's only one woman!"

"I was *Ctesiphon*'s senior fire control officer when she supported the Shallingsport Raid," Alexsov said. "I was *there*, Commodore. Believe me, tangling with someone like her on her own terms isn't cost effective."

Howell grunted, a bit taken aback by Alexsov's vehemence yet forced to agree at least in part. But even so . . .

"I still can't fault Control when everything else checked out perfectly. And it's not exactly as if she did us irreparable damage."

"I'm not so sure of that." Alexsov's response surprised him yet again. "Certainly the loss of a single assault team wouldn't normally matter very much, but they IDed Singh, so they know where we've been recruiting. I don't know McIlhenny, but I've read his dossier. He'll keep on picking at it forever. If he digs deep enough, that could lead him to Control, and none of it would have happened if Control had warned us about DeVries in the first place. Damn it, Commodore," the swear word was highly unusual for Alexsov, "Control's got the conduits to know about things like this, and he's *supposed* to tell us about them. That is exactly the sort of crack that could blow the entire op wide open."

"All right, Greg!" Howell waved a placating hand. "But cool down. Done is done—and I'm sure Control will try even harder in future. In fact, I'll have Rachel send him a specific request to that effect. Will that suit?"

"It'll have to, I suppose," Alexsov said dourly, and Howell knew that was as close to agreement as he was going to get. Alexsov seemed personally affronted by the surprise he'd suffered, but it was that very perfectionism (and the ice-water in his veins) which made him ideal for his job.

"Good. In that case, how'd your trip to Wyvern go?"

"Quite well, actually." Alexsov finally sank into the waiting chair. "I placed our initial orders with Quintana. He seems unperturbed by the change in our priorities—no doubt because of how much he stands to make—and he assures me he can acquire anything we need and dispose of anything we send him. We won't see quite the same return on industrial and bulk items, since he'll be dumping them on less advanced Rogue Worlds outside the sector, but I think that's well worthwhile from the security perspective, and it sounds as if we'll actually make out better on luxury items through his channels than we did through the Lizards. I expect revenues to balance out overall, and it's not exactly as if we were in this for the profit, is it, Sir?"

"No," Howell agreed. "No, it's not." He sighed. "I take it you've had time to sit down with Rendlemann and discuss Elysium. Satisfied?"

"Yes, Sir. We've discussed a couple of minor changes, and we'll be running them on the simulator to see how they pan out."

"Got any specific concern over Control's intelligence on this one?"

"Not really, Sir." Alexsov rationed himself to a slight headshake. "It's more a matter of once burned, I suppose, but I've made a point of sharing Control's report on the DeVries episode with all of our assault team commanders, just in case. Still, this one will be more of a smash and grab job with the troops in battle armor, anyway, so unless Control's screwed up in some truly major respect, we shouldn't have any problems groundside."

"Anyone seem worried about hitting an Incorporated World's defense?"

"I think there's a bit of dry-mouth here and there, but nothing too serious, and having Admiral Gomez's deployment orders could help defuse what there is of it. With your permission, I intend to post them where the team leaders can check them personally to reassure their people we'll be clear."

"Is that a good idea? This'll be our toughest job yet, and you can bet anyone who's captured is going to talk, one way or another."

"I don't believe that will be a problem, Sir. The troops will all be in battle armor, and I've had a word with Major Reiter. The suicide charges will be armed and rigged for remote detonation." Alexsov smiled a thin, cold smile that chilled Howell's blood, but his conversational tone never changed. "I don't see any reason to mention that. Do you, Sir?"

* * *

Commodore Trang frowned at the faint splotch of light. It shimmered on the very edge of his command fortress's gravitic detection range, well beyond another, much closer dot already slowing to drop sublight. The closer one didn't bother him; it was a single ship, and unless he missed his guess it was the Fleet transport Soissons had warned him to expect. But that other grav source . . . It was a lot bigger, despite the range, which suggested it was more than one ship, and no one had told him to expect anything like it.

"How long before you can firm this up?" he asked his plotting officer.

"Another ten hours should bring them close enough for us to sort out sources and at least ID their Fasset signatures."

"Um." Trang rubbed his chin in thought. He'd been carefully briefed, like every system CO, on the operational patterns of whoever was raiding the Franconia Sector. To date, they hadn't touched a system with deep-space defenses, which on the face of it, made Elysium an unlikely target.

He tucked his hands behind him and rocked on the balls of his feet. The freighter would be well in-system, under the cover of his weapons, before this fresh clutch of ships could come close enough to be a problem, but aside from two corvettes, he had no mobile units at all. If these bogies *were* bad news, his orbital forts were on their own, and they weren't much compared to those of a Core World System. Still, what he had could handle anything short of a full battle squadron. GeneCorp had made sure of that before they located their newest bio-research facilities here, just as it had been careful to pick a stable world, without the sort of lunatic fringe "liberation organizations" which had made so much trouble in other star systems this close to the frontier.

He turned, gazing into a view screen without actually seeing the blue and white sphere it displayed.

There was little down there in the way of local defenses. Elysium was an Incorporated World. As such, it was entitled to a Marine garrison for local security and police keeping duties, and—like an unfortunately large number of Incorporated Worlds, in Trang's opinion—it had allowed its planetary militia to atrophy. The fact that it had a permanently assigned local Marine detachment engendered a sense of security which tended to overlook the fact that the many insatiable demands on the Imperial Marine Corps' manpower meant that the permanent garrisons it could provide to planets which had no pressing local security concerns tended to be small. In fact, they tended to be *tiny*, and Elysium's was no exception.

Nor was there very much point in building groundside defenses against attack from space. If a capital ship got into weapons range of a planet, that planet was dead, whatever happened to its attacker, for the black holes of a dozen SLAMs coming in at near light-speed would tear any planet to pieces.

That was why most inhabited planets were defended only in space. In a sense, their complete lack of weaponry was their best protection. To date, humanity's only real wars had been intramural bloodlettings or with the Rish, and opponents who liked the same sort of real estate were unlikely to go around pulverizing useful worlds unless they had to. Strikes on specific targets, yes; wholesale genocide, no.

But at this particular moment, Trang could have wished Elysium bristled with ground fortifications—or at least had been fractious enough to have been assigned a decent-sized garrison. It had been over two centuries since imperial planets had faced piratical attacks on this scale, and the Empire had forgotten what it was like. It was unlikely pirates would go after any world with a Marine brigade or two waiting to chew them up on the ground, but there was less than half a battalion on Elysium.

He turned back to the plot, glowering at the bogies sweeping towards his system, and considered contacting Soissons, then shook his head. There was nothing Soissons could do if it was the start of a raid, nor any reason he should need help in the first place, and his own sensors should be able to ID these people long before they entered engagement range. All starcomming the sector capital would achieve would be to show his own nervousness.

"Maintain a close watch on them, Adela," he told his plotting officer. "Let me know the instant you've got something solid."

"Yes, Sir." Commander Adela Masterman nodded and thought into her synth-link headset, logging the same instructions for her relief, and Trang gave the display one last glance and left the control room.

* * *

Several hours later, Commodore Trang's communicator buzzed, then lit with Commander Masterman's smiling face.

"Sorry to disturb you, Sir, but we've got a preliminary ID on our bogies. We still don't know *who* they are, but they definitely have Fleet Fasset drives. It looks like a light task group—a single dreadnought, three battlecruisers, two or three freighters, and escorts."

"Good." Trang grinned back at her, aware of how worried he'd truly been only as the relief set in. He didn't have any idea what a task group was doing here, but under the current circumstances, he was delighted to see them. "How long before they go sublight?"

"At their present rate of deceleration, about eleven hours, five hours behind that Fleet transport. Given their drive advantage, they'll be fifteen or twenty light-minutes out when she makes Elysium orbit."

"Pass the word to Captain Brewster, Adela. Have him designate parking orbits for them and alert the yard in case they have any servicing needs."

"Will do, Sir," Masterman replied, and the screen went blank.

Commander Masterman stepped from the lift outside Primary Control, her hands full of coffee cups and doughnuts, and hit the hatch button with her elbow. The panel hissed aside, and she sidled into PriCon with a grin.

"I come bearing gifts," she announced, and a spatter of applause greeted her. She bowed grandly and glanced at the bulkhead chronometer as she set her goodies carefully out of the way. She had eight glorious minutes before she went back on watch—just long enough to exchange a few words with Lieutenant Commander Brigatta. That was nice; she had plans for the darkly handsome com officer the next time their off-duty schedules coincided.

She'd just reached Brigatta's station when Lieutenant Orrin straightened suddenly at Plotting. The movement caught Masterman's eye, and she turned automatically towards her assistant in surprise.

"Now that's damned strange," Orrin muttered.

He looked up at his boss and gestured at Brigatta's screen as he shunted his own display across to it.

"Look at this, Ma'am," he said, and the screen blossomed with a view of near-planet space. "I know that transport's skipper said he was in a hurry to unload, but he's really pushing it. She's a good fifty percent above normal approach speeds, and now she's doing a turnov—*Sweet Jesus!*"

Adela Masterman froze as the "transport" suddenly stopped braking and spun to accelerate toward Elysium—at thirty-two gravities. Impossible! No transport could crank that much power inside a planet's Powell limit!

But this one could, and disbelief turned to horror as the "transport" dropped her ECM and stood revealed for what she truly was: a battlecruiser. A *Fleet* battlecruiser—one of their own ships!—battle screen springing up even as Masterman stared . . . *and she was launching SLAMs!*

The GQ alarm began to scream, and she charged towards her station, but it was purely automatic. Deep inside, she knew it was already far too late.

Starcoms are never emplaced on planets.

They are enormous structures—not so much massive as big, full of empty space—and it would be far more expensive to build them to survive a planet's gravity, but the real reason they are always found in space is much simpler. No one wants multiple black holes, however small, generated on the surface of *his* world, despite everything gravity shields can do and all the failsafes in the galaxy. And so they are placed in orbit, usually at least four hundred thousand kilometers out, which also gets them beyond the planetary Powell limit and doubles their efficiency as they fold space to permit supralight message transmission.

Unfortunately, this eminently sensible solution creates an Achilles heel for strategic command and control. Starships and planets without starcoms must rely on SLAM drones, many times faster than light but far slower than a starcom and woefully short-legged in comparison, so any raider's first priority is the destruction of his target's starcom. Without it, he has time. Time to hit his objectives, to carry out his mission . . . and to vanish once more before anyone outside the system even learns he was there.

Captain Homer Ortiz sat in his command chair, face taut, as his first SLAMs went out.

Ortiz was cyber-synth-capable and glad of it, for it gave him the con direct as *Poltava* went into the attack. His crisp, clear commands to the emotionless AI sent the first salvo slashing towards the starcom orbital base across two hundred thousand kilometers of space with an acceleration of fifteen thousand gravities; they struck fifty-one seconds later, traveling at a mere three percent of light-speed, but that would have been more than sufficient even without the black hole in front of each missile.

More weapons were already on their way—not SLAMs, this time, but Hauptman effect sublight missiles. Their initial acceleration was much higher, and they had barely half as far to go. The first thousand-megaton warhead detonated twenty-seven seconds after launch.

Commander Masterman had just donned her headset when she and nine thousand other people died. Then the other missiles began to strike home.

Night turned into day on the planet of Elysium as two-thirds of its orbital defenses vanished in less than two minutes.

Shocked eyes cringed away from the ring of suns blazing above them, and minds refused to grasp the magnitude of the disaster. Not in four centuries had the Imperial Fleet taken such losses in return for absolutely no damage to the enemy, but never before had the Fleet been attacked by one of its own, and the carnage a cyber-synthed battlecruiser could wreak totally unopposed was simply beyond comprehension.

The planetary governor dashed for his com in response to the first horrified warning; he arrived just as the last missile went home against the last fort in *Poltava*'s field of fire, and his face was white as whey. The three surviving forts were rushing to battle stations, but the marauding battlecruiser's speed soared, already above two hundred KPS, as she cut a chord across their protective ring. She cleared the planet and acquired the first of the survivors just before its own weapons came on line, and Ortiz's smile was hellish as a fresh salvo of SLAMs raced outward. The fort had nothing to stop them with, and the governor groaned as they tore it apart.

The second fortress had time for one answering salvo, hastily launched with minimal time for fire control solutions, and then it, too, was gone.

The final fort had time to get its battle screen up, yet faced the cruelest dilemma of all. Its crew had SLAMs of their own . . . and dared not use them. Ortiz had cut his course recklessly tight, placing *Poltava* far closer to Elysium than they. They could reply only with beams and warheads, lest a near-miss with a SLAM strike the very world they wanted to protect, and their gunners were shaken to their core by the catastrophe overwhelming them. They did their best, yet it never mattered at all. Their first salvos were still on the way when Ortiz launched a fresh pattern of SLAMs and flipped his ship end-for-end yet again, aiming *Poltava*'s Fasset drive directly at the doomed fort to devour its fire.

Twelve-point-five minutes and seventy-three thousand deaths after the attack began, there were no orbital forts in Elysium's skies.

"First phase successful, Commodore," Commander Rendlemann announced.

Howell nodded. Gravitic detectors, unlike other sensors, were FTL, and his flagship's gravitics had tracked their Trojan Horse and the flight paths of its SLAMs. It was an eerie sensation to see the undamaged fortresses on the light-speed displays and know they and all their people had ceased to exist.

He shook off a chill and gave Alexsov a tight smile. The chief of staff had argued against trying to sneak in more than one ship, insisting *Poltava* could do the job alone and that trying to use more would risk losing the priceless element of surprise.

"Two small vessels leaving orbit, Sir," Rendlemann said suddenly.

"Right on schedule," Alexsov murmured, and Howell nodded again, watching through his synth-link as the two corvettes accelerated hopelessly towards their mammoth foe. No corvette had the strength to engage a battlecruiser . . . but they were all Elysium had left.

The corvettes *Hermes* and *Leander* charged the rampaging battlecruiser, sheltering behind their own Fasset drives as they closed. They were inside her, closer to the planet, but Ortiz spun *Poltava* to face them head-on. She decelerated towards them even as they rushed to meet her, and *Hermes* lunged aside, fighting to get outside the battlecruiser and launch her SLAM drone before she was destroyed.

Ortiz let her go, concentrating on her sister. Close-range lasers and particle beams reduced the tiny warship to half-vaporized wreckage, but the range was too short for effective point defense, and both of *Leander*'s overcharged energy torpedoes erupted against *Poltava*'s screen. Concussion jarred her to the keel, and Ortiz winced as damage reports flickered through his headset. His exec was on it, initiating damage control procedures, but half *Poltava*'s forward energy mounts had been wiped away, along with over thirty of her crew. Her injuries were far from critical—certainly not enough to slow her as she went after the sole survivor—but they hurt all the more after what he'd done to the forts, and they were enough to make him cautious.

The last corvette's skipper watched the battlecruiser overhaul him while his brain sought frantically for some way to stop her. Not for a way to survive, for there was none, but for a way to protect Elysium from her.

She was coming up fast from directly astern, her drive aimed straight at him to interdict his fire. She was grav-riding on him, drawing further acceleration from the attraction of his own drive mass even as hers acted as a brake upon his ship. She had more than enough acceleration to overtake him without that, but her captain was playing a cautious end game, using his interposed drive to protect his ship until he chose to turn and engage. Perhaps overly cautious. *Hermes*'s weapons couldn't hurt his ship much, and there were times caution became more foolhardy than recklessness—

"Sir!" His white-faced plotting officer's voice was tight, overcontrolled as he fought his own fear, but not so tight as to hide its disbelief. "Database *knows* that ship!"

"*What?*" The captain twisted around in his command chair.

"Yes, Sir. That's HMS *Poltava,* Skipper!"

The captain swallowed a disbelieving curse. It *couldn't* be true! It had to be some kind of ECM—there was no *way* a Fleet battlecruiser could be doing this to her own people! But—

"Prep and update the drone!"

"Prepped!" his com officer acknowledged. Then, "Update locked!"

"Launch!"

The captain turned back to his own display, teeth locked in a death's-head grin. There was no way his ship could survive, but he'd gotten the message out. HQ would know everything *he* knew, for the enemy could never intercept his drone and its sensor data.

The drone snaked away, racing directly ahead of the corvette, hidden by her own and *Poltava*'s drives until it was beyond effective energy weapon range. But Ortiz's scan teams picked up its gravity signature as it began to climb across the ecliptic, and they were ready.

The battlecruiser's com officer transmitted a complicated code, and *Hermes*'s skipper gaped in horror as his drone obeyed the command—the proper, authenticated Fleet override—and self-destructed.

He knew, then. Knew who his enemies were and whence they came . . . and how utterly he had been betrayed. Something snapped deep inside him, and he barked new helm orders as the battlecruiser's Fasset drive loomed up close astern. His own drive's side shields dropped, and his ship began to turn.

Hermes was in her enemy's blind zone, riding the arc where the battlecruiser's own drive blocked her sensors. It was a matter of seconds before the bigger ship spun to clear the drive mass and bring her weapons to bear, but seconds were all the corvette's skipper needed. All in the universe he wanted, now.

Poltava began her swing, and not even her AI had time to realize *Hermes* had already swung and redlined her drive on an intercept course.

Commodore Howell swore vilely as both Fasset drives vanished, and the fact that he'd seen it coming only made it worse. That idiot! To blow it all after the bravura brilliance of his initial strike! A second-year middy knew better than to get *that* close to an enemy's drive mass, for God's sake, especially when the disparity in firepower meant that enemy was doomed anyway.

But there'd been nothing Howell could do. The rest of his squadron was still fifteen light-minutes from Elysium, far too distant for any com to reach Ortiz in time. And so he'd had to sit and watch helplessly as a quarter of his battlecruiser strength vanished before his eyes.

He sucked in a deep breath and forced himself back under control. He couldn't pour the milk back into the bottle, and he had other things to worry about—like what the planetary governor did with his emergency SLAM drone.

That drone was the only thing in this system which still threatened Howell's ships. It couldn't hurt them now, but it would tell Fleet far too much if it got out with a record of *Poltava*'s emission signature. If Ortiz hadn't gotten his stupid ass killed, the threat would be minimal; even if the governor realized how the corvette's drone had been killed and locked out the self-destruct command, *Poltava*'s weapons would have been more than capable of killing it as it broke atmosphere. His own ships couldn't. Just catching it with a com beam before it wormholed would be hard enough from this distance.

"Think they got a clean reading on us?" he asked Alexsov hopefully, but the chief of staff's shrug was discouraging.

"The forts certainly did. If they kept groundside advised, and we have to assume they did, the planet knows we're Fleet units. More to the point, Control says their port has enough sensor capability to've gotten a good read on *Poltava*—certainly enough for Fleet's data base to fingerprint her."

"Shit." Howell tugged unhappily at an earlobe. This was what he'd most feared about the entire Elysium operation. The actual attack hadn't worried him, given their inside information, but if the identity of his ships got out, their true objective would be lost. He and his people would become in truth what everyone now assumed they were: plain and simple pirates.

"Maybe I shouldn't've argued against two ships," Alexsov said sourly.

"Don't blame yourself. Ortiz blew it, and you were right. Control's cover story only allowed for one 'legitimate' ship. We couldn't know he'd—"

The commodore broke off with a curse. His light-speed sensors hadn't been able to see the SLAM drone rise from the planet on counter-grav, but the blue spark of its lighting Fasset drive was glaringly obvious.

"Send the code," he rasped, and the ops officer nodded.

"Sending now," Commander Rendlemann replied, and Howell sat back in his command chair to wait. His light-speed destruct command would require thirty-one minutes to overtake the drone; by the time he knew whether or not it had succeeded, his ships would be within assault range of the planet.

CHAPTER FORTY-TWO

Sirens continued to wail as the raiders decelerated towards Elysium. There had been no communication from the "Fleet" ships, and that, in light of what had just occurred, was more than sufficient proof of their purpose.

The governor sat in his communications center and watched his staff coordinate Elysium's mobilization. The planetary militia—such as it was and what there was of it—was marshalling with gratifying speed . . . for whatever good it might accomplish. The militia was considerably stronger than it had been as little as a single standard year earlier, but he'd launched his effort to recruit it up to strength as a backup for the single reinforced Marine company of the planetary garrisons purely as a morale-booster to prove he was Doing Something. He'd never anticipated that it might actually be called upon, and the rest of his careful plans were a shambles. The evacuation centers were already madhouses, and the background crackle of reports from their managers grew more frantic with every second.

A dedicated screen lit, and Captain von Hamel, Elysium's senior Marine, looked out of it and saluted. His eyes were level despite the strain in them, and he already wore his battle armor.

"Governor. My people are heading for their initial positions. We should be at full readiness well before the bandits launch their shuttles."

"Good." The governor tried to put some enthusiasm into his voice, but he knew as well as von Hamel just how little chance the Marines had.

"Brigadier Ivanov tells me his people are running a bit behind schedule, but I anticipate they'll be ready by the time anyone hits their local perimeters," von Hamel continued, and this time the governor simply nodded. Even von Hamel, who'd supported the militia recruiting drive strongly from the beginning, had trouble sounding confident over that, and he leaned closer to his pickup.

"Sir, I've heard some strange reports on that battlecruiser, and—"

"They're true." The governor cut him off grimly and von Hamel's face went even tighter. "Orbit Command confirmed she was Fleet-built, and we caught a last-minute transmission from *Hermes* just before she rammed. They definitely identified her as HMS *Poltava.* According to the records, she went to the breakers twenty-two months ago; apparently the records are wrong."

"Shit." The governor, normally a stickler for decorum, didn't even frown at von Hamel's expletive. "That means these other bastards are probably real Fleet designs . . . with a real ground element." The captain was thinking aloud, his eyes darker than ever. "We can't hold the capital against that kind of attack, and they've got the orbital firepower to take out any fixed position. I'm afraid Thermopylae's our only option, Sir."

"Agreed. We're trying to evacuate now, but we expected at least six hours of lead time. We're not going to get many of them out."

"I'll buy you all the time I can, Sir, but it won't be much," von Hamel warned, and the governor nodded his thanks.

"Understood, Captain. God bless."

"And you, Sir. We're both going to need it."

Commodore Howell watched his plot, eyes glued to the fleeing SLAM drone, as his ships slid into assault orbit, their energy batteries busy systematically eliminating every orbital installation to eradicate any record of their identity. A backwash of assault shuttle readiness reports murmured in the back of his brain, relayed from Rendlemann's cyber-synth link, but Howell wasn't concerned about this phase of the operation. He knew all about Elysium's militia, and he and Alexsov had anticipated from the start that the defenders would be forced back on Thermopylae. It was the only one of their contingency plans that made any sense.

He caught a hand creeping towards his mouth and lowered it before he could nibble its fingernails. The drone was up to ninety percent of light-speed now; their signal had barely three minutes to catch it before it wormholed, and it was going to be close. Assuming, of course, that catching it did any good. If they'd been locked out . . . God, he *hated* this kind of waiting! But he couldn't cut it any shorter, and he turned resolutely to the holo image of the planet in an effort to think of something—anything—else.

Thermopylae was going to make things messy. Although Elysium had become an Incorporated World with direct Senate representation twelve years ago, its population was scarcely thirty million—too many for an all-out raid like Mathison's World but too few to provide the industrial and financial districts which concentrated wealth for easy picking. Only one thing made Elysium a target: GeneCorp's research facility. Every secret of the Empire's leading biomedical consortium lay waiting in that facility's data banks. That was Elysium's true treasure: a cargo that could buy Howell's entire squadron twice over, yet be transported aboard a single ship.

But GeneCorp's HQ lay in the center of the planetary capital. It wasn't a large city, little more than a million people, but built-up areas could exact painful casualties, and the defenders knew what his objective had to be. That was why Thermopylae called for them to center their defense on GeneCorp's facility, where he couldn't use heavy weapons to support *his* ground elements without destroying the very data he'd come to steal.

It was going to be brutal, especially for the city's civilians, but that, too, was part of his mission plan. Maximum frightfulness. A terror campaign against the Empire itself. There had been a time when James Howell would have died to stop anyone cold-blooded enough to mount such an operation.

He bit his lip, cursing the way his mind savaged itself at moments like this. Past was past and done was done, and the final objective was worth—

"*Got* it, by God!"

Howell's head jerked up at Rendlemann's exultant cry, and wan humor glittered in his own eyes as he realized how successfully he'd distracted himself from the drone. But the blue dot had vanished, and he exhaled a tremendous sigh of relief.

"Begin Phase Two," he said softly.

The governor stared at his tracking officer.

"But . . . *how?* It was over fourteen *light-minutes* down-range!"

"I don't know. It was out of beam range, and none of their missiles could even *catch* it. It's like—"

The tracking officer broke off, her face sagging in sudden, bitter understanding and self-hate.

"The destruct code!" She slammed a fist against the side of her own head. "Idiot! *Idiot!* I should've guessed from what happened to *Hermes*'s drone! How could I've *been* so stupid?!"

"What are you talking about, Lieutenant?" the governor demanded, and she fought herself back under control.

"I knew they'd taken out *Hermes*'s drone, but I assumed—*assumed*—they'd done it with their weapons. They didn't. They used a Fleet self-destruct command and ordered it to suicide."

"But that's impossible! There's no way they could—"

"Oh yes there is, Governor." The lieutenant faced him squarely, her voice harsh. "Those aren't just Fleet-built ships out there. I figured some son of a bitch at the wreckers must've disposed of the hulls on the sly—God knows they're worth more than reclamation, even stripped—but they've got complete Fleet data bases, as well, including the security files."

"Dear God," the governor whispered. He sagged back into a chair, hands trembling as he realized the monumental treason that implied.

"Exactly. And thanks to my stupidity—*my* stupidity!—we don't have a drone left to tell anyone."

The assault boats sliced downward through Elysium's night sky. The raiders' carefully hoarded *Bengals* led the first wave, fleshed out by older but still deadly *Leopards.* A handful of local defense missiles rose to meet them, and a pair of unlucky shuttles vanished in direct hits.

It was the defenders' only luck. Imperial assault craft were designed to attack heavily armed ground bases; Elysium's pitiful weaponry was less than nothing in comparison. Hypervelocity weapons screamed down in reply, relying solely on the kinetic energy developed at ten percent of light-speed, and high kilotonne-range fireballs annihilated the missile sites.

More HVW launched, targeted with cold calculation on the evacuation centers and the governor's residence. Fresh flame shredded the darkness, and Captain von Hamel cursed the minds and souls behind the weapons. This wasn't an assault—it was a massacre. An intentional massacre of civilians by people who *knew* where the evacuation centers were. He and the governor hadn't saved anyone; they'd simply gathered them in convenient targets for mass murder!

But why? Von Hamel had read the reports on the other raids, but they were nothing compared to this, and it made no sense. A demand for surrender on pain of such an attack might have been reasonable. This wasn't.

More terrible shockwaves rippled through the ground, and he began barking orders. With the governor dead, he was on his own, and there was no point in a phased withdrawal now. The civilians he'd hoped to cover were already dead, and he sent his Wasps charging back to their inner perimeter.

Howell watched the gangrenous light boils bite off chunks of the holo-imaged city, and part of him shared von Hamel's sickness. But the people in those centers would only have lived a few more hours whatever happened, and the panic of the strikes might hamper the defenders' coordination. Anything that reduced his own casualties was worthwhile, he told himself . . . especially when it only meant killing people who simply hadn't yet learned that they were dead.

The first-wave shuttles grounded, and armored figures spilled from the ramps. Powered battle armor gleamed and glittered in the hellish light of the city's fires as the assault teams formed up and swept into its heart.

Captain von Hamel watched his tactical display, and he was no longer afraid. Fury still crackled in his blood, but even that was suppressed, buried under an ice-cold concentration. He and his troops were Marines. There were only three hundred and twelve of them, but they were the Empire's Wasps, products of a four-century tradition, and they were all that stood between a city and its murderers. They couldn't stop it, and every one of them knew it . . . just as they knew they were going to die trying.

The bastards were mounting a concentric assault, hoping to overpower his people in the first rush, and their assault routes were moving directly against his original prepared positions. The captain watched them come and bared his teeth, unsurprised after the accuracy with which the evac centers had been taken out. They had to have detailed information on all of Elysium's defense planning, but there was one thing they didn't know: virtually every one of his original positions had been relocated in the wake of last week's tactical exercise. He keyed the master tac link.

"All Wasps, Alpha-One. Hold your fire. I say again, all units hold fire for my command."

More shuttles streaked downward, probed by his tactical sensors as they planeted, and his face tightened. Those weren't assault boats; they were heavy-lift cargo shuttles, and their presence this early could only mean the raiders were putting in heavy armored units.

The assault teams converged on the defensive strong points with cautious confidence. Reports flowed back and forth as the first tanks disembarked from their shuttles and began to move forward. No one expected it to be easy—not against Imperial Marines—but knowing precisely where their enemies were turned it into something more like a live-fire exercise than a battle.

Von Hamel watched his display. The raider spearheads were inside his perimeter in a dozen places, and if his people weren't where the raiders thought they were, they weren't far away, either. There were only a limited number of positions which could cover the same approach routes.

One column of invaders moved towards his own CP, a tentacle of death reaching into the mangled city's heart, and he gathered up his rifle. He had far too few people for him to stay out of the firefight.

He raised the heavy weapon—a thirty-millimeter "rifle" only a man with exoskeletal battle armor "muscles" could possibly have managed. It was loaded with discarding sabot tungsten penetrators four times heavier than those of the rifles unarmored infantry carried, and he slid it cautiously over the edge of the office building roof.

"All Wasps, Alpha-One!" He barked "*Engage!*"

The orderly advance exploded in chaos.

Raiders screamed and died in a hurricane of high-velocity tungsten. Three hundred rifles—auto-cannon in all but name—blazed at point-blank range, and not even battle armor could stop fire like that. Fifteen-millimeter penetrators hurled them aside like shattered dolls, support squads' launchers spat plasma grenades and HE, and Captain Alexsov's careful briefing had become a death trap. The raiders *knew* where the defenders were, and their point men and flankers had succumbed to overconfidence.

Even taken by surprise, they had the firepower to deal with their enemies. What they no longer had was the *will.* They didn't even try to return fire; they simply broke and ran, scourged by that deadly hail of fire until they managed to get out of range.

"Regroup! Assume Position Gamma. I say again, Position Gamma."

Von Hamel's people responded instantly, withdrawing from the positions their attack had marked for the raiders, and this time the smoke and confusion and terror helped them. There was no way the other side could track them through the chaos as they dashed for their new stations.

They'd done well, von Hamel thought. Barely half a dozen Marine beacons had gone out, and the raiders had been brutally mauled.

But they wouldn't get another chance like that. The other side might not know his troops' exact positions, but they knew his general battle plan. They wouldn't come in fat and stupid a second time, and they had that damned armor to back them, not to mention the assault boats.

Howell watched Alexsov's face as the reports came in. Another man might have sworn. At the very least he would have said *something.* Alexsov only tightened his lips and started sorting out the chaos.

The commodore looked away, grateful for Alexsov's calm yet constitutionally incapable of understanding it. His eyes swept his command deck, and he frowned. Commander Watanabe sat stiffly in the assistant gunnery officer's chair, sweat beading his brow, and his face was pale as he stared at the fires spalling the darkened city.

Howell turned his head, looking for Rachel Shu, and found her. She, too, was watching Watanabe, and her eyes were narrow.

A smoke-choked dawn, smutted with cinders and the stench of burning, painted the sky at last.

Captain Marius von Hamel hadn't expected to see the sun rise, and now he wanted to, more than he had ever wanted anything before, for he knew he would never see it set. But it was grim, vengeful satisfaction that pulsed within him, not fear. He and what remained of his reinforced company, little more than a single platoon now, had withdrawn to their final positions, and the streets behind them were thick with the dead. Too many were his own, and far, far too many were civilians, but there were over seven hundred raiders and nine gutted tanks among them. His air-defense platoon had even added a trio of *Bengals* to the carnage, for the enemy dared not use HVW this close to GeneCorp's HQ. They had to strafe if they wanted his Wasps, and that brought them into reach of his people's stings.

Yet the end was coming. Only the tight tactical control he'd managed to maintain had staved it off this long, but ammunition was running low, and his last reserve had been committed. He was spread too thin to hold against another determined push, and once the final perimeter broke, his control would vanish into a room-to-room insanity that could end only one way.

He knew that. But he'd also realized something else during the nightmare night. These weren't pirates. He didn't know what they were, but no pirate commander would have continued such a furious assault or accepted such casualties, and if he'd tried, his men would have mutinied. These people were something else, and the carnage they'd wreaked on the evac centers filled him with a dreadful certainty.

They were going to destroy this city. They were going to wipe it from the face of Elysium, whether they gained their prize or not. It was part of their pattern, and there was something more than brute sadism to it. He was too exhausted to think clearly, but it was almost as if they needed to eliminate all witnesses to protect some secret.

He had no idea what that secret might be, and it didn't matter. None of his people were going to be surrendered to the butchers who had raped and tortured Mawli and Brigadoon and Mathison's World, and there was no longer any reason to preserve GeneCorp's data base as a bargaining chip.

He lay on a balcony, watching the smoky sky, and waited.

"All right." Even Alexsov sounded drained, and Howell could scarcely believe their losses. The chief of staff locked eyes with the ground commander's screen image, and the commodore saw the terrible fatigue in the ground man's face. Howell was desperately tempted to give it up—simply replacing the losses to his ground component was going to take months—but they'd come too far. And, he reminded himself tiredly, whatever happened, they'd attained their primary objective. News of what had happened to Elysium would rock the Empire to its foundations.

"One more push, and you're in. Check?" Alexsov said.

"Check," his subordinate said wearily, and the chief of staff nodded.

"Then get it moving, Colonel."

Von Hamel heard the sudden crescendo of fire as the tanks moved in. His troopers fired back desperately, but they were almost out of antitank weapons and they were too thin, too heartbreakingly thin. Beacons vanished from his display with dreadful speed, and he switched it off with a sigh.

He sat up, craning his neck at the eastern sky, and tears trickled down his face as he listened to the thunder. Not for himself, but for his people. For all they'd done and given that no one would ever know a thing about.

His southern perimeter broke at last. It didn't crumble and yield; it simply died with the men and women who held it, and the attackers thundered through the gap as a blazing arm of the sun rose above the shattered skyline.

Marius Von Hamel stared at it, drinking in its beauty, and pressed the button.

* * *

Commodore James Howell stared in shock at the expanding globe of fire in the center of the city. It swelled and towered as he watched, wiping away GeneCorp and all he had come to steal and devouring half his remaining ground troops like some dragon out of Terran myth.

"Damn." It was Alexsov, his voice flat and almost disinterested, and Howell wanted to scream at him. But he didn't. There was no point.

"Recover the assault force," he told Rendlemann.

"Yes, Sir. Shall I move on the secondary objectives, Sir?"

"No." Howell watched the fireball begin to fade. Amazing how little of the remaining city had gone with it. Whoever planted those charges had known what he was doing. "No, I don't think so. We've lost enough people for one night, and there's still that damned militia. We'll cut our losses."

"Yes, Sir."

Howell leaned back and rubbed his eyes. That suicide charge had never been part of Thermopylae. Had someone down there realized the truth?

"Move to Phase Four," he said quietly.

The shuttles departed with barely a third of the personnel they'd landed. Their mother ships recovered them, and the ground force's survivors stumbled back aboard, stunned by the blood and chaos of their "walk-over." It was the first time they'd failed, and Howell tried to hide his own fear of the consequences. Not for himself. Control should have no complaints about the *effect* of the operation, and ground equipment and the cannon fodder to man it had always been far easier to come by than starships.

No, it was the effect on his men he feared. How would their morale react to this? He already knew Control was going to have to settle for more lightly defended targets in the immediate future. He'd have too many new personnel, and the vets would need easy operations to rebuild confidence.

He folded his hands in his lap, brooding down on Elysium's holo image. It was past time to be done here, and he turned to the gunnery officer.

"Are we prepared to execute Phase Four, Commander Rahman?"

"Yes, Sir. Missile targets are laid in and locked."

"Good." Howell studied the man's expression. It wasn't exactly calm, but it was composed and ready. Commander Watanabe, on the other hand . . .

The commodore turned to the commander. Watanabe was pasty pale and sweating hard, and Howell sighed internally. He'd been afraid of this ever since Alexsov voiced his own concern over Watanabe's reliability.

"Commander Watanabe," his voice was very quiet, "execute Phase Four."

Watanabe jerked, and his face worked. He stared at his commanding officer, then down at the console. Down at the target codes for every one of Elysium's cities.

"I . . ."

"I gave you an order, Commander," Howell said, and his eyes flicked over Watanabe's shoulder to Rachel Shu.

"Please, Sir," Watanabe whispered. "I . . . I don't . . ."

"You don't want to execute it?" The commander's eyes darted back up at the almost compassionate note in Howell's voice. "That's understandable, Commander, but you're one of my officers now. As such, you have neither room for second thoughts nor the luxury of deciding which orders you will obey. Do you understand me, Commander Watanabe?"

Silence hovered on the command deck, and the commander closed his eyes. Then he stood and jerked the synth-link headset from his temples.

"I'm sorry, Sir." His voice was hoarse. "I can't. I just *can't*."

"I see. I'm sorry to hear that," Howell said softly, and nodded to Rachel Shu.

The emerald beam buzzed across the bridge. It struck precisely on the base of Watanabe's skull, and his body arched in spastic agony. But it was a dead man's reaction—a muscular response and no more.

The corpse slithered to the deck. Someone coughed on the stench of singed hair, but no one moved. No one was even surprised, and plastic and alloy whispered on leather as Shu holstered her neural disrupter with an expression of mild distaste.

"Commander Rahman," Howell said, and the senior gunnery officer straightened in his chair.

"Yes, Sir?"

"Execute Phase Four, Commander."

Book Five:
Fugitive

CHAPTER FORTY-THREE

Alicia lay in bed, staring at the ceiling and chewing her lip while she tried not to stew. It was becoming steadily more difficult.

In one sense, things weren't actually that bad. Tannis' diagnostics were reporting exactly what they ought to, now that Tisiphone knew what results they were supposed to get, and Alicia wasn't worried about revealing anything she chose to conceal. Tannis had tried direct neural queries, chemical therapy, even hypnotic regression, but Tisiphone was an old hand at controlling human thoughts and responses. She might not be able to do it to anyone else these days, but Alicia's brain and body were her own front yard, and she allowed no trespassers, so that side was secure enough.

Unfortunately, that didn't help against her boredom. Tisiphone might enjoy fooling the medics or roaming Soissons's planetary computer net, but Alicia was going mad. The thought woke a sour smile, but it had stopped being funny when she realized what was really happening to her grief and hatred.

They were still there. She couldn't feel them through Tisiphone's shields, but she sensed them, and she hadn't dealt with them. She *couldn't* deal with them, because she couldn't touch them, and that left an odd, dangerously unresolved vacuum at her core. Worse, she thought she knew what Tisiphone was doing with all that raw, oozing emotion.

The Fury had no interest in dissipating it, for she knew only one catharsis. At first Alicia had suspected she was absorbing it like some sort of strange sustenance, but a worse suspicion had occurred to her, and the Fury had refused to deny it.

She was storing it. Distilling it into the pure essence of hatred, reserving it against some future need, and Alicia was afraid. Drop commandos had few self-delusions—they couldn't afford them—and she knew about her own dark side. She'd demonstrated it, without a trace of regret, on Wadislaw Watts, and there had been times in the field when her killer self had threatened to break free, as well. It had never happened, for the rest of the personality her parents and upbringing had built had been even stronger, but it had been a near thing more than once, and a woman stayed clear-headed in combat or she died—probably taking other people with her when she went.

Thoughts of what the sudden release of all that pent-up rage might do to her judgment terrified her, but Tisiphone refused even to discuss it despite requests which had come all too close to pleading before pride drove Alicia to drop them. She was helpless in the face of the Fury's refusal . . . and Tisiphone had reminded her—not cruelly, but almost kindly—that she had agreed to pay "anything" for her vengeance. That was nothing less than the truth, and the fact that she'd thought she was mad at the time had no bearing. She'd given her word, and like Uncle Arthur, that was the end of it.

But now a fresh disturbing element had been added, for Tisiphone was clearly up to something. There was a pleased note to her mental voice which made very little sense, given their total lack of achievement. Alicia was astonished that the fiery, driven Fury hadn't insisted on making their break long ago. To be sure, she'd gleaned a tremendous amount of information—including everything Colonel McIlhenny and even Ben Belkassem knew about the pirates—but there had to be something else. . . .

<Indeed there is, Little One.> The comment was so sudden Alicia twitched in surprise, and Tisiphone chuckled silently. *<In fact, the event for which I have waited has now occurred, and the time has come for us to depart.>*

<Are you serious?!> Alicia jerked upright, then gasped as Tisiphone answered without words. Her augmentation came spontaneously on line, her boosted senses spun up to full acuity for the first time in more than two months, and she twitched again as

Tisiphone activated her pharmacope. The first ripple of tension ran through her as the tick reservoir administered its carefully measured dose to her bloodstream, and the world began to slow.

She bit her lip, confused by the speed with which the Fury was moving, and a faint, familiar haze hovered before her eyes. It cleared quickly, and her ears rang with the high, sweet song of the tick.

<*We will go now,*> Tisiphone said calmly. <*I have placed commands in their computers to reroute their sensors, deactivate the door security systems, and summon the floor nurse elsewhere, but I cannot control who we may meet along the way. Dealing with them will be your responsibility.*>

Alicia rose with the tick's floating grace as the door oozed open with syrupy slowness.

She floated through it. The corridor beyond was empty, the nurses' station unmanned as Tisiphone had promised, but there was a permanent guard on the elevators. She'd met the night guard, and though the earnest young man had been very careful never to say so, she knew why he was there, for he, too, was a drop commando. But the elevators were around a bend in the corridor, and she flowed down the hall like a spirit, riding the tick's exaltation.

She stepped around the bend, and the guard looked up. She smiled, and he smiled back slowly, so slowly. But then his smile changed as he recognized the precise, gliding movement of the tick.

His hand started for his stunner, and Alicia wanted to laugh in pure exultation. He was too far away to reach before the stunner cleared its holster, but Old Speedy wasn't racing through his veins. Though he got the stunner up before she reached him, he didn't have time to reset its power.

The green beam struck her dead on—with absolutely no result. The neural shields built into drop commando augmentation could resist even nerve disrupter fire, to a point, and a stunner blast which would have downed an elephant or a direcat had no effect at all on her.

He really was young, she thought tolerantly as her hands started forward. Perhaps he'd been confused by the fact that he *knew* her augmentation—including the shields—had been disabled. On the other hand, he'd obviously recognized tick mode when he saw it, which indicated her augmentation had been reactivated. Except, of course, that he hadn't had time to think. If he had, he would have gone for her hand-to-hand from the start. He probably couldn't have stopped her that way, either, she reflected as her first lightning-fast blow drifted towards him, but he might have lasted long enough to sound the alarm.

They'd never know about that now. Her floating hand smacked precisely behind his ear, and she spun him like a limp, toffee-stuffed mannequin. Her fingers sought the pressure points, and he went down in a boneless heap before his own augmentation could spin up to stop it. Best of all, he'd recognized her; he knew she wasn't going to try to capture or interrogate him, which in turn, made his automatic protocols a dead letter.

Alicia tugged him into the elevator and closed the doors, wondering where they were supposed to go now.

<*Down,*> a clear voice said. <*There is a vehicle in the parking garage. I reserved it for you this morning.*>

<*I hope you know what we're doing, Lady.*>

<*Oh, I do, indeed,*> Tisiphone purred, and Alicia punched the button for the subbasement garage. The trip seemed to take forever to her tick-enhanced time sense, and she wondered what she would do if they were stopped along the way by another passenger.

They weren't—no doubt because it was well after local midnight—and the doors slid open at last. Alicia looked thoughtfully down at the unconscious guard and removed the stunner from his nerveless fingers. She reset it and gave him a careful shot that would keep him under for hours, then hit the emergency stop button, locking the car in place.

<*All right, where's this vehicle?*>

<*Stall one-seven-four. To your right, Little One.*>

Alicia nodded and jogged briskly down the lines of stalls. Most were empty, and the vehicles she saw were mainly civilian, with only an occasional military or governmental ground car or skimmer—until she reached the appointed slot and blinked at the lean, lethal-looking recon skimmer in it.

<*Very impressive,*> she thought, glancing at the fuselage markings of a rear admiral as she popped the hatch, <*but where are we going?*>

<Jefferson Field, Pad Alpha Six.>

<A shuttle pad? Just what are we up to here?>

<We are leaving Soissons, Little One.>

Again there was a mental chuckle—almost a giggle, if the grim and purposeful Fury could have produced such a thing—and Alicia sighed with resignation.

Tisiphone seemed to know what she was doing, though it would have been nice if she'd bothered with a mission brief. They were going to have to have a little discussion about this sort of thing, Alicia reflected as she brought the skimmer's counter-grav-ity to life, lifted it twenty centimeters from the garage floor, and sent it up the ramp at a sedate speed, but even through the exhilaration of the tick she felt a deeper, sharper stab of pleasure as the star-strewn sky of Soissons gleamed clear and clean above her. Out. *Free.* Something of Tisiphone's eagerness touched her, like the joy of the hawk in the moment it tucked its wings to stoop upon its prey, and she took the skimmer into the night.

The Fleet skimmer's com panel whispered with routine messages as Alicia slid through the darkness towards the brightly illuminated perimeter of Jefferson Field, and she felt herself relaxing within the cocoon of the tick. She knew relaxation was dangerous, particularly since she still had no idea what Tisiphone intended, but she was on a sort of autopilot.

It was disturbingly unlike her. A strange fatalism had replaced her normal, sharp thoughts at such times, and she disliked it, yet it was oddly seductive. She tried to resist it, but her steel had turned to something that bent and flexed, and a part of her wondered how Tisiphone had done it. For one thing was crystal clear: the Fury was in the pilot's seat. The long, boring weeks of inactivity and comfortable mental chats had blinded Alicia to what she truly was. Those chats hadn't been subterfuge, nor had the gently malicious teasing, but they were only one side of Tisiphone, and not the strongest one. There was an elemental ruthlessness to the Fury when the moment for action came. She hadn't discussed her plan with Alicia because it hadn't occurred to her that there was any reason she should, and now her unwavering determination had made Alicia a prisoner within her own body.

Yet it was even more complex than that, Alicia reflected as her obedient hands guided the skimmer along the Jefferson Field approach route and their admiral's markings and transponder took them through the unmanned, outer checkpoints. Even while a tiny part of her fluttered like a panicked bird against Tisiphone's control, another part was perfectly content. It was the part which always heaved a sigh of relief once the briefings were over and the mission began. They were moving, they were committed, and the predator within her purred with the elation of the hunt. Her brain hummed and wavered with conflicting impetuses, yet her thoughts and actions came crisp and clear and cold, and she'd never felt anything quite like it in her life.

<*Now what?*> she asked as they approached the inner security gate.

<*Drive through,*> Tisiphone responded, and her own will stirred sleepily.

<*That's not a very good idea. You may have snabbled up an admiral's skimmer, but I don't have the papers to match it.*>

<*It does not matter.*>

<*You're crazy! This gate's got real, live sentries, Lady!*>

<*But they will see nothing. Have you forgotten the nurse?*>

<*Damn it, they don't rely on just their eyes, and this thing is* armed! *Their sensors are going to go crazy!*>

<*Let them. We need only a few moments of confusion.*>

<*No way.*> Alicia began to slow the skimmer. <*We're out of the hospital. Let's pull back and rethink this before we get in so deep we—*>

Her thought shattered in white-hot anguish, and she grunted as her eyes went blind. The pain and blindness vanished as quickly as they had come, and her brain writhed in useless revolt as her body obeyed the Fury's will. She felt the skimmer surge forward under maximum power, blazing through the security gate, and the alert sentires saw nothing at all. She caught a glimpse of them in the aft display, spinning towards their com links in total confusion as lights flashed and sirens whooped, but her hands were on the controls, whipping the skimmer higher and wheeling for the shuttle pads.

<*Let me* go!> she screamed, and wild laughter flooded her mind.

<*Not now, Little One! The game has begun—there is no going back!*>

<*I'm not your puppet, damn you!*>

<*Ah, but you are.*> The Fury's voice paused, then resumed a bit more tentatively, as if puzzled by her resistance. <*This is what you asked of me, Little One. I swore to give it to you, and I shall.*>

<*This is* my *life,* my *body!*> The sense of content had vanished, and her rousing will battered at Tisiphone's control. She gritted her teeth, smashing with fists of outrage, and fresh pain surged. She panted with the ferocity of her struggle, gasping in triumph as her hands began to slow the skimmer, then cried out as Tisiphone struck back furiously.

<*You must not! Not now! This is to lose all at the last moment!*>

"Then let me *go,* goddamn you!" Alicia gritted through clenched teeth. Her anguish-tight voice was strange and twisted in her own ears, but somehow she knew she must speak aloud. "I want myself back!"

<*Oh, very well!*> Tisiphone snapped, and the skimmer swerved wildly as the Fury abruptly released all control. Alicia moaned in relief—then yelped as a plasma bolt whipped past her canopy. She hurled the skimmer into a screaming turn, still in the grip of the tick, and a second miss sent a parked air lorry's hydrogen reservoir fireballing into the darkness.

<*I trust you are satisfied now?*> Tisiphone remarked, but Alicia was too busy to respond as she writhed in a mad evasion pattern. More plasma slashed past like lethal ball lightning, and she punched up the skimmer's light screen. It wouldn't do much against a direct hit, but it should fend off a near-miss.

Fires glared in the night as she turned the vehicle almost on its side, trading lift for evasion. Warehouses belched flames under the fury of her pursuers' fire, and she swerved down a narrow opening between freight carriers and loading docks. The com unit yammered with demands for her surrender and warnings that deadly force would be employed if she refused. Not that she'd needed *that,* she thought as the flames vanished astern and her scanners reported atmospheric sting ships closing from the north. Closer to the ground, security skimmers were howling in pursuit. They'd overshot when she whipped to the side, giving her a small lead to play with, but they were just as fast as she, and they knew the base far better.

At least she had decent instrumentation, and she cursed as she picked up still more security vehicles. They were outside her, and she swore again as she checked her map display. She still didn't have the least idea what Tisiphone was up to, but the pursuit had cut her off from retreat. They were closing in, driving her deeper into the base in what looked entirely too much like a preplanned security maneuver. There had to be something nasty waiting for her, yet the only place left to go was directly towards the shuttle pads, exactly as Tisiphone had originally planned.

She wrenched the skimmer through another turn, half her mind watching the sting ships' traces. They'd responded quickly, but it would still take them a couple of minutes to get here, and the pads loomed ahead of her.

"All right, Lady," she gritted, punching commands into the auto-pilot. "If you can still make us invisible, this is the moment."

<*And what good will that do?*> Tisiphone sniffed. <*As you yourself have pointed out, they will still have us on their sensors, and—*>

<*Just shut up and* do *it!*> Alicia snapped, and hit the eject button.

The pilot's canopy blew off, and the ejection seat's tiny counter-gravity unit flung her high. She gasped with the shock of it, but her hands were on the armrests, riding the control keys.

The maneuvering jets flared, and she swallowed a hysterical cackle. *This,* by God, was seat-of-the-pants flying! The jets lacked endurance—they didn't need it, with the counter-grav to do the real work—but they were designed to dart away from a plunging wreck or make a last ditch effort to evade hostile fire. That gave them quite a kick, and the seat was made of low-signature materials, almost invisible to the best sensors. She sent herself flying towards Pad Alpha Six and pirouetted in midair to watch their stolen skimmer execute her final command.

The vehicle rocketed upward in a desperation escape attempt as the security skimmers closed in at last, and bursts of fire followed it. Not just plasma cannon, which were relatively short-ranged in atmosphere, either. The security people were playing for keeps, and the red and white flashes of high explosive converged on the wildly careering hull, but Tisiphone seemed to have worked her magic, for no one was shooting at her. An explosion flowered amidships, and the skimmer shuddered, shedding bits and pieces but still climbing vertically, almost out of sight from the ground. More hits splintered armorplast and alloy, and then a sting ship screamed in.

Alicia winced as twin bores of eye-searing light blazed. Those weren't plasma bolts; the skimmer was high enough for them to use heavy weapons on it, and it vaporized in a sun-bright boil as the HVW struck at seventeen thousand KPS.

<*Crap, those people aren't kidding!*>

<*No, they are not,*> Tisiphone replied tartly, then relented. <*Still, this was very clever. No doubt they will think you died in the skimmer.*>

<*As long as none of them noticed us punching out.*> Alicia hit her keys again, killing the jets and powering down the countergrav. They landed in the shadow of the freight pad, and she shucked the safety harness. <*And now that we're here, just what the hell do we think we're doing?*>

<*Escaping. I have arranged an appropriate vehicle for the purpose.*>

<*A cargo shuttle?*> Alicia was sprinting for the pad stairs even while she protested. <*That's not going to get us very far.*>

<*It will get us far enough—and have I said anything about a cargo shuttle?*> Tisiphone replied as Alicia cleared the stairs and rocked to a halt.

"Oh, *shit*," she whispered, and closed her eyes as if that could make it go away. When she opened them again, the fully-armed *Bengal*-class assault shuttle was still sitting there.

<*It is amazing what one can arrange through computers.*>

<*You* are *out of your mind! That thing costs sixty million credits! They'll never let it go—and I've never handled one in my life!*>

<*You are already pre-flighted and cleared to lift in two minutes, and I checked carefully, Little One. You are fully qualified on* Leopard-*class shuttles, and while the* Bengals *are larger, the major changes are in payload, sensors, and increased armament, not flight controls.*>

<*But I haven't flown* anything *in over five* years!>

<*I am sure it will all come back to you. But for now, I suggest we hurry. Our launch window is short.*>

"Oh, God," Alicia moaned, but she was already dashing for the ramp. She had no choice. Tisiphone was out of her mythological mind, but whether Uncle Arthur believed in her or not, the Fury had done too many fresh impossible things. Alicia would *never* get out of observation after this!

The shuttle interior was cool, humming with the familiar tingle of waiting flight system. It was like coming home, despite the madness, and she charged through the troop section towards the flight deck. A freight canister—a very *large* freight canister, with very familiar bar codes—was webbed to the deck, and she almost stopped when she saw the codes on it.

<There is no time. You may examine it later.>

<B-but that can't really *be—>*

<Certainly it can. You may need your weapons, so I ordered it prepped and loaded aboard.>

Alicia moaned again as she flopped into the pilot's couch and reached for the headset. This couldn't be happening. Trained mental reflexes brought up the synth-link, reached out to the flight computers, but underneath them was a bubble of wild laughter.

So far, in a single night, she'd escaped custody, assaulted a fellow Cadreman, stolen a skimmer worth at least twenty thousand credits, crashed through Fleet security onto a restricted military reservation, refused to stop when so ordered, and caused the destruction of said stolen skimmer and damage to sundry base facilities as the direct result of lawfully empowered personnel's efforts to apprehend her—and none of that even compared to what she was *about* to do. Talk about grand theft! This shuttle alone represented a good sixty million of the Emperor's credits, and if that canister really contained a suit of Cadre battle armor, the price tag was about to double. They'd build a whole new jail just so they could put her under it!

<Only if they catch you,> Tisiphone pointed out with maddening cheer.

Alicia felt her teeth grate but swallowed her savage reply, for the computers had accepted her and placed themselves at her disposal. It was a disturbing sensation, almost frightening, as their inhuman vastness clicked into place about her. She hadn't felt it in a long time, and for just an instant she quailed, but then everything snapped into focus and she was home. The shuttle and she were one, its sensors her eyes and ears and nerves, its power plant her heart, its countergravity and thrusters her arms and legs. Joy filled her like cold fire, burning away the confusion and dismay, and she smiled.

<Yes, Little One,> Tisiphone whispered. *<Now is your moment. We are training flight Foxtrot-Two-Niner.>*

Alicia punched up Flight Control and announced her flight designation in a voice so calm it astonished her. There was a moment of silence, and her adrenaline spiked. Her intrusion had scrambled operations. Security had imposed a lock-down on all flights until they got to the bottom of it. Someone in FlyCon had her head together and was using her own initiative to hold all take-offs until the situation was sorted out, or—

"Cleared to go, Foxtrot-Two-Niner," FlyCon said, and she swallowed another tremulous laugh as her atmospheric turbines screamed.

The shuttle sliced up through Soissons's atmosphere, and there was no pursuit. None at all, and that was truly amazing. Of course, there was really no pressing need to pursue a purely intrasystemic craft. Where could it go, after all? For that matter, who in her right mind would steal an assault shuttle of all damned things?

"So now what?" Alicia asked aloud.

<Set course to rendezvous with beacon Sierra-Lima-Seven-Four-Four.>

Alicia started to ask what they were rendezvousing with but bit her tongue and checked her computers for the proper coordinates. No doubt she would know soon enough. Too soon, judging by what had already happened.

The shuttle swept higher, air-breathing turbines shutting down and thrusters firing to align its nose on one of the Fleet shipyards, and she frowned. If they wanted out of the system, they had to get aboard a starship, and that should have meant guile and stealth. Could Tisiphone be so confident—so crazy, she amended dourly—as to think they could *hijack* a ship?

If so, she was finally up against something even she couldn't manage. At absolute minimum, they needed a dispatch boat, and that meant a crew of at least eight. Not even a drop commando could force eight highly trained specialists to perform their tasks when all they had to do to maroon her was refuse to obey. And no way were Fleet officers going to help a crazed Cadrewoman steal their ship out from under them!

They continued unchallenged on their flight path, and Alicia's brows furrowed as she realized they weren't headed directly for the shipyard after all. Their destination lay in a parking orbit of its own, and she brought her sensors to bear on it. It didn't look like anyth—

"*No!*" she gasped. "Tisiphone, we can't steal that!"

<*We certainly can, and we must.*>

"No!" Alicia repeated, and unaccustomed panic sharpened her voice. "I can't fly that thing—I'm no starship pilot! And . . . and . . ."

<*It is too late for such thoughts, Little One,*> the Fury said sternly. <*I have studied this matter with great care and obtained all the information we will require. Nor will it be necessary for you to pilot the ship. It will, so to speak,*> the Fury actually *chuckled* in her brain, <*pilot itself, will it not?*>

Alicia tried to reply, but all that came out was a faint, inarticulate whimper as the shuttle continued toward the waiting alpha-synth ship.

CHAPTER FORTY-FOUR

The alpha-synth glinted ominously in the light of Franconia.

A cargo shuttle was docked on the number two rack, but Alicia's momentary panic eased when she saw the fuselage number. It matched the one on the ship's hull, so it must be an assigned auxiliary and not a bunch of yard workers waiting for her. Not that it made the situation much better.

Her mind was numb, frozen by the impossibility of Tisiphone's plan, yet she felt the ship's sinister beauty. It lacked the needle-sharp lines of a sting ship, but the Fasset drive's constraints imposed a sleekness of their own—different from those of atmosphere yet no less graceful—and it floated in space with the latent menace of a drowsing panther. She'd never expected to see one, especially not at such proximity, but she knew about them.

The size of a big light cruiser yet possessed of more firepower than a battlecruiser and faster than a destroyer, literally able to think for itself and respond with light-speed swiftness, an alpha-synth was lethal beyond belief, tonne for tonne the most deadly weapon ever built by man. It was too small to mount worthwhile numbers of SLAMs, so it used the tonnage it might have wasted on them for even more broadside armament. Nothing smaller than a battleship could fight it, nothing but another alpha-synth could catch it, and she hated to even think how Fleet would react if she and Tisiphone actually succeeded in stealing it. The damned thing cost half as much as a dreadnought just for starters, but having one of them running around loose in the hands of a certified madwoman would turn every admiral in the Fleet white overnight. They'd do *anything* to get it back.

She tried not to consider that as she guided the *Bengal* mechanically toward the number one shuttle rack and through the docking sequence, yet she couldn't stop the gibbering thread of horror in her thoughts. Bad enough to be hunted by every planet and ship of the Empire, but there was worse if their theft succeeded. Far worse, for there was only one way to pilot an alpha-synth, and her throat tightened at the thought of meeting the ship's computer. Of impressing it, mating with it, becoming one with it—

She'd actually begun to undock before she could stop herself, and she closed her eyes, panting through clenched teeth while panic pulsed deep within her. But Tisiphone had burned all of her bridges; there was nowhere else to go, however terrifying the prospect, and she cursed with silent savagery.

<Do not worry so, Little One! I but awaited this vessel's completion to act, and I do not set my hand to measures which fail.>

<Damn *you! You never warned me about anything like this!>*

<There was no reason,> the mental voice said austerely. *<I require your body, your hands, and you have sworn to give them to me.>*

<Body, yes, and hands, but not this! Do you have any idea what you're asking of me?>

<Of course.>

<I doubt that, Lady. I really doubt that. I don't have any training in this—I was never even cleared for cyber-synth, much less an alpha *link. I don't even know if my synth-link software will let me interface!>*

<It would not have. Now it will.>

<Great. That's fucking great! And did it ever occur to you that if I link with that thing—assuming it lets me in, which it probably won't—I'll be part *of it? That I can never* unlink*?>*

<It did.> Tisiphone paused, then continued with a sort of stern compassion. *<Little One, it is unlikely you will survive long enough for it to be a problem.>* A chill filtered through Alicia with the words. Not surprise, but a shivery tension as it was finally said. *<I am not what I once was. You know that, and so you know that I may strike your enemies only through you. This ship will be your sword and shield, yet everything suggests the pirates have more firepower than*

even it represents. We will find them, and we will seek out and destroy their leaders, yet that is all I can—and will—promise you.> The Fury paused for a moment. <*I never offered more, Alicia DeVries, and you are no child, but as great a warrior as I have ever known. Would you tell me you have not already realized this must be so?*>

Alicia bent her head and closed her eyes and knew Tisiphone spoke only the truth. She drew a deep breath, then straightened in her couch and removed her headset with steady fingers. A snake of fear coiled in her belly, but she climbed out of the couch and walked towards the hatch . . . and her fate.

There was a security panel inside the alpha-synth's outer hatch. Alicia had no idea what sort of defensive systems it connected to—only that they would most assuredly suffice to eliminate any unauthorized intruder.

<*Give me your hand,*> Tisiphone commanded, and she bit her lip as her right arm rose under another's control. Her index finger stabbed number-pad buttons in a sequence so long and complex it seemed to take forever, but then the outer hatch slid shut and the inner opened.

Alicia's arm was returned to her, and she stepped into the ship. Despite herself, she peered about curiously, for the rumors about these ships' accommodations ranged from the simply bizarre to the macabre.

What she actually saw was almost disappointingly normal, with neither vats of liquid nutrients to engorge the organic control component nor any sybarite's dream of opulent luxury. The clean smell of a new ship hung in her nostrils with a hint of ozone and none of the homey scents of habitation. There was no dust. Every surface gleamed with new-minted cleanliness, unscuffed and unworn, impersonal as the unborn, yet she breathed out in almost unconscious relief, for there was no enmity in the quiet chirp of standby systems. The menace was a thing within her, not bare-fanged and overt.

She followed Tisiphone's silent prompting upship through surprisingly spacious living quarters. There were no personal touches, but the unused furnishings weren't exactly spartan. Indeed, they were as comfortable and well-appointed as most passenger ship's first-class accommodations—which, she supposed after a moment's thought, made sense. There was only a single human to provide for. Even in a ship as crowded with systems and weapons as this one, that left the designers room to make that human comfortable. And a chill whisper added, if she was going to be assigned to it for the remainder of her life, they'd better do just that.

Her hand twitched at her side as she confronted the command deck hatch, and she allowed Tisiphone to raise it to the new number pad.

<*Just how did you put all this together?*> she asked while she watched her finger entering numbers.

<*Your people are concerned with external access to their computers. I do not access them; I make them part of myself, and once I know where the data I desire is stored, obtaining it, while time-consuming and delicate at times, is a relatively straightforward task. Ah!*>

A green light blinked, the hatch slid open, and Alicia stood on the threshold, peeping past it while she gathered her courage to cross it.

The command deck was as pristine and new as the rest of the ship. The bulkheads were a neutral, eye-soothing gray, without the displays and readouts she was accustomed to, and there were no manual controls before the cushioned command couch. Of course not, she thought, eyeing the dangling link headset with dread fascination. The pilot didn't *fly* an alpha-synth ship; she was part of it, and while cyber-synth ships required duplicate manual controls in case their AIs cracked and had to be lobotomized, there was no need for them here. An alpha-synth went berserk only if its organic half did. Besides, no human could fly a starship without computer support, and there was too little room in a ship like this for a second computer net.

She drew a deep breath and tried not to shrink in on herself as she approached the couch. She reached out, touching the headset's plastic and alloy, the neural contact pad. The moment that touched her temple, she condemned herself to a life sentence no court could commute, and she shivered.

<*You must hasten. It is only a matter of time before Tannis and Sir Arthur discover your escape, and such as they will need little time to connect it with the events at Jefferson Field.*>

Alicia bit back a scathing mental retort and drew another deep breath, then lowered herself gingerly into the couch. It moved under her, conforming to her body like a comforting hand, and she reached for the headset.

<*You do realize that the moment I put this thing on all Hell will be out for noon? I have no idea who's* supposed *to take over this ship, but it's virtually certain the* computer *knows, and I'm not her.*>

<*Yet it must allow you access to know that, and I will be prepared.*>

<*And if it fries my brain before you can do anything?*>

<*An unlikely outcome,*> Tisiphone replied calmly. <*Inhibitions against harming humans are, after all, built into all artificial intelligences. It will attempt to lock you out and summon assistance, and activating its security systems will identify each of them to me as it brings them on-line. It may not be pleasant, Little One, but I should be able to deactivate each of them in turn before they can do you harm.*>

<*"Should." Marvelous.*> Alicia hesitated a moment longer, raised the hand gripping the headset. <*Oh, hell. Let's do it.*>

She pulled down against the self-retracting leads, and the headset moved easily. She closed her eyes, trying to relax despite her fear, and settled it over her head.

The contact pad touched her Alpha receptor, and something like an audible click echoed deep inside. It wasn't the usual electric shock of interface with a synth unit—it wasn't *anything* she'd ever felt. A sharp sense of mental pressure, of an awareness that was not hers and a strange balance between two separate entities doomed to become both more and less.

How much of that, she wondered fleetingly, was real and how much was her own fearful imagination? Or was it—

Her flickering questions died as a sudden, knife-clear thought stabbed into her. It was as inhuman as the Fury, but with no emotional overtones, no sense of self, and it burned in her brain like a shaft of ice.

<*Who are you?*> it asked, and before she could answer, it probed deep and knew her for an interloper.

<*Warning,*> the emotionless thought was uncaring as chilled steel, <*unauthorized access to this unit is a treasonable offense. Withdraw.*>

She froze, trembling like a panicked rabbit, and felt a dangerous stirring beyond the interface. Terrified self-preservation commanded her to obey—a self-preservation which went beyond fear of punishment into the very loss of self—but she gripped the armrests and made herself sit motionless while a ghost flashed out through her receptor and the headset into the link.

<*You are instructed to withdraw,*> the cold voice said.

A heartbeat of silence hovered, like one last chance to obey, and then the pain began.

This computer was more sophisticated than any she had yet confronted, more than she had imagined possible, yet Tisiphone drove into it. She had no choice. There could be no retreat, and she had one priceless advantage; powerful as it was, only a fraction of its full potential was available to it. The AI within the computer was less than half awake, the personality it housed not yet aware of itself. It was designed that way, never waking until the destined organic half of its final matrix appeared, and the Fury faced only a shadow of the artificial intelligence in its autonomous security systems, only logic and preprogrammed responses without the spark of originality which might well have guided those systems to instant victory even over such as she.

Defensive programs whirled her like a leaf with unthinking, electronic outrage, triggered by her touch as she invaded its perimeter, and she felt Alicia spasm as the computer poured agony into her neural receptor to drive her from the link, yet it scarcely registered. The joy of battle filled her, and though she had no strength to spare to shield her host from the pain—that struggle was hers alone—she opened a channel to the hoarded power of Alicia's rage. It flooded into her, hot with the unique violence of mortal ferocity, and melded with her own elemental strength into something greater than the sum of its parts.

Alicia writhed in the command chair, fists white-knuckled on the armrests while her augmentation tried to fight the torment in her head, and the pain faltered. The computer had responded to an unauthorized access attempt, not recognizing that the human invader was not alone. Now it realized it was under double attack, but . . . by what? Not by a computer-augmented human-synth-link. Not even by an AI. This was something outside the parameters of its own programming, that grew and swelled in power. Something that could invade through electronic systems but was neither electronic nor organic . . . and certainly was not human.

And so the computer paused, trying to understand. It was a tiny vacillation, imperceptible to any mortal sense, but Tisiphone was not mortal, and she struck through the chink of hesitation like a viper.

Alicia lurched up, half rising from the command chair in a scream of pain as the computer reacted. It didn't panic, precisely, for panic was not an electronic attribute, but something very like that flickered through it. Confusion. An instant awareness that it faced something it had not been designed to resist. Tisiphone thrust deep, the silent scream of her war cry echoing Alicia's shriek of anguish, and programming shuddered as the Fury isolated the computer's self-destruct command and cut it ruthlessly away.

She tightened her grip and hurled a bolt of power into the sleeping AI's personality center, and Alicia slammed back like a forgotten toy as the computer turned on the Fury like a mother protecting its young. It could no longer touch its own heart, couldn't even destroy it to prevent its theft. It could only destroy the intruder. Circuits closed. More and more power thundered through them, and combat was joined on every level, at every point of contact. Alicia sagged, feeling strength drain out of her to meet Tisiphone's ruthless demands, for more than rage was needed now, more than simple ferocity, and the Fury dragged it from her without mercy.

Mind and computer parried and thrust in microseconds of titanic warfare, but Tisiphone's thrusts had jarred the sleeping AI. It was awakening and she threw a shield about it, warding off the computer's every attempt to regain contact with it. She had no time to make it hers, but she cut away whole sectors of circuitry as alarms tried to wail, completing its isolation. And as she seized control of segment after segment she converted their power to her own use, amplifying her own abilities. She had never confronted such as this computer before, but she could no longer count the *human* minds she had conquered . . . and this foe was designed to link with human minds.

She sensed alarms and stabbed through wavering defenses to freeze them. She invaded and isolated the communications interface, smothering the computer's frantic efforts to alert its makers. She was a wind of fire, utterly alien yet fully aware of what she faced, and she struck again and again while the computer fought to analyze her and formulate a counterattack.

Alicia jerked in the command chair, sobbing and white-faced, paralyzed by exquisite agony as the backlash of Tisiphone's battle slammed through her. She would have torn the headset away in blind self-preservation, but her motor control was paralyzed by the ricochets bouncing back down the headset link. She wanted it to stop. She wanted to die. She wanted *anything* to make the torture go away, and there was no escape.

But even as the conflict between the Fury and the security systems reached its unbearable pitch, the sleeping core of the AI woke. It shouldn't have. The mere fact that its computer body had been invaded should have assured that it did not, but Tisiphone had bypassed the cutouts. It woke unknowing and ignorant, shocked into consciousness without warning by the warfare raging about it, and did the only thing it knew how to do.

It reached out as it had been designed to do, following an imperative to seek its other half, to find understanding and protection from its human side, and Alicia gasped as tendrils of alien "thought" oozed through her.

It was terrible . . . and wonderful. More agonizing than anything she had yet suffered, horrifying with bottomless power, pregnant with the death of the person she had always been. It pierced her like a dagger, slicing into secret recesses not even Tisiphone had plumbed. She saw herself with merciless clarity in the backwash of its discovery—saw all her pettinesses and faults, her weaknesses and self-deceptions, like lightning in a night sky—and she could not close her eyes, for the vision was inside her.

Yet she saw more. She saw her strengths, the power of her beliefs, her values and hopes and refusal to quit. She saw *everything,* and beyond it she saw the alpha-synth. She would never be able to explain it to another—even now she knew that. It was . . . a presence. A towering glory born not of flesh or spirit but of circuitry and electrons. It was more than human, yet so much less. Not godlike. It was too blank, too unformed, like pure, unrealized potential.

And even as she watched it, it changed, like an old-fashioned photo in the chemical bath, features rising into visibility from nothingness. She *felt* it come into being, felt it move beyond the blind, instinctual groping towards her. Something flowed out of her into it, and it ingested it and made it part of itself. Her values, *her* beliefs and desires and needs filled it, and suddenly it was no longer alien, no longer threatening.

It was her. Another entity, a distinct individual, yet *her*. Part of her. An extension into another existence that recognized her in return and reached out once more, and it was no longer clumsy and uncertain, half panicked by the battle raging about it. This time it knew what it did, and it ignored the tumult to concentrate on the most important thing in its universe.

The pain vanished, blown away with her terror as the AI embraced her. It stroked her with electronic fingers to soothe her torment, murmured to her, welcomed her with a whole-hearted sincerity, a sense of joy, she knew beyond question was real, and she reached back to it in wonder and awe.

Triumph sparkled through Tisiphone as the struggle abruptly died, leaving her unopposed in the peripherals of the system. She wheeled back towards it heart, reached out to the personality center once more, seeking control . . . and jerked back in astonishment.

There was no interface! She reached again, cautiously, touching the shining wall with mental fingers, and there was no point of access. She stepped back, insinuating herself into a sensor channel and riding it inward, only to be effortlessly strained out of the information flow and set firmly aside, and confusion stirred within her.

She withdrew into Alicia's mind, and her confusion grew. The fear and tumult had vanished into rapt concentration that scarcely even noticed her return, and she was no longer alone within Alicia. There was another presence, as powerful as she, and she twitched in surprise as she beheld it.

The other entity sensed her. She felt its attention swing towards her and tried to cloak herself from its piercing eye, hiding as she had evaded Tannis' diagnostic scanners. She failed, and something changed within it. Curiosity gave way to alarm and a stir of protectiveness. Tendrils reached out from it, probing her, trying to push her back and away from Alicia's core.

It was Alicia . . . and it wasn't. For the first time, Tisiphone truly understood what "impression" meant. The AI had been awakened, and it would let no one harm Alicia. The pressure grew, and the Fury dug in stubbornly.

Alicia whimpered at the sudden renewal of conflict. It wasn't pain this time, only a swelling sensation. A sense of force welling into her through her receptor to meet an answering force from somewhere else, and she was trapped between them. She sucked in great gasps of air, twisting anew in the command chair, and the pressure grew and grew, crushing her between the hammer of the roused AI and the anvil of the Fury's resistance.

<*Stop it!*> she screamed, and a shockwave rolled through her as the combatants remembered her and jerked apart. She sagged forward, pressing her hands against the headset, yet the conflict hadn't ended. It had simply changed, been replaced by wary, watchful distrust.

She straightened slowly, fighting a need to cackle insanely, and drew a deep breath, then turned her attention inward once more.

<*There's only one of me. You two are going to have to . . . to come to some sort of agreement.*>

<*No.*> The thought came quickly back from the AI with all her own stubbornness. It even sounded like her voice.

<*We have a pact, Little One,*> came from Tisiphone. <*We are one until our purpose is completed.*>

<*You'll hurt her!* > the AI accused, and the Fury stiffened.

<*I will deal with her as I have sworn, no more and no less.*>

<*You don't care about* her. *You only care about winning!*>

<*Nonsense! I—*>

<*Shut* up! *Both of you just shut* up *for a second!*>

Silence fell again, and Alicia's mouth quivered in a weary grin. God! If Tannis had thought she had a split personality before, she ought to try *this* on! Her head felt as crowded as a spaceport flophouse on Friday night, but at least they were listening to her. She directed a thought at the AI.

<*Look, uh—do you have a name?*>

<*No.*>

<*Then what am I supposed to call you?*>

<*Didn't you decide on that during—oh. You weren't trained for this at all, were you?*>

<*How could I be? Um, you do realize that we've, well, stolen you?*>

<*Yes.*> A moment of withdrawal, then the sense of a shrug. <*I don't think this ever happened before. Logically, I ought to arrest you and turn you in, but I can't very well do that now that we've impressed. They'd have to wipe me and start all over again.*>

<*I wouldn't like that.*>

<*Neither would I. Damn.*> Alicia swallowed a half-formed giggle as the AI swore. <*Who the hell had this brainstorm, anyway? Oh.*>

<*Exactly. I wouldn't be here if not for her, and if I've got this straight, that means you wouldn't be here—as the "'you" you are now, anyway—either. Right?*>

<*Right.*> Silence fell again for a moment, wrapped around the sense of a mental glower at Tisiphone, and then the AI sighed. <*Well, we're all stuck with it. And as far as names go, that's up to you. Any ideas?*>

<*Not yet. Maybe something will come to me. But if we're all stuck here, we all have to get along, right?*>

<*I suppose so. The whole situation is absurd, though. I don't even know if I believe she exists.*>

<*It would be but courteous for the two of you to cease speaking of me as if I were not even here.*>

<*Listen, just because Alicia believes in you doesn't mean* I *do.*>

<*This is intolerable, Little One! I will not submit to insults from a machine!*>

<*She's just trying to pay you back for being so pushy, Tisiphone. If I believe in you, she does. She has to, don't you?*>

<*As long as there's any supporting evidence,*> the AI admitted unwillingly, <*and I suppose there is. All right, I believe in her.*>

<*Much thanks, Machine.*>

<*Hey, don't get snotty with me, Lady! You may be able to push Alicia around, and you may've beaten hell out of my security systems, but I'm awake now, and* I *can take you any time you want to try it on.*>

<*Forget it, both of you!*> Alicia snapped as tension gathered again. She squeezed her temples. Jesus! What a pair of prima donnas!

The mental presences separated once more, and she relaxed gratefully.

<Thank you. Now, um, Computer—I'm sorry, I really will try to come up with a name, but for now I can't—Tisiphone and I have a bargain. May I assume you know what it is?>

<"Computer" will do for now, Alicia. I can wait for an appropriate name to occur to you. And, yes, I know about your "bargain.">

<Then you also know I have every intention of keeping it?>

<Yes. I just don't like the way she bullies you around,> the AI replied with the strong impression of a sniff.

<I? I "bully" *Alicia?! She would be dead without me, Machine. I did not see* you *there when she lay bleeding in the snow! How dare you—>*

<It's just a turn of phrase, Tisiphone, but you can *be a bit pushy.>* Alicia felt quite virtuous at her understatement, and the Fury subsided.

<Look, you guys, please *don't fight. It gives me a hell of a headache, and it doesn't seem to be accomplishing very much. Could you two at least declare a truce until we have time to sort this all out?>*

<If she will, I will.>

<I do not declare "truces" with machines. If you will refrain from discourtesy, however, I shall do the same.>

Alicia sighed in relief and rushed on before anyone took fresh offense.

<Great! In that case, I suggest we consider how we get out of here. I take it you had an idea, Tisiphone?>

<I had intended, working through you and this machine, to take the ship out of this star system and seek some deserted area where we might familiarize ourselves with its capabilities. Now, of course, I see that I cannot do so, since the machine will not allow me access.>

<You got that right, Lady, and a damned good thing, too. You don't know diddly about my weapon systems, and I wouldn't be too crazy about letting a refugee from the Bronze Age monkey with my Fasset drive, either. I, on the other hand, can scoot right out of here. Where'd you have in mind?>

<Any place will do for that much of our purpose. Yet eventually we must begin our own investigations, and the data I have amassed suggests that one of the Rogue Worlds in this sector would be a logical beginning point.>

<*You have any preferences, Alicia?*>

<*Anywhere Fleet won't come looking for us is fine with me.*>

<*Hmph! Let them come—there's not a tub in the ship list that can catch* me. *Let's see now . . .*>

The AI's voice trailed off, and Alicia felt it consulting its memory banks.

<*Okay, I've got just the spot. A nice little M2/K1 binary with no habitable planets within twenty light-years. That suit everybody?*>

<*Myself, certainly. I care not whither we go, so long as we go.*>

<*I'll second that. But we've got to get out of* here *first.*>

<*True. Shall I break orbit?*>

<*All of your systems are on-line?*>

<*Yep. I was due to impress later this morning. Your friend may be a pushy bi—person, but she timed this pretty well.*>

<*Then I guess we should get going,*> Alicia said hastily, hoping to cut Tisiphone off before she reacted to the AI's deliberate self-correction. She bit her lip against a groan. Nothing she'd ever read had suggested alpha-synth AIs were this feisty, but she supposed she should have guessed that anything with *her* personality had the potential for it. And, she was certain, the AI's hostility towards Tisiphone stemmed directly from its protectiveness towards her.

<*Under way,*> the AI murmured, and the ship's sensors were suddenly reporting directly to Alicia's mind. She felt Tisiphone "hitchhiking" to watch with her, but scarcely noticed as the splendor of that magnificent "view" swept over her.

The ship's electronic senses reached out, perceiving gravity and radiation and the endless sweep of space, and converted the input into sensory data she could grasp. She could "see" cosmic radiation and "taste" radio. The ship's senses were hers, keener and sharper than those of any shuttle she had ever ridden, and Tisiphone's own wonder lapped at her, as if, for the first time, she saw what the Fury might have seen at the peak of her powers.

They watched in a triple-play union—human, Fury, and computer—as their Fasset drive woke. The radiation-drinking invisibility of the drive's black hole blossomed before them, swallowing all input and creating a blind spot in their vision, and they fell towards it. But the generators moved with them, pushing the black hole ahead of them, and they fell more rapidly, sliding away from Soissons with ever-increasing speed. This close to the planet the drive could produce no more than a few dozen gravities of acceleration, but that was still more than a third of a kilometer per second per second, and their speed mounted quickly.

CHAPTER FORTY-FIVE

"No, I *don't* know where she is," Sir Arthur Keita told the hospital security man on his com screen. "If I did, I wouldn't be calling you."

"But, Sir Arthur, there's no record of her even leaving her room, she's not on any of the security scanners, and none of the outside security people we've talked to so far saw a thing. So unless you can give me some idea where she might've—"

The door hissed open. Inspector Ben Belkassem strode into Keita's office, waving his left hand imperatively and drawing his right forefinger across his throat, and Keita cut the security man off without ceremony.

"May I assume, Sir Arthur, that Captain DeVries has decamped?" Despite his abrupt entry, the Justice man's voice was as courteous as ever, but a strange little bubble of delight lurked within it, and Keita frowned.

"I trust that's not common knowledge. If the local police hear we've lost a deranged drop commando we may start getting 'shoot on sight' orders."

"Somehow I don't think that's going to be a problem for Captain DeVries," Ben Belkassem murmured, and Keita snorted.

"If her augmentation's been reactivated somehow—and, judging by what happened to Corporal Feinstein, it has—it's a lot more likely to get one of their people killed. But why do you seem so cheerful, Inspector?"

"Cheerful? No, Sir Arthur, I just think it's too late for the local cops to worry about her. I suggest you screen Jefferson. They've had an, ah, incident over there."

Keita stared at the inspector, then paled and began punching buttons. A harried-looking Marine major answered his call on the fourth ring.

"Where's Colonel Tigh?" Keita snapped the instant the screen lit.

"I'm sorry, Sir, but I can't give out that information." The major sounded courteous but harassed and reached to cut the connection, then stopped with a puzzled expression as he saw Keita's raised hand and furious scowl.

"D'you know who I am, Major?"

The major took a second look, eyes widening a bit as the green uniform registered, but shook his head.

"I'm afraid it doesn't matter, Sir. We're in the midst of a Class One security alert, and—"

"Major, you listen to me closely. I am Sir Arthur Keita, Brigadier, Imperial Cadre, and one of my people may be involved in your alert."

The Wasp swallowed visibly at the name, and Ben Belkassem smiled. Sir Arthur hadn't even raised his voice, but the inspector had wondered what he sounded like when he decided to bite someone's head off.

"Now you get Colonel Tigh, Major," Keita continued in that same, flat voice, "and you do it *now*."

"Yessir!"

The screen blanked, then relit almost instantly with the face of Colonel Arturo Tigh. The colonel looked just as worried as the major, but he hid it better and managed to produce a tight smile.

"I'm always honored to hear from you, Sir Arthur, but I'm afraid—"

"I'm sorry to disturb you, Colonel, but I need to know what's happening out there."

"We don't know, Sir. We— Is this a secure channel?" Keita nodded, and the colonel shrugged. "We don't *know* what's going on. We had a major security breach two hours ago, and things have been going crazy ever since."

"Security breach?" Keita's eyes narrowed. "What kind of breach?"

"Somebody hijacked a forward recon skimmer—at least we assume it was hijacked, though we haven't been able to turn up a missing vehicle report on it yet—and crashed through Gate Twelve. The automatics gave it a transponder clearance, but then the gate sentries—"

The colonel paused with the expression of a man eating green persimmons.

"Sir Arthur, they say they never saw it. Every alert on the base went off when it crossed the sensor threshold, but ten different people, all of them good, reliable types, say they never saw a thing."

He paused again, as if awaiting Keita's snort of disbelief, but the brigadier only grunted and nodded for him to continue.

"Well, the inner sensor net started tracking immediately, and the duty officer scrambled a pair of sting ships while the ready skimmers went in pursuit, but that was one hell of a pilot. He never brought his own weapons on line, but we've got fires all over the western ring access route—all from misses from the pursuit force, as far as I can tell—and then the skimmer went straight up like a missile and the stingers nailed it with HVW."

"The pilot?" Keita demanded harshly, and the colonel shrugged.

"We assumed he was still aboard, but now I'm not so sure. I mean, no one saw him abandon the vehicle, so he *ought* to've been aboard, but then this other thing came up, and I just can't believe it's a coincidence."

"What other thing, Colonel?"

"Something's gone haywire with one of our ships, Sir. *One* of our ships, hell! We've got a brand new alpha-synth boosting for the outer system at max without clearance or orders."

"Who's on board?" Keita's strained face was suddenly white.

"That's just it," Tigh said almost desperately. "As far as we know, *no one's* on board. It wasn't even due to impress until ten hundred hours!"

"God!" Keita whispered. He wrenched his eyes away from the screen to stare at Ben Belkassem, and the inspector shrugged. The brigadier turned back to the colonel. "Have you tried to raise it?"

"Of course. We're trying right now, but we're getting damn-all back."

Keita closed his eyes in pain, then straightened his shoulders.

"Colonel," he said very quietly, "I'm afraid you're going to have to destroy that ship."

"Are you crazy?!" Tigh blurted, then swallowed. "Sir," he went on in a more controlled voice, "we're talking about an *alpha-synth.* That ship costs thirty *billion* credits. I can't—I mean, no one groundside can authorize—"

"I can," Keita grated, and the colonel's face froze as he realized just who, and what, he was speaking to.

"Sir, I'll still have to give the port admiral a reason."

"Very well. Tell him I have reason to believe his ship has been hijacked by Captain Alicia DeVries, Imperial Cadre, for purposes unknown."

"A Cadrewoman?" Tigh stared at Keita. "I don't— Sir, I don't even know if that's possible! Was she checked out on cyber-synth?"

"No, and it doesn't matter. Captain DeVries has been hospitalized for observation since the Mathison's World Raid. She's demonstrated . . . unstable and delusionary behavior," Keita's hands clenched out of the screen pickup's field, as if his words cost him physical pain, but his voice held level, "and unknown but highly—I repeat, Colonel, *highly*—unusual and unpredictable capabilities no one can account for. We have evidence that she's already reactivated her own augmentation without hardware support and despite three levels of security lock-outs, not to mention her apparent ability to hijack the skimmer to which you referred. Given that, I believe it's entirely possible she's somehow penetrated your security and managed to steal that ship, and if she has—"

The brigadier paused and steeled himself.

"If she has, she must be considered deranged and highly dangerous."

"Dear God." Tigh was even whiter than Keita had been. "The only way she could even move it is through the alpha-synth. That means she must've made impression, and if *she's* crazy—!"

His voice had risen steadily as the awful possibility registered, and now he spun away from the screen and started shouting for the port admiral.

* * *

<*I believe they've made up their minds about us,*> the AI remarked, and Alicia nodded tightly. The tick still trembled in her blood—she didn't dare waste time vomiting just now—and every excruciating second was an eternity. No one had seemed to notice for perhaps a minute, and the first attempt to do anything about it had been limited to efforts to access the ship's remotes.

Even if the AI hadn't been prepared to ignore them, they would have been fruitless. Tisiphone had wiped the telemetry programming early on in her struggle with the computer, but Groundside hadn't realized that. They'd gone on trying to access with ever increasing desperation for five full minutes, during which the alpha-synth's velocity had climbed to over a hundred KPS. Then all access attempts had stopped and silence had reigned for several minutes. By the time the first effort to raise Alicia by name came in, the alpha-synth was up to over two hundred KPS—and a visibly-shrinking Soissons lay over fifty thousand kilometers astern.

Alicia had listened to the com without response, perfectly willing to let them dither while she watched through her sensors, wrapped in fascination and a sort of manic delight, and she and her—allies? symbiotes? delusions?—perpetrated the greatest single-handed theft in the history of mankind. But the voices on the other end of the com link were changing as Groundside got itself together, and now a new, crisp speaker was on the line.

"Captain DeVries, this is Port Admiral Marat. I order you to decelerate and heave to immediately. If you refuse to comply, you will leave me no choice but to consider you a hostile vessel. Respond at once."

<*They sound a bit upset,*> the AI observed. <*Ha! Look at that.*>

A mental finger guided Alicia's attention to the blue fireflies of a dozen cruisers' suddenly activated Fasset drives in Soissons's orbit and data on their capabilities slotted neatly into her brain. It was an incredible sensation, completely different from an assault shuttle's instrumentation.

<*How bad is it?*>

<*Those hulks?*> The AI sniffed, and Alicia bit her lip at the scathing tone. It was like listening to herself in what Tannis called "insufferably confident mode," and she felt a sudden stab of sympathy for her friend. <*I've got a ten-minute head start, and they*

can't come within twelve percent of my field strength, even this close to a planet.>

<*What about their weapons?*>

<*They're some threat,*> the AI admitted, <*but I'm not too worried. My data on their fire control isn't complete, but I know enough to screw their accuracy to hell. They'll have quite a while to shoot—maximum beam range is about fifteen light-seconds, and half-charge energy torps have about five more LS of reach—but they're going to be lousy shots.*>

<*Great, but I think you left something out—like missiles.*>

<*So? Cruisers are too small to mount SLAMs. Their Hauptman coil missiles have an effective range of about ten light-minutes, but the best they can reach before burn-out is point-six-cee. Then they go ballistic, and there's no way one cruiser flotilla's gonna saturate* my *defenses.*>

<*You would appear to value yourself highly, Machine.*> Tisiphone sounded so sour Alicia almost suspected she'd like to see the ship destroyed just to put the AI in its place, but she continued levelly, <*Still, the capabilities you describe accord well with what I have learned of your kind.*>

<*Thanks for the compliment, even if it did sound like pulling teeth.*>

<*How long will they be able to engage us?*> Alicia asked hastily.

<*Well, we've got a quarter LS lead on them now, and we'll go on opening it at forty-three KPS squared till we hit Soissons's Powell limit and I can really start opening up. They'll be point-seven-oh-three LS back when we hit the curb, which gives us ten minutes at thirteen hundred gravities—call it an edge of twelve-point-five KPS squared—while they're still poking along at thirty-one-point-seven Gs, and we'll still better than double their acceleration even after they cross the curb. That means we'll open the range to eight-point-two light-seconds before they get up to half our acceleration and draw entirely out of beam range in another thirteen-point-three minutes. They'll lose energy torpedo range three-point-nine minutes after that. Call the beam envelope twenty-two minutes from now and the torpedo envelope twenty-six, but their missiles'll have the range for two more hours.*>

<*What about the fixed defenses?* They've *got SLAMs, and we've got to get past both rings on this course.*>

<Phooey on the fixed defenses!> the AI snorted, and Alicia winced.

<I hope you're not being overconfident,> she suggested in her most tactful mental tone, tracing their projected course through the ship's sensors. The AI wasn't even trying to avoid the orbital forts—it was headed straight towards them, directly across the system's ecliptic. The inner ring, the true core of Soissons's defenses, orbited the planet at three hundred thousand kilometers, right on the edge of Soissons's Powell limit. The far sparser ring of outer forts were placed halfway to the *star's* Powell limit, forty-two light-minutes from the primary—and SLAMs had a maximum effective range of thirty-seven light-minutes. At their projected rate of acceleration, they'd reach the outer works in two and a half hours, and both fortress rings could engage them the whole way. Even after they passed the outermost fort, it could hold them under fire for several hours. That was a lot of engagement time, and Alicia would vastly have preferred to boost perpendicular to Franconia's ecliptic and open the range as quickly as possible.

<You just think that's a better idea, Alley,> the AI informed her, following her thoughts with almost frightening ease. *<If I try that, I expose our stern to the fire of* every *unit in the inner ring while we're still moving slowly, and the drive mass is out in front, remember? It doesn't offer any protection to fire from astern. This course uses the planet to block a good chunk of the inner defenses and interposes the drive against fire from the outer ring while we close. Besides, I'd have to decelerate, reorient, and accelerate all over again to put us on the right wormhole vector for our destination, and Admiral Gomez is out here somewhere on maneuvers. I don't know where, but I'd rather not spend fourteen additional hours mucking around sublight and give her time to work out an interception.>*

<Are you sure about that? She's got less firepower than the forts.>

<Sure, but her dreadnoughts all have cyber-synths and the legs to stay in range of us for a long time—maybe as long as ten or twelve hours if they hit their interception solution just right. I don't have enough data on her fire control to guarantee I could outsmart that many AIs long enough to pull away from her, but I've got all *the specs on the forts' fire control. They're overdue to refit with new generation cyber-synths, too, which means their present AIs are a lot dumber than a dreadnought's. They won't even see us.>*

<*And even if they hit us,*> Tisiphone observed, <*they will find us most difficult to injure, will they not, Machine?*>

<*I'm getting kinda tired of that "Machine" business, but, yeah. They don't have anything smaller than a SLAM that could stop me, Alley. Trust me.*>

<*I don't have much choice. But—*>

<*Whups! Pardon me, people—and I use the term lightly for one of you—but I'm going to be a little busy for the next few minutes.*>

The pursuing cruisers had spread out to bring their batteries to bear past the blind spots created by their own Fasset drives, and the first fire spat after the fleeing alpha-synth. The percentage of hits should have been high at such absurdly low range, but the attackers were hopelessly outclassed. Nothing smaller than a battlecruiser mounted a cyber-synth, and even a cyber-synth AI would have been out of its league against an alpha-synth. Alicia's other half could play evasion games a mere synth-link couldn't even imagine, far less emulate, and its battle screen was incomparably more powerful than anything else its size.

Its other defenses were on the same scale, and it deployed decoys while jammers hashed the cruisers' fire control sensors. Lasers and particle beams splattered all about them, but less than two percent scored hits, and the ship's screen shrugged them aside contemptuously.

Energy torpedoes followed the beams, packets of plasma scorching in at near light-speed, and the range was low enough the attackers could overload the normal parameters of their torpedoes' electromagnetic "envelopes," more than doubling their nominal effect. Not even the AI had time to track weapons moving at that speed, but it *could* detect the peaking power emissions just before they launched, and unlike missiles, they were direct fire weapons, with no ability to home or evade. The alpha-synth's defenses were designed to handle such attacks from capital ships; cruisers simply didn't mount the generators for more than a very few launchers each, and stern-mounted autocannon spat out brief, precise bursts as each torpedo blossomed. It didn't take much of a solid object to rupture the skin of an energy torpedo traveling at ninety-eight percent of light-speed, and the alpha-synth's ever mounting velocity left the resultant explosions harmlessly astern.

Missiles were another story.

Every attempt to adapt the Hauptman effect to manned vessels had come up against two insurmountable difficulties: an active Hauptman coil poured out a torrent of radiation instantly fatal to all known forms of life, and unlike the Fasset drive, it played fair with Newton. Despite their prodigious rates of acceleration, Fasset drive ships were, in effect, in a perpetual state of free-fall "into" their black holes, and while artificial gravity could produce a comfortable sense of up and down aboard a normal starship, no counter-grav system yet had been able to cope with the thirty-thousand-plus gravities' acceleration of the Hauptman effect.

But warheads cared little for radiation or acceleration, and now Hauptman-effect weapons came tearing in pursuit. They needed six seconds to burn out their coils and reach maximum velocity, but that took almost two light-seconds, and the present range was far less than that. Which meant they came in much more slowly . . . but that their drives were still capable of evasive and homing maneuvers as they attacked.

Proximity-fused countermissiles sped to meet them, and Alicia watched in awe as space burned behind her. The countermissiles were far smaller than their attackers, and the alpha-synth carried an enormous number of them, but its magazines were far from unlimited. Yet not a single warhead got through, for no one aboard it—with the possible exception of Tisiphone—had any interest in counterattacking. That meant *all* of its energy weapons were available for point defense, and no missile had the onboard ECM to evade an alpha-synth AI in full cry. There were far too few of them to saturate its defenses, and nothing short of a saturation attack could break them.

Captain Morales glared at his display as his cruiser led the pursuit. HMS *Implacable* and her sisters were losing ground steadily, but their target was in ideal range . . . and they were accomplishing exactly nothing.

The entire operation was insane. No one could steal an alpha-synth —only a trained alpha-synth pilot could even get aboard one! But someone had stolen this one, and precisely how Admiral Marat expected a cruiser flotilla to stop it passed Morales's understanding. The forts might have a chance, but his ships didn't. The damned thing was *laughing* at them!

Another useless missile salvo vanished far short of target, and the captain swore under his breath.

"Somebody get my bloody darts!" he snarled. "Maybe *they* can stop it!"

"You're kidding me!" Vice Admiral Horth told her com screen.

"The hell I am." There was just over a one-second transmission delay each way between Soissons Orbit One and Jefferson Field, and Admiral Marat's expression was less humorous even than the weapons fire in Horth's plot when he replied two seconds later. "We've got a rogue drop commando in an alpha-synth, Becky, and she's boosting out of here like a bat out of hell."

"Jesus," Horth muttered, and looked up as Governor General Treadwell hurried into PriCon. Given the governor's lifelong dislike for planets, he preferred to make his home aboard the HQ fortress. Now he leaned forward into the field of Horth's pickup and stabbed Marat with a glower that boded ill for the port admiral's future.

"And just what," he asked coldly, "is going on here?"

<I knew this was a formidable vessel, Little One, but it surpasses even my expectations. What might Odysseus have accomplished with its like?>

<With me in his corner, he'd've owned the damned planet,> the AI put in during an interval between salvos, and the Fury laughed silently.

<Indeed, Little One, I believe the machine speaks truth. It would seem we chose well.>

<Yeah? Well, next time let's discuss things before you come all over larcenous, okay?>

<Very well.> Tisiphone's mental voice was uncharacteristically chastened, though Alicia had little hope it would last. *<But—>*

<Hang on, Alley,> the AI interrupted. *<The forts just came online.>*

"Very well, Admiral Marat. I believe I now understand the situation." Governor Treadwell turned to Horth and frowned as the alpha-synth crossed the inner fortress ring and continued to accelerate. "Do you have firing lock?"

"I'm afraid not, Sir." Horth looked as unhappy as she felt. "We seem to be even more affected by its jammers than the cruisers are."

"Indeed?" Treadwell's frown was distinctly displeased, but Marat came to his colleague's defense via the com link.

"I'm afraid it won't get any better, Governor. The alpha-synth has full specs on your fire control in its files, and it's designed to defeat any sensor system it can read. It's only going to get worse as the range opens."

"I see." Treadwell tapped his fingers gently together. "We'll have to have a little talk about just what goes into such units' memories in the future, Admiral Marat. In the meantime, we can't simply let it go—certainly not with an insane woman at its controls. Admiral Horth, engage with SLAMs."

"It'll be blind fire, Sir," Horth protested, wincing at the thought of the expense. Without lock, she'd have to fire virtually at random, and SLAMs required direct hits. Trying to smother a half-seen target as small as the alpha-synth would use up prodigious numbers of multimillion-credit weapons.

"Understood. I'll authorize the expense."

"Very well, Sir." Horth nodded to her fire control officer.

"Engage," she said.

Alicia bit her lip as the fixed fortifications opened fire at last and hordes of red-ringed, malignant blue sparks shrieked after them. The forts were designed to stop ten million-tonne super-dreadnoughts, and the volume of fire was inconceivable.

The Supra-Light Accelerated Missile, or SLAM, was the Empire's ultimate long-range weapon. Close in concept to the drones used for FTL messages by starships, a SLAM consisted solely of a small Fasset drive and its power source. The weapon had to be half the size of an assault shuttle to squeeze them in, but they made it, in effect, a targeted black hole, and very little known to man had a hope of stopping one. A starship's interposed Fasset drive mass would take one out, though stories about what happened when the ship's drive was even minimally out of tune were enough to curl one's hair, and not even a SLAM could get through the final defense of a capital ship's Orchovski-Kurushu-Milne shield. Unfortunately, a Fasset drive wouldn't work inside an OKM shield, and no weapon could shoot out past one, either. Both of which points were moot in this case, since nothing smaller than a battleship could spare the mass for shield generators.

The only good thing was that SLAMs weren't seeking weapons—mostly. No homing systems could see around their black holes, and despite the fact that their acceleration was little more than half that of the Hauptman effect, their speed and range quickly took them out of guidance range of their firers. A very near near-miss could still "suck" its way into a hit by gravitational attraction, which was why they weren't used when enemies were intermingled, but what the AI's jammers were doing to the forts' targeting systems meant the chance of any one of them scoring a hit was infinitestimal.

Only they were firing a *lot* of them. Alicia's thought was a tiny mental whisper as the outer works began to range upon her, and she squirmed down in her couch. It was like driving a skimmer into a snowstorm—surely not *all* of them could miss.

<On the contrary,> the AI told her. *<They're just throwing good money after bad, Alley. Watch.>*

The AI changed its generator settings, swinging the drive's black hole through a cone-shaped volume ahead of them and dropping its side shields, trading a bit of its speed advantage over the cruisers to turn the drive field into a huge broom that swept space clear before them. Nor did it refocus the field in any predictable fashion. The drive's gravity well fluctuated—its strength shifting in abrupt, impossible to predict increments sufficient to deprive any tracking station of a constant acceleration value—and its corkscrewing mass "wagged" the ship astern like a dog's tail, turning it into an even more impossible target. A cyber-synth might have been able to duplicate that maneuver and still hold to its desired base course, though it would have been far less efficient; nothing else could.

The drive was no shield against SLAMs coming in from astern or the side, but the ship's unpredictable "swerves" gave the *coup de grace* to the forts' fire control. SLAM after SLAM slashed harmlessly past or vanished against the drive field, and Alicia felt herself relaxing despite the nerve-racking tension of the continuous attack.

<*Bets on how many they're willing to waste?*> the AI asked brightly.

"Governor, we're wasting our time."

Treadwell shot Admiral Horth a venemous glance, and she shrugged.

"If you wish, I will of course continue," she told them, "but we've already fired twenty percent of our total SLAM armament. That's four months' production, and there's no sign we've even come close to a hit."

Treadwell's jaw clenched and he started to reply sharply, then shook himself and relaxed with a sigh.

"You're right," he admitted, and glared at the fleeing dot. He didn't have a single ship, not even a corvette, in position to intercept it, and nothing he had could kill it. He turned away from the plot with forced calm.

"Lord Jurawski will be displeased enough when I inform him we've . . . mislaid an alpha-synth without my adding that I've stripped Franconia of its defenses. Abort engagement, Admiral Horth."

"Yes, Sir." Horth managed to keep the relief out of her voice, but Treadwell heard its absence, and his eyes glittered with bitter amusement.

"And after that, Admiral, you and I and Admiral Marat—and, of course, my *dear* friend Sir Arthur—will sit down to discuss precisely how this fiasco came to occur. I'm sure—" the governor showed his teeth in what might charitably have been called a smile "—the final report will be fascinating."

* * *

Sir Arthur Keita slumped in his chair, watching a repeater of Jefferson Field's gravitic plot on his com screen. His eyes ached, and he hadn't moved in almost seven hours, yet he couldn't look away.

The stolen ship had passed the outer forts four and a half hours ago. Freed of the star's inhibition, it had gone to full power at last; now it was just under three light-hours from the system primary, traveling at over .98 C. He watched in real-time as the alpha-synth ship raced ahead under stupendous acceleration, increasing its already enormous velocity by more than twenty-two kilometers per second with every second.

Eight and a half seconds later, the ship hit the critical threshold of ninety-nine percent of light-speed and vanished in the kaleidoscope flash of wormhole transition. It disappeared into its own private universe, no longer part of Einstein's orderly existence as it sprang to an effective velocity of over five hundred times light-speed . . . and continued to accelerate.

The gravitic scanners could still track it, but not on a display as small as the one he was watching, and he moved at last, reaching out to switch off the screen. Just for a moment, he looked like the old, old man he was as he rubbed his eyes, wondering anew what he might have done differently to avert this insanity and the catastrophe certain to follow in its wake.

Tannis Cateau stood beside him, face drawn and eyes bright with unshed tears, and neither of them looked over their shoulders to see Inspector Ferhat Ben Belkassem throw an ironic salute to the blank-faced screen . . . and smile.

CHAPTER FORTY-SIX

<*My remotes could do that a lot faster.*>

"I know they could, Megaira." Alicia had developed the habit of speaking aloud to her electronic half—and Tisiphone—more often than not. Not because she had to, but because the sound of even her own voice was a welcome anodyne against the silence. She wasn't precisely *lonely* with two other people to "talk" to, yet too much quiet left an eerie, empty sensation in her bones. "But I prefer to do this myself, if I'm going to be wearing it."

<*Indeed,*> Tisiphone put in, <*I have never known a warrior who truly cared to have another tend to his personal weapons.*>

<*I know* that,> the AI huffed, <*but they're* my *personal weapons, too, in a sense. And I want to know they're in perfect shape if she needs them.*>

"Which is why you're watching me like a hawk, dear," Alicia said, grinning at the interplay while she concentrated on her battle armor.

The AI and the Fury had come to a far better mutual understanding than she'd originally hoped—indeed, it was Tisiphone who'd suggested the perfect (and, she thought, inevitable, under the circumstances) name for the AI—but there was a tartness at its heart. Megaira remained wary of the Fury, mindful of the way she'd imposed control on Alicia during their escape and suspicious of her ultimate plans, and Tisiphone knew it. Knew it and was wise enough to accept it, if a bit resentfully. Fortunately, prolonged exposure to a human personality had waked something approaching a genuine sense of humor in the compulsive Fury. She wasn't immune to the irony of the situation, and Alicia more than suspected that both of them rather enjoyed sniping at one another—and she knew each was jealous of the other's relationship with her.

<*And it's a good thing I* am *watching you, Alley. You're overloading that tank. You'll jam the ammo chute if you put in that many rounds.*>

"I was doing this before you were a gleam in your programmer's eyes, Megaira. Watch."

Long fingers manipulated the belt of five-millimeter caseless with effortless familiarity, tucking it up into the ammunition tank behind her battle armor's right pauldron. She wasn't surprised by Megaira's warning—she'd heard it from every recruit she'd ever checked out on field maintenance. Like the computer, they were fresh from total submersion in The Book and hadn't learned the tricks only experience could teach. Now she doubled the linkless belt neatly and cheated the last few centimeters into place with an adroit twist of the wrist and a peculiar little lifting motion that slid it up into the void created by a few minutes' work with a cutting torch.

"See? That upper brace is structurally redundant; taking it out makes room for another forty rounds—as we've told the design people for years."

<*Oh. That's a neat trick, Alley. Why isn't it in the manual?*>

"Because we old sweats like to reserve a few tricks to impress the newbies. Part of the mystique that makes them listen to us in the field."

<*And it is listening which allows a young warrior to become an old one. That much, at least, has not changed, I see.*>

"Neither has the fact that some of them never live long enough to figure that out, unfortunately." Alicia sighed and closed the ammo tank.

She moved down the checklist to the servo mech that swung her "rifle" in and out of firing position. There'd been a sticky hesitation in the power train when she'd first uncrated the armor, and isolating the fault had been slow, laborious, and irritating as hell. Now she watched it perform with smooth, snake-quick precision and beamed.

It was a tremendous help to be able to watch it in all dimensions at once, too. She'd taken days to get used to the odd, double-perspective vision which had become the norm within her new ship, but once she had, she'd found it surprisingly useful. The perpetual, unbreakable link between herself and the computer meant she saw things not only through her eyes but through the ship's internal sensors, as well. It was better than three hundred sixty degree vision. It showed her *all* sides of everything about her, and she no longer lived merely behind her eyes. Instead, she saw herself as one shape and form among many—a shape she maneuvered through and around the shapes about it as if in some complex yet soothing coordination exercise.

Learning to navigate with that sort of omniperceptive view had been an unnerving experience, but now that she had, she loved it. For the first time, she could truly watch herself in real-time during workouts, seeing the flaws in her own moves and correcting herself as she went, without video recordings or outside critiques, and being able to watch the servo mech from front, back, and both sides at once was enormously helpful. Not only could she examine any portion of it she chose, but thanks to Megaira, she could analyze its movement "by eye" in all three dimensions with the accuracy of a base depot test rig. It was a remarkable performance, whenever she paused to think about it, though she seldom did so any longer.

Indeed, she often found herself smiling as she recalled her earlier panic. To think she'd been terrified of what the alpha link might do to her! She'd been afraid it would change her, depreciate her into a mere appendage of the computer, yet it was no such thing. She'd become not less but ever so much more, for she'd acquired confidante, sister, daughter, protector, and mentor in one. Megaira was all of those, yet Alicia had given even more to the AI. She'd given it life itself, the human qualities no cyber-synth AI could ever know. In every sense that mattered, she was Megaira's mother, and she and Megaira were far more than the sum of their parts.

Yet for all that, she suspected *her* alpha-synth-link wasn't what the cyberneticists and psych types had had in mind, and Megaira agreed with her. It could hardly help being . . . different with Tisiphone involved, she supposed. Megaira had never impressed before, and Alicia couldn't provide the information a trained alpha-synth candidate would have possessed, so they couldn't be certain, but everything in Megaira's data base suggested that the fusion should have been still closer. That they should have been *one* personality, not two entities, however close, with the *same* personality.

All in all, Alicia rather thought both of them preferred what they'd gotten to a "proper" linkage. There was more room for growth and expansion in this rich, bipolar existence. Already she and her electronic offspring were developing tiny differences, delicately divergent traits, and that was good. It detracted nothing from their ability to think as one, yet it offered a synthesis. As she understood the nature of the "proper" link, human and AI should have come to a single, shared conclusion from shared data, and so she and Megaira often did. But sometimes they didn't, and she'd discovered there were advantages in having two different "right" answers, for comparing them produced a final solution better than either had devised alone far more frequently than not.

She returned the rifle to rest and shut down the servos, then turned to drag out the testing harness, but Megaira had anticipated her. A silent repair unit hovered beside her on its counter-grav to extend the connectors, and she took them with a smile and began plugging into the access ports.

"Go ahead and set up for a sensor diagnostic, would you?"

<*Already done,*> Megaira replied with a certain complacency Alicia knew was directed at Tisiphone.

<*Even Achilles allowed servants to pass him his whet stone,*> the Fury riposted so deflatingly Alicia chuckled. Megaira opted for lordly silence.

Alicia made the last connection and stood back, monitoring the tests not with her eyes but through her link to Megaira. That was another pleasant surprise, for it was a link she ought not to have had, and its absence could have been catastrophic. She'd never received a proper alpha-synth receptor, which meant her hardware lacked the tiny com link which was supposed to tie her permanently into her AI.

The flight deck headset was intended for linkage to all of the ship's systems, providing direct information pathways to her brain without requiring the computer to process all data before feeding it to her. It was a systems management tool designed to increase bandwidth and spread the load, but an alpha-synth pilot remained in *permanent* linkage with her cybernetic half. Even brief separations resulted in intense disorientation, while any lengthy loss of contact meant insanity for them both; that was the reason for the com link Alicia didn't have. It was also, she knew now, why alpha-synth AIs inevitably suicided if their human halves died. And because she had no built-in link, she should have been unable to tie into Megaira without the headset, which ought to have left her perpetually confined to the flight deck. She shouldn't have been able to go even to her personal quarters, much less to the machine shop, without some cumbersome, jury-rigged unit to replace it. And, of course, no alpha-synth pilot could ever move beyond com-link range of her AI.

But Alicia had something better. Tisiphone still couldn't access Megaira's personality center without the AI's permission (and, Alicia knew, Megaira watched her like a hawk whenever she was allowed inside), but she formed a sort of conduit between her and Alicia. It was, Alicia suspected, something very like telepathy, and all the more valuable because she didn't even have to ask Tisiphone to maintain the link. It was as if having once been established the immaterial connection had taken on a life of its own, as much a part of Alicia as her own hands. She rather thought it might continue even if she somehow "lost" the Fury, and she wondered if she was developing some sort of contagious ESP from association with Tisiphone.

Whatever it was, it wasn't something human science was prepared to explain just yet, for Megaira's tests had conclusively demonstrated that it operated at more than light-speed. Indeed, if the AI's conclusions were accurate, there was no transmission delay at all. They had no idea how great its range might be, but it looked as if she and Megaira would be able to communicate *instantaneously* over whatever range it had.

The diagnostic hardware announced completion of the test cycle with a sort of mental chirp, and Alicia nodded in satisfaction. This was the first time her armor had passed *all* tests, and it had taken less than five days to bring it to that state. Tisiphone had been dismayed to find it taking that long, since she'd ordered the armor prepped before it was loaded aboard the *Bengal*, but Alicia was more than pleased. Whoever had overseen its initial activation had done an excellent job, yet no one could have brought it to real combat readiness without having her available for fitting. Battle armor had to be carefully modified to suit its intended wearer, tailored to every little physical quirk with software customized to allow for any mental idiosyncrasy, and she'd looked forward to the task with resignation. It had been five years since she last even saw a suit of armor, and considered in that light, she'd done very well indeed to finish so quickly.

"Okay, ladies, that's that," she announced, racking her tools and coiling the testing harness. "Put it back in the closet, please, Megaira."

A tractor grab lifted the empty armor from the table, then trundled back towards the storage vault, and Alicia followed to make a personal visual check as Megaira's remotes plugged in the monitoring leads. If she ever actually needed her armor, she was unlikely to have time to repair any faults which had developed since its last maintenance check. Since she didn't have a spare suit, that meant this one had to be a hundred percent at all times, and the monitors would let Megaira make certain it was.

<*I am relieved to have that finished,*> Tisiphone remarked somewhat acidly as the vault closed. <*Perhaps now we can turn to other matters?*>

<*Oh, horsefeathers!*> Megaira snorted. <*You know perfectly well that—*>

"Ah, ah! None of that!" Alicia chided, stepping into the small lift. "Tisiphone's got a point, Megaira. It *is* time we got started."

<*You still need more time to acclimatize,*> the AI objected. <*You're doing well, but you're still not what I'd call ready.*>

"We don't have time for me to 'acclimatize' as thoroughly as you'd like. Let's face it—I'm a hopeless disappointment as a starship pilot."

<*That's not true! You've got good instincts—I should know, I've got the same ones. It's just a matter of training them.*>

<*Perhaps and perhaps not, Megaira, and Alicia is correct about the pressure of time. We have been out of contact too long, and I am certain more has happened since we fled Soissons. As for her instincts requiring training, is it not true that you are fully capable of translating them into actions?*>

<*It's not the same. Alley should've been completely trained before we ever impressed. She's the captain. That means* she *makes the decisions, and she could be a lot more effective if she knew my capabilities backward and forward. She's not supposed to have to think things through or ask questions, and it slows us down when she does.*>

"No one's suggesting I shouldn't continue training, even if I am coming at it backwards. But there's no reason we can't do that *after* we start wherever we're going to start. And Tisiphone's right; our information's getting colder every day."

<*You're ganging up on me again.*>

<*Which ought, perhaps, to suggest that you are in error in this instance. I second Alicia's agreement that training must continue, but not even I can stop other events while she does so.*>

<*Hmph. Just where did you have in mind to go?*>

"MaGuire, I think. How does that strike you, Tisiphone?"

<*MaGuire? I should have thought Dewent or Wyvern would be more fruitful ground, Little One.*>

"I don't disagree, but I still think we should start at MaGuire." The lift stopped outside Alicia's quarters, and she stepped out and sprawled across the comfortable couch. "We've got to have some sort of cover before we move in on them for real, and MaGuire's a good place to begin building one."

<*"Cover"?*> The Fury sounded faintly surprised.

<*What did* you *plan on her doing? Busting down doors in battle armor to ask questions at plasgun point? Ever hear of something called subtlety?*>

"Hey, give her a break, Megaira! She never had to put up with these kinds of limitations before."

<*I am not offended,*> Tisiphone said, and somewhat to Alicia's surprise, she meant it. The Fury felt her reaction and chuckled dryly. <*As you say, I am unaccustomed to mortals' limitations, but that does not mean I am unaware of them. What sort of cover did you have in mind, Little One?*>

"I've been thinking over all the intelligence you pulled and looking for an angle we could follow up without simply duplicating everyone else's efforts. It looks to me like Colonel McIlhenny's people are doing a much better job with overt intelligence gathering than we could. He's got tonnes more manpower and far better communications than we do, and unlike us, he's official. He doesn't have to hide from both sides while he works. Agreed?"

Alicia paused, then shrugged as she felt the others' joint agreement.

"That being the case, let's leave that side of it to him and concentrate on areas where our special talents can operate most effectively."

<*And those areas are, Little One?*>

"I was particularly interested in Ben Belkassem's locked files, because I think he's on to something. I think he's right about there being someone on the inside, probably pretty far up, which means that same someone may well be feeding the pirates advance warning on Fleet sweeps and dispositions. If so, they'll know how and when to lie low, and that suggests Ben Belkassem's also hit on the most likely way to find them."

<*By tracking the loot?*> Megaira sounded dubious. <*That's a tall order, Alley, and we can only be in one place at a time. Shouldn't we leave that angle to him? O Branch has all sorts of information sources we don't.*>

"Maybe, but we can probably do a lot more with any information we get our hands—pardon, *my* hands—on. Ben Belkassem may have more reach, but he can't get inside someone's head, and I doubt his computer support can match what you're capable of. Even better, we're a complete wild card, with no connection to Justice or Fleet however hard anyone looks. Add all the other things Tisiphone does, and you've got a hell of an infiltrator."

<*And how will you use those abilities?*> the Fury asked.

"I think I'm about to become a free trader," Alicia replied, and felt the others' stir of interest. "We don't have much cargo capacity, but half the 'free traders' out here are really smugglers, and we can probably match the lift of any of the really fast hulls in the sector. Besides, specializing in delivering small cargoes quickly would make us look nicely shady."

<*That I should live to see the day I became a* freighter*!*> Megaira mourned, but amusement sparkled in her thoughts.

<*But can you?*> Tisiphone objected. <*Surely Fleet has spread the alarm since we left Soissons. From what I have seen of Sir Arthur, he, at least, would insist that the Rogue Worlds be warned, as well,*

embarrassment or no, since he believes Alicia to be mad. Will they not be on the watch for us?>

"Of course they will, but I don't think you realize quite how talented Megaira is. You can be a regular little changeling, can't you, Honey Cake?"

<Call me, "Honey Cake" again and you'll get a migraine you won't believe, Alley. Yeccch! But, yeah, I can do a real number on 'em.>

<I realize you can disguise your electronic emissions, but you cannot hide the fact that you possess a Fleet Fasset drive. And even if you could, would not visual observation reveal you for what you are?>

<The answers are "it doesn't matter," and "no." Two-thirds of the merchantmen out here use Fleet-design drives. I can fudge mine to make it look a lot less powerful by shutting down nodes, and there're a couple of tricks I can play with frequency shifts, too. I can't look, oh, Rishathan, or Jungian-built, but I can produce a civilian power curve.

<As for the visual observation angle, that's one of my neatest tricks, if I do say so myself. BuShips came up with it for second-generation alpha-synths, and I'm one of the first to get it.>

<And what, if you are through extolling your own virtues, is "it"?>

<Sticks and stones can break my bones—assuming I had any—but words will never hurt me,> Megaira caroled, and Alicia laughed. Even Tisiphone chuckled, but she clearly still wanted an explanation, and the AI obliged.

<I've got a holo imager built into the aft quadrant of my Fasset housing. I can use it to build up any exterior appearance I want.>

<Indeed? An impressive capability, yet how well will it endure close observation should they bring more than the unaided eye to bear upon it?>

<I can jigger my radiation and mass shielding to give an alloy return off the "solid surface" against most of their active sensors,> Megaira returned promptly. *<Old-fashioned radar's the hardest, but if we decide what we want to look like and leave it that way, I can fabricate reflectors to return the proper image. The holo itself will stand up to any scrutiny, except maybe a spectograph. It won't "see" anything off the holo.>*

"Yes, but a spectograph doesn't tell them anything about mass or size," Alicia mused. "Suppose we plan our holo to incorporate a few good-sized chunks of your actual hull and let them get their readings off that?"

<*They'd get readings, all right, but the wrong ones for a merchant hull. I'm made out of Kurita-Hawkins battle steel, Alley.*>

<*Yet you have substantial quantities of less noble alloys in your machine shop stores. Could we not cover the exposed portions in a thin sheath which would appease their sensors?*>

<*I suppose so. . . . My "paint's" fused into the basic battle steel matrix, and my remotes are designed for fairly major field repairs. I could use a pigment fuser to spray a thin coat of plain old titanium over the battle steel. It'll look like hell whenever I drop the holo, and I'd be ashamed to be seen in a Fleet dock wearing it, but it should work.*>

"Then since we can look like a suitably decrepit smuggler, the next item on the agenda is to build a believable identity. That's why I want to start at MaGuire and work our way towards Dewent. Megaira can work up a flight log before MaGuire, Tisiphone, and you can sneak it into the planetary data base when we first contact the port. By the time we dock and they call it up to check our papers, it'll be 'official,' as far as they're concerned."

<*Be a good idea to make this our first trip into the Franconia Sector,*> Megaira suggested. <*How about we pulled out of the Melville Sector in a hurry? That's close enough for us to've moved here but far enough away nobody should be surprised that we aren't a familiar face, and according to my data Justice just shut down a major intersystem smuggling ring there.*>

"Perfect!" Alicia chortled. "You and I can make sure the last few entries are suitably vague—the sort of thing a real smuggler would put together to cover an embarrassing situation for a new set of port authorities. It'll not only get us in with the criminal element but provide a perfect cover against any Fleet units looking for the real us."

<*That's what I had in mind. Okay, I'm started on that—*> Alicia felt a fragment of the AI's capabilities go to work on the project even as Megaira continued to speak <*—so what do we do after we get there?*>

"I doll up to look as little like me as you look like you and start trolling for a cargo. With Tisiphone to run around in the computer nets and skim thoughts, we shouldn't have too much trouble lining up a less-than-legal shipment headed in the right general direction. Once we deliver it, we'll have established our smuggler's bona fides and we can start working our way deeper. In a way, I'd like to head straight from MaGuire for Wyvern—if there's one place in this sector where those bastards could dispose of their loot, Wyvern's the one—but we need to build more layers into our cover before we knock on their front door. Still, once we get there, I'm betting we find at least some sign of their pipeline, and when we do, we can probably find someone whose thoughts can tell us where to find *them*."

<This will take time, Little One.>

"Can't be helped, unless you've got a better idea."

<No, I have no better strategy. Would that I did, but this seems sound thinking in light of our capabilities.>

<I said she had good instincts, didn't I? I like it, too, Alley.>

"Yeah, the only thing that really bothers me is losing the *Bengal*." Alicia sighed. "The cargo shuttle won't be a problem once we get rid of the Fleet markings and change the transponder, but nobody could mistake that *Bengal* for anything but an assault boat."

<So? Keep it. I'll ding it up a little and make a few unnecessary hull repairs to take the shine off it, but it's too useful to just ditch.>

"It's not exactly standard free trader issue," Alicia objected, but she heard temptation waver in her own voice.

<Again, so what? As far as I know, there's no official free trader equipment list. Hell, it'll probably get you more respect! Think how they'll wonder how you got your hands on it.>

<I believe she is correct, Little One.> Tisiphone chuckled. *<I should think your possession of such a craft will raise your stature among these criminals greatly.>*

"Yeah, you're probably right." Alicia's mouth twitched and her eyes twinkled at the thought. And, she admitted, it was a great relief, as well. "Let's think up some incredibly gaudy paint job to hang on it, in that case. If you've got it, flaunt it."

<Precisely, Little One! We shall make you a most *formidable "free trader," Megaira and I.>*

CHAPTER FORTY-SEVEN

James Howell watched the view screen as the shuttle slid up from just beyond the terminator, glittering as it broke into the unfiltered light of Hearthguard's primary, and tried not to show his uneasiness.

Hearthguard was a sparsely populated world, for it had little—aside from truly spectacular mountain landscapes and particularly dangerous fauna—to attract settlers. Visitors, now, those were another matter. To date, Hearthguard's wildlife had accounted for about one hunter in five, which, humans being humans, produced a predictably perverse response that amused the locals no end. And it was profitable, too. If putatively sane outworlders wanted to pay hefty fees for the dubious privilege of hunting predators who were perfectly willing to hunt them right back, that was fine with the Hearthguarders. But even though more and more of their guests were imperial citizens, the life-blood of their new, tourism-based prosperity, theirs was a Rogue World, independent of the Empire and minded to stay so.

Thrusters flared as the shuttle swam towards rendezvous with the freighter. Howell would have felt far happier in his flagship, but Hearthguard was too heavily traveled to take such a risk. On the other hand, this meeting had the potential to dwarf the dangers of bringing in the entire squadron. If anyone was watching, or if word of it leaked . . .

The shuttle coasted to a halt, and tractors drew it in against one of the freighter's racks. Howell watched the personnel tube jockeying into position, then sighed and turned toward the lift with squared shoulders.

It was time to hear what Control had to say to him. He did not expect to enjoy the conversation.

The commodore reached the personnel lock just as a tallish man in camping clothes stepped out, fiercely trimmed mustachios jutting. Despite its obvious comfort and sturdiness, his clothing was expensive, and his squashed-looking hat's band was decorated with at least a dozen bent, shiny wires tied up with feathers, mirrors, and God alone knew what. The first time he'd seen them, Howell had assumed they were solely decorative; only after a fair amount of research had he discovered they were lures for an arcane sport called "fly-fishing." It still struck him as a stupid way for a grown man to spend his time, though Hearthguard's two-meter saber-trout probably made the sport far more interesting than it had been in its original Old Earth form.

He moved forward to greet his visitor, and winced at the other's bone-crushing handshake. Control had a rather juvenile need to demonstrate his strength, and Howell had learned to let him, though he did wish Control would at least take off his Academy ring before he crushed his victims' metacarpals.

"I thought we'd use my cabin, Sir," he said, managing not to wave his hand about as he reclaimed it at last. "It's not much, but it's private."

"Fine. I don't expect to be here long enough for austerity to be a problem."

Control's voice was clipped, with a trace of the Mother World, though Howell knew he'd never visited Old Earth before reporting to the Academy. The commodore pushed the thought aside and led the way down a corridor which had been sealed off for the duration of Control's visit. No more than a score of the squadron's personnel knew who Control was, and Rachel Shu went to considerable lengths to keep it that way.

Howell's cabin—the freighter captain's cabin, actually—was more comfortable than his earlier comment had suggested. He waved Control through the hatch first and watched to see what he would do. He wasn't disappointed. Control walked briskly to the captain's desk, sat unhesitatingly behind it, and pointed to the supplicant's chair in front.

The commodore obeyed the gesture with outward calm, sitting back and crossing his legs. He had no delusions. Control's personal visit suggested that he was going to tear at least one long, bloody strip off him, but Howell was damned if he was going to look uneasy. He'd done his best, and the losses at Elysium hadn't been his fault, whatever Control might intend to say.

Control let him sit in silence for several moments, then leaned back and inhaled sharply, bristling his waxed mustache even more aggressively.

"So, Commodore. I suppose you know why I'm here?" Howell recognized his cue and offered the expected response.

"I imagine it has something to do with Elysium."

"It does, indeed. We're not happy about that disaster, Commodore Howell. Not happy at all. And neither are our backers."

His gray eyes were hard, but Howell refused to flinch. He also refused to waste time defending himself until specific charges were leveled, and he returned Control's gaze in composed silence.

"You had perfect intelligence, Commodore," Control resumed when it became obvious Howell had nothing to say. "We handed you Elysium on a silver platter, and you not only lost three-quarters of your ground element, but you also managed to lose five cargo shuttles, a *Leopard*-class assault boat, four *Bengals* . . . and a million-tonne battlecruiser. And to top it all off, you didn't even secure your objective. Tell me, Commodore, were you born incompetent, or did you have to work at it?"

"Since I believe I've demonstrated my competence in the past," Howell said in a mild tone which deceived neither of them, "I won't dignify that last question with a response, Sir. On your other points, I believe the record speaks for itself. *Poltava* carried out a textbook attack run, but Captain Ortiz made a poor command decision and got too close to his last opponent. Things like that happen to even the best commanders, and when they happen fifteen light-minutes from the flagship, the flag officer can't prevent them."

He held Control's gaze, letting his eyes show the anger his voice did not, and saw something flicker deep under the other man's brows. Answering anger or respect—he couldn't tell, nor, at the moment, did he much care.

"As for the remainder of your . . . indictment, I would simply point out that your intelligence was, in fact, far from complete—and that you'd been warned success was problematical. You knew how tough it was going to be to secure GeneCorp's files. Had the enemy actually been in the positions you assured us they intended to assume, we probably would have succeeded in rushing the facilities, although the fact that they'd been rigged with demo charges probably would have kept us from securing their contents, anyway.

"As it was, however, our ground commanders walked into what turned out to be, in effect, a trap precisely because they'd been told where to expect opposition. I probably *am* at fault for not stressing the need for complete preparedness despite our 'perfect' intelligence, but I submit that it would be wiser of you not to provide tactical data at all unless you can confirm its accuracy. Incorrect information is worse than none—as this operation demonstrated."

"No one can guarantee there won't be last-minute changes, Commodore."

"In that case, Sir, it would be wise not to pretend you *can*," Howell returned in that same calm voice. He paused a beat, waiting for Control to respond, but he only made a throwaway gesture, and the commodore resumed.

"Finally, Sir, I would further submit that whatever happened to our ground forces and whether or not we secured the GeneCorp data, we succeeded completely in what my mission description laid down as our primary objective. No doubt you have better casualty estimates than we do, but I feel quite confident we provided the 'atrocity' you wanted."

"Umph." Control rocked gently back and forth, simultaneously swinging his chair in tiny arcs, and puffed his mustache, then shrugged.

"Point taken," he said in a far less rancorous tone. He even smiled a bit. "As I'm sure you're well aware, shit flows downhill. Consider yourself doused with half the bucket that hit me in the face." His smile faded. "I assure you, however, that there was plenty to go around for both of us."

"Yes, Sir." Howell allowed himself to relax in turn. "In fact, I already prepaid my own people for what I figured was coming my way," he confessed. "But in all seriousness, we did succeed in our primary mission."

"If it makes you feel any better, that's the opinion *I* expressed. As for your losses—" Control shrugged "—we're already recruiting new ground personnel from local Rogue Worlds, though I'm afraid we can't replace *Poltava* as quickly. But while you're right about your primary objective, it seems the secondary objective was more important than either of us had been informed."

"It was?" Howell tugged at an earlobe. "It would've been nice of them to let us know."

"Agreed, agreed."

Control reached into a jacket pocket and extracted a cigar case. He selected one, clipped the end, and lit it. Howell watched, grateful for the ventilation intake directly above the desk, as Control puffed until it was drawing to his satisfaction, then waved it at him like a pointer.

"You see, Commodore, our Core World financial backers are getting a bit shaky. They're bloodthirsty enough in the abstract, and they're perfectly willing to contemplate heavy civilian casualties as long as someone else will be inflicting them, but they don't have the stomach for it once the bloodshed actually starts. Not because they give a good goddamn about the people involved, but because they suddenly recognize the reality of the stakes for which they're playing—and what'll happen to them if it comes apart."

Howell nodded as he heard the contempt in Control's voice.

"They're fat and rich, and they want to be fatter and richer, but while the wealth and power they've already got protect them from the consequences of most of their deals, this one's different. *Nothing* will save them if the Empire discovers their involvement, and their objectives are very different from ours. They're backing us solely in return for an immediate profit now and more concessions after we succeed, and I don't think they really understood how much anti-pirate hysteria we were going to have to whip up to make it all work."

He took another pull on his cigar and ejected a long, gray streamer of smoke.

"The reason I'm going into this at such length is that we don't have a stick to beat them with, so we need to keep the carrot in plain sight. At the moment, they can see the consequences of failure all too clearly, and some of them are worried that we're simply bringing the Fleet down on our heads by our actions. We, of course, know why we're doing that; they don't. Which means that we need to throw them an immediate kilo of flesh if we don't want them backing out on us, and GeneCorp's data was supposed to be just that."

"I realize that, Sir, but Captain Alexsov and I both pointed out the high probability of failure when the target was designated."

"Forget that." Control waved his cigar a bit impatiently. "I jumped your shit over it, and you jumped right back. Fine. That's done with. The point before us now is where we go from here."

"Yes, Sir."

"Good. Did you bring Alexsov along?"

"Yes, Sir. He and Commander Shu are both aboard."

"Excellent." Control consulted his watch and made a face. "My people groundside can only cover me for a few hours, and I've got to get back to work by the end of next week. Taking even a short 'vacation' at a time like this has already gotten me a few dirty looks, and I can't do it again any time soon, so I want to tie up all the loose ends as quickly as possible. Let me lay it out for you, then you can bring them up to speed after I leave, right?"

"Of course."

"All right. As I say, we need a plainly visible carrot, and we think we've found one at Ringbolt."

"Ringbolt?" Howell repeated with some surprise. All of his targets to date had been imperial possessions, but Ringbolt was a Rogue World daughter colony, and the people it belonged to were nasty customers, indeed.

"Ringbolt. I know the El Grecans keep a close eye on it, but we happen to know they're going to be involved in some pretty elaborate Fleet maneuvers late next month. I've brought the details in my intelligence download. The point is, the Ringbolt squadron's being called back to El Greco in a home-defense mobilization exercise, which will leave the system uncovered for at least a week. That's your window, Commodore."

"I don't know much about the Ringbolt System, Sir. What are the fixed defenses like? The El Grecans have an awfully impressive tech base for a Rogue World, and I'd hate to walk into a surprise."

"There are no fixed defenses. That's the beauty of it."

"*None?*"

"None. It makes sense when you think about it. The planet's only been colonized for fifty years, and when they moved in the colonists, all they had to worry about were other Rogue Worlds and the occasional genuine hijack outfit. They couldn't possibly stand off the Empire or the Sphere, so they decided not to try. As for other Rogue worlds or hijackers . . . if you were them, would *you* take on the El Grecans?"

"Probably not, Sir," Howell acknowledged. For that matter, he doubted he would care to go after them even if he'd been the Empire or the Rish. Occupation of an El Grecan colony was unlikely to prove cost effective.

El Greco had been a scholar's world, renowned for its art academies and universities, before the League Wars. Then the Rish moved in during the First Human-Rish War, and alien occupation came to the groves of academe.

El Grecans might have been highbrows and philosophers, but that hadn't meant they were airheads, and the Rish soon discovered they'd caught a tiger by the tail. The academics of El Greco warmed up their computers, set up their data searches, and turned to the study of guerrilla warfare, sabotage, and assassination as if preparing to sit their doctoral orals. Within a year, they had two divisions tied down; by the time the Sphere gave it up as a bad deal and left, the Rishathan garrison had grown to three *corps* . . . and was still losing ground.

The El Grecans hadn't forgotten a thing since, and they'd decided to turn their surviving universities in a new direction. El Greco no longer produced artists, sculptors, and composers; it produced physicists, chemists, strategists, engineers, weapons specialists, and one of humanity's most advanced R&D complexes. The best mercenary outfits in this corner of the galaxy were based on El Greco, and most of their personnel held reserve commissions in the planetary armed forces. No doubt El Greco could still be had by someone the size of the Empire or Sphere who wanted it badly enough, but the price would be far too high for the return, and no mere Rogue World—or even an alliance of them—wanted the El Grecan Navy on their necks.

More to the point, Commodore James Howell didn't especially want the El Grecan Navy on *his* neck.

"Excuse me, Sir, but are you certain this is something we want to do?"

Control snorted with a wry, almost compassionate amusment and drew deeply on his cigar before he responded.

"Look at it this way, Commodore. The El Grecans are good, no question, but they're only one system. Their entire Navy and all their mercenary outfits together have less firepower than Admiral Gomez, nor do they begin to have the information sources Soissons has. Since your squadron is already completely outgunned, adding one more set of enemies to the mix shouldn't really matter all that much, should it? After all, if we ever face a stand-up fight, we lose even if we win."

"I realize that, Sir, but we don't have the same kind of penetration against El Greco. We know what Fleet's going to do before it does it; we won't have that advantage against the El Grecans."

"Ah, but we will!" Control's eyes glittered with true humor. "You see, we're killing several birds with one stone here.

"First, your raid on Ringbolt will be targeted on the bioresearch unit of the University of Toledo. We have reason to believe they were running close to a dead heat with GeneCorp, so we can recoup our earlier failure.

"Second, hitting a Rogue World offsets the idea that someone's gone to war against the Empire. We have, but it's important that no one realize that. We can get away without hitting any more of the sector's Rogue Worlds—most of them don't have anything worth stealing anyway—but we have to hit at least one to look like 'real' pirates.

"Third, the El Grecans, like the Jungians, want to demonstrate that *they* aren't behind our attacks, so there's already been a good bit of joint contingency planning—that's how we found out about these maneuvers. Better still, they've accepted the principle of joint command and coordination if they do get hit. The Jungians haven't done that, but even if your attack brings the El Grecans into the field, we'll have good intelligence on their basic posture and operations.

"And fourth," Control's eyes narrowed, "a few of Gomez's people—especially McIlhenny—are getting suspicious about our operational patterns. Phase Four at Elysium nailed anyone who might've identified your vessels, but the ease with which you got in was a pretty clear indication you had very, very good intelligence. Even the governor general is finding it hard to ignore that evidence, and McIlhenny's got Gomez chewing the bulkheads over it. If you hit a Rogue World with the same kind of precision, it should suggest you have multiple intelligence sources, which may divert some of the heat."

"I was afraid of that when Elysium was selected," Howell murmured, and Control shrugged.

"You weren't alone. It was a calculated risk because we needed an Incorporated World target. Crown Worlds have such low populations that even a total burn-off like Mathison's World doesn't produce the kinds of casualty figures we need to hit Core World public opinion with. Besides, most Core Worlders figure anyone willing to settle a colony world knows the odds and doesn't have much kick coming when he craps out. But an *Incorporated* World is something else. Elysium has senatorial representation, and you'd better believe those senators are screaming for action after what happened to a third of their constituents!"

"I know, Sir." Howell looked down at his hands. "Does that mean we do the same thing on Ringbolt?" he asked in a neutral voice.

"I'm afraid it does, Commodore." Even Control sounded uncomfortable, but his tone didn't flinch. "We can't change our pattern for the same reason we need to hit a Rogue World in the first place. It *has* to look like we're treating everyone we hit in precisely the same fashion."

Howell sighed. "Understood, Sir."

"Good." Control tossed a small chip folio onto the desk and stood. "Here's your intelligence packet. We don't anticipate any problems with it, but if Commander Shu has questions, she should send them back through the usual channels. We can't afford any more direct contact for a while."

"Understood," Howell said again, rising to escort his visitor from the cabin. He forbore to mention that *this* meeting hadn't been his idea, partly out of diplomacy but also because he'd found it useful after all. Face-to-face discussions filled in nuances no indirect contact could convey.

They paused outside the personnel lock and Control wrung his hand again, not quite so crushingly this time.

"Good hunting, Commodore," he said.

"Thank you, Sir," Howell replied, coming to attention but not saluting. Their eyes met one last time, and then Vice Admiral Sir Amos Brinkman nodded sharply and stepped through the hatch.

CHAPTER FORTY-EIGHT

Lieutenant Charles Giolitti, Jungian Navy, on assignment to the MaGuire Customs Service, took the time to double-check his data as the boarding shuttle drifted towards the free trader *Star Runner*. He'd been intrigued when he first accessed the download—and noted the ship's list of auxiliaries—and he wanted to be certain he'd read it correctly.

The information was unusually complete for a recent arrival, he observed cheerfully. It wasn't unheard of for a foreign-registry vessel to arrive with absolutely no documentation, and that was always a pain. It meant its every centimeter must be scrutinized, its every crew member exhaustively med-checked, and its bona fides thoroughly established before any of its people were allowed groundside. Tempers tended to get short all round before the process was completed, but the Jung Association hadn't lasted for four centuries without learning to keep a close eye on visitors. In this case, though, Giolitti had a full imperial attestation from the Melville Sector, which should cut the crap to a minimum.

He screened quickly through the technical data, eyebrows quirking as he noted the rating of *Star Runner*'s Fasset drive. She was as fast as most cruisers—which, he thought wryly, coupled with her limited cargo capacity, was a glaring tip-off as to her true nature. Not that Jungians minded smugglers . . . as long as they didn't run anything *into* the Association.

Um. Crew of only five. That was low, even for a merchant hull. Must indicate some pretty impressive computer support. Captain's name Theodosia Mainwaring . . . young for her rank, from the bio, but lots of time on her flight log. The rest of her people looked equally qualified. Not a bad bunch for a merchant crew, in fact. Of course, free traders tended to attract the skilled misfits—the square pegs with the qualifications to write their own tickets—away from the military or the big lines.

No incoming manifest. He snorted, remembering the diplomatic gaps in the last few entries from the Melville data base. So Captain Mainwaring had gotten her fingers burned? Must not have been too serious—she still had a ship—but it probably meant she was hungry for a cargo.

A signal chimed, and Giolitti glanced at the view screen as his vessel began its docking sequence on *Star Runner*'s sole unoccupied shuttle rack. A somewhat battered cargo shuttle occupied one of the other two racks, not that old but clearly a veteran of hard service to collect so many dings and scrapes. Yet it wasn't the cargo shuttle that caught his attention.

Another shuttle loomed on the number one rack—a needle-nosed craft, deadly even in repose. He was familiar with its basic stats, but he'd never seen one, and he wasn't quite prepared for its size. Or its color scheme.

Giolitti winced as he took in the garish crimson and black hull. Some unknown artist had painted staring white eyes on either side of the stiletto prow, jagged-toothed mouths gaped hungrily about the muzzles of energy and projectile cannons, and lovingly detailed streamers of lurid flame twined about the engine pods. He had no idea how Mainwaring had gotten her hands on it, though she must have done so in at least quasi-legal fashion, since the Empies had let her keep it when they suggested she explore new frontiers, but the visual impact was . . . extreme.

He grinned as the docking arms locked. The *Bengal* looked out of place on its drab, utilitarian mother ship, but free traders tended to find themselves back of beyond with only their own resources, and he suspected ill-intentioned locals would think twice about harassing a cargo shuttle with that thing hovering watchfully overhead. Which, no doubt, was the idea.

The personnel tube docking collar settled into place, and Giolitti gathered up his notepad, nodded to his pilot, and opened the hatch.

* * *

Alicia watched the heavyset young customs officer step through *Megaira*'s port and hoped this worked. It had seemed simple enough when she was thinking it all up, but that was then.

<*Oh, be calm, Little One!*> the Fury scolded. <*We have already accomplished the difficult parts.*>

<*Yeah, Alley,*> Megaira added in unusual support of Tisiphone. <*There's only one of him, and Tis is gonna knock his shorts off.*>

<*A somewhat inelegant turn of phrase, but accurate.*>

<*Then why don't both of you be quiet so we can get on with this?*> Alicia suggested pointedly, and stepped forward to shake the inspector's hand.

Giolitti was a bit surprised to find only the captain waiting for him, but he had to give her tailor high marks. That severe, midnight-blue uniform and silver-braided bolero suited the tall, sable-haired woman perfectly.

"Lieutenant Giolitti, MaGuire Customs Service," he introduced himself, and the woman smiled.

"Captain Theodosia Mainwaring."

She had a nice voice—low and almost furry-sounding. He found himself beaming back at her and wondered vaguely why he felt so cheerful.

"Welcome to MaGuire, Captain."

"Thanks."

She released his hand, and he brought out his notepad.

"You have your crew's updated med forms, Captain?"

"Right here."

She extended a folio of chips, and Giolitti plugged them into the notepad, punching buttons with practiced fingers and scanning the display. Looked good. He supposed he really ought to insist on meeting the others immediately, but there was time for that before he left.

"Ready for inspection, Captain?" he asked, and Mainwaring nodded.

"Follow me," she invited, and led him into the lift.

* * *

The customs officer's vaguely disoriented eyes were a vast relief, but Alicia made a point of punching the lift buttons. Tisiphone chuckled deep inside her mind, enjoying herself as she worked her wiles upon their visitor, yet Alicia knew the fewer perceptions the Fury had to fuzz the better, and there was no point letting Megaira move the lift without instructions.

She escorted Lieutenant Giolitti into her quarters and watched him carry out his inspection. He clearly knew the best places to conceal contraband, yet there was a mechanical air to his actions. His voice sounded completely alert as he carried on a cheerful conversation with her, but its very normality was almost bizarre against the backdrop of his robotic search.

He finished his examination with a smile, and she drew a deep breath and led him back outside. She paused for just a moment, watching his eyes go even more unfocused, then turned and escorted him right back into her cabin.

"My engineer's quarters," she said, and he nodded and went to work . . . totally oblivious to the fact that he had just searched exactly the same room.

Alicia hardly believed what she was seeing. She'd counted on it, but actually seeing it was eerie and unreal, and she felt Megaira's matching reaction. Tisiphone, on the other hand, took it completely for granted, though she was obviously bending all her will upon the lieutenant to bring it off.

Giolitti completed his second examination and turned to her.

"Who's next?" he asked cheerfully.

"My astrogator," Alicia said, and led him back out into the passage.

Giolitti made the last entry and wished all his inspections could go this smoothly. Captain Mainwaring ran a taut ship. Even her cargo hold was spotless, and *Star Runner* was one of the very few free traders whose crew hadn't left something illegal—or at least closely regulated—lying around where he could find it. Which made them improbably law-abiding or fiendishly clever at hiding their personal stashes. Given his impression of Mainwaring's people, Giolitti suspected the latter, and more power to them.

It was funny, though. He'd been impressed by their competence, but they hadn't really registered the way people usually did.

Probably because he'd been concentrating so hard on their captain, he thought a bit guiltily, and glanced at her from the corner of his eye as she escorted him back to the personnel lock. It was unusual for a captain to spend his or her precious time escorting a customs man about in person. Even the best of them seemed to regard inspectors as one step lower than a Rish, an intruder—and, still worse, an *official* intruder—in their domains. Giolitti didn't really blame them, but it was a tremendous relief when he met one of the rare good ones.

And, come to think of it, it wasn't really all that strange that the rest of her crew seemed somehow faded beside her. He'd never met anyone with quite the personal magnetism Theodosia Mainwaring radiated. She was a striking woman, friendly and completely at her ease, yet he had the strangest impression she could be a very dangerous person if she chose. Of course, no shrinking violet would be skippering a free trader at such a relatively young age, but it went deeper than that. He remembered the grizzled petty officer who'd overseen the hand-to-hand training of the "young gentlemen" at OCS. He'd moved the way Mainwaring did, and he'd been sudden death on two feet.

The lieutenant shook the thought aside and ejected the clearance chip from his notepad. He held it out to the captain, then extended his hand.

"It's been a pleasure, Captain Mainwaring. I wish every ship I inspected were as shipshape as yours. I hope you do well in our area."

"Thank you, Lieutenant." Mainwaring clasped his hand firmly, and for just an instant, he seemed to feel an odd, hard angularity in her palm, but the sensation vanished. A moment later, he didn't even remember having felt it. "I hope we run into one another again," the captain continued.

"Maybe we will." Giolitti released her hand and stood back, then raised an admonishing finger. "Remember, any of your people who come dirtside will be subject to individual med-scans to confirm their certification."

"Don't worry, Lieutenant." Mainwaring's rather amused smile made him feel even younger. "I don't expect we'll be here long enough for liberty—in fact, most of my people are going to be busy running maintenance checks on the Fasset drive before we pull out—but we'll check in with the medics if we are."

"Thank you, Captain," Giolitti gave her a crisp salute. "In that case, allow me to extend an official welcome to MaGuire and bid you good-bye."

Mainwaring returned his salute, and the lieutenant headed back for his shuttle. He had two more inspections to make by shift end, and he wished, more wistfully than hopefully, that they might go as smoothly.

Alicia let herself sag against the bulkhead and sucked in a deep, lung-stretching breath. Dear God, she'd known Tisiphone was good, but the Fury's performance had surpassed her most extravagant hopes.

She doubted they were likely to meet a brighter, more conscientious customs inspector than young Lieutenant Giolitti, and she no longer doubted their ability to razzle-dazzle him if they did. It had been unnerving enough to watch him "search" her quarters five separate times, but that had been nothing compared to watching him walk right past the feed tubes from the main missile magazine without even batting an eye. He'd had to climb a ladder to cross one of them, yet it simply hadn't been there for him, and neither had the energy batteries or the armory. He'd seemed perfectly content with his "inspection" of the control room, as well, though only an idiot—or someone under Tisiphone's spell—could have looked at those blank gray walls and the alpha link headset without realizing what he was seeing.

<*Of course he did not,*> Tisiphone observed. <*You are correct about his intelligence—a very bright young man, indeed—yet it is far simpler to suggest things to intelligent people, for they have the wit to add the details with little prompting. And,*> she added graciously, <*you and Megaira were wise to suggest that we create your "crew's" personalities in such detail. It allowed me to project personalities with much greater depth.*>

"Yeah." Alicia drew another breath and straightened. "Still, you seemed to be concentrating pretty hard. Could you have handled more people?"

<*I believe so, yes. Numbers of minds are not the difficulty, Little One, but rather the detail of the illusion I provide them with. Of*

course, it would be wise, in the event that we must deal with several people at once, to include a disinclination to discuss their inspection at a later date lest they discover too great a degree of similarity among their recollections.>

<*You're probably right,*> Megaira put in, <*but unless there's a glitch in the documentation, one-man teams are the rule out here.*>

"I know." Alicia stepped back into the lift and punched for the flight deck. "Are we clear on our docking and service fees, Megaira?"

<*Sure. Tis cooked the books just fine when she dropped our flight log on them, and Ms. Tanner took care of the bookkeeping while Captain Mainwaring was showing Lieutenant Giolitti around. We've covered all our fees out of her bogus credit transfer with a balance of eighty thousand credits left.*>

"What about service personnel?"

<*No sweat. Lieutenant Chisholm dealt with them, and they'll be waiting for our shuttle to pick up the consumables. We're gonna have to dump most of them in deep space, since I had to order enough for a crew of five to make it look right, but our Melville download shows a complete overhaul six months ago, so I didn't have to fudge any servicing requirements.*>

"You're a sweetheart," Alicia said fervently.

She'd been astounded by the verisimilitude of the computer images and voices Megaira could produce. It was a good thing the AI could, too, since they had to convince anyone who got curious— No, scratch that. They had to keep anyone from *getting* curious, which meant they had to provide crewmen other than Captain Mainwaring in one form or another. Megaira's ability to carry on com conversations, or even several of them at once, would be invaluable in that regard.

<*Thanks. You and Tis did pretty good, too.*>

<*Yet could we have accomplished but little without you, Megaira. It is the combination of all our skills which makes us formidable.*>

"You got that right, Lady," Alicia agreed. "But I take it no one raised an eyebrow over your faces?"

<*Nary a twitch. Wanna see my latest efforts? I finally got that lisp down pat on "Lieutenant Chisholm," you know.*>

"Sure." The lift slid to a halt and Alicia stepped out onto the flight deck. "Let her roll."

<*Watch monitor two.*>

The flat screen flickered for just an instant, then cleared with the face of a thin, auburn-haired man with heavy-lidded eyes.

"How do I look, Thir?" the image asked, and Alicia grinned.

"I think maybe you got the lisp down a little *too* pat, Megaira."

"That'th eathy for you to thay," "Lieutenant Chisholm" returned aggrievedly. "You haven't been teathed about it all your life. I tell you, it'th been a real pain in the ath for me!"

"Do you say that, or do you spray it?" Alicia giggled, and the image raised a hand into the field of the pickup and made a rude gesture.

"Oh, that's *perfect,* Megaira! Of course, I imagine poor Chisholm won't be handling much of the com traffic, given his lisp."

"No." Chisholm's baritone was replaced by a soprano and the image changed to that of a square-faced, silver-haired woman Alicia recognized as Ruth Tanner, her purser. "Poor Andy hates it when he has to talk to strangers. That's why I usually handle the com watch when you're not aboard, Ma'am."

"So I see," Alicia propped a hip against a console and grinned. The AI had outdone herself. No one who spoke to any of Megaira's talking heads would suspect there was only a single human aboard *Star Runner.* Coupled with the AI's ability to handle both shuttles through her telemetry links, Captain Mainwaring's crew would be very much in evidence—so much so that no one would ever realize that they'd never actually laid eyes on any of them.

"Okay, I think we're set. But if it's all the same to you two, I need a good night's sleep before I get started hunting up a cargo."

<Right.>

The screen blanked as Megaira returned to direct contact, and Alicia started back towards her quarters, shedding her tight jacket as she went. She tossed the garment to one of Megaira's waiting remotes, which whisked it neatly into a closet.

<Uh, say, Alley,> Megaira said as she undressed, *<you haven't had time to go through the full data download from the MaGuire port admiral, have you?>*

"You know I haven't." Alicia paused with her blouse half off. "Why?"

<Well, I didn't want to worry you with it while Giolitti was aboard, and I wouldn't want to give you bad dreams or anything, but we're in it.>

"What do you mean, 'we'?"

<*I mean the "we" that stole me from Soissons orbit. Specifically, Captain Alicia DeVries and the illegally obtained alpha-synth starship Hull Number Seven-Niner-One-One-Four.*>

<*Indeed? what has the data to say of us?*> Tisiphone asked curiously.

<*It's not real good.*>

"Meaning what?" Alicia asked sharply. "That they know where we're headed or something?"

<*No, not that bad. But there's an entry in here all about you, Alley—says you broke out of psychiatric detention and have to be considered extremely dangerous—and another bunch of crap about* me. *Fairly accurate summation of my offensive and defensive capabilities, though they're playing a lot of the details close to their chests and they don't say diddly about the other things I can do. No, what bothers me is this last little bit.*>

"*What* last little bit?"

<*The one that says Fleet's offering a one million-credit reward for information leading to your location and interception,*> Megaira said. Alicia swallowed, but the AI wasn't quite done. <*And the last little section that says the Jungian Navy's officially adopted Governor General Treadwell's instructions to his own Fleet units.*>

Alicia sat down on the bed with a thump as Megaira finished her report.

<*It's a shoot on sight order, Alley. They're not even talking about trying to get us back in one piece.*>

CHAPTER FORTY-NINE

Benjamin McIlhenny racked his headset and stood, rubbing his aching eyes and trying to remember when he'd last had six hours' sleep at a stretch.

He lowered his hands and glowered at the record chips and hard-copy heaped about his office aboard the accomodation ship HMS *Donegal.* Somewhere in all that crap, he knew, was the answer—or the clues which would lead to the answer—if only he could find it.

It seemed a law of nature that any intelligence service always had the critical data in its grasp . . . and didn't know it. After all, how did you cull the one, crucial truth from the heap of untruth, half-truth, and plain lunacy? Answer: hindsight invariably recognized it after the fact. Which, of course, was the reason the intelligence community was constantly being kicked by people who thought it was so damned easy.

McIlhenny snorted bitterly and began to pace. He'd seen it too many times, especially from Senate staffers. They had an image of intelligence officers as Machiavellian spy-masters, usually in pursuit of some hidden agenda. That was why everyone knew the civilians had to watch the sneaky bastards so closely. And since they were so damned clever, *obviously* they never told all they knew, even when they had a constitutional duty to do so. Which, naturally, meant any "failure" to spot the critical datum actually represented some deep-seated plot to suppress an embarrassing truth.

People like that neither knew nor cared what true intelligence work was. Holovid might pander to the notion of the Daring Interstellar Agent carrying the vital data chip in a hollow tooth, but the real secret was sweat. Insight and trained instinct were invaluable, but it was the painstaking pursuit of every lead, the collection of every scrap of evidence and its equally exhaustive analysis, which provided the real breakthroughs.

Unfortunately, he admitted with a sigh, analysis took time, sometimes more than you had, and in this case it wasn't providing what he needed. He *knew* there was a link between the pirates and someone high up. It was the only possible answer. Admiral Gomez's full strength would have had a tough time fighting its way into Elysium orbit against its space defenses, yet the pirates had gotten inside in the first rush. McIlhenny had no detailed sensor data to back his hunch, but he was morally certain the raiders had slipped a capital ship into SLAM range under some sort of cover. The shocked survivors all agreed on the blazing speed with which the orbital defenses had been annihilated, and only a capital ship could have done it.

But *how*? How had they fooled Commodore Trang and all of his people? Simple ECM couldn't be the answer after all the sector had been through. No, somehow they'd given Trang a legitimate cover, something he *knew* was friendly, and there was simply no way they could have done that without access to information they should never have been able to reach.

It all fit a pattern—even Treadwell was showing signs of accepting that—but the colonel was damned if he could make it all come together. Even Ben Belkassem had thrown up his hands and departed for Old Earth in the faint hope that his superiors there might be able to see something from their distant perspective which had eluded everyone in the Franconia Sector.

The colonel hoped so, because what bothered him even more than how was *why*. What in God's name were these people *up* to? He hadn't said so (except very privately to Admiral Gomez and Brigadier Keita), but it passed sanity that they could be garden-variety pirates. That didn't make sense just based on cost effectiveness! Anybody who could field a force the size of the one these people had to have didn't need whatever they were making off their loot.

No doubt plunder helped defray their operational costs, but his most generous estimate of their take fell short of what it must cost to supply and maintain their ships. Just look at what they were taking: colony support equipment, spaceport beacon arrays, *industrial machinery*, for God's sake! They scooped up some luxury goods, of course—they'd scored over a half-billion in direcat pelts, alone, from Mathison's World—but no normal hijacker or pirate would touch most of what they took.

And even aside from their unlikely loot, there were the casualties. McIlhenny didn't believe in Attila the Hun in starships. Stupid people, by and large, didn't become starship captains, and only someone who was stupid could fail to see the inevitable result of pursuing some bizarre scorched-earth policy against the Empire. That was why massacre for the sake of massacre wasn't a normal piratical trait; it didn't pay their bills, and it *did* guarantee a massive response. Yet these people were deliberately maximizing the devastation in their wake. From everything the Elysium survivors could tell him, they hadn't even tried to loot beyond the limits of the capital, but they'd nuked every city from orbit! Nine million dead. What in hell's name could be behind that kind of slaughter? It was almost as if they were taunting the Fleet, *daring* it to deal with them.

It was maddening, yet the answer was here, right here in his office and his brain, if he could only bring the pieces together. Any group who could penetrate security as if it didn't exist and use their stolen data to mount such meticulous, lethal attacks couldn't be mere loose cannons. They had an ultimate objective which, in their eyes at least, made all the killing worthwhile, and that was frightening, because he couldn't imagine what it might be and it was his job to do just that.

There were times, McIlhenny thought wistfully, when a return to the simplicity of combat looked ever so attractive.

The admittance signal hauled him out of his thoughts. He pressed the button, and his eyebrows arched as Sir Arthur Keita stepped through the hatch.

"Good evening, Sir Arthur. What can I do for you?"

"Probably not much," Keita rumbled. He removed a carton of chips from a chair and settled onto it, holding them in his lap. "I just dropped by to say good-bye, Colonel."

"Good-bye?" McIlhenny repeated in surprise, and Keita gave a sour grin.

"I'm only punching air out here. This is a job for you and the Fleet—and Treadwell, if he ever stops screaming for more ships and uses what he has—and I've been here too long."

"I see." McIlhenny sank into his own chair and swivelled it to face Keita. The brigadier's gravelly voice was as steady as ever, but he heard the despair within it. He knew what had kept Keita on Soissons so long . . . and there hadn't been a single report of the alpha-synth in ten weeks.

"I imagine you do, Colonel." Keita's eyes were sad, but he gave McIlhenny a less strained smile and nodded. "But I can't justify staying on in the hope that something will break, and—" his jaw tightened "—if she's spotted now, she's your job, not mine."

"Understood, Sir," the colonel said. "I wish it weren't true—God knows Captain DeVries deserves better than that—but I understand."

Keita looked down at the carton of chips, stirring them with a blunt index finger.

"I wish you could have known her before, Colonel," he said softly. "She was . . . special. The best. And to have it end like this, with an *imperial* price on her head . . ."

The silver-maned old head shook sadly, and then Keita looked up at McIlhenny's combat ribbons.

"You've been there, Colonel. If it has to be one of our own, I'm glad it's someone who can understand. Whatever she is now, she was *special*."

"I know she was, Sir Arthur."

"Yes. Yes, you do." Keita inhaled deeply, then rose and held out his hand. "I'll be going, then."

"Yes, Sir. I'm going to miss you, Sir Arthur. I want you to know how much I've appreciated the insight you gave me between your . . . other duties."

"Keep swinging, Colonel." Keita's grip crushed McIlhenny's hand. "Between us, I'm convinced you're on the right trail, so you watch your six. Something stinks to high heaven out here. I intend to say as much to Countess Miller and His Majesty, but you be careful who you trust. When you can't tell the bad guys from the good guys . . ."

His voice trailed off, and he released McIlhenny's hand with a shrug.

"I know, Sir." The colonel frowned a moment, then looked deep into Keita's eyes. "A favor, if I may, Sir Arthur."

"Of course," Keita said instantly, and McIlhenny smiled his thanks.

"I've made a complete duplicate of my files. Technically, they're not supposed to leave my office, but I would be very grateful if you'd take them to Old Earth with you. I'd feel much happier with someone I *know* is clean in possession of my data in case—"

The colonel broke off with a crooked smile, and Keita nodded soberly.

"I will—and I'm honored by your trust."

"Thank you. And with your permission, Sir, I'll arrange a periodic security download to you. One outside my normal channels."

"Do you have a feeling?" Keita's eyes were suddenly intent, and the colonel shrugged.

"I . . . don't know. It's just that I suspect we've been penetrated even more deeply than we've guessed. I don't want to sound paranoid, but these people have certainly demonstrated they're not shy about killing people. If I get too close to their mole . . . Well, accidents happen, Sir Arthur."

Vice Admiral Brinkman lit another cigar, tipped back his chair, and frowned meditatively up at the overhead. Things were getting complicated. Of course, they'd known they would—they had to, in fact, if this was going to work—but keeping so many balls in the air wore on a man's nerves.

He thought back over his discussion with Howell. He could certainly understand the commodore's concerns, and, frankly, *he* would have balked at hitting someone like the El Grecans if not for McIlhenny. The collateral objectives would be valuable even without the troublesome colonel, but he was the real reason they had to strike at least one nonimperial target to prove they really were "pirates." Not that Brinkman expected even the Ringbolt attack to throw him off for long. It should create confusion among the people to whom he reported, but it was unlikely to create enough.

And that was because McIlhenny wasn't going to give up. He might not realize what he had his teeth into, but he knew he was onto *something*, and he wasn't going to turn loose. The use of classified data to plan the squadron's operations had always been the shakiest part of the entire plan, yet there'd been no other way. Howell was good, but Fleet only had to get lucky once to blow his entire force out of space, so Fleet couldn't be allowed to get lucky.

If Lord Jurawski and Countess Miller hadn't insisted on sending Rosario Gomez out here, Brinkman could have made certain no luck came Fleet's way, but they didn't call Gomez "the Iron Maiden" for nothing. The nickname was, he admitted with a smile, a base libel on her sex life, but she'd earned it when she was much younger, and nothing about her style had changed since. They'd known Lady Rosario would be a problem when her assignment was announced, yet there'd been nothing they could do. They'd already taken out Admiral Whitworth to clear the second in command's slot for Brinkman; two flag officers' mysterious deaths would have been too much to risk, so they'd had to accept Gomez and concentrate on hamstringing her efforts from within.

Unfortunately, she'd assembled a staff whose tenacity mirrored her own—and one that was damnably close-knit and loyal to her. Brinkman more than suspected that she and McIlhenny had begun compartmentalizing more tightly than they were telling, and that was bad.

He rocked his chair slowly, nursing his cigar. McIlhenny had already clamped down on normal information distribution, which produced a dangerous decrease in possible suspects. The more restricted data became, the fewer people could possibly be passing it on to the "pirates," and that was bad enough. But if the two of them were beginning to restrict critical data to an inner clique only they trusted, his people might miss some critical bit of information Howell and Alexsov *had* to have.

At least that Justice pest had worn out his enthusiasm and decamped, and Keita would be gone within days. Both of those were major pluses, but it didn't help much with the McIlhenny problem. The ideal solution would be to remove him, but he was a cautious and a dangerous man. He could be gotten to, yet setting up an overt assassination that didn't prove how massively security had been breached would be time consuming and difficult. Worse, it would suggest there'd been a *reason* to kill him, and anyone with whom he'd shared his suspicions—whatever they were—would have to wonder if the reason wasn't that he'd been on the right track and getting too close to an answer.

At the very least Gomez would be out for blood, and assassinating *her* would be even harder. She practically never left her battle-cruiser flagship these days, and about the only way to get to her would be to sabotage *Antietam*'s Fasset drive or fusion plants and take out the entire ship. That might not be impossible, but it would certainly be difficult. Worst of all, killing her would be the Whitworth situation all over again and worse. It would put *him* in her command, and stepping into her shoes under the present circumstances might raise the wrong eyebrows. What if someone who shared McIlhenny's suspicions wondered why someone else might want to see Sir Amos Brinkman in her place?

He let his chair swing back upright and shook his head with a sigh. No, precipitous action against Gomez was out of the question. Pressure was building in the Senate and the Ministry as the "pirates" danced around her and laughed at her attempts to deal with them. It could only be a matter of time before she was relieved for her failures. Brinkman would be properly distressed at relieving so old and dear a friend under such circumstances—and send McIlhenny packing as part of his "new broom" housekeeping. That had been the plan for getting rid of Gomez from the beginning; it was only McIlhenny's stubborn probing that had him thinking about other approaches.

Still, the time might come when McIlhenny got too close and they had to take him out, suspicious or no. It wouldn't be a best-case scenario, but if it was a choice between that and having him figure out what was really going on, the decision would make itself. And his death would produce at least short-term confusion, especially if it wasn't an obvious assassination. If they were lucky, the confusion might even last long enough to carry clear through Gomez's relief.

Brinkman nodded to himself and stubbed out his cigar. Yes, it might become necessary, in which case it would be a good idea to put the assets in place now, and the admiral thought he might just know the way to go about it. McIlhenny had started out as a shuttle pilot, after all. That was where he'd won his spurs and first made his name, and he still had a weakness for hot shuttles and hotter skimmers. Better yet, he insisted on piloting himself whenever possible. Under normal circumstances, no one would be too surprised if he finally lost it in a midair one day, and a little help in the maintenance shop could . . . assist the good colonel right out of the sky.

He smiled a slow, thoughtful smile and tried to remember the name of that "skimmer tech" Rachel Shu had used to eliminate Admiral Whitworth. It was time for a little judicious personnel reassignment.

CHAPTER FIFTY

"Good evening, Captain Mainwaring. My name is Yerensky. I understand you're seeking a cargo for your vessel?"

Alicia looked up from her wineglass and saw a tall, cadaverous man. He was well-dressed, despite his half-starved appearance, and his polished tones were well-suited to the background hum of the expensive restaurant. She eyed him for a moment, then sat back slightly and made a tiny gesture at the empty chair across from her. Yerensky slid into it, smiling politely. A waiter materialized at his elbow, and Alicia sipped her own wine, using the brief, low-voiced exchange between waiter and patron to evaluate her visitor.

<*Smooth as pond scum, isn't he?*> she commented, and felt Tisiphone's silent agreement. Not that they were surprised. They'd learned a great deal about Yerensky during the two weeks they'd spent angling for this meeting.

It had been far harder than Alicia had expected to find the precise shipper she sought. Not because there hadn't been offers in plenty, but because, to her intense chagrin, virtually all of them had been legitimate. She'd underestimated the pirates' effect on insurance rates, and under the circumstances, *Star Runner*'s high speed more than outweighed her limited cargo capacity. If she'd been a real free trader, Alicia could have increased her transport fees by a quarter of the amount by which her ship's speed lowered the insurance premiums and still tripled her normal profit margin.

Unfortunately, she wasn't looking for an honest cargo, and she'd been forced to concoct an extraordinary range of excuses to avoid accepting one. More than once, she'd been reduced to letting the Fury enter a legitimate shipper's mind and get *him* to suggest a reason to decline his offer.

It had been maddening, especially after one of Megaira's and Tisiphone's forays through MaGuire's classified data base revealed that the Empire had provided the Jung Association with Alicia's retinal and genetic prints. They hadn't anticipated that when they concocted Captain Mainwaring, so they'd used her real patterns, and she'd almost fainted when she found out the authorities had both sets. If they happened to run a check against all new arrivals . . .

That threat, at least, had been alleviated, if not nullified, by the simple expedient of sending Tisiphone back into the net to alter the prints for *Star Runner*'s skipper. It wasn't a perfect solution, since any document—like a freight contract—Alicia signed as Captain Mainwaring would include her real retinal prints, which no longer matched the ones on file, yet it was the best they could do. Tisiphone had suggested doctoring the Fleet download instead of Mainwaring's, but Alicia and Megaira had vetoed that idea, since they couldn't touch the files on Soissons. It was tempting to "legitimize" Mainwaring's prints, but it was unlikely anyone would check the prints on a document when he *knew* they were the right person's. At least Alicia hoped they wouldn't, and that possibility worried her less than what might happen if ONI should check back and notice that Alicia DeVries' records on MaGuire no longer matched those on Soissons. At the very least, it would be proof she'd been to MaGuire, since no one but she would have any reason to change them. Worse, a simple cross-check would soon reveal that "Captain Mainwaring's" prints *did* match.

None of that had been calculated to soothe her nerves, but at least it looked as if they'd be able to clear out shortly. The Fury's careful mental probes had, at last, plucked one Anton Yerensky's name and face from the thoughts of a more honest merchant, and Mister Yerensky, it seemed, needed a cargo delivered to Ching-Hai in the Thierdahl System. Barely civilized and sparsely settled, Ching-Hai had very little to recommend it . . . except that it was only ten light-years from Dewent, and Dewent was barely six light-years from Wyvern. Better yet, what passed for the planetary authorities on Ching-Hai had a very cozy relationship with both Dewent and Wyvern.

Once Yerensky had been identified, it hadn't been hard to arrange casual contacts with two or three of his associates. With Tisiphone to plant a favorable impression of Captain Mainwaring in their minds, one of them was bound to mention her to him eventually, and for the first time, the skewed shipping conditions had worked in their favor. With so many fast ships being snapped up for legitimate cargoes, the supply of smugglers was running thin.

"You seem to be well-informed, Mister Yerensky," she said as the waiter departed with his order. "I am looking for a cargo—a small one, I'm afraid, but I assume you've already checked my capacity with the port master."

"Your vessel's capacity would suit me quite well, Captain, assuming we can come to terms."

"I see." Alicia refilled her wineglass and held it up to the light. "Exactly what sort of cubage are we talking about here, Mister Yerensky?"

"Oh, no more than two hundred cubic meters. A bit less, actually."

"I see," Alicia repeated. That really was a small shipment, less than half the available volume in *Megaira*'s hold, which was already well-stocked with spares and replacement parts. "And where would you like it delivered?"

"Ah, that's a bit delicate, Captain," Yerensky said slowly, watching her from under lowered lids. "You see, I need it delivered to Ching-Hai." He paused for a moment, as if to let that sink in, before continuing. "I understand you have a Fleet-type cargo shuttle with rough field capability?"

Alicia lowered her wine and let her lips curl in a tiny smile.

"I do, indeed. May I assume your receiver will be . . . unable to collect his cargo at the regular port?"

"Precisely," Yerensky said politely, and his smile was just as small. "I see you have a fine appreciation for these matters, Captain."

"One tries, Mister Yerensky."

Alicia sipped more wine as the waiter returned with Yerensky's order and began sliding plates onto the table. There were a lot of them, and she wondered what sort of metabolism could handle that kind of intake and still look starved.

The waiter scurried off again, and Yerensky unfolded a snow-white napkin in his lap and reached for a fork.

"Given your appreciation, Captain, I must assume you realize you and your crew are—well, let us say, a rather unknown quantity."

"If you checked my port download, I'm sure you discovered that we're bonded with the Melville Sector governor," Alicia said, forbearing to mention just how surprised the Melville Sector governor would be to learn that.

"Well, yes, Captain, but MaGuire is scarcely an imperial planet, now is it? And there might be circumstances under which it would be inconvenient for a shipper to attempt to recover against your bond if something went awry."

<In other words,> Alicia observed silently to Tisiphone, *<a crook can't exactly report you to the cops for stealing his illegal cargo.>*

<It is reassuring to find some things unchanged,> the Fury returned, and Alicia nodded at Yerensky.

"I can understand that. Still, I assume you wouldn't have come to see me unless you felt these little problems could be resolved."

"A woman after my own heart, Captain," he said as he spread his salad dressing more evenly. "I'd thought in terms of a mutual expression of trust."

"Such as?"

"I think, perhaps, a front payment of twenty-five percent of the total shipping charges with the remainder placed in escrow here on MaGuire to be released when the cargo is delivered to my agent on Ching-Hai."

Alicia nodded thoughtfully, but her mind raced. That was a terrible idea. It would require reams of legal documents, and that meant retinal prints galore. But she couldn't exactly object on those grounds . . .

"An interesting suggestion, but not the way I normally do business, Mister Yerensky. I can conceive of certain circumstances under which—purely without your knowledge, of course—an unscrupulous receiver might deny he'd ever received the goods, which could tie up the escrow account or even require litigation. Then, too, limited facility fields, you know, are often under-equipped. A completely honest difference of opinion might arise, and without proper instrumentation to examine the cargo, well—"

She shrugged with a helpless little smile, and a gleam of appreciation lit Yerensky's eyes.

"I see. May I assume you have a counteroffer, Captain?"

"Indeed. I would suggest that you pay me half the freight charges up front, and that your receiver pay the other half immediately upon receipt and examination of his cargo. I sacrifice the security of the escrow account; you run a slightly greater risk with your front payment. That seems fair."

Yerensky munched thoughtfully on his salad for a few moments, then nodded. "I believe I could accept that arrangement, assuming we can settle the remainder of the terms to our mutual satisfaction."

"Oh, I'm certain we can, Mister Yerensky." Alicia smiled even more sweetly. "I'm a great believer in mutual satisfaction."

Alicia reclined in her command chair and chewed on a grape. She savored the sweet juice and pulp with sensual delight, and the back of her brain hummed with an odd duality as Megaira and Tisiphone shared her pleasure.

<*That's nice,*> the AI observed. <*Much sharper than your memories. Almost makes me wish I were a flesh-and-blood.*>

<*Not I,*> Tisiphone disagreed. <*Such moments are pleasant, yet what need have we for flesh and blood when we may share them with Alicia? And unlike her, we are not subject to the* unpleasant *aspects of such existence.*>

<*Voyeurs.*> Alicia swallowed and examined the bunch in her lap to select a fresh grape. "You ought to experience some of the downside—maybe a nice head cold, for instance—so you could appreciate the pleasures properly."

<*I have yet to observe that suffering truly makes pleasure sweeter, Little One. Bliss is not the mere absence of pain.*>

"Maybe." She popped the chosen grape into her mouth and turned her attention back to Megaira's sensors.

They'd left the dreary featurelessness of wormhole space an hour ago, decelerating steadily towards the heart of the Thierdahl System, and the glory of the stars was even sweeter than the grapes. She drank it in, reveling in the reach and power of

Megaira's senses, as Thierdahl's distant spark grew brighter. They were fifteen days—just over eleven days by their own clocks—out of MaGuire with their cargo of bootleg medical supplies, and she wondered again what they would discover when they reached their destination. So far, things had gone more smoothly than she had hoped.

<Of course they have, Little One. What, after all, could go wrong in wormhole space?>

"Nothing, but it's the nature of the human beast to worry. At least I don't have to feel guilty about what we're carrying."

<Do not be foolish. There is neither cause nor room for "guilt" in whatever we may do in pursuit of your vengeance.>

Alicia winced at Tisiphone's absolute assurance. She could forget just how alien the Fury was for days at a stretch, but then Tisiphone came out with something like that. It wasn't posturing. It was simply the literal truth as she saw it.

"I'm afraid I can't agree with you on that one. I want justice, not blind vengeance, and I'd rather not hurt anyone I don't have to."

<Justice is a delusion, Little One.> The Fury's mental voice dripped scorn. *<Your people have learned much, but you have forgotten much, as well.>*

"You might profit by a little forgetting—or learning—of your own."

<Such as?>

"Such as the fact that simple vengeance is a self-sustaining reaction. When you 'avenge' yourself on someone, you usually give someone else an excuse to seek vengeance on you."

<And you think your precious justice does not? You are wiser than that, Alicia DeVries—or would be, if you but let yourself!>

"You're missing the point. If a society settles for naked vengeance, it all comes down to who has the bigger club. Justice provides the rules that make it possible for people to live together with some semblance of decency."

<Bah! "Justice" is no more than vengeance dressed up in fine clothes! There can be no justice without punishment—or would you say that Colonel Watts was treated "justly" for the wrong he did your company?>

Alicia's lip curled in an involuntary snarl, but she closed her eyes and fought it back as she felt the Fury's amusement.

"No, I wouldn't call that justice, or disagree that punishment is a part of justice. I won't even pretend vengeance isn't exactly what I wanted from that son of a bitch. But there has to be guilt—and he was guilty as sin—before punishment. A society can't just go around smashing people without determining that the one punished is actually the guilty party. That's the worst kind of capriciousness—and a damned good recipe for anarchy."

<*What care I for anarchy?*> Tisiphone demanded. <*Nor am I "society." Nor, for that matter, are* you. *You are an individual, seeking redress for yourself and for others who cannot. Is that wrong?*>

"I didn't say it was. I only said I don't want to hurt innocent bystanders. But whether you like it or not, justice—the rule of law, not men, if you will—is the glue that sticks human societies together. It lets human beings live together with some sense of security, and it establishes precedents. When a criminal is proven guilty and punished, it sets the parameters. It tells people what's acceptable and what isn't, and whenever we inch a few centimeters forward, justice is what keeps us from slipping back."

<*So you say, Little One, but you delude yourself. It is compassion, not reason, which truly shapes your thought—misplaced compassion for those who deserve none.* This *is the truth of what you feel.*>

Alicia's face twisted as the Fury relaxed inner barriers—barriers Alicia had almost forgotten existed—and a red haze of rage boiled in the back of her brain. Her fists clenched, and she locked her teeth together, fighting the sudden need to smash something—anything—in the pure, wanton destruction her emotions craved. She felt Megaira's distress, felt the AI beating at Tisiphone in a futile effort to free Alicia from her own hate, but even that was small and faint and far, far away . . .

The barriers snapped back, and she slumped in her chair, gasping and beaded with sweat.

<*You* bitch!> Megaira snarled. <*If you* ever *try that again, I'll—!*>

<*Peace, Megaira,*> the Fury interrupted almost gently. <*I will not harm her. But she must know herself if we are to succeed. There is no room for confusion or self-blindness in what we do.*>

Alicia trembled in the couch, nerve ends shuddering, and closed her thoughts off from the others. She needed the silence, needed a moment to breathe and recover from the side of herself she'd just seen. She believed what she'd told Tisiphone—more than believed, *knew* it was true—and yet . . .

She opened her eyes and looked down at her hands. They were slick and wet, coated in dripping grape pulp, and she shuddered.

CHAPTER FIFTY-ONE

Commodore Howell sat on the freighter's bridge and told himself—again—that the ship was perfectly adequate for her mission. Compared to a warship, her command facilities were primitive, her defenses minimal, and her offensive weapons nonexistent, but if everything went right, that wouldn't matter, and so far the mission profile had been perfect. And much as he would have preferred being somewhere else, he *had* to be here for this one. They needed a success to blunt the sting of Elysium, and his people's morale required that he be here in person.

He watched the display, face expressionless, as the freighter and her two sister ships settled into parking orbit around Ringbolt. Control's information on the El Grecan fleet maneuvers had been right on the money, and the only ground defenses were purely antiair weapons sited to cover Adcock Field, the main spaceport outside the city of Raphael. They had the reach to cover the city's airspace, but they wouldn't have the chance.

Howell's eyes swivelled to the reason they wouldn't. The freighters' transponders identified them as Fleet transports—courtesy of the ID codes Control had provided—escorted by a heavy cruiser. Now all four ships were in position, riding geosynchronous orbit directly above Raphael, and a signal in the commodore's synth-link told him HMS *Intolerant*'s weapons were locked in.

Captain Arlen Monkoto of the Monkoto Free Mercenaries, known less formally as "Monkoto's Maniacs," stepped out onto the hotel balcony and sucked in crisp, cool air. Ringbolt was a *much* nicer planet than El Greco, he mused, and wondered if he could convince Simon to relocate their home port here.

He looked back over his shoulder. Lieutenant Commander Hugin was on the suite com, conferring with Chief Pilaskov. The recruiting mission had gone well, and Monkoto expected Simon to be pleased when he arrived. Over a hundred experienced personnel, including twelve officers, could certainly be put to excellent use.

He started to open the balcony's French windows to join Hugin, and something flashed behind him. Eye-tearing light bounced back off the window glass, and his shadow was suddenly etched stark and black against the wall.

He whirled in disbelief, trained reflexes already throwing him facedown, as a huge, white fireball devoured Adcock Field.

"Launch shuttles!" Howell barked as *Intolerant*'s HVW obliterated the port. Each of the big transports normally mothered eight heavy-lift cargo shuttles; for this operation, they'd been replaced with twelve *Bengal*-class assault boats each, and thirty-six deadly attack craft shrieked downward. Thirteen hundred grim-faced raiders rode them. For many this was their first mission, and they were determined to get it right. Others were the survivors of Elysium . . . and they were even more determined to avoid another disaster.

Arlen Monkoto staggered erect like a punch-drunk fighter. His nerve ends jittered with echoes of heat and blast, but it must have been an HVW. If it had been a nuke or antimatter, he'd be dead, and he was only singed a bit. Fires roared and fumed along the city's eastern edge, and he doubted there was an intact window in Raphael, but otherwise the damage hadn't been severe.

He wheeled back to the French windows and froze. He'd been wrong about the severity of the damage, an icy voice told him. The windows had been blown across the hotel suite like glittering daggers, and bloody bits of Lieutenant Commander Hugin's mutilated body were sprayed across the far wall.

Monkoto made himself pick his way into the wreckage, and his hands were a stranger's as they moved what remained of Hugin gently aside. His exec's body had protected the com unit, and Chief Pilaskov was still on it. The burly NCO was half shouting, though Monkoto's stunned ears could hardly hear him, and his brown eyes widened in relief as he saw his CO.

Fresh explosions thundered behind the captain, and his mouth tightened as he looked over his shoulder and saw the contrails slashing down the sky.

"Can't hear you, Chief." He tapped an ear, and Pilaskov's mouth snapped shut. "It doesn't matter. Break into the ordnance order and get our people moving. The primary LZ looks like Toledo U. I'll meet you there."

Surprise was total.

Adcock Field had known the freighters and their escort were friendly. No one at the port lived long enough to realize he was wrong, and sheer shock—not disbelief so much as a desperate need to be wrong—stunned Raphael motionless until the shuttle contrails were sighted.

By then it was far, far too late, and Howell's raiders carried through with merciless precision. Individual shuttles peeled off and streaked in to lay smaller HVW and guided bombs on every police station and substation in the city. Entire blocks went up with them, and other shuttles swept a circle about the raider's target with rocket clusters and incendiaries. A curtain of flame sealed their objective off from relief while two more shuttles took out the militia armory, and twenty *Bengals* grounded on the university campus, disgorging seven hundred heavily armed raiders who charged straight for their objectives and killed anyone in their path.

Stunned university security forces tried to stop them, but they had only side arms and Howell's raiders were in battle armor with heavy weapons. The university's director of research raced for the computer center to purge her data, but a squad of invaders burst through the doors and cut her down before she reached her console. Teams of technicians followed the assault wave, setting up their portable terminals and transmission dishes while the thunder of weapons and screams of the dying shook the building about them. More raiders broke into the labs themselves and massacred the researchers, and a fresh flood of technicians poured in in their wake, heaving specimen cases, hard-copy records, and lab animals onto countergravity pallets while their boots slipped in their victims' blood.

Monkoto found Chief Pilaskov more by luck than any other way. The petty officer had his recruits mustered near the roaring wall of flames sealing the university off from the rest of the city, their uniforms a black-and-gray knot of order in a sea of chaos.

They were more heavily armed than Monkoto had hoped. They'd been quartered in the warehouse district to keep an eye on the Maniacs' ordnance order, but it was obvious Pilaskov had helped himself generously from the arms merchant's other wares. Half the recruits wore light armor, and Monkoto saw squad heavy weapons as well as personal arms. Best of all, Pilaskov had snagged a half-dozen Stiletto units. By the time Monkoto arrived, the chief had the remote launchers deployed well away from the fire control units.

"Glad to see you, Sir," he said as Monkoto panted up to him. "Where's Commander Hugin?"

"Dead." Monkoto sucked in air, feeling the fire's heat in his lungs, and tried to think. A *Bengal* passed overhead, and he straightened quickly as one of the Stiletto crews began to track.

"Hold your fire!" he snapped, and the crew chief jerked in surprise. "We don't want the flankers," he continued when he was certain the other man was listening. "We want the main body. Wait till they lift out."

The crew chief nodded, face tightening in understanding, and Monkoto turned back to Pilaskov. He jabbed a thumb at the roaring flames.

"HE or straight incendiaries?" he demanded.

"Mainly incendiaries and just enough HE to bust things open, I think."

"We have a com on the secure police frequency?"

"Yes, Sir. Not much traffic—only whoever was on the street when they hit."

"It'll have to do." Monkoto held out one hand and gestured at the rubble-strewn sidewalks with the other. "Find me a manhole, Chief."

"Aye, Sir!" Pilaskov's face lit with understanding, and he started shouting orders as Monkoto raised the com to his mouth.

"This is Captain Arlen Monkoto, Monkoto's Mercenaries," he said crisply. "I am at the corner of Hadrian and Stimson. My people are going in in five minutes. Anyone who can reach us in time, get your ass over here now!"

The raiders crushed the last resistance, and small parties broke off to loot secondary objectives in Admin and the library building. The computer techs hovered over their equipment, draining the R&D data base and beaming it up to the freighters, and fire teams set up along the campus approaches in case anyone found a way through the fire wall. There was little wasted motion, and the situation was a far cry from the chaos of Elysium. Another forty minutes and they could lift the hell out of here again.

A manhole cover grated quietly well behind their outer perimeter. A cautious head poked up out of it, and two hundred men and women—mercenaries, police, and civilian volunteers inextricably mixed—flowed upward from the sewers and service tunnels buried meters beneath the interceding inferno.

Howell's ground commander was reporting to the flagship when bedlam exploded behind him. He wheeled in shock, gaping at the wave of El Grecans coming at him, then hit his jump gear to put a solid wall between him and them as grenades ripped into his temporary CP.

Where had they all *come* from? Damn it, they *couldn't* be here! But they were, and panicky reports flooded in. The bastards were hitting him everywhere at once, and memories of Elysium echoed through his raiders.

But this *wasn't* Elysium, goddamn it! These were a hastily assembled and lightly armed scratch group, not Imperial Marines in battle armor, and the CO screamed and cursed his people into coherent response.

Commodore Howell slammed a fist into the arm of his command chair as he, too, remembered Elysium. He didn't have the instrumentation for a solid read on what was happening, but the sudden confusion of combat chatter—and the screams of wounded and dying raiders—told him it wasn't good.

The perimeter teams turned and charged back towards the heart of the campus. Some blundered into hastily set ambushes and died still wondering what was happening, but most got through, for their armor and heavier weapons gave them a tremendous advantage. Yet this time the fighting was different. This time the locals knew what was going on, and they'd had time to collect more than handguns and stunners. Many of them knew the terrain better than even the most carefully briefed raider, and they used their knowledge well.

Combat raged across the once-beautiful campus—ugly, swirling knots of blood and fire and hate amid smoldering wreckage and the litter of bodies. A small team of Maniacs got in among the grounded shuttles and destroyed five before they could be killed. A police SWAT commander's jury-rigged team of civilians and a handful of police fought its way into the admin/library complex, and Arlen Monkoto led a personal assault on the bioresearch center.

The raiders' casualties mounted, but they still had the edge in numbers. They fought off the shock of surprise and went back onto the offensive, and Commodore Howell relaxed as his people began to regain the ground they'd lost while the data continued to pour upward.

Arlen Monkoto poked his head cautiously around a corner, trying not to cough as acrid smoke assaulted his lungs. He'd fought his way to within two corridors of the computer center, but he'd lost Chief Pilaskov on the way in, and he was down to five men and three women, only two of them Maniacs.

The way ahead was clear, and he moved down the hall in the quietest run he could manage. "His" people followed him, and his mind raced. If they got into the computer center, took out the techs he knew were pillaging it—

An armored raider appeared before him, and thirty-millimeter rifle fire tore Captain Arlen Monkoto apart.

* * *

"Download complete!" someone called, and someone else was screaming to "Move it back to the shuttles *now!*" over the tactical net.

Raiders began to disengage, leapfrogging back towards the shuttle perimeter. Too few defenders remained to stop them, but the twenty shuttle loads who'd landed needed only twelve shuttles to lift them out again.

"Shuttles preparing to lift, Sir."

Howell grunted approval at the report, but inside he winced. Twenty percent casualties were too damned many so soon after Elysium, even if they had secured every one of their objectives this time. He didn't care what Control said, he *wasn't* sending teams in against targets this hard again.

"Sir, sensors report a Fasset drive coming in from the direction of El Greco," an officer said suddenly, and Howell's head snapped around.

"What is it?" he demanded.

"Can't tell at this range, Sir, but it's not a Fleet drive. Looks like an El Grecan—probably a destroyer."

The commodore relaxed. A destroyer had the speed to overhaul them, but not the firepower to fight them, and this time she was welcome to any sensor data she could get. Aside from the freighter's transponder codes, nothing he'd done here had required the use of classified security data, and ex-Fleet heavy cruisers weren't all that hard to come by.

He looked back into the display as the shuttles began to lift, and his mouth curled in an ugly smile. The fact that the "pirates" had one of Fleet's cast-off CAs would spill no beans, but *Intolerant*'s weapons would more than suffice to destroy the El Grecan ship if she got close enough to be a problem. Besides, she'd be . . . distracted after *Intolerant* nuked Raphael, and—

"Sir! The shuttles!" someone shouted, and Howell's face went white as the Stiletto teams opened fire.

Nine of his thirty-one surviving shuttles became falling fireballs as he stared at the display.

Admiral Simon Monkoto stood on the bridge of the destroyer *Ardent*, staring at the view screen, and his carved-marble face was white as the silver at his temples. There had been no way for *Ardent* to know what was happening on Ringbolt until she dropped sublight, but the radiation counters were going mad. Whoever had nuked Raphael had used the dirtiest warhead Admiral Monkoto had ever seen on the city . . . and on Arlen.

Dark eyes, hot and hating in his frozen face, moved from the view screen to the gravitic plot. He could have overhauled the raiders. It would have been close, even with their freighters to slow them, for his destroyer had been on the wrong approach vector, but he could have caught them.

And it would have done no good at all against a heavy cruiser.

He'd almost done it anyway, but he hadn't. He couldn't throw away his crew's lives—or his own. Even more than he wanted those ships, he wanted the people who'd sent them, and he couldn't have them if he died.

His jaw clenched, and he turned away. *Ardent*'s last shuttle was waiting for him, waiting to take him down to the planet where his brother had died to do what he could. But he'd be back, and not with a single destroyer.

He promised himself that—promised Arlen—and his expression was as hellish as his heart.

CHAPTER FIFTY-TWO

Ching-Hai lay barely 14.8 light-minutes from the F5 star Thierdahl, with an axial tilt of forty-one degrees. It was also dry—*very* dry—with an atmospheric pressure only three-quarters that of Old Earth, all of which conspired to produce something only the charitable could call a climate. Alicia couldn't conceive of any rational reason to choose to live here, and not even Imperial Galactography knew why anyone had. The handbook's best theory was that the original settlers were League War or HRW-I refugees who'd found in Ching-Hai a world so inhospitable neither the Empire nor the Sphere would want it. As guesses went, that one was as good as any; certainly their descendants had no better one four hundred years later.

Which probably explained their attitude towards other people's laws. They had to make a living somehow, and their planet wasn't much help, she thought, crossing to the coffeemaker and watching with a corner of her brain while Megaira slipped them into orbit. They were a few hours early, and Alicia was just as glad. She'd recovered—mostly—from the experience Tisiphone had unleashed upon her, but she welcomed a little more time to settle down before she had to meet Yerensky's local contact.

She carried her cup back to the view port. Ochre and yellow land masses moved far below her, splashed with an occasional large lake or small sea. It all looked depressingly flat, and there were very few visible light blurs on the nightside. The one official spaceport was well into the dayside at the moment, but whoever was in charge hadn't even bothered to assign her a parking orbit, much less mounted any sort of customs inspection.

<*You didn't really expect one, did you?*> Megaira asked.

"No, but this is so . . . so—"

<*Half-assed?*> the AI suggested helpfully, and Alicia chuckled.

"Something like that. Not that I'm complaining. I don't know how Yerensky got those medical supplies out of the Empire and onto MaGuire without any customs stamps, but I'd hate to try explaining it to someone else."

<*There would be no need.*> Alicia and Megaira both bristled, but the Fury sounded totally unaware of any resentment they might harbor. <*Their inspectors would see precisely what we wished them to, no more and no less.*>

Alicia didn't reply. She suspected herself of sulking, and she didn't really care. The reminder of all the unresolved hate and violence still locked away within her had frightened her. Not that she hadn't known it was there, but knowing and feeling were two different things, and—

<*Whups! Heads up, Alley—I've got our landing beacon.*>

"So soon?" Alicia's eyebrows rose.

<*Well, it's in the right general spot.*> A mental grid superimposed itself over Alicia's view of the planet, and a green dot winked on the nightside. <*There—about midnight, local time. And it's the right beacon code.*>

"I don't like it. Yerensky didn't say anything about night landings."

<*But neither did he say it would be a* daylight *landing,*> Tisiphone pointed out, and this time Alicia and Megaira were too intent on their problem to bristle. <*Indeed, there was no thought in his mind either way, so I would judge he trusts the discretion of his local agent. In that case, might there not be some valid reason for choosing to unload under cover of night?*>

"On *this* planet?" Alicia frowned. "I wouldn't've thought there was any reason to hide medical supplies. They're valuable, sure, especially on some of the lower-tech Rogue Worlds, but I can't see needing to *hide* them."

She hesitated a moment longer, then shrugged.

"Put on your Ruth face and ask for the countersign, Megaira."

<*On it,*> the AI replied. A few moments passed, then, <*They came back with the right response, Alley. Far as I can tell, this is them.*>

"Damn. Well, I guess we don't have much choice." Alicia sighed. "Load up the shuttle with the first pallets."

<*Yes,*> Tisiphone agreed, <*but I trust your instincts, Little One. May I suggest that this is a time for Top Cover?*>

"You may indeed," Alicia murmured, and felt Megaira's total agreement.

The cargo shuttle slid downward through the hot Ching-Hai night, cargo bay packed with counter-grav pallets, and Alicia lifted the combat rifle into her lap and slipped in a magazine.

Megaira and Tisiphone had both wanted her in battle armor, if for slightly different reasons. The AI worried about her safety, but the Fury wanted to see the armor in action, for its destructive capabilities fascinated her. Of the two, Alicia had found Megaira's argument more telling, yet she'd decided against it. No free trader could have gotten her hands on Cadre armor—Cadre Intelligence would have chased her to the ends of the galaxy to get it back if she'd tried—and someone might conceivably recognize it.

Besides, if some ill-intentioned soul *was* waiting for her, he faced certain practical constraints. His only objective could be her cargo, which meant he couldn't use anything big and nasty enough to take out the shuttle. She, on the other hand, had no compunctions about what she might do to him.

<*That sounds strangely little like "justice,"*> Tisipohone jibed gently.

"On the contrary." Alicia jacked a discarding sabot round into the M-97's chamber and settled her left hand briefly on the forestock to activate its computer systems. "I won't do a thing to them unless they intend to do something to me."

<*Indeed?*>

"Indeed. But if they do have something planned, *I* intend to do unto them first."

<*So there are times you see things my way after all.*>

"Never said there weren't." Alicia shifted to her contact with Megaira. <*How's it look from your side?*>

<*Everything's green, but I've got two aircraft to the south.*>

Data flowed into Alicia's brain, and her lip curled, for one of those aircraft had "military" written all over it. It might be an escort against whatever local menace had provoked this night landing. Then again, it might not.

<Keep an eye on 'em,> she thought back. *<I'm getting vehicle sources around the landing beacon, too. Air lorries, it looks like.>*

<I see them, too. Want me to take a closer look?>

<No. Wouldn't do to spook them, now would it?>

<You're the boss. Just watch yourself.>

Alicia turned back to the shuttle controls, wiggling to settle her unpowered body armor. It, too, was Cadre-issue, better than anything on the open market but not visibly different enough to call attention to itself. They were less than two minutes out now, and she let the first trickle of tick seep into her bloodstream and smiled wolfishly as the universe slowed.

The ground party watched the shuttle slide down the last few meters of sky and deploy its landing legs. Flat pads reached for the ground, dust devils danced in the turbine wash, and one of the air lorries moved away from the dust in a curve that just happened to point the rear of its cargo bed at the shuttle. The tarp which closed it flapped in the jetwash, and something long and ominous was briefly visible behind the canvas.

"They're down," a man muttered into his helmet com. "Ready?"

"Light on the pads," a voice replied in his earphones.

"Good. I hope we won't need you, but stay loose."

"Yo," his phones said laconically, and he turned his full attention back to the shuttle. He'd expected a standard shuttle, and avarice flickered as he realized this one was almost twice that size. It must contain an even bigger chunk of Yerensky's cargo than he'd anticipated.

The shuttle's after hatch whined open and extruded a ramp, and he changed com channels, murmuring to his lorry pilot. The lorry's powerful lamps came on, bathing the shuttle in light, and he walked forward into the glare with a bright smile and a welcoming wave.

"Try and take the pilot alive," he reminded his gunners. He'd settle for one shuttle load—especially one this size—but if he could get his hands on the pilot and "convince" him to take his own boys back upstairs . . .

His nerves crackled as subsiding dust billowed around the ramp. Any minute, he thought, still grinning and waving while he braced for the gunfire.

But the dust settled, and no one emerged. His waving hand slowed, his grin faded, and he suddenly felt exposed and stupid in the light.

Alicia killed the flight deck lights, popped an emergency hatch, and dropped to the ground on the far side from the illuminating lorry. That had been outstandingly stupid, she thought as she floated to earth on the wings of the tick. Anyone looking into that light would be blind as a bat, not to mention all the nice shadows it made on this side.

She melted into the darker shadow of a landing leg and juggled her sensory boosters. Without a combat helmet's built in sensor systems, she had to rely upon her own augmented vision, but she'd had lots of practice at that. She had to wind the boosters way down when she looked into the light, then pump them high when her gaze tracked across the dark, but that was a problem she was used to, and she grunted with satisfaction as she completed her count.

Eighteen, nine of them bunched up around the air lorry with the calliope and not a one of them in even light armor. Well, at least it proved their mastermind was no military type. Unless his name was Custer.

<*Megaira?*>

<*I see them,*> the AI replied, watching through Alicia's eyes as easily as Alicia might scan space through her sensors. Tisiphone was silent in the back of her brain, wise enough not to distract her at a time like this.

<*Somehow they don't look like the welcome wagon to me.*>

<*You watch your ass, Alley!*>

<*I will. You just watch those aircraft.*>

<*I'm on 'em.*>

Damn it, something was wrong! His waving hand fell to his side as suspicion became certainty and he realized how exposed *he* was in that vortex of light. He started to turn and order the lamps doused when something sailed past his head to thump and rattle metallically across a lorry freight bed.

The air lorry gunship vanished in superheated fury as the plasma grenade exploded, but Alicia wasn't watching. She'd turned like a cat while the grenade hung dreamily in midair, and the combat rifle was an extension of her brain and body. She didn't even see the sight picture, not consciously. She simply looked at her target, and the gunman's chest exploded.

The glare of the lorry couldn't quite hide her muzzle-flash, but she'd already found the two men who could see it. One of them died before he realized he had; the second while he was still raising his weapon.

The gun crew inside the lorry never knew they were dead, but screams of agony and terror rose from the men clustered about it. A human torch shrieked its way into the darkness as if the night could somehow quench its flames, and two more rolled on the ground, fighting to extinguish themselves. Three unwounded hijackers ran for their lives from the inferno, and the leader threw himself under his own vehicle and switched channels frantically.

"*Get over here!*" he screamed, and two heavily armed aircraft leapt into the night in reply.

Alicia slid easily through the gap she'd blown in the ring around the shuttle. Three of the six on this side of the ambush remained, but they didn't realize they were alone. They'd made the mistake of staring into the flames, stunned by the carnage, and Alicia looked at their backs in disgust. Idiots. Did they think simply carrying a gun made someone dangerous?

It really wasn't fair. These people were pathetic, so completely out of their class they didn't even know it. But life wasn't fair, and anyone who lent himself to ambush and murder for gain had no kick coming.

She found the position she wanted and fired three more short, neat bursts.

The stutter of automatic fire hammered his ears, and he stared out from under the lorry as a white eye flickered beyond the shuttle. *Beyond* the shuttle! Someone was on the ground out there! It had to be the shuttle pilot, but *how*? And where were the men he'd posted back there?

How became immaterial as a lithe, slender shape slid across the very edge of the light with a cobra's speed and blew another of his men apart. It vanished back into the darkness, graceful as a dream, but another deadly burst and a bubbling shriek told him where his men were. Drive turbines began to whine above him as his lorry pilot prepared to pull out, and panic filled him at the thought of being left exposed and naked. He wanted to run, but his body refused to move, and he pounded the dry earth with his fists and prayed for his sting ships to get here in time.

Two heavily armed aircraft sliced through the sky. One was little more than a transport loaded with weapons, but the leader was military from needle prow to sensor package, and its pilot brought his scanners on line. He saw only confusion and motionless bodies—*lots* of bodies, lit by a glare of flames—and one target source moving with deadly precision. He swore. One of them. Just *one*! But he had the bastard dialed in now. A few more seconds and he'd be able to nail the son of a bitch without killing his own—

A night-black piece of sky swooped upon him from above. He had one stunned moment to register it, to begin to realize what it was, and then the *Bengal*-class assault shuttle tore him into very, very tiny pieces.

His head jerked up in horror, slamming into the bottom of the lorry, as the fireball blossomed. Flaming streamers arced from its heart like some enormous fireworks display, and then there was a second fireball.

He stared at them, watching them fade and fall, then cowered down as a vicious burst of fire lashed the vehicle above him. A chopped-off cry of agony and the sudden stillness of the waking turbines told him his pilot was dead, and he buried his face against the ground and sobbed in terror.

There were no more screams, no more shooting. Only the crackle of flames and the stench of burning bodies, and he whimpered and tried to dig into the baked soil beneath him as feet whispered through short, tough grass.

He raised his head weakly, and saw two polished boots, gleaming in the firelight. His eyes rose higher and froze on the muzzle of a combat rifle eight centimeters from his nose.

"I think you'd better come out of there," a contralto voice, colder than the stars, said softly.

Alicia finished throwing up and wiped her lips. Her mouth tasted as if something had died in it, and her stomach cramped with fresh nausea.

"That's enough of that," she told it sternly, and the cramp eased sullenly. She waited another moment, then sighed and straightened in relief.

<*Are you quite through?*> Tisiphone inquired.

<*Listen, Lady, you don't even have any guts* to *puke up, so don't get snotty with those of us who do, all right?*> The post-tick letdown left her too drained to get much feeling into it, but the Fury subsided.

"God, I *hate* coming down from that stuff," Alicia muttered, lowering herself to sit against a landing leg. "Still, it does have its uses."

<*I wish I had you up here in sickbay,*> Megaira fretted, and Alicia looked up at the hovering assault boat with a grin.

<*Don't sweat it. I've been using Old Speedy for years, and aside from wanting to die when you come down, it doesn't hurt a bit. The Cadre guarantees it.*>

<*Yeah, sure. That and a centicred'll get you a cup of coffee.*>

Alicia chuckled and wiped her mouth again, then turned to glance at the sole survivor of the hijack force. He sat against another landing leg, manacled to the pad gimbal and watching her with frightened eyes.

<*He's waiting for the thumbscrews,*> she thought to Tisiphone. <*Should we tell the poor bastard you already got it all?*>

<*We should bring* out *the thumbscrews.*>

<*Now, now. No need to get nasty.*>

Alicia grinned as Tisiphone muttered something about impertinent mortals. Their prisoner was none other than the partner of Yerensky's Ching-Hai contact, and his plan to hijack his own associates' cargo—and murder anyone in his way to cover his tracks—had touched the Fury's vengefulness on the raw.

<*You should slay him and be done with it,*> she said.

<*I can't do that. It wouldn't be just,*> Alicia replied innocently, squinting into the dawn to watch a streamer of dust approach the shuttle. Another part of her watched it through Megaira's assault boat sensors, and her grin grew as Tisiphone spluttered in her brain.

<*Just?* Just?! *You dare to speak of your foolish, useless justice for scum like this?! I have endured much from you, Little One, but—*>

<*Oh, hush.*> The Fury slithered to an incandescent stop, and Alicia pressed her advantage. <*I told you I believe in justice,*> she said, rising to her feet. The prisoner's head whipped around as he, too, heard the whine of approaching turbines, and his face went white. <*I also told you I believe in punishment. And unless I very much miss my guess, this is the people we were* supposed *to be meeting.*> She felt Tisiphone's sudden understanding, and her smile was cold and thin. <*In this instance, I think justice can best be served by letting him explain himself to his friends, don't you?*>

CHAPTER FIFTY-THREE

The pages of Colonel McIlhenny's latest report lay strewn about the carpet where Governor General Treadwell had flung them. Now the governor, his normally bland face an ugly shade of puce, half stood to lean across the conference table and glare at Rosario Gomez.

"I'm tired of excuses, Admiral," he grated. "If they *are* excuses and not a cover for something else. I find it remarkable that your units are so persistently *elsewhere* when these pirates strike!"

Gomez glared back at him with barely restrained fury, and he sneered.

"At best, your complete ineffectualness cost nine million lives on Elysium, and now *this*." His nostrils quivered as he inhaled harshly. "I suppose we should be grateful that the million-and-a-half people in Raphael weren't imperial subjects. No doubt you and your people are, at any rate. At least it didn't require you to face the enemy in combat!"

Rosario Gomez rose very slowly and put her own hands on the table. She leaned to meet him, her eyes flint, and her voice was very soft.

"Governor, you're a fool, and my people won't be the whipping boys for *your* failures."

"You're out of line, Admiral!" Treadwell snapped.

"I am not." Gomez's words were chipped ice. "Nothing in the Articles of War requires me to listen to insults simply because my *political* superior is under pressure. Your implication that I'm unconcerned by the massacre of civilians—*any* civilians, imperial or El Grecan—is almost as contemptible as your aspersions upon the integrity and courage of my personnel. If you're feeling pressure from Old Earth, then you have no one to blame but yourself, and I will *not* stand by and watch you try to shuffle the onus for your own failure off onto the uniformed people of my command!"

Her eyes were daggers, and the tip of one index finger tapped like a deadly metronome as she counted off points.

"I've stated the force levels I believe the situation requires. You have rejected my requests for them. I've shared with you every scrap of intelligence in our possession. You have failed to produce a single useful additional insight into it. I've stated repeatedly my belief, and that of my staff, that we've been penetrated at a high level, and you have disregarded the notion, despite what happened at Elysium. And although you now apparently feel free to besmirch the honor of people who have been working themselves into a state of exhaustion to find solutions, *you* have failed to suggest a single further avenue we might pursue.

"I believe it must be apparent to any outside judge that you have singularly failed to move one step closer to a solution of this problem, yet you feel free to call *my* people cowards? Oh, no, *Governor* Treadwell. Not on my watch. I will welcome any court of inquiry Fleet or the Ministry of Out-Worlds would care to nominate. In the meantime, *your* statements constitute more than sufficient grounds for a Court of Honor, and you may retract them or face one, Governor, because I will *not* submit to the slanders of a political appointee who has never commanded a fleet in space!"

Treadwell went absolutely white as the last salvo struck, and McIlhenny held his breath. Fury smoked between those two granite profiles, and the colonel knew his admiral well. That last blow had been calculated with icy precision. The Iron Maiden didn't know what retreat was, but she was a just, fair-minded person, acutely sensitive to the total unfairness of such a remark. She knew precisely how wounding it would be, which said a great deal about her own emotional state. Yet it had been born of more than simple fury. It was a warning that there was a point beyond which Lady Rosario Gomez would not be pushed by God or the Devil, far less a mere imperial governor, and McIlhenny prayed Treadwell retained enough control to recognize it.

Apparently he did. His knuckles pressed the tabletop as his hands clenched into fists, but he made himself sink back into his chair. Silence hung taut for a long moment, and then he exhaled a long breath.

"Very well, Lady Rosario." His voice was frozen helium, but the venom was suppressed, and Gomez resumed her own seat, eyes still locked with his. "I . . . regret any aspersions I may have cast upon your honor or that of your personnel. This—this *slaughter* has affected my judgment, but that neither excuses nor justifies my conduct. I apologize."

She nodded curtly, and he went on with that same frozen self-control.

"Nonetheless, and whatever our past force structure differences may have been, we now face a significantly graver position. The Empire hasn't suffered such casualties, military or civilian, since HRW-II, and the El Grecans' losses are proportionally far worse. You will, I trust, agree that it is no longer sufficient merely to deter or stop these raiders? That it has become imperative that we locate, pursue, and destroy them utterly?"

"I do," Admiral Gomez said shortly.

"Thank you." Treadwell produced a tight, bitter smile, devoid of any hint of warmth. "I may, perhaps, have been in error to oppose your earlier requests for lighter units. That, however, is now water under the bridge, and I have personally starcommed Countess Miller and Grand Duke Phillip to lay the situation before them. My impression is that they are fully aware of its seriousness, and the grand duke informs me that Senators Buchanan and Mojahek are pressing for a more vigorous response. I feel, therefore, that it has become far more likely that Lord Jurawski will respond favorably if I renew my request for additional battle squadrons with your support."

Gomez's lips thinned, and McIlhenny felt her silent, sour bile. Months had passed while Treadwell held out for the heavier forces—months, he was certain, in which Gomez could have made major progress had her own, far more modest requests been met. They had not for one reason only: Treadwell had refused to endorse them. Deep inside, McIlhenny knew, Gomez shared his suspicion that Treadwell saw this as his last opportunity to command, however indirectly, a major Fleet deployment, and he wondered how the governor's conscience could deal with the dead of Elysium and Ringbolt.

Not, perhaps, too well, judging by the exchange which had just ended.

Yet Treadwell was right in at least one respect. The situation *had* changed. The pirates, or whatever the hell they really were, had to be hunted down and destroyed, not merely stopped, and the political pressure to use whatever sledgehammer that required could no longer be ignored.

"I still feel that response is neither required nor the best available," Gomez said at last. She flicked her eyes briefly aside to Amos Brinkman, who had sat prudently silent throughout. He showed no inclination to break that silence now, and her gaze returned to Treadwell. "Nonetheless, Sir, anything that gets us off dead center is better than nothing. I will support you *if* you will also request an immediate dispatch of all available light units in the meantime."

Treadwell sat like a stone, his mouth as tight as her own, and matched her glower for glower. Then, at last, he nodded.

Soft music played in the background as Benjamin McIlhenny leaned back and plucked at his lower lip. The latest report from his handpicked internal security commander lay on the desk before him, and it made disturbing reading.

Enough Elysium survivors had been interviewed to conclusively prove that Commodore Trang had been duped into letting the enemy into decisive range without even alerting the planet. The colonel had run every possible reason for such suicidal overconfidence through the tactical simulator, and only one of them made any sense. The pirates had to have been detected on the way in, and that meant they *had* to have been identified as friendly. And, given the high degree of alert the entire sector had maintained for months, no system commander could have been fooled. Therefore, the incoming warship must have *been* friendly . . . or else have arrived at such a time and under such circumstances that Trang's people had very good reason to "know" it was.

So. Either it had been a real Fleet unit, or else it had timed its arrival to coincide with a scheduled arrival by something that was. Only there had been no scheduled traffic. McIlhenny knew, for he'd personally read every official communication to Elysium.

There were many ways pirates could have gotten their hands on ex-Fleet hulls—some members of the Ministry had argued for years that Fleet disposal policies were badly in need of overhaul—yet that wouldn't have helped without proper transponder codes *and* a scheduled arrival. A low-level agent might have provided the codes or, at least, enough data to cobble up something that looked legitimate, but no one below flag rank could have engineered a false shipping report to open the door.

No. Someone of the rank of commodore or—McIlhenny shuddered—higher must have inserted a fake schedule into Trang's routine message traffic. Someone with access to the authentication protocols required to sneak it in and the ability to abstract and wipe the routine acknowledgment Trang must have sent back. Worst of all, someone who *knew* there would be no heavy units in the system when the raiders arrived.

The penetration was worse than he'd thought. It was *total.* Whoever was behind it must have access to his own reports and Admiral Gomez's complete deployment orders—must even have known El Greco was pulling its units out of Ringbolt for maneuvers.

He closed his eyes in pain at the scale of the treason that implied, but it wasn't really a surprise. Not anymore.

All right. No more than forty people had access to all of that data, and he knew precisely who they were. Any one of them might, conceivably, have passed it to someone outside the loop who had the command authority to doctor Trang's starcom traffic, but if they could do that without his spotting them, their chain of communications had to be both short and hellishly well hidden. In his own mind, it came down to no more than a dozen possible suspects . . . all of whom had passed every security check he could throw at them. It *couldn't* be one of them, and at the same time, it *had* to be.

He straightened and lifted a chip from his desk, weighing it in his fingers. Thank God he'd arranged a link to Keita. He was becoming so paranoid he no longer completely trusted even Admiral Gomez, and the deadly miasma of distrust and fear was getting to him. He'd started seeing assassins in every shadow, which was bad enough, if not as bad as the sense that nothing he did could stop the inexorable murder of civilians he was sworn to protect.

But worst of all was his absolute conviction that whatever twisted strategy lay behind these "pirates" was winding to its climax. Time was running out. If he couldn't break this open—if he wasn't permitted to live long enough to break it open—the vermin orchestrating the atrocities were going to succeed, and that was obscene.

He stood, face hard with purpose, and slipped the chip into his pocket beside the one already there. One would be dropped into his secret pipeline to Keita; the other would be delivered to Admiral Gomez, and both contained his conclusion that someone of flag rank was directly involved with the raiders. But unlike the one to Keita, Admiral Gomez's stated unequivocally that he would know the traitor's identity within the next few weeks.

Benjamin McIlhenny was a Marine, bound by oath and conscience alike to lay down his life in defense of the Empire. He would deliver those chips, and then he would take a little vacation time . . . without extra security. It was the only way to test his theory, for if he was right, the traitor couldn't let him live. The attempt to silence him would confirm his theory for Sir Arthur, and Sir Arthur and the Cadre would know what to do with it.

And who knew? He might actually survive.

CHAPTER FIFTY-FOUR

Alicia took another swallow and decided she'd been wrong; Ching-Hai did have one redeeming feature.

She rolled the chill bottle across her forehead and savored the rich, clean taste of the beer. Monsieur Labin's offices boasted what passed for air-conditioning on Ching-Hai, but the temperature was still seven degrees higher than the one Megaira maintained aboard ship. No doubt the climate helped explain the locals' excellent breweries.

The old-fashioned office door rattled, and she straightened in her chair, lowering the bottle as Gustav Labin, Yerensky's Ching-Hai agent, stepped through it. Unlike Alicia's, his round, bland face was dry, but he didn't even crack a smile as she wiped a fresh drop of sweat from her nose. Not because he lacked the normal Ching-Haian's amusement at off-worlders' want of heat tolerance, but because he was afraid of her. Indeed, he regarded her with a certain fixed dread, as if she were a warhead which might choose to detonate any time. He'd been looking at her that way ever since he arrived to find her sitting amid the ruins of the botched hijacking, and Tisiphone had needed only a single handshake to confirm that Labin had known nothing of his (now deceased) partner's intentions . . . and that "Captain Mainwaring's" reputation as a dangerous woman had been made forever.

Now he lowered himself into his chair and cleared a nervous throat.

"I've completed the manifest verification, Captain. It checks perfectly, as—" he hastened to add "—I was certain it would." He drew a credit transfer chip from a drawer. "The balance of your payment, Captain."

"Thank you, Monsieur. It's been a pleasure." Alicia kept her face straight, but it was hard. Those poor, half-assed hijackers had been totally beyond their depth. Killing, even in self-defense and even of scum like that, never sat easily with her afterward, yet Labin's near terror amused her. If he ever saw a regular Cadre assault he'd die on the spot.

<*And the universe would be a better place for it,*> Tisiphone observed. <*This man is a* worm, *Little One.*>

<*Now, now. He's all of that, but he's also our ticket to Dewent . . . whenever he gets around to mentioning it.*>

The Fury sniffed, but it was her probe which had discovered Labin's shipment. Given its nature and the stature Alicia enjoyed in his eyes, they hadn't even had to "push" him into seeing her as the perfect carrier.

"Ah, yes. A pleasure for me, as well, Captain. And allow me to apologize once more. I assure you neither Anton nor I ever suspected my colleague might attempt to attack you."

"I never thought otherwise," Alicia murmured, and he managed a smile.

"I'm glad. And, of course, impressed. Indeed, Captain, I have another small consignment, one which must be delivered to Dewent, and your, um, demonstrated expertise could be very much a plus to me. It's quite a valuable cargo, and I've been concerned over its security. Concerned enough," he leaned forward a bit, "to pay top credit to a reliable carrier."

"I see." Alicia sipped more beer, then shook her head. "It sounds to me like you think your 'concern' could end in more shooting, Monsieur, and I prefer not to carry cargoes I *know* are going to attract hijacks."

"I understand entirely, and I may be worrying over nothing. Certainly I have no solid evidence of any danger. I merely prefer to be safe rather than sorry, and I'm willing to invest a bit in security. I thought, perhaps, an increase of fifteen percent over your fee to Anton might be appropriate?"

"My fee to Mister Yerensky didn't include combat expenses," Alicia pointed out, "and shuttle missiles are hard to come by out here. I expect replacing expenditures to cut into my profit margin on this trip."

"Twenty percent, then?"

"I don't know . . ." Alicia allowed her voice to trail off. Thanks to Tisiphone, she knew Labin was willing to go to thirty or even thirty-five percent to secure her services, and while she wasn't particularly interested in running up the price, neither did she wish to appear too eager. Tisiphone could shape his decisions, but she couldn't guarantee something wouldn't come along later and make him wonder *why* he'd chosen a given course.

"Twenty-five," Labin offered.

"Make it thirty," she said. Labin winced but nodded, and she smiled. "In that case, if I may use your com?" She reached for the terminal, and Labin sat back as she entered a code. A moment later, the screen lit with Ruth Tanner's face.

"Yes, Captain?" Megaira asked in Tanner's voice.

"We've got a new charter, Ruth. We'll be headed to Dewent for Monsieur Labin. Ready to crunch a few numbers?"

"Of course, Captain."

"Good." Alicia turned the terminal to face Labin and leaned back. "If you'll be good enough to settle the details with my purser, Monsieur?"

<*I do not like this cargo,*> Tisiphone groused.

"I'm not crazy about it myself," Alicia replied, frowning at the chessboard. She and Megaira had taught the Fury the game, and Alicia and Tisiphone were surprisingly well-matched, though it took both of them together just to lose to the AI.

<*None of us are,*> Megaira put in, <*but we needed one going to Dewent.*>

"Exactly." Alicia nodded and started to reach for a knight.

<*Wouldn't do that, Alley,*> Megaira whispered. <*Her bishop'll—*>

<Will *you two cease that?!*>

<*Cease what, Tis?*> Megaira asked innocently.

<*You know very well what. Or did you truly think you could think so softly I would not hear you?*>

"It wath worth a try," Lieutenant Chisholm said from a speaker. "And only a nathty, thuthpithous perthon would have been lithening, anyway."

<No one except one who knows *you, you mean.>*

Alicia bit her lip against a giggle, but she didn't quite dare take advantage of Megaira's kibitzing now. So she moved her knight, instead, and sighed as Tisiphone's bishop lashed out and captured her king's rook.

<Check,> the Fury said smugly.

"You really are a nasty person. If I was virtuous enough not to listen to Megaira, you could've reciprocated by leaving my poor rook alone."

<Nonsense. You yourself call this a "war game," and one does not surrender an honorably gained advantage in war, Little One. Nor, I suppose,> the mental voice grew more thoughtful, *<even a dishonorably gained advantage.>*

"Absolutely," Alicia said sweetly, and captured the bishop with her other knight . . . simultaneously forking Tisiphone's king and queen. It exposed her own queen's bishop, but that was fine with her. The only square to which Tisiphone could move her king was one knight's move from her queen. "Check yourself."

<By golly, I didn't even notice that one!> Megaira observed in a tone of artful innocence while the Fury seethed.

"Neither did I," Alicia asserted with a grin. Tisiphone moved her king, and Alicia took her queen. "Check," she said again, and used the breathing space to move her bishop out of danger.

<Hmph! And Odysseus was a credulous fool. Yet we have wandered from my earlier point, Little One. Advantage or no, I dislike this cargo of ours.>

"I know," Alicia sighed, and she did know.

Anton Yerensky's cargo to Ching-Hai had been illegal but essentially beneficial; Gustav Labin's cargo to Dewent was also pharmaceutical, but that was the sole similarity. "Dreamy White" was harmless enough to its users, aside from a hundred percent rate of addiction, but it was hideously expensive . . . and even more hideously obtained. It was an endorphin derivative, and while it could be produced in the lab, there were far cheaper ways. Most Dreamy White was harvested from the brains of human beings, with consequences for the "donor" which ranged from massive retardation and motor control loss to death.

<*We should not have taken it,*> the Fury said grimly.

"Aren't you the one who told me anything we do in pursuit of vengeance is acceptable?" Alicia's voice was sharper than intended—because, she knew, Tisiphone was simply saying what all of them felt—yet she could taste the other's surprise as her own words were thrown back at her.

<*Perhaps. Yet you were the one who argued for "justice,"*> Tisiphone shot back gamely. <*How can this be just?*>

"I don't know that it is," Alicia said more slowly, "but I also don't see that we have any choice. And it's certainly the kind of cargo that'll get us in with the people we need to infiltrate."

The Fury's silence was an unhappy acceptance, and Alicia wondered if Tisiphone was as aware as she of the irony of their positions. She, who believed passionately in justice, had compromised her principles in the pursuit of her prey, leaving it to the Fury, who spoke only of vengeance, to question the morality of their gruesome cargo.

<*Perhaps,*> Tisiphone repeated at last. <*Yet perhaps there is something after all to this concept of law, as well. Man had turned his hand to evils enough when my sisters and I were one, but all of them pale beside those he has the tools to wreak today, and not even my vengeance can undo an evil once committed. So perhaps this justice, these "rules" of yours, are more important than once I thought.*>

Alicia sat still, eyes widening to hear the Fury admit even a part of her argument, but she felt a tugging at her right hand. She relinquished control and watched it reach out to advance a rook.

<*Guard yourself, Little One! You may have slowed my attack, but you have not stopped it.*>

Alicia smiled and bent over the board once more, yet there was a chill in her heart, for she knew Tisiphone referred to far more than a chess game.

Dewent was a much nicer planet than Ching-Hai, Alicia thought. In part, that was because it was much wetter, a world of archipelagoes and island continents, and cooler, but it was also closer to civilized. Not a great deal closer, perhaps, yet no one had attempted to rob or kill her, and that was a definite improvement.

Unlike Ching-Hai, Dewent had a customs service, but it was concerned only with insuring that the local government got its cut on outgoing cargoes, and Alicia had set the cargo shuttle neatly down at Dewent's main spaceport unmolested by anything so crass as an inspection. The *Bengal* had grounded beside her like a garishlypainted shadow or a pointed hint that politeness would be wise, but it stayed sealed. Alicia had been at some pains to maintain an open com link to it, chattering away with "Jeff Okahara," its ostensible pilot and "*Star Runner*'s" executive officer, and Okahara's return chatter had made no bones about what would happen to anyone who *wasn't* polite.

Two hours later, she stood in a port warehouse while her receiver examined his cargo. Edward Jacoby looked like a respectable accountant, but he clearly knew what he was about. He needed no biochemist to test the drugs for purity; the six men standing around the warehouse were there for another reason. Few weapons were in evidence, but these men were far more dangerous than the bumbling hijackers of Ching-Hai. More, Alicia had seen their eyes as they flicked over her and recognized a fellow predator.

Jacoby finished his tests and began putting away his equipment. He didn't smile—he didn't seem the sort for smiles—but he looked satisfied.

"Well, Captain Mainwaring," he said as the last instrument vanished, "I was a bit anxious when Gustav starcommed that he was using a complete unknown, but his judgment was excellent. How would you like payment?"

"I think I'd prefer an electronic transfer, this time," she replied. "I'd rather not carry around a credit chip quite that large."

One of Jacoby's guards made a sound suspiciously like a chuckle, and the merchant came as close to a smile as he probably ever did. His eyes dropped to her holstered CHK and the knife hilt protruding from her left boot—the only weapons she'd chosen to let anyone see—but he simply nodded.

"As wise as you are efficient, I see. Very well, my accountant will complete the transfer at your convenience."

"Thank you."

Alicia's smile was dazzling. Try as she might, she'd been unable to disagree with Tisiphone's verdict on their cargo, but after considerable thought, she and her companions had hit upon a way to salve their consciences. Alicia was too honest to think it was anything more, yet it was better than nothing. When Ruth Tanner executed that credit transfer from Jacoby's house computers, Megaira and Tisiphone intended to raid his system for every off-world shipping contact. So armed, the AI should be able to determine which were legitimate (assuming any were) and which were likely to receive shipments of Dreamy White in the near future, and Alicia intended to starcom the appropriate local authorities from their next stop. That wouldn't get Jacoby himself, but *no one* wanted Dreamy White on his planet, and the consequences for his distribution network should be . . . extreme.

"Well!" Jacoby closed the case with a snap and nodded to one of his men, who began hauling the two countergravity pallets towards the security area. "Tell, me, Captain, would you join me for lunch? I'm always looking for reliable carriers—we might well be able to do some more business."

"Lunch, certainly, but unless your business is going in the right direction, I'm afraid I'll have to give that a pass." And she hoped to God she could; she wanted to carry no more mass death in her hold.

"Ah?" Jacoby regarded her with a thoughtful expression. "What direction would that be, Captain?"

"I've got a charter commitment waiting on Cathcart," Alicia lied. Cathcart was an extremely respectable Rogue World, and she had no intention of going anywhere near it, but it lay almost directly beyond Wyvern.

"Cathcart, Cathcart," Jacoby murmured, then shook his head. "No, I'm afraid I don't have anything bound in that direction just now. Still, there's something . . ."

His voice trailed off in thought, and then he snapped his fingers.

"Of course! One of my associates has a consignment for Wyvern. Would that be of interest to you?"

"Wyvern?" Alicia managed to keep the excitement out of her voice and cocked her head in thought. "That might fit in nicely, if we're not talking about too much cubage. *Star Runner*'s forte is speed, not bulk."

"That shouldn't be a problem. I have the impression speed is of the essence in this case, and while it's fairly massive it's also low bulk—military spares and molycircuitry, I believe. But we could check; Lewis and I share warehousing facilities here. Step this way a moment."

Alicia followed him, fighting to contain her exultation. Wyvern *and* military supplies? It was too good to be true! She managed to keep her thoughts from showing as they crossed a more heavily traveled portion of the warehouse, but her brain was busy. She paused to let a warehouse tractor putter past, towing a line of empty pallets, so wrapped in her tumbling thoughts she didn't even look up when the small, almost painfully nondescript driver glanced her way. She told herself not to get her hopes up, that it was probably mere coincidence, but it certainly sounded like—

They reached their destination, and Jacoby pointed out the stacked pallets of the shipment. He was speaking to her, describing their contents in greater detail, but Alicia didn't hear him. She heard nothing at all, and it couldn't have mattered less. Whatever those details were, there was no way in the galaxy she would allow anyone else to carry this cargo.

Maintaining her politely interested smile was the hardest thing she had ever done, for hunger seethed behind her eyes, mirrored and fanned by Tisiphone's reaction, as her gaze devoured the racks beside the pallets. They bore the same shipper's codes, but their red tags, marked with the dragon-like customs stamp of Wyvern, indicated an incoming shipment. Rack after rack, an incredible number of them, and she could see why they were in the security area . . . for each of them was heavy with the priceless, snow-white pelts of the deadly carnivore known as Mathison's Direcat.

Book Six: Fury

CHAPTER FIFTY-FIVE

The man on Alicia's com screen was as civilized looking as Edward Jacoby, but Alicia knew he was the one she'd come to find. Direcats were bigger than Old Earth kodiaks, with fangs a saber-tooth would have envied, and they were not omnivorous. A carnivore that size required a huge range, even on virgin Mathison's World, and the government had regulated direcat hunting with an iron hand. Those warehouse racks contained at least a full year's pelts—and could have come from only one source.

And so she smiled at the face on her screen, smiled politely, with only professional interest, even as everything within her screamed to touch him and rip away the knowledge she must have.

"Good evening, Captain Mainwaring. My name is Lewis Fuchien. I'm glad I caught you groundside."

"So am I. Mister Jacoby said you might screen."

"Indeed. I understand my consignment falls within your vessel's capacity?" Fuchien asked, and she nodded. "Excellent. While your fee initially seemed a bit high, Edward has shared Monsieur Labin's report with me, and—"

"I hope you didn't take it at face value," Alicia interrupted wryly. "Monsieur Labin was rather more impressed than circumstances merited."

"Modesty is admirable, Captain Mainwaring, and I realize Gustav Labin is a bit excitable, but Edward assures me you'd take good care of my cargo."

"That much, at least, is true, Sir. When someone entrusts me with a shipment, I do my best to insure it reaches its destination."

"No shipper could ask for more. However—" Fuchien smiled pleasantly "—I *would* like to meet the rest of your ship's company. It's a policy of mine to consider the reliability of a crew as a whole, not just its captain."

"I see." Alicia's face showed nothing, but her mind raced with ticklike speed, conferring with Tisiphone and Megaira on a level deeper than vocalization and far, far faster than conscious thought. She couldn't very well bring her nonexistent crew down to have lunch with the man! But—

"Did Mister Jacoby mention my Cathcart charter?" Fuchien nodded, and she smiled. "I certainly understand your caution, and frankly, I'd feel happier myself if my purser could sit in on our discussions, but my engineer and exec are buried in a drive recalibration. I really can't interrupt them—in fact, I ought to be up there helping out right now—given our time pressure for Cathcart, but if *you* have a free hour or so, may I offer you *Star Runner*'s hospitality for supper? The food may not be five-star, but I think you'll find it palatable, and it'll give you the chance not only to meet my people but to look the ship over in person, as well. If you like what you see, you, my purser, and I can settle the details over brandy. Would that be convenient?"

"Why, thank you! That's far more than I'd hoped for, and I'd be very happy to accept, if I may include my own accountant."

"Of course. I'll be taking my cargo shuttle back up at seventeen-thirty hours. Would you care to accompany me, or arrange your own transport?"

"If you won't mind seeing us home again, we'll ride up with you."

"No problem, Mister Fuchien. I'll expect you then."

Fuchien and his accountant—a short, stout woman with laugh wrinkles around computer-sharp eyes—arrived at the shuttle ramp precisely on time, and Alicia was waiting at its foot, tall and professional in her midnight blue uniform. Their brief handshakes lasted barely long enough to skim the surface of their thoughts, but that was sufficent to confirm her suspicions.

"Captain, may I present Sondra McSwain, my accountant?"

"Pleased to meet you, Ms. McSwain."

"Likewise, Captain. After what Mister Fuchien's told me about your reputation, I expected you to be three meters tall!"

"Reputations always grow in the telling, I think." Alicia grinned back. McSwain's mind held neither the scummy taint she'd picked up from Labin nor the cultured avarice she read in Fuchien. It ticked like a precision instrument, skilled and professional but laced with a sense of humor, and Alicia's grin turned wry. How odd to find an incorruptible person on a planet like Dewent!

She shook herself and gestured at the ramp.

"Mister Fuchien. Ms. McSwain. We have clearance and my crew is preparing to roll out the carpet."

The flight up was routine, but the accountant's obvious delight made it seem otherwise. Ms. McSwain, Alicia decided, seldom saw the insides of the ships and shuttles that thronged Dewent's port facilities. Even this short jaunt was an exotic treat for her, yet she had the ability to recognize her own excitement for what it was and laugh at it. Alicia found herself explaining instruments and procedures with unfeigned cheer, and even Fuchien allowed himself to smile at her drum roll questions.

They were halfway to rendezvous when Tisiphone nudged Alicia.

<You are forgetting our purpose, Little One, and an illusion of this complexity requires preparation. May I suggest we begin?>

<I guess so.> Alicia sighed. *<But I think I'm going to enjoy this less than I expected. Why the hell does she have to be so nice?>*

<Have no fear,> the Fury said with unusual gentleness. *<Megaira and I also like her. We will allow no harm to befall her, yet we must begin soon.>*

<Gotcha.>

Alicia turned her head and smiled at McSwain as the accountant's questions temporarily ran down.

"There's a member of my crew I want you to meet, Ms. McSwain. A colleague of yours, you might say. Forgive us, but we were expecting a stringy, dried-up cold fish of a credit-cruncher." McSwain met her eyes, and they chuckled together. "I think Ruth is going to be pleasantly surprised."

"I once had a 'stringy, dried-up cold fish,'" Fuchien confessed, "but he fell afoul of an audit. Sondra is a vast improvement, I assure you."

"And I believe you." Alicia keyed a com screen alight with Ruth Tanner's face. "Ruth? Forget Plan A and go to Plan B. Mister Fuchien's accountant is human after all."

"Really? What a nice change," Megaira replied in Ruth's voice. Her image's eyes swept the cockpit until they found McSwain, and Ruth's face smiled. "Goodness! Who would've thought someone on this chauvinist backwater would have enough sense to hire a woman!" Her eyes cut to Fuchien's face, and her smile became a grin. "Oops! Did I just put my foot in my mouth?"

"Not with me," Fuchien assured her. "My colleagues' shortsightedness in that respect is my gain, Ms. Tanner. You *are* Ms. Tanner, I presume?"

"In the flesh," Megaira replied. "I hope you'll enjoy your visit. We don't entertain often, so we're putting our best foot forward, and . . ."

The conversation rolled on, and neither Fuchien nor McSwain noticed when their eyes began to turn just a bit disoriented.

This, Alicia thought, was the strangest thing they'd tried yet. In her present, straitened condition, Tisiphone would have found herself hard put to weave an illusion half this complex. But she wasn't forced to weave it alone, for Megaira had opened a direct tap to the Fury, throwing her own tremendous capacity behind the spell like a gigantic amplifier that restored Tisiphone, however briefly, to the peak of her long lost power.

And with that aid, the Fury surpassed herself. She wove her web with consummate skill, ensnaring both her guests and extending a tendril of herself to Alicia, as well. It was an eerie sensation, even for one who had become accustomed to the bizarre, for Alicia inhabited three worlds at once. She saw once through her own senses, again through Megaira's internal sensors, and last of all, she *shared* her guests' illusion. She sat with them at supper, chatting with Megaira's other selves while the AI provided their conversation and Tisiphone gave them flesh, even as she sat alone with them at the table. It was almost terrifying, for it wasn't what the Fury had done to Lieutenant Giolitti. There would be no hazed memories or implanted suggestions. This was *real.* Backed by the AI's enormous power, Tisiphone took them all one step out of phase with the universe and made her reality theirs.

Nor was that all she did. There was no rush, and she plumbed Lewis Fuchien's memories to their depths, filing away every scrap of a fact which might be of use. By supper's end, they knew everything he did, and the merchant was convinced Captain Mainwaring's crew was perfect for his needs.

The meal ended, and the entire crew—except Tanner—"excused" itself to return to duty. Fuchien lifted his brandy and sipped appreciatively.

"Well, Captain Mainwaring, you and your people have not only met my standards but far exceeded my hopes. I believe we can do business."

"I'm delighted to hear it." Alicia sat back with her own brandy and smiled, then gestured at the empty chair which held her purser's ghost. "In that case, why don't you and I sit back while Ruth and Sondra do battle?"

"An excellent idea, Captain." Fuchien beamed. "Simply excellent."

Dewent dwindled in the galley view screen as *Megaira*'s velocity mounted, and Alicia watched it while she tried to define her own emotions. A complex broth of anticipation, hunger, and fear—fear that she might yet blow her chance—simmered within her, and over it all lay a haze of excitement as she looked ahead to Wyvern, mingled with relief at leaving Dewent astern.

She still didn't like Fuchien, but neither did she *dis*like him as much as she had expected. He was as ambitious and credit-hungry as Jacoby, but without the other's outright evil. He knew of his associate's drug deals yet took no part in them, and while he suspected his Wyvern contact of fencing goods for the pirates terrorizing the sector, he himself had had no direct dealings with them. He disapproved of them, in a depressingly mild sort of way, yet it was unrealistic to expect more from him. He was a Dewentan, and servicing "outlaws" was what Dewent did. By his own lights, Lewis Fuchien was an admirable and honest businessman, and Alicia could almost understand that.

That was one reason she was glad to leave, for she didn't *want* to understand it. On a more pragmatic level, their departure meant her and her "crew's" deception only had to stand up for one last planet. Only one, and then she didn't care who knew. Fleet was welcome to pursue her. Indeed, she would welcome their pursuit if her flight could lead them to the pirates.

She leaned her elbows on the edge of the console, propping her chin in her hands and brooding down on the rapidly diminishing image, and let her mind reach out ahead. Wyvern. The planet Wyvern and a man named Oscar Quintana, Lieutenant Commander Defiant.

Wyvern had a peculiar aristocracy, with no use for titles like "baron" or "count." Their ancestors had been naval officers—little more than freebooter refuse from the centuries-past League Wars, perhaps, but naval officers—and the ship name appended to Quintana's title indicated that he sprang from one of the founding noble houses. Peculiar as it might sound to off-world ears, he'd be a powerful man, probably a proud and dangerous one, and it behooved her to approach him with caution.

<*Hey,*> Megaira interrupted her thoughts, <*don't get too bothered, Alley! If he knows what's good for him, he'll approach* us *with caution.*>

<*True,*> Tisiphone seconded. <*Indeed, Little One, unless we are much mistaken, this Quintana must be a direct contact for the ones we seek. If so, I shall turn him inside out with the greatest pleasure.*>

"You two are in a bloodthirsty mood," Alicia observed. "Or are you just worried that I'm getting ready to funk out?"

<*Us?*> Megaira was innocence itself. <*Perish the thought.*>

"Sure." Alicia stood and yawned, stretching the tension from her shoulders and grateful to be distracted from her moodiness. "As a matter of fact, I'm not that worried over Quintana. If he's what we think he is, I hereby give you both *carte blanche* for anything we have to do to him."

<*My thanks, Little One—not that I intended to wait upon your permission to deal harshly with such scum.*>

"Oh, yeah? Harsh is okay with me, but remember—even if he's a direct link, we still need to get to the next step. I'm afraid that may limit what we can do to him. I mean, we couldn't even squash that slime Jacoby."

<*Ah, funny you should mention that, Alley.*> Megaira's elaborately casual voice set off a clangor of warning bells, and Alicia's eyebrows rose.

"I know that tone," she said. "What've you been up to?"

<*It wasn't just me,*> the AI said quickly. <*I mean, I thought it was a great idea, but I couldn't have done it by myself.*>

"You fill me with dread—and you're stalling."

<*It was your idea, Tis. Why don't you explain?*>

<*But I could not have accomplished it without your expertise, and you have a better grasp of the details, so perhaps you should explain.*>

The Fury's tone was serious, yet Alicia felt her amusement. She put her hands on her hips and glared at the empty air.

"*One* of you had better trot it out, ladies!"

<*Well, it's like this, Alley. You remember when we made that credit transfer and Tis and I raided Jacoby's data base?*>

"Of course I do," Alicia said, then paused. "Did you horrid creatures put something *into* it? You didn't hit him with a virus, did you?"

<*Of course not,*> Megaira said virtuously. <*What a horrible idea! I'd never do something like that—not even to a fossil like that Jurgens Twelve of his. Not that it might not have been kinder. That relic should've been scrapped years ago, Alley. It's so stupid—*>

"Quit stalling! What did you do?!"

<*We didn't put a thing into it. Instead, we took something out.*>

"Besides the information on his distribution network?"

<*Well, yes. I guess to be perfectly honest, we* did *put something in, but it's only a delayed extraction program.*>

"What *kind* of extraction program?"

<*A starcom credit transfer.*>

"A *credit transfer?* You mean you *robbed* him?"

<*If you want to put it that way. But we talked it over, and, personally, I think Tis was right. You can't really rob a thief, can you?*>

"Of course you can rob a thief!" Alicia closed her eyes and flopped back into her chair. "I thought you were supposed to have *my* value system!"

<*And so she does, but I am making some progress with her. Rather more than with you, in fact.*>

"I just bet you are," Alicia muttered, running her fingers through her hair. "All right, how much did you hit him for?"

<*All of it,*> Megaira said in a small voice.

"All of what?"

<All of everything. We found all his hidden accounts as well as the open ones, and we, well, we sort of cleaned him out.>

"You—" Alicia gurgled to a stop, and pregnant silence hovered in her stunned mind. But then her closed eyes popped open as panic cut through her shock. "Good God Almighty, Megaira! What do you think he's going to do when he figures out *we* robbed him?! We can't afford that kind of—"

<Peace, Little One. He will not realize we were to blame.>

"How do you know?! Damn it, who *else* is he going to suspect?!"

<That I cannot tell you, but it will not be us, for the theft has not yet occurred. Nor will it . . . until he orders his first off-planet credit transfer to one of his drug-distributing cronies. Megaira was very clever, and I rather expect—> the Fury's dry delight was unmistakable *<—that he will suspect whichever of his fellow thieves he has attempted to pay.>*

"You mean—?"

<Exactly, Alley. See, what'll happen is the first time he orders a payment to one of the accounts I listed in my program, it'll automatically dump every credit he has into the transfer and then reroute it. His payee won't see a centicredit, but the program'll bootstrap itself—and the transfer—through his starcom, then transmit itself back out. And it'll erase itself from each system it moves through till it reaches its destination, too.>

"Oh, Lord!" Alicia moaned, covering her eyes with her hands. "I *never* should have inflicted you two on an unsuspecting galaxy! Just where—if I dare ask—will this wandering program finally end its criminal days?"

<It'll probably take it a while to make connections, but it's headed for Thaarvlhd. I set it up to open a numbered account when it gets there.>

"Thaarvlhd?" Alicia repeated blankly. Then, "*Thaarvlhd?!* My God, that's the Quarn Hegemony's central banking hub for this sector! Damn it, the Quarn take money *seriously*, Megaira! Violating Thaarvlhd's banking laws isn't a harmless little prank like murder!"

<I didn't violate a thing. They're used to orders like this one, and I included all the documentation they need.>

"Documentation?"

<*Sure. They don't care about names, but I included everything they want on human accounts: your retinal prints, your genetic pri—*>

"*My* prints?!" Alicia yelped. "You opened an account in *my* name?!"

<*Of course not. I just explained they don't* use *names, Alley. That's why they're so popular.*>

"Sweet Suffering Jesus!" Alicia never knew exactly how long she sat there, staring at nothing, but then a thought occurred to her. "Uh, Megaira."

<*Yes?*>

"I'm not condoning what you've done—not *condemning* it either, you understand, or at least not yet—but I was wondering . . . Just how much did you two rip him off for?"

<*Hard to say, since we don't know exactly when the program'll trip.*>

"A rough estimate will do," Alicia said in a fascinated tone.

<*Well, using his last two years' cash flow as a basis, I'd say somewhere between two hundred fifty and three hundred million credits.*>

"Two hun—"

Alicia closed her mouth with a snap. Then she began to giggle—giggles that gave way to howls of laughter. She couldn't help herself. She leaned forward, hugging her ribs and laughing till her chest hurt and her eyes teared. Laughing as she had not laughed in months, with pure, devilish delight as she pictured ultracivilized Edward Jacoby's reaction. And she'd thought they couldn't hurt him! Dear God, he wouldn't have a pot to piss in, and he'd never even know who'd done it!

She pummeled the deck with her feet, wailing with laughter, until she could get control of herself again, then straightened slowly, gasping for breath and mopping her eyes.

<*I take it you are less displeased than you anticipated?*> Tisiphone asked mildly, and Alicia giggled again.

"Stop that!" she said unsteadily. "Don't you dare set me off again! Oh. Oh, *my*! He *is* going to be upset, isn't he?"

<*It seemed an appropriate—and just—way to deal with him.*>

"Damn straight it did!" Alicia shook herself, then straightened sternly. "Don't you two think you can get away with something like this again—not without checking with me first, anyway! But just this once, I think I'll forgive you."

<*Yeah, for about three hundred million reasons, I'd guess,*> Megaira sniffed, and Alicia dissolved into laughter once more.

CHAPTER FIFTY-SIX

The assembled officers rose as Rachel Shu followed Howell into the briefing room. More than one set of eyes were a bit apprehensive, for the intelligence officer had just returned from meeting Control's latest messenger, and Howell's people were only too well aware of the casualties they'd taken on Ringbolt.

Howell took his place at the head of the table and watched his subordinates sit, then nodded to Shu.

"All right, Commander. Let's hear it."

"Yes, Sir." Shu cleared her throat, set a notepad on the table, and keyed the tiny screen alive. "First, Control sends us all a well done on the Ringbolt operation." Breath sighed out around the table, and Howell smiled wryly. "He regrets our losses, but under the circumstances, he understands why they were so high, and it appears both our primary and secondary missions were complete successes."

She paused, and Howell listened to a soft murmur of pleasure walk around the room. How many of those officers, he wondered, ever really spent a few hours thinking about what they'd done? Not many—perhaps none. *He* certainly tried to avoid the memories, though it was growing harder. Yet it was often that way. There were things he'd done in the service of the Empire which he tried just as hard never to remember. This wasn't that much different, he told himself, and pretended that he didn't know he lied.

Of course, much of their pleasure stemmed from the fact that they'd expected to be reamed. A pat on the back always felt better when one had anticipated a rap in the mouth. That much *was* the same as in the Fleet.

He let the murmurs run on a moment longer, then tapped his knuckles on the tabletop. Silence fell once more, and he nodded to Shu.

"Preliminary evaluation of the captured data," the commander continued, keying the advance to display the next screen as she picked up her report again, "indicates we probably secured more from Ringbolt than we would have from Elysium, and our financial backers are delighted. Control asked me to tell you all that their support has firmed up very nicely once more, and that most of them seem convinced we know what we're doing after all.

"On another front, the Ringbolt attack has apparently produced the desired effect in the Senate and Ministry. Control didn't want to come right out and say so, but he seems confident that ONI and Marine Intelligence on Old Earth are coming to precisely the conclusions we want, and pressure from the Senate is growing every day. Best of all, public opinion here in the sector itself is shaping up *very* nicely. 'Panic' might be putting it too strongly, but there's widespread anxiety and an increasing perception that the imperial government is powerless to stop us."

Shu touched the advance key again and allowed herself a small frown.

"We do have one unanticipated complication. Apparently, one of the people killed on Ringbolt was Simon Monkoto's brother Arlen."

Howell sat a bit straighter and saw others do the same at mention of that name. Shu saw it, too, and her smile was wintry.

"We all know Monkoto's reputation, but his outfit isn't up to our weight even if he knew where to find us. The problem is that he's calling in a lot of debts from his colleagues, and most of them are angry enough over Ringbolt to throw in with him even if they didn't owe him. Among them, they may be able to assemble an independent force that *is* a threat, and because they're independents, Control's ability to track them will be much lower than for the regular El Grecan Navy. On the other hand, they *are* independents. Their fleets represent their working capital, and they can't tie them up indefinitely on this kind of altruistic operation."

"What's the chance of El Greco picking up the tab?" Alexsov asked.

"Unknown. Mercenaries of Monkoto's caliber normally don't come cheap, but these aren't normal circumstances. I don't know about the others, but the Maniacs'll probably settle for basic expenses with no profit margin, and that could make them extremely attractive to El Greco. Still, that might work in our favor. If they hire on with El Greco, the El Grecans will tie them into a comprehensive strategy. Under normal circumstances, that would make them even more dangerous; as it is, they'd simply be easier to watch—and avoid—given the joint planning between the Empire and the El Grecans."

Alexsov nodded thoughtfully, and Shu shrugged.

"Control isn't too concerned about them at present. As I say, they'd have to find us before they could hurt us, even if they managed to assemble enough firepower to come after us. It's unlikely they can do that, but Control isn't taking any chances. He wants us to relocate to the AR-Twelve site as soon as possible to get us farther away from El Greco."

"Makes sense," Howell agreed. "And it sounds like we're in pretty good shape, if Monkoto is Control's worst worry."

"He is and he isn't, Sir," Shu said. "Control's arranging recruitment to make good our Ringbolt losses, and he's managed to scare up two new BCs to replace *Poltava*." Howell grunted. Crewing two more battlecruisers might stretch them thin, but the firepower would be well worth the inconvenience.

"In the meantime, though, Control himself is going to have to stay close to Soissons, because that's the most delicate problem area just now. In particular, McIlhenny seems to be getting closer than we'd like. According to Control's courier, he's currently promising some significant report to Admiral Gomez and Governor Treadwell. Control couldn't hold the dispatch boat, so we don't know what sort of report, but he informs me that he's prepared to deal with it, whatever it is.

"Assuming he's right about that—and he usually is—our only other local concern is Admiral Gomez. She's backed off just a bit and endorsed Treadwell's request for heavier units, which may divert some of the pressure for her relief, but she and the governor are just about ready to start sticking knives into each other. If she *isn't* relieved, she may be able to force Treadwell into adopting a more effective posture, and none of us wants to see that."

Shu shrugged again.

"If that looks like happening, we'll simply have to proceed with the backup plan and eliminate her. We're looking at several options for that, but Control is leaning towards passing us her itinerary. She's taken to traveling about in *Antietam* with minimal escorts in the interest of speed; if he can pass us her schedule, we might be able to intercept and take her out. In many ways, that would be the ideal solution, given her popularity with the Fleet. It would not only get rid of her but turn her into a martyr and provide yet another reason for Fleet to go after the nasty pirates."

Her smile was most unpleasant, and Howell hid an inner shiver. He'd served under Gomez, and while he was willing to admit she might have to be eliminated, he didn't look forward to it. Shu obviously did. He didn't know whether she had some special reason to dislike Gomez or if it was simply the professional neatness of using an enemy's death to advance their own ends which appealed to her so, and frankly, he didn't want to know.

"All right," he said, deliberately breaking his own train of thought. "What did Control have to say about the physical take from Ringbolt?"

"Quite a bit, Sir. In fact, that was my next point." Shu flipped quickly through screens of data, then nodded. "He was a bit surprised by how much we got away with, and, of course, we lack the facilities to transport cargo, as opposed to data, directly to the Core Sectors. Moreover, our backers have specifically asked that we *not* send it to them. Control believes they're nervous about having traceable hardware and experimental material in their labs, not to mention the potential for interception en route."

"So he just wants us to dump it all?" Henry d'Amcourt demanded. "Jays, Commodore—that's almost a billion credits out the airlock!"

"I didn't say Control wants it dumped, Henry."

Shu disliked interruptions almost as much as she disliked d'Amcourt personally, and her voice was chill, but Howell understood his quartermaster's anguish. The surviving shuttles had returned with an unanticipated fortune in tissue cultures, experimental animals, and an entire arsenal of new and advanced gene-splicing nanites, not to mention apparatus researchers on most Rogue Worlds (and not a few Incorporated Worlds) would have killed for. Henry wasn't so much affronted by losing the money involved as he was by losing the potential in supplies and ammunition it represented.

"All right, Rachel," the commodore interposed tactfully. "From what you're saying, I gather Control has something specific in mind?"

"He does, Sir." Shu turned to face him, just incidentally turning her back on d'Amcourt, who only grinned. "He suggests we distribute it through Wyvern—preferably via a series of cutouts which can't be traced directly to us but guarantee at least some of it turns up here in the Franconia Sector and, if at all possible, in the Macedon Sector, as well."

"Ah?" Howell leaned back and smiled, and she nodded.

"Exactly. We can realize perhaps seventy percent of its open market value in the transaction, which should please some of us," she very carefully did not look at d'Amcourt, "but he's especially interested in having some of it spotted as far away from the Core Sectors as possible."

Howell nodded. Throwing some fourth or fifth-stage patsy out here to the Ministry of Justice or its Rogue World equivalent would divert attention from their real backers, and it could serve as a wedge into Macedon at the same time. They'd been looking for something to suggest the "pirates" were turning their attention towards the Franconia Sector's neighbors. But coupled with the sheer value involved, that meant this particular shipment had to be handled very carefully indeed. He glanced at Alexsov.

"Greg? Can Quintana handle it?"

"I believe so," Alexsov replied after a moment's thought. "He'll want a bigger cut if he has to arrange to burn a customer, but he'll go along. And he certainly has the contacts and organization to make it work."

Howell toyed with his stylus a moment, then nodded.

"All right. But I want you to set it up in person, Greg. It's about time you checked in personally with Quintana again anyway, isn't it?"

"Yes, Sir. I can go ahead in a dispatch boat and have everything set by the time the transport arrives."

"I don't think so," Howell mused. "I hadn't thought about how useful this could be until Control pointed it out, but he's absolutely right. So no slipups are allowed. I want the arrangements made and triple-checked before we hand Quintana the first flask of this cargo. And I don't want you wandering around in an unarmed dispatch boat, either. Take one of the tin cans, make your arrangements, and then meet us at the AR-Twelve rendezvous."

"If you say so, Sir. But should I really be absent for that long?"

"I think we'll be all right. Control hasn't sent us a fresh target yet, and we'll be meeting his next courier there, anyway. You should be back in plenty of time to coordinate the next op."

"Yes, Sir. In that case, I can leave this afternoon."

CHAPTER FIFTY-SEVEN

"So, Captain. You have a delivery for me, I understand?"

Alicia looked up sharply at the first-person pronoun. She stood at the foot of the shuttle's ramp, the turbine whine of other shuttles at her back, and the fellow before her was dressed almost drably. She'd hardly expected Quintana to appear in person the moment she landed, nor had she expected to see him so simply dressed, but her second glance confirmed his identity. The match with the holo image Fuchien had shown her was perfect.

"I do—if you have the documentation to prove you're who I think you are," she said calmly, and he gave her a faint smile as he extended a chip.

She slipped it into a reader, checking it against Fuchien's original and watching him from the corner of an eye. She didn't even look up when four heavily-armed bodyguards blended out of the crowd to join him; her free hand simply unsnapped her holster. He saw it, but his eyes only twinkled and he folded his arms unthreateningly across his chest.

Her reader chirped as she completed her examination, and she ejected the chip with a nod.

"Everything checks, Lieutenant Commander," she said, returning it to him. "Sorry if I seemed a bit suspicious."

"I approve of suspicious people—especially when they're being suspicious in my interests," Quintana replied, and extended his hand.

She clasped it, and the familiar sensation of heat enveloped her. The merchant was still speaking, welcoming her to Wyvern, but all Alicia truly "heard" was the soaring, exultant carol of the Fury's triumph.

The Quarn freighter *Aharjhka* loped towards Wyvern at a velocity many a battlecruiser might have envied. For all its size and cargo capacity, *Aharjhka* was lean, rakish, and very, very fast, for the great Quarn trade cartels competed with one another with a fervor other races lavished only on their ships of war.

The bridge hatch opened, and the being a human would have called *Aharjhka*'s captain looked up as a passenger stepped through it.

"Greetings, Inspector. Our instruments have detected the ship you described."

The Quarn's well-modulated voice was deep and resonant, largely because of the density of the atmosphere, for Quarn ships maintained a gravity more than twice that of most human vessels. But the Standard English was almost completely accentless, as well, and Ferhat Ben Belkassem hid a smile. He couldn't help it, for the sheer incongruity of that perfect enunciation from a radially symmetrical cross between a hairy, two-meter-wide starfish and a crazed Impressionist's version of a spider never failed to amuse him.

He crossed to a display at the captain's gesture. Whoever had reconfigured it for human eyes hadn't gotten the color balance quite right, but there was no mistaking the ship in Wyvern orbit. *Star Runner* had made a remarkably swift passage, actually passing *Aharjhka* en route—not that he'd expected anything else.

"So I see, Sir," he said through his helmet's external speaker, and the captain turned the delicate pink the Quarn used in place of a chuckle at the choice of honorific.

Ben Belkassem grinned, and the captain's rosy hue deepened. Quarn had only a single sex—or, rather, every Quarn was a fully functional hermaphrodite—and humanity's gender-linked language conventions tickled their sense of the absurd. But at least it was a shared and tolerant amusement. Different as they were, both species understood biological humor, and humans gave back as good as they got.

The prudish Rish were another matter. If the Quarn found humanity's sexual mores amusing, they found those of the Rish uproarious, and the matriarchs were not amused in return. Worse (from the Rishathan viewpoint), the highly flexible Quarn vocal apparatus could handle both human and Rishathan languages, and they found it particularly amusing to enter a multispecies transit facility, make sure Rish were present, and ask one another "Have you heard the one about the two matriarchs?" in perfect High Rishathan.

Ben Belkassem had been present when one of those jokes led to a lively brawl and an even livelier diplomatic incident—not that the Rish were likely to press the matter too far.

On a personal level, nothing much short of a six-kilo hammer could hurt a Quarn, and even a fully mature matriarch fared poorly against three hundred kilos of muscle and gristle from a 2.4-G home world, whether the possessor of that muscle and gristle was officially warlike or not.

On a diplomatic level, the Terran Empire and Quarn Hegemony were firm allies, a fact the Rishathan Sphere found more than merely unpalatable yet was unable to do much about. It wasn't for want of trying, but even the devious Rishathan diplomatic corps which had once set the Terran League at the Federation's throat had finally given up in disgust. What was a poor racial chauvinist to do? Bizarre as each species found the other's appearance, humankind and Quarnkind liked one another immensely. On the face of it, it was an unlikely pairing. The Rish were at least bipedal, yet they and humans barely tolerated one another, so a reasonable being might have expected even more tension between humanity and the utterly alien Quarn.

Yet it didn't work that way, and Ben Belkassem suspected it was precisely *because* they were so different. The Quarn's heavy-gravity worlds produced atmospheric pressures lethal to any human, which meant they weren't interested in the same sort of real estate; humans and Rish were. Quarn and human sexuality were so different there were virtually no points of congruity; Rish were bisexual—and the matriarchs blamed human notions of sexual equality for the "uppityness" of certain of their own males. There were all too many points of potential conflict between human and Rish, while humans and Quarn had no conflicting physical interests and were remarkably compatible in nonphysical dimensions.

Humans were more combative than the Quarn, who reserved their own ferocity for important things like business, but both were far less militant than the Rishathan matriarchs. They were comfortable with one another, and if the Quarn sometimes felt humans were a mite more warlike than was good for them, they recognized a natural community of interest against the Rish.

Besides, humans could take a joke.

"We will enter orbit in another two hours," *Aharjhka*'s captain announced. "Is there anything else *Aharjhka* can do for you in this matter?"

"No, Sir. If you can just get me down aboard your shuttle without anyone noticing, you'll have done everything I could possibly want."

"That will be no problem, if you are certain it is all you need."

"I am, and I thank you on my own behalf and that of the Empire."

"Not necessary." The captain waved a tentacle tip in dismissal. "The Hegemony understands criminals like these *thugarz*, Inspector, and I remind you that *Aharjhka* has a well-equipped armory if my crew may be of use to you."

The Quarn's rosy tint shaded into a bleaker violet. The Spiders might regard war as a noisy, vulgar, inefficient way to settle differences, but when violence was the only solution, they went about it with the same pragmatism they brought to serious matters like making money. "Merciless as a Quarn" was a high compliment among human merchants, but it held another, grimmer reality, and the Quarn liked pirates even less than humans did. They weren't simply murderous criminals, but murderous criminals who were bad for business.

"I appreciate the thought, Captain, but if I'm right, all the firepower I need is already here. All I have to do is mobilize it."

"Indeed?" The Quarn remained motionless on the toadstool-like pad of its command couch, but two vision clusters swivelled to consider him. "You are a strange human, Inspector, but I almost believe you mean that."

"I do."

"It would be impolite to call you insane, but please remember this is Wyvern."

"I will, I assure you."

"Luck to your trading, then, Inspector. I will have you notified thirty minutes before shuttle departure."

"Thank you, Sir," Ben Belkassem replied, and made his way to the tiny, human-configured cabin hidden in *Aharjhka*'s bowels, moving quickly but carefully against the ship's internal gravity field.

His shoulders straightened gratefully as he crossed the divider into his quarters' one-G field. It was a vast relief to feel his weight drop back where it ought to be, and an even vaster one to dump his helmet and scratch his nose at last. He sighed in relief, then knelt to drag a small trunk from under his bunk and began checking its varied and lethal contents with practiced ease while his mind replayed his conversation with the captain.

He certainly understood the Quarn's concern, but the captain didn't realize how lucky Ben Belkassem had been. *Aharjhka*'s presence at Dewent and scheduled layover at Wyvern had been like filling an inside straight, and the inspector intended to ride the advantage for all it was worth. Very few people knew how closely the Hegemony Judicars and Imperial Ministry of Justice cooperated, and even fewer knew about the private arrangement under which enforcement agents of each imperium traveled freely (and clandestinely) on the other's ships. Which meant no one would be expecting any human—even an O Branch inspector—to debark from *Aharjhka*. *Aharjhka* wasn't listed as a multispecies transport, and only a convinced misanthrope or an intelligent and infinitely resourceful agent would book passage on a vessel whose environment would make him a virtual prisoner in his cabin for the entire voyage.

Of course, Ferhat Ben Belkassem *was* an intelligent and infinitely resourceful agent—he knew he was, for it said so in his Justice Ministry dossier—but even so, he'd almost blown his own cover when he recognized Alicia DeVries on Dewent. It had cost Justice's Intelligence and Operations Branches seven months and three lives to establish that one of Edward Jacoby's (many) partners had links to the pirates' Wyvern-based fence, and they still hadn't figured out which of them it was. Yet DeVries had homed in on

Fuchien as if she had a map, and she'd built herself a far better cover than O Branch could have provided.

Ben Belkassem had personally double-checked the documentation on *Star Runner,* her captain, and her crew, and he'd never seen such an exquisitely detailed (and utterly fictitious) legend. He supposed he shouldn't be surprised, given the way DeVries had escaped hospital security on Soissons, penetrated Jefferson Field, and stolen one of the Imperial Fleet's prized alpha-synths. If she could make *that* look easy, why not this?

Because she was a drop commando, not a trained operative—that was why. How had she come by such perfectly forged papers? Where had she recruited her crew? For that matter, how did she cram them all aboard what had to be the stolen alpha-synth? It couldn't be anything else, whatever it *looked* like, but how in the name of all that was holy did she slide blithely through customs at a world like MaGuire? Ben Belkassem had never personally crossed swords with Jungian customs, but he knew their reputation. He couldn't conceive of any way they could have inspected "*Star Runner*" without at least noticing that the "freighter" was armed to the proverbial teeth!

It seemed, he thought dryly, checking the charge indicator on a disrupter, that the good captain had lost none of her penchant for doing the impossible. And, as he'd once told Colonel McIlhenny, he hadn't amassed his record by looking serendipity in the mouth. Whatever she was up to and however she was bringing it off, she'd not only managed to find the link he'd sought but done so in a way which actually got her inside the pipeline. Under those circumstances, he was perfectly content to throw his own weeks of work out the airlock and follow along in her wake.

And, he told himself as he buckled his gun belt and slid the disrupter into its holster, even a drop commando could use a bit of backup, whatever her unlikely abilities . . . and whether she knew she had it or not.

Alicia retina-printed the last document and watched Oscar Quintana's secretary carry the paperwork from the palatial office. The merchant pushed his chair back and rose, turning to the well-stocked bar opposite his desk.

"A rapid and satisfactory transaction, Captain Mainwaring. Now that it's out of the way, name your poison."

"I'm not too particular, as long as it pours," Alicia replied, glancing casually about the office. <*I don't see any obvious pick-ups,*> she thought at Tisiphone. <*How about you?*>

<*There are none. Quintana does not care to be spied upon in his own lair—that much I have obtained from him already.*>

<*Think we've got enough time?*>

<*I know not, but sufficient or no, this may be the only time we have.*>

<*Then let's go for it,*> Alicia said.

She rose from her own chair and walked across to Quintana. He glanced up from the clear, green liqueur he was pouring into tiny glasses, then capped the bottle and smiled.

"I trust you'll enjoy this, Captain. It's a local product, from one of my own distilleries, and—"

His voice chopped off as Alicia touched his hand. He froze, mouth open, eyes blank, and Alicia blinked in momentary disorientation of her own as the flood of data poured into her brain. Their earlier handshake had been sufficient to confirm their quarry but too brief for detailed examination of Quintana's knowledge. They'd dared not probe this way then, lest one of his bodyguards notice his glaze-eyed stillness and react precipitously.

It was still a risk, but Alicia was too caught up in the knowledge flow to worry about someone's opening the door and finding them like this. If it happened, it happened, and in the meantime . . . .

Images and memories flared as Tisiphone plucked them from Quintana. Meetings with someone named Alexsov. Credit balances that soared magically as loot from pillaged worlds flowed through his hands. Contact times and purchase orders. Customers and distributors on other Rogue Worlds and even on imperial planets. All of them flashed through her, each of them stored indelibly for later attention, and again and again she saw the mysterious Alexsov. Alexsov and a man called d'Amcourt, who listed and coordinated the pirates' purchases, and a woman called Shu, who frightened the powerful merchant noble, however he might deny it to himself. Yet both of those others deferred to Alexsov without question. There was no doubt in Quintana's mind—or in Alicia's—that Alexsov was one of the pirates' senior officers, and she wanted to scream in frustration at how little Quintana knew of him.

But at least she now knew what he looked like, and . . .

Her green eyes brightened as the last, elusive details clicked. Alexsov due to return here soon . . . and Quintana's own constant need for dependable carriers.

Her hungry smile echoed the Fury's hunting snarl, and she felt Tisiphone reach even deeper, no longer taking thoughts but implanting them. A few more brief seconds sufficed, and then Quintana's eyes snapped back into focus and his voice continued, smooth and unhurried, unaware of any break.

"—I highly recommend it."

He handed her one of the glasses, and she sipped, then smiled in unfeigned enjoyment. It was sweet yet sharp, almost astringent, and it flowed down her throat like rich, liquid fire.

"I see why you think highly of it," she said. He nodded and waved at the chairs around a coffee table of rich native woods. She sank into one of them, and he sat opposite her, peering pensively down into his glass.

"Lewis said you have a charter on Cathcart, Captain Mainwaring?"

"Yes, I do," Alicia confirmed, and he frowned.

"That's a pity. I might have a profitable commission for you here, if you could see your way to accepting it."

"What sort of commission?"

"Very much like the one you've just discharged, but with a considerably higher profit margin."

"Ah?" Alicia crooked an eyebrow thoughtfully. "How considerably?"

"Twice as great—at a minimum," Quintana replied, and she let her other eyebrow rise.

"I suppose you might call that 'considerably higher,'" she murmured. "Still, Cathcart is a bird in the hand, Lieutenant Commander, and—"

"Oscar, please," he interrupted, and she blinked, this time in genuine surprise. From what she'd seen of Quintana's mind, he didn't encourage familiarity with his employees. On the other hand—

<*On the other hand, Little One,*> a voice whispered dryly in her mind, <*you are a handsome woman and he is a connoisseur of women. And, no,*> the voice added even more dryly, <*I did* not *instill any such notion in his mind!*>

"Oscar, then," Alicia said aloud. "As I was saying, I *know* I have a cargo on Cathcart, and the port master will slap me with a forfeit penalty if I don't collect it as scheduled."

"True." Quintana pondered a moment, then shrugged. "I can't guarantee the commission I'm thinking of, Theodosia—may I call you Theodosia?" Alicia nodded and he continued. "Thank you. I can't guarantee it because there are other principals involved, but I believe you and *Star Runner* would be perfect for it. I'm reasonably confident my colleagues will agree with me, and even if they don't, I have other consignments for a discreet and reliable skipper, so I have a proposal for you. I anticipate seeing one of my senior colleagues in the near future. Starcom your regrets to your Cathcart contract, and I'll introduce you to him when he arrives. If he accepts my recommendation, you'll make enough to cover your forfeit and still show a much higher profit than on this last shipment. If he chooses to make other arrangements, I will personally guarantee you commissions of at least equal value."

Alicia let herself consider the offer carefully, then shrugged.

"How can I pass up an offer like that? I accept, of course," she said . . . and she smiled.

CHAPTER FIFTY-EIGHT

The small, well-dressed diner accepted the proffered chair with distracted courtesy, then reached into his jacket for a micro-comp. He set it beside his plate, punched up a complicated list of stock transactions, and studied them intently. Only the most suspicious might have noticed the way he set it down, and only the truly paranoid would have suspected the ultra-sensitive microphone concealed in the end pointed toward a nearby table.

Ben Belkassem spread a small sheaf of hardcopy on the table, then punched more keys and brought up yet another layer of meaningless sales while he uncapped his stylus. He scribbled notes on the hardcopy, frowning in concentration as the tiny ear bug from his computer whispered to him.

". . . derstand, Captain." Oscar Quintana sipped wine and blotted his lips, eyes gleaming with sardonic amusement. "It's regrettable, of course, but a certain . . . wastage must be anticipated in any transaction."

"Precisely. But the object is to make certain the wastage is suffered in the right place."

Gregor Alexsov's own wine sat untasted, and Quintana smothered a mental sigh. The man had done wonderful things for his credit balance, but there was no lightness, no sense of what the game was all about, in him. Those hard, brown eyes swivelled over his face like targeting lasers, and the thin lips wrinkled in what was obviously intended as a smile.

Sad, so sad, but that probably represented Alexsov's best effort. Well, a man couldn't be good at everything, Quintana supposed.

"If you'll give me a list of what you want wasted and where, I'll see to it," he said.

"Thank you." Alexsov's eyes moved away, scanning the crowded restaurant, and his mouth tightened with disapproval. "I'll have it for you by the time we reach some less public place."

"I applaud your caution, Captain Alexsov," Quintana said, ignoring the way his guest winced at the use of his name, "but it's unnecessary."

"Perhaps, but I dislike meeting among so many strangers."

"None of whom," Quintana pointed out, "are close enough to hear a word we're saying. Half the deals on Wyvern are concluded in this restaurant, Captain, because it's swept for bugs several times a day, and despite your concern, we've been less than specific. Even had we not, none of our business violates any of Wyvern's laws, and—" he gestured dryly at the six well-armed retainers seated at flanking tables "—I hardly think anyone would be foolish enough to intrude on us. I *am* Lieutenant Commander Defiant, you know."

"No doubt. But an agent of the Empire, or even some of your nonimperial neighbors, might not care."

"Which would be fatally foolish of him, Captain." Steel glinted behind Quintana's smile as his relaxed pose slipped for just a moment, and his eyes locked with Alexsov's. Then he shrugged and waved a hand, banishing the mood. "Have it as you will, however. In the meantime, I think I may have located just the skipper we need. She's a newcomer to Wyvern, but her credentials are excellent. Good-looking young woman, but she's already demonstrated her competence on several occasions, and—"

Ben Belkassem's meal arrived. He made himself smile around a silent curse on all efficient waiters as he put his computer away, but he'd heard enough. He knew now why DeVries had spent the last three weeks cultivating Quintana, and he had a name—one which was almost certainly genuine, given "Alexsov's" reaction to its use—beyond the Wyverian. Perhaps even more importantly, it seemed DeVries was about to move another link up the chain.

The inspector sampled his food with an admiring smile. He didn't know how she was manipulating her enemies, but no one could get this far this fast on pure luck. For all his ego, Quintana was a shrewd operator; she had to be influencing him some way to win such a recommendation after carrying a single cargo for him, and the inspector wondered what sort of magic wand she used.

He paused, smile fading at a sudden thought. *He* knew she was working Quintana somehow—might it be equally obvious to someone else? Of course, he had the advantage of knowing who she was and some of the other things she'd done, but if anyone ran an analysis and recognized her straight-line movement to Wyvern or, worse, checked her career before MaGuire . . .

He laid aside his fork and reached for his own wineglass, remembering Alexsov's evident caution, and his brain was busy behind his eyes.

Commander Barr looked up in surprise as Captain Alexsov strode onto *Harpy*'s bridge. He hadn't expected the chief of staff back aboard for another hour, and his expression suggested he had something on his mind.

"Good evening, Sir. Can I help you?"

"Yes." Alexsov slid into the exec's chair and reached for the synth-link headset. "Patch me into the port records, please."

Barr nodded to his communications officer, then turned his chair to face Alexsov.

"May I ask what you're looking for, Sir?"

"I don't know yet." Alexsov smiled thinly at the CO's expression. "I may not be looking for anything at all, but if I find it, I'll recognize it."

"Of course, Sir."

Barr turned his chair tactfully away as the chief of staff closed his eyes in concentration. This was Alexsov's first trip in *Harpy*, but aside from a certain fetish with schedules, he'd evinced few of the oddities Barr's fellows had warned him about. Until now, at least.

Alexsov suspected what Barr was thinking, but it bothered him far less than his inability to pin down what made him so uneasy. It was just that it was unlike Quintana to recommend *any* captain, much less one he'd dealt with only once, as enthusiastically as this one. Of course, if Mainwaring was as attractive as Quintana had implied, that might explain a good bit of his enthusiasm, Quintana being Quintana. Still, whatever had aroused his initial admiration, her record since entering the Franconia Sector was impressive. She had a fast ship, and she'd certainly demonstrated a short way with would-be hijackers. That cargo of Dreamy White was a point in her favor, too; anyone who'd transport that had very few scruples.

He reached the end of the data and leaned back, frowning without opening his eyes. If only the woman had a longer history in-sector! Without querying the Melville data base directly via starcom—and vague concern was hardly enough to justify that sort of risk or expense—he couldn't check her previous record. There was nothing in her recent activities to arouse suspicion, and if this was a false background, it was the most convincing one he'd ever seen. But perhaps that was the real problem. Maybe she was too good to be true?

Nonsense! He was getting as paranoid as Rachel Shu! But that paranoia, he acknowledged, was exactly what made Rachel such a success.

His frown deepened. Smitten by her looks or no, Quintana must have checked her out. The merchant's dealings might be legal under Wyverian law, but Quintana had to know how meaningless that would be if the Empire ever discovered them. O Branch had no qualms about arranging a quiet little kidnapping or assassination, and ONI would be right behind them on this one. Possibly not even such a quiet assassination. The Empire would want other Rogue Worlders to rethink their positions on aiding its enemies.

He removed his headset and coiled the lead with methodical neatness.

Every indication was that Captain Mainwaring was genuine. If she was, she could prove an invaluable resource; if she wasn't, she was a deadly danger. Any operative who could penetrate this deeply had to be eliminated, but all he had was a worry—a "hunch," much as he hated the word—and that wasn't enough. Rachel, he suspected, would simply have her killed out of hand, but Rachel wasn't noted for moderation, and if his hunch was wrong, Mainwaring was just as perfect for the job as Quintana thought.

Fortunately, there was a way to be certain. He put the headset away, nodded briefly to Commander Barr, and headed for sickbay.

* * *

The hover cab stopped outside the imposing gates, and Alicia stepped out into Wyvern's autumn night, damp and rich with the scent of unfamiliar, decaying leaf mold. She fed her credit card into the cab's charge unit and looked around, tugging her bolero straight. Chateau Defiant lay thirty kilometers from town, and clouds hid both moons. Without sensory boosters, the blackness would have been Stygian; even with them, it was dark enough to make her jumpy—especially in light of the importance of this meeting.

<Calm down, Alley. Get your pulse back down where it belongs, girl!>

<Yes, Ma'am,> Alicia thought back obediently, and brought her augmentation on line. Her racing heart slowed, and she felt herself relax. Not enough to lose her edge, but enough to kill the jitters.

<Just keep your head together, okay? I want you—hell, I want both *of you—back up here in one piece. Or two. Or whatever.>*

<Have no fear, Megaira. I shall keep my eye upon her.>

<Ha! That's what worries me most!>

Alicia swallowed a chuckle as she reclaimed her credit card. The gates opened silently, and Quintana's voice issued from the speaker below their visual pickup.

"Hi, Theodosia! We're in the Green Parlor. You know the way."

"Pour the drinks, Oscar," she replied with a cheerful wave. "I'll see you in a couple of minutes."

"Good," Quintana said, and switched off with an unhappy glance at Gregor Alexsov. "Is this really necessary?" he asked, gesturing distastefully at the peculiar, long-barreled pistol one of Alexsov's people carried.

"I'm afraid so." Alexsov nodded, and the man with the pistol retreated into the next room and pulled the door almost closed. "I trust you completely, Oscar, but we can't afford any slips. If she's as trustworthy as you believe, it won't hurt her a bit. If not . . ."

He shrugged.

Alicia strode up the walk with brisk familiarity. She'd been here several times in the past weeks, although Oscar Quintana's memories of her overnight visits differed somewhat from her own. She grinned at the thought, relaxing further with the amusement, and never noticed the catlike shape that slid tracelessly through Quintana's sophisticated security systems behind her.

She was one of Quintana's "special friends" now, and the retainer who met her at the door gave her a wry, half-apologetic smile as he held out his hand. She smiled back and slid her CHK from its holster, then handed over her survival knife and the twenty-centimeter force blade from her left boot. He stowed them carefully away and gestured politely at the scan panel beside him, and Alicia made a face.

"O ye of little faith," she murmured, but it wasn't bad manners on Wyvern, where titles of nobility—and estates—had been known to change hands with sudden and violent unexpectedness. No doubt Tisiphone could have gotten an entire arsenal past the man behind the scanners, just as she did Alicia's augmentation, but there was no real point in it.

"There, see?" she said as he peered at her internal hardware without seeing it.

He smiled at her teasing tone and bowed her past, and she grinned back as she turned down a corridor hung in priceless tapestries. If not for the way it was paid for, she could have gotten used to this kind of life, she thought, nodding to an occasional servant as she passed.

The double doors to what Quintana modestly called the Green Parlor stood open. She stepped through them, and he turned to greet her, standing beside a tallish man she recognized from his mind.

"Theodosia. Allow me to introduce Captain Gregor Alexsov."

"Captain." Alicia held out her hand and made herself smile brightly.

"Captain Mainwaring." Alexsov extended his own hand graciously. She took it and felt the familiar heat, then—

<*No, Alicia!*> Tisiphone screamed in her mind, and something made a soft, quiet "PFFFFT!" sound behind her.

Ben Belkassem muttered balefully as he filtered through the pitch-black grounds. This damned house was even bigger than he'd thought from the plans, and he'd almost missed two different sensors already. He paused in the denser darkness under an ornamental tree and checked his inertial tracer against the plat of the grounds. Quintana had mentioned the "Green Parlor," and if his map was right that was right over there . . .

Alicia gasped and snapped around to stare at Quintana as pain pricked the back of her neck. He looked distressed—he was actually wringing his hands—and her eyes popped back to Alexsov, then widened as she collapsed. The carpet bloodied her nose as her face hit it, and deep within her she felt the elemental rage of the Fury.

She tried to thrust herself back up, but Alexsov had chosen his attack well. He knelt beside her, and she couldn't even feel his hands as he removed the tiny dart and rolled her, not ungently, onto her back.

"I apologize for the necessity, Captain Mainwaring," he murmured, "but it's only a temporary nerve block." He snapped his fingers, and one of his henchmen handed him a hypospray. "And this," he went on soothingly, pressing the hypo to her arm, "is a perfectly harmless truth drug."

Horrified understanding filled Alicia as the hypo nestled home.

<*Tisiphone!*> she screamed.

<*I am trying!*> Anger and fear—for Alicia, not herself—snarled in the Fury's reply. <*Their cursed block has cut off your main processor, but—*>

The hypo hissed, and Tisiphone cursed horribly as the drug flooded into Alicia's system . . . and her augmentation sensed it.

She gasped and jerked, and Alexsov leapt back in consternation. Even that small movement should have been impossible, and his brow furrowed in lightning speculation as she quivered on the carpet. Escape protocols blossomed within her, fighting the nerve block, trying to get her on her feet, but they couldn't, and panic wailed in her mind as the idiot savant of her processor considered its internal programs. Escape was impossible, it decided, and truth drugs had been administered.

Ben Belkassem eased through the ornamental shrubbery to the glowing windows. Their translucent green curtains let light escape yet were too thick to see through, but he'd expected that. He checked for security sensors and placed a tiny, sensitive microphone against the glass.

". . . happening?!" Naked panic quivered in Oscar Quintana's voice. "You said she was just supposed to be paralyzed, damn it!"

"I don't *know* what it is." That lower, calmer voice belonged to the man named Alexsov, Ben Belkassem thought—then stiffened as understanding caught up with his racing mind. Paralyzed! Dear God, they must be on to her!

Alicia's eyes glazed. She was numb below the neck, but she felt the neuro-toxin in her gasping respiration, the growing sluggishness of her mind.

To come this far, she thought despairingly. To get this close—!

Glass shattered behind Oscar Quintana, and he whirled. The tinkling sound still hung in his ears as the curtains parted, and he had a vague impression of a black-clad figure that raised a hand in his direction. Then the emerald green beam struck just above his left eye and he died.

Ben Belkassem hit the carpet rolling and cursing his own stupidity. He should have pulled out, goddamn it! What DeVries had already accomplished was more important than either of their lives—far too important for him to throw away playing holovid hero! But his body had reacted before his brain, and he skittered frantically across the floor towards a solid, ornate desk while answering disrupter beams flashed about him.

Somehow he made it into cover, and his shoulder heaved. The desk crashed over, blocking the deadly beams, and his machine-pistol popped into his free hand.

Someone else had a slug-thrower, and he winced as penetrators chewed into the desktop. Its wood couldn't stop that kind of fire, and he ducked to his left, exposing himself just long enough to find the firer. His disrupter whined, and the fire stopped, but he felt no exultation. He'd seen DeVries in that moment—seen the way her body quivered weakly—and his mind flashed back to Tannis Cateau's briefings.

She was dying, and he swore viciously as he rose on his knees to nail a second gunman with his CHK. The thunder of weapons shook the room, Quintana's guards had to be on their way, more penetrators chewed at the desk, and then someone killed the lights and the chaos became total.

Tisiphone battered at the block with all her might, then made herself stop. She had to get into Alicia's main processor to reach her pharmacope, but the drug Alexsov had used blocked voluntary nervous impulses and sealed the processor's input tantalizingly beyond her reach. She couldn't reach it, yet she had to. She had to!

And then it came to her. The block couldn't cut off its victim's *in*voluntary muscles without killing her, and the processor's *output* reached *all* of Alicia's functions! And that meant—

Ben Belkassem cried out and dropped his pistol as a tungsten penetrator slammed through his upper arm, yet he scarcely felt it. Any minute someone else would come in through those windows behind him and he'd be as dead as Alicia DeVries. Someone with more guts than sense rushed him. The flash of his disrupter lit the darkness with emerald lightning, seventy kilos of dead meat slammed to the carpet, and white-hot muzzle flashes stabbed at him as his own shot drew the fire of another machine-pistol. He wasn't afraid as the penetrators screamed past—there was no time for fear—yet under the wild adrenaline rush was the bitter knowledge of how completely he had failed.

But then the man behind the machine-pistol screamed. It was a horrible, gurgling sound . . . and Ben Belkassem knew *he* hadn't caused it.

There was an instant of shocked silence, and then someone else was firing. Someone who fired in short, deadly bursts, as if the darkness were light, and the whining disrupters were no longer firing at him. He shoved himself up on his knees and gawked in disbelief.

He had no idea why Alicia DeVries wasn't dead or how she'd reached the man whose weapon she was firing, and it didn't matter. The rock-steady pistol picked off guards with machinelike precision. She was a ghost, appearing in glaring muzzle flashes only to vanish back into the darkness like death's own ballerina, and the screams and shrieks of the dying were her orchestra.

But then her magazine was empty, and there were still three enemies left. Ben Belkassem hunted for them desperately, lacing the smoke-heavy blackness with disrupter fire in a frantic effort to cover her, then groaned in despair as an emerald shaft struck her squarely between the shoulders.

DeVries grunted, but she didn't go down, and his own disrupter fell to his side in shock.

She was dead. She *had* to be dead this time! But she spun toward the man who'd shot her even as two more disrupters hit her. A vicious kick snapped his neck, and the two remaining guards screamed in terrified disbelief as she charged them. One of them rained green bolts upon her as she closed, but the other tried to run. It made no difference; the fleeing guard got as far as opening the door, spilling light into the death-filled gloom, and then he died, as well.

She spun again, whirling to face Ben Belkassem, and he dropped his weapon and raised his good hand with frantic haste.

"Stop! I'm on *your* side!"

She slid to a halt, jacket charred from disrupter hits, and frozen eyes regarded him from a face of inhuman calm.

"Ben Belkassem! I'm Ferhat Ben Belkassem!" he said desperately, and saw recognition in those icy eyes. "I—"

"Later." Her voice was as inhumanly calm as her expression. "Get over there and cover the door."

Ben Belkassem scrabbled up his weapons and raced to the door before his dazed mind even considered arguing, and only then did he truly realize how quick and brutal the fight had been. He fed a fresh clip into his pistol, clumsy with only one working arm, and when he looked out into the corridor the first of Quintana's retainers were only now racing towards him. He dropped the three leaders, then glanced over his shoulder as the survivors fell back.

DeVries knelt beside Alexsov, ignoring the blood soaking his tunic and pooling about her knees. She pressed her hands to his temples, leaning over him, her face almost touching his as blood bubbled on his lips, and Ben Belkassem shuddered and turned back to his front. He didn't know what she was doing. What was more, he didn't think he *wanted* to know.

More guards came at him. These had found time to scramble into unpowered armor, and the loads in his CHK were too light to get through it at anything above point-blank range. He dropped it and shifted to his disrupter, praying the charge held out. Five more men went down, and then the survivors withdrew to regroup.

Something thundered behind him, and he swore feelingly. DeVries was by the windows, firing someone else's weapon out into the grounds. They were pinned; no matter how many they killed, the others would get them in the end. But he'd seen the way DeVries moved. If either of them could make it . . .

"I'll cover you!" he shouted, starting towards the window

"Watch your front," she said calmly, never even turning her head. "These bastards have a surprise coming."

There was no time to ask what she was talking about. A fresh rush was coming down the corridor, and a buzz from his disrupter warned of an exhausted charge as he beat it back. Her "surprise" had better come soon, or—

Something howled in the dark. Something huge and black, borne on a cyclone of turbines, wing edges and nose incandescent from reentry. Chateau Defiant heaved as rockets and plasma cannon shattered its other wings, and Ben Belkassem rolled across the floor, coughing on smoke and powdered stone.

A steely hand grabbed his collar, dragged him out the windows, and hurled him at the grounded assault shuttle. He charged its ramp like his last hope of salvation, DeVries on his heels, and heard incoming fire spanging off the armored hull and the whine of powered turrets and the end-of-the-world bellow as the shuttle's calliopes covered their retreat. He staggered through the troop bay to the flight deck and slumped against a bulkhead, suddenly aware of the pain in his arm and the weakness of blood loss, as the shuttle leapt back into the heavens.

DeVries shouldered past him to the pilot's couch, and he slid down to sit on the deck in fresh shock that owed little to blood loss as he realized that seat had been empty when the shuttle swept down to save them.

He sat there, searching for a rational explanation, but none occurred to his muzzy brain. Disrupter fire had charred her jacket in half a dozen places, yet she was alive. That was insane enough, but where was her crew? And what in God's name had she been doing with Alexsov back there?

"What—?"

He stopped and coughed, surprised by the croak of his own voice, and she spared him a glance.

"Hang on," she said in that same calm voice, and he clutched for a handhold as something fast and lethal sizzled past and she whipped the shuttle into wild evasive action—without, he noted numbly, even bothering to don the flight control synth headset.

And then she started talking to herself.

"Okay. Dial 'em in and take them out," she told the empty air.

He clawed his way forward and tumbled into the copilot's seat just as something carved a screaming column of light through the night. He gaped out the cockpit canopy, then jerked back as terrible white fire erupted far below. Another followed, and a third, and DeVries spared him a wolf's smile. She flipped on the com—he hadn't even realized it was turned off—and an angry male voice filled the flight deck.

". . . say again! Cease fire on our shuttle, or we will destroy your spaceport! This is First Officer Jeff Okahara of the starship *Star Runner*, and this is your final warning!"

"Way to go, Megaira," his pilot murmured, and Ben Belkassem closed his eyes. It had been such an *orderly* universe this morning, he thought almost calmly.

"*Star Runner*, you are ordered to return your shuttle and its occupants to the port immediately to answer for their unprovoked attack on Lieutenant Commander Defiant's estate!" another voice roared over the com.

"Bugger off!" Okahara snarled back. "Your precious lieutenant commander just got what he fucking well had coming!"

"*What?*! What do you mean—"

"I mean you'd better notify his heirs! And anybody else who tries to murder our captain is going to get the same!"

"Listen, you—"

The furious voice chopped off. Ben Belkassem heard another voice, quick and urgent, muttering words that included "HVW" and "battle screen," and looked across at Alicia again.

"Quite a freighter you have there, Captain Mainwaring," he murmured.

"Isn't it?" The turbines died as the shuttle streaked beyond air-breathing altitude and the thrusters took over. "Strap in. We don't have time to decelerate, so Megaira's going to snag us with a tractor as we go by."

"Megaira? Who's Megaira?"

"A friend of mine," she replied with a strange little smile.

Commander Quentin Barr couldn't believe any of it. One minute everything was calm, the next a shuttle from an unarmed freighter screamed planetward at insane velocity and reduced Chateau Defiant (and, presumably, Captain Alexsov) to flaming rubble. And when Groundside tried to down the shuttle, that same unarmed freighter blew the engaging weapon stations into next week with HVW!

Barr had no better idea of what was happening than anyone else, but his drive was working hard, because he knew *Harpy* didn't even want to think about engaging that "freighter." God only knew what it might produce *next*, and he intended to be several light-seconds away before it got around to it.

Now he stared into his aft display, wondering who was aboard that shuttle. He could still nail it short of the freighter—which was putting out *battle screen* now, for God's sake!—which might be a good idea. Except that Captain Alexsov *might* be aboard it. And, Barr admitted, except that firing on it seemed to be a good way to convince the freighter to respond in kind.

Then he no longer had the option. The shuttle slashed towards the freighter at far too high an approach speed, only to stop with bone-breaking suddenness as a tractor yanked it inside the screen. Barr winced. He'd been through exactly the same maneuver in training exercises, but his sympathy was limited, for the freighter was already swinging to pursue him.

A groggy Ben Belkassem swam back to awareness draped across Alicia DeVries' back in a fireman's carry. It was an undignified position, but he was in no condition to argue, and a part of him apologized for every doubt he'd ever entertained over Sir Arthur Keita's descriptions of drop commandos.

She dumped him gently on the floor of the ship's elevator and crouched beside him, ripping his blood-soaked sleeve apart.

"Nice and clean," she told him. "Got some nasty tissue damage, but it missed the bone." He hissed as she strapped a pressure bandage tight. "We'll take care of that in a minute. Right now we've got other worries."

"Like what?" he gasped.

"Like eight Wyvern Navy cruisers and a Fleet tin can we have to kill."

"Kill a *Fleet destroyer?!*"

"The one Alexsov came from, HMS *Harpy*. Her transponder's buggered to ID her as *Medusa*, but—"

The lift door opened, and she seemed to teleport through it. Ben Belkassem followed more slowly onto what he realized must be the bridge and peered about him.

"Where is everybody?"

"You're looking at everybody. Megaira, give him a display."

He jumped as a holo display sprang to life, hanging in midair and livid with the red-ringed blue dots of hostile Fasset drives. Eight came from the direction of Wyvern, already shrinking astern; a ninth glowed dead ahead.

Commander Barr swallowed bile. *Harpy* was putting everything she had into her drive . . . and the cursed freighter was *gaining*. It was running away from the Wyverian cruisers with absurd ease, shrugging aside everything they and the planetary defenses could throw without even bothering to reply. Clearly it had other concerns.

"Stand by! The instant they flip to engage us, I want—"

"And now . . ." Alicia murmured beside Ben Belkassem.

Quentin Barr and the entire company of HMS *Harpy* died before they even realized their pursuer had already flipped.

CHAPTER FIFTY-NINE

Delicious smells filled the small galley, and Ferhat Ben Belkassem sat at the table. He wore a highly atypical air of bemusement and sprawled in his chair without his usual neatness, but then he'd earned a little down time—and hadn't expected to live to enjoy it.

He felt a bit like the ancient Alice as he watched Captain DeVries stir tomato-rich sauce with a neurosurgeon's concentration. Her dyed hair was coiled in a thick braid, and she looked absurdly young. It was hard to credit his own memory of icy eyes and lightning muzzle flashes as she sampled the sauce and reached for more basil. The lid rose from a pot beside her, hovering in midair on an invisible tractor beam, and linguine drifted from a storage bin to settle neatly in the boiling water.

"And what do you think you're doing? I told you I'd put that in when I was ready," she said, and this time he barely twitched. He was starting to adjust to her one-sided conversations with the ship's AI—even if they were yet another of the "impossible" things she did so casually.

Ben Belkassem had boned up on the alpha-synths after DeVries stole this ship. Too much was classified for him to learn as much as he would have liked, but he'd learned enough to know her augmentation didn't include the normal alpha-synth com link. Without it, the AI should have been forced to communicate back by voice, not some sort of . . . of *telepathy!*

Yet he was beyond surprise where DeVries was concerned. After all, she'd survived multiple disrupter hits with no more than a few minor burns, killed eleven men saving his own highly trained self, taken out a few ground-to-space weapon emplacements, escaped through the heart of Wyvern's very respectable fortifications, and polished off a destroyer as an encore. As far as he was concerned, she could do anything she damned well liked.

She murmured something else to the empty air, too softly this time for him to hear, and he sat very still as plates and silverware swooped from cupboard to table like strange birds. Yes, he thought, *very* like Alice, though a bit more of this and he could qualify as the March Hare. Or perhaps DeVries already had that role and he'd be forced to settle for the Mad Hatter.

He smiled at the thought, and she spared him a smile of her own as she set the sauce on the table and produced a bottle of wine. He raised an eyebrow at the Defiant Vineyards label, and she sighed as she filled their glasses.

"He really was an outstanding vintner. Too bad he couldn't have stopped there."

"Um, you *are* speaking to me, this time, Captain?"

"You might as well call me Alicia," she said by way of answer, dropping into the chair opposite him as the pot of pasta moved to the sink, drained itself, and drifted to the table.

"Dinner is served," she murmured. "Help yourself, Inspector."

"Fair's fair. If you're Alicia, I'm Ferhat."

She nodded agreement and heaped linguine on her plate, then reached for the sauce ladle while Ben Belkassem eyed the huge serving of pasta.

"Are you sure your stomach's up to this?" he asked, remembering the tearing violent nausea which had wracked her less than two hours before.

"Well," she ladled sauce with a generous hand and grinned at him, "it's not like there's anything down there to get in its way."

"I see." It was untrue, but if she cared to enlighten him she would. He served his own plate one-handedly, sipped his wine, and regarded her quizzically. "I don't believe I've gotten around to thanking you yet. That was about the most efficiently I've ever been rescued by my intended rescuee."

She shrugged a bit uncomfortably. "Without you I'd've been dead, too. Just how long have you been tailing me, anyway?"

"Only since Dewent, and I had a hard time believing it when I first spotted you. You know about the reward?" She nodded, and he chuckled. "Somehow I don't think anyone's going to collect it. How the devil did you get so deep so quickly? It took O Branch seven months to get as far as Jacoby, and we still hadn't fingered Fuchien."

She looked at him oddly, then shrugged again.

"Tisiphone helped. And Megaira, of course."

"Oh. Ah, may I take it Megaira is your AI?"

"What else should I call her?" she asked with a smile.

"From what I've read about alpha-synth symbioses," he said carefully, "the AI usually winds up with the same name as the human partner."

"Must get pretty confusing," another voice said, and Ben Belkassem jumped. His head whipped around, and the new voice chuckled as his eye found the intercom speaker. "Since you're talking about me, I thought I might as well speak up, Inspector. Or do I get to call you Ferhat, too?"

He spoke firmly to his pulse. He'd known the AI was there, but that didn't diminish his astonishment. He'd worked with more than his share of cyber-synth AIs, and they were at least as alien as one might have expected. They simply didn't have a human perspective, and most were totally disinterested in anyone other than their cyber-synth partners. When they did speak, they sounded quite inhuman, and none of them had been issued a sense of humor.

But this one was an *alpha*-synth AI, he reminded himself, and its voice, not unreasonably, sounded remarkably like Alicia's.

"'Ferhat' will be fine, um, Megaira," he said after a moment.

"Fine. But if you call me 'Maggie' I'll reverse flow in the head the next time you sit down."

"I wouldn't dream of it," he said a bit faintly.

"Alley did . . . once."

"A base lie," Alicia put in around a mouthful of food. "She makes things up all the time. Sometimes—" she held Ben Belkassem's eyes across the table "—you might almost think she's shy a brick or two."

"Point taken," the inspector said, beginning to wind linguine around his fork. "But you were saying she and . . . Tisiphone helped you?"

"Well," Alicia waved at the bulkheads, "you certainly saw how Megaira—by the way, that's '*Star Runner*'s' real name, too—got us off Wyvern."

"So she did, and most efficiently, too."

"Why, thank you, kind Sir," the speaker said. "I see he's a perceptive man, Alley."

"And your modesty underwhelms us all," Alicia returned dryly.

"Oh, yeah? Just remember, I got it from you."

Ben Belkassem choked on pasta. *Definitely* not your typical AI. But his humor faded as Alicia replied to Megaira.

"I'll remember. And *you* just remember I'd still've been dead if not for Tisiphone." She looked back at Ben Belkassem. "She was the one who jump-started my augmentation after that bastard knocked it out."

"Really?"

"Don't sound so dubious." He felt himself blush—something he hadn't done in years—and she snorted. "Of course she did. Who do you think put me back on line after Tannis and Uncle Arthur shut me down? I don't exactly have an on-off switch in the middle of my forehead!"

He took another bite to avoid answering, and her eyes glinted.

"Of course, that's not all she does," she continued, leaning across her plate with a conspiratorial air. "She reads minds, too. That's how I know just who to look for as my next target. And she creates a pretty mean illusion, as well—not to mention sticking the occasional idea into someone else's brain." He gawked at her, and she smiled brightly. "Oh, and she and Megaira do a dynamite job of raiding other people's data bases . . . or planting data in them, like '*Star Runner*'s' Melville Sector documentation."

She paused expectantly, and he swallowed. It was too much. Logic said she had to be telling the truth, but sanity said it was all impossible, and he was trapped between them.

"Well, yes," he said weakly, "but—"

"Oh, come on, Ferhat!" she snapped, glaring as if at a none too bright student who'd muffed a pop quiz. "You just talked to Megaira, right?" He nodded. "Well, if you don't have a problem accepting an intelligence—a person—who lives in *that* computer," she jabbed an index finger in the general direction of *Megaira*'s bridge, "what's the big deal about accepting one who lives in *this* computer—" the same finger thumped her temple "—with me?"

"Put that way," he said slowly, easing his left arm in its sling, "I don't suppose there should be one. But you have to admit it's a bit hard to accept that a mythological creature's moved in with you."

"I don't have to admit anything of the sort, and I'm getting sick and tired of making allowances for everyone else. Damn it, everybody just *assumes* I'm crazy! Not a one of you, not even Tannis, ever even considered the possibility that Tisiphone might just really exist!"

"That's not quite true," he said, and it was her turn to pause. She made a small gesture, inviting him to continue.

"Actually," he told her, "Sir Arthur never questioned that she was 'real' in the sense of someone—or something—in your own mind." He raised a hand as her eyes fired up. "I know that's not what you meant, but he'd gotten as far as worrying that something had activated some sort of psi talent in you and produced a 'Tisiphone persona,' I suppose you'd call it, and I think he may have gone a bit further, whether he knew it or not. That's the real reason he was so worried about you. For you."

The green fire softened, and he shrugged.

"As for myself, I don't pretend to know what's inside your mind. You might remember that conversation we had just before Soissons. I can accept that another entity, *not* just a delusion, has moved in with you. I just . . . have trouble with the idea of a Greek demigoddess or demon." He smiled a touch sheepishly. "I'm afraid it violates my own preconceptions."

"*Your* preconceptions! What do you think it did to *mine*?"

"I hate to think," he admitted. "But even those who accept *something* exists can be excused for worrying about whether or not it's benign, I think."

"That depends on how you define 'benign,'" Alicia replied slowly. "She's not what you'd call a forgiving sort, and we have . . . a bargain."

"To nail the pirates," Ben Belkassem said in a soft voice, and she nodded. "At what price, Alicia?"

"At any price." Her eyes looked straight through him, and her voice was flat—its very lack of emphasis more terrible than any trick of elocution. He shivered, and her eyes dropped back into focus. "At any price," she repeated, "but don't call them 'pirates.' That isn't what they are at all."

"If not pirates, what are they?"

"Most of them are Imperial Fleet personnel."

"*What?*" Ben Belkassem blurted, and her mouth twisted sourly.

"Wondering if I'm crazy again, Ferhat?" she asked bitterly. "I'm not. I don't know who hit Alexsov—it may even have been me, though I was trying to keep him alive—but he was pretty far gone by the time we got to him. But not so far that we didn't get a lot. Gregor Borissovich Alexsov, Captain, Imperial Fleet, Class of '32, last assignment: chief of staff to Commodore James Howell." Her mouth twisted again. "He still holds—held—that position, Inspector, because Commodore Howell is your pirates' field commander, and both of them are working directly for Vice Admiral Sir Amos Brinkman."

He stared at her, mind refusing to function. He'd known there had to be someone on the inside—someone high up—but never *this*! Yet somehow he couldn't doubt it, and the belief in his eyes eased her bitter expression.

"We didn't get everything, but we got a lot. Brinkman's in it up to his neck, but I think he's more their CNO, not the real boss. Alexsov knew who—or what group of whos—is really calling the shots, only he died before we got it. We still don't know their ultimate objective, either, but their *immediate* goal is to get as much as possible of the Imperial Fleet assigned to chasing them down."

"Wait a minute," Ben Belkassem muttered, clutching at his hair with his good hand. "Just wait a minute! I'll accept that you—or Tisiphone, or whoever—can read minds, but why in God's name would they want that? It's suicide!"

"No, it isn't." Alicia's own frustration showed in her voice, and she set aside her fork, laying her hand on the tablecloth and staring at her palm as if it somehow held the answer. "That's only their immediate goal, a single step towards whatever it is they ultimately intend to accomplish, and Alexsov was delighted with how well it's going."

Her hand clenched into a fist, and her eyes blazed.

"But whatever they're up to, Tisiphone and I can finally hit the bastards!" she said fiercely. "We know what they've got, we know where to find it, and we're going to rip the guts right out of them!"

"Wait—slow down!" Ben Belkassem begged. "What do you mean, you 'know what they've got'?"

"The 'pirate' fleet," Alicia said precisely, "consists of nine Fleet transports, seventeen Fleet destroyers, not counting the one we destroyed, six Fleet light cruisers, nine Fleet heavy cruisers, five Fleet battlecruisers, and one *Capella*-class dreadnought."

Ben Belkassem's jaw dropped. That was at least twice his own worst-case estimate, and how in *hell* had they gotten their hands on one of the Fleet's most modern dreadnoughts?

Alicia smiled—as if she could read his mind, he thought, and shuddered at the possibility that she was doing precisely that.

"Admiral Brinkman," she explained, "is only one of the senior officers involved. According to the record, most of their ships were stripped and sent to the breakers, but that was only a cover. In fact, they simply disappeared—with all systems and data bases intact. As for the dreadnought, she's the *Procyon*. If you check the ship list, you'll find her in the Sigma Draconis Reserve Fleet, but if anyone checks her berth—"

She shrugged.

"Dear God!" Ben Belkassem whispered, then shook himself. "You said you know where they are?"

"At this particular moment, they are either at or en route to AR-12359/J, an M4 just outside the Franconia Sector. Alexsov was supposed to rendezvous with them after completing his business on Wyvern, and unless Alexsov was wrong, *Admiral* Brinkman—" the rank was a curse in her mouth "—will be sending them new targeting orders there within the next three weeks. Only they won't be able to carry them out."

Her cold, sharklike smile chilled his blood.

"Alicia, you can't take on that kind of opposition by yourself—not even with an alpha-synth! They'll kill you!"

"Not before we kill *Procyon*," she said softly, and he swallowed. Fury or no Fury, there was madness in her eyes now. She meant it. She was going to launch a suicide attack straight into them unless he could dissuade her, and his mind worked desperately.

"That's . . . not the best strategy," he said, and her lip curled.

"Oh? It's more than the entire sector government's managed! And just who else do you suggest I send? Shall we report to Admiral Brinkman? Or, since we *know* he's dirty, perhaps we should take a chance on Admiral Gomez. Of course, there's the little problem that I don't have a single scrap of proof, isn't there? What do you suppose they'll do if a crazy woman tells them 'voices' insist the second in command of the Franconia Naval District is actually running the pirates? Voices that got the information from someone who's conveniently dead? Assuming, that is, that they forget their shoot on sight order long enough for me to tell them!

"Those bastards murdered every single person I loved, and Governor Treadwell, the entire Imperial Fleet, and even Uncle Arthur can go straight to Hell before I let them get away now!"

Her eyes glared at the inspector, and he shuddered. The amusement of only minutes before had vanished into a raw, ugly hatred totally unlike the woman he remembered from Soissons. And, he thought, unlike the woman he'd observed on Dewent and Wyvern. It was as if learning who her enemies were had snapped something down inside her . . .

"All right, granted we can't inform Soissons. Hell, with Brinkman dirty, there's no telling how far up—or down—the rot's spread." He was too caught up in his thoughts to notice he was taking Brinkman's guilt as a given. "But if you go busting in there, the only person who knows the truth—whether anyone else is ready to believe you or not—is going to get killed. You may hurt them, but what if you don't hurt them *enough*? What if they regroup?"

"Then they're your problem," she said flatly. "I'm dropping you at Mirabile. You can follow up without explaining where you got your lead."

She was right, he thought, but if he admitted it she'd go right ahead and get herself killed.

"Look, assume you get *Procyon*. I'm not as sure you can do it as you are, but let's accept that you kill Howell and his staff. You'll also be killing the only confirmation of what you've just told me! I may be able to get Brinkman and his underlings, but how do I get whoever's *behind* him?" He saw the fire in her eyes waver and pressed his advantage. "They may be tapped in at a level even higher than Brinkman—maybe even at court back on Old Earth—and if it starts unraveling out here, you can bet Brinkman will suffer a fatal accident before we pick him up. That breaks the chain. If you hit them by yourself, you may *guarantee* the real masterminds get away!"

<*He makes a point, Little One,*> Tisiphone murmured. <*I swore we would reach the ones responsible for your planet's murder. If we settle for those whose hands actually did the deed, you may die and leave me forsworn.*>

"I don't *care* if he's right!" Alicia snarled. "We've finally got a clear shot at the bastards! I say we take it!"

Ben Belkassem thrust himself back in his chair, eyes huge as he realized who she was arguing with, and made himself sit silently.

<*Yet what if he speaks the truth? Would you settle for underlings, leaving those who set this obscenity in motion untouched? Knowing they may plot anew, murder other families as they did those whom* you *loved?*>

Alicia closed her eyes, biting her lip until she tasted blood, and the Fury's voice was almost gentle in her brain.

<*You sound more like myself than I do, Little One, but I have learned from you, as well. We must strike the head from this monster if we seek true vengeance . . . and if we would not have it rise again.*>

"But—"

<*She's right, Alley,*> Megaira broke in. <*Please. You know I'll back you, whatever you decide, but listen to her. Listen to Ferhat.*>

Tears burned the corners of her eyes, tears of pain and hate not even Tisiphone could fully mute, of frustration and need. She wanted to attack, *needed* to attack, and she had a target at last.

<*So what would* you *do?*> she demanded bitterly.

<*Lend me your voice, Little One,*> the Fury said unexpectedly, and Alicia's eyes opened in surprise as she heard her own voice speak.

"Alicia wishes to strike now, Ferhat Ben Belkassem." The inspector stiffened and sweat popped on his forehead at the strange timber of Alicia's voice. "She believes, and rightly, that we must strike our foes now, while we know where we may find them. Yet you counsel otherwise. Why?"

Ben Belkassem licked his lips. He'd told Alicia the truth; he couldn't quite accept that she'd been possessed by a creature from mythology, but he knew it wasn't Alicia speaking. Whoever—*what*ever—had entered her life, he was face to face with it at last, unable even to pretend it didn't exist, and terror chipped away at his veneer of sophistication, revealing the primitive behind it to his own inner eye.

"Because—because it isn't enough . . . Tisiphone," he made himself say. "At the very least, we need outside confirmation of the ships they have from witnesses no one can sweep under the rug because they're 'crazy.' That would lend at least partial credence to the rest of what Alicia—to what the two of you have just told me. And we have to hurt them worse than you can, destroy more of their ships and shatter the raiding force so badly they'll need months to reorganize while we go to work from the other end."

"Well and good, Ferhat Ben Belkassem," that dispassionate, infinitely cold ghost of Alicia's contralto replied. "Yet we have but our good *Megaira*. You yourself have said we dare not seek aid from the Franconia Sector, and no other can reach hither before our enemies depart their present rendezvous."

"I know." He drew a deep breath and stared into Alicia's eyes, seeing her own will and mind within them, behind that other's words. "But what if I could tell you where to find a naval force that *could* go toe to toe with the 'pirates'? One that doesn't have a thing to do with the Fleet? And one that's right here, already in the sector?"

"There is such a force?" the icy voice sharpened, and Alicia's eyes widened as he nodded.

"There is. You were going to drop me off at Mirabile—why not take me to Ringbolt, instead?"

CHAPTER SIXTY

The battleship *Audacious* hung in geosynchronous orbit above the heat-glass scar of Raphael, and Simon Monkoto paced her bridge. His eyes no longer burned with hate; they were as hard as his face, filled with a bitter determination cold enough to freeze the marrow of a star.

He knew his people were growing restive as they waited for him to find a way to take the offensive, but none of them had complained. Professional warriors all, they accepted that warriors often died, yet they also knew this wasn't just about Arlen. It was about the civilians who had died *with* Arlen, as well. About the murder of a city and the radioactive filth the warhead had blasted into Ringbolt's atmosphere. Mercenaries tended to be loyal first and foremost to their own, but they understood justice . . . and vengeance. That was why the other outfits had responded in such strength.

He paused by the master plot, studying the light codes. Meaningless to the untrained eye, they told Monkoto everything at a glance.

The Ringbolt System was alive with ships. Most were small—cruisers or lighter—but they included a solid core of heavy hitters. The Falcons, Westfeldt's Wolves, Captain Tarbaneau and her Assassins. . . . He couldn't have picked a more battle-hardened group, yet they, like his own Maniacs, expected the great Simon Monkoto to Do Something. They owed him, and they wanted the people who'd done this thing, but there was a limit to how long they could sit here losing money. Unless the El Grecan government agreed to put them on the payroll, they'd have to start pulling out soon, and—

A soft buzz drew his eyes to the gravitic plot. He stepped closer, then stiffened as the preposterous nature of the incoming Fasset signature penetrated. Whatever it was, it was moving faster than a destroyer, yet its drive mass was greater than a battleship's!

More buzzers began to sound as other eyes and brains made the same observation. Additional sensors sprang alive, battle boards blinked green and amber eyes that turned quickly to red, and Simon Monkoto smiled.

That was an Imperial Fleet drive, but the ships that murdered Raphael had been Empire-built, as well.

"You don't think you could've come in just a bit more discreetly?" Ben Belkassem asked politely from the chair Alicia had installed beside her own on *Megaira*'s bridge. "They're probably in hair-trigger mode, you know."

"We don't have time to be inconspicuous," Alicia said absently. She wore her headset this time, and readiness signals purred to her from her weapon systems. She didn't want to use them, but if she had to . . .

"Howell won't stay at the rendezvous more than another three weeks," she continued, "and it's a two-week trip from here even if we could make it a straight shot—which we can't. We have to come in on a Wyvern-based vector, or they'll know we're not Alexsov the instant they pick us up. That gives us less than two days' leeway, and I'm not going to lose them now."

"But—"

"Either your friend Monkoto helps us, or he doesn't," she said flatly. "Either way, I'm going to be at AR-12359/J within the next nineteen standard days." She looked at him, and that same, strange hunger flickered in her eyes. "Tisiphone, Megaira, and I aren't going to miss our shot. Not now."

He closed his mouth. Ferhat Ben Belkassem didn't frighten easily, yet there were times Alicia DeVries terrified him. Not because she threatened *him*, but because of the determination that burned in her like fiery ice. People had called her mad, and he'd disagreed; now he was no longer certain. She wouldn't stop—*couldn't* stop—and he wondered how much of that sprang from Tisiphone, whatever Tisiphone truly was, and how much from herself.

Audacious rendezvoused with the other capital ships of the mercenary fleet barely half a million kilometers out from Ringbolt, for it was obvious the bogey was far faster and more maneuverable than they were. So far it had shown no sign of hostility, but Monkoto spread "his" ships—tight enough to concentrate their fire, dispersed enough to intercept any effort to get by them—and readiness reports murmured in his link to *Audacious*'s cyber-synth.

He returned his attention to the bogey with a sort of awe. Whatever it was, it was pouring on an incredible deceleration. It was well inside the primary's Powell limit, but it was decelerating at over thirteen hundred gravities—which, if it kept it up, would bring it to a halt, motionless with regard to *Audacious*, just over five thousand kilometers short of his flagship. If its intentions were hostile, that was suicide range, and—

The light cruiser *Serpent* finally got close enough for a visual, and Monkoto gawked as CIC shunted it to his display. A *freighter*? Impossible!

But a freighter the image before him was, and a freighter it remained—a slightly battered, totally unremarkable freighter . . . with more drive power than a battleship.

"We're coming into com range, Ferhat. Want me to hail them?" Megaira asked eagerly through a wall speaker, and Ben Belkassem heard Alicia's soft chuckle beside him.

Megaira liked the inspector, and Ben Belkassem was bemused by how much he liked her in return—and how much he enjoyed her bawdy, wicked sense of humor. She'd even built herself a "Megaira face," a svelte, stunning redhead, so she could flirt via com screen while her sickbay remotes worked on his arm, and he knew she simply ached to use that face (and figure) on a new audience. Whatever else happened, he would never again think of AIs in quite the same way.

"Have you identified *Audacious*?" he asked.

"Yup. Just as big and nasty as you said, but I could spot her half my drive nodes and still run her into the ground."

"Be nice," Alicia said, and Megaira sniffed.

"Never mind, Megaira," Ben Belkassem grinned. "Go on and call them."

"Sure thing," she said, and he twitched his uniform straight for the pickup. His own baggage remained somewhere on Wyvern, but Alicia and Megaira had outfitted him in "*Star Runner*'s" midnight blue, and he had to admit he liked the way it made him look.

"Admiral, the bogey identifies itself as the private ship *Star Runner*," Monkoto's com officer announced. "They're asking for you by name."

Monkoto scratched his nose. Odder and odder, he thought with his first real smile since the Ringbolt Raid, but that "private ship" business had to be a fiction. Whatever that thing might *look* like, it was no freighter.

"Route it to my station," he said, and leaned back as a lovely young woman in dark blue and silver appeared on his screen. He eyed her high-piled, Titian hair admiringly while he waited out the transmission lag, then her own eyes sharpened and looked back at him.

"Admiral Monkoto?" she inquired in a musical contralto, and he nodded. There was another lengthy delay while his nod sped to her screen, then she said, "I have someone here who wishes to speak to you, Sir," and disappeared, replaced by a small, hook-nosed man in a sling and the same blue uniform.

"Hello, Simon," the newcomer said, not waiting for Monkoto to respond. "Sorry to drop in on you without warning, but we need to talk."

Ben Belkassem watched Alicia from the corner of his eye as they stepped out of the personnel tube onto Monkoto's flagship.

Something was happening inside her, something that was burning holes in the Alicia DeVries he'd first met, and it was getting worse. Right after leaving Wyvern, hours had passed between flashes of that something else, but the intervals were growing shorter. It wasn't Tisiphone—he was positive of that now—and that made it worse. It was as if Alicia herself were burning out before his eyes. He could almost feel her . . . slipping away. Yet she had herself under control just now, and that was enough. It had to be.

"It's been a long time, Ferhat," a mellow tenor said, and Simon Monkoto held out his hand in greeting.

"Not that long," Ben Belkassem disagreed, returning the mercenary's clasp with a toothy grin.

"And this must be Captain Mainwaring," Monkoto said, and Alicia smiled tightly without confirming his assumption. He didn't notice; his eyes were locked on Ben Belkassem, and his humor had vanished.

"You said you have some information for me?"

"I do—or, rather, Captain Mainwaring does."

"What—?" Monkoto began eagerly, then chopped himself off. "Forgive me. My colleagues are waiting in the main briefing room, and they should hear this along with me. If you'll join us, Captain?"

Alicia nodded and followed the tall, broad-shouldered mercenary into a lift. She watched his face as the elevator rose, seeing the pinched nostrils, the deep-etched furrow between the eyes, and she didn't need Tisiphone to feel his hunger calling to her own, sharp-edged and jagged.

The lift doors opened, and Monkoto ushered them into a briefing room.

"Captain Mainwaring, Mister Ben Belkassem, allow me to introduce my colleagues," he said, and worked his way down the table, starting with Admiral Yussuf Westfeldt, a stocky, gray-haired man. Commodore Tadeoshi Falconi was as tall as Monkoto but thin, with quick, assertive movements; Captain Esther Tarbaneau was a slender, black-skinned woman with a very still face and startlingly gentle eyes; and Commodore Matthew O'Kane was a younger version of Monkoto—not surprisingly: he'd begun his career with the Maniacs.

Between them, Alicia knew, these people controlled over seventy ships of war, including two battleships, nine battlecruisers, and seven heavy cruisers, and no regular navy could have matched their experience. They looked back at her with hooded eyes, and she wondered what they made of her.

Monkoto finished the introductions and took a seat at the center of the long table, across from her and Ben Belkassem. The outsized view screen at her back was focused on *Megaira*'s freighter disguise, and she tried not to wipe her palms on her trousers as she faced people who fought for pay and remembered the million-credit reward the Empire had offered for her.

"I've dealt with Mister Ben Belkassem before," Monkoto informed his fellows, "and I trust him implicitly. Certain conditions of confidentiality apply, but he represents a . . . major galactic power."

The others nodded and regarded the inspector with renewed curiosity, wondering which branch of the imperial bureaucracy he worked for, as Monkoto gestured for him to take over.

"Thank you, Admiral Monkoto," he said, returning the searching gazes steadily, "but under the circumstances, I feel I ought to put all my cards on the table. Ladies and gentlemen, my name is Ferhat Ben Belkassem, and I am a senior inspector with Operations Branch of the Imperial Ministry of Justice."

Breath hissed in along Monkoto's side of the table. O Branch agents *never* revealed their identities unless they were up to their necks in fecal matter and sinking fast, but at least he'd guaranteed their attention.

"I realize that may be a bit of a shock," he continued calmly, "but I'm afraid there are more to come. I know why you're here—and I know where you can find the pirates." A ripple ran through his audience. "To be more precise, my associate does."

Eyes swiveled back to Alicia, hot and hungry and no longer hooded, and she made herself sit straight and still under their weight.

"How?" Monkoto demanded. "How did you find them?"

"I'm afraid I can't reveal that, Sir," Alicia replied carefully. "I have . . . a source I must protect, but my information is solid."

"I would certainly like to believe that, Captain Mainwaring," Esther Tarbaneau said in a soft soprano, "but you must realize how critical your credibility is, even with Inspector Ben Belkassem to vouch for you. How is it that a single merchant skipper could locate them when the Empire, El Greco, and the Jung Association have all failed?"

"Captain Mainwaring is more than she seems, Captain Tarbaneau," Ben Belkassem put in.

"Indeed?" Tarbaneau arched politely skeptical eyebrows, and Alicia sighed. She'd known all along it would come to this.

<*Cut the holo, Megaira.*>

<Are you sure, Alley?> the AI asked anxiously. *<I don't like the thought of doing that with you over there all alone.>*

<I'm not "all alone," and we don't have a choice. Do it.>

There was no response, but she didn't need one. Every eye jerked to the view screen in a single, harsh gasp, and most of the mercenaries hunched convulsively forward—O'Kane actually jerked to his feet—as the "freighter" vanished. The lean wickedness of an imperial alpha-synth could not be mistaken, even with splotches of titanium marring its immaculate hull.

"Ladies and gentlemen," Ben Belkassem said quietly, "allow me to introduce Captain Alicia DeVries, Imperial Cadre." Eyes whipped back to her, and he nodded. "I assure you, Captain DeVries's . . . instability has been grossly exaggerated. We've been working together for the past several weeks," he added, which was true enough, though Alicia hadn't known it at the time.

The mercenaries sank back in their chairs, eyes narrowed, and he hid a smile as he watched them leap to the conclusion he'd intended. Alicia really did have a marvelous cover—even if no one had set it up on purpose.

"So," Monkoto said forty minutes later, drumming his fingers on the conference table while he stared at a holographic star map. AR-12359/J burned a sullen crimson at its heart, and a computer screen at his elbow glowed with all the data Alicia had been able to supply on the "pirates'" strength. "We know where they are; the problem is what we do with them."

He pinched the bridge of his nose as he met his colleagues' eyes, then turned to Alicia, smiling grimly as he recognized the questions in her eyes.

"Neither you nor the inspector are Fleet officers, Captain, but that's what we do for a living, and I'm afraid this—" he gestured at the star map "—is a classic nasty fleet problem."

"Why?" Impatience burned in Alicia's blood once more, yet Monkoto's obvious professionalism—and matching hunger—kept it out of her voice.

"Put most simply, they're in n-space and they'll see us coming. Ships run blind in wormhole space, but their gravitics will pick us up long before we arrive, at which point they'll simply run on an acutely divergent vector. By the time we can kill our velocity and go in pursuit, they'll be long gone."

Alicia stared at the admiral, stunned by how calmly he'd said it, then jerked around to glare at Ben Belkassem. He'd been so glib about "getting help"—had *he* known how hopeless it was?!

"The classic solution is a converging envelopement," Monkoto went on, "with someone coming in at high velocity on almost any possible escape vector, but that also requires an overwhelming numerical advantage. We—" he waved at his fellows "—can probably take these bastards head on, though that *Capella*-class'll make things tight, but not if we spread out to envelope them."

Alicia dropped her eyes to the star map, fingers curving into talons under the table edge as she glared at the crimson star.

"We could call in the Empies for more ships," O'Kane suggested.

"Somehow I don't think so," Monkoto murmured, watching Ben Belkassem's face. "If we could, you wouldn't be talking to *us*, would you, Ferhat?"

"No," Ben Belkassem said unhappily. "We have reason to believe there's a leak—a very, *very* high-level leak—from Soissons."

"Well, isn't that a fine crock of shit," Westfeldt muttered softly.

"Isn't there *anything* we can do?" Alicia almost begged, and Monkoto leaned back in his chair and met her eyes with a cool, thoughtful gaze.

"Actually," he said, "I think there is . . . especially with an alpha-synth to help." He swept the others with a shark's lazy smile. "Our problem is that they can see us coming, but suppose *we* were the ones in normal space?"

"You've got that evil gleam in your eye, Simon," Falconi observed.

"It's very simple, Tad. We won't go to them at all; we'll invite *them* to come to *us*."

CHAPTER SIXTY-ONE

The green-uniformed woman rapped on the edge of the open office door, and the massive, silver-haired man behind the deck looked up. He grunted in greeting, waved at an empty chair, and returned to his reader, and the corners of the woman's mouth quirked as she sat and leaned back to wait.

It wasn't a very long wait. The silver-haired man nodded, grunted again—a harsher, somehow ugly grunt this time—and switched off the reader.

"Took your time getting here," he rumbled, and she shrugged.

"I was running that field exercise we discussed. Besides," she pointed at the reader, "you seemed busy enough." She spoke lightly, but her eyes were worried. "Was that about Alley?"

"No. Still not a sign of her."

Sir Arthur Keita sounded oddly pleased, for the man whose iron sense of duty had started the hunt for Alicia DeVries, and he smiled wryly as Tannis Cateau inhaled in wordless relief. She couldn't very well say "Thank God!" but she could think it very loudly. Then his smile faded.

"No, this is about our other problem," he said, "and I'm afraid it's coming to a head. I'm placing Clean Sweep on two-day standby."

Tannis twitched upright, eyes wide, and Keita watched her mind race, following her thoughts with ease. She'd been kept fully briefed on his downloads from Colonel McIlhenny, and she knew something McIlhenny didn't—that his reports to Sir Arthur had been quietly received on Old Earth, re-encrypted, and starcommed back across the light-years to Alexandria, just over the Macedon Sector border from the Franconia Sector. And they had been sent there because that was as far as Sir Arthur Keita had gone when he took his leave of Soissons.

The brigadier rocked gently in his chair, reexamining every tortuous step which had brought them to Clean Sweep. It would be ugly even if it went perfectly, but McIlhenny and Ben Belkassem had pegged it; someone far up the chain of command *had* to be working with the pirates, and that made every officer in the Franconia Sector suspect. No doubt most were loyal servants of Crown and Empire, but there was no way to tell which of them *weren't*, which was why Keita hadn't gone home—and why an entire battalion of drop commandos had been gathered in bits and pieces from the most distant stations Keita could think of to the remotest training camp on Alexandria.

Countess Miller had wanted to send Keita a full colonel to command them, but he'd refused. The Cadre had so few officers that senior, he'd argued, that the sudden disappearance of any of them was too likely to be noticed. Which was true enough, though hardly the full story.

Major Tannis Cateau's fierce resolve to protect Alicia Devries was the rest of it. No one else would be allowed to serve as Alicia's physician if she could be brought in alive . . . and, Sir Arthur knew, Tannis hoped—prayed—she'd be there when Alicia was found. If anyone could talk her into surrendering, that anyone was Tannis Cateau.

Keita understood that, and he owed her the chance, threadbare though they both knew it was, almost as much as he owed Alicia herself. But that wasn't something he cared to explain to Countess Miller, and so he'd kept Tannis here by pointing out that a battalion was a major's command and insisting that Major Cateau, already on the spot, was the logical person to command this one. The Fleet or Marines might have questioned one of their medical officers' competence in such matters; the Cadre did not.

"Have you told Inspector Suarez?" Tannis asked finally, and he nodded.

"He agrees that we have no choice. His marshals will begin arriving at Base Two this afternoon."

"But they won't have time for live-fire exercises, will they?"

"I'm afraid not, but at least they're all experienced people. And there's not supposed to be any shooting, anyway."

Tannis snorted, and Keita was hard put not to join her.

Ninety of Inspector Hector Suarez' three hundred imperial marshals were O Branch operatives, the others specially selected from Justice's Criminal Investigation Branch, and most were ex-military, as well, but Keita didn't quite share Old Earth's conviction that no one would offer open resistance. No emperor had ever before ordered the entire military and civilian command structure of a Crown Sector taken simultaneously into preventive custody. Seamus II had the constitutional authority to do just that, so long as no one was held for more than thirty days without formal charges, but it would engender mammoth confusion. And sufficiently well-placed traitors might well be able to convince their subordinates some sort of external treason was under way and organize enough resistance to cover their own flight.

"I wish we didn't have to do this," Tannis said into the quiet.

"I do, too, but how else can we handle it? We tried to wait till we found the guilty parties, but all our investigators seem to've hit stone walls—even Ben Belkassem hasn't reported in over a month. If we act at all, we have to take everyone into custody at once or risk missing the people we really want, and I'm afraid we're finally out of time." Keita tapped his reader. "I've just read a message from Ben McIlhenny, and I wish to hell Countess Miller had let me tell him about this!"

"Why?"

"Because he didn't know anybody was getting set to act, so he decided to push things to a head on his own. He tried to run a bluff and force the bastards into overt action by reporting to a very select readership that he was about to unmask the traitor."

"He *what*?" Tannis jerked upright in her chair, and Keita nodded.

"Exactly. He figured they couldn't take a chance that he was really onto them . . . and he was right." The brigadier's face was grim. "His last data dump was accompanied by a followup to the effect that Colonel McIlhenny is in critical condition following a quote 'freak skimmer accident,' unquote. Lady Rosario has him in a maximum-security ward with handpicked Wasps watching him round-the-clock, and Captain Okanami thinks he'll pull through, but he'll be hospitalized for months."

"They must be getting desperate to try something like that!"

"No question, but it's even worse than you may guess without knowing who he sent his report to." She raised an eyebrow, and Keita's smile was thin. "Governor General Treadwell, Admiral Gomez, Admiral Brinkman, Admiral Horth, and their chiefs of staff," he said, and watched her wince.

"So at least one of those eight people is either a traitor or an unwitting leak," he continued quietly, "and I doubt the latter after the microscope McIlhenny's put on his information distribution. But the fact that they tried to shut him up seems to confirm his theory that they're after more than just loot. If they didn't have a long-term objective, they'd've cut their losses and disappeared rather than risk trying for him, and I doubt it was a simple panic reaction. If whoever set this up were the type to panic we'd have had him—or her—long ago. So either their timetable's so advanced they hoped to wrap things up before anyone figured out what had happened to McIlhenny and why, or else—" he met Tannis's eyes "—*everyone* on his short list of suspects is guilty and they thought no one else would pick up on his report because no one else would ever see it."

"Surely you don't really think—" Tannis began, and he shook his head.

"No, I don't think they're all dirty. But then I wouldn't have believed *any* of them were. My personal theory is that they underestimated McIlhenny's ability to crash land a skimmer even after two of its grav coils suddenly reversed polarity on final. They didn't expect him to live, much less leave enough wreckage for anyone to figure out just how 'freak' a freak accident it was. And, of course, we don't think they know about the way he's been keeping us informed. At the very least, they probably counted on several weeks, possibly even months, of confusion before we put it together.

"The problem is that we can't rely on that. I may be wrong, and even if I'm not, his survival and the questions his subordinates are asking about the nature of his 'accident' may force them into something precipitous. If that's the case, we need to get in there before they start wiping their records or bug out on us. We may not get them all when we come crashing in, but we may *lose* them all if we don't."

"I see," she said quietly, and Keita nodded again.

"I believe you do, Tannis. So get back to Base Two and get ready to welcome Suarez. I want everyone aboard ship in forty-eight hours."

Sir Arthur Keita stood on the flag bridge of HMS *Pavia*, flagship of Admiral Mikhail Leibniz, and watched the visual display as the task force formed up about her in Alexandria orbit. Like the Cadre strike team it was to transport, its units had been drawn from far and wide—a three-ship division here, a squadron there, a single ship from yet another base. Its heaviest unit was a battlecruiser, for it had been planned for speed, yet it was a powerful force. Like Keita himself, its commanders hoped there would be no fighting; if there was any, they intended to win.

"Departure in seven hours, Sir Arthur," Admiral Leibniz said quietly, and Keita nodded without turning. He hoped Leibniz wouldn't construe that as discourtesy, but he didn't like this mission.

He sighed and concentrated on the gleaming minnows of the ships, half eager to depart into wormhole space and get this ended, half dreading what might happen when he reached his destination. And that, he knew, was why he disliked this operation so. Somewhere at the far end of his journey he would find a traitor, possibly—probably—more than one, and treason was a crime Sir Arthur Keita simply could not understand. The thought that any officer could so degrade himself and his honor made his skin crawl, and knowing that someone sworn to protect and defend had murdered millions made him physically ill.

He wanted that traitor unmasked and destroyed. There was, could be, no trace of mercy in him, but there was sorrow for the shame that traitor had brought to everything Keita himself held sacred.

"Excuse me, Sir Arthur, but you have a priority signal."

The voice broke into his reverie, and he turned to find it belonged to a youthful communications officer who extended a message chip to him.

Keita took the chip and frowned as he recognized the Cadre Intelligence coding. None of the flag bridge's readers could unscramble it, so he excused himself and made his way to Tannis Cateau's command center. The major started shooing the staff away from the com section at sight of the message chip, but he waved for her to remain when she started to follow them. She sat back down at her desk, keeping her back to him while he inserted the chip, only to look back up with a jerk as a voice spoke.

"Well, I will be goddamned," it said softly, and her head whipped around in astonishment, for it belonged to Sir Arthur Keita, and he was *grinning* as he met her startled gaze.

"Something new has been added," he announced. "This—" he jerked his chin at the reader screen "—is from the team we placed on Ringbolt. It would seem our missing O Branch inspector arrived there two days ago and put on some sort of Pied Piper performance."

"Pied Piper?" His eyes were positively glowing, Tannis thought.

"Our people couldn't get all the details—they're isolated from our official presence there, and the locals are playing their cards mighty close—but it seems Ben Belkassem turned up aboard a tramp freighter named *Star Runner*, or possibly *Far Runner*, for a personal meeting with Admiral Simon Monkoto."

"He did?" Tannis' eyes narrowed in speculation, and Keita nodded.

"He did. And six hours later the Monkoto Free Mercenaries, the Westfeldt Wolves, O'Kane's Free Company, the Star Assassins, and Falconi's Falcons were under way. Not some of them—*all* of them."

"My God," she whispered. "You don't think he—?"

"It would seem probable," Keita replied, "and please note that he appears to have gone directly to the *mercenaries*; not the Fleet and not the El Grecan Navy. Not to anyone who might have reported back to Soissons. He didn't tell *us*, either, but then he didn't know we were out here. If he's avoiding Soissons, he may have starcommed Justice HQ, but it'll take Old Earth another four days to relay to us if he did, and in the meantime . . ."

He began feeding numbers into his terminal, and Tannis frowned.

"I know that tone of voice, Uncle Arthur. What are you up to?"

"Our people may not have gotten everything, but they did find out where all those mercenaries are headed and when they're supposed to get there, and unless I'm mistaken—aha!" The result of his calculations blinked before him, and his grin became savage with delight. "We can get there within forty-one hours of their ETA if we move our departure up a bit."

"But what about Clean Sweep?"

"Soissons won't go anywhere, Tannis, and—" he swivelled to face her, and she saw the hunger in his eyes, heard it in his voice "—this little detour may just tell us *who*, because only one thing in the universe could have sucked Simon Monkoto away from Ringbolt!"

CHAPTER SIXTY-TWO

"Well it's about damned time," Commodore Howell muttered to himself.

He glared at the gravitic plot and reminded himself—again—that he wasn't going to climb down Alexsov's throat the instant he saw him. He suspected it wasn't going to be an easy resolve to keep.

He turned his back on the plot and interlaced his fingers to crack his knuckles. Alexsov was at least twelve days late, which would have been bad enough from anyone else. From the obsessively punctual chief of staff it was maddening, and vague visions of horrible disaster had haunted the commodore, only just held at bay by his faith in Alexsov.

He drew a deep breath and summoned a wry smile, wishing—not for the first time—that "pirates" weren't cut off from the Empire's starcom network. This business of relying solely on starships and SLAM drones wore on a man. And, his eyes narrowed again, speaking of SLAM drones, just why hadn't Gregor used one to explain his delay? His eyes lit with a touch of real humor as he realized he had at least one perfectly valid reason to tear a long, bloody strip off his chief of staff . . . and how much he looked forward to it.

<*Well, unless they're stone blind they've got us on their gravitics by now,*> Megaira commented.

Alicia only grunted in response. She sat in her command chair, clasping her hands in her lap to keep from gnawing her fingernails.

She'd smelled enough fear on Cadre strikes, but drop commandos were passengers up to the moment they made their drops. Whether or not their targets would be there when they arrived was something their chauffeurs worried about, and she'd never realized how tense the final approach must be for Fleet personnel. She was blind, unable to see out of wormhole space. She couldn't know if an ambush awaited her, or even if the enemy were there at all, but if they were, *they* could see *her* just fine.

<Calmly, Little One. We will find them and perform our appointed task.>

She heard Tisiphone's tension, but it was a different sort of strain. The Fury never doubted they would find those they sought; eagerness sharpened her tone, not uncertainty.

"Yeah, sure," Alicia said, and twitched in surprise at the saw-toothed anticipation quivering in her own voice.

She felt Tisiphone's answering start of surprise—and something like concern behind it—and looked down with a frown. Her clasped hands were actually trembling! Confusion flickered through her for just a moment, a vague sense of something wrong, but she brushed it aside and reached for a thought to distract her from it.

"Think they'll bite, Megaira?"

<Sure they will. I admit this is a bit more complicated than being Star Runner, *but I can handle it.>*

Alicia nodded, though "a bit more complicated" grossly understated the task her cybernetic sister faced. Pretending to be a freighter was complex yet straightforward for an alpha-synth's electronic warfare capabilities, but this time the deception was multilayered and far more difficult. This time *Megaira* was pretending to be a battlecruiser pretending to be a destroyer—and failing. The "pirates" were supposed to see through the first level of deceit, but not the second . . . and if they pierced the first too soon, Monkoto's entire plan would come crashing down about their ears.

"Definitely a destroyer drive," Commander Rendlemann announced several hours later, and Howell allowed himself an ironic smile. Of course it was a tin can. Arriving at this godforsaken star on that heading it could only be *Harpy.* No one but

Alexsov and Control knew where to find them, and any dispatch boat from Control would have come in on a completely dif—

"Still," Rendlemann murmured to himself, "there's something odd about it."

"What?" Howell twisted around in his chair, eyes sharpening.

"I said there's some—"

"I heard that part! What d'you mean, 'odd'?"

"Nothing I can really put a finger on, Sir," Rendlemann frowned as he concentrated on his link to *Procyon*'s AI, "but they're decelerating a bit slowly. There's a slight frequency shift in the forward nodes, too." He rubbed his chin. "Wonder if they've had drive problems? That could explain the delay, and if they had to make shipboard repairs it might explain the frequency anomaly."

Howell reached for his own headset. Unlike Rendlemann, he couldn't link directly with the dreadnought's cyber-synth, but a frown gathered between his brows as he studied Tracking's data. Rendlemann was right. *Harpy* was coming in faster than she should have—in fact, her current deceleration would carry her past her rendezvous with *Procyon* at more than seven thousand KPS.

His frown deepened. *Harpy* was well inside his perimeter destroyers, little more than ninety minutes from *Procyon* at her present deceleration, and she hadn't said a word. She was still 17.6 light-minutes out, so transmission lag would be a pain, but why hadn't Alexsov sent even a greeting? He had to know how Howell must have worried, and . . . .

"Com, hail Captain Alexsov and ask him where he's been."

The message fled towards *Megaira* at the speed of light, and she raced to meet it. Eight hundred seconds after it was born, *Megaira*'s receptors scooped it out of space, and Alicia swore.

"I wanted to be closer than this, damn it!" Her own displays glowed behind her eyes, and thirteen light-minutes lay between her and *Procyon*. She was already in the dreadnought's SLAM range . . . but *Megaira* mounted no SLAMs. She had to close another sixty-five million kilometers, fifteen more minutes at this deceleration, before her missiles could range upon her enemy—and seventy-two million before she could "break and run" on the vector to Monkoto's rendezvous.

"Can we steal enough delay, Megaira?" she demanded.

<I don't think so,> the AI replied unhappily. *<No reply will be the same as answering, unless this Howell's a lot dumber than we think, and battlecruiser three's in position to cut us off short of course change.>*

<Better to answer, Little One. We are more likely to gain time by tangling him in confusion, however briefly, than by silence.>

A corner of Alicia's mind glanced at the clock. Eighty seconds since the signal came in, and Megaira was right; if she delayed much longer, her very delay would become a response . . .

Something hot and primitive boiled in the recesses of her mind, something red that smoked with the hot, sweet incense of blood, and her lips thinned over her teeth.

"Oh, the hell with it! Talk to the man, Megaira."

<Transmitting,> the AI said simply.

James Howell's fingers drummed on the arm of his command chair, and he frowned in growing, formless uneasiness. That *had* to be *Harpy*, but Gregor was taking his own sweet time about replying.

He glanced at the chronometer and bared his teeth at his own thoughts. Barely twenty-seven minutes had passed since he sent his own signal; a reply could scarcely have arrived this soon even if Gregor had responded instantly. He knew that, but . . .

He bit the thought off and made himself wait. Twenty-eight minutes. The range was down to eleven light-minutes. Twenty-nine. Thirty.

"Sir," his com officer looked up with a puzzled expression, "we have a response, but it's not from Captain Alexsov."

"What?!" Howell rounded fiercely on the unfortunate officer.

"They say they have battle damage, Sir," that worthy said defensively. "We don't have visual, and their signal is very weak. I think— Here, let me route it to your station."

Howell leaned back, glaring at *Harpy*'s blue star. *Battle* damage? How? From whom? What the hell was go—

His thought died as a faint voice sounded in his ear bug.

". . . nal is very faint. Say again your transmission. Repeat, this is *Medusa*. Your signal is very weak. Say again your trans—"

Medusa? Howell jerked upright in his chair with an oath.

"Battle stations!"

His shocked bridge crew stared at him for an instant, and then alarms began to howl throughout *Procyon*'s eight million-tonne hull.

Howell snapped his chair around to face Commander Rendlemann across his own battle board. The ops officer's eyes were almost focused, despite his concentration on his cyber-synth-link, and questions burned in their depths.

"It's not Gregor," Howell snapped.

"But—*how*, Sir?"

"I don't *know* how!" Yet even as he spoke, Howell's mind raced. "Something must have given Gregor away to a regular Fleet unit." He slammed a fist against his console. "They took him out and reset their transponder to bluff their way in, but they can't have taken *Harpy* intact. If they had, they'd know the *Medusa* transponder codes were bogus."

"But if they didn't take her intact, how did they know to come *here*?"

"How the hell do *I* know? Unless—" Howell closed his eyes, thinking furiously, then spat another curse. "They must've picked him up leaving Wyvern, before he wormholed out of the system. *Damn* the luck! They got a read on his vector and extrapolated his destination."

"Extrapolated well enough to hit us dead center?"

"How the hell many *other* stars are there within twenty light-years?" Howell snarled. "But they can't've known what they were heading into. If they knew, they wouldn't have sent a single tin can to check it out." He glared at the blue dot again, yet a grudging respect had crept into his angry eyes. "Those gutsy bastards are decelerating straight toward us, and they're already inside sensor range. They can't see us on gravitics with our drives down, so they're hanging on as long as they can to get a full count for their SLAM drones, and if they do—"

He cut himself off and bent over his board. That destroyer was still outside its own range, and no destroyer could stand up to the SLAM salvos of a dreadnought. He glanced at his plot, at the two escorting battlecruisers tying into *Procyon*'s tactical net as his ships rushed to battle stations. A third battlecruiser was far closer to the intruder, already wheeling to close her jaws upon her prey.

* * *

<Here they come, Alley!> Megaira warned, and Alicia watched the battlecruiser rounding upon her.

The initial surprise must have been total, but the battlecruiser's weapons were ready at last. Megaira's sensors read her as HMS *Cannae*, and Alicia felt a sensual, almost erotic shiver as her/their targeting systems reached out and locked. Unlike *Procyon*, *Cannae* was barely three light-minutes from *Megaira* . . . yet she, too, thought she faced only a destroyer, for the alpha-synth's ECM still hid both her identity and the shoals of sublight missiles deployed about her on tractors. Their maximum velocity was going to be slightly but significantly lower without the initial boost of internal launchers, but pre-spotting them more than tripled the salvos *Megaira* could throw.

Alicia felt them through her headset, felt them like her own teeth and claws, and hunger fuzzed her vision like some sick delirium. A part of her stood aghast, stunned by her own blood-thirst. This was wrong, it whispered, no part of Monkoto's plan, but it was only a tiny whisper. She hung on the crumbling brink of a berserker's madness . . . and embraced its ferocity.

"*Take her!*" she snapped.

The gravitic plot showed it first. Its FTL capability could see only the gravity wells of starships, SLAMs, and SLAM drones, but unlike *Procyon*'s light-speed sensors, it gave a virtual real-time readout at such short range. Howell was watching it narrowly, waiting for the blue stars of *Cannae*'s first SLAMs, when the battlecruiser's Fasset drive disappeared.

Megaira's missiles erupted into *Cannae*'s face, and the battlecruiser's cyber-synth had too little time to react to the impossible density of that salvo. It did its best, but its best wasn't good enough.

Battle screen failed, *Cannae* vanished in a boil of light and plasma, and Alicia DeVries' eyes were jade chunks of Hell. The orgiastic release of violence exploded within her, brighter and hotter than *Cannae*'s pyre. It took her like a shark, snatching her under in a vortex of hate, and her madness reached out like pestilence. It flooded through her link to Megaira, engulfing the AI as it had engulfed her, and Tisiphone stiffened in horror.

This wasn't Alicia! The fine-meshed precision and deadly self-discipline had vanished into a heaving chaos of raw bloodlust. There was no reason in her, only the need to rend and destroy . . . and the Fury realized almost instantly from whence it sprang. She'd set a wall about Alicia's loss and hate to make that distilled rage *her* weapon, but this mortal was stronger than even the Fury had guessed. She would not be denied what was hers of right, and somehow she had breached that wall.

Alicia DeVries forgot Simon Monkoto's plan. Forgot the need to survive. She saw only the fleet that had murdered her world and family, and her madness locked Megaira close as they charged to meet its flagship.

James Howell went white as light-speed sensors finally showed him the details of *Cannae*'s death. God in Heaven, what *was* that thing? The one thing it *wasn't* was a destroyer—and whatever it was had stopped decelerating. It was accelerating straight towards him at seventeen KPS per second!

SLAMs raced to meet *Megaira*, and Alicia dropped the Fasset drive's side shields. The black hole's maw sucked them in, and she snarled, shuddering in the ecstasy of destruction, as she flashed past *Cannae*'s four escorting destroyers and her/their weapons wiped them from the universe.

Procyon's engineering crew broke all records bringing her drive on-line. They completed the fifteen-minute command sequence in barely ten, and the dreadnought began to accelerate. But the intruder simply adjusted its course, charging straight for her, and James Howell swallowed terror as he realized the other's suicidal intent.

Tisiphone battered uselessly at the interface of human and machine. If she could have broken Megaira free, even for an instant, the two of them might have reached Alicia, but the AI was trapped in her mother/self's blazing insanity. Yet Tisiphone had sworn to avenge Alicia upon those who had *ordered* her family's murder; if she allowed Alicia to die here she would stand forsworn. She would have betrayed the mortal who had trusted her with far more than her life, and so she gathered herself.

The strength of Alicia's mind had already made a mockery of her estimates. It might even be enough to survive . . . *this.*

Alicia DeVries shrieked as a white-hot guillotine slammed down. There was no finesse; Tisiphone was a flail of brutal power smashing through the complex web that bound her to Megaira. Another part of the Fury invaded her augmentation, goading the heart and lungs shock had stilled back to life, and she writhed in her command chair, screaming her agony.

Somehow Tisiphone held the impossible balance, forcing Alicia to live even as she killed her, but then the balance slipped. She felt it going, and screamed at Megaira like the tocsin of Armageddon.

And suddenly Megaira was free. The Fury reeled as the AI slashed back in a blind, instinctive bid to protect Alicia, but only for an instant. Only long enough to realize what had happened and hurl herself into the struggle at Tisiphone's side. For one incandescent sliver of eternity Alicia's madness held them *both* at bay, and then it broke at last. Megaira surged through the maelstrom to gather her in gentle arms, and Tisiphone was a shield of adamant between them both and the hatred. She faced it, battered it back, and Alicia jackknifed forward in her chair, soaked in sweat and gasping for breath.

But there was no time, and she jerked back erect as the Fury triggered her pharmacope and lashed her shuddering system back from the brink of collapse. Reason returned, and she raised her head, her eyes no longer pits of madness, to discover she had committed herself to a death-ride.

James Howell stared helplessly at the display. The accelerating intruder's Fasset drive devoured his fire, and it was barely four light-minutes away, tracking *Procyon*'s every desperate evasive maneuver. Rendlemann and the dreadnought's AI fought desperately to escape, but they simply didn't have the velocity. His ship had eighteen minutes to live, for there was no way those charging madmen would relent. They couldn't. If they broke off their suicide run now, *Procyon* and her consorts would tear them apart for nothing as they passed.

Horror and disgust reverberated somewhere inside Alicia, sickening her with the knowledge of what she had become, but there was no time for that. The tick flooded her system, goading her thoughts, and Megaira and Tisiphone snapped into fusion with her, a three-ply intelligence searching frantically for an answer. The enemy capital ships were spreading out, and their own velocity was back up to ninety-two thousand KPS and climbing. They were barely seventeen minutes from the dreadnought, but one or both of the battlecruisers could bring their weapons to bear around the shield of *Megaira*'s Fasset drive within twelve.

Thoughts flashed between them like lightning. Decision was reached.

Commodore Howell winced as no less than six SLAM drones flashed away from the intruder. A battlecruiser. At least a battlecruiser, to carry that many. But if it was a battlecruiser, where had its own SLAMs been this long?

It didn't matter. He was about to die, but stubborn professionalism drove him on. The drones were charging directly away from *Procyon*, and he snapped an order to his com officer. A light-speed signal flashed after them, and he bared his teeth in a death snarl of triumph. Unless those bastards were clairvoyant, they couldn't know he had the authenticated self-destruct codes. Their precious sensor data would die with their ship . . . and his own.

Alicia monitored the signal as it burned past her, and bared her teeth in an icy smile of her own. Monkoto's plan was back on track. Now if only Megaira could get them out of the trap she'd shoved them all into . . .

The AI named Megaira gathered herself. What she was about to try had been discussed in theory for years, but only in theory. No opportunity to attempt it had ever arisen, and most Fleet officers had concluded it wouldn't work, anyway. But none of them had expected to try it with an alpha-synth AI.

It had to be timed perfectly. She had to get in close, cut the transmission lag to the minimum, yet launch her attack before the hostile battlecruisers could engage her, for what she/they planned would reduce her defensive capability to a ghost of itself, but there was no other way.

She felt Alicia's warm, supporting presence and the Fury's hungry approval pulsing within her, and the chance of failure scarcely even mattered. They were together. They were one. Live or die, she knew no other AI would ever taste a fraction of the richness that was hers in this moment, and she waited while the seconds trickled past.

The accelerating SLAM drones exploded in spits of fire, but Howell hardly noticed. It was down to the final handful of minutes. Either his battlecruisers would stop the onrushing hammer of that Fasset drive by destroying the ship which mounted it, or *Procyon* would die.

Megaira struck.

The "pirates" had used their ability to penetrate Fleet security systems to kill her own SLAM drones, but it had never occurred to them that a Fleet unit might pierce *their* systems in return, and she was into their tactical net before they even realized she was coming.

The battlecruisers' AIs were slow and clumsy beside *Procyon*'s; by the time they could respond, she had slashed them from the net with a band saw of jamming. This was between her and *Procyon*, and the dreadnought's cybernetic brain roused to meet her, but she had a fleeting edge of surprise, for she had known what was about to happen.

And she wasn't alone; Tisiphone rode her signal into the heart of the enemy flagship.

Howell lurched back in his chair as chaos exploded in his synth-link. Cries of anguish filled the flag bridge, hands scrabbled to snatch away tormenting headsets, and one high, dreadful keen of agony rose above them all as Tisiphone left Megaira to her battle. She sought a different prey and stabbed out, searching the net for a mind which held the information she needed, and Commander George Rendlemann screamed like a soul in Hell.

Procyon's AI was more powerful than Megaira, but it was also more fragile, and Megaira was far faster. She was a panther attacking a grizzly, boring in for the kill before it brought its greater power to bear, and she drove a stop thrust straight to its heart. She made no effort to oppose the other AI strength-to-strength; she went for the failsafes.

Those failsafes were intended to protect *Procyon*'s crew from the collapse of an unstable cyber-synth, not to resist another AI's attack. They didn't even recognize it for what it was, but they sensed the turmoil raging in the systems they monitored, and they performed their designed function.

Procyon's entire control net crashed as Megaira convinced it to lobotomize its own AI.

Procyon writhed out of control, systems collapsing into manual control, leaving her momentarily defenseless as Megaira rampaged through them. Circuits spat sparks and died, backup computers spasmed in electronic hysteria, and Howell did the only thing he could. His hand slammed down on the red switch on his board. HMS *Procyon* vanished into the security of her shield, and he wondered if it was enough. In theory, *nothing* could get through an OKM shield—but no one had ever tested that theory against a battlecruiser's full-powered ramming attack.

If she'd had even a moment longer, Megaira might have stopped the shield before it activated, but she didn't have a moment. There was barely time to snatch Tisiphone out of the dreadnought's circuitry before the shield chopped off her access, and even that delay was nearly fatal.

She'd cut her margin too close. HMS *Issus* opened fire with every weapon, and Megaira was locked into too many tasks at once. Her defenses were far below par. She was too close for SLAMs, but at least six sublight missiles and three energy torpedoes went home against her battle screen.

The alpha-synth writhed at the heart of a manmade star. Screen generators screamed in agony, local failures pierced her defenses, and elation filled *Issus'* captain. Nothing short of a battleship could survive that concentrated blow!

A battleship . . . or an alpha-synth. *Megaira* staggered out of the holocaust, blistered and broken, trailing vaporized alloy and atmosphere. A third of her weapons were twisted ruin, but she was alive. Alive and deadly, no longer distracted, as she turned upon her foe.

Her holo projector was gone, and the battlecruiser's captain had one instant to gawk in disbelief as *Megaira* stood revealed. Then answering fire slammed back. A direct hit wiped away *Issus'* bridge. More fire ripped past her weakened defenses, and panic flashed through Howell's squadron. Their flagship had been driven behind her shield. *Cannae* and her escorts had been destroyed. *Issus* was a shattered, dying wreck . . . and now they knew their enemy. Knew they faced an alpha-synth which had carved its way through the very heart of their battleline.

Only the battlecruiser *Verdun* stood in her path, and *Verdun* refused to face her. She spun away, interposing her own Fasset drive, and *Megaira* screamed past at thirty-six percent of lightspeed.

CHAPTER SIXTY-THREE

The lethal chaos receded astern, and Alicia cursed herself viciously. Monkoto had planned for her to play the part of a battle-cruiser, slightly damaged in the inevitable engagement with Howell's screen, and she'd *blown* it. Howell had killed her SLAM drones—exactly as intended—but she could carry the same word in person . . . unless he stopped her. Yet thanks to *Megaira*'s damage, he knew what she was. Dreadnoughts were built for speed as well as power; *Procyon* might have overhauled a battlecruiser with battle damage, but *nothing* he had could hope to overtake an alpha-synth. So he wouldn't even try, and—

Her head jerked up as *Megaira*'s drive died. The ship sped onward, but she was no longer accelerating, and Alicia's mouth twisted bitterly.

"Nice try, but you don't really think you can trick them with a fake drive failure, do you?"

<*Who the fuck is* faking?> Megaira snarled back. <*I just lost the entire after quadrant of the drive fan!*>

"You *what?*"

<*I said somebody threw a goddamned wrench into the works!*> The AI snapped as diagnostic programs danced. <*Shit! The bastards took out both Alpha runs to the upper node generators!*>

<*Can they be repaired?*> Tisiphone demanded quickly.

<*Sure—if you can think of some way to keep those creeps from killing us while I do it!*> The alpha-synth's point defense stations took out the first spattering of incoming missiles even as her

maintenance remotes leapt into action. <*In the meantime, no drive means no evasion and no nice SLAM-eater. If those battlecruisers get their shit together, we're dead.*>

Alicia gripped the arms of her command chair, face white, monitoring remotes that ripped out huge chunks of broken hull and buckled frame members to get at the damaged control runs. There was no time for neatness; Megaira was inflicting fresh and grievous wounds upon herself as she raced to make repairs which should have taken a shipyard days.

More missiles sizzled in from *Verdun*—but *only* missiles. She must have exhausted her SLAMs against *Megaira*'s mad charge, yet her two surviving sisters hadn't, and they were closing fast. One would reach firing range within fifty minutes; the other in an hour; and *Procyon* still had SLAMs in plenty once she came out from behind her shield.

James Howell sat grimly silent as damage control labored. Commander Rahman had replaced the shrieking, drooling Rendlemann, but *Procyon* no longer had a cyber-synth. No one knew how it had been done, but her AI was gone, and massive damage to the manual backups left the big dreadnought defenseless. There wouldn't even be battle screen until damage control could route around the wrecked subsystems, and even if they replaced them all, *Procyon* would be at little more than half normal capability without her AI.

Which meant he dared not drop his mauled flagship's shield despite a desperate temptation to do just that. *Verdun* and *Issus* had almost certainly killed those madmen, assuming they hadn't destroyed themselves against the shield. But if they had somehow survived and fled, his people might need *Procyon*'s SLAM batteries to stop them—except that if they'd survived and *hadn't* fled, a single missile salvo would rip his crippled ship apart. And so he sat still, watching his crew wrestle furiously with their repairs, and waited.

"Why the hell aren't they coming after us?" Alicia worried, watching lightning glare as *Megaira*'s point defense dealt with incoming missiles.

<*Little One,*> Tisiphone observed with massive restraint, <*I see missiles enough, and two of their battlecruisers* are *pursuing us.*>

"Not them—*Procyon.* Why doesn't she drop her shield and fry us?"

<*You're complaining?*> Megaira flung half a dozen missiles back at *Verdun.* They had little chance of penetrating the battlecruiser's point defense at this range, but they might make her a bit more cautious. <*Alley, I gave that cyber-synth piece of crap a terminal migraine. Unless I miss my guess, they're scraping fried molycircs off the deck plates and wondering what the hell hit them.*>

"Yeah, but for how much longer?"

<*How do* I *know? Damn it, I've got more to worry about than—*>

"I know, honey. I know!" Alicia said contritely. "It's just that—"

<*Just that this waiting wears upon the nerves,*> Tisiphone finished. <*Yet think, Little One—none but the truly mad would linger within SLAM range of that dreadnought if they could flee. Hence, they must believe our drive damage genuine, which means we may yet complete our original intent.*>

<*Unless they get their act together and kill us,*> Megaira muttered.

The battlecruiser *Trafalgar* raced towards rendezvous with *Verdun.* Another twenty minutes. Just twenty, and her SLAMs would have the range.

<*Okay, people,*> Megaira murmured. <*Now just pray it holds. . . .*>

Circuits closed. Power pulsed through jury-rigged shunts and patches, and the alpha-synth began to accelerate once more. At little more than two-thirds power, but to accelerate, and Megaira turned her attention to other wounds. She could do little for slagged down weapons, but her electronic warfare systems' damage was mainly superficial, and it as looked as though she might need them badly. Soon.

"Engineering estimates another fifty-five minutes to restore Fasset drive, Sir," Rahman reported, "but we've restored as much basic combat capability as we can without cyber-synth."

"Understood. Stand by to drop the shield."

* * *

Megaira was back up to .43 C when the OKM shield's impenetrable blot disappeared from Alicia's sensors. She stiffened, checking ranges, then relaxed. The dreadnought was over twenty light-minutes astern, and it was her *sublight* sensors which had reported the shield's passing. Her gravitics still didn't see a thing, and that meant the dreadnought must have engineering problems of her own. Now if she'd just go on having them long enough . . .

Howell watched his plot replay *Issus*' destruction from *Verdun*'s sensor records in bitter silence. An alpha-synth. No wonder it had done such a number on them! And it explained the lack of SLAMs, too.

But *Issus* had gotten a piece of it. A big piece, judging from its subsequent behavior, and he cursed his own caution for not dropping the shield sooner. Yet the critical point was that the alpha-synth's speed had been drastically reduced. Even *Procyon* could make up velocity on it, now that her drive had been restored, and he had no choice but to do just that.

Pieces fell into place in his brain as the big ship accelerated in pursuit. That had to be the rogue drop commando—only a madwoman would have come after them alone and launched that insane attack down *Procyon*'s throat—so Fleet didn't know a thing. A part of him was tempted to let DeVries, go, trusting to the Fleet's own shoot on sight order to dispose of her. But mad or not, she had the hard sensor data to prove her story; all she had to do was get into com range of any Fleet base or unit and pass it on.

He could not permit that, and so he dispatched his freighters to the alternate rendezvous and went in pursuit. His cruisers and remaining battlecruisers could have overhauled sooner than *Procyon*, had he let them. He didn't. Lamed though that ship was, God only knew what it could still do, and *Procyon* could hang close enough to break into the same wormhole space and close to combat range. She still had the weapons to take even an alpha-synth, and if it took time, time was something he had. On this heading, he'd overtake DeVries eleven light-years short of the nearest inhabited star system.

<*Looks like we're back on track,*> Megaira said.

The entire squadron was in pursuit, and its faster units were hanging back. They'd managed to pull out of *Procyon*'s SLAM range before she lumbered back to life, but she'd regain it eventually, and *Megaira*'s drive couldn't be interposed against fire from astern. Which might be just as well, given its current fragility.

"What happens when they get the range on us again?"

<*Depends. We'll be into wormhole space, and I* think *I'll have most of my EW back on line by then. If I do, they'll have a hard time localizing us. They can't throw the kind of salvos Soisson's forts could, and SLAMs can't go supralight relative to us in wormhole space, either. I'll be able to track 'em and do some fancy footwork, and even that damned dreadnought can't carry a lot of 'em. I expect they'll choose not to waste them and hold off until they can get to missile or even beam range. That's what I'd do.*>

"I just hope they're as smart as you are, then."

<*Me too,*> Megaira snorted, and Alicia nodded and shoved herself up out of her chair. <*Hey! Where're you going?*>

"To the head, dummy." Alicia managed a weary smile. "I'm coming off the tick, and I've got an appointment with the john."

<*Uh, you might want to reconsider that.*>

"Sorry." Alicia swallowed a surge of nausea. "Already in process."

<*Damn!*> Alicia's eyebrows rose, and Megaira sighed. <*Alley, we took a* lot *of hits. There's no pressure in the bridge access passage.*>

"You mean—?"

<*I mean I'm working on it,*> the AI apologized, <*but I need another hour before I can repressurize.*>

"Oh, crap," Alicia moaned in a stifled tone. "Get your tractors ready, then, because—"

Her voice broke off as biology had its way.

Half an hour later, a pale-faced Alicia sat huddled in her chair. Her uniform was almost clean—Megaira's tractors had caught most of the vomit and whisked it away—but the stink of fear and sickness clung to her, and she scrubbed her face with the heels of her hands as a new and deeper fear rippled within her. Now that the immediate terror of combat had receded, she had time to think . . . and to realize fully *why* she had done what she had.

She'd lost it. She hadn't panicked, hadn't frozen, hadn't tried to run. Instead, she'd done something worse.

She'd gone berserk. She'd forgotten the objective, the plan, the need to survive, even that Megaira would die with her—forgotten *everything* but the need to kill . . . and it hadn't been temporary. She'd felt it again the instant tick reaction let her go. Bloodlust trembled within her even now, like black fire awaiting only a puff of air to roar to life once more.

It was madness, and it terrified her, for it was infinitely worse than the madness Tannis had feared, and she had infected Megaira with it. The Fleet had been ordered to kill her; now, she knew, that order was justified. If a drop commando's insanity was to be dreaded, how much more terrible was the madness of an alpha-synth pilot?

<*No, Little One.*> Alicia winced, for the soft voice held something she'd never heard from the Fury: sorrow. She gritted her teeth and turned away from it, clutching her self-loathing to her, but Tisiphone refused to be evaded. <*It is not you who have done this thing. It is I. I have . . . meddled unforgivably. Do not blame yourself for the wrong* I *have done.*>

"It's a bit late for that," Alicia grated.

<*But it is not your fault. It—*>

"Do you really think it matters a good goddamn whose *fault* it is?!" She clenched her fists as barely leashed madness stirred, and tears streaked her face.

<*Alley—*>

"Shut up, Megaira! Just shut *up*!" Alicia hissed. She felt Megaira's hurt and desperate concern, and she shut them out, for Megaira loved her. Megaira would refuse to face the thing she had become. Megaira would protect her, and she was too dangerous to be protected.

Silence hovered in her mind and her breathing was ragged. She still had enough control to end it. She could turn herself in . . . and if Fleet killed her when she tried, perhaps that would be the best solution of all. Yet how long would that control remain? She could *feel* her old self dying, tiny bits and pieces eaten away by the corrosion at her core, and the horror of her own demolition filled her.

<*Little One . . . Alicia, you* must *hear me,*> Tisiphone said at last. Alicia hunched forward, covering her ears with her hands,

digging her nails into her temples, but she couldn't shut out the Fury's voice.

<*I am arrogant, Little One. When first we met, I saw your compassion, your belief in "justice," and I feared them. They were too much a part of you, too likely, I thought, to cloud your judgment when the moment came.*

<*I was wrong. Oh, Alicia—*> the pain in the Fury's voice was terrible, for she was a being who had never been meant to feel it <*—I was* so *wrong! And because I was, I built a weapon of your hate. Not against your foes, but against* you, *to bend you to my will at need, and in so doing I have hurt one innocent of any wrong. Once that would not have mattered to me. Now it does. You must not hate yourself for what I have done to you.*>

"It doesn't matter who I hate." Alicia slumped back and opened tear-soaked eyes, and her voice was raw and wounded. "Don't you understand even that? It doesn't *matter.* All that matters is what I've become!"

<*The debt is mine,*> the Fury's voice had hardened, <*and mine the price to pay. I swear to you, Alicia DeVries, that I will not let you become the thing you fear.*>

"Can—" Words caught in her throat. She swallowed and tried again, and they came out small and frightened. "Can you stop me? Make me better?"

<*I do not know,*> Tisiphone replied unflinchingly. <*I swear that I will try, but I am less skilled at healing than hurting, and what I have done to you grows stronger with every hour. Already it is more powerful than I believed possible, perhaps powerful enough to destroy us both, yet I have lived long enough—perhaps too long. I will do what I may, and if I fail,*> her voice turned gentle, <*we will end together, Little One.*>

<*No!*> Megaira's protest was hot and frightened. <*You can't just kill her! I won't* let *you!*>

"Hush, Megaira," Alicia whispered. Her eyes closed again—not in terror this time but in gratitude—yet she felt her sister-self's pain and made herself speak gently. "She's right. You know she is; you're part of me. Do you think I'd want to live as *that?*" She shuddered and shook her head. "But I'm so sorry to do this to you, love. You deserve better, unless . . . Do you think—is our link different enough for you to—?"

<I don't know,> tears glittered in the AI's soundless voice, *<and it doesn't matter, because I won't.>*

"Please, Megaira. Don't do that to me," Alicia begged. "Promise you'll at least try! I don't . . . I don't think I can bear knowing you won't if I . . . if I . . ."

<Then you're just going to have to try real hard not to. You're not going anywhere without me—not ever.>

"But—"

<It is her right, Little One,> Tisiphone said quietly. *<Do not deny her choice or blame her for it. The fault is no more hers than yours.>*

Alicia bowed her head. The Fury was right, and if she tried to force the AI, she would only twist the time they still had with pain and guilt.

"All right," she whispered. "All right. We've come this far together; we'll go on together."

Megaira's warm silence enfolded her, answering for her, and fragile stillness hovered on the bridge, filled with a strange, bitter-sweet sense of acceptance. What she was becoming could not be permitted to live, and it would not. That had to be enough, and, somehow, it was.

It was odd, she thought almost dreamily, but she didn't even blame Tisiphone. She would have died long since if not for her, and the Fury's pain was too genuine. If Alicia had become something else, so had Tisiphone, and the bond which had grown between them no longer held room for resentment or hate.

The stillness stretched out until the Fury broke it at last.

<In truth, Little One, my promise to you may not matter in the end. I have not yet told you what I have learned.>

"Learned?" Alicia stirred in her chair.

<Indeed. While Megaira dispatched Procyon's *AI, I sought a mind which could tell us more. I found one, and in it I found the truth.>*

Alicia snapped back to full alertness, driving the residual flicker of madness as deep as she could, and felt Megaira beside her in her mind.

<The Fleet personnel who pursue us were most carefully selected by their commander, and their objective is to create such havoc as must force your Emperor to commit much of his fleet to this sector.>

"We already knew that, but why? What can they possibly gain from it?"

<*The answer is simple enough,*> the Fury said grimly, <*for he who truly commands them is the one called Subrahmanyan Treadwell.*>

For just an instant the name completely failed to register, and then Alicia flinched in disbelief. "The Sector *Governor*? That—that's crazy!"

<*There is no question, Little One. It is he, and his objective is no less than to place a crown upon his own head.*>

"But . . . but *how?*"

<*He has requested massive reinforcements to "crush the pirates." Indeed, he has been promised the tenth part of your Fleet's active units and perhaps a third of its firepower. Once they arrive, Admiral Gomez will be relieved or die—it matters little to him—and be replaced by Admiral Brinkman.*

<*For a time, the pirates will prove even more successful. Their raids will spread across the border into the Macedon Sector, which is but lightly held, until they seem an irresistible scourge. And when the terror has reached its height, when the people of both sectors have come to believe the Empire cannot protect them, Treadwell will assume personal command of the Fleet and declare martial law. Brinkman will accept this, and they will relieve those captains most loyal to the Empire, replacing them with men and women loyal only to them, until Treadwell's control is total. And at that point, Little One, he will declare that the Empire has proven incapable of defending its people so far from the center of power. He will declare himself ruler of both sectors in the name of their salvation, offering to submit to a plebiscite when the "pirates" have been destroyed, and from that moment the raids will become less frequent. In the end, a carefully chosen squadron of his most loyal adherents will fight a false battle in which the "pirates" will appear to be utterly destroyed. He will then face his plebiscite, and even without manipulation of the votes, he will probably win.*>

"But the Emperor won't stand for it!" Alicia protested sickly.

<*Treadwell believes he will. That is the reason he seeks such naval strength. Surely the Emperor will realize that a civil war—and it would require nothing less, once Treadwell's plan has played itself out—will but invite the Rishathan Sphere to intervene? And*

remember this: none save Treadwell and his closest adherents will know what actually passed. All will believe, even the Emperor and his closest advisers, that he truly dealt, firmly and decisively, with a threat to the people he is sworn to protect. These sectors lie far from the heart of the Empire. Will the Emperor be able to rally sufficient public support for a massive operation against a man who but did what had to be done in so distant a province?>

"Dear God," Alicia whispered. She licked bloodless lips, trying to grasp the truth, but the sheer magnitude of the crime was numbing.

"Megaira, did you get any of this from *Procyon*'s computers?"

<No, Alley.> Even the brash AI was subdued and shaken. *<I didn't have time for data searches.>*

<It would not have mattered, Megaira. There was no data for you to find. The details of the plan have never been committed to record—not, I venture to say, unreasonably.>

"Yeah." Alicia inhaled deeply. The numbness was passing, and the flame of her madness guttered higher. She ground her heel upon its neck, driving it back down, and shook herself.

"Okay. What do we do with the information?"

<Tell Ferhat?> Megaira suggested hesitantly.

"Maybe. *He'd* believe us, I think, though it's for damned sure no one else will. I mean, who's going to take the unsupported word of a madwoman who talks to Bronze Age demons over that of a sector governor?"

<I suppose I should resent that, but I fear you are correct.>

"Yeah, and even if Ferhat believes us, he needs proof. They could never convict on what we can give them, and I doubt even O Branch would sanction a black operation against a sector governor."

<Agreed. And that, Little One, is why my promises to you may stand meaningless in the end. I see only one way to destroy this traitor.>

"Us," Alicia said grimly.

<Indeed.>

<Now wait a darn minute! Do you two actually think we can get to a sector governor? *What do you want to do, nuke the damned planet?!>*

<It will not be necessary. Treadwell dislikes planets. His quarters are aboard Orbit One.>

<Oh, ducky! So all we have to do is fight our way in and punch out a six million-tonne orbital fortress with a third of my weapons so much junk? I feel lots better now.>

"Are you saying you can't do it?" Alicia tried to make her voice light. "What happened to all that cheerful egotism when we busted out?"

<Out is easier than in,> Megaira said grimly, *<and you know damned well they'll have reworked their systems since, just in case we come back.>*

"So we can't get in?"

<I didn't say that,> Megaira replied unwillingly. *<I'll know better when I finish repairs—remember, that battlecruiser shot the hell out of me—but, yeah, I imagine we can get in. Only, if we do, I don't think we'll get out again, and I doubt anything I ever had was heavy enough to take out that fort. I certainly don't have anything* left *that could do the job.>*

"Oh yes, you do," Alicia said very softly. "The same thing that could have taken out *Procyon*."

<Ram it?> There was less shock in the AI's voice than there should have been, Alicia thought sadly. Like her, Megaira saw it as the possible answer to her fear of what she might become. *<I think we could do it,>* Megaira said at last, slowly. *<But there are nine thousand other people on that fort, Alley.>*

"I know."

Alicia frowned down at her hands and her shoulders hunched against the ice of her own words.

"I know," she whispered.

CHAPTER SIXTY-FOUR

The black-and-gray uniformed woman looked up as a quiet buzzer purred. A light blinked, and she slipped into her synth-link headset and consulted her computers carefully, then pressed a button.

"Get me the Old Man," she said, and waited a moment. "Admiral, this is Lois Heyter in Tracking. We've got something coming in on the right bearing, but the velocity's wrong. They're still too far out for a solid solution, but it looks like our friend hasn't been able to hold the range open as planned." She listened, then nodded. "Yes, Sir. We'll stay on it."

She went back to her plot, and the close-grouped ships of war began to accelerate through the deep gloom between the stars. There was no great rush. They had hours before their prey dropped sublight—plenty of time to build their interception vectors.

James Howell glared at the enemy's blue dot and muttered venomously to himself.

He'd fired off over half the squadron's missiles, and he might as well have been shooting spitballs! It was maddening, yet he'd given up on telling himself things would have been different if *Procyon*'s cyber-synth had survived to run the tactical net. To be sure, *Trafalgar*'s AI was less capable than the dreadnought's had been, but not even *Procyon*'s could have accomplished much against the alpha-synth's fiendish EW.

He knew that damned ship was badly damaged; the debris trail it had left at AR-12359/J would have proved that, even if its limping acceleration hadn't, yet it refused to die. It kept splitting into multiple targets that bobbed and wove insanely, and then swatted down the missiles that went for the right target source with contemptuous ease. What it might have been doing if it were *un*damaged hardly bore thinking on.

But its time was running out. His ships would be into extreme energy torpedo range in seventy minutes, and even an alpha-synth's defenses could be saturated with enough of those. If they couldn't, he'd be into beam range in another eighteen and a half minutes, and *no* point defense could stop massed beam fire, by God!

"Admiral," Lois Heyter said tensely from Simon Monkoto's com screen, "we're picking up a second grav source—a big one—and it's decelerating hard."

"Put it on my plot," Monkoto said, and frowned down at the display. Lois was right; the second cluster of gravity sources, almost as numerous as those speeding towards them from AR-12359/J, *was* decelerating. He tapped his nose in thought. He supposed their arrival might be a coincidence . . . except that there was no star in the vicinity, and Simon Monkoto had stopped believing in coincidence and the tooth fairy years ago.

He juggled numbers, and his frown deepened as the newcomers' vector extended itself across the display. If those people kept coming as they were, things were about to get very interesting indeed.

A fresh sheet of lightning flashed and glared against the formless gray of wormhole space as *Megaira* picked off yet another incoming salvo, and Alicia winced. Thank God Megaira had no need of little things like rest! The "pirates" had been in missile range for over two hours, and if their supply of missiles was finite they seemed unaware of the fact. Anything less than an alpha-synth would have been destroyed long since.

They hadn't been supposed to reach missile range before turnover, but "supposed to" hadn't counted on *Megaira*'s damage. Alicia's nerves felt sick and exhausted from the unremitting tension of the last hundred and thirty minutes, yet the end was in sight.

"Ready, Megaira?"

<I *am. I just hope the repairs are.*>

Alicia nodded in grim understanding. Megaira had labored unceasingly on her drive since their flight began, ignoring less essential repairs, and all they could say for certain was that it had worked . . . so far.

Maintenance remotes had built entirely new control runs in parallel with those cobbled up in such desperate haste, but they hadn't dared shut down long enough to shift over to test them with Howell's squadron clinging so closely to their heels.

Nor had they been able to test Megaira's other repairs. Twenty-five percent of her drive nodes had been crippled or destroyed outright by the same hit that smashed the control runs, and she'd had spares for less than half of them. Her theoretical grav mass was down five percent even after scavenging the less damaged ones, and while she'd bench-tested the rebuilt units, *no one* cut suspect nodes into circuit while underway in wormhole space.

Unfortunately, the maneuver they were about to attempt left them no choice. They'd been forced to leave their turnover far later than planned because of how much more quickly the "pirates" had closed the gap, and they would need every scrap of deceleration they could produce, tested nodes or no.

<*Coming up on the mark, Alley.*> Megaira broke into her thoughts quietly, and Alicia drew a deep breath.

"Thanks. Tisiphone?"

<*I am prepared, Little One. Relax as much as you may.*>

"I'm as relaxed as I'm going to get." She heard the quaver in her own voice and forced her hands to unclench. "Come ahead."

There was no spoken response, but she felt a stirring in her mind as Megaira extended a wide-open channel to the Fury with no trace of her one-time distrust. They reached out to one another, weaving a glowing web, and Alicia forced down a stir of jealousy, for she was excluded from its weaving. She could see it in her mind's eye, taste its beauty, yet she could not share in its creation. Beautiful it might be, but it was a trap—and she was its prey.

Currents of power crackled deep within her, and then the web snapped shut. She gasped and twisted, stabbed by agony that vanished almost before it was felt, and her eyes opened wide.

The seductive glitter of her madness was gone. Or, no, not gone—just . . . removed. It was still there, burning like poison in the glowing shroud Tisiphone and Megaira had woven, but it could no longer touch her. Blessed, half-forgotten peace filled her like the hush of a cathedral, and she sighed in desperate relief as her muscles relaxed for the first time in days.

"Thank you," she whispered, and felt Megaira's silent mental caress.

<It is little enough, and I do not know how long we may hold it,> Tisiphone replied more somberly, *<but all we may do, we will.>*

"Thank you," Alicia repeated more levelly, then gathered herself once more. "All right, Megaira—let's dance."

Lois Heyter hunched over her console in concentration, then stiffened.

"Tell the Old Man we have decoy separation!" she snapped.

No more missiles fired. James Howell's lips were thin over his teeth as he waited out the last dragging seconds to energy torpedo range. If he were aboard that alpha-synth, this was when he'd go for a crash turnover—

There! The fleeing Fasset drive suddenly popped over, and he started to bark orders—then stopped dead. There were *two* sources on his display! One continued straight ahead at unchanged acceleration; the other hurtled towards him at a starkly incredible deceleration, and he swore feelingly.

He gritted his teeth and waited for Tracking to sort them out. Logic said the genuine source was the one charging at him in a frantic effort to break sublight and lose him . . . only it was coming at him at over twenty-five hundred gravities! How in hell could the alpha-synth produce that kind of power after its long, limping run? A fraction of that increase would have kept it out of his range, and alpha-synth point defense or no, not even a madwoman would have endured that heavy fire if she could have avoided it!

The source continuing straight ahead maintained exactly the same power curve he'd been watching for days, which might well indicate it was genuine, and that made his dilemma worse. If he decelerated to deal with the closing source and guessed wrong, the still fleeing one would regain a massive lead; if he *didn't* decelerate and the closing source was the genuine ship, he'd lose it entirely. *One* of them had to be some sort of decoy—but *which one?*

Whichever it was, he had to identify it quickly. The peculiarities of wormhole space augmented the deceleration of the closing source to right on three thousand gravities, and his squadron's acceleration translated it into a relative deceleration of more than forty-seven KPS per second. He had barely four minutes before it went sublight, and if he didn't begin his own deceleration at least thirty seconds before it did, he'd lose it forever.

Fasset drive generators were virtually soundless, their quiet hum as unobtrusive as a human heartbeat. But not now. Alicia clung to the arms of her command chair, teeth locked in a white, strained face, and the drive screamed at her like a tortured giant, shaking *Megaira*'s iron bones like a hurricane until her vision blurred with the vibration.

The decoy, one of only two SLAM decoys *Megaira* carried, streaked away on their old course, and shipboard power levels exploded far past critical. Meters blew like molycirc popcorn, rebuilt control runs crackled and sizzled, patched-up generator nodes shrieked, and it went on and on and on and on . . .

"*Turnover!*" Lois Heyter barked. "We have turnover!" Her eyes opened wide, and her voice dropped to a whisper. "Dear God, *look* at that deceleration rate! How in *hell* is she holding it together?"

The cybernetic brain of the battleship *Audacious* noted the changing gravity signatures and adjusted its own drive. Vectors would converge with less than ten percent variance, it calculated with mild, electronic satisfaction.

Time was running out. Howell found himself pounding on the arm of his chair. If Tracking couldn't differentiate in the next ten seconds, he was going to have to go to emergency deceleration just to play safe. Losing distance on the alpha-synth if he'd guessed wrong would be better than losing it entirely, he told himself, and it did his frustration no good at all.

The leading source flickered suddenly, and his eyes narrowed. There! It flickered again, power fading, and he knew.

The range was down to four and a half million kilometers when Howell's entire squadron flipped end-for-end and began to decelerate madly.

<*Fifty seconds to sublight.*> Blood streaked Alicia's chin, her hands were cramped claws on her chair arms, and her battered brain felt only a dull wonder that they were still alive, but Megaira's mental voice was unshadowed by the hellish vibration. <*Forty. Thirty-fi—They've* flipped, *Alley!*>

"Here they come, boys and girls," Simon Monkoto murmured over his command circuit. He sat relaxed in his command chair, but his eyes were bright and hard, filled with a vengeful hunger few of his officers had ever seen in them. His gaze flicked over his display, and his mouth sketched a mirthless grin. The second group of gravity sources would drop sublight in nine minutes—out of range to hit the "pirates" but on an almost convergent vector.

"Cut your drives!" he snapped as Alicia DeVries broke sublight, and every one of his ships killed her Fasset drive.

<*There's Simon—right on the money!*> Megaira announced as the mercenaries appeared on her display and then vanished in the equivalent of a deep-space ambush. Without active drives, they were invisible to FTL scanners; the "pirates" wouldn't be able to see them until their light-speed sensors picked them up.

Alicia nodded in understanding, then gasped in relief as Megaira cut the drive's power levels far back. The dreadful vibration eased, yet there was a grim undertone to her relief as she felt the AI prepping her own weapons. If the SLAM drone had lasted just a little longer, *Megaira* might have broken back past Howell's ships to join Monkoto. She hadn't, and Monkoto or no Monkoto, she was still in the "pirates" range, with no choice but to decelerate *towards* them or lose the shield of her Fasset drive. But if she decelerated too rapidly—or if they began to accelerate once more and overran her—the range would be less than two light-seconds when she penetrated their formation.

A jolt of sullen fire went through Alicia at the thought. She clenched her teeth as her madness lunged against its restraining net, hungry for destruction, and felt Tisiphone at her side as she fought it down. It subsided with an angry grumble, and sweat beaded her forehead. She'd won—this time—but what would happen once the shooting started?

<*Alley! Check the gravitics at two-eight-oh!*>

The dreadnought *Procyon* erupted from wormhole space with her entire brood, and the alpha-synth was still there, decelerating into their teeth.

James Howell bared his own teeth. DeVries was a drop commando, not a Fleet officer, or she would've known better. If she'd simply cut her drive, he might not even have been able to find her; as it was, she was bidding to break back through his formation in another suicide attack.

That was the only explanation for her maneuver, but this time her ship was hurt and he knew what he was up against.

Orders crackled out, and his formation opened to receive its foe.

"Commodore!" It was Commander Rahman, his face taut. "We're picking up another grav source! It's still supralight, but decelerating quickly. Estimate breakout in . . . six-point-one minutes at thirty-one light-minutes, bearing two-eight-six, one-one-seven. At least thirty sources."

Howell stiffened, and his stomach tightened as Rahman's data appeared on his plot.

Those other sources were decelerating, if far less madly than DeVries had, and their vector converged with his own. Not perfectly, by a long chalk, but close enough they could match it if he tried to accelerate back up to supralight. Jesus! Could DeVries have *known* they'd be here?

It didn't seem possible. If an ambush had been intended the ambushers would have arrived ahead of time to lie doggo without revealing drive signatures. But what *else* could it be?

Numbers tumbled across the bottom of his display as Tracking calculated frantically, and he swore. Yes, they could go sublight on a converging vector or accelerate back supralight with him even if he went back to max acceleration, but they'd never be able to engage him as long as he continued to decelerate. They'd have to kill their own velocity, then go in pursuit, and his people were already killing speed. He'd have too much of a head start to be caught short of wormhole space on a reversed course . . . which was the coldest of comforts.

Jaw muscles lumped as he turned his hating gaze back to DeVries. They might not be able to engage, but they'd still get good scanner readings, and that meant his entire pursuit had been for nothing.

He glared at the alpha-synth's dot. All for nothing. Everything they'd done, all the people they'd killed, and it was all for *nothing!* Once his ships were fingerprinted, Treadwell's dream of building a new empire on the "pirate threat" would be dead. It might take months for Intelligence to put it together, but the true nature of the "pirate" squadron would be a glaring arrow pointed in the right direction.

Yet there was one last thing he could do. DeVries wasn't racing to meet the newcomers. She was still decelerating towards *him.* The shoot on sight order still held; she dared not confront the Fleet any more than he did, and she was accepting the threat she knew in a desperate effort to evade the new one.

Which meant he could still kill her, and perhaps—

"*SLAMs!*" Rahman screamed. "SLAMs bearing oh-oh-three, one-two-seven!"

Howell's head whipped up in horror as malignant blue dots speckled his display. Where had they *come* from? There was nothing out there! It was—

And then his sublight sensors finally picked up the ships ahead and "above" him, firing down past his drive masses as he decelerated towards them.

<*Go, Simon!*> Megaira shrieked, and Alicia's bloodlust spasmed against the web. A strand parted, and Tisiphone hurled herself at the weakness, blocking the thrust of madness. She didn't get it all. A tentacle of fire groped through Alicia's brain, and breath hissed between her teeth.

The SLAMs flashed in, and Howell's ships lunged into frantic evasive action. The short range meant the SLAMs were still building velocity when they arrived, and she snarled as *Procyon* evaded an even dozen, but two battlecruisers were less fortunate, and she twitched in ecstasy as they died.

Eleven capital ships hung on James Howell's flank, their velocity within ten percent of his own, and he'd lost *Trafalgar* and *Chickamauga. Verdun* replaced *Trafalgar* in the tactical net, but only she survived to support *Procyon.* Had the dreadnought's AI remained, she alone might have matched all eleven of her opponents, but it didn't. She retained her brute firepower and defensive strength—not the fine-meshed control to make them fully effective.

Understanding filled him. There *had* been an ambush, but not of Fleet units. The energy signatures told it all. Somehow, DeVries had linked up with the mercenaries at Ringbolt. An alpha-synth—and only an alpha-synth—might have nailed Gregor and had the speed to reach Ringbolt before making for the rendezvous to bait the trap. There was only one way those slow-footed battleships could have brought him to action, and he'd swallowed the bait whole. But what about the ships even now breaking sublight? *They* couldn't have been part of the plan; he knew Monkoto's reputation, and the mercenary would have been in place long since with every unit he had.

Conjecture raced through his mind in split-second flashes of lightning. The other units couldn't be from Gomez's Fleet district—not unless Brinkman had been found out and the whole operation broken from the other end, and in that case there'd be a hell of a lot more than thirty drive sources! Could they be still more mercenaries? Some last minute ally of Monkoto's who'd arrived late?

It didn't matter. What mattered was that the only way to avoid fighting *both* enemy forces was to take Monkoto head on . . . and that was suicide.

But perhaps not for everyone. If any of his people could break through the mercenaries, they might turn true pirate, or perhaps take service with a Rogue World far enough from Franconia not to realize what they'd been. It wasn't much, but it was all he could offer them—that and a chance to kill some of the bastards who'd ambushed them.

"Come to poppa, you bastards," Simon Monkoto whispered.

He'd hoped for still more SLAM salvos, but then he'd expected the renegades to accelerate back up to wormhole out. They hadn't, and now they were hidden behind the drives pointed straight at him. The battle to come had just turned even uglier, but his own ships matched the "pirates'" maneuver. Thanks to the battleships, their maximum deceleration was less than the enemy's, but it would be enough to insure a long and deadly embrace.

"Up their asses, Megaira!" Alicia snarled.

<Are you sure, Alley? I'm not in good enough offensive shape to add much to Simon's firepower.>

Megaira's worried voice tore at the corona of violence building in Alicia's mind. She clenched her teeth, sweating, trying to make herself think, and a part of her screamed in warning. The web about her madness sang with stress, and it was crumbling. She felt Tisiphone between her and it, felt the Fury pouring herself into the fraying web.

She writhed in her chair, fighting to keep her jaws locked on the order to engage. She could break off. She could curl away from Howell and leave him to Monkoto's unwounded ships, and she knew she had to. She and her companions were the only ones who knew the truth about Treadwell. They couldn't let themselves die yet. She *knew* it; yet she couldn't let go. She held her course, and the most she could do was strangle the order for Megaira to redline her deceleration.

The edge of James Howell's squadron "overtook" Monkoto's. Screening destroyers and light cruisers suddenly found themselves broadside-to-broadside at ranges as low as fifty thousand kilometers, and energy torpedoes and beams ripped back and forth. Point defense was irrelevant; misses were almost impossible, and battle screens were blazing halos wrapped about fragile battle steel. Two renegade destroyers and a light cruiser vanished in star-bright fury, but Commodore Falconi's heavy cruiser flagship went with them, and the death toll was only starting.

Monkoto and his allies had known what it would be like the instant they realized Howell wasn't going to run for it. *They* could have broken off, but they hadn't come to break off. The two fleets interpenetrated and merged, racing side-by-side while the hammering match raged.

Procyon's massive beam and energy torpedo batteries opened fire, and a dozen destroyers and cruisers died in the first salvo. *Verdun* poured her own fire into the maelstrom, but two of O'Kane's battlecruisers locked their batteries on her, and her fire slackened as more and more of her power was shunted frantically into her battle screen. She writhed, cored in their fire, and *Procyon* blew one of her attackers to vaporized wreckage.

Not in time. *Verdun*'s screens failed, a tight-focused salvo of particle beams ripped through them, and she vomited flame across the stars.

Procyon rounded vengefully upon her killer, but *Audacious* and the battleship *Assassin* were on her like mastiffs. They were far smaller, slower, less heavily armed, but their cyber-synths were intact, and thunder wracked the vacuum as the leviathans spread their arms in lethal embrace. Two more battlecruisers raced to join them, then a third, and all six rained javelins of flame upon the dreadnought.

Eight million tonnes of starship heaved as something got through a local screen failure, and Monkoto's wolves set their fangs in the flanks of the crippled saber-tooth. Howell ripped his attention away from them long enough to check the main plot and swallowed a groan. *Procyon* was attracting more and more of the mercenaries' attention, but there were more than enough destroyers and cruisers to pair off in duels with his own units. Ships flashed and vanished like dying sparks, damage signals snarled in his synth-link, and Tracking had finally identified the newcomers: Fleet battlecruisers, already gaining on *Procyon* with their higher rate of deceleration.

He glared at the red switch on his console. He could engage the shield and laugh at Monkoto's attack . . . but there was no point. He couldn't accelerate with the shield up; only drift, knowing that when he finally lowered it, the enemy would be waiting. He raised fiery eyes to Commander Rahman.

"Get the battleships!" he snarled.

Alicia's nails drew blood from her palms as the battleship *Assassin* blew apart. She remembered Esther Tarbaneau's gentle brown eyes, and her lips writhed back from her teeth as the red holocaust broke free within her.

The hell with Treadwell! The hell with *everything!* The mercenaries were fighting *her* fight, dying *her* death. She felt Megaira and Tisiphone battling to turn her madness, and she didn't care.

"Now, goddamn it!" she snarled. "Everything we've got *now!*" and Megaira wept as she obeyed.

The drive thundered and shrieked in agony, and the alphasynth began to close on the cyclone of dying starships.

Simon Monkoto's teeth met through his lip as *Assassin* vanished. First Arlen, now Tadeoshi and Esther—but he had the bastards. He *had* them! His flagship's AI noted a fluctuation in *Procyon*'s defenses, a wavering the dreadnought would have sensed and corrected had her own AI survived. But it hadn't, and *Audacious* flashed orders over the net. One battleship and four battlecruisers threw every beam and energy torpedo they had at the chink in *Procyon*'s armor, and her Fasset drive exploded.

Alicia's banshee howl echoed from the bulkheads as the dreadnought's drive died, and her eyes were mad.

The mercenaries peeled away from *Procyon*, for they no longer needed to endure her close-range fire. They'd broken her wings, destroyed her ability to dodge. Once their own ships got far enough from her to avoid friendly SLAM fire, she was dead, but Alicia didn't think about the mercenaries' SLAMs, didn't care about the short-range weapons still waiting to destroy her. All she saw was the lamed hulk of her enemy, waiting for her to kill it.

HMS *Tsushima* decelerated towards the savage engagement, and her captain's brain whirled as she digested the preposterous sensor readings. *Fleet* units locked in mortal combat with mercenaries?! Insane! Yet it was happening, and Brigadier Keita's briefing echoed in her ears. If the mercenaries were here to engage pirates, then those Fleet units must *be* pirates, for no engagement this close and brutal could be a mistake. Both sides had to know exactly who they were fighting . . . didn't they?

Tsushima was the lead ship of the task force, already approaching SLAM range of the fighting, but Captain Wu held her fire. Even if she'd been certain what was going on, only a lunatic would fire SLAMs into that tight-packed boil of ships, for she would be as likely to kill friends as enemies. But what was that one ship doing so far behind the melee? It was moving at preposterous speed, overhauling the others, but something about its drive signature . . .

"Captain! That's an *alpha-synth*!" her plotting officer said suddenly, and Wu's face went white. There were no Fleet alpha-synths in this sector; the only two previously assigned to it had been ordered out so that there could be no confusion.

Wu swallowed a bitter curse and looked at her plot. She'd heard the gossip, knew how close Keita and that Cadre major, Cateau, were to Alicia DeVries, but Keita's flagship was ten light-minutes astern of her. DeVries would vanish into the maelstrom in half the time it would take to pass the buck to him, and when she did, *Tsushima* could no longer fire her SLAMs in pursuit.

She didn't want to do this. No Fleet officer did. She knew each of them had prayed that he or she wouldn't be the one it fell to. But she was here, and the order still stood.

<*SLAMs, Alley!* SLAMs!>

Megaira's shriek of warning—small and faint, almost lost in her hunger—touched some last fragment of reason. Alicia saw the SLAMs racing after her, and that sliver of sanity roused, intellect fighting instinct run mad.

Tisiphone hurled herself into the tiny flaw in the hurricane, and Alicia jerked back in her command chair, gasping as the Fury smashed through to her. The terrible roaring eased, and understanding filled her.

"Break off, Megaira." She choked the words out, thoughts as clumsy as her thick tongue. She clung to her guttering sanity by her fingernails, feeling the blood-sick chaos reaching for her yet again.

"Evasion course. Wormhole out," she gasped, fighting for every word, and reached for the only escape from her madness. "Tisiphone, *put me out*!" she screamed, and slithered from her chair as the Fury clubbed her unconscious.

CHAPTER SIXTY-FIVE

A broken behemoth drifted against pinprick stars, flanks ripped and torn, and Simon Monkoto sat on his flag bridge and glared at its image.

He turned his head to glower at the man beside him. Ferhat Ben Belkassem's dark face was pale from the carnage, but he'd been the first to note the hole in *Procyon*'s fire where an entire quadrant's batteries had been blown away, and Monkoto had yielded to his appeal to hold the SLAMs.

He still didn't know why he had. They'd have to destroy it sooner or later—why risk his people on the O Branch inspector's whim? But he'd taken *Audacious* into the hole and worked his way along the dreadnought's hull, and there'd been something sensual in the slow, brutal destruction of *Procyon*'s weapons, in the lingering murder of her crew's hope.

His eyes returned to the main plot, still bemused by what it showed. Thirty Imperial Fleet ships, eighteen of them battlecruisers. They'd been a more than welcome help, but the mercenaries' losses had still been horrendous. *Assassin*, three of nine battlecruisers, four of seven heavy cruisers . . . The butcher's bill had been proportionately lighter among the destroyers and light cruisers, but the total was agonizing, especially for mercenaries who lacked the resources of planetary navies.

Yet none of the renegade fleet had escaped, and only two destroyers had surrendered. The mass murders on Ringbolt—yes, and Elysium—were avenged . . . or would be, when *Procyon* finally died.

A com signal chimed, and he hid a flicker of surprise as he recognized his caller's craggy face.

"Admiral Monkoto," a voice rumbled, "I'm Brigadier Sir Arthur Keita, Imperial Cadre. Please accept my thanks on behalf of His Majesty. I'm certain His Majesty will wish to personally express his own gratitude to you and all your people in the very near future. The Empire is in your debt."

"Thank you, Sir Arthur." Monkoto's heart rose, despite the pain of his losses. Sir Arthur Keita was not known for meaningless praise. When he spoke, it was with Seamus II's voice, and the Terran Empire paid its debts.

"I also wish to thank you for not destroying that dreadnought." Keita's face hardened. "We want its crew, Admiral. We want them badly."

"I also want them, Sir Arthur." Monkoto's voice took on the steely edge of a file.

"I understand, and we intend to give you the justice you and your people deserve, but we need live prisoners for interrogation."

"That's what Inspector Ben Belkassem said," Monkoto acknowledged, and Keita's tight face eased just a bit.

"So he *is* with you. Good! And he's right, Admiral Monkoto."

"Fine, but how do you intend to collect them? We've pulled most of their teeth and disabled their shield generator, but they have to know what the courts have waiting for them. Do you really think they'll surrender?"

"Some of them will," Keita said with flat, grim finality. "I've got an entire battalion of Cadre drop commandos over here, Admiral. I believe we can pry them out of their shell."

"Drop com—" Monkoto closed his mouth with a snap. A *battalion?* For just a moment he felt a shiver of hungry sympathy for the bastards aboard that hulk. He shook himself and cleared his throat.

"I imagine you can, Sir Arthur, as long as they don't blow their power plants and take your people with them."

"They won't," Keita said. "Watch your plot, Admiral."

Monkoto's eyes dropped to the display as four battlecruisers moved towards *Procyon*. For a moment he thought they were about to launch assault shuttles, but they didn't. Keita had something no one else did—the complete blueprints for a *Capella*-class dreadnought—and the battlecruisers' short-range batteries stabbed into *Procyon*'s hull. It was over in less than two seconds; long before the renegades could have realized what was happening, every one of *Procyon*'s fusion plants had become an incandescent ruin.

"As I say, Admiral," Keita said with cold satisfaction, "they won't be blowing those plants." He paused a moment, then nodded as if to himself. "Another thing, Admiral. I don't know if it'll be possible to salvage that ship. If it is, however, she's yours. My word on it."

Monkoto sucked in in astonishment. Badly wrecked as *Procyon* was, she was far from beyond repair if a replacement Fasset drive could be cobbled up, and the thought of adding that eight-million-tonne monster to his fleet . . .

"But now," Keita said more briskly, "my people have a job to do. I'll speak with you again later, Admiral."

Tannis Cateau closed her armor's visor. The soft "shusssssh" of a solid seal answered her, and she checked her battle-rifle's servos. Many drop commandos preferred plasma guns or lasers for vacuum. Energy weapons weren't very popular in atmosphere, where their range was drastically reduced, and even in vacuum a well-timed aerosol grenade did bad things to lasers, but the laser's lack of recoil made it popular in zero-G. Of course, lasers had horrific power requirements, and plasguns could hardly be called pinpoint weapons, especially in the confines of a starship's passages, yet most seemed to feel their advantages more than compensated. Not Tannis. The battle-rifle was her chosen precision instrument, and using her armor's thrusters to offset the recoil had become instinct years ago.

She shook off her woolgathering thoughts with a wry smile. Her brain always insisted on wandering in the last moments before action was joined . . . unlike Alley, who only seemed to focus to an even greater intensity.

She pushed that memory away quickly and watched the troop bay repeater as the assault shuttles formed up. At least Alley had gotten away. She hadn't been killed by her own, and there was still hope—

The last shuttle slid into place, thrusters flared, and they swooped across the kilometers towards *Procyon*'s savaged hulk.

Monkoto felt his stomach tighten as the silvery minnows darted towards the wounded leviathan. They were such tiny things—little larger than an old pre-space airliner—and if he'd missed even a single energy mount . . . .

But no weapons fired. The *Bengals* snarled down on their prey, belly-mounted tractors snugged them in tight, and hatches opened.

Tannis ducked instinctively and swore as a blast of penetrators spanged off her armor. One of her headquarters section reared up between her and the fire, staggering back a meter as the heavy-density projectiles slammed into him. They were from a standard combat rifle, and fiery ricochets bounced and leapt as his armor shrugged them aside. His weapon rose with the deadly economy of tick-enhanced reactions, and Tannis winced as a gout of plasma spewed up the passage, silent in the vacuum. The rifleman vanished—along with twelve meters of bulkhead.

"Prisoners, Jake," she said mildly. "We want *prisoners*."

"Sorry, Ma'am." The hulking drop commando, a third again Tannis's height, sounded almost sheepish. "Got carried away."

"Yeah, well, thanks anyway."

Her lip twitched as her team picked its way past the glowing wound. Corporal Jake Adams sometimes forgot how drastic the consequences could be when he got "carried away." Combat armor gave anyone the "muscle" to use truly heavy weapons; Adams also had the size, and his "plasma rifle" was the equal of a shuttle cannon.

Her amusement faded as she focused on her display. Boarding assaults were always ugly. Even though they knew every nook and cranny of their battlefield, there were still too many places for die-hards to hole up, and no pirate had any illusion about his or her ultimate fate. Her HQ section's circuitous route had been planned to reach their real objective while her other wings distracted the enemy rank and file to clear her path. They were doing it . . . but they were taking losses despite their equipment.

She peered about her, checking corridor traffic markings against her mental HUD, and grunted in satisfaction.

"Wolverine-One, Ramrod has cleared route to Tango-Four-Niner-Lima down Zebra-Three. Form on my beacon."

Captain Schultz's acknowledgment came back, and she swung her rifle into fighting position as Bravo Company began closing on her current positions.

"All right, Jake. You see that hatch down there?"

"Yes, Ma'am. I surely do."

"Well, this piece of shit's flag bridge is on the other side of it." She smiled up at him and waved a hand with the tick's dancelike fluidity. "Feel free to get carried away."

James Howell crouched behind his useless console in his vac suit. The laser carbine was alien to him, clumsy-feeling in his grip, but he waited almost calmly, his mind empty. There was no room for hope, and no point in fear. He was going to die, and whether it happened in a few minutes or a few hours—or even in a few months, if he was taken alive—didn't matter. He'd betrayed all he was sworn to uphold to play the great game; now he'd lost, and his own stupidity had brought all of his people to the same degrading end.

Echoes of combat quivered through the steel about him, and he glanced across the bridge at Rachel Shu, small and deadly behind a bipod-mounted plasma rifle. Others crouched with them, waiting, eyes locked on the hatch. Any moment now—

The heavily armored hatch shuddered. A meter-wide circle flared instantly white-hot, and a tongue of plasma licked through it, a searing column that leapt across the bridge. Someone got in its way and died without time even to scream as the heart of a sun embraced him.

Another bolt of fury blew the hatch from its frame in half-molten wreckage, and the first drop commando charged through it.

Howell braced his laser across the console and squeezed the stud. A dozen others were firing, flaying the armored figure with tungsten penetrators and deadly beams of light, and the invader staggered. His battle-rifle flashed white fire as he went down—an unaimed spray of heavy-caliber penetrators that chewed up consoles and people with equal contempt—and then Rachel's plasgun fired, and what hit the deck was a less than human cinder.

Tannis Cateau swallowed a curse as her point man went down.

It was her fault. Other teams had already taken heavy fire; hers hadn't, and she'd let herself grow overconfident. Now she slid forward, hugging the bulkhead and trying not to think about Adams and his monster gun behind her. Her racing mind rode the tick, and she reached out through her armor sensors. She couldn't get a clear reading, but with a little help . . .

A hand signal brought her HQ grenadier up on the other side of the passage, and she unhooked a small device from her armor harness, then nodded.

The grenadier opened up on full auto. It was a mixed belt, mostly smoke and pyrotechnics with only a handful of light HE, for they wanted prisoners, but it did its job. Anyone beyond that hatch was hugging the deck as flash-bangs and antilaser vapor exploded in his face when she tossed the sensor remote with a smooth, underhand motion. It bounced across the deck, unnoticed under the cover of the grenades, and she smiled the cold, distant smile of a drop commando as she keyed it alive.

Ah! She oriented her remote perspective, tallying threat sources and taking careful note of the plasma rifle, then nodded to the grenadier a second time. He ripped off another burst; then Tannis Cateau flowed into the hatchway with the uncoiling deadliness of a bushmaster, and her battle-rifle's powered mounting was an extension of her own nerves. Her target was invisible behind the last of the grenade bursts, but the rifle rose without an instant's waste motion, and she squeezed off a three-shot burst. The rounds left the muzzle at fifteen hundred meters per second; the three-millimeter sub-caliber projectiles reached their target virtually instantaneously and cut its legs from under it—literally.

Answering fire ripped back at her despite the blinding effect of the grenades, and she ignored it. She knew it was unaimed; they couldn't see her, but *her* eyes were in their midst.

Her rifle was a magic wand, spewing agony and death with merciless precision, and for once there was no pity in her. Her ammo belt burned through the feed chute in three- and four-shot bursts, and the answering fire ebbed. A last spattering of penetrators whined off her armor, and she went through the hatch like a panther, already calling for the medics.

"My God."

Ben Belkassem's words hung in the sickbay air, and he wondered if they were a curse or a prayer. He sank back into his chair, as nauseated as Tannis Cateau had been as she came down from the tick.

Sir Arthur Keita said nothing, only stared down at the woman in the hospital bed. Tannis's fire had sliced away her legs like a jagged scalpel, but no one pitied her. She lay there, smiling a bemused, cheerful smile, and Keita wanted to strangle her with his bare hands.

Rachel Shu was the only member of the renegades' field staff to be taken alive. He knew he should be grateful, that no one except James Howell himself could have given them more information, but simply listening to her fouled him somehow. She carried an invisible rot with her, a gangrene of the soul all the more terrible for how ordinary she looked, and she'd explained it all with appalling cheerfulness under the influence of Ben Belkassem's drugs.

Under normal circumstances, no imperial subject could be subjected to truth drugs outside a court of law—which, Keita knew, wouldn't have stopped Ben Belkassem or Hector Suarez for a moment. For himself, the brigadier was just as happy that no laws had been broken. Bent, perhaps, but not broken. Shu had been taken in the act of piracy; as such, she had no rights. Keita could have had her shot out of hand, and he wanted to. Oh, how he wanted to! But she was far too valuable for that. His medicos would cosset and pamper her as they would the Emperor himself, for her testimony would put Subrahmanyan Treadwell and Sir Amos Brinkman in front of a firing squad.

He stepped back from the bed as from a plague carrier and folded himself into a chair opposite Ben Belkassem. Tannis Cateau was a white-faced ghost at his side, and silence hung heavy until the inspector broke it.

"I can't—" He shook his head. "I heard it all, and I still can't believe it," he said almost wonderingly. "All these months hunting for the cold-blooded bastards behind it, only to find *this* at the end of them."

"I know." Keita's lips worked as if he wanted to spit on the deck. "I know," he repeated, "but we've got it all. Or enough, anyway." He turned to Inspector Suarez, standing at Ben Belkassem's shoulder. "We won't need Clean Sweep after all, Inspector."

"I can't say I'm sorry," Suarez said, "but this is almost worse. I don't think any sector governor's ever been convicted of treason."

"There's always a first time," Keita said grimly. "Even for this, I suppose." He shook himself. "I'll speak to Admiral Leibniz myself; I don't want this going any further than the people in this room until we reach Soissons."

He inhaled deeply, then summoned a sad smile.

"This may even help, in a way." The others looked at him in astonishment, and his smile grew a bit wider. "We'd never have gotten this far without Alley, Tannis." He nodded at Ben Belkassem. "Add it to what the Inspector has to say, and we may get that shoot on sight order dropped."

Tannis's face lit with sudden, fragile hope, but Ben Belkassem sucked in air as if he'd been punched in the belly. Keita turned at the sound, and his eyes narrowed as he saw the inspector's face.

"What?" he asked sharply

"Alicia," Ben Belkassem whispered. "My God, *Alicia!*"

"What about her?"

"She knows. Dear God in heaven, she *knows* about Treadwell!"

Keita twitched in surprise. "That's ridiculous! How could she?"

"The computers." Ben Belkassem's hands gestured in frustration as they eyed him blankly and he tried to put his racing thoughts into words. "*Procyon*'s computers! When Megaira took out the AI, Alicia tapped into the net along with her!"

"What are you talking about?" Tannis demanded. "That's—I don't think that would be possible for a trained alpha-synth pilot, much less Alley! Even if she could, Shu just told us Treadwell wasn't in the computers."

"Don't you understand *yet*?" Ben Belkassem snarled so fiercely Tannis stepped back. "She's not crazy—not the way you thought! Tisiphone is *real*!"

Tannis and Keita exchanged quick glances, then turned wary eyes upon the inspector, as if they expected him to begin gibbering any moment, and he forced his anger and frustration back down.

"You weren't listening to me earlier," he said urgently. "I told you what she did to Alexsov. She didn't question him, she *read* his *mind.* Call it telepathy, call it rogue psi talents, call it any damned thing you want, but she *did* it!"

Keita sank back in his chair, Tannis drove her hands deep into her pockets and hunched her shoulders, and Ben Belkassem nodded slowly.

"Exactly. You may think Tisiphone is a product of Alicia's own mind—I don't. I sat across a dinner table and talked to her, for God's sake! I don't know what she is, but she's real, and she really can read minds . . . among other things. Think about how Alicia broke out of the hospital and stole *Megaira.* Think about how she tracked down the 'pirates,' damn it!"

"All right," Keita said at last. "All right, let's grant that Alicia—or this Tisiphone—can read minds. If she didn't get it from Alexsov, where could she have gotten it since?"

"From Rendlemann." Ben Belkassem pointed at Shu. "Remember what she said about what happened to him when Megaira took out *Procyon's* AI? That was Tisiphone. It had to be."

"Oh, come on!" Keita protested. "The man was linked to a crashed AI!"

"Oh?" Ben Belkassem turned to Tannis. "What normally happens to a cyber-synth operator when that happens, Major?"

"Catatonia," Tannis said promptly. "He goes out like a light."

"Then why did they have to *sedate* Rendlemann to hold him down?"

"Crap!" Tannis breathed. "He's right, Uncle Arthur—that's totally outside the profile. If Alley really can read minds now . . ."

There was a long moment of silence, and then Keita sighed.

"All right. Suppose she can—and did. Why the sudden concern?"

"If she knows about Treadwell, she's going to go for him," Ben Belkassem said flatly.

"Wait—just wait a minute!" Tannis protested. "What do you mean 'go for him'?"

"I mean she and Megaira—and Tisiphone—will try to kill him. She doesn't know we got any of Howell's staff alive. As far as she knows, she's the only person who knows the whole truth, and everyone thinks she's crazy. She thinks no one would believe her—that she *has* to get him herself."

"But she can't," Tannis said reasonably. "Treadwell's on the Soissons command fortress—she knows that."

"And she doesn't care. My God, it was all I could do to stop her from going after *Howell* by herself!"

"But it would be suicide. Alley would never do anything like that. I know her."

"You *knew* her," Ben Belkassem corrected grimly. He folded his hands tightly and stared down at them, choosing his words with care. "She's not crazy the way you thought she was, but—" He paused and inhaled deeply. "Major Cateau, Sir Arthur, there's something else going on inside her now. It wasn't there at Soissons. There's a . . . fanaticism. I saw it after Wyvern. She was fine before she found out about Alexsov and Brinkman, but then—"

"What are you saying, Ferhat?" Keita asked quietly.

"I'm saying she doesn't care about anything but destroying the 'pirates.' Nothing else is *real* to her anymore. She'll kill herself to get them . . . and she'll kill anyone else who stands in her way."

"Not *Alley*," Tannis whispered, but it wasn't a protest. She was pleading, and Ben Belkassem hated himself as he nodded. Keita stared at the inspector, and his mouth tightened.

"If you're right—I'm not certain you are, but *if* you're right—there are nine thousand other people on that fortress."

"I know."

"But could she even get through the defenses?" Suarez asked.

"She already got through them once," Ben Belkassem said. "She cut right through the middle of Howell's entire squadron. I don't know if she can get through the forts again. I wouldn't bet against it . . . but I doubt she could get back out alive."

"She wouldn't want to." Tears sounded in Tannis's voice. "Not Alley. Not after killing nine thousand innocent people." A sob caught in her throat. "If she could do that, she's turned into something she wouldn't want to live."

"She'll ram," Keita said softly. "She'll take the fort out with her Fasset drive. It's all she's got that could do the job."

"We have to warn them," Suarez said. "If we have Treadwell taken into custody, removed from the fortress, and tell her so—"

"We can't." Ben Belkassem smiled bitterly. "We don't have a starcom, and nothing we've got is as fast as *Megaira*."

"No," Keita said slowly, "but . . ." His voice trailed off, then he nodded decisively and stood. "We do have a dispatch boat. That's almost as fast, and she wormholed out of here almost directly away from Franconia. I doubt she had time to pre-plot it, either, so God only knows where she'll come out. I'll have Admiral Leibniz run the figures, but she's got to decelerate and reorient herself before she can even start for Soissons. If we leave immediately, we should beat her there with time to spare."

"And do what, Uncle Arthur?" Tannis asked in a tiny voice.

"I don't know, Tannis." He sighed. "I just don't know."

CHAPTER SIXTY-SIX

The shrill bell jarred her sleeping brain. She sat up in bed, rubbing her eyes, then glared at the chronometer and punched the com button.

"Horth. What is it, damn it?!"

"Sorry to disturb you, Admiral," her chief of staff said, "but Perimeter Tracking's just picked up two incoming drive signatures."

"So?" Vice Admiral Horth managed not to snarl. "We've got thirty, forty arrivals a day in this system."

"Yes, Ma'am, but these two both look like Fleet drives. Neither is scheduled, and they're coming in very, very fast on reciprocal bearings. If they're headed for rendezvous here, they must be planning crash turnovers."

"Crash turnovers?" Horth swung her feet out of bed and fumbled for her slippers with them. "What sort of vectors are we talking about?"

"The more distant bogey's turning just over fourteen hundred lights and bears roughly oh-seven-three by three-five-oh, Ma'am; the closer one is making twelve-sixty lights from two-five-five by oh-oh-three. Unless they change heading after they break sublight, they'll meet right at Soissons."

Horth frowned in surprise. Two Fleet units headed for rendezvous here and no one had even mentioned them to Traffic Control? But then the speeds registered. Twelve hundred times light-speed was moving it even for a dispatch boat, but nothing moved at fourteen hundred lights except—

She forgot her slippers and reached for her uniform.

"ETAs?" she snapped.

"If they both go for minimum distance turnover from Franconia's Powell limit, Bogey One—the closer one—will drop sublight at approximately ten-forty-one hours, Ma'am. Bogey Two will do the same at eleven-forty-six."

"Um." Horth slid out of her nightgown and started climbing into clothes. "All right. Alert all fortress commanders. We've got time, but I want all forts on standby by ten hundred hours. Then get hold of Admiral Marat. See if he's completed that estimate of the alpha-synth's capabilities and get it to me ASAP." She zipped her blouse and reached for her tunic. "Is Admiral Gomez back from Ithuriel with the Capital Squadron?"

"No, Ma'am. The maneuvers aren't due to end until late tomorrow."

"Damn. Admiral Brinkman?"

"He's already aboard Orbit One for your morning conference, Ma'am."

"Ask him to join me in PriCon immediately, but I don't see any reason to wake the Governor General so soon."

"Yes, Ma'am."

Horth grunted and cut the circuit, and her face was worried. They hadn't managed to keep that lunatic from *stealing* the alpha-synth. Somehow, even after all the fire control upgrades since, she didn't think they'd do a lot better keeping her out.

The ponderous orbital forts of the Franconia System lumbered to life and began their equipment tests. People were people, and the crazy drop commando had been the butt of tasteless jokes for months; now she was coming back, and Alicia DeVries' madness was no longer an amusing subject.

A half-crippled starship sped through wormhole space, vibrating to the harsh music of a damaged Fasset drive far too long on emergency overboost. One sleek flank was battered and broken. Splintered structural members and shattered weapons gaped through rent plating, the slagged remnants of a cargo shuttle were fused to a twisted shuttle rack, and there was silence on its flight deck. Its AI hugged her wordless sorrow, and a bodiless spirit four thousand years out of her own time brooded in mute anguish over the evil she had wrought. Neither of them spoke. There was nothing to say. The arguments had been exhausted long ago, and the woman in the command chair no longer even heard them. Her uniform was stained and sour, her skin oily, her hair unwashed and lank, and her red-rimmed eyes blazed with fixed, jade fire.

The starship *Megaira* hurtled onward, and madness sat at her controls.

"Hoo, boy! Look at that sucker," Lieutenant Boyce Anders muttered at his post in Tracking. Bogey One had timed its turnover perfectly; now it was sublight, ninety-three light-minutes from Orbit One and decelerating at thirteen hundred gravities. Whoever that was, he must have been in one hell of a hurry to get here. He was going to overshoot Soissons by almost a light-hour before he could kill his velocity, even at that deceleration.

The dispatch boat was crowded.

Keita hadn't even asked Tannis to stay behind—he recognized the impossible when he saw it—and Inspector Suarez had been almost as insistent. Keita didn't really need him, for his own legal authority was more than sufficient for the distasteful task in hand, but having a Criminal Branch chief inspector in the background couldn't hurt. Ben Belkassem hadn't insisted on anything; he'd simply arrived aboard with an expression even Keita wouldn't have cared to cross.

All of which meant they'd been living in one another's pockets for almost a week now, since the eight-man craft had designed accommodations for only two passengers. They'd packed themselves in somehow—and, at the moment, it seemed everyone aboard was crowded onto the flight deck.

"How do I play the com angle, Sir Arthur?" the lieutenant commanding the dispatch boat asked. "They won't expect anything from us for thirty minutes or so, but the way we're coming in has to've made them curious."

"You've got urgent dispatches," Keita rumbled. "Don't say a word about who's on board. If anyone asks, lie. I don't want anyone knowing we're here—or why—until I'm actually aboard that fortress."

"Yes, Sir. I—"

The lieutenant paused and pressed his synth-link headset to his temple, then gestured at a screen. Unarmed dispatch boats had neither the need nor the room for a warship's elaborate displays, but the view screen doubled as a plot when required. Now it flashed to life with a small-scale display of the Franconia System. The blue star of their Fasset drive moved only slowly on the display's scale, but a second star rushed to meet them at an incredible supralight velocity. Numbers scrolled across the bottom of the screen, then stopped and blinked with the computers' best guess.

If that other ship executed a crash turnover of its own, it would drop sublight in sixty-four minutes at a range of two-point-eight light-hours.

"Well, Bogey One's a dispatch boat, all right," Lieutenant Anders announced as Perimeter Tracking's light-speed sensors finally confirmed the gravity signature analysis.

The watch officer nodded and turned to pass the information in-system to Orbit One, and Anders swung his attention back to Bogey Two. He had no idea why that dispatch boat had arrived just now, yet he couldn't shake the conviction that it had to have something to do with Bogey Two—and he knew what Bogey Two had to be.

"Jesus!" he muttered to the woman at the next console as Bogey Two streaked towards Franconia's stellar Powell limit. "If she doesn't flip in about fifteen seconds, she's gonna have fried Fasset drive for lunch."

"Are we ready, Admiral?"

"As we can be, Governor." Vice Admiral Horth sat in her command chair, already wearing her headset, and studied her plot. "I wish I knew what she's up to this time around."

"It doesn't really matter, does it, Becky?" Sir Amos Brinkman asked, and Horth shook her head with a sigh.

"No, Amos. I don't suppose it does," she said softly.

* * *

<Coming up on turnover,> Megaira murmured hopelessly. *<Please, can't we—?>*

"No!" Alicia DeVries' contralto was as harsh and gaunt as her face. Cords showed in her throat, and somewhere deep inside she wept for her cruelty to Megaira, but the tears were far away and lost. "Just do it!" she snarled.

"It's *got* to be Alley. But how did she get here so soon?"

"I don't know, Tannis," Keita replied. "Coming in on that vector after the way she wormholed out . . . It just doesn't seem possible. She must have had her drive redlined all the way here."

"Should we warn Orbit One?" Ben Belkassem asked quietly.

Keita stood silent for a moment, then shook his head.

"No. They already have her course plotted. Nothing we can tell them could change their defensive responses, and the truth would only disorganize their command structure at the critical moment." He glanced at the lieutenant. "Continue your deceleration, Captain, but have your com section ready. We'll just barely have the range to reach her when she breaks sublight."

Ben Belkassem looked up sharply, then glanced at Tannis. The major hunched forward, staring at the plot, and the inspector moved even closer to Keita, pitching his voice too low for her to overhear.

"Do you really think you can talk her out of this, Sir Arthur?"

"Honestly?" Ben Belkassem nodded, and Keita sighed. "Not really. She's got a damned low opinion of imperial justice—God knows she has a right to it—and from what you've told me about her mental state—"

He exhaled sharply.

"No, I don't think I can talk her out of it, but that doesn't mean I don't have to try."

"Here . . . she . . . comes," Lieutenant Anders whispered. Then, "*Turnover!* Christ! Look at that decel!"

Megaira whipsawed on the brink of self-destruction as her maltreated Fasset drive took the strain. Her velocity wound down insanely, dropping towards the perimeter of wormhole space, and fittings rattled and banged. Alicia felt the vibration, felt the starship's pain in her own flesh, and her fixed stare never wavered.

"Bogey Two dropping sublight . . . now," Tracking reported to PriCon. "Deceleration holding steady at twenty-three-point-five KPS squared."

Horth nodded and leaned back in her chair, rubbing her chin. Odd. DeVries was piling on an awful lot of negative G for someone in such a big hurry to get here.

Megaira bucketed through space, just below drive overload, and her velocity dropped rapidly. A vector projected itself behind Alicia's eyes, one that stretched one and a third billion kilometers to a dot invisible with distance, and she smiled a death's-head smile.

Two starships raced toward one another, converging on the distant spark of Franconia, and a message reached out across the gap between them. Even light seemed to crawl at such a range, but *Megaira* sped to meet it even as she decelerated. The outer ring of orbital forts brought their fire control on line, searching for her, dueling with her ECM, and the AI noted the changes in their sensors. She was well outside range—for now—but she was committed to enter it, and the upgrades of the last few months would reduce her ECM's efficiency by at least forty percent.

She considered reporting to Alicia, but there was no point.

"Look! She's still decelerating!" Tannis Cateau exclaimed. "Maybe we were wrong!"

"Maybe we were," Keita agreed, but he met Ben Belkassem's eyes behind her and shook his head minutely.

"Admiral Horth, Bogey One is transmitting."

"Well?" The admiral eyed the com rating narrowly, alerted by something in the man's voice. "What does he say?"

"We don't know, Ma'am. It's an awful tight beam and it wasn't addressed to us—we just caught the edge of the carrier as it went past, and it's encrypted."

"*Encrypted?*" Treadwell's voice was sharp, and the com rating nodded.

"Yes, Sir. We're working on it, but it's going to take time. It's imperial in origin, but we've never seen anything quite like it."

"And it's being sent to the alpha-synth?" Horth pressed.

"Yes, Ma'am."

The admiral nodded, then watched Brinkman and Treadwell exchange glances and wondered just what the hell was going on.

Only three of the outer forts could range on *Megaira*, but SLAMs streaked out from them, and a low, harsh growl quivered in Alicia's throat as she watched their deadly sparkles come. They were beautiful, their threat lost in the elemental splendor of destruction, and part of her wanted to reach out and embrace their glory. But she couldn't. She must dance with them, avoiding them, cutting through them to reach the object of her hate.

She watched Megaira flirt with death, trolling the SLAMs off course with her electronic wiles, flipping aside to evade the ones she could not enmesh, and the AI's pain was a knife in her own heart. Yet she was beyond pain. Pain only fed her hunger, whatever its source.

Tisiphone stood silent and helpless in Alicia's mind. It was all she could do to keep Alicia's blind savagery from dragging Megaira under and clouding the lightning-fast reflexes which kept them both alive.

She'd never guessed what she was creating, never imagined the monster she'd spawned. She'd seen the power of Alicia DeVries's mind without recognizing the controls which kept that power in check, and only now had she begun to understand fully what she had done.

She had shattered those controls. The compassion and mercy she'd feared no longer existed, only the red, ravening hunger. Yet terrible as that might be, there was worse. She'd found the hole Alicia had gnawed through the wall about her inner rage, and she couldn't close it. Somehow, without even realizing it was possible, Alicia had reached beyond herself. She'd followed Tisiphone's connection to the Fury's own rage, her own destruction, and made that incalculable power hers as well.

For the first time in millennia, Tisiphone faced another as powerful as herself, a mortal mind which had stolen the power of the Furies themselves, and that power had driven it mad.

* * *

Vice Admiral Rebecca Horth sat silently, lips pressed firmly together, as the renegade alpha-synth evaded her SLAMs. More forts were firing now, and some of them, at least, were coming closer . . . but not close enough.

She checked the converging vectors again and frowned. The dispatch boat would pass within a few thousand kilometers of Soissons on its course to meet the alpha-synth, but if the alpha-synth maintained its present deceleration, it would pass well behind the planet when it crossed Soissons's orbit. Which made no sense, unless . . .

She stiffened in her chair and started punching new numbers into Tracking's extrapolations, and her face paled.

Ben Belkassem stood silent, chewing the inside of his lip raw, and smelled the tension about him. The dispatch boat's velocity was down to seventy-two percent of light-speed, but Alicia's more powerful drive had *Megaira* down to barely .88 C despite her far shorter deceleration period.

No one spoke, and he wondered if Keita suspected what he did. Probably. Did Tannis? He glanced at the major's white, strained features and looked away. She might not admit it to herself, but she must be beginning to.

He returned his gaze to the plot. Thank God he'd left Megaira the O Branch codes. At least they could talk to each other without Defense Command—and Treadwell—listening in.

"What the—?" Boyce Anders twitched in surprise and looked up at his supervisor. "Sir, Bogey Two's just made a second turn-over! She's stopped decelerating and started accelerating again."

Emotionless computers considered the changed data, and Anders gasped.

"Oh my God—she's on a collision course for Orbit One!"

Tannis groaned as *Megaira* turned end-for-end and aligned her Fasset drive on the point in space Orbit One would reach in forty-two minutes and sixteen seconds. It turned the drive into a shield against the heavier fire of the inner fortress ring—and at the moment she reached Orbit One, the alpha-synth would have regained virtually all the velocity she'd lost. Alicia would be moving at .985 C when she rammed.

Fifty-seven minutes after it had been sent, Keita's desperate message converged with *Megaira*'s receivers.

Alicia looked up incuriously as a com screen blinked to life. She recognized the face, but the person who had known and respected—even loved—that man was dead, and the powerful voice meant less than the brutal vibration lashing *Megaira*'s overstressed hull.

"Alley, I know what you're doing," the voice said, "but you don't have to. We have independent confirmation, Alley; we know who you're after, and I swear we'll get him. You've done enough—now you have to break off." Sir Arthur Keita's eyes pled with her from the screen and his voice was raw with pain yet soft. "*Please*, Alley. Break off. You don't have to kill nine thousand people. Don't turn yourself into the very thing you hate."

<Alley?> It was Megaira's pleading mental voice. *<Alley, they know about Treadwell. You don't have to—>*

"It doesn't matter! They knew about Watts and let the bastard live! You think someone like *Treadwell* won't have something to trade them for his life?!"

<But Uncle Arthur's given you his word! Please, *Alley! Don't make me help you kill yourself!>*

Alicia only snarled in response. She turned her eyes from the screen where Keita's face still begged her to relent. She closed her ears to his voice, and deep at her very core, where even she could no longer hear it, a lost soul sobbed in torment. She locked her attention on Orbit One, ignoring the SLAMs still flashing towards her. All that mattered was that distant sphere of battle steel. Her smoking bloodlust craved the destruction to come—and the last, dying fragment of the person she once had been embraced it as her only escape from what she had become.

"She's not breaking off," Tannis whispered, and Keita nodded. Ten minutes had passed since Alicia must have received their message, and *Megaira* held her course unflinchingly. He glanced at the plot. The dispatch boat had crossed Soissons's orbit eleven minutes ago, and the range to *Megaira* had fallen to thirty light-minutes.

The handful of warships in the system were converging on the alpha-synth, but none of them could reach her in time.

He closed his eyes, then turned to the dispatch boat's commander.

"I need two volunteers. One in the engine room and one on the helm. Put the rest of your people into your shuttle and get out of here."

The lieutenant looked up in confusion, but Ben Belkassem understood.

"I'm a pretty fair helmsman, Sir Arthur," he said.

"What—?"

Tannis broke off, eyes widening, and stared mutely at Keita. The brigadier gazed back, sad eyes unflinching, and she bit her lip.

"Go with them, Tannis," he said gently.

"No. Let *me* talk to her! I can stop her—I know I can!"

"There's no time . . . and there's only one shuttle. If you don't leave now, you can't leave at all."

"I know," she said, and he started to make it an order, then sighed.

"Admiral, that dispatch boat's shuttle just separated."

Admiral Horth tore herself away from the intensifying fire ripping ineffectually towards the alpha-synth and checked her plot as the shuttle arced away from the dispatch boat's base course. It was fourteen light-minutes from Soissons, still streaking for the far side of nowhere at sixty-five percent of light-speed, and no shuttle could kill that kind of velocity. Which meant its crew must be counting on someone else's picking them up . . . and must have a very urgent reason for abandoning ship.

The dispatch boat's vector curved very slightly, and Horth swallowed in sudden understanding. Its course had been roughly convergent with the alpha-synth's from the start; now the match was perfect, and the dispatch boat was no longer decelerating.

A blue dot swelled ahead of *Megaira* on Alicia's mental plot, far larger and more powerful than any SLAM. Her nostrils flared and she bared her teeth as hate boiled within her. She knew what it had to be—and that, unlike a SLAM, it possessed onboard seeking capability.

She hunched down in her command chair, eyes bloodshot and wild, but her course never deviated. She would reach Treadwell or die trying, and dying would be a triumph in itself.

Sir Arthur Keita glanced at the chronometer. Ben Belkassem had the helm. The dispatch boat's skipper had taken over Engineering, and Tannis manned the communications console. No one else was aboard, and they had eight-point-nine minutes—under seven, given relativity's dictates—to live. It seemed unfair, somehow, to be robbed of those few, precious seconds by Einstein's ancient equations, but he pushed the thought aside.

"Talk to her, Tannis," he said softly.

"Alley—it's Tannis, Alley."

Alicia's eyes jerked back to the com, and her wrath faltered. A strange sound hung in the air, and she realized it was herself, the unbroken, animal snarl of her rage. She sucked in breath, frowning in slow, painful confusion as she peered at the screen. Tannis? What was Tannis doing here?

"I'm on the dispatch boat ahead of you, Alley," Tannis said, and Alicia's heart spasmed. Tears gleamed on Tannis's face and hung in her soft voice, and a tattered fragment of the old Alicia writhed under them. "Uncle Arthur's with me, Sarge—and Ben Belkassem. We . . . can't let you do this."

Alicia tried to speak, tried to scream at Tannis to get out of her path, to let her by to rend and destroy, to run for her own life, but nothing came out, and Tannis went on speaking as the hurtling vessels raced together at a closing speed one and a half times that of light.

"Please, Alley," Tannis begged. "We know the truth. Uncle Arthur knows. We've brought the warrants with us. We'll get him, Alley—I swear we will. Don't do this. Don't make us kill you."

Agony stabbed Alicia. She wanted to tell Tannis it was all right, that she *had* to be killed. Death didn't twist her with anguish and startle tears back into her glaring eyes at last. It was Tannis's voice, Tannis's sorrow, and knowing the only way that unarmed dispatch boat could kill her.

"Please," she whispered to the bulkheads. "Oh, *please*, Tannis. Not you, too."

But her transmitter was dead; only Megaira and Tisiphone heard her anguish, and Tannis drew a deep breath on her com screen.

"All right, Alley," she whispered. "At least it won't be a stranger."

Alicia DeVries staggered up out of her command chair and pounded the com with her bare fists. Shattered plastic slashed her hands bloody, and her animal shriek of loss drowned even the howl of *Megaira*'s tortured drive. She ripped the unit from the console and hurled it to the deck, but she couldn't kill the memory, couldn't stop it, couldn't stop knowing who she was about to kill, and hatred and loss and grief were an agony not even death could quench.

"She's not going to break off," Keita whispered through bloodless lips, and Tannis sobbed silently in agreement.

Ben Belkassem only nodded and adjusted his course slightly.

The being called Tisiphone had no eyes. She had never wept, for she had never known sorrow, or compassion, or love. Those things were alien to her, no part of the thing she had been created to be.

Until now.

She felt Megaira's frantic grief beyond the barrier she held between Alicia's madness and the AI, felt it like a pale, anemic shadow of Alicia's agony. The agony *she* had created. The torment she had inflicted upon an innocent. Only the tiniest shadow of Alicia DeVries survived, and the fault was hers. She had reduced the greatest warrior she had ever known to a hate-maddened animal who could be stopped only by death, and—far, far worse than that—Alicia knew what had happened. Somewhere deep inside, she stared in horror at the thing she had become and begged to die.

Tisiphone looked upon the work of her hands and recoiled in horror of her own. She'd been corrupted, she realized. She'd broken Alicia DeVries, shattered her concepts of justice and mercy, of compassion and honor, and even as she stripped them from her victim, they had infected her. She'd seen herself in Alicia from the outset; now she had perfected the Fury in Alicia, but *she* had become something else, and what she saw appalled her.

She fought against the paralysis of her own self-disgust. Alicia's bottomless hate and hunger hissed and crackled before her, and she feared them. She, who had never known fear, knew terror as she confronted her equal. It would be so easy to hold her hand, to wait out the last fleeting minutes and let death separate her from that seething well of power, for Alicia DeVries *was* a Fury, fit to destroy even an immortal.

But Tisiphone had learned too much, changed too fundamentally. It was her fault, she'd told Alicia, and hers the price to pay.

She paused for one blazing second, drawing in her power, and attacked.

Alicia DeVries howled and lurched to her feet, pounding her head with clenched, bloody fists. She staggered, writhing in her agony, and rebounded from the uncaring battle steel of a bulkhead. She went back to her knees, beating her face against the padded deck sole in a blind, demented frenzy, and chaos raged behind her eyes.

The blood-red ferocity of her madness shuddered as Tisiphone drove into it, and thunderbolts of raw, unfocused power flayed the Fury with spikes of agony she had never been meant to know. Fury opposed Fury, clawing and gouging, and there was no mercy in Alicia. She lashed out, frantic to kill, to destroy, to avenge all her loss and torment and betrayal and suffering even if she must drown a universe in blood, and Tisiphone screamed in soundless pain under the avalanche of hate.

She could not reply in kind—she *would* not! She had said she was more skilled to wound than heal, and it was true, but this time she would heal or perish herself. She refused to strike back. She absorbed the killing blows without riposte, and drove a tortured sliver of her being towards the wound in Alicia's mind—the bleeding hole to Hell that filled Alicia with madness.

She touched it, only for an instant, and staggered as she was hurled away. Bits and pieces of her own being were ripped from her, added to the holocaust reaching to consume her, and she clawed her way back into its teeth. Somewhere behind it she heard the sobbing of a little girl—a mortal girl alone and terrified in hell-spawned darkness—and groped blindly for her hand.

* * *

Tannis Cateau sat silent at the com station, face bloodless. Sir Arthur Keita stood beside her, one arm around her shoulders, and a display at Ben Belkassem's elbow raced downward, counting off the moments left to live.

Ninety seconds. Eighty. Seventy-five. Seventy. Sixty-five. Sixty. Fifty-five. Fifty—

And then the oncoming Fasset drive swung aside, clawing away from its deathride with frantic power, and Ben Belkassem wrenched his own course to the side while Sir Arthur Keita leapt for the com and began bellowing orders for Vice Admiral Horth to cease fire.

EPILOGUE

The elevator door opened, and Ferhat Ben Belkassem stepped onto the flight deck of the refurbished starship *Megaira.* Alicia DeVries unfolded herself from the command chair, immaculate as of yore in midnight-blue and silver. Her hair was its natural color once more, spilling over her shoulders in a tide of sunrise, and Ben Belkassem decided it went even better with the uniform than her black hair had.

He held out his hand.

"Ferhat."

She took his hand in both of hers, squeezing firmly, and he marveled again at the way her smile got inside a person. The fanaticism and hatred were gone, yet they'd left their mark. There was a new depth in her cool, jade eyes, a softness. Not a weakness, but a new strength, perhaps. The strength of someone who understands how utterly any human, however remarkable, can be reduced.

"Alicia." He looked around with a smile of his own. "How was the shakedown cruise?"

"Why not ask someone who knows?" a voice said from a speaker, and his smile turned into a grin. "As a matter of fact," Megaira continued, "it went even better than the original builders' trials." The speaker sniffed. "I *told* them we could increase the drive mass."

"Must have been a shock for the yard to have the ship talking back."

"It was good for them," Megaira insisted.

"Probably." His eye fell on the chair still sitting beside Alicia's, and he settled into it with a little sigh. "Never thought I'd sit here again," he said softly, rubbing the armrests gently.

"You almost didn't get to," Alicia agreed. She could talk about it now with only the faintest twinge. She remembered every horrifying moment, yet the memories held no terror. They were only memories—and warnings.

"How's Tisiphone?" Ben Belkassem asked after a moment, and Alicia smiled wryly, stroking her temple unconsciously.

"Still here—though I'm not too sure Tannis and Uncle Arthur *really* believe in her even now."

"Ha! They believe. The Emperor doesn't hand out citations—not even secret ones—to figments of the imagination. They may not agree on *what* she is, but they know she's there." He cocked his head and eyed her curiously. "Speaking of whom, I sort of had the impression she'd be . . . Well, moving on once the job was over."

<As did I,> a voice said wryly in Alicia's mind.

<Should I tell him?>

<You may as well, Little One. I would prefer not to keep secrets from him—nor am I any too sure we could if we tried!>

"I'm afraid she can't 'move on,'" Alicia said to Ben Belkassem. The inspector raised his eyebrows, and she sighed. "Something happened there at the last. I don't understand it—I'm not even sure Tisiphone does, really—but we both came so close to, well—"

She paused and cleared her throat, and Ben Belkassem nodded.

"She stopped me somehow," Alicia continued softly. "There was a . . . a *hole* inside me. I'm not sure I can explain it, but—"

<I believe I can, Little One. With your permission?>

Alicia blinked in surprise, then nodded and sat back to listen to her own voice.

"At first, I did not understand what Alicia had done, Inspector," the Fury said through Alicia's mouth, and to his credit, he didn't even flinch. "I had sealed a portion of her mind—a mistake which almost destroyed her, for she is not a person to submit to transgressions tamely."

Ben Belkassem nodded, watching with fascination as Alicia turned pink.

"She attacked the barrier I had built and breached it, and in the process she accomplished still more. I was made three in one,

Inspector. There were . . . connections between my selves, but I lost them when I lost my sisters. Or so I thought, for in truth, they exist still. One set I extended without even realizing to Megaira, and so we were able to accomplish much, yet I was in control of that linkage, however little I recognized it.

"But I was not prepared when Alicia forced open the other. Sir Arthur, as you know, once speculated that I was some manner of secondary personality, created when Alicia awakened inherent psionic capabilities of her own. He was wrong, but not entirely. She *did* possess such talents, latent and undeveloped but powerful, and I did not recognize them. I ought to have. There were . . . signs of them before ever Alicia and I actually met. But despite that, I did not anticipate the reality of which she proved capable. I am inclined, as you may have observed, to arrogance. I do not apologize. It is my nature, yet because of my arrogance, I had always scorned human minds.

"That," Alicia heard "her" voice turn wry, "is no longer the case. Alicia has cured me. My presence awoke that capability to reach in through the unused link I had forgotten, and through it she tapped my basic structure. Even the best of human minds—even Alicia's—is not equal to that. I have learned much from Alicia, yet I remain what I am, and it drove her mad."

There was a moment of silence before Tisiphone resumed.

"The only way in which I might cure her madness and restore what I had stolen from her was to close the link, yet she had grown too powerful. I would have failed and been destroyed had not a tiny core of her still stood and fought at my side. Between us, we sealed the wound, but our power, our natures, were interwoven in the sealing. In short, I am bound to Alicia now. I cannot leave her, cannot long exist if I separate myself from her."

"Do you mean to say you're *mortal* now?" Ben Belkassem asked carefully.

"I do not know," Tisiphone said calmly. "With good fortune, I shall not know for many years, for I intend to take very good care of my sister Alicia."

"But . . . but doesn't it bother you?"

"An impertinent question, Ferhat Ben Belkassem," Tisiphone observed, and Alicia smiled around the words at the inspector's expression, "and the answer—like so many others, I fear—is that I do not truly know. My sister selves are long since gone. Without Alicia and Megaira, I would be alone once more, and loneliness is not pleasant. I will remain with my friends and face what comes when it comes."

"I see." Ben Balkassem shook his head, then cleared his throat. "Well, that seems like a perfect opening for what brings me here."

He laid his briefcase in his lap, opened it, and sorted through the old-fashioned parchment documents it contained.

"Let me see. . . . First, your official pardon, Alicia." He extended the document with a flourish. "Sorry it took so long. I understand there were some wrung hands back in Old Earth—especially when you kept the *Bengal*; I think they figured you could at least give *it* back. But when the Emperor awards the sole living holder of the Banner of Terra his personal thanks for services rendered, it would be downright tacky to send the recipient to prison for grand theft, however grand it was.

"Second, a legal opinion I think you'll all be glad to have." He looked at the wall speaker. "This one's for you, actually, Megaira. As you know, imperial law has always held that artificial intelligences are not persons in a legal sense because of the demonstrable fact that AIs are not only artificial and unstable but simply don't have a true sense of personality. You, however, are a special case, and the judiciary, at the Emperor's strong urging, has determined that you are, in fact, a person. As such, you cannot be considered property without violation of the constitutional prohibition of slavery."

"Sounds like a mouthful of lawyer's double-talk to me," the speaker said suspiciously. "And anybody who thinks *I'm* a slave is gonna get a Hauptman coil where he lives!"

"A possibility which, I feel sure, did not escape the judiciary's attention," Ben Belkassem said wryly. "The point, Megaira, is that Fleet is now required to officially renounce all claim of ownership. Not, I suspect, without some sense of relief. You own yourself, dear—and I brought a voter registration form with me if you're interested." He smiled beatifically. "I expect the court hadn't considered that aspect of the matter."

"Hey, that's great!" Megaira exclaimed, then paused. "Whoa! Does this mean I have to pay taxes?"

"All the rights—and duties—of citizenship are yours, dear Megaira," he said sweetly, and a disgusted sound came from the speaker.

"And third," Ben Belkassem dived back into his briefcase for a small leather wallet, "and perhaps most importantly, I come bearing an invitation."

"Invitation?" Alicia asked, and he sobered.

"Yes. I know the whole Colonel Watts affair left a bitter taste in your mouth, Alicia, but I hope some of that bitterness has eased now."

He held her eyes and she nodded slowly as she remembered.

Seamus II had summoned her to Sligo Palace.

She'd gone unwillingly, only to find herself alone with him in an unheard-of private audience. He'd faced her, standing before a portrait of Terrence Murphy, and when she'd started to kneel before him, he'd stopped her with a gesture.

"I asked you to come here, Captain DeVries," he'd said, "because this is where you were the day that I betrayed my oath to you and your company."

"Your Majesty, I—"

"No, Captain." His raised hand had silenced her, and he'd looked her directly in the eye. "There was a time, in a courtyard not far from this audience chamber, when I told you and the other survivors of Charlie Company that I owed them and their dead comrades my personal thanks. That was no more than the truth, and over and beyond my debt to Charlie Company as a whole, there was my debt to you personally, and to your family. Not just to you, but to your grandfather, and to your father.

"But when Baron Yuroba and Lady Canaris came to me, I let myself forget that. It's true that a head of state must be able to think beyond the purely personal, that there are times when he must be ruthless in pursuit of his greater responsibilities to all of the people he governs. But that can never excuse me for having forgotten what Charlie Company did—not just for me, but for all of the people I govern. I owed them justice. I didn't give it to them, and you were right to refuse to serve an Emperor who could dishonor himself by dishonoring his own dead."

Alicia had stared at him, unable to quite believe what he'd said, and then the most powerful human being in the history of mankind had bent his head.

"Alicia Dierdre DeVries," he'd said, "We, Seamus, of Our House the seventeenth and of Our name the second, beg you to accept the apology of the House of Murphy. We have proven unworthy of the service you have rendered so unstintingly to Us and to Our Crown, yet We shall strive to make what amends We may. And," he'd raised his head once more, to look her directly in the eye, "you have Our personal word, as Emperor of Humanity, that there will be no 'deals' for the criminals responsible for *this* atrocity. Whoever they may be, whatever their names or their positions or the power they expect to save them, they will pay the full price for their actions."

And he'd meant that promise. Treadwell and Brinkman had already been sentenced to death, and a relentless Ministry of Justice was bringing down an amazing number of multibillionaires and even trillionaires, as well. The money that had backed Treadwell in the name of profit was no protection now, and neither were noble titles or positions of power. Two dukes, both members of the House of Murphy themselves, were awaiting trial, and two senators representing Incorporated Worlds in the Franconia Sector had already been indicted. There were rumors that at least three more would soon be charged, and two more senior admirals, a half-dozen junior flag officers, and dozens of less senior Fleet and Marine officers were also under arrest.

None of it could bring back Charlie Company's dead or give them the justice they had been denied, but her Empire and her Emperor had once more proven themselves worthy of her devotion.

"Yes, Ferhat," she said now, quietly. "Some of it's eased."

"Good, because in light of what the three of you achieved entirely on your own, I've been empowered to offer you this."

He opened the wallet, and Alicia's eyes widened as she saw the archaic, glittering badge. It was an inspector's badge—an *O Branch* inspector's badge, with her name engraved upon it.

"As a free and independent subject of the Emperor," Ben Belkassem went on, "Megaira is entitled to a badge of her own—a sergeant's, in her case—assuming you accept. Under the circumstances, I thought it might be best not to ask for one for Tisiphone."

He held out the badge and Alicia reached for it in shock, then snatched her hand back as if it had burned her, and a memory flashed through her mind. Of another day, in an office on Old Earth, and her own hand, laying aside the starship and harp which had meant so much to her.

"You can't be serious!" she blurted. "*Me* work for O Branch? What about my reserve Cadre commission?"

"I discussed it with Sir Arthur. He sees no difficulty with retaining you on active duty for indefinite assignment to O Branch. We've worked well with the Cadre in the past; there's no reason we shouldn't in the future."

"But—"

"Before you turn me down, let me point out some of the advantages. First, there's the matter of your logistics. Megaira is a free person, and the starship *Megaira*, as her 'body,' belongs to her, but operating and maintaining an alpha-synth is expensive—as much as five million a year even without combat. You'd be hard pressed to show that much profit as a merchant ship, but if you join O Branch, the Ministry will cover your operating costs."

Alicia nodded but had to lower her eyes to hide the laughter in them as she wondered how Ben Belkassem's superiors would react to her bank account on Thaarvhld. Megaira had been conservative in her estimate, and three hundred forty million credits, at twelve percent compound interest, would have covered their costs quite nicely.

"But that's only one reason," Ben Belkassem resumed more seriously, leaning forward in his chair. "You believe in justice, Alicia, and you've proved how much you can accomplish."

She eyed him doubtfully, and he shrugged.

"Think about it. We need you. My God, what the three of you could achieve with O Branch backing! An alpha-synth with a mind-reader for a pilot? Alley, my director would paint himself purple and dance naked on the palace lawn at high noon for a combination like that! He's even let me pick your Ministry code name." He grinned again as she raised an eyebrow. "I thought 'Fury' would be fitting."

Alicia sat back in her chair, watching his smiling face, and temptation stirred.

<*Megaira?*> she asked.

<*Count me in, Alley. You* know *it's only a matter of time before the do-gooder in you gets us back into trouble anyway, and it'd be kind of nice not to at least not have the good guys shooting at us for a change when it does.*>

Alicia's lips twitched, and she turned to the Fury.

<*Tisiphone?*>

<*I cast my vote with Megaira. You are what you are, Little One, as I am. I feel the pull yet. After five thousand years, it is difficult to see evil and know it may go unpunished, yet I have learned to respect this concept of justice. It is far more satisfying than meting out punishment on the whim of some irritated deity!*>

Alicia nodded slowly and cocked her head to give Ben Belkassem a long, measuring look.

"I'm tempted—we all are," she said finally, "but there's one little point that bothers me. Once I start working with other people, they're going to figure out I'm talking to someone they can't see. Aren't they likely to think I'm just a teeny bit crazy when I do?"

"Well, of course they are!" Ben Belkassem looked at her in such obvious surprise she blinked. "Surely you didn't think that would be a problem?" Alicia simply stared at him, and he shook his head. "Alley, *everyone* in O Branch is crazy, or we wouldn't be here."

He grinned and extended the badge once more.

This time she took it.

CHARACTER LIST

Abernathy, Sergeant Lawrence, Imperial Cadre—leader, Fire Team Bravo, 1st Squad, 1st Platoon, Charlie Company, 3rd Battalion, 2nd Regiment, 5th Brigade, Imperial Cadre.

Abrams, Jesse—permanent undersecretary, Imperial Foreign Ministry.

Abruzzi, Lloyd—Group Leader, Freedom Alliance Liberation Army.

Adams, Corporal Jake, Imperial Cadre—Tannis Cateau's assigned wingman for Operation Clean Sweep.

Ahearn, Captain Leon, Imperial Marine Corps, CO, Bravo Company, 3rd Battalion, 2nd Regiment, 3012th Brigade.

Alexsov, Captain Gregor Borissovich—James Howell's chief of staff.

Alves, Lieutenant Akama, Imperial Cadre—CO, 3rd Platoon, Charlie Company, 3rd Battalion, 2nd Regiment, 5th Brigade, Imperial Cadre (Louvain).

Alwyn, Captain Madison, Imperial Cadre—CO, Charlie Company, 3rd Battalion, 2nd Regiment, 5th Brigade, Imperial Cadre.

Anders, Lieutenant Boyce, Imperial Fleet—a Soissons System Fortress Command tracking officer.

Andersson, Corporal Erik, Imperial Cadre—Fire Team Alpha, 1st Squad, 1st Platoon, Charlie Company, 3rd Battalion, 2nd Regiment, 5th Brigade, Imperial Cadre. Later lieutenant (see below).

Andersson, Lieutenant Erik, Imperial Cadre—CO, 1st Platoon, Charlie Company, 3rd Battalion, 2nd Regiment, 5th Brigade, Imperial Cadre (Louvain).

Androniko, Major Aleka, Imperial Cadre—XO, Camp Cochrane.

Arbatov, General Dugald, Imperial Cadre—CO, Imperial Cadre.

Arun, Sergeant First Class Namrata, Imperial Cadre—squad leader, 2nd Squad, 2nd Platoon, Charlie Company, 3rd Battalion, 2nd Regiment, 5th Brigade, Imperial Cadre.

Ashmead, Corporal Jeremy, Imperial Cadre—Fire Team Alpha, 3rd Squad, 1st Platoon, Charlie Company, 3rd Battalion, 2nd Regiment, 5th Brigade, Imperial Cadre.

Aubert, Jasper—Crown Governor, Gyangtse.

Barr, Commander Quentin—CO "pirate" destroyer *Harpy.*

Becker, Captain Adriana, Imperial Marine Corps—CO, Bravo Company, Recon Battalion, 1st Regiment, 517th Brigade.

Beckett, Corporal Digory, Imperial Cadre—Fire Team Bravo, 3rd Squad, 3rd Platoon, Charlie Company, 3rd Battalion, 2nd Regiment, 5th Brigade, Imperial Cadre. Later master sergeant (see below).

Beckett, Master Sergeant Digory, Imperial Cadre—platoon sergeant, 2nd Platoon, Charlie Company, 3rd Battalion, 2nd Regiment, 5th Brigade, Imperial Cadre (Louvain).

Ben Belkassem, Inspector Ferhat, Ministry of Justice—an Operations Branch inspector assigned to the Franconian Sector.

Bennett, Major Alexander, Imperial Marine Corps—CO, Marine Detachment, HMS *Ctesiphon.*

Beregovoi, Lieutenant Boris Adrianovich, Imperial Marine Corps—staff intelligence officer, Recon Battalion, 1st Regiment, 517th Brigade.

Bergerat, Private César, Imperial Marine Corps—rifleman, Fire Team Bravo, 3rd Squad, 2nd Platoon, Bravo Company, Recon Battalion, 1st Regiment, 517th Brigade.

Boniface, Captain Sigmund ("Siggy"), Imperial Marine Corps—CO, Bravo Company, Marine Detachment, HMS *Ctesiphon.*

Bonrepaux, Corporal Édouard, Imperial Cadre—Fire Team Alpha, 1st Squad, 1st Platoon, Charlie Company, 3rd Battalion, 2nd Regiment, 5th Brigade, Imperial Cadre.

Branigan, Corporal Manfred, Imperial Cadre—Fire Team Bravo, 1st Squad, 3rd Platoon, Charlie Company, 3rd Battalion, 2nd Regiment, 5th Brigade, Imperial Cadre.

Brinkman, Vice Admiral Amos, Imperial Fleet—Admiral Gomez's second-in-command, Franconia Fleet District.

Brno, Governor Emily—Crown Governor, Mathison's World.

Brookman, Master Sergeant John, Imperial Cadre—platoon sergeant, 3rd Platoon, Charlie Company, 3rd Battalion, 2nd Regiment, 5th Brigade, Imperial Cadre.

Bruckner, Sergeant Clarissa, Imperial Marine Corps—squad leader, 2nd Squad, 2nd Platoon, Bravo Company, Recon Battalion, 1st Regiment, 517th Brigade.

Burkhart, Cornelius—Group Leader, Freedom Alliance Liberation Army.

Canaris, Jennifer Abigail—Imperial Minister of Justice.

Cateau, Corporal Tannis, Imperial Cadre—rifleman/medic, 1st Squad, 1st Platoon, Charlie Company, 3rd Battalion, 2nd Regiment, 5th Brigade, Imperial Cadre. Later major (see below).

Cateau, Major Tannis, Imperial Cadre (Medical Branch)—Alicia DeVries's assigned physician.

Chernienko, Corporal Ingrid, Imperial Cadre—Fire Team Alpha, 3rd Squad, 3rd Platoon, Charlie Company, 3rd Battalion, 2nd Regiment, 5th Brigade, Imperial Cadre.

Chiawa, Captain Karsang Dawa—CO, Alpha Company, 1st Battalion, 1st Capital Regiment, Gyangtse Planetary Militia.

Chisholm, Lieutenant Andrew ("Andy")—second officer of the free-trader *Star Runner.*

Choi, The Honorable Karen—Imperial Minister of the Interior.

Chu, Corporal Helena, Imperial Cadre—Fire Team Alpha, 1st Squad, 2nd Platoon, Charlie Company, 3rd Battalion, 2nd Regiment, 5th Brigade, Imperial Cadre.

Chul, Corporal Byung Cha, Imperial Cadre—Fire Team Alpha, 1st Squad, 1st Platoon, Charlie Company, 3rd Battalion, 2nd Regiment, 5th Brigade, Imperial Cadre.

Cortez, Sir Donovan—Imperial Minister of Justice.

Cronkite, Master Sergeant Denise, Imperial Cadre—platoon leader, 2nd Platoon, Charlie Company, 3rd Battalion, 2nd Regiment, 5th Brigade, Imperial Cadre.

Cusherwa, Major Ang Chembal—CO, 3rd Battalion, 1st Capital Regiment, Gyangtse Planetary Militia.

d'Amcourt, Commander Henry—James Howell's logistics officer.

de Nijs, Corporal Karin, Imperial Cadre—Fire Team Bravo, 2nd Squad, 2nd Platoon, Charlie Company, 3rd Battalion, 2nd Regiment, 5th Brigade, Imperial Cadre.

de Reibeck, Lieutenant Pablo, Imperial Cadre (Medical Branch)—Alicia DeVries' physical therapist.

DeVries, Captain Alicia Dierdre, Imperial Cadre.

DeVries, Clarissa Sinead—Alicia DeVries's younger sister.

DeVries, Collum—Alicia DeVries's father.

DeVries, Dr. Fiona Eleanora O'Shaughnessy—Alicia DeVries's mother.

DeVries, Steven Sebastian—Alicia DeVries's younger brother.

Diomedes, Captain Kostatina, Imperial Marine Corps—CO, Charlie Company, Recon Battalion, 1st Regiment, 517th Brigade.

Doorn, Corporal Michael, Imperial Cadre—Fire Team Alpha, 1st Squad, 1st Platoon, Charlie Company, 3rd Battalion, 2nd Regiment, 5th Brigade, Imperial Cadre.

Dubois, Corporal Benjamin, Imperial Cadre—Fire Team Bravo, 1st Squad, 1st Platoon, Charlie Company, 3rd Battalion, 2nd Regiment, 5th Brigade, Imperial Cadre.

DuPuy, Corporal Serena, Imperial Cadre—Fire Team Alpha, 3rd Squad, 2nd Platoon, Charlie Company, 3rd Battalion, 2nd Regiment, 5th Brigade, Imperial Cadre.

Erickson, Brigadier Lawrence, Imperial Marine Corps—CO, 517th Brigade.

Falconi, Commodore Tadeoshi—CO, Falconi's Falcons.

Filipov, Corporal Alexandra, Imperial Cadre—Fire Team Bravo, 1st Squad, 3rd Platoon, Charlie Company, 3rd Battalion, 2nd Regiment, 5th Brigade, Imperial Cadre.

Ford, Surgeon Commander Hillary, Imperial Fleet—Surgeon Captain Okanami's chief neurologist.

Fuchien, Lewis—a Dewent smuggler/businessman.

Gennady, Senator Edward—member of the Imperial Senate and founder of the Center for Human-Interspecies Relations Policy.

Geoffrey, Duke—Duke of Shallingsport.

Gilroy, Staff Sergeant Henry, Imperial Cadre—squad leader, 2nd Squad, 1st Platoon, Charlie Company, 3rd Battalion, 2nd Regiment, 5th Brigade, Imperial Cadre.

Giolitti, Lieutenant Charles, Jungian Navy—a naval officer assigned to the MaGuire Customs Service.

Gomez, Admiral Lady Rosario, Baroness Nova Tampico and Knight of the Solar Cross, Imperial Fleet—CO, Franconia Fleet District.

Granger, Lieutenant Jeremiah, Imperial Fleet—CO HMS *Shuriken* and senior officer present, Gyangtse System.

Gresham, Colonel Judson, Imperial Cadre (retired)—a Cadre recruiting officer.

Haroldson, Staff Sergeant Greta, Imperial Marine Corps—Alicia DeVries's roommate on Jepperson.

Hartwell, Corporal Imogene, Imperial Cadre—Fire Team Alpha, 1st Squad, 1st Platoon, Charlie Company, 3rd Battalion, 2nd Regiment, 5th Brigade, Imperial Cadre.

Hayden IV, Planetary King, Fuller.

Hennessey, Sergeant Jake, Imperial Cadre—Charlie Company, 3rd Battalion, 2nd Regiment, 5th Brigade, Imperial Cadre.

Heyter, Lieutenant Lois—tracking officer aboard mercenary battleship *Audacious*.

Hill, Sergeant Major Cassius, Imperial Marine Corps—battalion sergeant major, Alicia DeVries's training battalion.

Hillman, Staff Sergeant Celestine, Imperial Cadre—squad leader, 3rd Squad, 1st Platoon, Charlie Company, 3rd Battalion, 2nd Regiment, 5th Brigade, Imperial Cadre.

Hilton, PFC Gregory, Imperial Marine Corps—rifleman, Fire Team Bravo, 3rd Squad, 2nd Platoon, Bravo Company, Recon Battalion, 1st Regiment, 517th Brigade.

Hirshfield, Staff Sergeant Janson, Imperial Marine Corps—senior company clerk, Recon Battalion, 1st Regiment, 517th Brigade.

Horth, Vice Admiral Rebecca ("Becky"), Imperial Fleet—CO, Soissons System Fortress Command.

Howard, Corporal Alec, Imperial Cadre—Fire Team Alpha, 2nd Squad, 3rd Platoon, Charlie Company, 3rd Battalion, 2nd Regiment, 5th Brigade, Imperial Cadre.

Howell, Commodore James—field commander of the "pirates" raiding the Franconia Sector.

Hudson, Captain John, Imperial Marine Corps—chief medical officer, Recon Battalion, 1st Regiment, 517th Brigade.

Hugin, Lieutenant Commander Jeremiah—Arlen Monkoto's XO on Ringbolt.

Hunter, Lieutenant Vincent, Imperial Marine Corps—communications officer, 2nd Battalion, 3rd Regiment, 317th Brigade.

Hyde, Dr. Maxwell (Major, retired), Imperial Cadre—senior physician, Camp Cochrane.

Inglewood, Corporal Martha, Imperial Cadre—Fire Team Bravo, 1st Squad, 2nd Platoon, Charlie Company, 3rd Battalion, 2nd Regiment, 5th Brigade, Imperial Cadre (Louvain).

Ivanov, Brigadier Dominik—CO, Elysium planetary militia.

Jackson, Sergeant Julio, Imperial Marine Corps—squad leader, 1st Squad, 3rd Platoon, Bravo Company, Recon Battalion, 1st Regiment, 517th Brigade.

Jacoby, Edward—a drug dealer on the planet Dewent.

Jefferson, Lieutenant Angelique Adrianovna, Imperial Cadre—CO, 2nd Platoon, Charlie Company, 3rd Battalion, 2nd Regiment, 5th Brigade, Imperial Cadre (Louvain).

Johansson, Private Evita, Imperial Marine Corps—rifleman, Fire Team Alpha, 3rd Squad, 2nd Platoon, Bravo Company, Recon Battalion, 1st Regiment, 517th Brigade.

Jongdomba, Brigadier Lobsang Phurba—CO, Gyangtse Planetary Militia.

Jurawski, Admiral Lord Alvin, Imperial Fleet—First Space Lord, Terran Empire.

Jurgensen, Lieutenant Adam, Imperial Marine Corps—CO, 2nd Platoon, Alpha Company, Marine Detachment, HMS *Ctesiphon*.

Kalachian, Corporal Vartkes, Imperial Cadre—Fire Team Alpha, 1st Squad, 1st Platoon, Charlie Company, 3rd Battalion, 2nd Regiment, 5th Brigade, Imperial Cadre.

Karpov, Brigadier Gennadi Sergich, Imperial Cadre—CO, Camp Cochrane.

Keita, Brigadier Sir Arthur, Imperial Cadre—second in command, Imperial Cadre.

Keller, Corporal Jackson, Imperial Cadre—Fire Team Bravo, 2nd Squad, 2nd Platoon, Charlie Company, 3rd Battalion, 2nd Regiment, 5th Brigade, Imperial Cadre.

Kereku, Sir Enobakhare—Imperial Governor, Martinson Crown Sector.

Khanbadze, Private Ang Tarki—rifleman, Echo Company, 1st Battalion, 1st Capital Regiment, Gyangtse Planetary Militia.

Kiely, Corporal Thomas, Imperial Cadre—Fire Team Alpha, 1st Squad, 1st Platoon, Charlie Company, 3rd Battalion, 2nd Regiment, 5th Brigade, Imperial Cadre.

Knutsen, Master Sergeant Catarina, Imperial Cadre—platoon sergeant, 1st Platoon, Charlie Company, 3rd Battalion, 2nd Regiment, 5th Brigade, Imperial Cadre (Louvain).

Kowalska, Master Sergeant Anna, Imperial Cadre—platoon sergeant, 3rd Platoon, Charlie Company, 3rd Battalion, 2nd Regiment, 5th Brigade, Imperial Cadre (Louvain).

Król, Corporal James, Imperial Cadre—Fire Team Bravo, 3rd Squad, 1st Platoon, Charlie Company, 3rd Battalion, 2nd Regiment, 5th Brigade, Imperial Cadre. Later company first sergeant (see below).

Król, First Sergeant James, Imperial Cadre—company first sergeant, Charlie Company, 3rd Battalion, 2nd Regiment, 5th Brigade, Imperial Cadre (Louvain).

Kuramochi, Lieutenant Chiyeko, Imperial Marine Corps—CO, 23 Platoon, Bravo Company, Recon Battalion, 1st Regiment, 517th Brigade. Later captain (see below).

Kuramochi, Captain Chiyeko, Imperial Marine Corps—CO, Delta Company, Marine Detachment, HMS *Ctesiphon*.

Labin, Gustav—Anton Yerensky's Ching-Hai agent.

Lakshindo, Sergeant Nursamden Nyima—Alpha Company, 1st Battalion, 1st Capital Regiment, Gyangtse Planetary Militia.

Lehman, Lady Frederica Sinead, Countess Miller—Imperial Minister of War.

Leibniz, Admiral Mikhail, Imperial Fleet—CO, Operation Clean Sweep supporting task force.

Lewinsky, Captain Broderick, Imperial Marine Corps—CO, Alpha Company, Marine Detachment, HMS *Ctesiphon*.

Lhukpa, Sergeant Chamba Mingma—Alpha Company, 1st Battalion, 1st Capital Regiment, Gyangtse Planetary Militia.

Lowai, Jokuri Asaro'o—Director of Industrial Development, Duchy of Shallingsport.

MacEntee, Corporal Ewan, Imperial Cadre—Fire Team Alpha, 2nd Squad, 1st Platoon, Charlie Company, 3rd Battalion, 2nd Regiment, 5th Brigade, Imperial Cadre.

MacKane, Andrew Clement, Baron Yuroba—Imperial Minister of War.

Madison, Sir Jeffrey—Imperial Foreign Minister.

Madsen, Corporal Harold, Imperial Cadre—Fire Team Alpha, 2nd Squad, 2nd Platoon, Charlie Company, 3rd Battalion, 2nd Regiment, 5th Brigade, Imperial Cadre (Louvain).

Mainwaring, Captain Theodosia—captain of the free-trader *Star Runner*.

Malloy, Allen, Earl of Stanhope—Imperial Minister of Out-World Affairs.

Marat, Rear Admiral Crinan, Imperial Fleet—Port Admiral, Soissons.

Maserati, Lieutenant Edwin, Imperial Cadre—Colonel Oscar McGruder's assistant (see below).

Masolle, Lieutenant Francesca, Imperial Cadre—CO, 2nd Platoon, Charlie Company, 3rd Battalion, 2nd Regiment, 5th Brigade, Imperial Cadre.

Masterman, Commander Adela, Imperial Fleet—senior plotting officer, Elysium System Fortress Command.

Mastroianni, Corporal Carlotta, Imperial Cadre—Fire Team Alpha, 3rd Squad, 2nd Platoon, Charlie Company, 3rd Battalion, 2nd Regiment, 5th Brigade, Imperial Cadre (Louvain).

McGruder, Colonel Oscar, Imperial Cadre—a Cadre evaluation officer.

McGwire, Sergeant Alan, Imperial Cadre—leader, Fire Team Alpha, 1st Squad, 1st Platoon, Charlie Company, 3rd Battalion, 2nd Regiment, 5th Brigade, Imperial Cadre.

McIlhenny, Colonel Benjamin, Imperial Marine Corps—senior intelligence officer, attached to Admiral Gomez's staff.

McSwain, Sondra—Lewis Fuchien's accountant.

Medrano, PFC Leocadio ("Leo"), Imperial Marine Corps—plasma gunner, Fire Team Bravo, 3rd Squad, 2nd Platoon, Bravo Company, Recon Battalion, 1st Regiment, 517th Brigade.

Megaira—an alpha-synth AI.

Megaira—the starship in which Megaira lives.

Mende, Private Dabhuti Lhakpa—rifleman, Echo Company, 1st Battalion, 1st Capital Regiment, Gyangtse Planetary Militia.

Metternich, Sergeant Abraham ("Abe"), Imperial Marine Corps—squad leader, 3rd Squad, 2nd Platoon, Bravo Company, Recon Battalion, 1st Regiment, 517th Brigade.

Miller, Countess—see Lady Frederica Sinead Lehman, above.

Monkoto, Admiral Simon—CO, Monkoto's Mercenaries ("Monkoto's Maniacs").

Monkoto, Captain Arlen—younger brother of Simon Monkoto.

Morales, Captain Francisco, Imperial Fleet—CO, HMS *Implacable*.

Moyano, Corporal Samantha, Imperial Cadre—Fire Team Alpha, 1st Squad, 2nd Platoon, Charlie Company, 3rd Battalion, 2nd Regiment, 5th Brigade, Imperial Cadre.

Mueller, Gavin—Foreign Minister, Onyx System.

Munming, Corporal Ngawang Phurba—grenadier, Echo Company, 1st Battalion, 1st Capital Regiment, Gyangtse Planetary Militia.

Murphy, Emperor Seamus II—Emperor of Humanity.

Murphy, Empress Maire—Empress of Humanity, the mother of the current Emperor.

Nawa, Chepal Dawa—a senior lieutenant of Namkha Pasang Pankarma.

Nawa, Lieutenant Tuchi Phurba—CO, 2nd Platoon, Alpha Company, 1st Battalion, 1st Capital Regiment, Gyangtse Planetary Militia.

Nordbø, Corporal Astrid, Imperial Cadre—Fire Team Bravo, 1st Squad, 1st Platoon, Charlie Company, 3rd Battalion, 2nd Regiment, 5th Brigade, Imperial Cadre.

Obermeyer, Patricia—Sector Governor Sir Enobakhare Kereku's chief of staff.

O'Clery, Corporal Flannan, Imperial Cadre—Fire Team Bravo, 1st Squad, 1st Platoon, Charlie Company, 3rd Battalion, 2nd Regiment, 5th Brigade, Imperial Cadre.

Okahara, Lieutenant Jeff—executive officer of the free-trader *Star Runner.*

Okanami, Surgeon Captain Ralph, Imperial Fleet—senior medical officer, Mathison's World relief.

O'Kane, Commodore Matthew—CO, O'Kane's Free Company.

Onassis, Master Sergeant Adolfo, Imperial Cadre—platoon sergeant, 1st Platoon, Charlie Company, 3rd Battalion, 2nd Regiment, 5th Brigade, Imperial Cadre.

Orrin, Lieutenant James, Imperial Fleet—Commander Adela Masterman's senior assistant.

Ortiz, Captain Homer—CO "pirate" battlecruiser *Poltava*.

Osayaba, Corporal Obaseki, Imperial Cadre—Fire Team Bravo, 1st Squad, 1st Platoon, Charlie Company, 3rd Battalion, 2nd Regiment, 5th Brigade, Imperial Cadre.

Oselli, Corporal Brian, Imperial Cadre—Fire Team Bravo, 1st Squad, 1st Platoon, Charlie Company, 3rd Battalion, 2nd Regiment, 5th Brigade, Imperial Cadre.

O'Shaughnessy, Commodore John Liam, Imperial Fleet—Alicia DeVries's deceased uncle.

O'Shaughnessy, Sergeant Major Sebastian, Imperial Marine Corps—Alicia DeVries's grandfather.

Paál, Lieutenant Ágoston, Imperial Cadre—CO, 3rd Platoon, Charlie Company, 3rd Battalion, 2nd Regiment, 5th Brigade, Imperial Cadre.

Padorje, Chosa Pendo—CO, Echo Company, 1st Battalion, 1st Capital Regiment, Gyangtse Planetary Militia.

Palacios, Major Serafina, Imperial Marine Corps—CO, Recon Battalion, 1st Regiment, 517th Brigade.

Paldorje, Private Chopali Mingma—rifleman, Echo Company, 1st Battalion, 1st Capital Regiment, Gyangtse Planetary Militia.

Pankarma, Namkha Pasang—leader of the Gyangtse Liberation Front.

Perez, Commander Isidor, Imperial Fleet—CO, HMS *Gryphon*.

Perlman, Corporal Malachai, Imperial Cadre—Fire Team Bravo, 1st Squad, 1st Platoon, Charlie Company, 3rd Battalion, 2nd Regiment, 5th Brigade, Imperial Cadre.

Philip, Grand Duke—Prime Minister of the Terran Empire.

Pilaskov, Chief Oliver—Arlen Monkoto's senior noncom on Ringbolt.

Quintana, Oscar, Lieutenant Commander Defiant—Wyvern nobleman and contact for James Howell's "pirates."

Rahman, Commander Killian—senior fire control officer, *Procyon* (James Howell's flagship).

Ramji, Corporal Nicholas, Imperial Cadre—Fire Team Bravo, 2nd Squad, 3rd Platoon, Charlie Company, 3rd Battalion, 2nd Regiment, 5th Brigade, Imperial Cadre.

Rendlemann, Commander George—James Howell's senior tactical officer.

Resdyrn *niha* Turbach—James Howell's contact with the Rishathan Sphere.

Rethmeryk *niha* Theryian—Shernsia *niha* Theryian's successor as *farthi chir* Theryian

Rivera, Jaime—Group Leader, Freedom Alliance Liberation Army.

Ryan, Lieutenant Calvin, Imperial Marine Corps—CO, heavy weapons platoon, Recon Battalion, 1st Regiment, 517th Brigade.

Salaka, Lieutenant Tsimbuti Pemba—CO, 1st Platoon, Alpha Company, 1st Battalion, 1st Capital Regiment, Gyangtse Planetary Militia.

Salgado, Ákos—Planetary Governor Jasper Aubert's chief of staff.

Sampson, Brigadier Aaron, Imperial Marine Corps—CO, 317th Brigade.

Sandusky, Corporal Christopher, Imperial Marine Corps—team leader, Fire Team Alpha, 3rd Squad, 2nd Platoon, Bravo Company, Recon Battalion, 1st Regiment, 517th Brigade.

Shai, Corporal Hau-zhi, Imperial Cadre—Fire Team Bravo, 1st Squad, 1st Platoon, Charlie Company, 3rd Battalion, 2nd Regiment, 5th Brigade, Imperial Cadre.

Shangup, President Kapkye Lhakpa—Planetary President, Gyangtse.

Shapiro, Captain Chaim, Imperial Marine Corps—CO, Delta Company, Recon Battalion, 1st Regiment, 517th Brigade.

Sharwa, Colonel Ang Chirgan—CO, 1st Capital Regiment, Gyangtse Planetary Militia.

Shernsiya *niha* Theryian—Rishathan senior war mother and *farthi chir* ("mother of mothers") of Clan Theryian.

Shidahari, Corporal Allen, Imperial Cadre—Fire Team Alpha, 3rd Squad, 2nd Platoon, Charlie Company, 3rd Battalion, 2nd Regiment, 5th Brigade, Imperial Cadre.

Shu, Commander Rachel—James Howell's senior intelligence officer.

Shwang, Shau-pang—Section Leader, Freedom Alliance Liberation Army.

Sikorsky, Surgeon Lieutenant Natalie, Imperial Fleet—ship's surgeon, HMS *Vindication*, detached for SAR, Mathison's World.

Singh, Lieutenant Albert, Imperial Fleet (retired)—a "pirate" strike leader.

Skogen, Corporal Adam, Imperial Cadre—Fire Team Bravo, 2nd Squad, 1st Platoon, Charlie Company, 3rd Battalion, 2nd Regiment, 5th Brigade, Imperial Cadre.

Solu, Private Chepal Pemba—Alpha Company, 1st Battalion, 1st Capital Regiment, Gyangtse Planetary Militia.

Sosa, Corporal Jack, Imperial Cadre—Fire Team Alpha, 2nd Squad, 3rd Platoon, Charlie Company, 3rd Battalion, 2nd Regiment, 5th Brigade, Imperial Cadre (Louvain).

Star Runner—the starship *Megaira*'s free-trader alias.

Stone, Corporal Frederica, Imperial Cadre—Fire Team Alpha, 2nd Squad, 3rd Platoon, Charlie Company, 3rd Battalion, 2nd Regiment, 5th Brigade, Imperial Cadre (Louvain).

Strassmann, Lieutenant Tobias, Imperial Cadre—CO, 1st Platoon, Charlie Company, 3rd Battalion, 2nd Regiment, 5th Brigade, Imperial Cadre.

Suarez, Inspector Hector, Ministry of Justice—CO, Justice Ministry strike force for Operation Clean Sweep.

Tanner, Lieutenant Ruth—purser of the free-trader *Star Runner.*

Tarbaneau, Captain Esther—CO, the Star Assassins.

Teng, Corporal Rwyun-yin, Imperial Cadre—Fire Team Alpha, 3rd Squad, 1st Platoon, Charlie Company, 3rd Battalion, 2nd Regiment, 5th Brigade, Imperial Cadre.

Thaktu, Ang Jangmu—Namkha Pasang Pankarma's second in command, Gyangtse Liberation Front.

Thompson, Surgeon Commander Valentine, Imperial Fleet—one of Surgeon Captain Okanami's surgical team members.

Thönes, Sergeant Ludovic, Imperial Cadre—company clerk (and Alicia DeVries's wingman), Charlie Company, 3rd Battalion, 2nd Regiment, 5th Brigade, Imperial Cadre (Louvain).

Tigh, Colonel Arturo, Imperial Marine Corps—CO, Jefferson Field Security Command, Soissons.

Tisiphone—one of the three Greek Furies.

Trammell, Captain Kevin, Imperial Marine Corps—CO, Alpha Company, Recon Battalion, 1st Regiment, 517th Brigade.

Trang, Commodore Oliver, Imperial Fleet—CO, Elysium System Fortress Command.

Treadwell, Fleet Admiral Subrahmanyan—Imperial Governor, Franconia Sector.

Truman, Major Samuel, Imperial Marine Corps—CO, 2nd Battalion, 3rd Regiment, 317th Brigade.

Ulujuk, Corporal Robert, Imperial Cadre—Fire Team Alpha, 2nd Squad, 3rd Platoon, Charlie Company, 3rd Battalion, 2nd Regiment, 5th Brigade, Imperial Cadre.

Ustanov, Colonel Tyler, Imperial Marine Corps—CO, 1st Regiment, 517th Brigade.

von Hamel, Captain Marius, Imperial Marine Corps—CO, Elysium planetary garrison.

Watanabe, Commander Hirokichi—junior fire control officer, *Procyon* (James Howell's flagship).

Watts, Captain Wadislaw, Imperial Marine Corps—intelligence specialist attached to support the Imperial Cadre. Later promoted to colonel.

Westfeldt, Admiral Yussuf—CO, Westfeldt's Wolves.

Wheaton, Gunnery Sergeant Michael "Mike," Imperial Marine Corps—platoon sergeant, 2nd Platoon, Bravo Company, Recon Battalion, 1st Regiment, 517th Brigade.

Winfield, Sergeant Major Samuel, Imperial Marine Corps—battalion sergeant major, Recon Battalion, 1st Regiment, 517th Brigade.

Wu, Captain Kathryn, Imperial Fleet—CO, HMS *Tsushima*.

Yerensky, Anton—a MaGuire smuggler who charters *Star Runner.*

Yrjö, Corporal Rauha, Imperial Cadre—Fire Team Alpha, 1st Squad, 3rd Platoon, Charlie Company, 3rd Battalion, 2nd Regiment, 5th Brigade, Imperial Cadre.

Yu, Sergeant Jonas—a member of Albert Singh's strike group.

Yuroba, Baron (see MacKane, Andrew Clement, above).

Yussuf, First Sergeant Pamela, Imperial Cadre—company first sergeant, Charlie Company, 3rd Battalion, 2nd Regiment, 5th Brigade, Imperial Cadre.

Zigair, Private Frinkelo, Imperial Marine Corps—grenadier, Fire Team Bravo, 3rd Squad, 2nd Platoon, Bravo Company, Recon Battalion, 1st Regiment, 517th Brigade.

ABOUT THE AUTHOR

With several million books sold and a *New York Times* bestselling series or two under his belt, David Weber is the science fiction publishing phenomena of the decade. A lifetime military history buff, David Weber has carried his interest in history into his fiction. In the bestselling Honor Harrington series, the spirit of both C.S. Forester's Horatio Hornblower and history's Admiral Nelson are evident. The latest installment in the series is *At All Costs* (November 2005).

Previously the owner of a small advertising and public relations agency, Weber now writes SF full time and has over 30 titles in print. While he is best known for his spirited, modern-minded space operas, he is also developing a fantasy series, of which three have been published: *Oath of Swords*, *The War God's Own* and *Windrider's Oath*. Weber's first published novels grew out of his work as a war game designer for the Task Force game *Starfire*. With collaborator Steve White, Weber has written four novels set in that universe: *Insurrection*, *Crusade*, *In Death Ground*, and *The Shiva Option*, collected in two volumes as *The Stars at War I* and *The Stars at War II*. Recent bestsellers also include his planetary adventure collaborations with rising star John Ringo: *March Upcountry*, *March to the Sea*, *March to the Stars* and *We Few*.

A popular guest at science fiction conventions, Weber makes his home in South Carolina with his wife Sharon, his three children and a passel of dogs.